David Morrell was born in Canada. He is a former Professor of American Literature at the University of Iowa. He is a multiple bestselling author, with over fifteen million copies of his books in print, translated into twenty-two languages. His novels include FIRST BLOOD, TESTAMENT, THE TOTEM and BLOOD OATH and his most recent bestsellers have been THE FIFTH PROFESSION, THE COVENANT OF THE FLAME, ASSUMED IDENTITY, DESPERATE MEASURES, EXTREME DENIAL, DOUBLE IMAGE, BLACK EVENING, BURNT SIENNA, LONG LOST and THE PROTECTOR. Morrell is a graduate of the National Outdoor Leadership wilderness survival school. He is also an honorary lifetime member of the Special Operations Association and an honorary member of the Association of Former Intelligence Officers. With his wife, he lives in Santa Fe, New Mexico.

Also by David Morrell

FICTION

First Blood (1972)
Testament (1975)
Last Reveille (1977)
The Totem (1979)
Blood Oath (1982)
The Brotherhood of the Rose (1984)
The Fraternity of the Stone (1985)
The League of Night and Fog (1987)
The Fifth Profession (1990)
The Covenant of the Flame (1991)
Desperate Measures (1994)
The Totem (Complete and Unaltered) (1994)
Double Image (1998)
Black Evening (1999)
Burnt Sienna (2000)
Long Lost (2002)
The Protector (2003)

NON-FICTION

John Barth: An Introduction (1976)
Fireflies (1988)
American Fiction, American Myth (Essays by Philip Young)
edited by David Morrell and Sandra Spanier (2000)
Lessons from a Lifetime of Writing:
A Novelist Looks at His Craft (2002)

Assumed Identity
Extreme Denial

David Morrell

headline

ASSUMED IDENTITY first published in Great Britain in 1993
by HEADLINE BOOK PUBLISHING

EXTREME DENIAL first published in Great Britain in 1996
by HEADLINE BOOK PUBLISHING

First published in this omnibus edition in 2004
by HEADLINE BOOK PUBLISHING

A HEADLINE paperback

10 9 8 7 6 5 4 3 2 1

ISBN 0 7553 2257 6

Typeset in Plantin by Avon DataSet Ltd,
Bidford on Avon, Warwickshire

Printed and bound in Great Britain by
Clays Ltd, St Ives plc

Papers and cover board used by Headline are natural,
recyclable products made from wood grown in sustainable
forests. The manufacturing processes conform to the
environmental regulations of the country of origin.

HEADLINE BOOK PUBLISHING
A division of Hodder Headline
338 Euston Road
London NW1 3BH

www.headline.co.uk
www.hodderheadline.com

Assumed Identity

To Martin E. Wingate (d. 1986),
"the rock,"
a good friend and a special teacher

No mask like open truth cover lies,
As to go naked is the best disguise.

William Congreve
The Double Dealer

And, after all, what is a lie?
'Tis but the truth in masquerade.

Lord Byron
Don Juan

PROLOGUE

Mexico, 1562.
Less than forty years after the Spanish conquerors arrived in the New World, the systematic extermination of the natives was well under way. Much of the genocide required no effort inasmuch as diseases to which the Europeans had become accustomed . . . smallpox, measles, mumps, and influenza, for example . . . did not exist in the New World and hence had a rapid effect on the natives, who had no immunity to them. Those who did not die from disease (perhaps as few as ten percent of the original population survived) were beaten into submission and forced into slavery. Villages were destroyed, the inhabitants herded into labor camps. Every effort, especially torture, was used to compel the survivors to abandon their culture and convert to that of their European dominators.

In Mexico's southeastern extreme, the Yucatán peninsula, a Franciscan missionary whose name was Diego de Landa reacted with shock to the evidence of snake worship and human sacrifice within the Mayan faith. Determined to eradicate these pagan barbarities, Landa organized the destruction of temples, statues, frescoes, any object with religious connotations . . . and in so doing, he not only separated the Maya from symbols of their beliefs but prevented modern historians from discovering the clues they needed to decipher the remaining hieroglyphs that described the lost, ancient ways.

Landa's greatest triumph of destruction occurred at the village of Maní, where he exposed a secret library of Mayan books. These irreplaceable texts – bound like thin, small accordions and known as codices – 'contained nothing in which there was not to be seen superstitions and lies of the devil,' Landa reported to his superiors. 'We burned them all.'

We burned them all.

A present-day lover of antiquity exhales with despair at the self-righteous, narrow-minded confidence in those words. Bookburners throughout time have shared Landa's purse-lipped, squinty-eyed, jut-jawed, absolute belief in his correctness. But Landa was deceived.

In several ways.

The codices contained historical and philosophical truths in addition to what Landa called lies.

And not all the codices were destroyed. Three of them, salvaged by Spaniards in charge of the burning and smuggled home to Europe as souvenirs, were eventually uncovered in private collections and recognized for their incalculable value.

Known as the Dresden Codex, the Codex Tro-Cortesianus, and the Codex Persianus, they are owned by libraries in Dresden, Madrid, and Paris. A fourth – known as the Grolier Codex and located in Mexico City – has been declared by one expert a fake and is currently under investigation.

But rumors persist that there is a fifth, that it is authentic, that it has more truths than any other, especially *one* truth, a crucial truth.

A modern observer wonders how Friar de Landa would react if he could be summoned from Hell and made to witness the bloodbath comparable in intensity if not in magnitude to the one Landa caused in the fifteen-hundreds, the bloodbath that could have been avoided if Landa had never begun his inquisition or else if he had been the professional he claimed to be and had actually accomplished his hateful job. Maní, the name of the village where Landa found and destroyed the codices, is the Mayan word for 'it is finished.'

But it wasn't finished at all.

ONE

1

Chicago, Illinois.

'Now I realize you all want to hear about human sacrifice,' the professor said, allowing just the right mischievous glint in his eyes, signaling to his students that to study history didn't mean they had to suppress their sense of humor. Each time he taught this course – and he'd been doing so for thirty years – he always began with the same comment, and he always got the reaction he wanted, a collective chuckle, the students glancing at each other in approval and sitting more comfortably.

'Virgins having their hearts cut out,' the professor continued, 'or being thrown off cliffs into wells – that sort of thing.' He gestured dismissively as if he were so familiar with the details of human sacrifice that the subject bored him. Again his eyes glinted mischievously, and the students chuckled louder. His name was Stephen Mill. He was fifty-eight, short and slender, with receding, gray hair, a thin, salt-and-pepper mustache, square-framed, wire-rimmed bifocals, and a brown wool suit that gave off the scent of pipe smoke. Liked and respected by both colleagues and students, he was beginning the last seventy minutes of his life, and if it were any consolation, at least he would die doing what he most enjoyed, talking about his life's obsession.

'Actually the Maya didn't have much interest in sacrificing virgins,' Professor Mill added. 'Most of the skeletons we've retrieved from the sacred wells – they're called *cenotes*, by the way; you might as well begin learning the proper terms – belong to males, and most of *those* had been children.'

The students made faces of disgust.

'The Maya did cut out hearts, of course,' Professor Mill said. 'But that's the most boring part of the ritual.'

Several students frowned and mouthed 'boring?' to each other.

'What the Maya would do is capture an enemy, strip him, paint him blue, take him to the top of a pyramid, break his back but not kill him . . . not yet at least, the temporary objective was to paralyze him . . . then cut out his heart, and *now* he'd die, but not before the high priest was able to raise the victim's pulsing heart for everyone to see. The heart and the blood dripping from it were smeared onto the faces of gods carved into the walls at the top of the temple. It's been theorized that the high priest may also have consumed the heart. But this much we know for certain – the victim's corpse was subsequently hurled down the steps of the pyramid. There a priest cut off the victim's skin and danced in it. Those who'd witnessed the ceremony chopped the corpse into pieces and barbecued it.'

The students swallowed uncomfortably, as if they felt sick.

'But we'll get to the dull stuff later in the term,' Professor Mill said, and the students laughed again, this time with relief. 'As you know, this is a multi-discipline course.' He switched tones with expert ease, deepening his voice, abandoning his guise as an entertainer, becoming a lecturer. 'Some of you are here from art-history. Others are ethnologists and archaeologists. Our purpose is to examine Mayan hieroglyphics, to learn to read them, and to use the knowledge we obtain to reconstruct Mayan culture. Please turn to page seventy-nine of Charles Gallenkamp's *Maya: The Riddle and Rediscovery of a Lost Civilization.*'

The students obeyed and immediately frowned at a bewildering diagram that looked like a totem pole with two descending columns of distorted, grimacing faces flanked by lines, dots, and squiggles. Someone groaned.

'Yes, I realize the challenge is daunting,' Professor Mill said. 'You're telling yourselves that you can't possibly learn to read that maze of apparently meaningless symbols. But I assure you, you *will* be able to read it and many others like it. You'll be able to put sounds to those glyphs, to read them as if they were sentences.' He paused for dramatic effect, then straightened. 'To speak the ancient Mayan language.' He shook his head with wonder. 'You understand now what I meant. Stories about human sacrifice are dull. This' – he pointed toward the hieroglyphs in Gallenkamp's book – 'this is the true excitement.' He directed a keen gaze toward each of his twenty students. 'And since we have to start somewhere, let's start as we did when we were children, by making lines and dots. You'll note that many of the columns of glyphs – which depict a date, by the way – look like this.' Grabbing a piece of chalk, Professor Mill drew hurried marks on the blackboard.

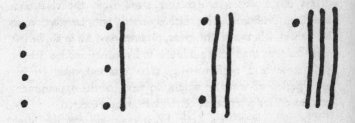

'Each dot has a value of one. A line – or what we call a bar – signifies five. Thus the first group I drew equals four, the second equals eight, the third is twelve, and the fourth . . . Well, why should *I* do all the talking?' Professor Mill drew his right index finger down his list of students. 'Mr Hogan, please tell me the value of . . .'

'Sixteen?' a tentative, male voice responded.

'Excellent, Mr Hogan. You see how easy it is? You're already learning to read Mayan symbols. But if you put all the numbers on those glyphs together, the date they depict wouldn't make any sense to you. Because the Maya used a different calendar than we do. Their calendar was almost as accurate as our own. It was also considerably more complicated. So, as our first step in understanding Mayan civilization, we'll have to understand their concept of time. For our next class, read chapters one and two in *A Forest of Kings: The Untold Story of the Ancient Maya* by Linda Schele and David Friedel. Meanwhile I'll summarize what you'll be reading.'

And so Professor Mill continued, taking obvious delight in his subject matter. With less than twenty minutes remaining in his life, he was enjoying every second. He concluded the class with a joke that he always used at this point in the course, elicited another anticipated chuckle, answered a few questions from students who lingered, then packed his books, notes, syllabus, and list of students into his briefcase.

His office was a five-minute stroll from the classroom building. Professor Mill breathed deeply, with satisfaction, as he walked. It was a bright, clear, pleasant day. All in all, he felt splendid (less than fifteen minutes to live now), and his delight with how he'd performed in class was enhanced by his anticipation of what he would do next, of the appointment he'd made for after class, of the visitor he expected.

The office was in a drab, brick building, but the bleak surroundings had no effect on Professor Mill's sense of well-being and eagerness. Indeed he felt so full of energy that he passed students at the elevator and walked rapidly up the two flights of stairs to the dimly lit corridor halfway along which he had his office. After unlocking the door (ten minutes to go) and setting his briefcase on his desk, he turned to walk down to the faculty lounge but paused, then smiled, when he saw his visitor appear at the open doorway.

'I was just going for some coffee,' Professor Mill said. 'Would you care for some?'

'Thanks but no.' The visitor nodded in greeting and entered. 'My stomach and coffee don't get along anymore. I have heartburn all the time. I think I'm developing an ulcer.'

The visitor was a distinguished-looking man in his middle thirties. His neatly trimmed hair, custom-made white shirt, striped silk tie, hand-tailored double-breasted suit, and thin-soled calfskin shoes were in keeping with his occupation as a highly paid, corporate executive.

'Ulcers come from stress. You'd better slow down.' Professor Mill shook hands with him.

'Stress and speed are part of my job description. If I start worrying about my health, I'll find myself out of work.' The visitor sat.

'You need a vacation.'

'Soon. They keep promising me soon.'

'So what have you got for me?' Professor Mill asked.

'More glyphs to be translated.'

'How many?'

The visitor shrugged. 'Five pages.' He frowned as a group of students went by in the corridor. 'I'd prefer to keep this confidential.'

'Of course.' Professor Mill got up, shut the door, and returned to his desk. 'Mayan pages or contemporary pages?'

The visitor look puzzled, then realized, 'Right, I keep forgetting Mayan pages are bigger. No, contemporary pages. Eight-by-ten photographs. I assume the fee we negotiated the last time is still acceptable.'

9

'Fifty-thousand dollars? *Very* acceptable. As long as I'm not rushed,' Professor Mill said.

'You won't be. You can have a month, the same as before. The same terms of payment – half now, half when you're finished. The same conditions pertain. You may not make copies of the pages. You may not reveal what you are doing or discuss your translation with anyone.'

'Don't worry. I won't, and I haven't,' Professor Mill said, 'although there's nothing so interesting in the translation that anybody except you and me and your employer would care. No matter. You pay me so well that I'd be insane to break the terms of the agreement and jeopardize my future relationship with you. I have a sabbatical next year, and the money you've generously paid me will allow me to devote the entire year to studying the Hieroglyphic Stairway in the Mayan ruins at Copán in Honduras.'

'It's too hot down there for me,' the visitor said.

'When I'm at the ruins, I'm too excited to think about the weather. May I see the pages?'

'By all means.' The visitor reached into an alligator-skin briefcase, pulling out a large, manila envelope.

With less than a minute to live, Professor Mill took the envelope, opened it, and removed five photographs that showed numerous rows of hieroglyphs. He shifted books to the side of his desk and arranged the photographs so that the rows of glyphs were vertical.

'All part of the same text?'

'I have no idea,' the visitor said. 'All I was told was to make the delivery.'

'They appear to be.' Professor Mill picked up a magnifying glass and leaned close to the photographs, studying the details of the glyphs. Sweat beaded on his brow. He shook his head. 'I shouldn't have run up those stairs.'

'Excuse me?' the visitor asked.

'Nothing. Just talking to myself. Does it feel warm in here?'

'A little.'

Professor Mill took off his suit coat and resumed his inspection of the photographs. Fifteen seconds to live. 'Well, leave them with me, and . . .'

'Yes?'

'I . . .'

'What?' the visitor asked.

'Don't feel so good. My hands . . .'

'What about them?'

'Numb,' Professor Mill said. 'My . . .'

'What?'

'Face. Hot.'

Professor Mill abruptly gasped, clutched his chest, stiffened, and slumped, sagging backward in his creaky, swivel chair, his mouth open, his head drooping. He shivered and stopped moving.

The small office seemed to contract as the visitor stood. 'Professor Mill?' He felt for a pulse at a wrist and then the neck. 'Professor Mill?' He removed rubber gloves from his briefcase, put them on, then used his right hand to collect the photographs and slide them into the manila envelope, which he held steady with his left hand. Cautiously he used the left hand to peel off the glove on his right hand, and vice versa, in each case making sure that he didn't touch any area that had touched the photographs. He dropped the gloves into another manila envelope, sealed it, and put both envelopes into his briefcase.

When the visitor opened the door, none of the students or faculty passing in the corridor paid much attention to him. An amateur might have walked away, but the visitor knew that excitement could prime memories, that someone would eventually remember seeing a well-dressed man come out of the office. He didn't want to create a mystery. He was well aware that the best deception was a version of the truth. So he walked rapidly to the secretary's office, entered it in distress, and told the secretary, 'Hurry. Phone nine one one. Professor Mill. I was visiting . . . I think he just had a heart attack.'

2

Guatemala City.

Despite his thirty-six-hour journey and his sixty-four years, Nicholas Petrovich Bartenev fidgeted with energy. He and his wife had flown from Leningrad —

Correction, he thought. St Petersburg. Now that Communism has collapsed, they've abolished Lenin.

— to Frankfurt to Dallas to here, by invitation of the new Guatemalan government, and indeed if it hadn't been for the Cold War's end, this journey would not have been possible. Guatemala had only recently, after forty years, resumed diplomatic relations with Russia, and the all-important Russian exit visas, which for so long had been impossible to obtain, had been issued with astonishing efficiency. For most of his life, Bartenev had one consuming dream – to travel to Guatemala, not because he was eager to leave Russia, rather because Guatemala obsessed him. But he'd persistently, repeatedly been denied permission, and all of a sudden it was merely a matter of filling out some government forms and coming back a few days later to get the necessary travel papers. Bartenev couldn't believe his good fortune. He feared that all of this would turn out to be a cruel hoax, that he'd be refused permission to enter Guatemala, that he'd be deported back to Russia.

The jet – a stretch 727 owned by American Airlines . . . American! For a Russian citizen to be a passenger on a jet labeled American would have been unthinkable not many years ago – descended through clouds, past mountains, toward a city sprawled in a valley. The time was eight-fifteen in the evening. Sunset cast a crimson glow across the valley. Guatemala City's lights gleamed. Bartenev gazed spellbound out his window, his heart pounding with the eagerness of a child.

Beside him, his wife clasped his hand. He turned to study her beautiful, wrinkled face, and she didn't need to say anything to communicate the pleasure she felt because he would soon fulfill his dream. From the age of eighteen, from the first time he'd seen photographs of the Mayan ruins at Tikal in Guatemala, he had felt an eerie identification with the now-almost-vanished people who had built them. He felt as if he had been there, as if he had been one of the Maya, as if his strength and sweat had helped erect the great pyramids and temples. And he had become fascinated with the hieroglyphs.

All these years later, without ever having set foot on a Mayan ruin, without ever having climbed a pyramid, without ever having stared face-to-face at the hook-nosed, high-cheeked, slope-browed visages of the Maya in the hieroglyphs, he was one of the top five Mayan epigraphers in the world (perhaps the top of the top, if he believed his wife's flattery), and soon – not tonight, of course, but tomorrow perhaps or certainly the day after – he'd have managed yet another flight, this one to a primitive airstrip, and have accomplished the difficult journey through the jungle to Tikal, to his life's preoccupation, to the center of his world, to the ruins.

To the hieroglyphs.

His heartbeat increased as the jet touched down. The sun was lower behind the western mountains. The darkness thickened, pierced by the glint of lights from the airport's terminal. Nervous with anticipation, Bartenev unbuckled his seat belt, picked up his briefcase, and followed his wife and

13

other passengers along the aisle. A frustrating minute passed, seeming to take much longer, before the aircraft's hatch was opened. He squinted past the passengers ahead of him and saw the murky silhouettes of buildings. As he and his wife descended stairs to the airport's tarmac, he breathed the thin, dry, cool, mountain air and felt his body tense with excitement.

The moment he entered the terminal, however, he saw several uniformed, government officials waiting for him, and he knew that something was wrong. They were somber, pensive, brooding. Bartenev feared that his premonition had been justified, that he was about to be refused permission to enter the country.

Instead a flustered, thin-lipped man in a dark suit stepped away from them, nervously approaching. 'Professor Bartenev?'

'Yes.'

They spoke in Spanish. Bartenev's compulsive interest in Guatemala and the Mayan ruins throughout Mesoamerica had prompted him to acquire a facility in the local language since much of the scholarship being done on the hieroglyphs was published in Spanish.

'My name is Hector Gonzales. From the National Archaeological Museum here.'

'Yes, I've received your letters.' As they shook hands, Bartenev couldn't help noticing how Gonzales guided him toward the government officials. 'This is my wife, Elana.'

'I'm very pleased to meet you, Mrs Bartenev. If you'll please come through this door . . .'

Abruptly Bartenev noticed stern soldiers holding automatic rifles. He cringed, reminded of Leningrad during the worst of the Cold War. 'Is something wrong? Is there something you haven't told me, something I should know?'

'Nothing,' Gonzales said too quickly. 'A problem with your accommodations. A scheduling difficulty. Nothing serious.

14

Come this way. Through this door and down this hallway. Hurry, or we'll be late.'

'Late?' Bartenev shook his head as he and his wife were rushed along the corridor. 'Late for what? And our luggage? What about—?'

'It's being taken care of. Your luggage will be brought to your hotel. You don't need to go through Immigration and Customs.'

They passed through another door, into the night, onto a parking lot, where a jeep filled with armed soldiers waited in front of a black limousine behind which there was another jeep filled with armed soldiers.

'I demand to know what is going on,' Bartenev said. 'In your letters, you claimed that I would feel welcome here. Instead, I feel like a prisoner.'

'Professor Bartenev, you must understand that Guatemala is a troubled country. There is always much political uneasiness here. These soldiers are for your protection.'

'Why would I need—?'

'Please get in the car, and we can discuss it.'

The moment an escort shut the door on Bartenev, his wife, Gonzales, and two government officials, Bartenev again demanded, 'Why would I need protection?'

The limousine, flanked by the jeeps, sped away.

'As I told you, politics. For many years, Guatemala has been ruled by right-wing extremists.' Gonzales glanced uneasily at the government officials, as if he suspected that they would not approve of his vocabulary. 'Recently moderates have come into power. The new government is the reason that your country now is permitted to have diplomatic relations with ours. It also explains why you were invited here. A visit from a Russian academician emphasizes the good will that the Guatemalan government wants with your country. You were an ideal man to invite because you are not a politician and because your

15

expertise relates to Guatemalan history.'

'The way you speak . . .' Bartenev hesitated. 'It makes me think you work less for the National Archaeological Museum than you do for the government. What is the name of the dynasty that ruled Tikal?'

Gonzales didn't answer.

'In what century did Tikal reach its zenith of power?'

Gonzales didn't answer.

Bartenev scoffed.

'You are in danger,' Gonzales said.

'What?'

'The right-wing extremists strongly disapprove of your visit,' Gonzales explained tensely. 'Despite the collapse of Communism in Russia, these extremists see your visit as the beginning of a corrupting influence that will make this country Marxist. The previous government used death squads to enforce its rule. Those death squads are still in existence. There have been threats against your life.'

Bartenev stared, despair spreading through him. His wife asked what Gonzales was saying to him. Grateful that she didn't understand Spanish, Bartenev told her that someone had forgotten to make a reservation for them at the hotel, that their host was embarrassed about the oversight, and that the mistake was being corrected.

He scowled at Gonzales. 'What are you saying to me? That I have to leave? I refuse. Oh, I will send my wife to safety. But I did not come all this way only to leave before I see my dream. I'm too old. I will probably not have this chance again. And I'm too close. I will go the *rest* of the way.'

'You are not being asked to leave,' Gonzales said. 'That would be almost as ruinous a political act as if someone attempted to kill you.'

Bartenev felt blood drain from his face.

Gonzales said, 'But we must be extremely careful. Cautious.

16

We are asking you not to go out in public in the city. Your hotel will be guarded. We will transport you to Tikal as quickly as possible. And then we request that after a prudent length of time – a day, or at the most two – you feign illness and return to your home.'

'A day?' Bartenev had difficulty breathing. 'Perhaps two? So little time after so many years of waiting for . . .'

'Professor Bartenev, we have to deal with political realities.'

Politics, Bartenev thought, and wanted to curse. But like Gonzales, he was accustomed to dealing with such obscene realities, and he analyzed the problem with desperate speed. He was out of Russia, free to go anywhere – that was the important factor. There were numerous other major Mayan ruins. Palenque in Mexico, for example. He'd always been fond of photographs of it. It wasn't Tikal. It didn't have the emotional and professional attraction that Tikal had for him, but it was accessible. His wife could accompany him there. They would be safe there. If the Guatemalan government refused to pay for further expenses, that wouldn't matter – because Bartenev had a secret source of funds about which he hadn't told even his wife.

Indeed secrecy had been part of the business arrangement when the well-dressed, fair-haired American had arrived at Bartenev's office at St Petersburg State University. The American had shown him several photographs of Mayan glyphs. He had asked in perfect Russian how much Bartenev would charge to translate the glyphs and keep the assignment confidential. 'If the glyphs are interesting, I won't charge anything,' Bartenev had answered, impressed by the foreigner's command of the language. But the American had insisted on paying. In fact, his fee had been astonishingly generous: fifty-thousand dollars. 'To ensure your silence,' the American had said. 'I've converted some of it to rubles.' He gave Bartenev the equivalent of ten thousand dollars in

17

Russian currency. The remainder, he explained, would be placed in a Swiss bank account. Perhaps one day Bartenev would be free to travel, in which case the money could easily be obtained. Failing that, couriers could be arranged to transport prudent amounts into St Petersburg for him, amounts that wouldn't be so large that the authorities would ask questions about their source. Since that visit, the American had come two more times, in each case with more photographs of Mayan glyphs and with the same fee. Until now, the money had not been as important to Bartenev as the fascinating, although puzzling message (like a riddle within a code) that the glyphs revealed.

But now the money was *very* important, and Bartenev bitterly meant to get full value from it.

'Yes,' he told Gonzales. 'Political realities. I will leave whenever you want, whenever I have served your purpose.'

Gonzales seemed to relax. But only for a moment. Abruptly the limousine arrived at a hotel, the steel-and-glass modern design of which was jarringly unHispanic. The soldiers escorted Bartenev and his wife quickly through the lobby, into an elevator, and to the twelfth floor. Gonzales came with them as a government official spoke to a clerk at the check-in desk.

The phone was ringing as Gonzales unlocked the door, turned on a light, and guided Bartenev and his wife into the suite. Actually there were two phones, one on a table next to a sofa, the other on a bar.

Gonzales locked the door behind them. The phone kept ringing. As Bartenev stepped toward the one by the sofa, Gonzales said, 'No, let me answer it.' He chose the closer phone, the one on the bar. 'Hello.' He turned on a lamp. 'Why do you wish to speak with him?' He stared at Bartenev. 'Just a moment.' He placed a hand over the telephone's mouthpiece. 'It's a man who claims to be a journalist. Perhaps it would be wise to give an interview. Good public relations. I'll listen on this phone while you use that one.'

Bartenev pivoted toward the phone on the table beside the sofa. 'Hello,' he said, casting a shadow against the window.

'Go to hell, you Goddamned Russian.'

As the window shattered inward, Bartenev's wife screamed. Bartenev did not. The bullet that struck his skull and mushroomed within it killed him instantly. The bullet burst out the back of his head, spraying blood across the flying glass.

3

Houston, Texas.

The space shuttle, *Atlantis*, was on the second day of its current mission . . . a no-problem launch, an all-systems-go performance so far . . . and Albert Delaney felt bored. He wished that something would happen, anything to break his tedious routine. Not that he wanted excitement exactly, because he associated that word with a crisis. The last thing NASA needed was more foul-ups and bad publicity, and at all costs, another *Challenger* disaster had to be avoided. One more like that and NASA would probably be out of business, which meant that Albert Delaney would be out of a job, and Albert Delaney preferred boredom any day to being unemployed. Still, if anybody had told him when he'd been accepted by NASA that his enthusiasm for what he assumed would be a glamorous career would all too quickly change to tedium, he'd have been incredulous. The trouble was that NASA prechecked the details of a mission so often, testing and retesting, going over every variable, trying to anticipate every contingency that by the time the mission occurred, it was anticlimactic. No, Albert Delaney didn't want excitement, but he certainly wouldn't have minded an occasional positive surprise.

A man of medium height and weight, with average features, in that cusp of life where he'd stopped being young but wasn't yet middle-aged, he'd noticed that more and more he'd been feeling dissatisfied, unfulfilled. His existence was ordinary. Predictable. He hadn't yet reached the stage of his syndrome where he was tempted to cheat on his wife. Nonetheless he was afraid that what Thoreau had called 'quiet desperation' might drive him to do something stupid and get more excitement than he'd bargained for by ruining his marriage. Still, if he didn't find some purpose, something to interest him, he didn't know if he could rely on his common sense.

Part of his problem, Albert Delaney decided, was that his office was at the periphery of NASA headquarters. Away from the mission-control center, he didn't have the sense of accomplishment and nervous energy that he imagined everyone felt there. Plus, even *he* had to admit that being an expert in cartography, geography, and meteorology (maps, land, and weather, as he sometimes put it bluntly) seemed awfully dull compared to space exploration. It wasn't as if he got the chance to examine photographs of newly discovered rings around Saturn or moons near Jupiter or active volcanoes on Venus. No, what he got to do was look at photographs of areas on earth, sections that he'd looked at dozens of times before.

It didn't help that the conclusions of the research he was doing had already been determined. Did photographs from space show that the alarming haze around the earth was becoming worse? Did high-altitude images indicate that the South American rain forest continued to dwindle due to slash-and-burn farming practices? Were the oceans becoming so polluted that evidence of the damage could be seen from three hundred miles up? Yes. Yes. Yes. You didn't need to be a rocket scientist to come up with those conclusions. But NASA wanted more than conclusions. It wanted specifics, and even though the photographs that Albert Delaney examined would eventually be sent to other government agencies, it was his job to make the preliminary examination, just in case there was something unique in them so that NASA could get the publicity.

The shuttle's current mission was to deploy a weather satellite over the Caribbean Sea and perform various weather-related observations and experiments as well as transmit photographs. The photograph currently in front of Delaney showed a portion of Mexico's Yucatán peninsula. For several years, a blight had been attacking the palm trees in that area, and one of Delaney's jobs was to determine how far the blight had spread, something that could easily be seen in the photographs since the sick, denuded trees created a distinct, bleak pattern. The theory was that substantial loss of vegetation in the Yucatán would disturb the oxygen/carbon-dioxide ratio in the area and affect weather patterns just as the disappearance of Brazil's rain forest did. By measuring the area of blight and factoring that information with temperature and wind variations in the Caribbean, it might be possible to predict the creation of tropical storms and the direction of hurricanes.

The blight had definitely spread much farther than photographs of the Yucatán taken last year indicated. Delaney placed a transparent, scale-model map over the photograph, aligned topographical features, recorded measurements, and continued to another photograph. Perhaps it was his need for a break in his routine. Perhaps it was his need to be surprised. For whatever reason, he found that he was examining the photographs far more diligently than usual, paying attention to matters that weren't related to the palm-tree blight.

Abruptly something troubled him, a subconsciously noticed detail, a sense that something was out of place. He set down the photograph he was examining and went back to the one he'd just finished looking at. Frowning, he concentrated. Yes, he thought. There. At once he felt a stimulating flow of adrenaline, a warming in his stomach. That small area in the bottom left corner of the photograph. Those shadows among the denuded palm trees. What were those shadows doing there?

The shadows formed almost perfect triangles and squares. But triangles and squares did not exist in nature. More, those shadows could be made only by sunlight that struck and was blocked by objects above the ground. Large objects. Tall objects. Normally, shadows didn't pose a mystery. Hills made them all the time. But these shadows were in the Yucatán's northern lowlands. The descriptive name said it all. Lowlands. There *weren't* any hills in that region. Even if there were, the shadows they cast would have been amorphous. But these were *symmetrical*. And they occupied a comparatively wide area. Delaney made quick calculations. Thirty square kilometers? In the middle of an otherwise dramatically flat section of the Yucatán rain forest? What the hell was going on?

4

'For our final report, something old discovered by something new. Computer-enhanced photographs received from the space shuttle, *Atlantis*, have revealed what appears to be a large area of unsuspected Mayan ruins in a remote section of Mexico's Yucatán peninsula. The rain forest in that region is so dense and inaccessible that it could take months before a preliminary assessment of the ruins can be completed, but a spokesperson for the Mexican government indicated that the apparent scope of the ruins suggests that they have the potential to rival the pyramids, palaces, and temples at legendary Chichén Itzá. To paraphrase F. Scott Fitzgerald, and so we move on – into the past. This is Dan Rather. For CBS news, good evening.'

5

The Virgin Islands.

The visitor noted that several more artifacts – figurines, ceramics, and masks – had been added to the collection. All were authentic, expensive, and illegally obtained examples of ancient Mayan craftsmanship. 'The woman disappeared.'

'*What?*' The old man, who'd been distracted as he attached an intravenous line to a needle in his arm, snapped his head up. '*Disappeared?* You assured me that wasn't possible.'

'I believed it wasn't,' the fair-haired man said. His tone was somber. 'She was being paid so well and treated so lavishly that I thought it highly unlikely she would want to leave.'

The old man glowered, his thin body rigid with fury. Seated in a leather chair in the main cabin of his two-hundred-foot-long yacht, flanked by displays of his current passion, Mayan art, he stretched his gaunt frame to its maximum. His gaze intensified by his glasses, his pinched expression emphasized by his thick, white hair, he dominated the cabin, even though he wasn't tall. 'Human nature. Damn it, that's always been your problem. You're excellent when it comes to tactics. But your emotional range is so limited that you don't understand . . .'

'She was lonely,' the pleasant-faced man said. 'I anticipated that possibility. My people were watching her in case she attempted to do something foolish. Her maid, her butler, her chauffeur, the doorman at her condominium building in Manhattan – all of them worked for me. Every exit from that building was constantly watched. On those rare occasions when she had permission to leave it, she was followed.'

23

'And yet,' the old man rasped, his nostrils flaring with angry sarcasm, 'she managed to disappear.' His white hair contrasted with the pewter tint of his skin, which in turn was emphasized by the gray of his robe, the left sleeve of which was rolled up to admit the intravenous tube leading into his arm. 'You. I blame *you*.' He pointed his bony, right index finger. 'Everything depends on her. *How in God's name did this happen?*'

The well-dressed man gestured in frustration. 'I don't know. My people don't know. It happened last night. Between two a.m. when the maid last saw her and noon when the maid decided to check on her, the woman managed to get out of the condo and the building. We have no idea how. When I learned what had happened, I decided I'd better report to you in person rather than use the telephone. I caught the first available flight.' He gestured toward the starboard windows of the cabin and the numerous other yachts in St Thomas' hotel-rimmed, sunset-tinted harbor.

The old man squinted. 'Willingness to face blame. I respect that. It's rare for a sociopath to have character. *Does she have access to her bank account?*'

'No. Since she was provided with all the comforts she wanted, she had no need to spend money. Hence she didn't realize that the bank statements she was shown, the ones that indicated her salary deposits, were for an account that required me to cosign for withdrawals. The money's inaccessible to her.'

'Jewelry?'

'She took it all. The diamond necklace alone is worth four-hundred-thousand dollars. In theory. But of course, the stones aren't genuine. Still, there are only certain establishments in the New York area that would have the resources to buy such an item, if it weren't a copy. And since she doesn't know it's a copy, she'll have to go to them. My people are watching those establishments.'

The old man frowned. 'Assuming she's able to obtain money, and I suspect she will, given the ingenuity she showed in escaping your people, where would she go? What can she do?'

'She'd be a fool to go back to her former patterns. She has to assume that we'll watch her relatives, her friends, and her previous business associates, that we'll tap their phones, et cetera. If she's smart, and she's proven she is, she'll go to ground. The last thing she wants is trouble from us.'

'Us?'

'From you.'

The old man gestured with a wrinkled hand, his eyes harsh with disapproval yet glinting with superiority. 'Human nature. You still haven't learned the lesson. If loneliness made her run, the one thing she *won't* do is go to ground. She'll want companionship. She'll want the security and satisfaction of a life that *she* creates, not one that's forced upon her. She won't trade one cage for another.'

'Then what will . . . ?'

The old man stared at his intravenous line and brooded. 'She'll get help.'

'From?'

'There are only two reasons for someone to help someone else,' the old man said. 'Money and love. We can't possibly anticipate who would work for her. But I wonder if she would trust a stranger who is loyal to her only for money. I suspect that someone in her position would prefer to depend on love, or at least friendship. Who in her background has the skills to help her?'

'As I told you, her family, friends, and former contacts are under surveillance.'

'No. Look deeper. She wouldn't have fled unless she had a plan. Somewhere there's someone who knows about this sort of thing and whom *she* knows she can ask for help. Someone who isn't obvious. Someone she trusts.'

'I'll get started immediately.'

'You've disappointed me,' the old man said. 'Your success in Chicago and Guatemala was so encouraging that I'd arranged a reward for you. Now, I'm afraid, I'll have to withhold it.'

An intercom buzzed on a table beside the old man's chair. He pressed a button. 'I told you not to interrupt me.'

'Sheik Hazim is returning your telephone call, Professor,' a female voice said.

'Of course. I'll speak to him.' The old man rested his hand on the telephone beside the intercom. But before he picked it up, he told his visitor, his voice stern and flinty, 'Don't disappoint me again.' He adjusted the flow of red liquid that drained from an intravenous bottle into his arm – blood treated with hormones from unborn lambs. 'Find the bitch before she ruins everything. If Delgado discovers she's loose, if he discovers she's out of control, he'll go after her and possibly us.'

'I can deal with Delgado.'

'Of that, I have no doubt. Without Delgado, however, I can't do business. I can't get access to the ruins. And *that* would make me very unhappy. You do not want to be near me when I am unhappy.'

'No, sir.'

'Get out.'

TWO

1

Cancun, Mexico.

All the hotels were shaped like Mayan temples, a row of terraced pyramids along the four-lane highway dividing the sandbar that until twenty-five years ago had been uninhabited. Buchanan ignored them and the red, brick sidewalk along which, concentrating, he walked with deceptive calm. As twilight thickened into night, what he paid attention to were the disturbing proximity of tourists before and behind him, the threatening rumble and glare of traffic passing him on the right, and the ominous shadows among the palm trees that flanked the hotels on his left.

Something was wrong. Every instinct and intuition warned him. His stomach felt rigid. He tried to tell himself that he was merely experiencing the equivalent of stage fright. But his experience of too many dangerous missions had taught him the hard way to pay attention to the visceral, warning signals that alerted him when something wasn't as it should be.

But what? Buchanan strained to analyze. Your preparation was thorough. Your bait for the target is perfect. Why in God's name are you so nervous?

Burn-out? Too many assignments? Too many identities? Too many high-wire, juggling acts?

No, Buchanan mentally insisted. I know what I'm doing. After eight years, after having survived this long, I recognize the difference between nerves and . . .

Relax. You're on top of things. Give yourself a break. It's hot. It's muggy. You're under stress. You've done this a hundred times before. Your plan is solid. The bottom line is quit second-guessing. Get control of your doubts, and do your job.

Sure, Buchanan thought. But he wasn't convinced. Maintaining his deceptively leisurely pace in spite of the pressure in his chest, he shifted leftward, relieved to escape the threatening traffic. Past the equally threatening shadows of the dense, colorfully flowered shrubs that lined the driveway, he proceeded warily up the curving entrance toward the glistening, Mayan-temple shape of Club Internacional.

2

Buchanan's appointment was for nine-thirty, but he took care to arrive ten minutes early in order to survey the meeting place and verify that nothing about the site had changed to jeopardize the rendezvous. For the past three evenings, he'd visited this hotel exactly at this time, and on each occasion, he'd satisfied himself that the location was perfect.

The problem was that *this* night wasn't those other nights. A plan that existed perfectly on paper had to match the 'real world,' and the real world had a dangerous habit of changing from day to day. A fire might have damaged the building. Or the site might be so unusually crowded that a discreet, nonetheless damning conversation could be easily overheard. An exit might be blocked. There were too many variables. If anything disturbed him, Buchanan would disguise his concern and drift back into the night. Then by prior agreement, when his contact arrived at nine-thirty and didn't see Buchanan, the contact would know that the circumstance wasn't ideal, a euphemism for 'get your ass out of here,' that the meeting had been postponed until eight tomorrow morning at breakfast at another hotel, and of course Buchanan had arranged a further backup plan in case that second meeting, too, was postponed. Because Buchanan had to assure his contact that every precaution was being considered, that the safety of the contact was Buchanan's primary consideration.

So Buchanan strolled past the two Mexican porters at the entrance to Club Internacional. Inside the lobby, he eased beyond a group of jovial American tourists on their way to Cancun's Hard Rock Cafe and tried not to breathe the perfumed, acrid odor of insecticide that the hotel periodically sprayed along its corridors to discourage the area's considerable population of cockroaches. Buchanan wondered which the guests hated more – the offending spray or the ubiquitous insects which after a while seemed as commonplace as the area's numerous lizards. While a maid unobtrusively swept up dead insects, Buchanan hesitated at the rear of the lobby just long enough to notice a Japanese guest coming through a door beside the gift shop on the left. That door, Buchanan knew, led to balconies, rooms, and stairwells to the beach. One of many exits. In working order. So far so good.

To his right, he proceeded along a short hallway and came to steps that went down to a restaurant. As on previous nights, the restaurant was moderately busy, just enough for Buchanan and his contact to be inconspicuous but not so busy that they'd be surrounded by potential eavesdroppers.

Again so far so good. Perhaps I'm wrong, Buchanan thought. Perhaps everything's going to be fine.

Don't kid yourself, a warning voice insisted.

Hey, I'm not about to cancel a meeting just because I've got a case of nerves.

He felt briefly reassured when a Mexican waiter came over and agreed to sit him at the table he requested. That table was ideally situated in the far right corner, away from the other diners, near the exit to the hotel's gardens. Buchanan chose a chair that put his back to the wall and gave him a view of the stairs leading down to the restaurant. The air conditioning cooled his sweat. He glanced at his watch. Nine twenty-five. His contact would be here in five minutes. Pretending to study a menu, he tried to seem calm.

At once, pulse increasing, he noticed two men appear at the top of the stairs that led to the restaurant.

But Buchanan had expected to meet only *one* man.

Both were Hispanic. Both wore beige, linen suits that were stylishly wrinkled, their yellow, silk shirts open to their breastbones. Each had a gold Rolex watch as well as several gold neckchains and bracelets. Each was thin, in his thirties, with chiseled, narrow, severe features and thick, dark, slicked-back hair gathered in a ponytail. Their hooded eyes were as dark as their hair, and like their hair, their eyes glinted. Predator's eyes. Hawk's eyes. Merciless eyes. The men were *gemelos*, twins, and as they descended toward the restaurant, they braced their shoulders, puffed out their chests, and exuded confidence, the world at their command.

Buchanan tried to look relaxed while he intensified his awareness. The men immediately headed in his direction. Their footsoldiers would have given them his description, Buchanan knew. More, there would have been surreptitious photographs taken of him. He dreaded being photographed.

As the twins reached his table, Buchanan stood to shake hands with them. He deliberately hadn't worn a jacket, wanting them to see that he wasn't armed. They would note that his navy shirt was tucked under his belt rather than hanging loose and possibly concealing a pistol. They would also note that his shirt was somewhat tight, sufficiently so that if he were hiding a tape recorder or a transmitting device, the outline would be obvious. Of course, state-of-the-art transmitters were so miniaturized that one could easily be disguised as a button on his shirt, just as a small handgun could be secured above his ankle beneath his pants. Not that Buchanan would need a handgun at this proximity. The ballpoint pen in his shirt pocket could be equally lethal. Nonetheless Buchanan knew that these hawk-eyed men would appreciate his gesture of apparent openness. At the same time, he took for granted that, despite their display of confidence, they would maintain the wariness that had kept them alive this long.

They greeted him in English.

Buchanan replied in Spanish, 'Thank you for meeting me.' He used '*ustedes*,' the formal word for '*you*.'

'*De nada*,' the first man said and gestured for Buchanan to sit.

Both glanced around the restaurant, seemed satisfied by the meeting place, and sat as well. No doubt, Buchanan thought, they'd ordered subordinates to check the restaurant's suitability before they'd arrived. Presumably they also had stationed guards inconspicuously outside the hotel and in the corridor that led to the restaurant. As a further precaution, they took napkins from the table, spread them on their laps, and made a smooth, practiced motion with their right hands that told Buchanan they'd slid a pistol beneath each napkin.

Finally settled, they studied him.

'You have *cojones*,' the first twin said.

'*Gracias*.'

'And the luck of a fool,' the second twin said. 'We could have dealt with you permanently at any time.'

'*Claro que si*,' Buchanan said. 'Of course. But I hoped that you would listen to reason. I have confidence in the business opportunity I came to offer you.'

31

'Our business is already satisfying,' the first twin said.

'So what makes you think that you can make our business even *more* satisfying?' The second twin squinted.

Buchanan spoke softly. 'Because you know how satisfying my own business has become. I take for granted that I'm reasoning with disciplined businessmen. Professionals. The proof is that you didn't respond to my efforts by . . . as you put it . . . dealing with me permanently. You saw how . . .'

Buchanan coughed discreetly in warning and cocked his head to the left.

Their waiter approached and gave them menus. He compared his two Hispanic guests to the solitary *norteamericano* and obviously decided that since Cancun was Mexico's most popular resort for Americans, he would give Buchanan the most attention. 'Would you like a drink, *señores?*'

'Tequila for me. *Y para mis compadres?*' Buchanan turned to them.

'The same,' the first twin said. 'Bring lime and salt.'

'Make it doubles for everyone,' the second twin said.

As the waiter departed, the first twin scowled, leaned over the table, almost touching Buchanan, and whispered hoarsely, 'No more bullshit, Señor Potter,' the first time he'd used Buchanan's pseudonym. 'What do you want from us? This is your one and only chance.' He reached toward the napkin that covered his lap and patted his pistol. 'Give us a reason not to kill you.'

3

The briefing had been at a safe site in Fairfax, Virginia, an apartment on the second story of a sprawling complex into which Buchanan could easily blend. He had rented it under his then pseudonym of Brian MacDonald. He had a driver's license, a passport, a birth certificate, and several credit cards in that name as well as a detailed fictional background for that temporary identity. His telephone bills indicated that he phoned a number in Philadelphia every Sunday evening, and if anyone investigating Brian MacDonald had called that number, a cheery female receptionist would have answered, 'Golden Years Retirement Home.' That establishment did in fact exist, a profitable cover organization for Buchanan's employers, and its records indicated that a Mrs MacDonald, Brian's 'mother,' was in residence. She wasn't in her room at the moment, but she'd be pleased to return a call, and soon an elderly woman who worked for Buchanan's employers *would* return the call, the destination of which would of course be traced, the conversation recorded.

Buchanan's fictitious occupation at that time, three months earlier, had been that of a computer programmer. He had an interest in and talent for computers, so that part of his assumed identity was easy to establish. He worked at home, he told anyone who happened to ask, and the powerful IBM in his apartment, supplied by his employers, validated his claim. As a further proof of his bogus identity, each Thursday he sent backup computer disks via Federal Express to New Age Technology in Boston, another profitable cover organization for Buchanan's employers, but to maintain the skills of his true occupation, each evening for three hours he exercised at the local Gold's Gym.

Mostly he waited, trying to be patient, maintaining discipline, eager to do his real work. So when an executive from New Age Technology at last phoned, announced that he'd be in Fairfax on business, and wondered if he could pay a visit, Buchanan thought, *Soon. Soon I'll be useful. Soon I won't be bored.*

His controller knocked on the door on schedule. That was

four p.m. on a Friday, and when Buchanan-MacDonald glanced through the door's security eye, then let him in, the short, gaunt man in a rumpled suit placed his briefcase on the living room's coffee table, waited for Buchanan-MacDonald to close and bolt the entrance, then studied his surroundings and asked, 'Which would you prefer? To go for a walk or stay here?'

'The apartment's clean.'

'Good.' The hollow-cheeked controller opened his briefcase. 'I need your driver's license, your passport, your birth certificate, your credit cards, all of your documents for Brian MacDonald. Here are the release forms for you to sign, and here's my signed receipt.'

Buchanan complied.

'Now here are your further documents,' the thin-lipped controller continued, 'and the acceptance form for you to sign. Your new name is Edward Potter. You used to be employed as a . . . Well, it's all in this file. Every detail of your new background. Knowing how retentive your memory is, I assume that as usual you'll be able to absorb the information by the time I come back to retrieve the file tomorrow morning. What's wrong?'

'What took you so long to get in touch with me?' Buchanan asked. 'It's been two months.'

'After your last assignment, we wanted you to disappear for a while. Also we thought we'd have a use for you as Brian MacDonald. Now that scenario's been discarded. We've got a much more interesting project for you. I think you'll be pleased. It's as important as it is risky. It'll give you quite a rush.'

'Tell me about it.'

His controller studied him. 'I sometimes forget how intense field operatives can be, how anxious they are to . . . But then, of course, that's why you're field operatives. Because . . .'

'Because? I've asked myself that many times. What's the answer?'

'I should have thought that was obvious. You enjoy being someone else.'

'Yes. Exactly. So indulge me. Pretend I'm a method actor. What's my new character's motivation?'

4

In the restaurant in Cancun's Club Internacional, Buchanan showed no fear when the first twin threatened him. Instead he replied matter-of-factly, 'Give you a reason not to kill me? I can give you several million of them.'

'We have many millions as it is,' the first twin said. 'What makes you think a few more would make us risk trusting you?'

'Human nature. No matter how much money a person has, it's never enough. Besides,' Buchanan said, 'I didn't offer a *few* million. I offered *several*.'

'Hard to spend in prison. Impossible to spend in the grave,' the second twin said. 'The practical response to your offer is to eliminate your interference. We resent a competitor, and we have no need for a partner.'

In the background, the drone of conversing diners muffled their exchange.

'That's just the point,' Buchanan said, still showing no apprehension. 'I don't want to be your competitor, and you do need a partner.'

The second twin bristled. 'You have the nerve to tell us what we need. Your eggs are truly hardboiled.'

'But they can be cracked,' the first twin growled.

'Definitely,' Buchanan said. 'I knew the danger when I set up shop here.'

'Not only here, but in Mérida, Acapulco, and Puerto

Vallarta,' the second twin said angrily.

'Plus a few other resorts where you apparently don't know I've established contacts.'

The first twin's eyes narrowed, emphasizing their hawklike intensity. 'You have the impudence to brag to our faces.'

'No.' Buchanan shook his head emphatically. 'I'm not bragging. I'm being candid. I hope you'll appreciate my honesty. I assure you, I'm not being disrespectful.'

The twins considered his apology, frowned at each other, nodded with sullen reluctance, and leaned back in their chairs.

'But by your own admission, you've been extremely industrious,' the second twin said. 'And at *our* expense.'

'How else could I have attracted your attention?' Buchanan spread his hands deferentially. 'Consider the risk *I* took, a *norteamericano*, suddenly conducting business not only in Mexico, but in your backyard, in your country's resorts, especially here in Cancun. Even with my special knowledge, I had no idea who to approach. Fernandez, I suspected you,' Buchanan told the first man. 'But I had no idea you had a twin, and to tell the truth' – Buchanan switched his attention to the second man – 'I don't know which of you is Fernandez. When you entered this restaurant, I confess I was stunned. *Gemelos*. Twins. That explains so much. It was never clear to me how Fernandez could be in two places, Mérida and Acapulco, for example, at one time.'

The first man twisted his thin lips in what passed for a grin. 'That was our intention. To cause confusion.' Abruptly he sobered. 'But how did you know that even one of us had the first name of Fernandez?' He spoke with increasing speed and ferocity. 'What is this special information to which you refer? When our subordinates paid you our courtesy of warning you to stop interfering with our business, *why did you ask for this meeting and give our subordinates the names on this sheet of paper?*'

36

To demonstrate, the first twin reached into his wrinkled, linen suit coat and produced a folded page. He slapped it onto the table. 'The names on this paper are some of our most trusted associates.'

'Well' – Buchanan shrugged – 'that just goes to show.'

'Show *what*?'

'How mistaken you can be about trusted associates.'

'Fucker of your mother, what are you talking about?' the second twin demanded.

So the bait really worked, Buchanan thought. I'm in! I've got their attention! Hell, they wouldn't have both shown up if they weren't afraid. That list of names spooked them more than I hoped.

'What am I talking about?' Buchanan said. 'I'm talking about why you should trust me instead of those bastards. I used to belong to the . . .'

Again Buchanan coughed in warning.

The twins stiffened as their waiter returned, carrying a tray from which he set onto the table a plate of sliced limes, a bowl of salt, a small spoon, and six shot glasses filled with amber tequila.

'*Gracias*,' Buchanan said. 'Give us ten minutes before we order dinner.'

He used the tiny, metal spoon to place salt on his left hand, on the web of skin between his thumb and first finger. '*Salud*,' he told the twins. He licked the salt from his hand, quickly swallowed the contents of one of the glasses, and as quickly bit into a slice of lime. The sour juice of the lime spurted over his tongue, mixing with the sweet taste of the tequila and the bitterness of the salt, the various flavors combining perfectly. His mouth puckered slightly. His eyes almost watered.

'Never mind drinking to *our* health. Just worry about yours,' the first twin said.

'I'm not worried,' Buchanan said. 'I think we're going to

have a productive relationship.' He watched them lick salt, swallow tequila, and chew on wedges of lime.

Immediately they placed more salt on their hands and waited for him to do the same.

As Buchanan complied, it occurred to him that his was one of the few occupations in which the consumption of alcohol was a mandatory requirement. His opponents wouldn't trust anyone who didn't drink with them, the implication being that an abstainer had something to hide. So it was necessary to consume quantities of alcohol, for the purpose of gaining trust from those opponents. By vigilant practice, Buchanan had learned the limit of his tolerance for alcohol, just as he'd learned how believably to pretend that he'd exceeded that tolerance and to convince his opponents that he was drunk and hence saying the truth.

The narrow-faced twins raised their second glass of tequila, clearly expecting Buchanan to do the same. Their dark eyes glowed with the anticipation that he would soon lose control and reveal a weakness.

'You were saying,' the first twin said, 'that you suspect the loyalty of our associates because you used to belong to . . .'

5

'The Drug Enforcement Administration,' Buchanan's controller had told him three months earlier. They'd sat opposite each other in the living room of the safe-site apartment in the sprawling complex in Fairfax, Virginia. Between them, on the coffee table, the gray-haired controller had spread documents, the details of Buchanan's new identity, what was known in the trade as his legend. 'You have to convince your targets that you used to be a special agent for the DEA.'

Buchanan, who was already assuming the characteristics of Edward Potter, deciding how the man would dress and what foods he preferred, pressed the tips of his fingers together almost prayerlike and raised them meditatively to his chin. 'Keep talking.'

'You wanted to know your character's motivation? Well, basically he's sick of seeing the war against drug dealers turn into a joke. He thinks the government hasn't provided sufficient funds to prove that it's serious about fighting the war. He's disgusted with CIA interference whenever the DEA gets close to the really big dealers. According to your new character, those big dealers are on the CIA payroll, supplying information about the politics in the volatile Third World countries from which they get their product. So naturally the CIA clamps down on the DEA whenever one of the agency's informants steps in shit.'

'Well, that part won't be hard to fake. The CIA does have the biggest Third World dealers on its payroll,' Buchanan said.

'Absolutely. However, that's about to change. Those Third World dealers have become too smug. The information they've been supplying isn't worth squat. They think they can take the agency's money, do virtually nothing in return, and in effect give the agency the finger. Apparently they didn't learn from our invasion of Panama.'

'Of course not,' Buchanan said. 'After we grabbed Noriega, other dealers took his place. Nothing changed, except children starved to death because of the economic embargo.'

'Good. You're beginning to sound like your new personality,' Buchanan-Potter's controller said.

'Hey, I lost friends in the Panama invasion. At the start, I believed the invasion was necessary. But when I saw the pathetic follow-up – *why doesn't the American government do things all the way?* – I wanted to vomit.'

39

'Even better. You're convincing me, and I know you're acting, so obviously you've got a damned fine chance of convincing your targets.'

'But I'm not acting.'

'Buchanan, give it a rest, okay? We've got a lot of details to cover. So save your method-acting techniques until later.'

'Don't call me "Buchanan." My name is Edward Potter.'

'Sure, right, Edward. Maybe it'll give you further motivation to know that your assignment is intended to compensate for the half-hearted follow-up to what happened in Panama. Your ultimate objective is to scare the living beJesus out of the agency's Third World drug-lord informants who still make jokes about the American lives lost in the useless invasion of Panama.'

'No. That's Buchanan's motivation. I don't want to hear that. I don't want my mind to be contaminated. Just tell me about Edward Potter. What's *his* motivation?'

The pallid controller lowered his head, shook it, and sighed. 'I have to tell you, Buchanan—'

'Potter.'

' —sometimes you worry me. Sometimes I think you absorb yourself too much in your assumed identities.'

'But you're not risking your ass if I forget who the hell I'm supposed to be. So don't fool with my life. From now on, talk to me with the assumption that I'm Edward Potter.'

Again the controller sighed. 'Whatever you want, Edward. Your wife divorced you because you were too devoted to your job and not enough to her and your two sons. She remarried. Because of the numerous threats you've received from drug dealers, she asked for and was granted a court order that forbids you to come anywhere near her and your children without prior approval from her and without guarantees of safety. Her new husband earns two hundred thousand a year as an owner of several health spas. You, by comparison, earn a

40

paltry forty thousand, or rather used to earn that amount, a salary that's especially humiliating in contrast with the millions earned by the scum you arrested and saw released on bail and eventually plea-bargained to a short-term sentence in a minimum-security prison. You're convinced that if you'd accepted the bribes you were offered, your wife would have been satisfied with a new house, et cetera, and wouldn't have left you. When everything you believed in collapsed, you got pissed. You decided that by God, if you couldn't beat the drug lords, you'd join them. You'd show your fucking wife that you could earn a hundred times as much as her faggot new husband. *Your* dick was bigger than his.'

'Yes,' Buchanan-Potter said. 'My dick *is* bigger.'

The controller stared. 'Amazing.'

Buchanan-Potter's cheek muscles hardened. 'So how do I get even?'

6

'*You used to be an agent for the Drug Enforcement Administration?*' In the restaurant in Cancun's Club Internacional, the first Hispanic twin spoke softly yet with paradoxical force. Shocked, he and his brother jerked back in their chairs.

'Take it easy,' Buchanan said. 'I'm on *your* side now.'

'Certainly,' the second twin said derisively. 'By all means. Of course.'

'And you truly expect us to believe this?' the first twin demanded. 'To accept that you're a defector and to trust you?'

'It's not as if I haven't made a gesture of good faith,' Buchanan said. 'That folded sheet of paper beneath your hand. If you put pressure on the Bahamian bank officials you hire to launder money, you'll find that the supposedly loyal associates

I mentioned on that list all have secret, offshore bank accounts. Now I realize that graft is a way of life down here. But I think you'll agree that the amounts your supposedly loyal associates put away for a rainy day are considerably higher than payoffs and kickbacks alone would explain.'

The second twin squinted. 'Assuming for the moment that your information is correct . . .'

'Oh, it is. That goes without saying. After all, I'm guaranteeing it with the best collateral imaginable.'

'And what is that?' The first twin tapped his fingers on the table.

'My life. If I'm lying about those bank accounts – and it won't be hard for you to discover if I am – you'll have me killed.'

'But in the meantime, perhaps you'll be able to accomplish whatever you intend and drop out of sight before we can get our hands on you.' The second twin squinted more severely.

'What could I possibly accomplish?' Buchanan gestured. 'Until you investigate the men on that list and decide if my information is valuable, you won't let me into your confidence. You won't do business with me.'

'We might not do business with you, even if you're telling the truth.' The first twin kept tapping his fingers on the table.

'There's always that possibility.' Buchanan shrugged. 'But the way I see it, I'm taking all the risks and you're taking none. Certainly there's nothing risky about your meeting me here – at a mutually agreeable, neutral place – for drinks and dinner. At the worst, you've been inconvenienced. From *my* point of view, however, at the worst, I get dead.'

Without looking at each other, the twins seemed to reach a mutual conclusion.

'*Exactamente.*' The second twin turned toward the half-filled restaurant, caught their waiter's attention, pointed toward the glasses on their table, held up two fingers, and then waved his hand in a circle, indicating he wanted another round of tequila, doubles for everyone. Seeing the waiter nod, he pivoted toward Buchanan. 'You interrupted before I could finish my earlier question.'

'*Perdón*. So ask it now.'

'Assuming you're telling the truth about these offshore bank accounts, how do you explain the considerable amounts you claim our associates have hidden from us? What is the source of those funds? They must be bribes from drug-enforcement officers for supplying information. Because the only other explanation would be that they're stealing a portion of our merchandise or else the money we collect, and I assure you we can account for every kilo we send to the United States and every dollar we get back.'

Buchanan shook his head. 'Bribes alone won't explain the tremendous sums in these offshore accounts. As you're aware, drug-enforcement officers have never been known for being overly generous with their bribes. Their budget's stretched too thin. But as it happens, you're wrong about having protected yourselves against theft. Your men are running an extremely sophisticated skim operation.'

'*What?*' The second twin looked stunned. '*No es posible.*'

'It's not only possible. It's a fact.'

'I'm telling you, we'd know!'

'Not this way. Not the way they're doing it. They're using rogue DEA officers to help them skim. How many shipments did you lose last year? An approximate percentage. Ten percent?'

'More or less,' the first twin said. 'It's inevitable that some of our shipments will be discovered. Couriers get nervous and make mistakes. Or DEA officers happen to be at the right place at the right time. We expect a certain percentage of losses. It goes with the business.'

'But what if some of those couriers weren't as nervous as

they pretended?' Buchanan asked. 'And what if those DEA officers had advance warning to be at the right place at the right time? And what if those couriers and DEA officers were in business for themselves?'

As the waiter brought the second round of drinks, the group became silent. The moment the waiter departed, they assessed the restaurant's customers, assured themselves that no one was close enough to overhear, then faced each other, raising glasses, going through the ritual of consuming salt, tequila, and lime.

'Finish what you were saying.' The first twin clearly hoped that the alcohol would affect Buchanan's judgment and reveal a weakness.

'Their system's quite clever.' Buchanan set down the slice of lime from which he'd chewed. 'The rogue agents from the DEA have to satisfy their superiors that they're doing their job. So they surrender a portion of what they confiscate. Then the government brags about how it's winning the war on drugs, and the American television networks report the latest victory on the evening news. But what the government doesn't know, and of course the American public, is that other shipments were confiscated and that *those* shipments were sold to American drug dealers. The money from those sales – millions – is divided between the rogue DEA officers and the trusted associates you've put in charge of sending the shipments. As far as you're concerned, those shipments have been accounted for. By your own admission, you expect those losses. As long as you receive your usual profit, why would you think you were being cheated?'

Both twins glowered.

'*How do you know this?*' the second twin rasped.

'Because, as I told you, I used to belong to the DEA. I wasn't on the take. I was one of the good guys. That's how I thought of myself, dummy that I was. I did my job. But I'm not blind. I

44

saw what was going on. The thing is, drug enforcement is the same as any other police work. You don't turn against your fellow officers. If you do, they have ways to make your life a nightmare. So I had to keep quiet. And then . . .'

Scowling, Buchanan gulped his further glass of tequila.

'Yes? And then?' The second twin leaned toward him.

'That's none of your business.'

'With respect, given our reason for meeting here, it's very much our business.'

'I had personal problems,' Buchanan said.

'Don't we all? We're men of the world. We understand personal problems only too well. There's no need to be defensive. Unburden yourself. It's good for the soul. What problems could have . . . ?'

'I prefer not to talk about it.' Buchanan made his elbow slip off the table, as if the tequila had started to work on him. 'I've told you what I came to say. You know how to reach me. Use your contacts to investigate your associates' offshore bank accounts. When you find out I was telling the truth, I hope you'll decide that the three of us can cooperate.'

With heart-stopping recognition, Buchanan glanced toward the stairs that led down to the restaurant and noticed a man, an American, in company with an Hispanic woman who wore a revealing dress and too much makeup, approach a waiter and ask for a table. The American was in his forties, tall, with extremely broad shoulders and a bulky chest, his sandy hair trimmed upward in a brush cut. His ample stomach protruded against his too-small, green T-shirt and hung over the waist on his low-slung jeans. He wore sneakers and puffed on a cigarette as he gave orders to the waiter.

Oh, Jesus, Buchanan thought. His mind raced. *How am I going to—?*

The first twin shook his head. 'Too many things about you trouble us.'

45

Desperate to avoid the man who'd entered the restaurant, Buchanan concentrated on his targets.

'Crawford!' a booming voice called.

Buchanan ignored it. 'What exactly troubles you?'

'Crawford! By Jesus, long time no see!' The booming voice cracked crustily and became a smoker's cough.

Buchanan continued to direct his attention straight toward his targets.

'Crawford!' the voice boomed louder. 'Have you gone deaf? Don't you hear me? Where by Jesus did you get to after Iraq?' The voice was made more conspicuous because of its heavy, drawling Texas accent. 'When they flew us to Germany and we touched down in Frankfurt, I wanted to buy you a drink to celebrate gettin' out of that Arab hell hole. But one minute you was there in the terminal with all them officials greetin' us and reporters aimin' their cameras. The next minute you dropped out of sight like one of our broken drill bits down a dry well.'

The drawling voice boomed so close that Buchanan couldn't possibly pretend to ignore it. He shifted his gaze from his fidgeting targets toward the looming, sun-and-alcohol-reddened face of the beefy American.

'I beg your pardon?' Buchanan asked.

'Crawford. Don't you recognize your ol' buddy? This is Big Bob Bailey talkin' to you. Come on, you can't have forgotten *me*. We was prisoners together in Kuwait City and Baghdad. Jesus, who'd have ever figured that nutcase would actually believe he could get away with invadin' Kuwait? I've worked my share of tough jobs, but when those Iraqi tanks pulled onto our drillin' site, I don't mind admittin' I was so shittin' scared I . . .'

Buchanan shook his head in confusion.

'Crawford, have you got post trauma whatever the hell the shrinks who talked to me in Germany called it? Have you been drinkin' more than *I* have? This is Big Bob Bailey speakin' to

46

you. We and a bunch of other American oil workers was held hostages together.'

'I'm pleased to meet you, Bob,' Buchanan said. 'But apparently you've confused me with someone else.'

The twins watched Buchanan intensely.

'Give me a break. Your name is Crawford,' the beefy American said. 'Jim Crawford.'

'Nope. Sorry. My name's Ed Potter.'

'But—'

'Honestly I'm not Jim Crawford. I'm Ed Potter, and I've never seen you before. Whoever Jim Crawford is, I must resemble him.'

'More than resemble, and that's a damned fact.'

'But you're mistaken. I'm not him.'

The twins watched Buchanan with greater intensity.

'Well, I'll be a . . .' The American looked uneasy, his sun-and-alcohol-reddened face becoming redder with embarrassment. 'Sorry, pal. I would have sworn . . . I must have been partyin' too much. Here, let me make up for interruptin' and buy you and your friends a drink. Honest to God, I didn't mean to bother you.' The American backed off, staggering slightly as he retreated.

'No problem,' Buchanan said.

7

But it *was* a problem. A *big* problem. One of the nightmares Buchanan dreaded was the risk that a contact from a previous assignment would wander into a present one. Twice in Buchanan's career, fellow specialists had happened to enter locations (a pub in London, a cafe in Paris) where Buchanan was using false identities to recruit informants who might help him infiltrate terrorist networks. In each case, Buchanan had noticed the subtle look of recognition in his fellow operative's eyes. Briefly, Buchanan had felt nervous. However, his counterpart – obeying an absolute rule of tradecraft – had ignored Buchanan and soon, when it seemed natural, had left the location.

But while Buchanan could count on the tact of a professional, there was no way to guard against the spontaneity of a civilian whom he'd encountered on another mission, a civilian who had no idea of Buchanan's true occupation. The beefy American – now retreating in confusion to a table where his female escort waited – had indeed known Buchanan in Kuwait City as well as in Baghdad, and Buchanan's name at that time had indeed been Jim Crawford. Prior to the Allied counterstrike, Buchanan had been inserted at night via a high-altitude, low-opening parachute drop into Kuwait to reconnoitre Iraqi defenses. Buchanan had buried his jump equipment in the desert, then hiked through the dark toward the lights of Kuwait City. He wore civilian clothes – a soiled workshirt and jeans – and carried documents that identified him as an American oil worker from Oklahoma. If stopped, his cover story would be that he'd gone into hiding when the Iraqis invaded. His scraggly beard, unkempt hair, and haggard appearance would reinforce that story. For three weeks, aided by Allied sympathizers, he was able to use a small, two-way radio to broadcast important information to his superiors, but prior to his extraction by submarine, an Iraqi patrol had discovered him on the way to the beach.

It wasn't any wonder that Big Bob Bailey shook his head in confusion as he joined his female escort at a table in the restaurant. After all, Buchanan had spent a month with Bailey and other captive oil workers, first in the confinement of a demolished, Kuwait City hotel, then in one of several trucks that transported the Americans from Kuwait to Iraq, and finally in a warehouse in Baghdad.

Saddam Hussein eventually set free the Americans 'as a Christmas present to the United States.' They were flown via Iraqi Airlines to various destinations, one of which was Frankfurt, Germany. Big Bob Bailey sat next to Buchanan during the latter flight. Big Bob Bailey chattered endlessly, with nervous relief, about how when they touched down he intended to get good and drunk with his good ol' pal, Jim Crawford. But when they entered the terminal, Jim Crawford disappeared among the crowd, shielded by plain-clothed, Special Operations personnel who hurried Buchanan to a safe site and intensely debriefed him.

That had been twelve assignments ago, however, and Big Bob Bailey had become just another vaguely remembered contact to whom Buchanan had played one of his numerous roles.

Big Bob Bailey. Damn it, he was from another life. From several lives past. Iraq's invasion of Kuwait was ancient history. Big Bob Bailey was just a minor character in . . .

But at the moment, Big Bob Bailey was very much a major character in *this* life, Buchanan thought in dismay.

And Big Bob Bailey wouldn't stop looking over at Buchanan, all the while squinting and shaking his head as if he wasn't just confused now but angry, convinced that Buchanan *was* Jim Crawford and insulted because Buchanan wouldn't admit it.

Jesus, Buchanan thought, he looks pissed off enough that he might come over again! If he does, my cover will be absolutely destroyed. These two Mexican drug distributors didn't stay alive this long by being idiots. Check their eyes. They're already wondering what's going on. I've got to . . .

'I guess it's a variation on an old joke,' he told the first twin. 'South of the border, all Americans look alike, sometimes even to each other.'

'Yes,' the first twin replied.

'Very amusing,' the second twin said flatly.

'But he certainly attracted attention to us,' Buchanan continued.

'I think the sooner we get out of here, the better,' the second twin said. 'Especially before that man comes back here, which I suspect he's about to do.'

'Fine with me. Let's go.' Buchanan stood to walk toward the stairs that led up from the restaurant.

'No, *this* way,' the second twin said. He touched Buchanan's arm and gestured toward the rear entrance, a sliding glass door that gave access to the hotel's night-shrouded gardens.

'Good idea,' Buchanan said. 'It's faster. Less conspicuous.' He signaled the waiter that he'd left money on the table and turned toward the glass door.

As Buchanan stepped from the restaurant into the humid, fragrant gardens, as he heard the glass door being slid shut behind him, he noticed that the twins had positioned themselves on either side of him. He noticed as well that they held the napkins beneath which each had earlier concealed a pistol in his lap, and the napkins didn't look empty. Finally, he noticed a piece of the night step from between tall bushes to the left of the door, bushes that would have given the bodyguard a hidden view through the glass while Buchanan spoke with the twins.

The bodyguard was Hispanic, unusually tall and large-boned.

Like the twins, he held a pistol. Hard to tell in the shadows, but it looked like a Beretta 9-millimeter equipped with a sound-suppressor.

And imitating the expression on his employers' faces, the bodyguard scowled.

'Who the fuck *are* you?' the first twin demanded, jabbing Buchanan's chest.

'Hey, what are you—?' Buchanan tried to object.

'We're too close to the windows of the restaurant. Someone inside will see,' the second twin cautioned his brother. 'We need to go down to the beach.'

'Yes,' the first twin said. 'The beach. The fucking beach.'

'*Todavía no*. Not yet,' the bodyguard warned. He unhooked a handheld metal detector from his belt and quickly but thoroughly scanned it over Buchanan.

The metal detector beeped three times.

'His belt buckle. His keys. A pen,' the bodyguard said, not needing to explain that the buckle might conceal a knife, that the keys and pen could be used as weapons.

'Take off your belt,' the first twin ordered Buchanan. 'Drop your keys and the pen on the ground.'

'What's wrong? I don't understand,' Buchanan insisted.

The second twin showed his pistol, a Browning 9-millimeter. 'Do what you're told.'

The bodyguard jabbed his Beretta into Buchanan's left kidney. '*Rápido. Ahora*. Now.'

Buchanan complied, removing his belt, dropping it along with his keys and his pen.

The first twin snatched them up.

The second twin shoved Buchanan away from the restaurant toward the gardens.

The bodyguard kept the Beretta low, inconspicuous, and followed.

The gardens were spacious, filled with flowering shrubs, trickling pools, and meandering paths. Here and there, small lights of various colors projected from the ground, illuminating the walkways, tinting the shrubs, reflecting off the pools. Nonetheless, compared to the glare from the windows of the towering hotel, the garden was cloaked in darkness. Anyone who happened to look out would see merely the vague, moving shadows of four men out for a stroll, Buchanan thought. Certainly an observer wouldn't be able to see that three of the men held pistols by their sides. Not that it mattered. If anyone did see the weapons and felt compelled to phone the police, whatever was going to happen would have ended by the time the police arrived.

As Buchanan proceeded along a walkway toward the splash of waves on the beach, he assessed his options. One was to take advantage of the garden's darkness, overpower his captors, and escape, using the shrubs for cover in case any of his captors survived his attack and starting shooting. Or at least Buchanan could *attempt* to escape. The problem was that his captors would be anticipating the likelihood of his using the darkness. They'd be primed for a sudden movement, and as soon as he made one, he'd be shot. The sound-suppressor on the bodyguard's Beretta would prevent anyone in the hotel from hearing the weapon's report. By the time Buchanan's corpse was discovered, the three Hispanics would be far from the area.

That wasn't the only problem, Buchanan thought. If he did manage to catch the Hispanics by surprise, the darkness that initially helped him might then work against him. All he needed to do was collide with an unseen object as he fought with his captors. If he lost his balance . . .

But a further problem — and the one to which Buchanan

gave the most importance – was that the Hispanics might be threatening him merely to test him. After all, he couldn't expect the twins to believe his cover story simply because his manner of presenting it was confident and convincing. They'd need all sorts of proof about his authenticity. *All* sorts. Every detail of his fictitious background would bear up under investigation. Buchanan's controllers had made sure of that. A female operative was posing as Ed Potter's ex-wife. A male operative was posing as her new husband. Each had a well-documented fictitious background, and each had been coached about what to say if anyone asked questions. Certain members of the DEA were prepared to claim that they'd known Ed Potter when he was an agent. In addition, the details of Ed Potter's DEA career had been planted in a dossier in government computers.

But perhaps Buchanan's opponents would take the solidity of his cover story for granted. Then what other way did they have to verify his authenticity? The more Buchanan thought about it, the more the issue became: were the twins truly furious or only pretending to be? Would the twins question his credibility just because a drunken American had claimed to have known him as Jim Crawford, or was it more likely that the twins would take advantage of the drunken American's claim and use it as a pretense for intimidating Buchanan, for trying their best to frighten him, for doing their damnedest to find a weakness in his confidence?

Layers within layers. Nothing was ever self-evident, Buchanan thought in turmoil, as his captors nudged him along a path toward the muted lights of an outdoor bar at the edge of the beach.

The bar had a sloping, thatched roof supported by wooden pillars. There weren't any walls. Bamboo tables and chairs surrounded the oval counter, giving several groups of drinkers a view of white-capped waves in the darkness. Sections of the

53

hotel bordered the gardens, so that the only way for Buchanan and his captors to get to the beach was to pass near the bar.

'Do not expect those people to help you,' the first twin murmured on Buchanan's right as they neared the bar. 'If you make a commotion, we will shoot you in front of them. They do not matter to us.'

'They are drunk, and we are in shadows. As witnesses, they are useless,' the second twin added on Buchanan's left.

'And they cannot see my pistol. I have covered it with my jacket. But be assured I am aiming it at your spine,' the bodyguard said behind Buchanan.

'Hey, let's lighten up, okay? I'm missing something here. Why all this talk about shooting?' Buchanan asked. 'I wish the three of you would relax and tell me what's going on. I came to you in good faith. I wasn't armed. I'm not a threat to you. But all of a sudden, you—'

'Shut up while we pass the people in the bar,' the first twin murmured in Spanish.

'Or the next words you speak will be your last,' the second twin said. '*Entiende*? Understand?'

'Your logic is overwhelming,' Buchanan said.

A few tourists glanced up from their margaritas as Buchanan and the others walked by. Then one of the tourists finished telling a joke, and everybody at that table laughed.

The nearby outburst in reaction to the joke was so loud and unexpected that it made the twins flinch and jerk their heads toward the noise. Presumably the bodyguard was also surprised. There wasn't any way for Buchanan to know for certain. Still, the odds were in his favor. He could have done it then. He could have taken advantage of the distraction, smashed the side of his hands against the larynx of each twin, kicked backward with his left foot angled sideways to break the bodyguard's knee, and spun to snap the wrist that held the Beretta. He could have done all that in less than two seconds.

The light from the bar made him able to see clearly enough that he wouldn't have had to worry about the accuracy of his blows. The agonizing damage to the throats of the twins would have prevented them from breathing. In their panic to fill their lungs with air, they would not have had time to think about shooting Buchanan, not before he'd finished the bodyguard and swung back to finish them. That would have taken another second or two. All told, four seconds, max, and Buchanan would have been safe.

But as confident as he was of success, Buchanan didn't do it. Because his safety wasn't the point. If all he cared about was his safety, he wouldn't have accepted this mission in the first place. The mission. *That* was the point. As the laughter of the tourists subsided, as the twins and their bodyguard regained their discipline, as Buchanan and his captors finished passing the bar and reached the murky beach, Buchanan told himself, How would you have explained it to your superiors? I can imagine the expression on their faces if you told them the mission failed because you got so nervous you killed your contacts. Your career would be over. This isn't the first time someone's aimed a pistol at you. You know damned well that on this assignment it would have happened sooner or later. These guys aren't dummies. Plus, they'll never trust you until they learn if you can handle stress. So let them find out. Be cool. Play out the role.

But what would Ed Potter do? Buchanan wondered. Wouldn't a corrupt ex-DEA officer try to escape if he thought the drug distributors from whom he was taking business had decided that killing him was less risky and less trouble than becoming partners with him?

Maybe, Buchanan thought. Ed Potter *might* try to run. After all, he isn't me. He doesn't have my training. But if I behave the way Ed Potter truly would, there's a good chance I'll get myself killed. I've got to modify the character. Right now, my audience is testing me for weakness.

But by God, they won't find any.

Club Internacional had a sidewalk that ran parallel to the beach. The stars were brilliant, although the moon had not yet risen. A cool breeze came off the ocean out of the darkness. Hearing the distant echo of more laughter from the bar, which was shielded from him by a row of tall shrubs and a waist-high wall, Buchanan paused at the edge of the sidewalk.

'All right,' he said. 'Here's the beach. It's nice. Real nice. Now would you put those guns away and tell me what in God's name this is all about? I haven't done anything to—'

10

'God's name?' the first twin asked and shoved Buchanan off the sidewalk onto the sand. 'Yes, a name. *Many* names. *That's* what this is all about. Ed Potter. Jim Crawford.'

Buchanan felt his shoes sink into the sand and spun to face the twins as well as their bodyguard, where they stood slightly above him on the sidewalk. 'Hey, just because some drunk thinks he knows me? Haven't *you* ever been mistaken for—?'

'The only person I have ever been mistaken for is my brother,' the second twin said. 'I do not believe in coincidence. I do not believe that in the middle of a conversation about my business and my safety, I can ignore anyone — drunk or not — who interrupts to tell me the man I am speaking to is not the man he claims to be.'

'Come on! That drunk admitted he was wrong!' Buchanan insisted.

'*But he did not look convinced,*' the first twin snapped.

Two murky silhouettes approached along the beach. Buchanan and his antagonists became silent. The Hispanics stiffened, wary. Then the silhouettes walked near enough for

Buchanan to see a man and a woman – American, early twenties – holding hands. The couple seemed oblivious to their surroundings, conscious only of each other. They passed and disappeared into the darkness farther along the beach.

'We can't stay here,' the second twin said. 'Other people will come. We're still too close to the hotel, especially to the bar.'

'But I want this matter settled,' the first twin said. 'I want it settled *now*.'

The bodyguard scanned the beach and pointed. '*Por allí*. Over there.'

Buchanan looked. Near the white-capped waves, he saw, were the distinctive outlines of several *palapa* sun shelters. Each small structure had a slanted, circular top made from palm fronds and held up by a seven-foot-tall, wooden post. Plastic tables and chairs, as white as the caps on the waves, were distributed among them.

'Yes,' the first twin said. 'Over there.'

The Hispanic stepped from the concrete onto the sand and shoved Buchanan hard enough that Ed Potter could not have resisted the thrust, so Buchanan allowed himself to stumble backward.

'Move! Damn you and your mother, move!' the first twin said.

Continuing to stumble, Buchanan turned toward the deserted shelters. Immediately the Hispanic shoved him again, and Buchanan lurched, concentrating to maintain his balance, his shoes slipping in the sand.

The effect of adrenaline made his stomach seem on fire. He wondered if he'd been right not to defend himself earlier. Things had not yet gotten out of control. But the first twin was working himself into a rage. The insults and shoves were occurring more forcefully, more often, and Buchanan had to ask himself, Is this an act? Or is it for real?

If he's acting, I'll fail the test by ignoring some of those insults. If this guy shoves me any harder, if I don't anticipate and absorb the impact, he'll knock me down. He'll dismiss me as unworthy of respect if I don't make a pretense of resisting.

But how much resistance can I show and still be Ed Potter? And how much resistance is enough to satisfy the twin without truly making him angry?

And—

The question kept nagging at Buchanan.

—*what if this is for real?*

As Buchanan reached a shelter, the first twin shoved him again, knocking him across a plastic table.

Buchanan straightened and spun. 'Now that's enough! Don't shove me again! If you've got questions, *ask* them. I'll explain whatever's bothering you. I can settle this misunderstanding! But damn it, keep your hands off me!'

'Keep my hands off you?' The first twin stepped close to Buchanan, grabbed Buchanan's shirt and twisted it with his fist, then raised the shirt so that Buchanan felt suspended by it. 'What I'd like to do is shove my hand down your throat and pull out your guts.'

Buchanan smelled the tequila on his breath.

Abruptly the twin released his grip on Buchanan's shirt.

Buchanan allowed himself to topple, sprawling again across the table, this time on his back instead of his chest. It took all his discipline to restrain himself from retaliating. He kept reminding himself, The mission. You can't jeopardize the mission. You can't fight back until you're certain he intends to kill you. So far all he's done is shove, insult, and threaten you. Those aren't good enough reasons for you to abort the mission by responding with deadly force.

Surrounded by darkness, glimpsing the lights of the hotel beyond the twins and their bodyguard, Buchanan stared up at the first twin, who grabbed him again, jerked him to his feet, and thrust him into a chair. Buchanan's spine banged against

58

the plastic. Waves splashed behind him.

'You promise that you can explain? Then do so. By all means, explain. It will be amusing to hear' – the twin suddenly pressed the muzzle of his Browning 9-millimeter pistol against Buchanan's forehead – 'how you intend to settle what you call this misunderstanding.'

That almost made the difference. Buchanan's pulse quickened. His muscles compacted. Inhaling, he prepared to—

But the twin hasn't cocked the pistol, Buchanan noticed, and the Browning doesn't have a sound-suppressor. If he intends to kill me, isn't it more likely that he'd want to avoid causing a commotion? He'd use the bodyguard's Beretta, which does have a sound-suppressor, so he wouldn't attract a crowd from the bar.

It's still possible that this is an act.

Sweating, mustering resolve, Buchanan watched the second twin approach.

The man stopped beside his brother and peered down. Even in the gloom, his eyes were vividly hawklike. 'Listen carefully,' he told Buchanan. 'We are going to talk about names. But not the name that the drunken American called you in the restaurant. Not Jim Crawford, or at least not only Jim Crawford. And not just Ed Potter. Other names. *Many* other names. In fact, so many that I find it impossible to remember them all.' He pulled a folded piece of paper from his suit coat. 'You gave us a list of names of our associates whom you claim betrayed us. Well, I have a different list, one with other names.' He unfolded the paper and aimed a penlight at it so he could read. 'John Block. Richard Davis. Paul Higgins. Andrew Macintosh. Henry Davenport. Walter Newton. Michael Galer. William Hanover. Stuart Malik.'

Oh, shit, Buchanan thought.

The second twin stopped reading, scowled at the sheet of paper, shook his head, and sighed. 'There are several other names. But those will do for purposes of illustration.' He refolded the piece of paper, returned it to his suit-coat pocket, and at once thrust the penlight close to Buchanan's face, aiming it into Buchanan's right eye.

Buchanan jerked his face away to avoid the light.

But the bodyguard had shifted behind Buchanan and abruptly slammed his hands against the sides of Buchanan's head, making Buchanan's ears ring. The sudden, stunning pressure of the hands was like a vice. Buchanan tried, but he couldn't turn his face away. He couldn't avoid the blinding glare of the slender beam of light aimed into his eye. He reached up to grab the bodyguard's smallest fingers and snap them in order to make the bodyguard release his grip.

But Buchanan froze in mid-gesture as the first twin cocked the Browning, the muzzle of which was now pressed against Buchanan's left temple. Christ, Buchanan thought, he just might do it.

'*Bueno. Muy bueno,*' the first twin said. 'Don't make trouble.'

The penlight kept glaring at Buchanan's eye. He blinked repeatedly, then scrunched his eyelid shut, but could still see the light through the eyelid's thin skin. He scrunched the eyelid shut tighter. A rough hand grabbed the side of his face, clawing at the eyelid, forcing it up. The light again glared. Buchanan's eyeball suddenly felt hot, dry, and swollen. The light felt like a bright, hot needle that threatened to lance his eyeball as if it were a festering boil. Buchanan needed all his self-control not to struggle, not to attempt to break away from the hands that bound him – because he knew without doubt that if he struggled again, the first twin would blow his brains out.

'*Bueno,*' the first twin repeated. '*Muy bueno. Excelente.* Now, if you wish to live, you will tell us what all of those names that my brother read to you have in common. Think well before

60

you answer.' He nudged the muzzle of the Browning harder against Buchanan's temple. 'I cannot respect, do business with, or tolerate a liar. The names. What is their secret?'

Buchanan swallowed. His voice was hoarse. 'They're all me.'

11

Except for the splash of the waves and the pounding of Buchanan's heart, the night became silent. Then, in the distance, laughter echoing from the hotel's outside bar broke the quiet. The twins and the bodyguard seemed frozen. At once they moved, the first twin lowering his pistol, the second twin releasing his grip on Buchanan's right eyelid, then shutting off the penlight, the bodyguard removing his vice-like hands from the sides of Buchanan's head.

The first twin studied Buchanan. 'I did not expect the truth.' He sat on a chair near Buchanan, placing his Browning on the table so its muzzle was pointed at Buchanan, leaving his hand on the weapon. 'I asked you earlier. I'll ask you again. Who *are* you?'

'Ed Potter.' Buchanan closed his right eyelid, massaging it, still seeing the painful glare from the penlight.

'And not John Block? Or Richard Davis? Or Paul Higgins?' the first twin asked.

'Or Jim Crawford?' the second twin insisted.

'I never *heard* of Jim Crawford,' Buchanan said. 'I don't know what the hell that drunk in the restaurant was talking about. But as far as John Block, Richard Davis, and Paul Higgins are concerned, they're . . . How did you find out about my aliases?'

'You do not have the right to ask questions.' The first twin tapped the barrel of his pistol on the table. 'Why did you assume those names?'

'I'm not a fool,' Buchanan said. His right eye watered. He kept it closed and squinted at his captors with his remaining functional eye. 'You expect me to come to Mexico, start smuggling drugs north and weapons south, and use my real name? I'd use a false name if I were dealing drugs in the United States. Here in Mexico, where a *yanqui* is conspicuous, I had all the more reason to use a false name.'

The second twin turned his penlight on and off as if in warning. 'A false name is understandable.'

'But so *many* false names?' The first twin persisted in tapping the side of his pistol on the table.

'Look, I told you I was doing business in more places than Cancun,' Buchanan said. 'I have bases in Mérida, Acapulco, Puerto Vallarta, several resorts I haven't mentioned.'

'But you will,' the second twin said. 'You will.' His voice thickened with emotion. 'The names. I want to hear about these names.'

Buchanan slowly opened his right eye. The glare from the penlight was still seared upon his vision. If his gambit didn't work, they would try to kill him. There'd be a fight (if he was lucky and had the opportunity to try to defend himself), but he didn't have much chance of surviving a struggle against three men while his vision was impaired.

'Answer!' the second twin barked.

'I take it as a given that when an American does illegal business in a foreign country, natives of that country have to be recruited,' Buchanan said. 'Those natives can go places and do things that the American wouldn't dare to without the risk of being conspicuous. The local authorities have to be bribed. The drugs need to be picked up from the suppliers. The weapons need to be delivered to those suppliers. There's no way *I'm* going to try to bribe the Mexican police. Even as bribable as they are, they might decide to make an example of a *gringo* and stick me in jail for a hundred years. I'd just as soon

62

someone else took the risk of picking up the drugs and delivering the weapons, especially when it comes to dealing with those crazy bastards in the Medellín cartel. Let's face it – Mexico's so poor there are plenty of young men who are glad to risk their lives if I pay them what they think is a fortune but what to me is nothing. Of course, I need recruits in every resort where I do business, and while I'm in those resorts, I need a cover story to account for my presence. A tourist attracts attention if he comes back every three weeks. But a businessman doesn't, and one of the most commonplace American businessmen at Mexican resorts is a timeshare condominium salesman. American tourists don't trust Mexican salesmen to lease them real estate. But they'll trust an American. Under assumed names in all the resorts where I have a base, I've convinced the authorities that I'm legitimate. Naturally I use a different name in each resort, and I have false documents in that name. But here's the trick. If my Mexican recruits in each resort get picked up by the police or questioned by suppliers who have turned against me, my recruits don't know the assumed name I'm using. They don't know where I live or where I do business. Except on terms of my own choosing, they have no way to get in touch with me or to lead the police or a drug supplier to me. The name by which each recruit knows me is also assumed, but of course I don't need identification papers for those other names.'

The first twin leaned forward, his hand on his pistol. 'Keep talking.'

'Each of the characters I pretend to be has a particular style of clothes, a preference for different foods, an individual way about him. One might slouch. Another might stand rigidly straight as if he used to be in the military. Another might have a slight stutter. Still another might comb his hair straight back. Or have spectacles. Or wear a baseball cap. There's always something about the character that's memorable. That way, if

63

the police start asking questions about a man with a certain name and certain mannerisms, it'll be difficult to find that man because the mannerisms are as false as the name. I mentioned after that drunken American confused me with someone else back at the restaurant – his mistake is a variation of an old saying that all foreigners look the same to Americans. Well, that saying can be turned around. Most Americans resemble each other as far as Mexicans are concerned. We weigh too much. We're clumsy. We've got too much money, and we're not very generous with it. We're loud. We're rude. So any American who has easy-to-describe, individual characteristics will be remembered by my recruits, and if they're forced to give that description – "he has spectacles and always wears a baseball cap" – to an enemy, all I have to do is assume a different set of characteristics, blend with other Americans, and become invisible.'

Buchanan watched the twins, wondering, Are they buying it?

The first twin frowned. 'Since you use so many false names, how do we know that Ed Potter is your true identity?'

'What motive would I have for lying? I had to tell you my real name or else you wouldn't be able to investigate my background and satisfy yourselves that I'm not a threat to you.'

Buchanan waited, hoping that he'd overcome their misgivings. He'd followed a rule of deep-cover operations. If someone challenges you to the point that you're about to be exposed, the best defense was the truth, or rather a version of the truth, a special slant on it that doesn't compromise the mission and yet sounds so authentic that it defeats skepticism. In this case, Buchanan had established a cover, as he'd explained to the twins, but then he had yet another cover, that of Ed Potter. The latter cover was intended to manipulate the twins into accepting him as a partner. But the false names he used as a time-share condominium salesman in various resorts, and the further false names that he used with his recruits, had not been intended as a way to impress the twins and demonstrate that he would be an asset to them. Rather those false identities had been a way for Buchanan to protect himself against the Mexican government and, equally important, to prevent the Mexican authorities from tracing his illegal activities to a covert branch of the United States military. The last thing Buchanan's controllers wanted was an international incident. Indeed, even if Buchanan were arrested while he was posing as Edward Potter, his activities could still not be traced to his controllers. Because he had yet another cover. He would deny to the authorities that he had ever belonged to the DEA, and in the meantime, his controllers would remove or erase all the supporting details for that assumed identity. Buchanan would claim that he had invented the DEA story in order to infiltrate the drug-distribution system. He would insist, and there would be supporting details for this cover as well, that he was a freelance journalist who wanted to write an exposé about the Mexican drug connection. If the Mexican authorities tried to investigate beyond that cover, they would find nothing that linked Buchanan to U.S. special operations.

'Perhaps,' the first twin said. 'Perhaps we can work together.'

'Perhaps?' Buchanan asked. '*Madre de Dios*, what do I have to do to convince you?'

'First we will investigate your background.'

'By all means,' Buchanan said.

'Then we will determine if some of our associates have betrayed us as you claim.'

'No problem.' Buchanan's chest flooded with triumph. I've turned it around, he thought. Five minutes ago, they were ready to kill me, and I was trying to decide if I'd have to kill them. But I did the right thing. I kept my cool. I talked my way out of it. The mission hasn't been jeopardized.

'You will stay with us while we verify your credentials,' the second twin said.

'Stay with you?'

'Do you have a problem with that?' the first twin asked.

'Not really,' Buchanan said. 'Except that making me a prisoner is a poor way to begin a partnership.'

'Did I say anything about making you a prisoner?' The second twin smiled. 'You will be our guest. Every comfort will be given to you.'

Buchanan forced himself to return the smile. 'Sounds fine with me. I could use a taste of the life style I want to become accustomed to.'

'But there *is* one other matter,' the first twin said.

'Oh? What's that?' Buchanan inwardly tensed.

The second twin turned on his penlight and flicked its glare past Buchanan's right eye. 'The drunken American in the restaurant. You will need to prove to our satisfaction that you were not in Kuwait and Iraq at the time he claims he spent with you there.'

'For Christ sake, are you still fixated on that drunk? I don't understand how I'm supposed to—'

12

'Crawford!' a man's voice boomed from the darkness near the hotel's bar. The voice was deep, crusty from cigarettes, thick from alcohol.

'What's that?' the first twin quickly asked.

Oh, no, Buchanan thought. Oh, Jesus, no. Not when I've almost undone the damage from the first time.

'Crawford!' Big Bob Bailey yelled again. 'Is that you flashin' that light over there?' A hulking silhouette lurched from the hotel's gardens, a beefy man who'd had too much to drink and now had trouble walking in the sand. 'Yes, *you*, damn it! I mean *you*, Crawford! You and them Spics you're talkin' with under that fancy beach umbrella or whatever the hell it is.' He stumbled closer, breathing heavily. 'You son of a bitch, I want a straight answer! I want to know why you're lyin' to me! 'Cause you and me *both* know your name's Jim Crawford! We both know we was prisoners in Kuwait and Iraq! So why won't you admit it? How come you made a fool of me? You think I'm not good enough to drink with you and your Spic pals or somethin'?'

'I don't like the feel of this,' the first twin said.

'Something's wrong,' the second twin said.

'*Very* wrong.' The first twin snapped his gaze away from Big Bob Bailey's awkwardly approaching shadow and riveted it upon Buchanan. 'You're trouble. You Americans have an expression. "Better safe than sorry." '

'Come on, he's just a drunk!' Buchanan said.

'Crawford!' Big Bob Bailey yelled.

I don't have another choice, Buchanan thought.

'Shoot him,' the first twin told the bodyguard.

(I've got to—!)

'I'm talkin' to you!' Big Bob Bailey stumbled. 'Crawford! By Jesus, answer me!'

'Shoot them both,' the second twin told the bodyguard.

But Buchanan was already in motion, lunging from the plastic chair, diving toward the left, toward the first twin and the Browning pistol he'd set on the table, his hand spread over it.

Behind Buchanan, the bodyguard fired. With the sound-suppressor on the barrel, the guard's Beretta made a muffled pop. The bullet missed the back of Buchanan's head.

However, it didn't miss Buchanan entirely. As he rose and lunged, his right shoulder appeared where his head had been, and the bullet sliced, burning, through the muscle at the side of that shoulder. Before the bodyguard could shoot a second time, Buchanan had collided with the first twin, toppling him over his chair, simultaneously grabbing for the first twin's weapon. But the first twin would not let go of it.

'Shoot!' the second twin told the bodyguard.

'I can't! I might hit your brother!'

'Crawford, what the hell's goin' on?' Big Bob Bailey yelled.

Rolling in the sand, Buchanan strained to keep the first twin close to him as he fought for a grip on the pistol.

'Move closer!' the second twin told the bodyguard. 'I'll shine my light!'

Buchanan's shoulder throbbed. Blood streamed from the wound, slicking the first twin and himself, making it hard for Buchanan to keep a grasp on the twin and use him as a shield. As he rolled, sand scraped into his wound. If he'd been standing, the blood would have streaked down his arm to his hand, causing it to become so slippery that his fingers wouldn't have been able to wrench the pistol from the first twin's hand. But he was prone, and his hand stayed dry as he struggled in the sand. He sensed the bodyguard and the second twin rushing toward him. He heard Big Bob Bailey again yell, 'Crawford!' And all at once, the first twin fired his pistol. Unlike the bodyguard's weapon, the twin's Browning did not have a sound-suppressor. Its report was shockingly loud. The bodyguard and the second twin cursed, scrambling to get out of the line of fire. Buchanan's ears — already ringing from when the bodyguard had slammed his hands against the sides of Buchanan's head — now rang louder from the proximity of the shot. Buchanan's right eye still retained a harsh afterimage from the glare of the penlight that the second twin had aimed at the eye. Relying more on touch than on sight, Buchanan rolled and struggled with the first twin to get control of the pistol. His shoulder ached and began to stiffen.

The first twin fired the pistol again. As much as Buchanan

could tell, the bullet went straight up, bursting through the palm fronds at the top of the shelter. But Buchanan's already compromised vision was assaulted by the pistol's muzzle flash. 'Jesus!' he heard Big Bob Bailey yell. Despite the ringing in his ears, he also heard distant exclamations from the hotel's outside bar. He sensed the bodyguard and the second twin surging toward him once more, and suddenly he managed to grab the first twin's right thumb, twisting it, yanking it backward.

The thumb snapped at the middle joint with a sound that was soft, gristly, not so much a crack as a crunch. The first twin screamed and reflexively loosened his hold on the pistol, needing to relax his hand, to reduce the stress on his thumb. In that instant, Buchanan wrested the pistol away and rolled, sand sticking to his bloody shoulder. The bodyguard fired. As Buchanan kept rolling, the bullet struck next to him, and Buchanan shot four times in rapid succession. His vision was still sufficiently impaired that he had to rely on other senses – the touch of sand that the bodyguard scattered while he rushed closer to Buchanan, the sound of the muffled pop from the sound-suppressed Beretta – to help him estimate the bodyguard's position. Three of Buchanan's bullets struck the bodyguard, knocking him backward. Buchanan immediately twisted, aiming to his left, firing twice, hitting the second twin in the stomach and the chest. Blood spurting from between his unbuttoned silk shirt, the target doubled over and fell.

But the bodyguard was still on his feet, Buchanan realized. The man had been hit three times and yet seemed only dazed. Buchanan abruptly understood that all three bullets had struck the bodyguard's chest and that the Hispanic had seemed so unusually large-boned because he was wearing a concealed, bullet-resistant vest. As the bodyguard straightened and aimed yet again, Buchanan shot him in the throat, the left eye, and the forehead. Even then, he feared that the bodyguard might spastically squeeze off a shot. Buchanan tensed, desperate to squirm backward. But instead of firing, the bodyguard rose as if trying to balance on his tiptoes, leaned back as if balancing now on his heels, and toppled across the table. At the same time, Buchanan felt thrashing to his right, twisted onto his side, and shot the first twin through his left temple. Blood, bone, and brain – hot and sticky – spattered over Buchanan's face.

The first twin shuddered, dying.

Buchanan in turn inhaled deeply and trembled, overwhelmed by adrenaline. The repeated shots from the unsilenced Browning had intensified the agony of the ringing in his head. Due to years of habit, he'd mentally counted each shot as he'd pulled the trigger. Four toward the bodyguard. Two toward the second twin. Three more toward the bodyguard. One toward the first twin. Earlier the first twin had fired twice. That made twelve all told. Buchanan hadn't worried about using all his ammunition because he knew that the Browning was capable of holding thirteen rounds in the magazine and one in the chamber. Normally he wouldn't have needed to shoot so many times, but in the darkness, he couldn't guarantee precision. But now his remaining bullets would not be enough if the shots had attracted the twins' other bodyguards. In a rush, Buchanan crouched behind the table, aiming toward the gloom of the beach, the glow of the lights at the outdoor bar, and the gleam of the lights at the hotel. A loud, nervous crowd had gathered on the sidewalk that flanked the beach. Several men were pointing in Buchanan's direction. He didn't see any armed men rushing toward him. Quickly he made sure that the bodyguard and the first twin were dead. While stopped at the first twin, he searched the body, retrieving his belt, his keys, and his pen. He didn't want anything associated with him to remain on the scene. In a greater rush, he checked the second twin, groped inside his

70

suit coat, and pulled out the list of names – Buchanan's pseudonyms – that the second twin had read to him. He left the other list, the names of supposedly disloyal associates that he'd given the twins. The authorities would investigate those names and try to implicate them in these killings.

Or so Buchanan hoped. He wanted to accomplish at least *some* of what he'd been sent here to do, to inflict as much damage on the drug-distribution network as he could. If only this mission hadn't gone to hell, if only . . .

Buchanan suddenly froze. *Big Bob Bailey.* Where *was* he? What had happened to—?

'Crawford?' an unsteady voice murmured from the darkness.

Buchanan strained his vision to study the night, his eyes now less impaired by the glare of the penlight and the strobelike flash of the shots.

'Crawford?' Bailey's voice sounded oddly muffled.

Then Buchanan realized – Bailey had been stumbling toward this table the last time Buchanan had seen him. When the shooting started, Bailey must have dropped to the beach. His voice was muffled because he was pressed, face downward, against the sand.

'Jesus Christ, man, are you all right?' Bailey murmured. 'Who's doin' all the shootin'?'

Buchanan saw him now, a dark shape hugging the beach. He shifted his gaze toward the crowd on the sidewalk near the hotel's outdoor bar. The crowd was larger, louder, although still afraid to come anywhere near where guns had been fired. He didn't see any bodyguards or policemen rushing in his direction. They will, though. Soon, he thought. I don't have much time. I have to get out of here.

The pain in his shoulder worsened. The wound swelled, throbbing more fiercely. Urgent, he used an unbloody section of his shirt to wipe his fingerprints from where he'd touched the top of the table and the sides of a chair. He couldn't do anything about the prints he'd left on the glasses in the restaurant, but maybe the table would have been cleared by now, the glasses taken to the kitchen and washed.

Hurry.

As he started to swing toward the first twin, wipe fingerprints from the pistol, and leave it in the twin's hand, he heard Bailey's voice become stronger.

'Crawford? Were you hit?'

Shut up! Buchanan thought.

Near the hotel's bar, the crowd was becoming aggressive. The glow from the hotel was sufficient to reveal two uniformed policemen who sprinted off the sidewalk into the sand. Buchanan finished wiping the pistol clean of fingerprints and forced it into the first twin's fingers. He pivoted, stayed low, and ran, making sure he kept his right shoulder close to the splashing waves. That shoulder and indeed his entire right side were covered with blood. He wanted the blood to fall into the water so that the police couldn't track him by following splotches of his blood in the sand.

'*Alto*!' a man's gruff voice ordered. 'Halt!'

Buchanan raced harder, staying low, charging parallel to the waves, hoping the night would so envelop him that he'd make a poor target.

'*ALTO*!' the gruff voice demanded with greater force.

Buchanan sprinted as fast as he could. His back muscles rippled with chills as he tensed in dread of the bullet that would—

'Hey, what do you think you're—? What are you shovin' me for? I didn't do nothin'!' Big Bob Bailey objected with drunken indignation.

The police had grabbed the first person they came to.

Despite his pain and his desperation, Buchanan couldn't help grinning. Bailey, you turned out not to be completely useless, after all.

72

THREE

1

Baltimore, Maryland.
Pushing a squeaky cart along a dark, drizzly, downtown alley, the woman dressed as a bag lady felt exhausted. She hadn't slept in almost forty-eight hours, and that period of time (as well as several days before it) had been filled with constant dread. Indeed, for months, since she'd first met Alistair Drummond and had agreed to his proposal, she'd never been free from apprehension.

The assignment had seemed simple enough, and certainly the fee she earned was considerable, her accommodations lavish. As a bonus, she seldom had to perform. Mostly all she had to do was stay in the Manhattan condominium with its splendid view of Central Park and let servants take care of her, occasionally deigning to accept a telephone call but making it short, pretending to be hoarse because of a throat problem that she claimed her doctor had diagnosed as polyps and that might require surgery. Rarely she went out in public, always at night, always in a limousine, always wearing gems, a fur, and an exquisite evening gown, always with protective, handsome escorts. Those outings were usually to the Metropolitan opera or to a charity benefit, and she stayed just long enough to insure that her presence was noticed, that she'd be mentioned in a society column. She permitted no contact with her character's former friends or former husband. She was, as she'd indicated in a rare magazine interview, beginning a period of self-assessment which required isolation in order for her to commence the second act of her life. Her performance was one of her best. No one thought her behavior unusual. After all, genius was subject to eccentricities.

But she was terrified. The accumulation of fear had been gradual. At first, she had attributed her unease to stage fright, to becoming accustomed to a new role, to convincing an unfamiliar audience, and of course, to satisfying Alistair Drummond. The latter particularly unnerved her. Drummond's gaze was so intense that she suspected he wore spectacles not to improve his vision but rather to magnify the cold glint in his eyes. He exuded such authority that he dominated a room, regardless of how crowded it was or how many other notables were present. No one knew for certain how old he was, except that he was definitely over eighty, but everyone agreed that he looked more like an eerie sixty. Numerous face lifts, combined with a macrobiotic diet, massive amounts of vitamins, and weekly infusions of hormones, seemed to have stopped the evidence of his advancing age. The contrast between his tightened face and his wizened hands troubled her.

He preferred to be called 'professor,' although he had never taught and his doctorate was only honorary, the result of a new art museum that bore his name and that he'd had constructed as a gift to a prestigious but financially-embattled, Ivy League university. One of the conditions of her employment had been that the 'professor' would have access to her at all times and that she would appear in public with him whenever he dictated. As vain as he was rich, he cackled whenever he read his name − in company with her character's − in the society columns, especially if the columnist called him 'professor.'

The sound of his brittle, crusty laughter chilled her.

But as frightening as she eventually found Alistair Drummond, even more frightening was his personal assistant, a pleasant-faced, fair-haired, well-dressed man whom she knew only as Raymond. His face never changed expression. It always bore the same cheery countenance, regardless if he helped Drummond inject himself with hormones, looked at her in a low-cut evening gown, watched a weather report on television, or was sent on an assignment. Drummond was careful never to discuss the specifics of his business transactions while she was present, but she took for granted that anyone who had accumulated so much wealth and power, not to mention world-wide notoriety, by definition had to be ruthless, and she always imagined that the assignments Drummond gave to Raymond would have repugnant consequences. Not that Raymond gave any indication. Raymond always looked as cheery when he left as when he returned.

What had made her uneasiness turn into dread was the day she realized that she wasn't merely pretending to be in seclusion – she was a prisoner. It was unprofessional of her, she admitted, to have wanted to break character and take an unescorted afternoon walk in Central Park, perhaps go over to the Metropolitan art museum. The moment the thought occurred to her, she repressed it. Nonetheless, briefly she'd felt liberated, and subsequently she'd felt frustrated. I can't, she thought. I made an agreement. I accepted a fee – a *large* fee – in exchange for taking on a role. I can't break the bargain. But what if . . . ?

That tantalizing question had made her impatient with her narrow world. Except for a few sanctioned outings and an occasional performance on the telephone, she spent most of each day exercising, reading, watching video tapes, listening to music, eating, and . . . It had sounded like a vacation until she was forced to do it. Her days had become longer and longer. As much as Alistair Drummond and his assistant made her uneasy, she almost welcomed their visits. Although the two men were frightening, at least they were a change. So she had asked herself, What if I did break character? What if I did go out for an afternoon walk in Central Park? She had no intention of actually doing so, but she wondered what would happen if . . . ? A bodyguard had suddenly appeared at the end of the corridor outside her unit and had prevented her from getting on the elevator.

She was an experienced observer of audiences. She'd known from the start – the first time she was allowed from the condominium, escorted into Drummond's limousine – that the building was being watched: a flower seller across the street, a hot-dog vendor on the corner, no doubt the building's doorman, and no doubt someone like an indigent at the rear exit from the building. But she had assumed that these sentries were there to prevent her character's former acquaintances from arriving unexpectedly and catching her unprepared. At once, now, she had realized that the building was under watch to keep her *in* as much as to keep others out, and that had made her world even smaller, and that had made her even more tense, Drummond had made her more tense, Raymond had made her more tense.

When will I be able to get out of here? she'd wondered. When will the performance end? Or *will* it end?

One evening as she put on her diamond necklace – which Drummond had told her would be her bonus when the assignment was completed – she'd impulsively scraped the necklace's largest stone across a glass of water. The stone had not made a scratch. Which meant that the stone was not a diamond. Which meant that the necklace, her bonus, was worthless.

So what else was . . . ? She examined the bank statement she was sent each month. A gesture of good faith from Drummond, each statement showed that Drummond had, as he had promised, deposited her monthly fee. Since all her necessities were provided, she had no need to use that money, Drummond had explained. Thus, when her assignment was over, she'd be able to withdraw the entire, enormous sum.

The bank statement had an account number. She knew that she didn't dare use the telephone in her condominium (it presumably was tapped), so she had waited for the rare opportunity when she was allowed to leave the condominium during the day, and when the bank would be open. It had given her enormous pleasure that during a pause in the political luncheon's program of speakers, she had whispered to Alistair Drummond, who had brought her, that she needed to go to the ladies' room. Taut-faced, Drummond had nodded his permission, gesturing with a wrinkled hand for a bodyguard to accompany her.

She had leaned close, pressing a breast against him. 'No, I don't want your permission,' she had whispered. 'What I want is fifty cents. That's what it costs to get into the toilets here.'

'Don't say "toilets".' Drummond had pursed his lips in disapproval of her vulgarity.

'I'll call them "rose bowls" if you want. I still need fifty cents. Plus two dollars for the attendant with the towels. I wouldn't have to ask you if you'd give me some actual money once in a while.'

'All your needs are taken care of.'

'Sure. Except when I have to go to the ladies' room – excuse me, the rose bowl.' She pressed her breast harder against his bony arm.

Drummond turned toward Raymond beside him. 'Escort her. Give her what she asks.'

So she and Raymond had proceeded through the crowd, ignoring the stares of celebrity worshippers. Raymond had discreetly given her the small sum of money she had requested, and the moment she had entered the powder-room part of the ladies' room, she had veered toward a pay phone, inserted coins, pressed the numbers for the bank into which Drummond deposited her fee, and asked for Accounting. Several society women who sat on velvet chairs before mirrors and freshened their makeup turned in recognition of someone so famous. She nodded with an imperious 'Do you mind? Can I have some privacy?' look. Conditioned to pretend not to be impressed, the society matrons shrugged and resumed applying lipstick to their drooping lips.

'Accounting,' a nasally male voice said.

'Please check this number.' She dictated it.

'One moment . . . Yes, I have that account on my computer screen.'

'What is the balance?'

The nasally voice told her. The sum was correct.

'Are there any restrictions?'

'One. For withdrawals, a second signature is required.'

'Whose?'

Raymond's, she learned, and that was when she knew that Drummond didn't intend for her to get out of this role alive.

It took several weeks of preparations, of calculations, of watching and biding her time. No one suspected. She was sure of that. She made herself seem so contented that it was one of the best performances of her career. Last night, after going to her bedroom at midnight, after keeping her eyes shut when the maid looked in on her at two, she had waited until four to make sure that the maid was asleep. She had quickly dressed, putting on her sneakers and gray, hooded exercise suit. She had stuffed her purse with the necklace, bracelets, and ear-rings that Drummond had promised her, the jewelry that she now knew was fake. She had to take them because she wanted Drummond to think that she still believed the diamonds and other gems to be real and would try to sell them. His men would waste time

78

questioning the dealers she was most likely to approach. She had a small amount of money — what she'd been given for the attendant in the ladies' room, a few dollars that she'd stolen in isolated dimes and quarters from her maid's purse while her maid was distracted by a task in another room, twenty-five dollars that she'd brought with her the first day she'd started this assignment. It wouldn't take her far. She needed more. A great deal more.

Her first task had been to leave the condominium. As soon as she'd realized that she was a prisoner, she'd automatically assumed that the door would be rigged to sound an alarm and warn her guards if she tried to escape in the night. The alarm was one of the reasons she had waited several weeks before leaving. It had taken her that long, whenever the maid wasn't watching, to check the walls behind furniture and paintings and find the alarm's hidden switch. Last night, she had turned it off behind the liquor cabinet, silently unlocked the door and opened it, then peered left down the corridor. The guard who watched the elevator could not be seen. He usually sat in a chair just around the corner. At four in the morning, there was a strong possibility he'd be drowsing, relying on the sound of the elevator to make him become alert.

But she had no intention of using the elevator. Rather she left her door slightly ajar — she didn't dare close it all the way and risk making an avoidable noise — then turned to the right, walking softly along the carpet toward the fire door. That door wasn't guarded on this floor, but in the lobby, the exit from the stairwell was. With painstaking care, she eased the fire door open, closed it as carefully behind her, and exhaled, wiping sweat from her hands. That had been the part she most dreaded, that she'd make a noise when she opened the fire door and alert the guard. The rest, for a time, would be easy.

She hurried down the cold, shadowy stairwell, the rubber soles on her sneakers making almost no sound. Forty stories later, energized rather than fatigued, she reached the lobby door but didn't stop and instead continued to the basement. As she made her way through dusty storage areas and the noisy furnace area, passing a clutter of pipes and circuit breakers, she feared that a custodian would confront her, but no one seemed on duty, and eventually she found stairs that led to a rear exit from the building, one that was far enough from the conventional exit that anyone watching the other exit wouldn't notice someone leaving the basement.

Still cautious, she turned off the nearest light before she opened the door so that no illumination would spill out and reveal her. Then she was in an alley, feeling the chill of late October, hurrying along. She wished that she'd been able to bring a coat, but all the coats in her character's closet had been expensive, designed to be worn with evening clothes. There'd been nothing as inconspicuous as a windbreaker. No matter. She was free. But for how long? Fear and urgency gave her warmth.

Without her wig, special makeup, and facial-altering devices, she no longer resembled her character. But even though the public wouldn't recognize her, Alistair Drummond had a photograph of her original appearance. So she didn't dare use a taxi. The driver, if questioned, would remember picking her up at this hour and in this vicinity, especially since she was Hispanic. The driver would also remember where he'd dropped her off. That destination would be a safe distance from where she intended to go. It would not reveal anything that put her in danger. Nonetheless she considered it better if she permitted Drummond no leads whatsoever, false or true, and instead just seemed to vanish. Besides, given the little money she had, she didn't dare waste it on a taxi.

So she ran, to all appearances an early morning jogger on the nearly deserted streets. She went hunting, skirting Central Park, trying to look like an easy target. Finally two kids with knives emerged from shadows. She broke both their arms and took the fourteen dollars she found on them. By dawn, her exercise clothes dark with sweat, she rested in a twenty-four-hour hamburger joint in Times Square. There she sacrificed part of her meager funds on several steaming cups of coffee and a breakfast of scrambled eggs, hash browns, sausage, and English muffins. Not the sort of breakfast she usually ate and certainly not recommended by the American Heart Association, but given the frantic, furtive day she expected to have, she needed all the calories and carbohydrates her stomach would hold.

She sacrificed more of her meager funds to go to a theater that showed movies around the clock. The only woman present, she knew that she'd attract predators in the almost-deserted seats at seven in the morning. She wanted to. When the movie ended and she left the theater, she carried fifty more dollars, money that she'd taken from three men whom she'd knocked unconscious, using her elbow, when each – a half hour apart – had sat next to her and tried to molest her.

By then, a few cut-rate clothing stores were open, and she bought a plain wool cap, a pair of wool gloves, and an insulated, black nylon jacket that blended with her gray exercise clothes. She tucked her hair beneath her cap, and with her slightly baggy exercise clothes hiding her voluptuous breasts and hips, she appeared overweight and androgynous. Her costume was almost perfect. Except that her clothes were new (and she remedied that by dragging her cap, gloves, and jacket in the gutter), she looked like most of the other street people.

Next, it was time to pick her spot among the hucksters beginning to set up shop on the curb along Broadway. It took two hours, a watchful eye for the police or anyone else who showed undue interest in her, and several prudent shifts of location, but she finally used her powers of performance to sell all of her jewelry to tourists, amassing two hundred and fifteen dollars.

That gave her enough to travel – not enough to fly, of course (which she wouldn't have done anyhow because the airports would be among the first places that Drummond's men would check), but certainly enough to take a train, and a bus would be even cheaper. Plus, the way she was dressed, she thought she'd be more invisible on a bus, so she ate a hamburger while she walked to the junkie-infested Port Authority Bus Terminal, and by noon she was on her way to Baltimore.

Why Baltimore? Why not? she thought. It was close enough that a ticket there wouldn't use all her money. At the same time, it was comfortably far. She had no previous associations with Baltimore. It was simply a random selection, impossible for Drummond to predict, although if he eliminated the cities with which she'd been associated and if he arbitrarily chose the remaining big cities within a certain radius of Manhattan, he might make a lucky guess. Nothing was guaranteed. She had to be careful.

En route to Baltimore, while she studied the other passengers to determine if any was a threat, she had ample opportunity to think about her options. She didn't dare fall back into old patterns. Her family and friends were a danger to her. Drummond's men would be watching them. She had to construct a new persona, one unrelated to any character she'd assumed before. She had to make new friends and create new relatives. As far as employment was concerned, she would do whatever was most tolerable, as long as it wasn't anything she'd done previously. She had to make a complete break with the past. Getting the proper documents for a new false identity wasn't a problem. She was an expert.

But as she considered her existential condition, she wondered if she was prepared to make the sacrifice. She *liked* the person she'd been before she met Alistair Drummond. She wanted to be that person again. Had she been foolish? Had she misjudged Drummond's intention? Perhaps she should have been patient and continued to live in luxury.

Until you served your purpose and your performance was no longer necessary.

And then?

Remember, the gems were fake, and there was no way you were ever going to get the money Drummond claimed to be paying you. The only explanation for the way he rigged that bank account was that he planned to have you killed and take back the money.

But why would he want me killed?

To hide something.

What, though?

The bus arrived in Baltimore at nine in the evening. A cold drizzle made the downtown area bleak. She found a cheap place to eat – more caffeine, calories, and carbohydrates, not to mention grease (she rationalized that the fat might help insulate her from the cold). She didn't want to waste her remaining money on a hotel room – even a cheap one would be disastrous to her reserves. For a time, she roamed the back streets, hoping that someone would accost her. But the man who grabbed her and whose collar bone she broke had only fifty cents in his pocket.

She was tired, cold, wet, and depressed. She needed to rest. She needed a place where she'd feel reasonably safe, where she could think and sleep. When she found a shopping cart in an alley, she decided on her next role. After wiping dirt on her face, she threw trash into the cart. With her shoulders slumped and with an assumed, crazy, empty look in her eyes, she pushed the cart, wheels squeaking, through the drizzle, a bag lady on her way to a shelter for the homeless that she had just passed.

What am I going to do? she thought. The confidence she'd felt when escaping had drained from her. The rigors of her new life weighed upon her imagination. Damn it, I *liked* who I was. I want to be her again.

How? To do that, you've got to beat Drummond, and he's too powerful to be beaten.

Is he? Why did he hire me? Why did he want me to put on that performance? What's his secret? What's he hiding? If I can find *that* out, maybe he *can* be beaten.

One thing's sure. Without money and resources, you need help.

But who can I ask? I don't dare turn to my friends and family. They're a trap. Besides, they haven't the faintest idea of what to do, of what this involves.

So what about the people you trained with?

No, they're a matter of public record. Drummond can use his influence to learn who they are. They'll be watched in case I approach them – as much a liability as my family and friends.

The drizzle increased to a downpour. Her soaked clothes drooped and clung to her. In the gloom, she felt every bit the spiritless bag lady she pretended to be.

There's got to be *someone*.

The cart she pushed kept squeaking.

You can't be that alone! she wanted to scream.

Face it. The only person you could trust to help you would have to be someone so anonymous, so chameleonlike, so invisible, without a trace or a record that it would be like he'd never existed. And he'd have to be damned good at staying alive.

He? Why would it have to be a man?

But she suddenly knew, and as she reached the entrance to the shelter for the homeless, a man in a black suit with a white, ministerial collar stepped out.

'Come, sister. It's not a fit night to be out.'

Playing her role, she resisted.

'Please, sister. It's warm inside. There's food. A place to sleep.'

She resisted less stubbornly.

'You'll be safe, I promise. And I'll store your cart. I'll protect your goods.'

That did it. Like a child, she allowed herself to be led, and as she left the gloom of the night, as she entered the brightly lit shelter, she smelled coffee, stale donuts, boiled potatoes, but it might as well have been a banquet. She'd found sanctuary, and as she shuffled toward a crowded, wooden bench, she mentally repeated the name of the man whom she had decided to ask for help. The name filled her mind like a mantra. The problem was that he probably no longer used that name. He was constantly in flux. Officially he didn't exist. So how on earth could she get in touch with a man as formless and shifting as the wind? Where in hell would he be?

2

Until 1967, Cancun was a small, sleepy town on the northeastern coast of Mexico's Yucatán peninsula. That year, the Mexican government – seeking a way to boost the country's weak economy – decided to promote tourism more energetically than ever. But instead of improving an existing resort, the government chose to create a world-class holiday center where there was nothing. Various requirements such as suitable location and weather were programed into a computer, and the computer announced that the new resort would be built on a narrow sandbar in a remote area of the Mexican Caribbean. Construction began in 1968. A modern sewage-disposal system was installed as well as a dependable water-purification system and a reliable power plant. A four-lane highway was built down the middle of the sandbar. Palm trees were planted next to the highway. Hotels designed to resemble ancient Mayan pyramids were constructed along the ocean side of the island while night clubs and restaurants were built along the inner lagoon. Eventually, several million tourists came each year to what had once been nothing but a sandbar.

Cancun's sandbar had the shape of the number seven. It was twelve miles long, a quarter mile wide, and linked to the mainland by a bridge at each end. Club Internacional – where Buchanan had shot the three Hispanics – was located at the middle of the top of the seven, and as Buchanan raced away from it through the darkness along the wave-lapped beach, he ignored the other hotels that glistened on his left and tried to decide what he would do when he reached the bridge at the northern end of the sandbar. The two policemen who'd arrived at the scene of the killings would use two-way radios to contact their counterparts on the mainland. Those other policemen would block the bridges and question all Americans who attempted to leave. No matter how much effort it took, the police would respond promptly and thoroughly. Cancun prided itself on appearing safe for tourists. A multiple murder demanded an absolute response. To reassure tourists, a quick arrest was mandatory.

Under other circumstances, Buchanan would not have hesitated to veer from the beach, pass between hotels, reach the red-brick sidewalk along the highway, and stroll across the bridge, where he would agreeably answer the questions of the police. But he didn't dare show himself. With his wounded shoulder and his blood-drenched clothes, he'd attract so much attention that he'd be arrested at once. He had to find another way out of the area, and as the beach curved, angling to the left toward the looming shadow of the bridge, he stared toward the glimmer of hotels across the channel that separated the sandbar from the mainland, and he decided he would have to swim.

Unexpectedly he felt lightheaded. Alarming him, his legs bent. His heart beat too fast, and he had trouble catching his breath. The effects of adrenaline, he tried to assure himself. It didn't help that he'd drunk four ounces of tequila before fighting for his life and then racing down the beach. But adrenaline and he were old friends, and it had never made him lightheaded. Similarly his profession was such that on several occasions he'd been forced into action after his deep-cover identity required him to gain a contact's trust by drinking with him. On none of those occasions, however, had the combination of exertion and alcohol made him lightheaded. A little sick to his stomach, yes, but never lightheaded. All the same, he definitely felt dizzy now, and sick to his stomach as well, and he had to admit the truth – although his shoulder wound was superficial, he must be losing more blood than he'd realized. If he didn't stop the bleeding, he risked fainting. Or worse.

Trained as a paramedic, Buchanan knew that the preferred way to stop bleeding was by using a pressure bandage. But he didn't have the necessary first-aid equipment. The alternative was to use a method that at one time had been recommended but had now fallen out of favor – applying a tourniquet. The disadvantage of a tourniquet was that it cut off the flow of blood not only to the wound but also to the rest of a limb, in this case Buchanan's right arm. If the tourniquet were applied too tightly or not relaxed at frequent, regular intervals, the victim risked damaging tissue to the point where gangrene resulted.

But he didn't have another option. Sirens wailing, lights flashing, emergency vehicles stopped on the bridge. As Buchanan paused at the edge of the channel between the sandbar and the mainland, he glanced warily toward the darkness behind him and neither saw nor heard an indication that he was being pursued. He *would* be, though. Soon. Hurriedly, he reached inside his pants pocket and pulled out the folded belt that the second twin had taken from him and that Buchanan had retrieved after shooting the man. The belt was made from woven strips of leather, so there wasn't any need for eyelets. The prong on the buckle could slide between strands of leather anywhere along the belt. Buchanan hitched the belt around his swollen right shoulder, above the wound, and cinched it securely, tugging at the free end with his left hand while he bent his right arm painfully upward and with sweating effort used his trembling right fingers to push the buckle's prong through the leather. His legs wobbled. His vision blackened. He feared that he would pass out. But at once, his vision returned to normal, and with tremendous effort, he compelled his legs to move. Already he sensed, without being able to see the effect clearly, that the flow of blood had lessened significantly. He didn't feel as lightheaded. The trade-off was that his right arm now felt disturbingly prickly and cold.

Concerned that his blue canvas deck shoes would slip off his feet when filled with water, he removed them, tied their laces together, and wound the laces tightly around his right wrist. Then he took out the list of his pseudonyms that he'd removed from the second twin's corpse. After tearing the sheet into tiny pieces, he quickly waded into the darkness of the channel, the surprisingly warm water soaking his knees, his thighs, and his abdomen. As white-capped waves struck his chest, he pushed his feet off the sandy bottom and surged outward. A strong current tugged at him. In small amounts, he released the bits of torn paper. Even if someone managed impossibly to find all the pieces, the water would have dissolved the ink.

Relying on the kick of his muscular legs to give him momentum, he turned so his right side was below him, allowed his wounded right arm to rest, and used his left arm to stroke sideways through the water, adding to the power of his legs. The shoes attached to his right wrist created drag and held him back. Determined, he kicked harder.

The mouth of the channel was a hundred yards wide. As

Buchanan pulled with his left arm and thrust with his legs, the water soaked the belt around his right shoulder, stretched the leather, and caused the tourniquet to loosen, decreasing the pressure above his wound. His right arm − no longer cold and prickly − now felt warm and sensitive to the tug of the current. Salt in the water made his wound sting.

Maybe the salt will disinfect it, he thought. But then he smelled the film of oil and gasoline on the water, left by the numerous power boats that used the channel, and he realized that the water would contaminate his wound, not disinfect it.

He realized something else − the loose tourniquet meant that his wound would be bleeding again. Blood might attract . . .

He swam with greater urgency, knowing that barracuda were often seen among the area's numerous reefs, knowing as well that sharks were sometimes reported to have swum up the channel and into the lagoon between the island and the shore. He had no idea how large the sharks had been or whether they were the type that attacked swimmers, but if there were predators in the water, the blood could attract them from quite a distance.

He kicked. His foot touched something. A piece of wood perhaps. Or a clump of drifting seaweed. But it might be . . .

He thrust himself faster, his foot again touching whatever was behind him.

He was a quarter of the way across the channel, far enough into it that he felt small, swallowed by the night. Abruptly he heard the drone of a motor to his left and frowned in that direction. The drone became a roar. He saw the lights of a swiftly approaching power boat. It came from the lagoon, sped beneath the bridge, and hurried through the channel toward the ocean. A police boat? Buchanan wondered and strained to get out of its way. As he kicked, he again felt something behind him. He weakened from further loss of blood. Staring frantically toward the approaching boat, he suddenly recognized the silhouette revealed by its lights. The vessel didn't belong to the police. It was a cabin cruiser. Through its windows, he saw several men and women drinking and laughing.

But the vessel was still a threat. It kept speeding toward him. Halfway across the channel, feeling the vibration of the cruiser's engines through the water, so close that within a few seconds he would either be seen by someone on board or else struck, Buchanan took a deep breath and submerged, veering downward, forced to use his injured arm to help him gain more speed, to avoid the passing hull and the spinning propellers.

The rumble of the cruiser's powerful engines assaulted Buchanan's eardrums. As he dove farther, deeper, the shoes attached to his right wrist impeded the already awkward motion of his injured arm. He heard the cruiser's rumble pass over him.

The moment it diminished, he arched fiercely upward, feeling lightheaded again, desperate to breathe. Beneath him, something brushed past his feet. Hurry, he told himself. The decreasing pressure against his ears alerted him that he was almost to the surface. His lungs seemed on fire. Any second now, he anticipated, his face would be exposed to the night. He'd be able to open his mouth and—

Whack! His skull struck something large and solid. The impact was so unexpected, so painful, so stunning that Buchanan breathed reflexively, inhaling water, coughing, gagging. He might have briefly passed out. He didn't know. What he did know was that he inhaled more water, that he fought to reach the surface. He grazed past the object he'd struck, burst into the open, and greedily filled his lungs, all the while struggling not to vomit.

What had—?

His head felt squeezed by swelling pain. In agony, desperate to get his bearings, he found himself facing the receding stern of the brightly lit cabin cruiser. Ominous, a long low shadow stalked the cruiser. The object must have been what Buchanan had struck. But he didn't understand what—

And then he did. A dinghy. The cruiser's towing it. I had no way of knowing about—

Something brushed past his legs again. Startled into action, ignoring the pain in his shoulder and now in his skull, Buchanan twisted onto his stomach and swam without regard for his wounded shoulder, using both arms, kicking with both legs, striking whatever it was that bumped past his feet. The opposite shore, the gleaming hotels past the beach, grew rapidly closer. As Buchanan stroked deeply with his left hand, his fingers suddenly touched sand. He was into the shallows. Standing, he lunged toward the beach, his knees plunging through the waves. Behind him, something splashed, and as he reached the shore, he spun toward the gloom of the channel, seeing the phosphorescent wake that something in the water had made. Or perhaps it was only his imagination.

Like hell.

Breathing heavily from pain, he wanted to slump onto the sand, to rest, but he heard the blaring rise and fall of more police sirens, and he knew that he didn't dare remain in the open, even in the darkness, so he mustered discipline, drew from the depths of his resolve, and turned his back to the bridge, staggering away from the channel, proceeding along the curve of the beach, studying the glow at the rear of the various hotels.

3

Here, as at Club Internacional, the beach was deserted, tourists preferring to go to bed early or else to party at Cancun's many night spots. Buchanan chose a hotel that didn't have an outdoor bar behind it and trudged from the sand. Remaining in the shadows, he found a lounge chair beneath a palm tree and slumped. There were other chairs, but what had attracted him to this particular chair was that a guest had left a towel upon it.

He slipped the belt from the top of his right shoulder, pressed the folded towel over his wound, and looped the belt several times over the towel, securing it tightly, attempting to make a pressure bandage. Although the towel became wet and dark in places, it seemed to reduce his loss of blood. For how long, he couldn't tell. Right now, all he wanted to do was rest.

But there was too much to do.

He unlooped the laces that attached his deck shoes to his right wrist. The canvas of his shoes was pliant because of the water. It shouldn't have been difficult putting them on his feet. But doing so and lacing them was among the hardest tasks he'd ever attempted.

His skull throbbed from its impact against the dinghy. The sharp pain remained as severe. Gingerly raising his left hand to his wet hair, he touched a gash and felt a large area of swelling. The water in his hair prevented him from determining if the gash was bleeding and if so, how much.

At the same time, the salt in the water had severely aggravated the pain in his wounded right shoulder. That injury, too, was swollen. It pulsed against the pressure bandage. In addition, disturbingly, the fingers of Buchanan's right hand trembled.

He told himself that the trembling must be the result of the trauma to his shoulder or of the struggle with the first twin and his subsequent swim across the channel. Relief after stress. Something like that. Hey, when you exercise with weights, he reminded himself, your hands sometimes shake afterward. Sure.

But only his right hand trembled, not both of them, and the fingers seemed to have a will of their own. He couldn't help worrying that something serious was wrong.

Move. You're acting like you've never been in a firefight before.

With effort, he stepped closer to the back of the hotel, leaving the shadows of the beach, moving warily onto concrete, passing more palm trees, approaching muted lights around a small, oval swimming pool.

The pool, surrounded by tropical bushes and patio furniture, was deserted. Staying close to the cover of shrubs, Buchanan reached the first, dim, overhead light, where he noticed that his wet shoes left prints on the concrete. He noticed as well that his shirt and pants still dripped water. What interested him most, though, was that the blood on his clothes had been rinsed away. A small blessing in a night of disasters. As soon as his shirt and pants dried, they wouldn't attract attention. But the blood on the towel strapped to his shoulder would certainly make people look twice.

He needed something to loop over his shoulder and conceal the towel. A jacket would be ideal, but the only way he could think to get one was by breaking into a room, and that was out of the question. Oh, he could pick a lock with ease if he had the equipment, which in this case he didn't, but only amateurs smashed windows and caused a disruption, which in this case he'd be forced to do.

So what *are* you going to do?

The pain from his injured skull aggravated the pain in his wounded shoulder. The combination was excruciating. Again he felt dizzy.

While he still had strength, he had to hurry.

He veered to the left toward a tunnel. Concrete stairs led up to the right toward the rooms on the upper floors. But his interest was directed inside the tunnel toward stairs on the left that went down. He couldn't imagine that a hotel with as impressive a design as this would be crude enough to lodge tourists below ground. So the only reason the hotel would have rooms down there would be for storage and maintenance.

He squinted at his digital Seiko watch, the sort of time piece he'd decided an ex-DEA officer would wear. It was still functioning after his swim, and when he pressed a button on the side, the LED display showed 11:09. This late, he doubted that the maintenance staff would still be working. He listened carefully for any voices or footsteps that echoed up the stairwell. Hearing none, he started down.

His rubber-soled deck shoes made almost no sound on the stairs. At a platform, the stairs reversed direction and took him to a dimly illuminated corridor. It smelled mouldy and damp. The odor would be a further reason for workers not to remain down here. Peering cautiously from the bottom of the stairwell, seeing no one at either end of the corridor, he stepped from cover, proceeded arbitrarily to the right, came to a metal door, listened, heard no sound behind it, and turned the knob. It was locked.

He continued to another door, and this time after he listened and tried the knob, he exhaled as the knob moved. Slowly pushing the door open, he groped along the inside wall, found a light switch, and flicked it on, relaxing when he saw that the room was unoccupied. The light bulb that dangled from the ceiling was as sickly yellow as those in the corridor. The room was lined with metal shelves upon which tools and boxes had been stored. A small, rusted, metal desk was wedged in one corner, and upon the desk—

– despite his pain, Buchanan felt a surge of excitement –
—sat a black, rotary telephone.

He shut the door, locked it, and picked up the phone. His heart pounded as he heard a tone. He quickly dialed a number.

A man answered. Buchanan's case officer. To be near Buchanan at this phase of the mission, he'd rented an apartment in the mainland part of Cancun. Normally he and Buchanan communicated by means of coded messages left at prearranged dead-drop locations on a predetermined schedule. Rarely, because of the risk of electronic eavesdropping, did they speak on the telephone, and only then between pre-selected pay phones. Never, while Buchanan was under deep cover, had they met. Buchanan had access to a protective backup team if he suspected he was in danger, but given the paranoia of the men he'd arranged to meet tonight, it had been decided that the benefit of the backup team's presence in and around Club Internacional would be offset by the danger that the drug distributors and *their* backup team would sense they were being watched. After all, the mission had been progressing according to plan. There'd been no reason to suspect that the meeting would not go smoothly. Until Big Bob Bailey showed up. Now Buchanan didn't have to worry about jeopardizing his cover if he phoned his case officer. What worse could happen? Buchanan's contacts were dead. The mission was blown.

What worse could happen? Oh, something worse could happen, all right. The Mexican police could capture him, and his superiors could be implicated in three murders. He had to disappear.

'Yes,' Buchanan's case officer said.

'Is that you, Paul?'

'I'm sorry. No one by that name lives here.'

'You mean this isn't . . . ?' Buchanan gave a telephone number.

'You're not even close.'

'Sorry.'

Buchanan hung up and rubbed his throbbing forehead. The number he'd given his controller was a coded message for which an expanded translation would be that the mission had to be aborted, that an absolute disaster had occurred, that he'd been injured, was on the run, and had to be extracted from the area as soon as possible. By prior agreement, his case officer would try to rendezvous with Buchanan ninety minutes after Buchanan's call. The rendezvous location was on the mainland in downtown Cancun, outside a cantina near the intersection of Tulum and Coba Avenues. But every plan had to allow for contingencies, had to have numerous alternative agendas. So if Buchanan didn't make the rendezvous, his case officer would try again at eight tomorrow morning outside a coffee shop on Uxmal Avenue, and if Buchanan still did not arrive, the case officer would try once more at noon outside a pharmacy on Yaxchilan Avenue. If that third contact failed to happen, Buchanan's case officer would return to his apartment and wait for Buchanan to get in touch with him. Forty-eight hours later, if the case officer still hadn't heard from Buchanan, he would assume a worst-possibility scenario and get out of the country, lest he too become a liability. A delicate investigation would be set into motion to learn what had happened to Buchanan.

Ninety minutes from now, Buchanan thought. I have to get to that cantina. But spasms in his right hand distracted him. He stared down and saw the fingers of his right hand – and only those fingers, not those on his left hand – twitching again. They seemed not to belong to him. They seemed controlled by a force that wasn't his. He didn't understand. Had the bullet that slashed his shoulder injured the nerves that led down to his fingers?

He suddenly had trouble concentrating. The pain in his skull increased. His bullet wound throbbed. He felt something warm and wet seep from the towel that formed a pressure bandage over his wound. He didn't need to look to know that the towel, held in place by his belt, was becoming saturated and starting to leak.

His vision became alarmingly hazy. At once, it cleared as he tensed, hearing footsteps beyond the door.

The footsteps echoed slowly, hesitantly, along the concrete

corridor, increasing in volume. They stopped outside the door. Buchanan sweated, frowning when he saw and heard the doorknob being turned. As a matter of course, he had locked the door after he'd entered the room. Even so, whoever was out there presumably worked for the hotel and might have a key. Someone out there pushed at the door. When it wouldn't open, the person shoved harder, then rammed what probably was a shoulder against it. No effect.

'Who is in this room?' a gruff male voice demanded in Spanish. Knuckles rapped on the door. 'Answer me.' A fist pounded. 'What are you doing in there?'

If he's got a key, now is when he'll use it, Buchanan thought. But what made him come down here and check this particular room? The hesitant footsteps I heard along the corridor . . . the man seemed almost to be looking for something.

Or following something?

As Buchanan shifted quietly toward the side of the door where he could shut off the light and grab the man if he used a key to enter, he glanced down and realized that the man had indeed been following something. Buchanan's drenched clothes had dripped on the concrete, making a trail.

Buchanan listened nervously for the metallic scrape of a key that the man would shove into the lock. Instead what Buchanan heard was more pounding, another indignant 'What are you doing in there?', and sudden silence.

Maybe he doesn't have a key. Or else he's afraid to use it.

Abruptly the footsteps retreated, clattering along the corridor, diminishing up the stairway.

I've got to get out of here before he has time to come back with help, Buchanan thought. He freed the lock, opened the door, checked the dim corridor, and was just about to leave when he noticed what seemed like rags on one of the shelves. The rags were actually a rumpled, soiled, cotton work-jacket and a battered, stained baseball cap from which the patch had been torn. He grabbed them. After using the jacket to wipe his fingerprints from everything he'd touched, he hurried along the corridor and up the staircase, seeing the wet trail he'd made.

The trail didn't matter now. All that did was getting away from the hotel before the worker came back with help. They'll probably call the police about a prowler. The police will be so frantic to arrest a suspect for the three killings that they might decide this incident is related. They'll focus their search in this area.

Buchanan swung toward where the shadowy beach would eventually take him near downtown Cancun. Heading north, he ran midway between the white-capped waves and the gleaming hotels. A fragrant sea breeze cooled the sweat on his brow and cleared the utility room's foul smell from his nostrils. The breeze had sufficient strength that it might even dry his wet clothes.

But abruptly he stumbled, losing his balance enough that he almost fell. It wouldn't have worried him so much if he had tripped over an unseen object. However, he had stumbled for the worst reason he could imagine. Because he was weaker. His wound pulsed, soaking the towel with blood. His skull throbbed from the sharpest headache of his life.

Wedged between his right arm and his side, he had the rumpled, cotton work-jacket and the stained, baseball cap. Gingerly, he set the cap on his head. The cap was battered enough that it might attract attention, but without it, the blood that it hid would certainly attract a lot more attention. Breathing with effort, he draped the soiled work-jacket over his right shoulder, hiding the blood-stained towel strapped over his wound. Now he could take the chance of showing himself in public. But as he pushed a button on his watch and looked at the digital time display, he discovered to his shock that almost an hour had passed since he'd phoned his case officer. *That's impossible! I left the utility room just a little while ago.*

You think.

Pal, you must be having blackouts.

Buchanan's thoughts became more urgent. He would have to veer between hotels and get a taxi on the throughway. Otherwise he'd never be able to reach the rendezvous site in time to meet his case officer. Unsteady, he left the beach.

He'd been right about one thing at least – the breeze from the sea had dried his clothes sufficiently that they didn't stick to him.

But the breeze no longer had any effect on the sweat that dripped from his brow.

4

'Jesus,' Buchanan's case officer said, 'that wound needs stitches. Take off your cap. Let me look at . . . Yeah, oh, man, that gash on your skull needs stitches, too.'

They were stopped at an abandoned gas station on Highway 180, thirty kilometers west of Cancun. After taking a taxi into the downtown part of the city, Buchanan had waited no more than half a minute at the rendezvous site before his case officer stopped a rented Ford Taurus in front of the busy cantina and Buchanan got in.

The case officer was in his fifties, slightly balding, slightly overweight. His clothes . . . sandals, a lemon-colored polo shirt, and lime-colored shorts . . . matched his cover as a tourist. He and Buchanan hadn't worked together before. Buchanan knew him only as Wade, which Buchanan assumed was neither his real name, nor his usual cover name.

After Buchanan explained, Wade exhaled. 'Shit. It's completely unsalvageable. Damn it to hell. God . . . Okay, let's think a minute.' He tapped his fingers on the steering wheel. 'Let's make sure we . . . The police'll be watching the airport in town and probably the one on Cozumel. That leaves us the next closest option.'

'Mérida,' Buchanan said.

Wade increased speed as he drove from Cancun. 'That's assuming our best move is to get you out of the country. Maybe you ought to hole up somewhere. Go to ground. Hey, all the police have is a description that fits a lot of Americans. It's not like they have a photograph. Or fingerprints. You said you took care of that.'

Buchanan nodded, feeling nauseous. 'Except for the glasses I drank from in the restaurant. I couldn't do anything about them. The odds are they were taken to the kitchen and washed before the police thought to check them.' Buchanan raised his uninjured left arm and wiped increasing sweat from his brow. 'The *real* problem is, everybody in the restaurant heard Bailey call me Crawford, and me insist that I was Ed Potter. So the police have a name that Mexican emigration officers can watch for at airports.'

'That doesn't bother me,' Wade said. 'I brought an alternate passport and tourist card for you. Another pseudonym.'

'Good. But the police also have Bailey himself. They'll insist he help one of their artists prepare a sketch, and once copies of that sketch are faxed to every airport and every emigration officer, anybody who resembles the sketch will be stopped when he turns in his tourist card and pays his exit fee. I have to get out of the country before that sketch is distributed. Plus . . .' Buchanan stared at the fingers of his right hand. They were twitching again, an unwilled motion as if they weren't a part of him. His wounded arm seemed on fire. Blood soaked the towel strapped to his arm. 'I need a doctor.'

Wade glanced in his rearview mirror. 'I don't see any headlights behind us.' He peered ahead along the narrow forest-lined highway. 'This deserted gas station is as good a place as any.' He pulled off the road, got out, took something from the back seat, and came around to Buchanan's side of the car.

But after he opened Buchanan's door, exposed Buchanan's injuries, and aimed a narrow-beamed flashlight at them, he muttered, 'No shit you need a doctor. You need stitches.'

'I can't depend on somebody local not to notify the police about a gunshot wound,' Buchanan said.

'No problem,' Wade replied. 'I have contact with an American doctor in the area. He's worked for us before. We can trust him.'

'But I can't waste time going to him.' Buchanan's voice was raspy, his mouth dry. 'The police will soon have that sketch ready. I have to reach Mérida. I have to get on a plane out of Mexico. Hell, Florida's just a couple of hours away by jet. When I said I need a doctor, I meant *stateside*. The quicker I'm out of here, the quicker I can . . .'

'You'll bleed to death before then,' Wade said. 'Didn't you hear me? I said you need *stitches*. At the least. I don't know about the gash in your head, but the wound in your arm – it's hard to tell with so much blood – it looks infected.'

'The way it feels, it probably is.' Buchanan struggled to rouse himself. 'What's that you set on the ground?'

'A first-aid kit.'

'Why didn't you say so?'

'Hey, what you've got wrong with you is more than any first-aid kit's going to help.'

'I keep forgetting. You're a civilian. One of those guys from the Agency.'

Wade straightened, defensive. 'You don't expect me to reply to that, do you? Besides, what difference does it make?'

'Just open the kit,' Buchanan said. 'Let's see what you've got. Good. *My* people prepared it. Pay attention. Do what I tell you. We've got to get the bleeding stopped. We have to clean the wounds.'

'We? Come on I don't know anything about this. I haven't been trained to—'

'*I* have.' Buchanan tried to stop his mind from swirling. 'Take that rubber tube and tie it above the wound in my shoulder. For five minutes, a tourniquet won't do much damage. Meanwhile . . .' Buchanan tore open a packet and dumped out several gauze sponges.

Wade finished tying the rubber tube around Buchanan's exposed shoulder. The bleeding lessened dramatically.

'That plastic container of rubbing alcohol,' Buchanan said. 'Pour some of it onto those gauze sponges and start wiping the blood away from the bullet wound.' It seemed to Buchanan that his voice came from far away. Fighting to remain alert, he pried a syringe from a slot in a block of protective styrofoam and squinted at the label, satisfying himself that the contents were an antibiotic. 'Use a clean sponge and wipe some of that alcohol on the upper muscle of my right arm.'

Wade did what he was told, then quickly resumed cleaning the bullet wound.

Buchanan injected the antibiotic into his right arm. As soon as he withdrew the needle, the fingers of his right hand starting jerking again. Clumsily he returned the syringe to the slot in the styrofoam block.

'There,' Wade said. 'I finished cleaning the edges of the wound.'

'Now pour that hydrogen peroxide into it,' Buchanan said.

'Pour?' Wade asked. 'That'll hurt like—'

'Nothing compared to dying from blood poisoning. The wound has to be disinfected. *Do it*.'

Wade unscrewed the top from the hydrogen peroxide, pursed his lips, and poured what amounted to several tablespoons of the clear liquid into the long slash of the wound.

In the glow from the flashlight propped on the seat, Buchanan saw the liquid enter the slash. He saw his flesh and blood begin to bubble, like boiling acid. The pain suddenly hit him, even worse than the pain he'd already been feeling. It gnawed. It stabbed. It burned.

His vision doubled. He wavered.

'Buchanan?' Wade sounded alarmed.

'Do it again,' Buchanan said.

'You can't be serious.'

'Do it again. *I've got to be sure the wound's clean.*'

Wade poured. The wound bubbled, its edges turning white, clots of blood welling out. Sweat slicked Buchanan's face.

'And some on the gash on my head,' Buchanan murmured.

This time, Wade surprised Buchanan by complying without objection. Good, Buchanan thought through his pain. You're tougher than I expected, Wade. You're going to need to be when you hear what you have to do next.

The hydrogen peroxide felt as if it ate through Buchanan's skull and into his brain.

He shuddered. 'Fine. Now you see that tube in the first-aid kit? That's a triple-antibiotic ointment. Squeeze some on the gash on my head and a lot more into my bullet wound.'

Wade's movements became more confident.

Buchanan felt the tourniquet digging into his right shoulder. Apart from the agony of the wound, the arm seemed swollen and had no sensation. 'Almost done,' Buchanan told Wade. 'There's only one more thing you have to do.'

'One more? What's that?'

'You were right. I need stitches.'

'What are you talking about?'

'I want you to sew me up.'

'Sew you—? Jesus Christ.'

'Listen to me. Without stitches, once that tourniquet's released, I'll hemorrhage. There's a sterile surgical needle and thread in that foil pouch. Wash your hands with rubbing alcohol, open the pouch, and *sew me up*.'

'But I've never done anything like—'

'It isn't complicated,' Buchanan said. 'I don't give a damn about neatness, and I'll tell you how to tie the knots. *But it has to be done.* If I could reach that far around my shoulder, I'd do it myself.'

'The pain,' Wade objected. 'I'll be so clumsy . . . You need anesthetic.'

'Even if we had some, I couldn't risk using it. I have to stay alert. There's so little time. While we drive to Mérida, you have to coach me about the identity you're giving me to get out of the country.'

'Buchanan, you look as if you're ready to pass out as it is.'

'You son of a bitch, don't ever do that to me again.'

'Do what? What are you—?'

'You called me "Buchanan". I forgot about Buchanan. I don't know who Buchanan is. On this assignment, my name's Ed Potter. If I respond to the name "Buchanan," I could get myself killed. From now on . . . No, I'm wrong. I'm not Ed Potter anymore. I'm . . . Tell me who I am. What's my new identity? What's my background? What do I do for a living? Am I married? Talk to me, damn it, while you sew me up.'

Cursing, insulting, commanding, Buchanan forced Wade to use the curved surgical needle and stitch the bullet wound shut. With each thrust of the needle, Buchanan gritted his teeth harder until his jaw ached and he feared that his teeth would crack. The only thing that kept him from losing consciousness was his desperate need to acquire his new persona. He was Victor Grant, he learned. From Fort Lauderdale, Florida. He customized cabin cruisers and yachts, specializing in installing audio-visual electronics. He'd been in Cancún to speak with a client. If he had to, he could give the client's name and local address. The client, cooperating with Buchanan's employers, would vouch for Victor Grant.

'Okay,' Wade said. 'It looks like hell, but I think it'll hold.'

'Smear antibiotic cream on a thick gauze pad. Press the bandage onto the stitches. Secure the pad with a wraparound bandage, several layers, and wrap the bandage with tape.' Buchanan sweated from pain, his muscles rigid. 'Good,' he said. 'Now release the tourniquet.'

He felt a surge of blood into his arm. As the numbness lessened, his flesh prickling, the already severe pain became worse. But he didn't care about that. He could handle pain. Pain was temporary. But if the stitches didn't hold and he hemorrhaged, he didn't need to worry about remembering his new identity or about getting to the Mérida airport before a police sketch of him was faxed there or about being questioned by an emigration officer at the airport. None of those worries would matter. Because by then he'd have bled to death.

For a long minute, he stared at the bandage. No blood seeped through it. 'Okay, let's move.'

'Just in time,' Wade said. 'I see headlights coming behind us.' He shut the first-aid kit, slammed Buchanan's door, ran around to get in the driver's side, and veered onto the road before the headlights came near.

Buchanan tilted his head back, breathing hoarsely. His mouth was terribly dry. 'Have you got any water?'

'Sorry. I didn't think to bring any.'

'Great.'

'Maybe there'll be a place open where we can buy some.'

'Sure.'

Buchanan stared ahead through the windshield, watching the glare of the car's headlights pierce the night. He kept repeating to himself that his name was Victor Grant. From Fort Lauderdale. A customizer of pleasure boats. Electronics. Divorced. No children. The tropical forest crowded each side of the narrow road. On occasion, he glimpsed machete-scarred trees from which chicle had been drained to make chewing gum. On occasion, too, he saw groups of thatched huts, aware that the inhabitants were Maya, with the broad features, high cheekbones, and folded eyelids of their ancestors who had built the great monuments at Chichén Itzá and other ancient cities now turned to ruin in the Yucatán peninsula. Rarely, he saw a dim light through the open door of a hut and a family sleeping in various hammocks, the hammocks helping them to stay cool and to keep them safe from reptiles prowling in the night, for Yucatán meant 'place of snakes.' Mostly what he noticed was that every time the car approached a group of thatched huts, evidently a village, a sign at the side of the road said *TOPE* – slow down – and then, no matter how slowly Wade drove, the car lurched over a traffic bump in the road and jolted Buchanan enough that his head jerked off the back of the seat, brutally intensifying the pain in his skull and in his shoulder. His right hand again became spastic. Away from the sea, the humidity on the peninsula felt smothering. But the air was so still, so laden with bugs that the car's windows had to be closed. Victor Grant. Fort Lauderdale. Pleasure boats. Electronics.

He passed out.

5

Despite a ground-mist that obscured the illumination from the moon and stars, Balam-Acab had little difficulty moving through the rain forest at night. Part of his skill was due to his having been born in this region. After thirty years, he was thoroughly at home in the jungle. Nonetheless, the jungle was a living thing, ever shifting, and another reason that Balam-Acab knew his way so well through the crowding trees and drooping vines was the feel of stones beneath his thin sandals. After all, he had made this particular journey many times. Habit was in his favor.

In the dark, he let the flat, worn stones guide his footsteps. During the day, the pattern of the stones would not be evident to an inexperienced observer. Trees thrust up among them. Bushes concealed them. But Balam-Acab knew that a thousand years ago, the stones would have formed an uninterrupted path that the ancients had called a *sacbe*: 'white road.' The name was not strictly accurate inasmuch as the large, flat stones were more gray than white, but even in its dilapidated condition, the walkway was impressive.

How much more so would it have been during the time of the ancients, before the Spanish conquerors, when Balam-Acab's ancestors had ruled this land? There had been a time when Mayan roads had crisscrossed the Yucatán. Trees had been cut, swaths hacked through the jungle. In the cleared section, stones had been placed, forming a level that was two to four feet above the ground. Then rubble had been spread over the stones, to fill the gaps between them, and finally the stones and rubble had been covered with a concrete made from burned, powdered limestone mixed with gravel and water.

Indeed the path that Balam-Acab followed had once been a smooth road that was almost sixteen feet wide and sixty miles long. But since the extermination of so many of his ancestors, there had been no one to attend to the road, to care for and repair it. Centuries of rain had dissolved the concrete and washed away the rubble, exposing the stones, and the area's numerous earthquakes and the sprouting vegetation caused them to shift. Now only someone as aware of the old ways and as attuned to the spirit of the forest as Balam-Acab was could follow the path so skillfully in the misty darkness.

Stepping from stone to stone, veering around unseen trees, sensing and stooping to avoid vines, alert for the slightest unsteadiness underfoot, Balam-Acab maintained perfect balance. He *had* to, for if he fell, he couldn't use his arms to grab for support. His arms were already occupied, carrying a precious bowl wrapped in a soft, protective blanket. He hugged it to his chest. Given the circumstances, he didn't dare take the risk of packing the bowl in his knapsack along with his other important objects. Too often, the knapsack was squeezed against a branch or a tree. The objects within the knapsack were unbreakable. Not so the bowl.

The humidity in the underbrush added to the sweat that slicked Balam-Acab's face and stuck his cotton shirt and pants to his body. He wasn't tall — only five foot three, typical for the males of his tribe. Although sinewy, he was thin, partly from the exertions of living in the jungle, partly from the meager diet provided by his village's farms. His hair was straight and black, cut short to keep it free from insects and prevent it from being entangled in the jungle. Because of the isolation of this region and because the Spanish conquerors had disdained to have children with the Maya, Balam-Acab's facial features bore the same genetic traits as his ancestors when Mayan culture was at its zenith centuries before. His head was round, his face broad, his cheekbones pronounced. His thick, lower lip had a dramatic downward curve. His eyes were dark, with the shape of an almond. His eyelids had a Mongolian fold.

Balam-Acab knew that he resembled his ancestors because he had seen engravings of them. He knew how his ancestors had lived because his father had told him what *his* father had told him what *his* father had told him, as far back as the tribe had been in existence. He knew how to perform the ritual he intended because as the ruler and shaman of the village he had been taught by his predecessor, who revealed to him the sacred mysteries that had been passed on to *him* just as they'd been passed on to *his* predecessor and that dated back to 13.0.0.0.0. 4 *Ahau* 8 *Cumku*, the beginning of time.

The direction of the stones changed, curving toward the left. With perfect balance, Balam-Acab squeezed between more

108

trees, stooped beneath more vines, and felt the pressure of the stones beneath his thin sandals, following the curve. He had nearly reached his destination. Although his progress had been almost silent, he now had to be even *more* silent. He had to creep with the soundless grace of a stalking jaguar, for he would soon reach the edge of the jungle, and beyond, in the newly created clearing, there would be guards.

Abruptly Balam-Acab smelled them, their tobacco smoke, their gun oil. Nostrils widening, he paused to study the darkness and judge distance as well as direction. In a moment, he proceeded, forced to leave the ancient, hidden pathway and veer farther left. Since the new conquerors had arrived to chop down the trees and dynamite the rocky surface, to smooth the land and build an airstrip, Balam-Acab had known that the disaster predicted by the ancients was about to occur. Just as the *first* conquerors had been predicted, these had as well, for time was circular, Balam-Acab knew. It turned and went around, and each period of time had a god in charge of it.

In this case, the thunder of the dynamite reminded him of the thunder of the fanged rain god, Chac. But it also reminded him of the rumble of the area's numerous earthquakes that always signified when the god of the Underworld, who was also the god of Darkness, was angry. And when that god was angry, he caused pain. What Balam-Acab had not yet been able to decide was whether the new conquerors would make the god of the Underworld and of Darkness furious, or whether the new conquerors were the *result* of that god's already excessive fury, a punishment for Balam-Acab and his people.

All he could be certain of was that placating rituals were demanded, prayers and sacrifices, lest the prediction in the ancient *Chronicles of Chilam Balam* again come true. One of the signs, the sickness that was killing the palm trees, had already come true.

* * *

On that day, dust claims the earth.
On that day, a blight covers the earth.
On that day, a cloud hangs low.
On that day, a mountain soars.
On that day, a strong man clutches the land.
On that day, things collapse into ruin.

Balam-Acab was fearful of the sentries, but he was also hopeful of succeeding in his mission. After all, if the gods did not want to be placated, if they were truly furious, they would have punished him before now. They would never have allowed him to get this far. Only someone favored by the gods could have walked through the darkness and not been bitten by any of the area's numerous, swarming serpents. In the daylight, he could see and avoid the snakes or else make noises and scare them away. But walking silently and blindly at night? No. Impossible. Without the protection of the gods, he should have stepped not on stones but on death.

At once the density of the darkness changed. The mist seemed less thick. Balam-Acab had reached the edge of the jungle. Hunkering, inhaling the fecund odors of the forest in contrast with the rancid, sweat smell of the sentries, he focused on the night, and suddenly, as if an unfelt breeze had swept across the clearing, the fog dissipated. Unexpectedly able now to see the illumination from the moon and stars, he felt as if night had turned into day. At the same time, he had the eerie certainty that when he crept from the jungle into the clearing, the sentries would not be able to see him. From their point of view, the fog would still exist. It would envelop him. It would make him invisible.

But he wasn't a fool. When he stepped from the jungle, he stayed low, close to the ground, trying not to reveal his silhouette as he hurried forward. In the now-evident light from the moon and stars, he could see and was disturbed by the extent of the work that the invaders had accomplished in the mere two days since he had last been here. A vast new section of forest had been leveled, exposing more brush-covered mounds and hillocks. Without the trees to obscure the skyline, the murky contours of considerably higher breaks in the terrain were also evident. Balam-Acab thought of them as mountains, but none of them was the mountain predicted as one of the signs of the end of the world in the ancient *Chronicles of Chilam Balam*.

No, *these* mountains were part of the spirit of the universe. Granted, they weren't natural. After all, this part of the Yucatán was called the flatlands. Mounds, hillocks, and certainly mountains did not exist. They had all been built here by human beings, by Balam-Acab's Mayan ancestors, more than a thousand years ago. Although the brush that covered them camouflaged their steps, portals, statuary and engravings, Balam-Acab knew that the elevations were palaces, pyramids, and temples. The reason they were part of the spirit of the universe was that the ancients who had built them knew how the Underworld, the Middleworld, and the glorious arch of the heavens were linked. The ancients had used their knowledge of the secrets of the passing sun to determine the exact places where monuments in honor of the gods needed to be situated, and in so doing, they focused the energy of both the Underworld and heavenly gods toward the Middleworld and this sacred precinct.

Wary of the armed intruders, Balam-Acab came to the tallest mountain. The excavators had been quick to clear the vegetation from the level ground, but whenever they had come to an elevated area, they had left it undisturbed, presumably intending to return and violate it later. He studied the shadowy bushes and saplings that had somehow found places to root between the huge, square, stone blocks that formed this consecrated edifice. If the bushes and saplings weren't present,

Balam-Acab knew that what looked like a mountain would actually reveal itself to be an enormous, terraced pyramid, and that at the top there would be a temple dedicated to the god, Kukulcan, the meaning of whose name was 'plumed serpent.'

Indeed the weathered, stone image of a serpent's gigantic head – mouth open, teeth about to strike – projected from the bushes at the bottom of the pyramid. Even in the dark, the serpent's head was manifest. It was one of several that flanked the stairs that ascended through the terraces on each side of the pyramid. Heart swelling, reassured that he had managed to get this far unmolested, becoming more convinced that the gods favored his mission, Balam-Acab held the blanket-covered bowl protectively to his chest and began the slow, painstaking ascent to the top.

Each step was as high as his knee, and the stairway was angled steeply. During daylight, the arduous climb could be dizzying, not to mention precarious because the bushes, saplings, and centuries of rain had broken the steps and shifted the stones. He needed all his strength and concentration not to lose his balance in the dark, step on a loose rock, and fall. He didn't care about his own safety. Otherwise he wouldn't have risked being bitten by snakes or shot by sentries in order to come here. What he *did* care about were the precious objects in his knapsack and in particular the sacred, blanket-wrapped bowl he clutched to his chest. He didn't dare fall and break the bowl. That would be inexcusable. That for certain would prompt the fury of the gods.

As he climbed, his knees aching, his body drenched with sweat, Balam-Acab mentally counted. It was the only way he could measure his progress, for the bushes and saplings above him prevented him from distinguishing the outline of the square temple at the otherwise pointed top of the pyramid. Ten, eleven, twelve . . . One hundred and four, one hundred and . . . He strained to breathe. Two hundred and eighty-nine.

Two hundred and . . . Soon, he thought. By now he could see the top against the stars. Three hundred and . . . At last, his heart pounding, he reached the flat surface in front of the temple.

Three hundred and sixty-five. That sacred number represented the number of days in the solar year and had been calculated by Balam-Acab's ancestors long before the Spanish conquerors first came to the Yucatán in the fifteen-hundreds. Other sacred numbers had been incorporated into the pyramid – the twenty terraces, for example, which signified the units of twenty days into which the ancients had divided their shorter, two-hundred-and-sixty-day ceremonial year. Similarly there originally had been fifty-two stone images of serpents along the top of the temple, for time revolved in a fifty-two-year circle.

Circles were very much in Balam-Acab's thoughts as he gently set down the blanket, unwrapped it, and exposed the precious bowl. It didn't look remarkable. As wide as the distance from his thumb to his elbow, as thick as his thumb, it was old, yes, obviously very old, but it had no brilliant colors, just a dull, dark interior coating, and an outsider might have called it ugly.

Circles, Balam-Acab kept thinking. No longer impeded by his need to protect the bowl, he moved swiftly, taking off his knapsack, removing an obsidian knife, a long cord stitched with thorns, and strips of paper made from the bark of a fig tree. Quickly he removed his sweat-soaked shirt, exposing his gaunt chest to the god of the night.

Circles, cycles, revolutions. Balam-Acab positioned himself so that he stood at the entrance to the temple, facing east, toward where the sun each day began its cycle, toward the direction of the symbol of rebirth. From this high vantage point, he could see far around the pyramid. Even in the dark, he detected the obvious large area that the invaders had denuded of trees. More, he could distinguish the gray area that marked the airstrip a quarter-mile to his right. He could see the numerous large tents that the invaders had erected and the log buildings that they were constructing from the fallen trees. He saw several campfires that he hadn't been able to notice from the jungle, armed guards casting shadows. Soon more airplanes would arrive with more conquerors and more machinery. More gigantic helicopters would bring more heavy vehicles. The area would become more desecrated. Already a road was being bulldozed through the jungle. Something had to be done to stop them.

Cycles. Revolutions. Balam-Acab's father had told him that his name had a special history in the village. Centuries before, when the conquerors had first arrived, Balam-Acab's namesake had led a band of warriors that attempted to repulse the Spanish from the Yucatán. The struggle had persisted for several years until Balam-Acab's namesake was captured and hacked into pieces, then burned. But the glory of the rebel persisted beyond his death, indeed until the present generation, and Balam-Acab was proud to bear the name.

But burdened as well. It wasn't a coincidence that he'd been given this name instead of another. History moved in circles, just as periodically the Maya had again revolted against their oppressors. Stripped of their culture, yoked into slavery, the Maya had rebelled during the sixteen hundreds, again in the eighteen hundreds, and most recently in the early part of this century. Each time, they had been fiercely defeated. Many were forced to retreat to the remotest parts of the jungle in order to avoid retribution and the terrible sicknesses brought by the outsiders.

And now the outsiders had come again. Balam-Acab knew that if they weren't stopped, his village would be destroyed. Circles, cycles, revolutions. He was here to make a sacrifice to the gods, to ask for their wisdom, to pray for their counsel. He needed to be guided. His namesake had no doubt conducted this same ritual during the fifteen hundreds. Uncontaminated, it would be repeated.

He raised his obsidian knife. Its black, volcanic glass – 'the fingernail of the lightning bolt' – was sharpened to a stiletto-like point. He raised it to the underside of his outstretched tongue, struggling to ignore the pain as he thrust upward, piercing. The only way he could manage the task was by clamping his teeth against his tongue to hold it in place so that the exposed, slippery flesh could not resist the blade. Blood gushed from his tongue, drenching his hand. He trembled from shock.

Nonetheless, he continued thrusting upward. Only when the obsidian point came completely through his tongue and scraped along his upper teeth did he remove it. Tears welled from his eyes. He stifled the urge to moan. Continuing to clamp his tongue with his teeth, he lowered the knife and raised the cord stitched with thorns. As his ancestors had done, he shoved the cord through the hole in his tongue and began to pull upward. Sweat burst from his face, no longer from humidity and exertion but from agony. The first thorn in the cord reached the hole in his tongue. Although it snagged, he pulled it through. Blood ran down the cord. He persisted in pulling, forcing another thorn through his tongue. And another. Blood cascaded down the cord and soaked the strips of paper where the bottom of the cord rested in the precious bowl.

Inside the temple behind him, there were images of Balam-Acab's ancestors performing this ritual. In some cases, the king had impaled his penis, then thrust the cord of thorns through that organ instead of his tongue. But whatever part of the body was used, the objective was the same – through pain and blood, to achieve a vision state, to communicate with the Otherworld, to understand what the gods advised and indeed demanded.

Weakened, Balam-Acab sank to his knees as if he worshipped

the blood-soaked strips of paper in the bowl. As soon as the cord of thorns had been pulled completely through his tongue, he would place it in the bowl with the strips of paper. He would add more paper and a ball of copal incense. Then he would use matches – the only adulteration of the rite that he permitted – and set fire to his offering, adding more paper as necessary, the flames boiling and eventually burning his blood.

His mind swirled. He wavered, struggling to maintain a delirious balance between consciousness and collapse, for his ancestors would not have performed this rite without assistance whereas he would have to rouse himself and proceed alone through the jungle back to the village.

He thought that the gods began to speak to him. He heard them, at the edge of hearing. He felt them, felt their presence, felt—

The tremor spread through him. But it wasn't a tremor caused by shock or pain. The tremor came from outside him, through the stones upon which he knelt, through the pyramid upon which he conducted his ritual, through the earth beneath which lay the god of Darkness to whom he appealed.

The tremor was caused by the shockwave from dynamite as a crew continued their devastation despite the night. The rumble sounded like a moan from a restive god.

He raised a book of matches, struck one, and dropped it onto the strips of paper that lay above his blood in the sacred bowl.

Circles.

Again time had turned.

This holy place was being defiled.

The conquerors had to be conquered.

FOUR

1

When Buchanan wakened, he was soaked with sweat, his lips so parched that he knew he had a fever. He swallowed several aspirins from the first-aid kit, almost gagging, forcing them down his dry throat. By then, it was after dawn. He and Wade were in Mérida, 322 kilometers west of Cancun, near the Gulf of Mexico side of the Yucatán peninsula. Unlike Cancun, Mérida evoked an Old World feeling, its great mansions dating from the turn of the century. Indeed the city had once been called the 'Paris of the Western World,' for in former, richer times, millionaire merchants had deliberately tried to make Mérida like Paris, where they often went on vacation. The city still retained much of its European charm, but Buchanan was too delirious to care about the tree-lined avenues and the horse-drawn carriages. 'What time is it?' he asked, too listless to peer at his watch.

'Eight o'clock.' Wade parked near a not-yet-open market. 'Will you be okay if I leave you alone for a while?'

'Where are you going?'

Wade answered, but Buchanan didn't hear what he said, his mind drifting, sinking.

When he wakened again, Wade was unlocking the Ford, getting in. 'I'm sorry I took so long.'

117

So long? Buchanan thought. 'What do you mean?' His vision was bleary. His tongue felt swollen. 'What time is it now?'

'Almost nine. Most stores still aren't open. But I managed to get you some bottled water.' Wade untwisted a cáp from a bottle of Evian and tilted it toward Buchanan's parched lips.

Buchanan's mouth seemed like a dry sponge, absorbing most of the water. Some trickled down his chin. Frustrated, he tried again and this time managed to swallow. 'Give me more of those aspirins.' His throat sounded as if it were wedged with stones.

'Still feverish?'

Buchanan nodded, grimacing. 'And this bitch of a headache won't stop.'

'Hold out your hand. I'll give you the aspirins.'

Buchanan's left hand felt weak, and his right hand suddenly became spastic again. 'Better put them in my mouth.'

Wade frowned.

Buchanan swallowed the aspirins with more water.

'You have to keep your strength up. You can't survive on just water,' Wade said. 'I brought donuts, milk, and coffee.'

'I don't think my stomach would tolerate the donuts.'

'You're scaring me,' Wade said. 'We should have gone to the doctor I know in Cancun.'

'We've been over this,' Buchanan murmured. 'I have to get out of the country before the police sketch is circulated.'

'Well, what about orange juice? At least try the orange juice I brought.'

'Yes,' Buchanan murmured. 'The orange juice.'

He managed three swallows.

'I found a woman unpacking boxes, getting ready for when the market opens,' Wade said. 'She sold me this straw hat. It'll hide the gash on your head. Also I bought this serape. You can drape it over the bandage on your arm when you pass through emigration.'

'Good,' Buchanan said weakly.

'Before that, I phoned several airlines. For a change, you're in luck. Aeromexico has a seat available on a flight to Miami.'

Buchanan inwardly brightened. Soon, he thought. Soon I'll be out of the country. I can sleep when I'm on the plane. Wade can phone ahead and have a team waiting to take me to a clinic.

'There is a problem, though,' Wade said.

'Problem?' Buchanan frowned.

'The flight doesn't leave until twelve-fifty.'

'Until? But that's . . . what? . . . four hours from now.'

'It was the first flight I could get. Another one left earlier for Houston. It had a seat, but it also made a stop en route.'

'What do I care about a stop? Why didn't you book me on it?'

'Because the stop was back in Cozumel, and the man I spoke to said you had to get off the plane and then reboard.'

Shit, Buchanan thought. Cozumel, near Cancun, was one of the airports he needed to avoid. If he had to leave the plane and pass through a checkpoint, a guard might . . .

'All right, the twelve-fifty flight to Miami,' Buchanan said.

'At the airport, I can't buy your ticket for you. It draws attention. Besides, the clerk will want to see Victor Grant's passport. Very few people give somebody else their passport, especially when they're about to leave the country. If the police have told the attendants to be on the lookout for anybody who acts suspiciously, that might be enough for them to wait for you to arrive and question you.'

'Question both of us.' Buchanan fought to focus his vision. 'You made your point. I'll buy the ticket.' He peered out the window, seeing traffic increase, frowning at the pedestrians crowding past the Ford. 'Right now, I think we'd better drive around town. I get nervous staying parked like this.'

'Right.'

As Wade steered into a break in traffic, Buchanan used his

trembling right hand to reach behind him and pull a waterproof, plastic pouch from his back pocket. 'Here's Ed Potter's ID and passport. Whatever pseudonym I'm using, I always carry his documents. There's no way of predicting when they might come in handy.'

Wade took the plastic pouch. 'I can't give you an official receipt. I don't have any with me.'

'Screw the receipt. Just give me Victor Grant's documents.'

Wade handed him a brown, leather, passport folder.

As Buchanan took it, he felt Ed Potter drain from him and Victor Grant seep into his consciousness. Weak and far from alert, he nonetheless responded to habit and began to imagine traits (Italian food, Dixieland jazz) for his new character. At the same time, he opened the folder and examined its contents.

'Don't worry. Everything's there,' Wade said. 'Including the tourist card.'

'But I do worry.' Buchanan searched through the documents. 'That's how I've stayed alive this long. I never take anyone's word for . . . Yes. Okay, the tourist card and everything else is here. Where's that aspirin bottle?'

'Don't tell me you've still got a headache.' Wade looked troubled.

'And it's getting worse.' Buchanan didn't trust his trembling right hand. Raising his left hand, which felt wooden, he put more aspirins in his mouth and swallowed more orange juice.

'You're sure you want to do this?'

'Want to? No. Have to? Definitely. Okay,' Buchanan said, 'let's go through the drill. I left plenty of loose ends in Cancun.' Breathing was an effort. He fought for energy. 'Here are my keys. When you get back to Cancun, close up my time-share condominium office. You know who I rented it from. Call him. Tell him I've gone out of business. Tell him he can keep the remainder of the rent, that you'll send him the keys as soon as you pick up my belongings.'

'Right.'

'Do the same thing about my apartment. Erase me. You know the places I used in Acapulco, Puerto Vallarta, and the other resorts. Erase me from all of them.' Buchanan's head throbbed. 'What else? Can you think of—?'

'Yes.' As Wade drove along the Paseo de Mayo, Mérida's main thoroughfare, Buchanan ignored the grass-covered island that separated the several lanes of traffic on each side, anxious for Wade to continue.

'The contacts you recruited in each area,' Wade said. 'They'll wonder what happened to you. They'll start asking questions. You have to be erased from their lives, too.'

Of course, Buchanan thought. Why didn't I think of that? I'm more light-headed than I guessed. I have to concentrate harder. 'Do you remember the dead-drop locations I was using to pass each of them messages?'

Wade nodded. 'I'll leave each contact a note, some excuse about problems with the police, along with a final payoff that's generous enough to encourage them to keep their mouths shut.'

Buchanan brooded. 'Is that it, then? Is that everything? There's always something else, a final detail.'

'If there is, I don't know what—'

'Luggage. When I buy my ticket, if I don't have a bag, I'll attract attention.'

Wade steered off the Paseo de Mayo, stopping on a side street. The stores were now open.

'I don't have the strength to carry anything heavy. Make sure the suitcase has rollers.' Buchanan told Wade his sizes. 'I'll need underwear, socks, T-shirts . . .'

'Yes, the usual.' Wade got out of the Ford. 'I can handle it, Buchanan. I've done this before.'

'You son of a bitch.'

'What?'

'I told you don't call me "Buchanan". *I'm Victor Grant.*'

'Right, Victor,' Wade said dryly. 'I wouldn't want you to forget who you were.' He started to close the door, then paused. 'Hey, while you're practicing your lines . . . that is, when you're not calling me names . . . why don't you try eating some of those donuts, so you're not so weak that you fall on your face when you get to the airport?'

Buchanan watched the slightly bald, slightly overweight man in the lemon colored polo shirt disappear into the crowd. Then he locked the doors, tilted his head back, and felt his right hand tremble. At once his whole body shivered. The fever, he thought. It's really getting to me. I'm losing control. Wade's my life line. What am I doing? Don't make him mad.

Buchanan's shoes nudged the bag of donuts on the floor. The thought of eating made him nauseous. As did the pain in his shoulder. And in his skull. He shuddered. Just a few more hours, he told himself. Hang on. All you have to do is get through the airport. He forced himself to drink more orange juice. The acidic sweetness made his stomach queasy. Victor Grant, he told himself, concentrating, struggling to chew on a donut. Victor Grant. Divorced. Fort Lauderdale. Customizes pleasure boats. Installs electronics. Victor . . .

He jerked as Wade unlocked the driver's door and put a suitcase in the back.

'You look terrible,' Wade said. 'I brought a toilet kit: a razor and shaving soap, toothpaste . . .'

2

They drove to a wooded park that had a public washroom. Wade bolted the door and stood behind Buchanan, holding him steady while Buchanan hunched over the sink, trembling, doing his best to shave. He tried to comb his blood-matted hair

122

but didn't have much success, deciding that he'd definitely have to use the straw hat that Wade had bought for him. He used bottled water to brush his teeth, feeling marginally better now that he was partially cleaned up. His shirt and pants, which the sea had cleaned sufficiently of blood to stop people from staring at him last night, were unacceptably soiled and wrinkled in the daylight. He changed into a fresh shirt and pair of pants that Wade had bought, and after they left the washroom, Buchanan crammed the dirty clothes into the suitcase in the Ford's back seat. Associating his Seiko watch with the now-defunct character of Ed Potter, he traded it for Wade's Timex, anything to get the feel of a new identity.

By then, it was eleven o'clock.

'Traveling time,' Wade said.

In contrast with the large, picturesque city, the airport was surprisingly small and drab. Wade managed to find a parking space in the lot in front of the low terminal. 'I'll carry your suitcase to the entrance. After that . . .'

'I understand.'

As they walked toward the entrance, Buchanan glanced casually around, studying the area. No one seemed to be paying attention to him. He concentrated on walking in a straight line, not wavering, not betraying his weakness. At the sidewalk in front of the doors, he shook hands with Wade. 'Thanks. I know I was a little grumpy a couple of times. I . . .'

'Forget it. This isn't a popularity contest.' Wade continued to grip Buchanan's right hand. 'Something's wrong with your fingers. They're jerking.'

'It's not a problem.'

Wade frowned. 'Sure. I'll be seeing you, Victor.' He emphasized the pseudonym. 'Have a good flight.'

'I'm counting on it.'

Buchanan made sure that the serape was hitched firmly to his right shoulder, hiding his wound. He gripped the pull-strap on the suitcase and entered the terminal.

3

Several impressions struck him simultaneously. The terminal was stark, hot, tiny, and crowded. Everyone, except for the few Anglos, seemed in slow motion. As one of those few Anglos, Buchanan attracted attention, Mexican travelers studying him as he inched through the claustrophobia-producing crowd. He sweated as much as they did, feeling faint, wishing the terminal were air-conditioned. At least I'll have a reason for looking sick, he thought, trying to muster confidence. He stood in a frustrating line at the Aeromexico ticket counter. It took him thirty minutes before he faced an attractive female attendant. Using Spanish, he told her what he needed. For a moment his heart lurched when she appeared not to know anything about a reservation for Victor Grant, but then she found the name on her computer screen and with painstaking care made an impression of his credit card, asked him to sign the voucher, and peeled off his receipt.

'*Gracias*.' Hurry, Buchanan thought. His legs were losing their strength.

With even greater care, she tapped keys on the computer and waited for the printer, which also seemed in slow motion, to dislodge the ticket.

But at last Buchanan had it, saying '*Gracias*' again, turning away, pulling the suitcase, inching again through the crowd, this time toward the X-ray machine and the metal detector at the security checkpoint. He felt as if he struggled through a nightmare in which he stood in mud and tried to walk. His vision dimmed for a moment. Then a sudden surge of adrenaline gave him energy. With effort, he used his left hand to lift the suitcase onto the X-ray machine's conveyor belt and proceeded through the metal detector, so off balance that he almost bumped against one of its posts. The detector made no sound. Relieved that the security officers showed no interest in him, Buchanan took his suitcase from the opposite end of the conveyor belt, set it with effort on the floor, and patiently worked his way forward through the crowd. The heat intensified his headache. Whenever someone bumped against his right shoulder, he needed all his discipline not to show how much pain the impact caused him.

Almost there, he thought. Two more checkpoints and I'm through. He stood in a line to pass through a customs inspection. Mexico was lax about many things but not about trying to stop ancient artifacts from being smuggled out of the country.

The haggard customs agent pointed at Buchanan's suitcase. '*Abralo*. Open it.' He didn't look happy.

Buchanan complied, his muscles in agony.

The agent pawed through Buchanan's clothes, glowered when he didn't find anything suspicious, then gestured dismissively.

Buchanan moved onward. Only one more checkpoint, he thought. Emigration. All I have to do is hand in my tourist card, then pay the fifteen-dollar exit fee.

And hope that the emigration officer doesn't have a police sketch of me.

As Buchanan moved tensely through the crowd, he heard a slight commotion behind him. Turning, he saw a tall American shove his way past an Hispanic woman and three children. The American had a salt-and-pepper beard. He wore a gaudy, red-and-yellow-splotched shirt. He held a gym bag and muttered to himself, continuing to push ahead, causing a ripple in the crowd.

The ripple spread toward Buchanan. Trapped by people on every side, he couldn't avoid it. All he could do was brace himself as a man was nudged against another man, who in turn was nudged against Buchanan. Buchanan's legs were so weak that he depended on the people around him to keep him steady, but when the ripple struck him, he suddenly found that the person ahead of him had moved forward. Shoved against his back, Buchanan felt his knees bend and reached ahead to grab for someone to steady him. But at that moment, another ripple in the crowd nudged against his left shoulder. He fell, his mind so dazed that everything seemed a slow blur. When his right shoulder struck the concrete floor, the pain that soared from his wound changed his impression, however, and made everything fast and sharply focused. Sweat from his forehead spattered the concrete. He almost screamed from the impact against his wound.

He struggled to stand, not daring to attract attention. As he came to his feet and adjusted the serape over his wound, he peered ahead through the crowd and noticed that officers at the emigration checkpoint seemed not to have cared about what had happened, concentrating only on collecting tourist cards and exit fees.

He came closer to the checkpoint, breathing easier when he didn't see a police sketch on the counter. But the terminal was so stifling that sweat oozed from his body, slicking his chest and his arms, beading on his palms.

He wiped his left hand on his slacks, then reached in his shirt pocket, and gave the officer a yellow card and the fifteen-dollar exit fee. The officer barely looked at him as he took the card and the money. At once, though, the officer paid more attention, squinted, frowned, and raised his hand. '*Pasaporte, por favor.*'

Why? Buchanan thought in dismay. He didn't compare my face to a sketch. Hell, I don't even see a sketch that he can refer to. If there is a sketch, it's back in the emigration office, but after looking at so many faces, surely the officer can't have a clear memory of the sketch. Why on earth is he stopping me?

Buchanan used his left hand to surrender the passport. The officer opened it, compared the photograph to Buchanan's face, read the personal information, and frowned again at Buchanan. '*Señor Grant, venga conmigo.* Come with me.'

Buchanan tried to look respectfully puzzled. '*Por que?*' he asked. 'Why? Is something wrong?'

The officer squinted harder and pointed toward Buchanan's right shoulder. Buchanan looked and showed no reaction, despite his shock.

Crimson soaked his serape. What he'd thought was sweat was actually blood trickling down his arm, dripping from his fingers. Jesus, he thought, when I fell on my shoulder, I must have opened the stitches.

The officer gestured toward a door. '*Venga conmigo. Usted necesita un medico.* You need a doctor.'

'*Es nada. No es importante,*' Buchanan said. 'It's nothing. A small injury. The bandage needs to be changed. I'll fix it in the bathroom and still have time to catch my plane.'

The officer placed his right hand on his holstered pistol and repeated, this time sternly, 'Come with me *now.*'

Buchanan obeyed, walking with the officer toward a door, trying to look relaxed, as if it were perfectly natural to have blood streaming from his shoulder. He had no hope of fleeing, certain that he'd be stopped before he could push his way through the crowd and reach an exit from the terminal. All he could do was try to bluff his way out, but he doubted that the explanation he was concocting would satisfy the officer after the officer got a look at the wound on his shoulder. There'd be questions. Plenty of questions. And perhaps the police sketch would have arrived by then, if it hadn't already. For sure, he would not be on the 12:50 flight to Miami. So close, he thought.

Unlike the United States, where a suspect is presumed to be innocent until proven guilty, Mexico bases its laws on the Napoleonic Code in which a suspect is guilty until proven innocent. Prisoners are not warned that they have a right to remain silent or told that if they cannot afford an attorney, one will be provided. There is no *habeas corpus*, no right to a speedy trial. In Mexico, such notions are ludicrous. A prisoner has no rights.

Buchanan shared a mildewed, flea-infested, leaky-roofed, pocked-concrete cell that was twenty feet long and fifteen feet wide with twenty other, foully clothed prisoners in what amounted to the tank for thieves and drunkards. To avoid bumping into anyone and causing an argument, Buchanan made sure he stayed in one place with his back to the wall. While the others took up every space on the floor, sleeping on soiled straw, he sank down the wall until he dozed with his head on his knees. He waited as long as he could before using the open hole in a corner that was the toilet. Mostly, despite his lightheadedness, he struggled to remain on guard against an attack. As the only *yanqui*, he was an obvious target, and although his watch and wallet had been taken from him, his clothes and in particular his shoes were better than those of any other prisoner – hard to resist.

As it happened, a great deal of time Buchanan wasn't in the cell, and the attacks didn't come from his fellow prisoners but from his guards. Escorted from the cell to an interrogation room, he was pushed, tripped, and shoved down stairs. While being questioned, he was prodded by batons and beaten with rubber hoses, always in places where clothes would hide the bruises, never around the face or skull. Why his interrogators retained this degree of fastidiousness, Buchanan didn't know. Perhaps because he was a U.S. citizen, and fears about political consequences made them feel slightly constrained. They nonetheless still managed to injure his skull when it struck concrete after they knocked over the wooden chair to which they had tied him. The pain — added to the pain from the gash he'd received when he'd struck the dinghy while swimming across the channel at Cancun — made him nauseous and created a worrisome double vision. If a doctor hadn't redressed and restitched his wounded shoulder at Mérida's jail, he probably would have died from infection and loss of blood, although of course the doctor had been supplied not out of compassion but simply for the practical reason that a dead man couldn't answer questions. Buchanan had encountered this logic before and knew that if the interrogators received the answers they wanted, they would feel no further necessity to provide him with medical courtesies.

That was one reason — the least important — for his refusal to tell his interrogators what they wanted. *The* reason, of course, was that to confess would have been a violation of professional conduct. In refusing to talk, Buchanan had three advantages. First, his interrogators were employing clumsy, brutal methods, which were easier to resist than the precise application of electrical shock combined with such inhibition-reducing drugs as sodium amytal. Second, because he was already weakened by the injury to his head and the wound in his shoulder, he had a tendency to pass out quickly while being tortured, his body supplying a kind of natural anesthesia.

And third, he had a script to follow, a role to play, a scenario that gave him a way to behave. The primary rule was that if captured, he could never admit the truth. Oh, he could use portions of the truth to concoct a believable lie. But the whole truth was out of the question. For Buchanan to say that, yes, he'd killed the three Mexicans, but they were drug dealers after all, and besides he was working under cover for a covert branch of the U.S. military would have temporarily saved his life. However, that life would not have been worth much. As an object lesson to the United States for interfering in Mexican affairs, he might have been forced to serve a lengthy sentence in a Mexican prison, and given the severity of Mexican prisons, especially for *yanquis*, that sentence in all probability would have been the same as a death sentence. Or if Mexico released him to the United States as a gesture of good will (in exchange for favors), his superiors would make his life a nightmare because he had violated his pact with them.

5

'Victor Grant,' an overweight, bearded interrogator with slicked-back dark hair said to Buchanan in a small, plain room that had only a bench upon which the interrogator sat and a chair upon which Buchanan was tied. The round-faced, perspiring interrogator made 'Victor Grant' sound as if the name were a synonym for diarrhea.

'That's right.' Buchanan's throat was so dry that his voice cracked, his body so dehydrated that he'd long ago stopped sweating. One of the tight loops of the rope cut into his stitched, wounded shoulder.

'Speak Spanish, damn you!'

'But I don't *know* Spanish.' Buchanan breathed. 'At least, not very well.' He tried to swallow. 'Just a few words.' Ignorance about Spanish was one of the characteristics he'd chosen for this persona. That way he could always pretend that he didn't know what he was being asked.

'*Cabrón*, you spoke Spanish to the emigration officer at the airport in Mérida!'

'Yes. That's true.' Buchanan's head drooped. 'A couple of simple phrases. What I call "survival Spanish".'

'Survival?' a deep-voiced guard asked behind him, then

grabbed Buchanan's hair and jerked his head up. 'If you do not want your hair pulled out, you will survive by speaking Spanish.'

'*Un poco.*' Buchanan exhaled. 'A little. That's all I know.'

'*Why did you kill those three men in Cancun?*'

'What are you talking about? I didn't kill anyone.'

The overweight interrogator, his uniform stained with sweat, pushed himself up from the bench, his stomach wobbling, and plodded close to Buchanan, then shoved a police sketch in front of his face. The sketch was the same as the one the emigration officer at Mérida's airport had noticed beside a fax machine on a desk in the room to which he had taken Buchanan to find out why he was bleeding.

'Does this drawing look familiar to you?' the interrogator growled. '*Ciertamente*, it does to me. *Dios, sí.* It reminds me of *you.* We have a witness, a fellow *yanqui* in fact, who saw you kill three men in Cancun.'

'I told you I don't know what you're talking about.' Buchanan glared. 'That drawing looks like me and a couple of hundred thousand other Americans.' Buchanan rested his hoarse voice. 'It could be anybody.' He breathed. 'I admit I was in Cancun a couple of days ago.' He licked his dry lips. 'But I don't know anything about any murders.'

'You lie!' The interrogator raised a section of rubber hose and whacked Buchanan across the stomach.

Buchanan groaned but couldn't double over because of the ropes that bound him to the back of the chair. If he hadn't seen the overweight man clumsily start to swing the hose, he wouldn't have been able to harden his stomach enough to minimize the pain. Pretending that the blow had been worse than it was, he snapped his eyes shut and jerked his head back.

'Don't insult me!' the interrogator shouted. 'Admit it! You *lie.*'

'No,' Buchanan murmured. 'Your witness is lying.' He

trembled. 'If there *is* a witness. How could there be? I didn't kill anybody. I don't know anything about . . .'

Each time the interrogator struck him, it gave Buchanan a chance to steal opportunities, to wince, to breathe deeply and rest. Because the police had already taken his watch and wallet, he didn't have anything with which to try to bribe them. Not that he thought a bribe would have worked in this case. Indeed, if he did try to bribe them, under the circumstances his gesture would be the same as an admission of guilt. His only course of action was to play his role, to insist indignantly that he was innocent.

The interrogator held up Buchanan's passport, repeating with the same contemptuous tone, 'Victor Grant.'

'Yes.'

'Even your passport photograph resembles this sketch.'

'That sketch is worthless,' Buchanan said. 'It looks like a ten-year-old did it.'

The interrogator tapped the rubber hose against the bandage that covered the wound on Buchanan's shoulder. 'What is your occupation?'

Wincing, Buchanan told him the cover story.

The interrogator tapped harder against the wound. 'And what were you doing in Mexico?'

Wincing more severely, Buchanan gave the name of the client he supposedly had come here to see. He felt his wound swell under the bandage. Every time the interrogator tapped it, the injury's painful pressure increased, as if it might explode.

'Then you claim you were here on business, not pleasure?'

'Hey, it's always a pleasure to be in Mexico, isn't it?' Buchanan squinted toward the rubber hose that the interrogator tapped even harder against his wound. From pain, his consciousness swirled. He would soon pass out again.

'Then why didn't you have a business visa?'

Buchanan tasted stomach acid. 'Because I only found out a

couple of days ahead of time that my client wanted me to come down here. Getting a business visa takes time. I got a tourist card instead. It's a whole lot easier.'

The interrogator jammed the tip of the hose beneath Buchanan's chin. 'You entered Mexico illegally.' He stared deeply into Buchanan's eyes, then released the hose so Buchanan could speak.

Buchanan's voice thickened, affected by the swelling in his throat that the hose had caused. 'First you accuse me of killing three men.' Breathing became more difficult. 'Now you blame me for failing to have a business visa. What's next? Are you going to charge me with pissing on your floor? Because that's what I'm going to have to do if I'm not allowed to use a bathroom soon.'

The man behind Buchanan yanked his hair again, forcing tears from Buchanan's eyes. 'You do not seem to believe that this is serious.'

'Not true. Take my word, I think this is *very* serious.'

'But you do not act afraid.'

'Oh, I'm afraid. In fact, I'm terrified.'

The interrogator glowered with satisfaction.

'But because I haven't done what you claim I did, I'm also furious.' Buchanan forced himself to continue. 'I've had enough of this.' Each word was an effort. 'I want to see a lawyer.'

The interrogator stared in disbelief, then bellowed with laughter, his huge stomach heaving. 'Lawyer?'

The guard behind Buchanan laughed as well.

'*Un jurisconsulto?*' the interrogator asked with derision. '*Que tu necesitas está un sacerdote.*' He whacked the rubber hose across Buchanan's shins. 'What do you think about that?'

'I told you I hardly know any Spanish.'

'What I said is, you don't need a lawyer, you need a priest. Because all that will help you now, Victor Grant, is prayers.'

'I'm a U.S. citizen. I have a right to . . .' Buchanan couldn't help it. His bladder was swollen beyond tolerance. He had to let go.

Urinating in his pants, he felt the hot liquid stream over the seat of the chair and dribble onto the floor.

'*Cochino!* Pig!' The interrogator whacked Buchanan's wounded shoulder.

Any second now, Buchanan thought. Dear God, let me faint.

The interrogator grabbed Buchanan's shirt and yanked him forward, overturning the chair, toppling him to the floor.

Buchanan's face struck the concrete. He heard the interrogator shout in Spanish to someone about bringing rags, about forcing the gringo to clean up his filth. But Buchanan doubted he'd be conscious by the time the rags arrived. Still, although his vision dimmed, it didn't do so quickly enough to prevent him from seeing with shock that his urine was tinted red. They broke something inside me. I'm pissing blood.

'You know what I think, gringo?' the interrogator asked.

Buchanan wasn't capable of responding.

'I think you are involved with drugs. I think that you and the men you killed had an argument about drug money. I think . . .'

The interrogator's voice dimmed, echoing. Buchanan fainted.

6

He found himself sitting upright once more, still tied to the chair. It took several moments for his vision to focus, for his mind to become alert. Pain definitely helped him sharpen his consciousness. He had no way of knowing how long he'd been out. The room had no windows. The fat interrogator seemed to be wearing the same sweaty uniform. But Buchanan noticed that the blood-tinted urine had disappeared from the floor. Not even a damp spot. Considerable time must have passed, he concluded. Then he noticed something else — that his pants remained wet. Hell, all they did was move me to a different room. They're trying to screw with my mind.

'We have brought a friend to see you.'

'Good.' Buchanan's voice broke. He fought not to lose his strength. 'My client can vouch for me. We can clear up this mistake.'

'Client? Did I say anything about a client?' The interrogator opened the door.

A man, an American, stood flanked by guards in a dim hallway. The man was tall, with broad shoulders and a bulky chest, his sandy hair in a brushcut. He wore sneakers, jeans, and a too-small, green T-shirt, the same clothes he'd been wearing when he'd come into the restaurant at Club Internacional in Cancun. The clothes were rumpled, and the man looked exhausted, his face still red but less from sun and alcohol than from strain. He hadn't shaved. Big Bob Bailey.

Yeah, I bet you're sorry now that you didn't stay away from me at the restaurant, Buchanan thought.

The interrogator gestured sharply, and the guards nudged Bailey into the room, guiding him with a firm hand on each of his elbows. He walked unsteadily.

Sure, they've been questioning you since they caught you on the beach, Buchanan thought. They've been pumping you for every speck of information they can get, and the pressure they put on you encourages you to stick to your story. If they get what they want, they'll apologize and treat you royally to make certain you don't change your mind.

The guards stopped Bailey directly in front of Buchanan.

The interrogator used the tip of the rubber hose to raise Buchanan's face. 'Is this the man you saw in Cancun?'

Bailey hesitated.

'Answer,' the interrogator said.

'I . . .' Bailey drew a shaky hand across his brushcut. 'It could be the man.' He stank of cigarettes. His voice was gravelly.

'*Could be?*' The interrogator scowled and showed him the police sketch. 'When you helped the artist prepare this sketch, I am told that you were definite in your description.'

'Well, yeah, but . . .'

'*But?*'

Bailey cleared his throat. 'I'd been drinkin'. My judgment might have been clouded.'

'And are you sober now?'

'I wish I wasn't, but yeah, I'm sober.'

'Then your judgment should be improved. Is this the man you saw shoot the three other men on the beach behind the hotel?'

'Wait a minute,' Bailey said. 'I didn't see anybody shoot nobody. What I told the police in Cancun was I saw a friend of mine with three Mexicans. I followed 'em from the restaurant to the beach. It was dark. There were shots. I dove for cover. I don't know who shot who, but my friend survived and ran away.'

'It is logical to assume that the man who survived the shooting is responsible for the deaths of the others.'

'I don't know.' Bailey pawed at the back of his neck. 'An American court might not buy that logic.'

'This is *Mexico*,' the interrogator said. '*Is this the man you saw run away?*'

Bailey squinted toward Buchanan. 'He's wearin' different clothes. His hair's got blood in it. His face is dirty. His lips are scabbed. He hasn't shaved, and he generally looks like shit. But yeah, he looks like my friend.'

'*Looks like?*' The interrogator scowled. 'Surely you can be more positive, Señor Bailey. After all, the sooner we get this settled, the sooner you can go back to your hotel room.'

'Okay.' Bailey squinted harder. 'Yeah, I think he's my friend.'

'He's wrong,' Buchanan said. 'I never saw this man in my life.'

'He claims he knew you in Kuwait and Iraq,' the interrogator said. 'During the Gulf War.'

'Oh, sure. Yeah, right.' The pain in Buchanan's abdomen worsened. He bit his lip, then struggled to continue. 'And then he just happened to bump into me in Cancun. Hey, I was never in Kuwait or Iraq, and I can prove it. All you have to do is look at the stamps on my passport. I bet this guy doesn't even know my name.'

'Jim Crawford,' Bailey said with sudden anger. 'Except you lied to me. You told me your name was Ed Potter.'

'Jim Crawford?' Buchanan grimaced at the interrogator. 'Ed Potter? Get real. Does this guy know my name's Victor Grant? Show him my passport. From the sound of things – he admitted as much – he was so drunk I'm surprised he doesn't claim he saw Elvis Presley. I'm not whoever he thinks I am, and I don't know *anything* about three men who were murdered.'

'In Cancun,' the interrogator said, 'my brothers on the police force are investigating Ed Potter. Assuming that you did not lie when you gave Señor Bailey that name, you will have left some evidence in the area. You had to stay somewhere. You had to store your clothes. You had to sleep. We will find that place. There will be people who saw you at that place. We will bring those people here, and they will identify you as Ed Potter, proving that Señor Bailey is right.' The interrogator shook the piece of rubber hose in front of Buchanan's face. 'And then you will explain not only why you shot those three men but why you carry a passport with a different name, why you use so *many* names.'

'Yeah. Like Jim Crawford,' Bailey said. 'In Kuwait.'

The interrogator looked extremely satisfied now that Bailey was cooperating again.

Throughout, Buchanan showed no reaction except pain-aggravated anger. But his thoughts, despite his excruciating headache, were urgent. He worked to calculate how protected he was. He'd used the mail to negotiate for and to pay the rent on his office. The only times he'd spoken to the landlord had been on the telephone. The same methods had been employed with regard to his apartment in downtown Cancun. Recommended tradecraft. So far so good. It was also to Buchanan's advantage that the police would take quite a while to contact every hotel manager and landlord in Cancun. Still, eventually they would, and although Buchanan's landlords couldn't describe him, they would tell the police that they recognized the name 'Ed Potter,' and the police would question people who frequented the area where Ed Potter worked and lived. Eventually someone would be brought here who would agree with Big Bob Bailey's claim that the man who called himself Victor Grant looked very much like Ed Potter, and things would get very sticky after that.

'Let them,' Buchanan said. 'They can waste all the time they want investigating Ed Potter, whoever he is. I'm not worried. *Because I'm not that man.*' Pain gnawed at his abdomen. He had to relieve his bladder once more, and he feared that his urine would be an even darker red. 'The trouble is, while they're wasting their time, I'm getting the hell beat out of me.' He shuddered. 'And it's not going to stop — because I swear to God I won't confess to something I didn't do.' He glared at the beefy, nervous Texan. 'What did this cop say your name is? Bailey? Is that what—?'

Bailey looked exasperated. 'Crawford, you known damned well my name's—'

'Stop calling me "Crawford". Stop calling me "Potter".

138

You've made a terrible mistake, and if you don't get your memory straight . . .'

Buchanan couldn't restrain his bladder any longer. Indeed he didn't want to. He'd suddenly decided on a new tactic. He released his abdominal muscles, urine dribbling onto the floor, and he didn't need to look down to know that the liquid was bloody.

Because Bailey turned pale, raised a hand to his mouth, and mumbled, 'Holy . . . Look at . . . He's . . . It's . . .'

'Yeah, Bailey, take a good look. They worked me over until they broke something inside me.' Buchanan was almost breathless. He had to fight to muster the strength for every word. 'What happens if they kill me before they find out you made a mistake?'

Bailey turned paler.

'Kill you? That is ridiculous,' the interrogator interrupted. 'Obviously you have suffered other injuries besides those to your shoulder and your head. I did not know this. I realize now that you need further medical attention. As soon as Señor Bailey signs this document, identifying you as the man he saw run from the three victims, he can leave, and I can send for a doctor.'

The interrogator thrust a pen and a typed statement toward Bailey.

'Yeah, go ahead and sign it,' Buchanan murmured hoarsely. 'And then pray to God that the police realize there's been a mistake . . . before they beat me worse . . . before I hemorrhage so bad I . . .' Buchanan breathed. 'Because if they kill me, you're next.'

'What?' Bailey frowned. 'What are you talkin' about?'

'Don't be dense, Bailey. Think about it. You're the one who'll be blamed. We're talking about the death of an American citizen in a Mexican jail. Do you think this cop will admit to what happened? My corpse will disappear. There'll be no record of my arrest. And the only person who can say different is you.'

Bailey suddenly looked with suspicion toward the interrogator.

The interrogator grasped Bailey's arm. 'The prisoner is obviously delirious. We must allow him to rest. While you sign this document in the outer office, I will see that he gets medical attention.'

Hesitant, Bailey allowed the interrogator to turn him toward the door.

'Sure,' Buchanan said. 'Medical attention. What he means is another whack with that rubber hose because I made you realize how much trouble *you're* in. Think, Bailey. You admitted you were drunk. Why won't you admit that there's every chance I'm not the man you saw in Cancun?'

'I have had enough of this.' The interrogator jabbed Buchanan's injured shoulder. 'Any fool can see that you are guilty. How do you explain this bullet wound?'

Writhing in pain against the pressure of the ropes that bound him to the chair, Buchanan spoke through gritted teeth. 'It's not a bullet wound.'

'But the doctor said—'

'How would *he* know what caused it? He didn't do tests to look for gunpowder in the wound. All he did was restitch it.' Buchanan grimaced. 'I got this injury and the one on my skull in a boating accident.' Lightheadedness again overcame him. He feared he'd pass out before he could finish. 'I fell off my client's yacht as we left port. My skull hit the hull . . . One of the propellers cut my shoulder . . . Lucky I didn't get killed.'

'This is a fantasy,' the interrogator said.

'Right.' Buchanan swallowed. 'Prove it. Prove I'm lying. For God's sake, do what I've been begging you to do. Bring my client here. Ask him if he knows me. Ask if he can explain how I hurt myself.'

'Yeah, maybe that ain't a bad idea,' Bailey said.

'*What?*' The interrogator jerked toward the beefy Texan. 'Are you telling me that the description you gave in Cancun, that the drawing on this police sketch – *which you helped prepare* – does not match the prisoner? Are you telling me that the identification you made five minutes ago . . . ?'

'All I said was he *looks* like the man I saw.' Pensive, Bailey rubbed a callused, large fist against his beard-stubbled chin. 'Now I ain't so sure. My memory's fadin'. I need time to think. This is pretty serious business.'

'Anybody can make a mistake,' Buchanan said. 'Your word against mine. That's all this is until we get my client to vouch for me.'

Bailey narrowed his eyes toward the bloody urine on the floor. 'I ain't signin' nothin' till this man's client proves I'm right or wrong.'

Jubilant despite his pain, Buchanan managed to squeeze out a few more words. 'Charles Maxwell. His yacht's moored near the Columbus dock in Cancun.'

With that, Buchanan gave in to the dizziness that insisted. He'd done everything possible. Drifting, he heard the interrogator and Big Bob Bailey exchanging angry words.

7

He was taken back to his cell. Staggering across it, trying not to bump into the other prisoners and cause an incident, he noticed that many of the faces scowling at him were different from those who had scowled at him when he'd first arrived, however long ago that was. His weary guess was that new drunks had replaced those who'd sobered but that the thieves and other predators had been left here until somebody got motivated enough to take the trouble to put them on trial. He knew that in his weakened condition, it wouldn't be long before the predators moved against him, so he found a space against a wall and sat, straining to remain awake, staring in response to their stares, hiding his pain, calculating how best to defend himself. He didn't realize right away that two guards had unlocked the cell and were gesturing for him to come out.

They didn't take him toward the interrogation room, however. Instead they took him in the opposite direction toward a section of the jail that he hadn't seen.

What now? Is this when I disappear?

The guards opened a door, and Buchanan blinked in confusion. He'd expected the interrogator, but what he faced was a sink, a toilet, and a shower stall. He was told to strip, bathe, shave, and put on the white cotton shirt and pants that were stacked on a chair along with a pair of cheap, rubber sandals. Confused, he obeyed, the lukewarm water not only making him feel welcomely clean but bolstering his meager energy. The guards stood watch. Later, as Buchanan finished dressing, another guard came in and set a tray upon the sink. Buchanan was astonished. The tray held a plate of refried beans and tortillas, the first food that he had received since he'd been brought here. Weakness and pain had stifled his appetite, but he didn't need any encouragement to grab something else that was on the tray. A bottle of purified water. In a rush, he broke the seal, unscrewed the cap, and swallowed several large mouthfuls. Not too much. You'll get sick.

He studied the food, the aroma of which both attracted and repelled him. The food might be contaminated, he thought, the shower and the fresh clothes a trick to make him ignore his suspicion and eat. But I have to take the risk. Even if my stomach doesn't want it, I've got to force myself to eat.

Again he reminded himself, Not too much at once. It took him a long time to chew and swallow the first mouthful of beans. When his stomach didn't revolt, he was encouraged to drink more water and bite off a piece of tortilla.

He never was able to finish the meal. Holding his spoon in his right hand, he almost dropped it because his fingers began to twitch again, alarmingly. When he switched the spoon to his left hand but before he could raise more food, another guard arrived, and the four of them, looking somber, took him past his crowded cell, toward the interrogation rooms. *Why?* Buchanan thought. Why would they let me clean up and give me something to eat if they're planning to give me another session with the rubber hose? That doesn't make sense. Unless . . .

The guards escorted him into a room that Buchanan had never seen, a dingy, cluttered office in which the interrogator sat stiffly behind his desk and faced a stern, pinch-lipped American who sat with equal stiffness across from him. When Buchanan appeared, each man directed a narrow gaze at him, and Buchanan's hidden elation at the hope that he might be released turned into abrupt suspicion.

The American was in his middle forties, of middle height and weight, with a pointed chin, a slender nose, and thick, dark eyebrows that contrasted with his sunbleached, thinning hair. He was deeply tanned and wore an expensive, tropical-blend, blue suit with a red-striped, silk tie and a gleaming, white shirt that not only accentuated his tan but seemed to reflect it. He wore a Harvard ring, a Piaget watch, and Cole Haan shoes. Distinguished. Impressive. A man to have on your side.

The trouble was that Buchanan had no idea who the man was. He didn't dare assume that the interrogator had responded to his demand and contacted his alibi, Charles Maxwell. The emergency alibi had been established hastily. Normally, every detail of a plan was checked many times, but in this case, Buchanan didn't know what on earth Maxwell looked like. It was reasonable to assume that Maxwell, having been contacted, would come here to support Buchanan's claims. But what if the interrogator had found an American to impersonate Maxwell? What if the interrogator wanted to trick Buchanan into pretending to know the American and thus prove that Buchanan was lying about his alibi?

The American stood expectantly.

Buchanan had to react. He couldn't just keep peering blankly. If this really was Maxwell, the interrogator would expect Buchanan to show grateful recognition. But what if this *wasn't* Maxwell?

The interrogator withdrew his chin into the numerous folds of his neck.

Buchanan sighed, approached the American, placed an unsteady hand on his shoulder, and said, 'I was getting worried. It's so good to see . . .'

To see who? Buchanan let the sentence dangle. He might have been referring to his relief at seeing his friend and client, Charles 'Chuck' Maxwell, or he might have been saying that he was delighted to see another American.

'Thank God, you're here,' Buchanan added, another statement that could apply either to Maxwell or to a fellow American whom Buchanan didn't know. He slumped on a chair beside the battered desk. Tension increased his pain.

'I came as soon as I heard,' the American said.

Although the statement implied a strong relationship between the American and Buchanan, it still wasn't forthright enough for Buchanan to treat him as Charles Maxwell. Come on, give me a clue. Let me know who you are.

The American continued, 'And what I heard alarmed me. But I must say, Mr Grant, you appear in better condition than I expected.'

Mr Grant? Buchanan thought.

This man definitely wasn't Charles Maxwell. So who *was* he?

'Yeah, this is a regular country club.' The severity of Buchanan's headache made his temples throb.

'I'm sure it's been frightful,' the American said. His voice was deep and mellifluous, slightly affected. 'But all of that is finished now.' He shook hands. 'I'm Garson Woodfield. From the American embassy. Your friend, Robert Bailey, telephoned us.'

The interrogator glowered.

'Bailey isn't a friend,' Buchanan emphasized. 'The first time I met him was here. But he's got some delusion that he saw me in Cancun and knew me before in Kuwait. He's the reason I'm in this mess.'

Woodfield shrugged. 'Well, apparently he's trying to make amends. He also telephoned Charles Maxwell.'

'A client of mine,' Buchanan said. 'I was hoping he'd show up.'

'Indeed, Mr Maxwell has a great deal of influence, as you're aware, but under the circumstances, he thought it would be *more* influential if he contacted the ambassador and requested that we solve this problem through *official* channels.' Woodfield peered closely at Buchanan's face. 'Those abrasions on your lips. The bruise on your chin.' He turned pensively toward the interrogator. 'This man has been beaten.'

The interrogator looked insulted. 'Beaten? Nonsense. When he came here, he was so unsteady from his injuries that he fell down some stairs.'

Woodfield turned to Buchanan, obviously expecting a heated denial.

'I got dizzy,' Buchanan said. 'I lost my grip on the stairwell railing.'

Woodfield looked surprised by Buchanan's response. For his part, the interrogator looked astonished.

'Have they threatened you into lying about what happened to you here?' Woodfield asked.

'They certainly haven't been gentle,' Buchanan said, 'but they haven't threatened me into lying.'

The interrogator looked even more astonished.

'But Robert Bailey claims he saw you tied to a chair,' Woodfield said.

Buchanan nodded.

'And struck by a rubber hose,' Woodfield said.

Buchanan nodded again.

'And passing bloody urine.'

'True.' Buchanan clutched his abdomen and winced, a reaction that he normally would not have permitted.

'You realize that if you've been brutalized, there are a number of diplomatic measures I can use to try to obtain your release.'

Buchanan didn't like Woodfield's 'try to' qualification. He decided to continue following his instincts. 'The blood in my urine is from my accident when I fell off Chuck Maxwell's boat. As for the rest of it' – Buchanan breathed – 'hey, this officer thinks I killed three men. From his point of view, what he did to me, trying to get me to confess, that was understandable. What I'm angry about is that he wouldn't let me prove I was innocent. He wouldn't call my client.'

'All of that's been taken care of,' Woodfield said. 'I have a statement' – he pulled it from his briefcase – 'indicating that Mr Grant here was with Mr Maxwell on his yacht when the murders occurred. Obviously,' he told the interrogator, 'you have the wrong man.'

'It is not obvious to me.' The interrogator's numerous chins shook with indignation. 'I have a witness who puts this man at the scene of the murders.'

'But surely you don't take Mr Bailey's word over a statement by someone as distinguished as Mr Maxwell,' Woodfield said.

The interrogator's eyes gleamed fiercely. 'This is Mexico. Everyone is equal.'

'Yes,' Woodfield said. 'The same as in the United States.' He turned to Buchanan. 'Mr Maxwell asked me to deliver this note.' He pulled it from his briefcase and handed it to Buchanan. 'Meanwhile,' he told the interrogator, 'I need to use your facilities.'

The interrogator looked confused.

'A bathroom,' Woodfield said. 'A restroom.'

'Ah,' the interrogator said. 'A toilet. *Si*.' He hefted his enormous body from the chair, opened the office door, and directed a guard to escort Mr Woodfield to *el sanitario*.

As Woodfield left, Buchanan read the note.

Vic,
Sorry I couldn't be there in person. I'll show up if I have to, but let's exhaust other options first. Check the contents of the camera bag Woodfield brought with him. If you think what's inside will be effective, give it a try. I hope to see you stateside soon.

Chuck

Buchanan glanced down toward the briefcase beside Woodfield's chair, noticing the gray, nylon camera bag.

Meanwhile the interrogator shut the office door and frowned at Buchanan, his voice rumbling, his ample stomach quivering. He was obviously interested in the contents of the note. 'You lied about being beaten. *Por qué?*' He came closer. 'Why?'

Buchanan shrugged. 'Simple. I want you and me to be friends.'

'Why?' The interrogator stepped even closer.

'Because I won't get out of here without your cooperation. Oh, Woodfield can cause you a lot of trouble from your superiors and from politicians. But I still might not be released until a judge makes a ruling, and in the meantime, I'm at your

147

mercy.' Buchanan paused, trying to look defeated. 'Sometimes terrible accidents happen in a jail. Sometimes a prisoner can die before a judge has time to see him.'

The interrogator studied Buchanan intensely.

Buchanan pointed toward the camera bag. 'May I?'

The interrogator nodded.

Buchanan set the bag on his lap. 'I'm innocent,' he said. 'Obviously Bailey is confused about what he saw. My passport proves I'm not the man he thinks I am. My client says I wasn't at the scene of the crime. But you've invested a great deal of time and effort in this investigation. In your place, I'd hate to think that I'd wasted my energy. The government doesn't pay you enough for all the trouble you have to go through.' Buchanan opened the camera bag and set it on the desk.

He and the interrogator stared at the contents. The bag was filled with neat piles of used, hundred-dollar American bills. As Buchanan removed one of the stacks and leafed through it, the interrogator's mouth hung open.

'I'm only guessing,' Buchanan said, 'but this seems to be fifty thousand dollars.' He replaced the stack next to the others in the bag. 'Don't misunderstand. I'm not rich. I work hard, the same as you, and I certainly don't have this kind of money. It belongs to my client. He's loaning it to me to help me pay my legal expenses.' Buchanan grimaced. 'But I don't see why a lawyer should get it when I'm innocent and he won't have to earn his fee to get me released. He definitely won't have to work as long and hard as I will to pay the money back or as long as *you* would to receive this much.' Buchanan sighed from pain and frowned toward the door. 'Woodfield will be coming back any second. Why don't you do both of us a favor, take the money, and let me out of here?'

The interrogator tapped his fingers on the battered table.

'I swear to you. I didn't kill anybody,' Buchanan said.

The door swung slowly open. The interrogator shielded the

camera bag with his massive body, shut the bag, and with a remarkably fluid motion for so huge a man, set the bag out of sight behind the desk as he scrunched his wide hips into his creaking chair.

Woodfield entered.

'To pursue this matter any farther would be a mockery of justice,' the interrogator said. 'Señor Grant, your passport and belongings will be returned. You are free.'

8

'You look like you need a doctor,' Woodfield said.

They walked from the jail across a dusty street toward a black sedan parked beneath a palm tree.

'I know an excellent physician in Mérida,' Woodfield said. 'I'll drive you there as quickly as possible.'

'No,' Buchanan said.

'But . . .'

'No,' Buchanan repeated. He waited for a fenderless pickup truck to go by, then continued toward the car. After having been in the jail for so long, his eyes hurt from the glare of the sun, adding to his headache. 'What I want is to get out of Mexico.'

'The longer you wait to see a doctor . . .'

Buchanan reached the car and pivoted toward Woodfield. He didn't know how much the diplomat had been told. Probably nothing. One of Buchanan's rules was never to volunteer information. Another rule was don't break character. 'I'll see a doctor when I feel safe. I still can't believe I'm out of jail. I *won't* believe it until I'm on a plane to Miami. That jerk might change his mind and re-arrest me.'

Woodfield put Buchanan's suitcase into the back of the car. 'I doubt there's any danger of that.'

'No danger to *you*,' Buchanan said. 'The best thing you can do is drive me to the airport, get me on a plane, then phone Charles Maxwell. Tell him I asked him to arrange for someone to meet me and to take me to a hospital.'

'You're certain you'll be all right until then?'

'I'll have to be,' Buchanan said. He was worried that the police in Cancun would still be investigating his previous identity. Eventually they'd find Ed Potter's office and apartment. They'd find people who'd seen Ed Potter and who'd agree that the police sketch looked like Ed Potter. A policeman might decide to corroborate Big Bob Bailey's story by having those people take a look at Victor Grant.

He *had* to get out of Mexico.

'I'll telephone the airport and see if I can get you a seat on the next flight,' Woodfield said.

'Good.' Buchanan automatically scanned the street, the pedestrians, the noisy traffic. He tensed, noticing a woman in the background, among the crowd on the sidewalk beyond Woodfield. She was American. Late twenties. A redhead. Attractive. Tall. Nice figure. She wore beige slacks and a yellow blouse. But Buchanan didn't notice her because of her nationality or her hair color or her features. Indeed he couldn't get a look at her face. Because she had a camera raised to it. She stood at the curb, motionless among the passing Mexicans, taking photographs of him.

'Just a minute,' Buchanan told Woodfield. He started toward her, but the moment she saw him approaching, she lowered the camera, turned, and walked away, disappearing around a corner. The oppressive sun intensified his headache. Festering pressure in his wound made him weaker. Dizziness halted him.

'What's the matter?' Woodfield asked.

Buchanan didn't answer.

150

'You looked as if you were about to go somewhere,' Woodfield said.

Buchanan frowned toward the corner, then turned toward the car. 'Yeah, with you.' He opened the passenger door. 'Hurry. Find a phone. Get me on a flight to Miami.'

All the way to the airport, Buchanan brooded about the red-haired woman. Why had she been taking photographs of him? Was she just a tourist and he merely happened to be in the foreground of a shot of a scenic building? Maybe. But if so, why had she walked away when he started toward her? Coincidence? Buchanan couldn't afford to accept that explanation. Too much had gone wrong. And nothing was ever simple. There was always a deeper level. Then if she wasn't just a tourist, what *was* she? Again he asked himself, Why was she taking pictures of me? The lack of an answer disturbed him as much as the threatening implications. He had only one consolation. At least, when she'd lowered the camera, turning to walk away, he'd gotten a good look at her face.

And he would remember it.

9

Acapulco, Mexico.

Among the many yachts in the resort's famous bay, one in particular attracted Esteban Delgado's attention. It was brilliant white against the gleaming green-blue of the Pacific. It was approximately two hundred feet long, he judged, comparing its length to familiar landmarks. It had three decks with a helicopter secured to the top. It was sculpted so that the decks curved like a hunting knife down to the point of the bow. Behind the decks, at the stern, a large sunning area – designed to allow voyeurs to peer down unobserved from the upper windows of the looming decks – was terribly familiar. If

151

Delgado hadn't known for certain, if his assistant hadn't given him verified information less than an hour ago, Delgado would have sworn that the distinctive yacht didn't just resemble the source of his sleepless nights and his ulcerated stomach but was in fact the very yacht, owned by his enemy, that figured so prominently in his nightmares. It didn't matter that *this* yacht was called *Full House* whereas the yacht he dreaded was called *Poseidon,* for Delgado felt sufficiently persecuted to have reached the stage of paranoia where he suspected that the yacht's name had been altered in order to surprise him. But Delgado's assistant had been emphatic in his assurance that as of noon today, the *Poseidon* with Delgado's enemy aboard had been en route from the Virgin Islands to Miami.

Nonetheless Delgado kept staring from the floor-to-ceiling window of his mansion. He ignored the music, laughter, and motion of the party around the pool on the terrace below him. He ignored the women, so many beautiful women. He ignored the flowering shrubs and trees that flanked the expensive, pink vacation homes similar to his, carved into the slope below him. Instead he focused his gaze beyond the Costera Miguel Aleman boulevard that rimmed the bay, past the deluxe hotels and the spectacular beach. The yacht alone occupied him. The yacht and the yacht it resembled and the secret that Delgado's enemy used to control him.

Abruptly something distracted him. It wasn't unexpected, although it was certainly long anticipated, a dark limousine reflecting sunlight, coming into view on the slope's curving road, veering through the gates past the guards. He brooded, squinting, hot despite the room's powerful air conditioning. His surname had always been coincidentally appropriate for him inasmuch as Delgado meant 'thin,' and even as a boy, he'd been tall and slender, but lately he had heard whispered, concerned remarks about his appearance, about how much weight he had recently lost and how his carefully tailored suits now looked loose on him. His associates suspected that his weight loss was due to disease (AIDS, it was rumored), but they were wrong.

It was due to torment.

A knock at the door interrupted his distraction and jerked him back to full awareness. 'What is it?' he asked, betraying no hint of tension in his voice.

A bodyguard replied huskily beyond the door, 'Your guest has arrived, Señor Delgado.'

Wiping his clammy hands on a towel at the bar, assuming the confident demeanor of the second-most-powerful man in Mexico's government, he announced, 'Show him in.'

The door was opened, a stern bodyguard admitting a slightly short, balding, uncomfortable-looking man who was in his late forties and wore a modest, rumpled business suit. He carried a well-used briefcase, adjusted his spectacles, and looked even more uncomfortable as the bodyguard shut the door behind him.

'Professor Guerrero, I'm so pleased that you could join me.' Delgado crossed the room and shook hands with him. 'Welcome. How was the flight from the capital?'

'Uneventful, thank heavens.' The professor wiped his sweaty forehead with a handkerchief. 'I've never been comfortable flying. At least I managed to distract myself by catching up on some paper work.'

'You work too hard. Let me offer you a drink.'

'Thank you, Minister, but no. I'm not used to drinking this early in the afternoon. I'm afraid I . . .'

'Nonsense. What would you like? Tequila? Beer? Rum? I have some excellent rum.'

Professor Guerrero studied Delgado and relented, swayed by the power of the man who had summoned him. Delgado's official title was Minister of the Interior, but that influential position in the President's cabinet didn't indicate his even greater influence as the President's closest friend and advisor. Delgado and the President had grown up together in Mexico City. They'd both been classmates in law school at Mexico's National University. Delgado had directed the President's election campaign, and it was widely understood that the President had chosen Delgado to be his successor.

But all of that – and especially the chance to acquire the fortune in bribes and kickbacks that was the President's due – would be snatched from him, Delgado knew, if he didn't do what he was ordered, for in that case his blackmailer would reveal Delgado's secret and destroy him. At all costs, that had to be prevented.

'Very well,' Professor Guerrero said. 'If you insist. Rum with Coke.'

'I believe I'll join you.' As Delgado mixed the drinks, making a show of what a man of the people he was by not sending for a servant, he nodded toward the music and laughter drifting up from the pool-side party on the terrace below. 'Later, we can join the festivities. I'm sure you wouldn't mind getting out of your business clothes and into a bathing suit. And I'm *very* sure that you wouldn't object to meeting some beautiful women.'

Professor Guerrero glanced self-consciously toward his wedding ring. 'Actually, I've never been much for parties.'

'You need to relax.' Delgado set the moisture-beaded drinks on a glass-and-chrome table, then gestured for Guerrero to sit in a plush chair across from him. 'You work too much.'

The professor sat stiffly. 'Unfortunately our funding isn't large enough to allow me to hire more staff and reduce my responsibilities.' He didn't need to explain that he was the director of Mexico's National Institute of Archaeology and History.

'Then perhaps additional funding can be arranged. I notice you haven't touched your drink.'

Reluctant, Guerrero took a sip.

'Good. *Salud*.' Delgado sipped from his own. At once, his expression became somber. 'I was troubled by your letter. Why didn't you simply pick up the telephone and call me about the matter? It's more efficient, more personal.' He silently added, And less official. Bureaucratic letters, not to mention the inevitable file copies made from them, were part of the public record, and Delgado preferred that as little as possible of his concerns be part of the public record.

'I tried several times to talk to you about it,' Guerrero insisted. 'You weren't in your office. I left messages. You didn't return them.'

Delgado looked disapproving. 'I had several urgent problems that demanded immediate attention. At the first opportunity, I intended to return your calls. You need to be patient.'

'I've *tried* to be patient.' The professor wiped his forehead, agitated. 'But what's happening at the new find in the Yucatán is inexcusable. It has to be *stopped*.'

'Professor Drummond assures me—'

'He is *not* a professor. His doctoral degree is honorary, and he has never taught at a university,' Guerrero objected. 'Even if he did have proper credentials, I don't understand why you have permitted an archaeological find of this importance to be investigated exclusively by Americans. This is *our* heritage, not theirs! And I don't understand the secrecy. Two of my researchers tried to visit but weren't allowed to enter the area. It's been sealed.'

Delgado leaned forward, his expression harsh. 'Professor Drummond has spared no expense to hire the best archaeologists available.'

'The best experts in Mayan culture are citizens of this country and work in my institute.'

'But you yourself admitted that your funds aren't as ample as

155

you would like,' Delgado said, an edge in his voice. 'Think of Professor Drummond's generous financial contribution as a way of making your own funds go farther. Your researchers were denied permission to enter the site because the staff there is working so hard that they don't have time to be distracted by social obligations to visitors. And the area has been sealed off to guarantee that the site isn't plundered by the usual thieves who steal irreplaceable artifacts from newly discovered ruins. It's all easily explainable. There's no secrecy.'

Guerrero became more agitated. 'My institute—'

Delgado held up a hand. ' "Your" institute?'

Guerrero quickly corrected himself. 'The National Institute for Archaeology and History,' he said breathlessly, 'should have the sole right to determine how the site should be excavated and who should be permitted to do it. *I do not understand why regulations and procedure have been violated.*'

'Professor, your innocence troubles me.'

'What?'

'Alistair Drummond has been a generous patron of our country's arts. He has contributed millions of dollars to constructing museums and providing scholarships for aspiring artists. Need I remind you that Drummond Enterprises sponsored the recent worldwide tour of the most extensive collection of Mexican art ever assembled? Need I also remind you, the international respect that collection received has been an incalculable boost to our public relations? Tourists are now arriving in ever greater numbers, not just to visit our resorts but to appreciate our heritage. When Professor Drummond offered his financial and technical assistance to excavate the ruins, he added that he would consider it a favor if his offer were accepted. It was politically expedient to give him that favor because the favor was in *our* favor. Financially, we come out ahead. I strongly suspect that his team will finish the job long before your own understaffed group would have. As a

156

consequence, tourists can begin going there sooner. Tourists,' Delgado repeated. 'Revenue. Jobs for the natives. The development of an otherwise useless section of the Yucatán.'

'Revenue?' Professor Guerrero bristled. 'Is that all our heritage means to you? Tourists? Money?'

Delgado sighed. 'Please. It's too pleasant an afternoon to argue. I came here to relax and thought that you might appreciate the chance to relax as well. I have a few telephone calls to make. Why don't you go out by the pool, enjoy the view, perhaps introduce yourself to some young ladies – or not, whatever you prefer – and then later we can renew this conversation over dinner when we've had the chance to calm ourselves.'

'I don't see how admiring the view is going to make me change my mind about—'

Delgado interrupted, 'We can continue this conversation later.' He motioned for Guerrero to stand, guided him toward the door, opened it, and told one of his bodyguards, 'Escort Professor Guerrero around the property. Show him the gardens. Take him to the reception at the pool. Make sure all his needs are satisfied. Professor' – Delgado shook hands with him – 'I'll join you in an hour.'

Before Guerrero had a chance to reply, Delgado eased him out of the room and shut the door.

At once, his smile dissolved. His features hardened as he reached for the telephone on the bar. He'd done his best. He'd tried to do this in an agreeable, diplomatic fashion. Without being insultingly blatant, he'd offered every bribe he could imagine. Uselessly. Very well, other methods were now required. If Professor Guerrero didn't cooperate he would discover that he was no longer the director of the National Institute of Archaeology and History. The new director, whom Delgado had selected and who was already obligated to Delgado for various favors, would see no problem about allowing Alistair Drummond's archaeological team to continue excavating the recently discovered Mayan ruins. Delgado was certain about the new director's compliance because that compliance would be a condition of the new director's appointment. And if Professor Guerrero persisted in being disagreeable, if he attempted to create a political scandal, he would have to be killed in a tragic, hit-and-run, car accident.

How could anyone so educated be so stupid? Delgado wondered with fury as he picked up the telephone. He didn't dial, however, for a light began to flash on the phone's multi-line console, indicating that a call was coming through on another number. Normally Delgado would have let a servant answer the call by using one of the many extensions throughout the estate, but this particular line was so private that it didn't have extensions. Only this phone was attached to it, and very few people knew that Delgado could be reached on this line. Its number was entrusted only to special associates, who had instructions to use it only for matters of utmost importance.

Under the circumstances, Delgado could think of only one such matter and immediately jabbed the button where the light was flashing. 'Arrow,' he said, using the code word that identified him. 'What is it?'

Amid long-distance static, a gruff voice – which Delgado recognized as belonging to a trusted aide – responded with the code word, 'Quiver. It's about the woman.'

Delgado felt pressure in his chest. 'Is your line secure?'

'I wouldn't have called unless it were.'

Delgado's phone system was inspected daily for taps, just as his estate was inspected for electronic eavesdropping devices. In addition, a small monitor next to the phone measured the voltage on the line. Any variance from the norm would indicate that someone had patched into the line after the telephone system had been inspected.

'What about the woman?' Delgado asked tensely.

'I don't think Drummond controls her any longer. Her security has been removed.'

'For God sake, speak clearly. I don't understand.'

'You told us to watch her. But we can't get close because Drummond has his own people watching her. One of his operatives pretending to be homeless sits in a cardboard box and watches the rear of her building. Various vendors, one selling hot dogs, another T-shirts and umbrellas, watch the entrance from the park across the street. At night, they're replaced by other operatives pretending to be indigents. The building's doorman is on Drummond's payroll. The doorman has an assistant who keeps watch in case the doorman is distracted. The woman's servants work for Drummond as well.'

'I already know that!' Delgado said. 'Why are you—?'

'They're not on duty any longer.'

Delgado exhaled sharply.

'At first, we thought that Drummond had arranged for other surveillance,' the aide continued. 'But we were wrong. The doorman no longer has an assistant. The woman's servants left the building this morning and didn't return. The operatives outside the building have not been replaced.'

Next to the air-conditioning duct, Delgado sweated. A crush of conflicting implications made him feel paralyzed. 'She must have taken a trip.'

'No,' the aide said. 'My team would have seen her leave. Besides, on previous occasions when she did take a trip, her servants went with her. Today they left alone. Yesterday morning, there was an unusual flurry of activity, Drummond's men going in and out, especially his assistant.'

'If she hasn't taken a trip, if she's still in the building, why has the security team been removed?'

'I don't believe she's still in the building.'

'Make sense!' Delgado said.

'I think she broke her agreement with Drummond. I think she felt threatened. I think she managed to escape, probably the night before last. That explains the flurry of activity the next morning. The security team isn't needed at the building, so they've been reassigned to join the search for her. The servants aren't needed either, so they've been dismissed.'

'God have mercy.' Delgado sweated more profusely. 'If she's broken her bargain, if she talks, I . . . Find her.'

'We're trying,' the aide promised. 'But after this much time, the trail is cold. We're reviewing her background, trying to determine where she would go to hide and who she might ask for help. If Drummond's men locate the woman, I'm certain that Drummond will send his assistant to bring her to him.'

'Yes. Without her, Drummond has less power over me. He'll do everything possible to get her back.'

But what if she goes to the authorities? Delgado wondered, frantic. What if she talks in order to save herself?

No, Delgado thought. Until she's absolutely forced to, she won't trust the authorities. She'll be too afraid that Drummond controls them, that they'll release her to him, that he'll punish her for talking. I've still got some time. But eventually, when she doesn't see another way, she *will* talk. She knows the price is so great that Drummond won't stop hunting her. She can't run forever.

Delgado's aide had continued speaking.

'What?' Delgado demanded.

'I asked you, if we find her or if Drummond's men lead us to her, what do you want us to do?'

'I'll decide that when the moment comes.'

Delgado set down the phone. No matter how thoroughly his estate had been checked for hidden microphones and how well his telephone system had been examined for taps, he wasn't about to say anything more on this topic in this fashion. The conversation had not been incriminating, but it would certainly raise questions if the wrong people heard a recording of it. Delgado didn't want to raise even more questions and indeed supply the answers by providing the full instructions that his aide requested. For Delgado had forcefully decided what needed to be done. By all means. To soothe his ulcerated stomach. To dispel his nightmares and allow him to sleep.

If his men located the woman, he wanted them to kill her. And then kill Drummond.

FIVE

1

Miami, Florida.

The man's voice echoed metallically from the airport's public-address system. 'Mr Victor Grant. Mr Victor Grant. Please go to a courtesy telephone.'

Buchanan had just arrived at Miami International, and as he blended with the Aeromexico passengers leaving the immigration-customs area, he wondered if Woodfield had gotten the message through to Maxwell and how the rendezvous would be arranged. Amid the noise and congestion of the terminal, he barely heard the announcement and waited for it to be repeated, making sure before he walked across to a white phone marked AIRPORT mounted on a wall near a row of pay phones. There wasn't any way to dial. When he picked it up, he heard a buzz, then another as a phone rang at another station. A woman answered, and when he explained that he was Victor Grant, she told him that his party would be waiting for him at the information counter.

Buchanan thanked her and replaced the phone, then analyzed the rendezvous tactic. A surveillance team is watching the courtesy telephones, he concluded. After Victor Grant's name was called, they waited for a man to go to one of the phones. The team has either studied a photograph of me or been given a description. In any case, now they've identified me, and they'll hang back to see if anyone is following me while I go to the information counter.

But as pleased as Buchanan was about the care of the rendezvous procedure and as delighted as he was to have escaped the authorities in Mexico, to be back in the United States, he was also troubled. His controllers obviously thought that the situation remained delicate. Otherwise, they wouldn't have involved so many operatives in making contact with him.

At a modest pace, giving the surveillance team ample chance to watch the crowd (besides, he was in too much pain to walk any faster), Buchanan pulled his suitcase and proceeded toward the information counter.

A pleasant, athletic-looking, casually dressed man in his thirties emerged from the commotion of passengers. He held out his hand, smiled, and said, 'Hello, Vic. It's good to see you. How are you feeling? How was the flight?'

Buchanan shook hands with him. 'Fine.'

'Great. The van's right this way. Here, I'll take your bag.'

The man, who had brown hair, blue eyes, and sun-leathered skin, touched Buchanan's elbow and guided him toward an exit. Buchanan went along, although he didn't feel comfortable since he hadn't received some kind of identification code. When the man said, 'By the way, both Charles Maxwell and Wade want us to phone and let them know you're okay,' Buchanan relaxed. Several people knew about his claimed relationship with Charles Maxwell, but only his controllers knew that Buchanan's case officer in Cancun had used the pseudonym of Wade.

Across from the terminal, in the airport's crowded parking ramp, the man unlocked a gray van, the side of which was stenciled with white: BON VOYAGE INC., PLEASURE CRAFTS REFITTED, REMODELED. Until then, they'd been making small talk, but now Buchanan became silent, waiting for the man to give him directions, to let him know if it was safe to speak candidly and to tell him what scenario he was supposed to follow.

As the man drove from the parking ramp, he pressed a button on what looked like a portable radio mounted under the dash. 'Okay. The jammer's on. It's safe to talk. I'll give you the quick version and fill in the fine points later. I'm Jack Doyle. Used to be a SEAL. Took a hit in Panama, had to resign, and started a business, outfitting pleasure boats in Fort Lauderdale. All of that's true. Now this is where you come in. From time to time, I do favors for people I used to work for. In this case, they've asked me to give you a cover. You're supposed to be an employee of mine. Your controllers supplied all the necessary background documentation, social security, taxes, that sort of thing. As Victor Grant, you used to be in the SEALS as well, so it was natural that I'd treat you like more than just a hired hand. You live in an apartment above my office. You're a loner. You travel around a lot, doing jobs for me. If my neighbors get asked about you, it won't be surprising that they're not familiar with you. Any questions?'

'How long have you employed me?'

'Three months.'

'How much do I earn?'

'Thirty thousand a year.'

'In that case, I'd like a raise.'

Doyle laughed. 'Good. A sense of humor. We'll get along.'

'Sure,' Buchanan said. 'But we'll get along even better if you stop at that gas station up ahead.'

'Oh?'

'Otherwise I'll be pissing blood inside your van.'

'Jesus.'

Doyle quickly turned off the freeway toward a gas station. When Buchanan came out of the men's room, Doyle was leaving a pay phone. 'I called one of our team who's acting as communications relay at the airport. He's positive no one followed you.'

Buchanan slumped against the van, his face cold with sweat. 'You'd better get me to a . . .'

2

The doctor stood beside Buchanan's bed, read Buchanan's chart, listened to his heart and respiration, checked his intravenous bottle, then took off his bifocals and scratched his salt-and-pepper beard. 'You have an amazing constitution, Mr Grant. Normally I don't see anybody as banged up as you unless they've been in a serious car accident.' He paused. 'Or . . .'

He never finished his statement, but Buchanan was certain that what the doctor meant to add was 'combat' just as Buchanan was certain that Doyle would never have brought him here unless the small hospital had affiliations with his controllers. In all likelihood, the doctor had once been a military physician.

'I have the results of your X-rays and other tests,' the doctor continued. 'Your wound is infected, as you guessed. But now that I've redressed and resutured it and started you on antibiotics, it ought to heal with reasonable speed and without complication. Your temperature is already coming down.'

'Which means − given how serious you look − the bad news is my internal bleeding,' Buchanan said.

The doctor hesitated. 'Actually that bleeding seems more serious than it is. No doubt, it must have been quite a shock when you discovered blood in your urine. I'm sure you've been worried about a ruptured organ. The reassuring truth is that the bleeding is caused by a small, broken blood vessel in your bladder. Surgery isn't necessary. If you rest, if you don't

166

indulge in strenuous activity, the bleeding will stop and the vessel will heal fairly soon. It sometimes occurs among obsessive joggers, for example. If they take a few weeks off, they're able to jog again.'

'Then what is it?' The doctor's somber expression made Buchanan more uneasy. 'What's wrong?'

'The injury to your skull, Mr Grant. And the periodic tremors in your right hand.'

Buchanan's chest felt icy. 'I thought the tremors were caused by shock to the nerves because of the wound in my shoulder. When the wound heals, I assumed . . .'

The doctor squinted, concerned. 'Shock. Nerves. You're partially correct. The problem does involve the nerves. But not in the way you imagine. Mr Grant, to repeat, you have an amazing constitution. Your skull has been fractured. You've suffered a concussion. That accounts for your dizziness and blurred vision. Frankly, given the bruise I saw on the CAT-scan of your brain, I'm amazed that you were able to stay on your feet, let alone *think* on your feet. You must have remarkable endurance, not to mention determination.'

'It's called adrenaline, Doctor.' Buchanan's voice dropped. 'You're telling me I have neurologic damage?'

'That's my opinion.'

'Then what happens now? An operation?'

'Not without a *second* opinion,' the doctor said. 'I'd have to consult with a specialist.'

Restraining an inward tremor, appalled by the notion of willingly being rendered unconscious, Buchanan said, 'I'm asking for *your* opinion, Doctor.'

'Have you been sleeping for an unusual amount of time?'

'Sleeping?' Buchanan almost laughed but resisted the impulse because he knew that the laugh would sound hysterical. 'I've been too busy to sleep.'

'Have you vomited?'

'No.'

'Have you experienced any unusual physical aberrations, apart from the dizziness, blurred vision, and tremors in your right hand?'

'No.'

'Your answers are encouraging. I'd like to consult with a specialist in neurology. It may be that surgery isn't required.'

'And if it isn't?' Buchanan asked rigidly. 'What's my risk?'

'I try not to deal with an hypothesis. First we'll watch you carefully, wait until tomorrow morning, do another CAT-scan, and see if the bruise on your brain has reduced in size.'

'Best case,' Buchanan said. 'Suppose the bruise shrinks. Suppose I don't need an operation.'

'The best case is the worst case,' the doctor said. 'Damaged brain cells do not regenerate. I'd make very certain that I was never struck on my skull again.'

3

The one-story house was in a suburb of Fort Lauderdale called Plantation, its plain design disguised by abundant shrubs and flowers. Someone obviously took loving care of the property. Buchanan wondered if Doyle made a hobby of landscaping. Their conversation during the drive from the hospital to Doyle's home indicated that the recession had affected Doyle's business and he was hardly in a position to afford a gardener. But after Doyle parked in a carport and led Buchanan through the side screen door into the house, it quickly became obvious who was taking care of the grounds.

Doyle had a wife. Buchanan hadn't been sure inasmuch as Doyle didn't wear a wedding ring, and Buchanan seldom asked personal questions. But now he faced an energetic, pixyish woman a little younger than Doyle, maybe thirty. She had happy eyes, cheerleader freckles, and an engaging, spontaneous smile. Buchanan couldn't tell what color her hair was because she had it wrapped in a black-and-red-checkered handkerchief. She wore a white, cotton apron, and her hands were covered with flour from a ball of dough that she was kneading on a butcher-board counter.

'Oh, my,' she said with a pleasant Southern accent (Louisiana, Buchanan thought), 'I didn't think you'd be here this soon.' Appealingly flustered, she touched her face and left a flour print on her freckles. 'The house is a mess. I haven't had time to—'

'The house looks fine, Cindy. Really,' Doyle said. 'Traffic wasn't as bad as I figured. That's why we're early. Sorry.'

Cindy chuckled. 'Might as well look on the bright side. Now I don't have to wear myself out, rushing to clean the house.'

Her smile was infectious. Buchanan returned it.

Doyle gestured toward him. 'Cindy, this is my friend I told you about. Vic Grant. I used to know him in the service. He's been working for me the past three months.'

'Pleased to meet you.' Cindy held out her hand. Then she remembered the flour on it, blushed, and started to retract the hand.

'No, that's okay,' Buchanan said. 'I like the feel of flour.' He shook hands with her.

'Classy guy,' she told her husband.

'Hey, all my friends are classy.'

'Tell me another one.' She studied Buchanan, pointing at the thick bandage around his skull. 'I've got another black-and-red handkerchief that'll sure look better than that.'

Buchanan grinned. 'I'm not supposed to take this off for a while. It doesn't do much good. It's not like a cast or anything. But it reminds me to be careful of my head.'

'Fractured skull, Jack told me.'

Buchanan nodded, his head still aching.

He expected her to ask him how he'd injured it. That would be a natural, logical next statement, and he was preparing to repeat his lie about falling off a boat, but she surprised him, suddenly switching topics, gesturing toward the dough on the counter. 'I'm making you a pie. I hope you like Key lime.'

He hid his puzzlement and told her, 'I seldom taste homemade pie. I'm sure anything you cook would be wonderful.'

'Jack, I like this guy better and better.'

'I'll show you to the guest room,' Doyle said.

'Anything you need, just ask,' Cindy added.

'Hey, I bet everything is fine,' Buchanan said. 'I really appreciate your taking me in like this. I don't have a family or anything, and the doctor thought it would be better if . . .'

'Shush,' Cindy said. 'For the next few days, *we're* your family.'

As Doyle led Buchanan from the kitchen toward a sunlit hallway, Buchanan glanced back toward Cindy, still puzzled about why she hadn't asked him the obvious question about what had happened to his skull.

By now, she had turned from him and resumed kneading the ball of dough on the butcher-board counter. Buchanan noticed that she had flour handprints on the trim hips of her jeans. Then he noticed something else. A snub-nosed .38 revolver was mounted to a bracket beneath the wall-phone next to the screen door, and Buchanan knew that Jack Doyle would never have chosen that type of weapon for himself. Doyle would have considered it a toy, preferring a semi-automatic 9-millimeter or a .45. No, the snub-nosed revolver was for Cindy, and Buchanan was willing to bet that she knew how to use it.

Was the gun there as a precaution against burglars? Buchanan wondered. Had Doyle's experience with the SEALS made him extra security conscious in civilian life? As

Buchanan followed Doyle down the hallway, he remembered Doyle's comment about sometimes doing favors for people he used to work for, and immediately he decided that the revolver wasn't the only weapon he'd find around the house and that Doyle intended the weapons to be a protection for Cindy against the possible consequences of some of those favors.

'Well, here it is.' Doyle led Buchanan into a pleasant, homey bedroom with lace curtains, an antique rocking chair, and an oriental carpet on a hardwood floor. 'The bathroom's through there. You don't have to share it. We've got our own. No tub, though. Just a shower.'

'No problem,' Buchanan said. 'I prefer a shower.'

Doyle set Buchanan's bag on a polished bench at the foot of the bed. 'That's about it for now, I guess. Unpack. Have a nap. There's plenty of books on that shelf. Or watch TV.' He pointed toward a small set on a bureau in the corner. 'Make like the place is yours. I'll come back and let you know when lunch is ready.'

'Thanks.'

Doyle didn't leave, though. He looked preoccupied.

'What's the matter?' Buchanan asked.

'I don't know your real background, and it isn't right for me to know it, but I figure, considering the people who asked me to give you cover, we must be brothers of a sort. I appreciate your thanks. It isn't necessary, though.'

'I understand.'

Doyle hesitated. 'I've been following the rules. I haven't asked you any questions. All I need to know I assume I've been told. But there is one thing. What happened and why you're here . . . If you're able to . . . Is there any danger to Cindy?'

Buchanan suddenly liked this man very much. 'No. To the best of my knowledge, there isn't any danger to Cindy.'

The muscles in Doyle's cheeks relaxed. 'Good. She doesn't know anything about the favors I do. When I was in the

SEALS, she never knew where I was being sent or how long I'd be gone. Never asked a single question. Took everything on faith. Never even asked why I wanted her to learn how to shoot or why I've got guns mounted around the house.'

'Like the revolver beneath the phone on the wall in the kitchen?' Buchanan asked.

'Yeah, I saw you noticed it. And like this one.' Doyle raised the cover from the side of the bed and showed Buchanan a Colt 9-millimeter in a holster attached to the bedframe. 'Just in case. You ought to know about it. I don't care what happens to me, but Cindy . . . Well, she's a damned fine woman. I don't deserve her. And *she* doesn't deserve any trouble I bring home.'

'She's safe, Jack.'

'Good,' Doyle repeated.

4

The muffled ringing of a phone wakened him. Buchanan became alert immediately, and that encouraged him. His survival instincts were still functioning. He glanced from the bed toward the end table, didn't see a phone, then gazed toward the closed door of the guest room beyond which he again heard the phone, its ring muted by distance, presumably down the hall in the kitchen. He heard a murky voice, female, Cindy's. Then he heard Jack. The conversation was brief. The house became silent again.

Buchanan glanced at his watch, surprised that it showed half-past noon, that what had felt like a fifteen-minute nap had lasted almost two hours. The doctor had warned him about sleeping more than usual. Past noon? He frowned. Lunch should be ready by now, and he wondered why Cindy or Jack hadn't roused him. He stretched his arms, testing the stiffness in his shoulder where his wound had been restitched, then put on his shoes and got up from the bed.

He heard a soft rap on the door.

'Vic?' Cindy whispered.

'It's all right. I'm up.' Buchanan opened the door.

'Lunch is ready.' She smiled engagingly.

Buchanan noticed that she'd removed her flour-dusted apron but still wore the red-and-black-checkered handkerchief on her head. Her hair must need fixing, and she didn't have time, he thought as he followed her along the sunny hallway into the kitchen.

'The pie's for supper. We don't eat big meals at lunch,' she explained. 'Jack's a fanatic about his cholesterol. I hope you like simple food.'

A steaming bowl of vegetable soup had been set at each place along with a tuna sandwich flanked by a plate of sliced celery, carrots, cauliflower, and tomatoes.

'The bread's wholewheat,' she added, 'but I can give you white if you . . .'

'No, wholewheat's fine,' Buchanan said and noticed that Doyle, who was already sitting at the table, seemed preoccupied by the tip of his fork.

'Did you have a good nap?' Cindy asked.

'Fine,' Buchanan said and took a chair only after she did, waiting until she dipped her spoon into the soup before he started to eat. 'Delicious.'

'Try the raw cauliflower.' Cindy pointed. 'It's supposed to help purify your system.'

'Well, mine could definitely stand some purifying,' Buchanan joked and wondered why Doyle hadn't spoken or eaten yet. Obviously something was bothering him. Buchanan decided to prompt him. 'I bet I'd still be asleep if I hadn't heard the phone.'

'Oh, I was afraid that might have happened,' Cindy said.

173

'Yeah.' Doyle finally spoke. 'You know how I've got the office phone rigged so if someone calls there and we're out, the call is relayed to here?'

Buchanan nodded as if that information were obvious to him, trying to maintain the fiction in front of Cindy that he'd worked for her husband these past three months.

'Well, that was someone calling the office to talk to you,' Doyle said. 'A man. I told him you wouldn't be available for a while. He said he'd call back.'

Buchanan tried hard not to show his concern. 'It was probably someone I did a job for. Maybe he's got questions about a piece of equipment I installed. Did he leave his name?'

Doyle somberly shook his head.

'Then it mustn't have been very important.' Buchanan tried to sound casual.

'That's what I thought,' Doyle said. 'By the way, after lunch I ought to go down to the office. I need to check on a couple of things. If you're feeling all right, you want to keep me company?'

'Jack, he's supposed to be resting, not working,' Cindy said.

Buchanan chewed and swallowed. 'Not to worry. Sure. My nap did a world of good. I'll drive along with you.'

'Great.' Doyle finally started to eat, then paused, frowning toward Cindy. 'You'll be all right while we're gone?'

'Why wouldn't I be?' Cindy's smile was forced.

'The soup's excellent,' Doyle said.

'So glad you like it.' Cindy's smile became even more forced.

5

'Something's wrong,' Buchanan said.

Doyle didn't respond, just stared straight ahead and pretended to concentrate on traffic.

Buchanan decided to push it. 'Your wife's so good-natured I get the sense she's working at it. Working hard. She doesn't ask questions, but she picks up overtones – about that phone call, for example. If her smile got any harder, her face would have cracked. She doesn't believe for a minute that you and I are friends. Oh, she tries to pretend, but the truth is I make her nervous, and at lunch, she finally wasn't able to hide it anymore. If she gets any *more* nervous, I might have to leave.'

Doyle kept staring ahead, driving over bridges that spanned canals along which pleasure boats were moored next to palm trees and expensive homes. The sunlight was fierce. Doyle seemed to squint less from the sun and more from the topic, however, as he put on dark glasses.

Buchanan let him alone then, eased the pressure, allowing Doyle to respond at his own pace. Even so, Doyle took so long to reply that Buchanan began to think that he never would unless Buchanan prompted him again.

That wasn't necessary.

'You're not the problem,' Doyle said, his voice tight. 'How I wish life could be that simple. Cindy's glad to have you at the house. Really. She wants you to stay as long as necessary. When it comes to the favors I do, her nerves are incredible. I remember once . . . I was stationed at Coronado, California . . . Cindy and I lived off base. I said goodbye to her in the morning, drove to work, and suddenly my team was put on alert. No communications to anyone off base. So naturally I couldn't tell her I was being airlifted out. I could imagine what she'd be feeling when I didn't come home that night. The confusion. The worry. No emotional preparation for what might be the last time we saw each other.' Doyle's voice hardened. He glanced toward Buchanan. 'I was away for six months.' Buchanan noted that Doyle didn't say where he'd been sent, and Buchanan would never have asked. He let Doyle continue.

'I found out later that a reporter had managed to discover that I was a SEAL and Cindy was my wife,' Doyle said. 'The reporter showed up at our apartment and wanted her to tell him where I'd been sent. Well, at that point, Cindy still didn't know I was gone, let alone to where, which of course – the where part – she never would have known anyhow. But someone not as strong as Cindy couldn't have helped being surprised to find a reporter blurting questions at her and telling her I'd been sent on a mission. The natural response would have been for her to show her surprise, admit I was a SEAL, and ask him how much danger I was in. Not Cindy, though. She stonewalled him and claimed she didn't know what he was talking about. Other reporters showed up, and she stonewalled them as well. Her answer was always the same. "I don't know what you're talking about." Amazing. She never phoned the base, wanting to know what was happening to me. She just acted as if everything was normal, and Monday through Friday, she went to her job as a receptionist for an insurance company, and when I finally got back, she gave me a long, deep kiss and said she'd missed me. Not "Where were you?", just that she'd missed me. I left on plenty of missions, and I never for a second doubted that she was faithful to me, either.'

Buchanan nodded, but he couldn't help wondering, If Cindy wasn't nervous because of his presence, what was the source of the tension he sensed?

'Cindy has cancer,' Doyle said.

Buchanan stared.

'Leukemia.' Doyle's voice became more strained. 'That's why she wears that kerchief on her head. To hide her scalp. The chemotherapy has made her bald.'

Buchanan's chest felt numb. He understood now why Cindy's cheeks seemed to glow, why her skin seemed translucent. The chemicals she was taking – combined with the attrition caused by the disease – gave her skin a non-corporeal, ethereal quality.

'She just got out of the hospital yesterday after one of her three-day treatments,' Doyle said. 'All that fuss about the food at lunch today. Hell, it was all she could do to eat it. And the pie she was making . . . The chemotherapy does something to her sense of taste. She can't bear sweets. While you were napping, she threw up.'

'Christ,' Buchanan said.

'She's determined to make you feel at home,' Doyle said.

'You've got trouble enough without . . . Why didn't you turn this assignment down? Surely my controllers could have found someone else to give me cover.'

'Apparently they couldn't,' Doyle said. 'Otherwise, they wouldn't have asked me.'

'Did you tell them about . . . ?'

'Yes,' Doyle said bitterly. 'That didn't stop them from asking me. No matter how much she suspects, Cindy can't ever be told that this is an assignment. All the same, she knows it is. I'm positive of that, just as I'm positive that she's determined to do this properly. It gives her something to think about besides . . .'

'What do her doctors say?' Buchanan asked.

Doyle steered onto a highway along a beach. He didn't answer.

'Is her treatment doing what it's supposed to?' Buchanan persisted.

Doyle spoke thickly, 'You mean, is she going to make it?'

'. . . Yeah, I guess that's what I mean.'

'I don't know.' Doyle exhaled. 'Her doctors are encouraging but non-committal. One week she's better. The next week she's worse. The next week . . . It's a roller coaster. But if I had to give a yes-or-no answer . . . Yes, I think she's dying. That's why I asked if what we're doing puts her in danger. I'm afraid she's got so little time left. I couldn't stand it if something else killed her even sooner. I'd go out of my mind.'

6

'Who do you think phoned your house? Who asked for Victor Grant?'

Doyle – who'd been silent for the past five minutes, brooding, preoccupied about his wife – now turned toward Buchanan. 'I'll tell you who it wasn't. Your controllers. They told me they'd contact you by phoning either at eight in the morning, three in the afternoon, or ten at night. A man would ask to speak to me. He'd say that his name was Roger Winslow, and he'd suggest a time to meet at my office to talk about customizing a boat. That would mean you were supposed to go to a rendezvous an hour before the time they mentioned. A wholesale marine-parts supplier I use. It's always busy. No one would notice if you were given a message via brush contact from someone passing you.'

Buchanan debated. 'So if it wasn't my controllers who phoned ... The only other people who know I claim to be Victor Grant and work in Fort Lauderdale customizing pleasure boats are the Mexican police.'

Doyle shook his head. 'The man I spoke to didn't have a Spanish accent.'

'What about the man from the American embassy?' Buchanan asked.

'Could be. He might be phoning to make sure you arrived safely. He'd have access to the same information – place of employment, et cetera – that you gave the Mexican police.'

'Yeah, maybe it was him,' Buchanan said, hoping. But he couldn't avoid the suspicion that he wasn't safe, that things were about to get worse.

'Since you're supposed to be working for me and living above my office,' Doyle said, 'you'd better see what the place looks like.'

Doyle turned off the highway, taking a side street across from the beach. Past tourist shops, he parked beside a drab, two-story, cinder-block building in a row of similar buildings, all of which were built along a canal, the dock of which was lined with boats under repair.

'I've got a machine shop in back,' Doyle said. 'Sometimes my clients bring their boats here. Mostly, though, I go to them.'

'What about your secretary?' Buchanan asked, uneasy. 'She'll know I haven't been working for you.'

'I don't have one. Until three months ago, Cindy did the office work. But then she got too sick to . . . That's why she can make herself believe you came to work for me after she stayed home.'

As Buchanan walked toward the building, he squinted from the sun and smelled a salt-laden breeze from the ocean. A young woman wearing a bikini drove by on a motorcycle and stared at his head.

Buchanan gingerly touched the bandage around his skull, realizing how conspicuous it made him. He felt vulnerable, his head aching from the glare of the sun, while Doyle unlocked the building's entrance, a door stenciled BON VOYAGE, INC. Inside, after Doyle shut off the time-delay switch on the intrusion detector, Buchanan surveyed the office. It was a long, narrow room with photographs of yachts and cabin cruisers on the walls, displays of nautical instruments on shelves, and miniaturized interiors of various pleasure craft on tables. The models showed the ways in which electronic instruments could be installed without taking up undue room on a crowded vessel.

'You got a letter,' Doyle said as he sorted through the mail.

Buchanan took it from him, careful not to break character by expressing surprise that anyone would have written to him under his new pseudonym. This office was a logical place for someone investigating him to conceal a bug, and unless Doyle assured him that it was safe to talk here, Buchanan didn't intend to say anything that Victor Grant wouldn't, just as he assumed that Doyle wouldn't say anything inconsistent with their cover story.

The letter was addressed to him in scrawled handwriting. Its return address was in Providence, Rhode Island. Buchanan tore open the flap and read two pages of the same scrawled handwriting.

'Who's it from?' Doyle asked.

'My mother.' Buchanan shook his head with admiration. His efficient controllers had taken great care to give him supporting details for his new identity.

'How is she?' Doyle asked.

'Good. Except her arthritis is acting up again.'

The phone rang.

7

Buchanan frowned.

'Relax,' Doyle said. 'This is a business, remember. And to tell the truth, I could *use* some business.'

The phone rang again. Doyle picked it up, said, 'Bon Voyage, Inc.,' then frowned as Buchanan had.

He placed his hand across the mouthpiece and told Buchanan, 'I was wrong. It's that guy again asking to speak to you. What do you want me to say?'

'Better let *me* say it. I'm curious who he is.' Uneasy, Buchanan took the phone. 'Victor Grant here.'

The deep, crusty voice was instantly recognizable. 'Your name ain't Victor Grant.'

Heart pounding, Buchanan repressed his alarm and tried to sound puzzled. 'What? Who *is* this? My boss said somebody wanted to speak to . . . Wait a minute. Is this . . . ? Are you the guy in Mexico who . . . ?'

'Bailey. Big Bob Bailey. Damn it, Crawford, don't get on my nerves. You'd still be in jail if I hadn't called the American embassy. The least you can do is be grateful.'

'Grateful? I wouldn't have been *in* jail if you hadn't misidentified me. How many times do I have to say it? My name isn't Crawford. It's Victor Grant.'

'Sure, just like it was Ed Potter. I don't know what kind of scam you're runnin', but it looks to me like you got more names than the phone book, and if you want to keep usin' them, you're gonna have to pay a subscriber fee.'

'Subscriber fee? What are you talking about?'

'After what happened in Kuwait, I'm not crazy about workin' in the Mideast oil fields anymore,' Bailey said. 'Stateside, the big companies are shuttin' down wells instead of drillin'. I'm too old to be a wildcatter. So I guess I'll have to rely on my buddies. Like you, Crawford. For the sake of when we were prisoners together, can you spare a hundred thousand dollars?'

'A hundred . . . ? Have you been drinking?'

'You betcha.'

'You're out of your mind. One last time, and listen carefully. My name isn't Crawford. My name isn't Potter. My name's Victor Grant, and I don't know what you're talking about. Get lost.'

Buchanan broke the connection.

Doyle stared at him. 'How bad?'

Buchanan's cheek muscles hardened. 'I'm not sure. I'll know in a minute.' He kept his hand on the phone.

But it took only ten seconds before the phone rang again.

Buchanan scowled and let it ring three more times before he picked it up. 'Bon Voyage, Inc.'

'Crawford, don't kid yourself that you can get rid of me that easy,' Bailey said. 'I'm stubborn. You can fool the Mexican police, and you can fool the American embassy, but take my word, you can't fool me. I know your real name ain't Grant. I know your real name ain't Potter. And all of a sudden, I'm beginnin' to wonder if your real name is even Crawford. Who *are* you, buddy? It ought to be worth a lousy hundred-thousand to keep me from finding out.'

'I've run out of patience,' Buchanan said. 'Stop bothering me.'

'Hey, you don't know what being bothered is.'

'I mean it. Leave me alone, or I'll call the police.'

'Yeah, the police might be a good idea,' Bailey said. 'Maybe *they* can figure out what's goin' on and who you are. Go ahead. Prove you're an innocent, upstandin' citizen. Call the cops. I'd love to talk to them about those three Spic drug dealers you shot in Mexico and why you're usin' so many different names.'

'What do I have to do to convince—?'

'Buddy, you don't have to convince me of anything. All you have to do is pay me the hundred-thousand bucks. After that, you can call yourself Napoleon for all I care.'

'You haven't listened to a word I've—'

'The only words I want to hear are, "Here's your money". Crawford or whoever the hell you are, if you don't get with the program soon, I swear to God I'll phone the cops myself.'

'Where are you?'

'You don't really expect me to answer that. When you've got the hundred-thousand . . . and I want it by tomorrow . . . *then* I'll let you know where I am.'

'We have to meet. I can prove you're wrong.'

'And just how are you gonna do that, buddy? Cross your heart and hope to die?' Bailey laughed, and this time, it was *he* who slammed down the phone.

9

Buchanan's head throbbed. He turned to Doyle. 'Yeah, it's bad.'

He had to keep reminding himself that Bailey or somebody else might have planted a microphone in the office. So far he hadn't said anything incriminating. Whatever explanation he gave Doyle, it had to be consistent with Victor Grant's innocent viewpoint. 'That jerk who caused me so much trouble in Mexico. He thinks I shot three drug dealers down there. Now he's trying to blackmail me. Otherwise he says he'll call the cops.'

Doyle played his part. 'Let him try. I don't think the local cops care what happens in Mexico, and since you didn't do anything wrong, he'll look like a fool. Then you can have him charged with extortion.'

'It's not that easy.'

'Why?'

Buchanan's wound cramped as he suddenly thought of something. The phone had rung just after Buchanan and Doyle entered the office. Was that merely a coincidence? Jesus.

Buchanan hurried to the front door, yanked it open, and glanced tensely both ways along the street. A woman was carrying groceries toward a cabin cruiser. A car passed. A jogger went by. Two boat mechanics unloaded a crate from the back of a truck. A kid on a bicycle squinted at the bandage around Buchanan's head.

Buchanan pulled it off and continued staring along the street. His head pounded from the fierce sunlight. There! On the left. At the far end. Near the beach. A big man with strong shoulders and a brushcut – Bailey – was standing outside a phone booth, peering in Buchanan's direction.

Bailey raised his muscular right arm in greeting when he saw Buchanan notice him. Then, as Buchanan started up the street toward him, Bailey grinned – even at a distance, his smile was obvious – got in a dusty car, and drove away.

10

'Cindy?' Doyle hurried into the house.

The kitchen was deserted.

'Cindy?'

No answer.

Doyle turned to Buchanan. 'The door was locked. Her car's still here. Where would she go on foot? Why would—? Cindy?' Doyle hurried deeper into the house.

Buchanan stayed in the kitchen, frowning out a side window toward the driveway and the street.

'Cindy?' he heard from a room down the hall.

At once Doyle's voice softened. 'Are you . . . ? I'm sorry I woke you, honey. I didn't know you were sleeping. When I found the door locked, I worried that something might have . . .'

Doyle's voice softened even more, and Buchanan couldn't hear it. Uneasy, he waited, continuing to stare outside.

When Doyle came back to the kitchen, he leaned against the refrigerator and rubbed his haggard cheeks.

'Is she all right?' Buchanan asked.

Doyle shook his head. 'After we left, she threw up her lunch. She felt so weak she had to lie down. She's been sleeping all afternoon.'

'Did any strangers phone her or come around and bother her?'

'No.'

'Then why was the house locked?'

Doyle looked confused by the question. 'Well, obviously so she'd feel safe while she was napping.'

'Sure,' Buchanan said. 'But when you got here, you were surprised to find the door locked. You assumed she'd gone somewhere, which means she's not in the habit of locking the door while she's home.' Buchanan walked toward him. 'And *that* means the reason she locked the door is *I'm* here. She senses I brought trouble. And she's right. I did bring trouble. I don't belong here. You can't worry about me while you're worried about—'

The ringing of the phone seemed extra-loud.

Doyle flinched.

Buchanan gestured for him to pick it up. 'This is *your* house. If I answer, it'll seem unusual. We have to pretend everything's normal. Hurry, before Cindy—'

Doyle grabbed the phone. 'Hello? . . . Who *is* this? What do you want him for? . . . Listen, you son of a bitch. My wife might have answered. If you bother her, if—'

It's going to pieces quickly, Buchanan thought. We're almost to the point where anybody listening to a recording of what we said would have to wonder if I'm really the man I claim to be. He motioned sharply for Doyle to be quiet and wrested the phone from him. 'I told you to stop.'

'Crawford, your buddy sounds as if he's losin' it,' Bailey said. 'I guess that's because his wife is sick, huh? Too bad. A nice-lookin' gal like that.'

Yeah, you did your homework, Buchanan thought. You've

185

been watching. You must have flown to Miami right after I did. You drove to Fort Lauderdale and staked out where I'm supposed to be working. You found out where the man who pretends to employ me lives. You waited for me to get out of the hospital, and if I didn't show up for work, that would prove I wasn't who I claimed to be. Then you could really make trouble.

'A hundred-thousand dollars. Tomorrow, Crawford. If you don't think I'm serious, you're in for a surprise. Because, believe me, I *will* call the cops.'

At once, Buchanan heard the dial tone.

Pensive, he set down the phone.

Doyle's face was crimson. 'Don't ever yank a phone out of my hand.'

'Jack, honey?'

They spun.

Cindy wavered at the entrance to the kitchen. She gripped the doorjamb. Her skin was pale. The black-and-red handkerchief had slipped, exposing her hairless scalp. 'Who was that? Who were you yelling at?'

Doyle's throat made a sound as if he were being choked. He crossed the room and held her.

11

The Intracoastal Waterway stretches along the eastern United States from Boston to Brownsville, Texas. An inland shipping route composed of linked rivers, canals, lagoons, bays, and sounds, it runs parallel to the Atlantic Ocean and is protected from the severity of the ocean's waves and weather by buffering strips of land. In the north, it is used mostly by commercial vessels, but in the south, particularly in Florida, the waterway's major traffic is composed of pleasure craft, and one of its most attractive sections is at Fort Lauderdale.

At eight a.m., Buchanan parked Doyle's van at the side of Bon Voyage, Inc. and unlocked the building. The previous night, he had driven to a shopping mall, where he had used a pay phone in a bar to get in touch with his controllers. Now, as the sun's heat strengthened, he carried several boxes of electronic components to a powerboat that Doyle kept moored at the dock behind the office. Buchanan's wounded shoulder throbbed and his injured head felt caught in a vice due to exertion, forcing him to make several trips. But at last he had the boxes safely stowed, and after locking the building, he unmoored the boat and steered it from the canal into the long expanse of the waterway.

Restaurants, hotels, and condominium buildings flanked it on each side. So did many luxurious homes whose spacious grounds were landscaped with shrubs and palm trees. No matter what type of building stood along each shore, however, docks and boats were constant. Following Doyle's instructions, Buchanan headed south, admired a three-masted sailboat that passed him going the opposite way, and studied a mural of dolphins that someone had painted along the concrete buttress of a bridge. He pretended to enjoy the breeze and the bracing salt-smell of the water. At no time did he stare behind him to see if he was being followed. It was essential that he appear to be innocent, untutored in such matters, and that he not seem preoccupied by Bailey's threats. Bailey had phoned twice more, at midnight and at two a.m., in each case waking Cindy. Furious, Doyle had disconnected the phones, the fierce look in his eyes disturbing. The more Buchanan thought about it, the more he realized that Bailey wasn't his only problem.

Continuing south in accordance with Doyle's instructions, Buchanan passed beneath more bridges, pretending to admire other buildings and boats, and finally steered to the east toward an exclusive area of docks called Pier 66. It took him a while to find the right section, but at last he came abreast of a one-hundred-foot, dark-wood yacht called *Clementine*, where two men and a woman stood from deck chairs and peered down at him from the stern. One of the men was tall and trim with severe features and short, graying hair. In his fifties, he wore white slacks and a monogrammed, green, silk shirt. The second man was younger, in his forties, less tall, less expensively dressed, and more muscular. The woman, a blonde, was in her thirties and gorgeous. She wore a short, blue, terrycloth robe that was open and revealed a stunningly filled, red bikini, the glossy color of which matched her lipstick.

The tall man, obviously in charge, asked, 'Are you from . . . ?'

'Bon Voyage, Inc.,' Buchanan answered. He removed his Ray-Ban sunglasses and his Miami Dolphins cap so they could have a better look at him. 'I've got the equipment you ordered. I was told this was a good time to install it.'

'Bring it aboard,' the tall man said. He gestured for the younger, muscular man – evidently a bodyguard – to help.

Buchanan threw up a bow and stern line so the powerboat could be held steady, a thick rubber rim along its gunwales preventing the boat from scratching the yacht. Then he handed the boxes to the bodyguard, all the while ignoring his lightheadedness and the pain in his wounded shoulder, taking care to maintain his balance as the powerboat tilted slightly. The bodyguard dropped a rope ladder. When Buchanan climbed on deck, he tried not to look at the woman.

'Where does the equipment go?'

'Through here,' the bodyguard said. He pointed toward a cabin in the stern, and this time he didn't bother to help Buchanan carry the boxes.

Inside the compartment, which had mahogany walls, antique furnishings, and a baby grand piano, Buchanan stacked the boxes, watched the muscular man close the entrance, noticed that the draperies were already closed, and waited. He didn't know how they wanted to do this.

'Captain,' the tall, severe man said.

So it would be formal.

'Colonel.' Buchanan saluted.

'This is Major Putnam.' The tall man gestured toward the muscular man pretending to be a bodyguard. 'And this is Captain Weller.' He gestured toward the woman, who had closed her robe the instant she was out of sight from anyone observing the yacht.

'Major. Captain.' Buchanan saluted them both.

'Now what the hell is going on?' the colonel demanded. 'These past few days have been an administrative nightmare, a political minefield. Langley is having a fit about the screwup in Cancun. Your exposure to the Mexican authorities and our embassy down there could have jeopardized, not to mention exposed, everything.'

'Sir, I assumed you'd been informed about what happened in Mexico. When I was in the hospital, I was debriefed.'

'By the Agency. I prefer to get my information not from civilians but from one of my own.'

It took ninety minutes. Periodically Buchanan was interrupted and asked to expand on a detail. As his report became more current, his debriefers became more somber.

'A hundred-thousand dollars,' the colonel said.

'I assume it wouldn't satisfy him,' Buchanan said. 'Once he got me to pay and incriminate myself, he'd keep coming back for more and more.'

'Bailey's on a fishing expedition,' the muscular man, Major Putnam, said. 'Unless you pay, he's got nothing.'

The colonel studied Buchanan. 'Is that what you think, Captain?'

'Bailey's crude, but he isn't a fool, sir. He's caught me

playing three different identities. He *knows* there's something not right about me, even though he can't prove it. So he's testing me to see if I'll panic and give him the proof he needs.'

'Well, obviously you're not going to panic,' Major Putnam said. 'He's wasting his time.'

The gorgeous woman, Captain Weller, finally spoke. 'But Bailey can still play hell with the operation if he decides to make good on his threat and talk to reporters and the police.'

Buchanan gestured. 'True. The police have got problems enough right here without bothering themselves about killings in Mexico. But multiple identities might be sexy enough to attract their attention, and if they decide I'm a drug dealer, if they call in the DEA and the FBI . . .'

'Your cover documents are perfect,' the colonel said. 'Hell, your passport came directly from the State Department. So did all the others. And each of your files is erased after you discard that identity. The DEA and the FBI wouldn't learn squat. As far as the records are concerned, there's no way to tie Jim Crawford and Ed Potter to Victor Grant.'

'Still,' the woman persisted, 'Captain Buchanan would be exposed to considerable official attention and in effect taken out of duty.'

The colonel tapped his fingers together. 'I agree. So the question is, what do we do with our inconvenient Mr Bailey? It's an admission of guilt to pay him. But if the captain ignores him and Bailey calls the authorities, the FBI might put the captain under surveillance.'

'The stakes are important enough,' the woman said, 'we have to consider the possibility . . .'

The colonel looked puzzled. 'Say what's on your mind.'

'Should Bailey be terminated?'

The cabin became silent.

The muscular man finally spoke. 'I'd be reluctant to advise sanctioning it. After all, termination can cause more problems than it solves. For one thing, we don't know if Bailey has someone working with him. If he does, the threat won't go away with Bailey's death. In fact, it'll get worse because the accomplice could use Bailey's death as an additional means with which to try to interest the police.'

'If. Damn it, if,' the colonel said impatiently. 'We don't have enough information. Major, I want our people to do a thorough background check on Bailey. I want to know who we're dealing with. Also, I want the local hotels and boarding houses checked. Find out where he's staying. Put him under surveillance. Maybe he *doesn't* have an accomplice. In that case, if he persists in causing trouble . . .'

They waited.

' . . . termination might not be out of the question,' the colonel said.

Again the cabin became silent.

'Sir, with respect, a background check on Bailey will take a lot of time,' Buchanan said. 'So will establishing surveillance on him. But there *isn't* time. Bailey said he wants his money today. He was emphatic about that. I assume he's rushing things to prevent me from having the opportunity to move against him. However we deal with him, it has to be done by tonight.'

They looked uncomfortable.

'And there's another problem,' Buchanan said.

The colonel looked even more uncomfortable. 'Oh?'

'Jack Doyle.'

'You have reservations about him?'

'I'm sure he was a damned fine soldier,' Buchanan said.

'He was,' the colonel said. 'And the contract work he's done for us has been equally impressive.'

'Well, he's not the same man,' Buchanan said. 'His wife has cancer. She isn't responding to treatment. She's probably going to die.'

191

'Die?' The colonel's face tightened. 'I read about her illness in the file, but there was nothing about an imminent fatality.'

'It probably *isn't* imminent,' Buchanan said. 'But Doyle's extremely protective of her. Understandably. He's under a great deal of stress. He thinks Bailey is a threat to her. He . . . Let's put it this way. I believe Doyle will lose control sufficiently to attack him if Bailey keeps phoning the house and putting on pressure and disturbing Doyle's wife, especially if Bailey comes near the house. I have to get out of Fort Lauderdale, far away from Jack Doyle and his wife. Because if Doyle does attack Bailey, it won't be planned, and it won't be tidy. The attack will be absolute, and it won't be something we could cover up. God only knows what the authorities would learn about Doyle's background and his contract work for you as they prepared to go to trial.'

'Shit,' the muscular man said.

'That's what I've been thinking,' Buchanan said. 'I landed in a real mess. I think Victor Grant ought to move on.'

'But wouldn't that be the same as an admission of guilt?' the woman asked. 'Wouldn't that make Bailey all the more determined to hound you?'

'He'd have to find me first. And after I disappeared, after I assumed a new identity, he'd never be able to.'

'That still leaves Jack Doyle,' the major said. 'Bailey could come back and put pressure on Doyle.'

'Doyle's story then becomes that he doesn't know anything about me, except that I'm an old military friend who showed up three months ago and asked for work. Doyle complains to the police about Bailey's harassment. Finally Doyle and his wife take a trip – courtesy of some former friends – to a vacation spot that has an excellent cancer-treatment facility.'

'Possibly,' the colonel said, pensively tapping his fingers on the sides of his chair. 'That's certainly one option that we'll consider.' He glanced at his watch. 'We'll discuss it thoroughly. For now, you'd better leave. If someone's watching the yacht, it'll seem unusual that all of us are inside this long.' He glanced at the woman in the bathing suit and the man who might have been a bodyguard. 'It's important to maintain cover.'

'But what about Bailey?' Buchanan asked.

'We'll give you our decision later.'

'Sir, there isn't much time.'

'We know that, Captain.' The colonel looked irritated. 'I said we'll get back to you.'

'But in the meanwhile, what do I do?'

'Isn't it obvious? Whatever you think Victor Grant would do.'

The answer was vague and slippery. Buchanan suddenly felt apprehensive.

12

Favoring his wounded right arm, Buchanan climbed down the rope ladder into the powerboat. The moment he'd emerged from the shadowy cabin into the glaring sunlight, his head had started pounding again. He put on his cap and sunglasses while the two men and the woman peered down at him, the latter again opening her blue, terrycloth robe to reveal the stunningly filled, red bikini of the rich enchantress she was portraying.

'Just send us the bill,' the colonel said.

'Yes, sir. Thanks.' Buchanan caught the bow and stern lines that the major tossed to him. Then he started the powerboat's engine and steered away from the yacht.

Tension cramped his muscles.

Jesus, he thought. They don't know what to do. I need a decision, and they didn't give me one. I can't act without

193

orders. But if I don't hear from them by tonight, how am I going to stall Bailey?

Preoccupied, Buchanan drove past a dock on one side and a palm-tree-shaded mansion on the other, approaching the end of a canal, about to re-enter the expanse of the waterway. Abruptly the problem of Bailey became more immediate. Buchanan's veins swelled from sudden pressure, for ahead, on his left, near a channel marker, Bailey sat in a powerboat similar to Buchanan's, its engine off, the boat motionless except for the bobbing caused by the wake of passing vessels. He wore an orange, FORT LAUDERDALE IS THE GREATEST BEACH IN THE WORLD T-shirt and was leaning back in the seat behind the wheel, his canvas shoes up on the console, one beefy arm spread out as if he were relaxing on a sofa while with his other hand he smoked a cigarette.

Buchanan eased back on the throttle.

Bailey drew his hand across his brushcut, smiled, and tossed his cigarette into the water.

Buchanan eased farther back on the throttle, noticing the camera with the telephoto lens that was slung around Bailey's massive neck. Buchanan's instructions had been to do exactly what Victor Grant would do, and right now, he decided, Victor Grant wasn't going to ignore this son of a bitch.

He steered toward Bailey, pulled the throttle back all the way, felt the bow sink, floated next to Bailey, and grabbed the side of his boat.

'How ya doin', Crawford?'

'How many times do I have to tell you? *My name isn't Crawford.*'

Bailey pulled the pop tab on a can of Blue Ribbon. 'Yeah, I'm beginnin' to think you're right about that. It's probably somethin' else besides Crawford. Sure as hell, though, it ain't Victor Grant.'

'Look, I've done everything I can to prove it to you. That's my limit. I've run out of patience. I want you to quit following me. I want you to quit—'

'Almost forgot. Pardon me for bein' rude. I got another beer if you'd like—'

'Shove it up your ass.'

'Now is that any way to talk to an ol' buddy? Not to mention a business associate?'

'Give it a rest! I never saw you before you showed up in that jail in Mexico.'

'Well, that's where you're wrong.' Bailey lowered his shoes from the powerboat's console and straightened behind the wheel. 'I've got a product to sell, and you're gonna buy it. When you joined those folks on that yacht, I figured you meant to get the hundred thousand from them, but you didn't carry anythin' off. Time's flyin'. You better find that money some place. 'Cause after midnight tonight I . . . By the way, that gal on the yacht is some looker, ain't she? Through this big lens on my camera, I could see her so close . . . What's that phone commercial? "Reach out and touch someone"? I got some real good pictures of her, those two guys and you on the deck. Nice and clear. Photography's a hobby of mine. Matter of fact, I got some pictures here in this envelope—'

'I'm not interested.'

'Oh, but I guarantee you'll find these pictures *real* interestin'. I have to confess I didn't take 'em, though. Had 'em lifted off a tape and then cleaned up. But if you didn't know the difference, you'd swear—'

'What are you talking about?'

'*Just look at the damned pictures, Crawford.*'

Hesitant, Buchanan accepted the manila envelope. Chest tight, he was preoccupied by the threat of the pictures that Bailey had taken of him with the colonel, the major, and the captain. The officers weren't public figures. Bailey wouldn't know who they were. But if Bailey gave the pictures to the police and someone got curious about who was on that yacht, if the colonel were identified, the consequence would be disastrous. Somehow Buchanan had to get his hands on the film.

But as he withdrew the photographs – eight-by-ten, black-and-white glossies – as he sorted through them, he suddenly realized that he had much more to worry about than the pictures Bailey had taken of him with the colonel on the yacht. *Much* more. Because the photographs he now examined depicted a scene from December of 1990 in Frankfurt, Germany. They'd been lifted from a television news tape. They showed American hostages, newly released from Iraq, arriving at the Frankfurt airport. And there, in long shots and close-ups, was Big Bob Bailey getting off the plane with . . .

'A mighty good likeness of you, Crawford,' Bailey said. 'I've got copies of the original tape, so nobody can say the pictures have been fooled with. If you piss me off by not payin' up, I swear to God I'm gonna send 'em to the cops along with the Mexican police sketch for Ed Potter and those bottom photographs of Victor Grant.'

Photos of Victor Grant? Buchanan asked himself with puzzled alarm. He shuffled to the bottom of the pile and felt his chest turn cold as he stared at three photographs of him outside the Mexican prison, where he talked to Garson Woodfield from the American embassy.

'Another good likeness,' Bailey said. 'In case you miss the point, that guy from the embassy had to be in the picture so there'd be an absolutely straight-arrow witness to identify you as Victor Grant. I've got you as three different people, Crawford. Got you good.'

Stalling for time while he thought, Buchanan kept staring at the pictures. The ones in Mexico. How had—? At once Buchanan remembered. While he'd been talking to Woodfield across from the Mexican prison, he'd noticed a woman in the background, among the crowd on the sidewalk beyond Woodfield. She'd been American. Late twenties. A redhead. Attractive. Tall. Nice figure. Wearing beige slacks and a yellow blouse. But the reason he'd noticed her hadn't been her appearance.

She'd been aiming a camera at him.

Buchanan peered up from the photographs, and there wasn't any question now that Bailey had an accomplice. Possibly more than one. Dealing with him would be extremely complicated. *I have to warn the colonel.*

'Keep those pictures. I've got plenty like them in a real safe place, along with the negatives,' Bailey said. 'Plus, I've also got copies of the TV news tape from Germany. Hey, it isn't often I'm on television. A buddy taped me and made me a present of it. I never thought it would be worth anythin'.' Bailey leaned forward. 'Admit it, Crawford, you're screwed. Stop actin' innocent. Accept the penalty for gettin' caught. Pay the hundred-thousand dollars. I won't even ask you why all the names. That's *your* business. *My* business is gettin' paid.'

Buchanan suddenly noticed: throughout their conversation, Bailey had kept his face angled to the left, as if he had a stiff neck, forcing Buchanan to shift his boat and angle his own face a similar way in order to confront Bailey eye-to-eye.

Stiff neck?

Buchanan spun toward the concrete dock across from him, and there – between two moored sailboats – was the redhead, a camera in front of her face, taking pictures of Bailey and him. Her clothes weren't the same. This time, they were sneakers, jeans, and a denim shirt, but even though her face was obscured by the camera, there was no mistaking that athletic figure and that long, dramatic, flame-red hair.

'So you noticed my friend.' Bailey exhaled from his

cigarette. 'I guess it's obvious that gettin' rid of me won't solve your problem. She's got plenty of pictures of you and me, and if anythin' happens to me — which you better hope doesn't happen, not even an accident, like me gettin' drunk and fallin' down a flight of stairs and breakin' my neck — those pictures'll be sent to the cops. Plus, she helped me make copies of the pictures you're holdin', and she also took pictures of you with them folks on that yacht. It might be interestin' to find out who they are.'

The red-haired woman lowered the camera and stared across the water toward them. Definitely the same person, Buchanan thought. Strong forehead. Excellent cheekbones. Sensuous lips and chin. She reminded him of a cover model for a fashion magazine. But from the stern way she watched him, Buchanan guessed that a fashion photographer would have a hell of a hard time to get her to smile.

'Crawford, you had plenty to say until now. What's the matter?' Bailey asked. 'Cat got your tongue? Or maybe you can't think of any more bullshit. Pay attention. *I want my money.*'

Buchanan hesitated, then made a choice. 'When and where?'

'Stay close to your buddy's phone. I'll call his place at eight-thirty tonight and give you directions.'

13

It was dark outside. Buchanan kept the guest room's light off as he packed, relying on the slight illumination from the hallway. After he finished and made sure that he hadn't left anything behind, he considered taking the 9-millimeter pistol from the holster attached to the side of the bed but decided against it. If there were trouble, the police might trace the gun to Doyle, and Buchanan didn't want to involve him any worse than he already was.

Leaving the guest room, Buchanan almost turned left toward the lights in the kitchen but changed his mind and instead turned right toward a door farther along the dimly lit hallway. He knocked, received no answer, noticed that the door was slightly ajar, and decided to take a chance. Pushing the door farther open, he knocked again. 'Cindy?'

' . . . What is it?' her weary voice asked from the darkness.

Buchanan entered, crossed the murky room, and knelt beside the bed, able to see her shadowy contour under the sheets but not her face. 'I missed you at supper.'

'Tired,' she whispered. 'The casserole . . . ?'

'Was excellent. You didn't need to use up your energy making it. Jack and I could have eaten take-out.'

'Not in *my* home.' Cindy managed to emphasize the word despite her fatigue.

'Well,' Buchanan said, 'I just wanted to let you know I appreciate it and to thank you for everything.'

She moved slowly, evidently turning toward him. 'You sound as if . . . Are you leaving?'

'I have to.'

She tried to sit up but couldn't. 'I hope not because of me.'

'What would make you think that?'

'Because people feel self-conscious about me being sick. It's hard to be around . . .'

'I don't feel that way,' Buchanan said. 'It's just that I have things to do. It's time for me to move on and do them.'

She didn't reply.

'Cindy?'

'I sort of hoped you'd stay so you could be company for Jack.' She inhaled in a way that made Buchanan suspect she was crying. 'Seems like most of the time I'm either in the hospital or here in bed. I'm not afraid for me, but I feel so sorry for Jack.'

'He loves you very much.'

'Sure.'

'He told me that several times. He told me how proud he was of you, the way you put up with being married to him when he was in the service and how you stonewalled those reporters.'

She chuckled slightly, then sniffled. 'Yeah, I was tough. The good times. Except Jack was gone so much then, and now that we're together . . .'

'Right. You just said it. You're together. And you don't need me around to make a crowd. In a few minutes, I'll be on my way.'

'Take my car.'

Buchanan cocked his head in surprise.

'I get the feeling you'll be needing it.' She touched his hand. '*I* sure won't. I haven't driven it since before I was in the hospital this last time. Take it. Please.'

'I'll get it back to you when I'm settled.'

'There isn't any rush, believe me.'

'Cindy?'

'Yes?'

'I'm sorry.'

'Yeah. Me, too.'

Buchanan leaned down and kissed her gently on the cheek, his lips salty from her tears. 'Take care.'

'I always tried to. Didn't do me any good, though. *You* take care.'

'I'll have to.' He stood from beside the bed. 'Maybe some time I'll be back this way.'

She didn't respond.

'I'd better let you get some sleep.' Buchanan touched her cheek, then backed from the room and closed the door.

Doyle sat, playing solitaire at the kitchen table. He didn't look up when Buchanan entered the room. 'I overheard.'

'And?'

'Thanks. Friends mean a lot. These days, she doesn't have too many. Most of them ran when they found out how sick she was. They didn't know enough to say what you just did to Cindy.'

'What was that?'

' "I'm sorry." ' Doyle looked up from the cards. 'Cindy's right. I think it's a good idea to take her car instead of my van. Less conspicuous. When you're done with it, just let me know where to pick it up. And this is another good idea.' Doyle reached under the table, where there must have been a bracket – because when his hand reappeared, it held a Beretta 9-millimeter pistol.

Buchanan glanced toward the windows. The blinds were pulled so no one outside could see the weapon. But he was still wary of possible hidden microphones. Instead of talking, he shook his head in refusal.

Doyle mouthed, *Why not?*

Buchanan picked up a notepad on the counter and wrote, *What if I had to dump it?*

Doyle took the pen and wrote on the notepad, *I took it from a dead soldier in Panama. It can't be linked to me.*

Buchanan studied Doyle, then nodded. He removed the magazine to make sure it was loaded, reinserted the magazine, worked the slide back and forth to chamber a round, lowered the hammer, then stuck the weapon beneath his belt at his spine, and covered it by putting on a dark, brown, nylon windbreaker that he'd borrowed from Doyle.

Doyle assessed the effect. 'Fits you perfect.'

Buchanan glanced toward the clock on the stove. Eight

twenty-five. Bailey was due to call in five minutes. Doyle shrugged as if to say, Be patient. Self-conscious because the kitchen might be bugged, neither man spoke. Doyle ripped up the sheet of paper, burned the pieces in a saucer, and washed the ashes down the sink, more for something to do, it seemed, than for the sake of destroying an incriminating object. Then he returned to his game of solitaire, appearing to understand that Buchanan needed to focus his mind and not clutter it with small talk.

Eight-thirty. Buchanan kept staring toward the phone. Five minutes passed. Then ten. His head began to throb. At last, at a quarter to nine, the phone rang.

Buchanan grabbed it before the noise could wake Cindy.

'There's a mini-mall near you on Pine Island Road. The intersection of Sunrise Boulevard,' Bailey's crusty voice said.

'I know the place. I've driven past it.'

'Go over to the pizza joint. Stand to the right of the entrance. Be there at nine. Come alone.'

Before Buchanan could acknowledge the message, Bailey hung up.

Buchanan frowned and turned to Doyle. 'Got to run an errand.'

'The keys to the car are in that drawer.'

'Thanks.' Buchanan shook his hand.

That was all the sentiment Buchanan could allow. He took the keys, lifted his suitcase, grabbed a small, red, picnic cooler off the counter, and nodded as Doyle opened the door for him.

Ninety seconds later, he was driving away.

15

The small, red, picnic cooler contained an apple and two bologna sandwiches on a white, plastic tray. A lower tray contained ice cubes. Beneath that tray were a hundred-thousand dollars in hundred-dollar bills. In the dark, driving, Buchanan glanced toward the cooler on the seat beside him. Then he checked for headlights in his rearview mirror to see if he was being followed.

He'd received the cooler and the money that afternoon while he was parked at a stop light on his way back to Doyle's. The money was in response to a call that he'd made from a pay phone immediately after returning from his conversation with Bailey. The colonel had told Buchanan to wait at the Bon Voyage office until three o'clock and, when he drove away, to leave his passenger window open. At the stop light, a motorcyclist had paused, pushed the cooler through the open window, and driven on.

Now, his pulse quickening, Buchanan parked at the crowded mini-mall on Pine Island Road. Beneath hissing sodium lights, he carried the picnic cooler to the pizza shop and stood to the right of the entrance. Customers went in and out. A delivery boy drove hurriedly away. Scanning the night, Buchanan waited. This time, Bailey made contact exactly when he'd said he would.

'Is your name Grant?' a voice asked.

Buchanan turned toward the open door to the pizza shop, seeing a gangly, pimply-faced young man wearing a white apron streaked with sauce.

'That's right.'

'A guy just called inside. Said he was a friend of yours. Said you'd give me five bucks if I relayed a message.'

'My friend was right.' Buchanan gave the kid the five dollars. 'What's the message?'

'He said you're supposed to meet him in twenty minutes in the lobby of the Tower Hotel.'

Buchanan squinted. 'The Tower Hotel? Where's that?'

'The east end of Broward Boulevard. Near Victoria Park Road.'

Buchanan nodded and walked quickly toward his car, realizing what was ahead of him. Bailey – afraid that he'd be in danger when he showed himself to get the money – intended to shunt Buchanan to various places throughout the city, carefully watching each potential meeting site for any indication that Buchanan had not come alone.

Bailey's instincts were good, Buchanan thought, as he checked a map in his car and steered from the mini-mall, heading toward his next destination. The truth was, Buchanan did have a team keeping track of him. Their mission was to follow Bailey after the money was handed over and to try to find where he was keeping the video tape, the photographs, and the negatives, especially the ones depicting Buchanan on the yacht with the colonel, the major, and the captain. The colonel had been very emphatic about that point when he'd hastily returned Buchanan's phone call. The images of Buchanan with the colonel had to be destroyed.

As Buchanan headed east on Broward Boulevard, he again glanced in his rearview mirror to see if he was being followed. He looked for Bailey, not the team that was keeping track of him, for there was no way he could spot the team, he knew. They had a way to follow him and later Bailey that permitted them to stay far back, out of visual contact, and that method was the reason Bailey's protective tactic, no matter how shrewd, wouldn't work. Bailey would never see the team at any of the potential rendezvous sites. He could never possibly detect the team as they followed him after he received the money. No matter what evasion procedures he attempted, he would not be able to elude them.

Because they didn't need to keep him in sight. All they had to do was study an audio-visual monitor and follow the homing signals they received from a battery-powered location transmitter concealed within the plastic bottom of the small picnic cooler that contained the money.

Friday night traffic was dense. Amid gleaming headlights, Buchanan reached the glass-and-steel Tower Hotel two minutes ahead of schedule. Telling the parking attendant that he would probably need the car right away, he darted inside the plush lobby and found his jeans, nylon jacket, and picnic cooler being sternly assessed by a group of men and women wearing tuxedos and glittering evening gowns. Sure, Buchanan thought. There's a reception going on. Bailey found out and took advantage of it. He wants me and especially anyone following me to be conspicuous.

Used to being *in*conspicuous, Buchanan felt self-conscious as he waited in the lobby. He looked for Bailey among the guests, not expecting to find him, wondering how Bailey would contact him this time. The clock behind the check-in counter showed twenty after nine, exactly when Buchanan was supposed to . . .

'Mr Grant?' a uniformed bellhop asked.

Buchanan had noticed the short, middle-aged man moving from guest to guest in the lobby, speaking softly to each. 'That's right.'

'A friend of yours left this envelope for you.'

Finding a deserted corner, Buchanan ripped it open.

At quarter to ten, be at the entrance to Shirttail Charlie's restaurant on . . .

16

Three stops later, at eleven o'clock, Buchanan arrived at the Riverside Hotel on Las Olas, a street that seemed the local equivalent of Beverly Hills' Rodeo Drive. From information in the terracotta-floored lobby, he learned that the hotel had been built in 1936, a date which was very old by Fort Lauderdale standards. A few decades before, this area had been wilderness. The wicker furniture and coral fireplaces exuded a sense of history, no matter how recent.

Buchanan had a chance to learn these facts and notice these details because Bailey didn't contact him on schedule. By twenty after eleven, Bailey still hadn't been in touch. The lobby was deserted.

'Mr Grant?'

Buchanan looked up from where he sat on a rattan chair near glass patio doors, a location that he'd chosen because it allowed him to be observed from outside. A woman behind the small reception counter was speaking to him, her eyebrows raised.

'Yes.'

'I have a phone call for you.'

Buchanan carried the picnic cooler to the counter and took the phone from the receptionist.

'Go out the rear door, cross the street, and walk through the gate, then past the swimming pool.' Bailey's curt instructions were followed by the sudden hum of the dial tone.

Buchanan handed the telephone back to the receptionist, thanked her, and used the rear exit. Outside, he saw the gate across the street and a walkway through a small, murky park beside the swimming pool, although the swimming pool itself was deserted, its lights off.

Moving closer, enveloped by the shadows of palm trees, he expected Bailey's voice to drift from the darkness, to give him instructions to leave the money on a barely visible poolside table and continue to stroll as if he hadn't been contacted.

The only lights were ahead, from occasional arclamps along the canal as well as from a cabin cruiser and a houseboat moored there. He heard an engine rumbling. Then he heard a man call, 'Mr Grant? Is that you over there, Mr Grant?'

Buchanan continued forward, away from the swimming pool, toward the canal. He immediately realized that the rumbling engine belonged to a water taxi that was temporarily docked, bow first, between the cabin cruiser and the houseboat. The water taxi was yellow, twenty feet long with poles along the gunwales supporting a yellow and green, striped canvas roof. In daylight, the roof would shade passengers from the glare and heat of the sun. But at night, it shut out the little illumination that the arclamps along the canal provided and prevented Buchanan from seeing who was in there.

Certainly there were passengers. At least fifteen. Their shadowy outlines were evident. But Buchanan had no way to identify them. The canvas roof muffled what they said to each other, although their slurred rhythms made him suspect they were on a Friday-night round of parties and bars.

'That's right. My name is Grant,' Buchanan said to the driver, who sat at controls in front of the passengers.

'Well, your friend's already aboard. I wondered if you were going to show up. I was just about to leave.'

Buchanan strained to see through the darkness beneath the water taxi's roof, then stepped onto the gangplank that extended from the canal to the bow. With his right hand, he gripped a rope railing for balance while he held the picnic cooler in his left and climbed down a few steps into the taxi. Passengers in their early twenties, dressed casually but expensively for an evening out, sat on benches along each side.

The stern remained shrouded by darkness.

'How much do I owe you?' Buchanan asked the driver.

'Your friend already paid for you.'

'How generous.'

'Back here, Vic,' a crusty voice called from the gloomy stern.

As the driver retracted the gangplank, Buchanan made his way past a group of young men on his left and stopped at the

207

stern, his eyes now sufficiently adjusted to the darkness to see Bailey slouched on a bench.

Bailey waved a beefy hand. 'How ya doin', buddy?'

Buchanan sat and placed the picnic cooler between them.

'You didn't need to bring your lunch,' Bailey said.

Buchanan just stared at him as the driver backed the water taxi from between the cabin cruiser and the houseboat, then increased speed along the canal. Slick, Buchanan thought. I'm separated from my backup team. They couldn't have gotten to the water taxi in time, and certainly they couldn't have hurried on board without making Bailey suspicious.

Now that Buchanan's eyes had become even more accustomed to the darkness, the glow from condominiums, restaurants, and boats along the canal seemed to increase in brightness. But Buchanan was interested in the spectacle only because the illumination allowed him to see the cellular telephone that Bailey folded and placed in a pouch attached to his belt.

'Handy things,' Bailey said. 'You can call anybody from anywhere.'

'Like from a car to a pizza parlor. Or from a water taxi to a hotel lobby.'

'You got it,' Bailey said. 'Makes it easy to keep in touch while I'm on the go or hangin' around to see if extra company's comin'.' Bailey lowered his voice and gestured toward the cooler. 'No joke. That better not be your lunch, and it better all be here.'

The other passengers on the boat were talking loudly, obscuring what Bailey and Buchanan said.

'There's no more where that came from,' Buchanan murmured.

Bailey raised his bulky shoulders. 'Hey, I'm not greedy. All I need is a little help with my expenses, a little reward for my trouble.'

'I went through a lot of effort to get what's in this cooler,' Buchanan said. 'I won't go through it again.'

'I don't expect you to.'

'That definitely eases my mind.'

The water taxi arrived at a restaurant-tavern, where a sign on the dock said PAUL'S-ON-THE-RIVER. The stylish building was long and low, its rear section almost completely glass, separated by segments of white stucco. Inside, a band played. Beyond the large windows, customers danced. Others strolled outside, carrying drinks, or sat at tables amid flowering bushes near palm trees.

The taxi's driver set down the gangplank. Four passengers got up unsteadily to go ashore.

At once Bailey stood and clutched the picnic cooler. 'This is where we part company, Crawford. Almost forgot, I mean Grant. Why don't you stay aboard, see the sights, enjoy the ride?'

'Why not?' Buchanan said.

Bailey looked very pleased with himself. 'Be seein' you.'

'No. You won't.'

'Right,' Bailey said and carried the picnic cooler off the water taxi onto the dock. He strolled across the colorfully illuminated lawn toward the music, 'Moon River', and disappeared among the crowd.

17

Thirty minutes later, the water taxi brought Buchanan back to the Riverside Hotel. He wouldn't have returned there, except that he needed to retrieve his suitcase from the trunk of Cindy's car. The car was parked on a quiet street next to the hotel, and after Buchanan placed the keys beneath the driver's floor mat, he carried his suitcase into the hotel, where he phoned for a taxi. When it arrived, he instructed the driver to take him to an all-night car-rental agency. As it happened, the only one that was open was at the Fort Lauderdale airport, and after Buchanan rented a car, he drove to a pay phone to contact Doyle and tell him where to find Cindy's car. Next, he bought a twelve-pack of beer at a convenience store, drove to a shadowy, deserted street, poured every can of beer over the front seat and floor of the car, then tossed the empty cans onto the floor, and drove away, keeping all the windows open lest he get sick from the odor of the beer.

By then, it was quarter after one in the morning. He headed toward the ocean, found a deserted park next to the Intracoastal Waterway, and smashed the car through a protective barrier, making sure he left skid marks, as if the car had been out of control. He stopped the car, got out, put the automatic gearshift into drive, and pushed the car over the seawall into the water. Even as he heard it splash, he was hurrying away to disappear into the darkness. He'd left his suitcase in the car along with his wallet in the nylon jacket he'd borrowed from Doyle. He'd kept his passport, though. He didn't want anyone to do a background check on that. When the police investigated the 'accident' and hoisted the car from the water, they'd find the beer cans. The logical conclusion would be that the driver – Victor Grant, according to the ID in the wallet and the car-rental agreement in the glove compartment – had been driving while under the influence, had crashed through the barricade, and helpless because of alcohol, had drowned. When the police didn't find the body, divers would search, give up, and decide that the corpse would surface in a couple of days. When it didn't, they'd conclude that the remains had been wedged beneath a dock or had been carried by the tide out to sea. More important, Buchanan hoped that Bailey would believe the same thing. Under stress from being blackmailed, fearful that Bailey would keep coming back for more and more money, Crawford-Potter-Grant had rented a car to flee the area, had gotten drunk in the process, had lost control of the vehicle, and . . .

Maybe, Buchanan thought. It just might work. Those had been the colonel's instructions at any rate – to make Victor Grant disappear. Buchanan hadn't told Doyle and Cindy what he intended to do because he wanted them to be genuinely surprised if the police questioned them. The disappearance would break the link between Buchanan and Bailey. It would also break the link between Buchanan and what had happened in Mexico. If the Mexican authorities decided to reinvestigate Victor Grant and asked for the cooperation of the American authorities, there'd be no one to investigate.

All problems solved, Buchanan thought as he hurried from the shadowy park, then slowed his pace as he walked along a dark side street. He'd find a place to hide until morning, buy a razor, clean up in a public restroom, take a bus twenty-five miles south to Miami, use cash to buy an Amtrak ticket, and become an anonymous passenger on the train north to Washington. Now you see me, now you don't. Definitely time for a new beginning.

The only troubling detail, Buchanan thought, was how the colonel could be sure that he got his hands on all the photographs and the negatives. What if Bailey went into the first men's room he could find, locked a stall, removed the money from the cooler, and left the cooler next to the waste bin? In that case, the surveillance team wouldn't be able to trail Bailey to where he was staying and where presumably he kept the photos. Another troubling detail was the woman, the redhead who'd taken photographs of Buchanan outside the Mexican prison while he talked with the man from the American embassy, the same woman who'd also taken photographs of Buchanan with the colonel on the yacht and later with Bailey on the waterway. What if Bailey had already paid her off and never went near her again? The surveillance team wouldn't be able to find her.

So what? Buchanan decided as he walked quickly through the secluded, exclusive neighborhood, prepared to duck behind any of the numerous flowering shrubs if he saw headlights approaching. So what if Bailey did pay the woman and never went near her again? He'd have made sure he got the pictures and the negatives first. He wouldn't have confided in her. So it won't matter if the surveillance team can't locate her. It won't even matter if Bailey ditches the cooler and the surveillance team can't find the photographs and the negatives. After all, the pictures are useless to Bailey if the man he's blackmailing is dead.

18

EXPLOSION KILLS THREE

FT LAUDERDALE – A powerful explosion shortly before midnight last night destroyed a car in the parking lot of Paul's-on-the-River restaurant, killing its occupant identified by a remnant of his driver's license as Robert Bailey, 48, a native of Oklahoma. The explosion also killed two customers leaving the restaurant. Numerous other cars were destroyed or damaged. Charred fragments of a substantial amount of money found at the scene have prompted authorities to theorize that the explosion may have been the consequence of a recent, escalating war among drug smugglers.

19

MURDER-SUICIDE

FT LAUDERDALE – *Responding to a telephone call from a frightened neighbor, police early this morning investigated gunshots at 233 Glade Street in Plantation and discovered the bodies of Jack Doyle (34) and his wife, Cindy (30), both dead from bullet wounds. It is believed that Mr Doyle, despondent about his wife's cancer, shot her with a .38-caliber, snub-nosed revolver while she slept in their bedroom, then used the same weapon on himself.*

20

The Yucatán peninsula.

Struggling to concentrate amid the din of bulldozers, trucks, jeeps, chainsaws, generators, and shouting construction workers, Jenna Lane drew another line on the surveyor's map she was preparing. The map was spread out, anchored by books, on a trestle table in a twenty-by-ten-foot tent that was her office. Sweat trickled down her face and hung on the tip of her chin as she intensified her concentration and made a note beside the line she'd drawn on the map.

A shadow appeared at the open entrance to her tent. Glancing up, she saw McIntyre, the foreman of the project, silhouetted by dust raised by a passing bulldozer. He removed his stetson, swabbed a checkered handkerchief across his sunburned, dirty, sweaty brow, and raised his voice to be heard above the racket outside. 'He's coming.'

Jenna frowned and glanced at her watch, the metal band of

which was embedded with grit. 'Already? It's only ten o'clock. He's not supposed to be here until—'

'I told you he's coming.'

Jenna set down her pencil and walked to the front of her tent, where she squinted in the direction that McIntyre pointed, east, toward the sun-fierce cobalt sky and a growing speck above the jungle. Although she couldn't hear it because of the rumble of construction equipment, she imagined the helicopter's distant drone, its gradual increase to a roar, and then as the chopper's features became distinct, she did hear it setting down on the landing pad near camp, the churning rotors adding their own, distinctive, rapid whump-whump-whump.

Dust rose – shallow soil that had been exposed when that section of forest was cut down, stumps blasted away or uprooted by bulldozers. Drivers and construction workers momentarily stopped what they were doing and stared toward the landing pad. This wasn't one of the massive, ugly, industrial helicopters that the crew had been using to lift in the vehicles and construction equipment. Rather, this was a small, sleek, passenger helicopter, the kind that movie stars and sports celebrities liked to be seen in, or in this case one that could be anchored on top of a yacht and was owned by one of the richest businessmen in the world. Even from a distance, the red logo on the side of the helicopter was evident: DRUMMOND INDUSTRIES. The force of the name was such that the sight of it compelled the workmen back to their tasks, as if they feared Drummond's anger should he think that they weren't working hard enough.

But not the guards, Jenna noticed. Constantly patrolling with their rifles, they hadn't paid attention to the helicopter. Professionals, they kept their attention riveted on the surrounding forest.

'We'd better not keep him waiting,' McIntyre said.

'He doesn't wait,' Jenna said. 'Hell, look at him. He's already out of the chopper. He'll beat us to the main office. I hear he swims two miles every morning.'

'Yeah, the old bastard's probably got more energy than both of us,' McIntyre grumbled as Jenna rolled up the surveyor's map and tucked it under her arm.

They walked quickly toward the most substantial structure in the camp. A one-story, wooden building made from logs, it contained essential supplies – food, fuel, ammunition, dynamite – items that needed to be protected from the weather or scavenging animals, and especially from humans. The building also contained an administrative center where McIntyre stored the project's records, kept in radio contact with his employer, and conducted daily meetings with his various subforemen.

Jenna had been right. As she and McIntyre approached the building, she saw Alistair Drummond reach it before them. His exact age wasn't known, but he was rumored to be in his early eighties, although except for his severely wrinkled hands he looked twenty years younger, his facial skin unnaturally tight from cosmetic surgery.

In fact, rumors were the essence of Drummond's notoriety. How much wealth had he amassed? How great was his influence with the premier of the People's Republic of China? What had been his part in the 1973 Arab oil embargo? What had been his part in the Iran-contra arms scandal? In his middle years, had he really been sexually involved with Ingrid Bergman, Marlene Dietrich, and Marilyn Monroe? Much more recently, what was his relationship with his frequent companion the great opera diva, Maria Tomez? Divorced six times, spending more days each year on his jet than he did at the estates he owned in eleven nations, devoting the pharmaceutical portion of his financial empire to AIDS research, able to boast of a first-name friendship with every

Russian, British, and American leader since the 1940s, Alistair Drummond exhibited a combination of outrageous success and shameless self-promotion that gave him a larger-than-life stature in an arena of world-renowned figures. The rumors and riddles about him made him a blend of contradictions, capable of being interpreted in various ways. His commitment to AIDS research, for example. Was that for humanitarian reasons or for the opportunity to earn boundless profits? Or both? He was a powerful enigma, and for that reason, anyone who'd ever met him never forgot the experience, regardless if the meeting had demonstrated his calculated charm or ruthless manipulation.

Certainly *I* won't forget him, Jenna thought, and I sure as hell won't forget this job. When she'd been interviewed for the project, Drummond had assessed her honey-colored hair, her high, firm breasts, her trim, equally firm hips, and with his raspy voice that caused her nerves to quiver, he had made his employment offer sound like a sexual proposition. Perhaps it *had* been a sexual proposition; perhaps Drummond considered all the people who worked for him to be the same as prostitutes. But high-class prostitutes, Jenna thought. While Drummond was without a doubt the coldest, meanest bastard she'd ever known, he was also the most generous. Her salary for this project was the equivalent of what she'd earned from her last ten projects combined. Deservedly. For this assignment was obscene, and if she were going to sell her professional soul, she didn't intend to do it cheaply.

As she and McIntyre entered the dirt-floored office, Jenna's gaze immediately gravitated toward Drummond, who was already surrounded by a group of crew leaders, blurting questions to them and snapping orders. He took charge so rapidly that even with his English-made, blended-wool, blue-striped suit in contrast with the sweat-stained, dirt-encrusted, rumpled work clothes of the crew leaders, he seemed perfectly in place, in his element. By contrast, the fair-haired, well-dressed man standing next to Drummond appeared aloof, not at all comfortable in these primitive conditions. His name was Raymond, and the cold expression in his eyes warned Jenna not to believe that his pleasant features were an indication of his personality. She suspected that Raymond was truly in his element only when he was causing pain.

Dear God, what have I gotten myself into?

'No,' Drummond told a supervisor, his voice brittle but forceful. 'No. You understood the rules before you agreed to be hired. You signed a document binding you to certain conditions. Under no circumstances are you or any member of your crew permitted to leave camp until all the work is completed. I'm paying everyone handsomely to work seven days a week, and I expect to receive maximum value for my money. Bring women in? Nonsense. No outsiders are allowed in camp. Permission to use the two-way radio for private communications? Absolutely not. What happens down here is *my* business, and I don't want your men telling *my* business to outsiders. You know how I feel about privacy. In every way possible, this camp is sealed. Don't raise this subject again.'

Drummond turned dismissively from the group and noticed Jenna and McIntyre just inside the open door. 'Good, I want to see both of you.' He motioned for Raymond to take the supervisors outside, then gestured for Jenna and McIntyre to approach. 'Have you found it?'

Jenna and McIntyre looked away.

'I don't know why I bothered asking,' Drummond said. 'If you *had* found it, those idiots would have been jabbering hysterically about it. They wouldn't have been able to restrain themselves. Which means they still don't suspect,' Drummond said. 'Is that true?'

McIntyre cleared his throat. 'Yes. That's true.'

Having taken the supervisors outside, Raymond re-entered

217

the building, shut the door, and leaned against it, crossing his arms, coldly assessing Jenna. She felt his arrogant gaze upon her.

'I'm not pleased, not pleased at all,' Drummond said. 'I gave you all the necessary information. The job shouldn't be that difficult. You practically have step-by-step instructions. But you still haven't found it.'

McIntyre mumbled something.

'What?' Drummond glared. 'Damn it, man, speak up. Muttering won't trick me into thinking my ears are failing me.'

'I didn't mean to . . .'

'Don't apologize. I hate a whimperer. Maybe that's why you haven't achieved your objective. Because you're not man enough to direct the job.'

'The instructions weren't as specific as you claim,' Jenna interrupted.

'Oh?' The old man swung toward her. 'At least *you* don't mutter. But I don't recall asking you for a comment.'

'If I need to be asked, that would mean I'm not a very good employee, wouldn't you agree?'

'An excellent answer.' Drummond studied her. 'Continue.'

'A vague and possibly flawed translation isn't what I'd call step-by-step instructions.'

Drummond bristled. 'The translation wasn't flawed. The best experts for the maximum price were hired to decipher the text.'

'But even the experts don't understand all the Mayan symbols.'

'And you yourself are expert enough to know that?'

'Perhaps you've forgotten.'

'I forget *nothing*.'

'I'm not only a surveyor,' Jenna said. 'I'm an *archaeological* surveyor. My expertise is mapping sites like this one, and I may not be able to translate Mayan symbols, but I know several people who can, and they're the first to admit that there's a great deal more to be accomplished in their specialty.'

'Perhaps. Or perhaps you're trying to justify a poor performance. Perhaps I should hire someone else and deduct that person's fee from yours.'

Panic muted Jenna's anger. Stop. Keep your opinions to yourself. Don't antagonize him.

'Work harder,' Drummond said. 'Quit making excuses. The translation is as perfect as it can be. And it's explicit. What we're looking for is here. But why can't you find it?'

'Topography doesn't have much variation in the Yucatán,' Jenna said. 'The site described in the text could be anywhere. Plus, the geology in this area isn't stable. In the thousand years since the landscape was described, earthquakes could have obliterated some of the features we're searching for.'

Drummond scowled and returned his attention to McIntyre. 'I don't have time for delays. The jungle has to be cleared, but your men haven't accomplished anywhere near as much as they were supposed to by now. You haven't kept up with the schedule.'

'The schedule didn't allow for sabotage,' McIntyre said.

Drummond jerked his head back. 'Sabotage?'

'Someone's been tampering with the bulldozers and the trucks. Dirt in the fuel tanks. Radiator hoses cut. Tires slashed.'

Drummond became livid. '*Why wasn't I told?*'

'We thought we could handle the problem without troubling you. We fixed the vehicles and posted guards around them,' McIntyre said.

'*And?*'

'Posting guards around the vehicles meant we had to lessen the number of men watching the perimeter of the camp. The next night, a lot of our tools were stolen. Our water supply was contaminated. Our fuel-storage barrels were punctured. That's why we've got barrels stored in here. As an emergency backup. The helicopters have been working double time bringing in spare parts and replacement supplies instead of new equipment.'

'Replacing supplies isn't the answer!' Drummond snapped. 'Find whoever's causing the damage. What about those supervisors who were in here complaining? Could it be someone who wants to shut down work so he can spend a weekend getting drunk in Mérida?'

'We thought of that,' McIntyre said. 'No. The men are tired and grumpy, but they're also eager to finish the job ahead of schedule so they can get their bonus. None of them would do anything to force them to spend more time here.'

'Then who?'

'Natives,' Jenna said. 'Maya.'

Drummond looked astonished. 'You're telling me a handful of ignorant Indians are capable of out-thinking you and paralyzing the project?'

'There might be more of them than you think. And as for being ignorant, this is *their* backyard, not ours. They know this territory a lot better than we do.'

'Excuses.'

'I'm sure they're watching our every move from the jungle,' Jenna said, 'and I strongly suspect that this site has religious importance to them, that they're furious about what we're doing here.'

'Superstition and nonsense. I'm amazed that you've let it interfere with the project.' Drummond scowled. 'But you've given me an idea. You're right. This *is* their backyard.' He turned to the fair-haired, pleasant-faced, well-dressed man who leaned against the closed door. 'Raymond, how would you like to go hunting?'

'I'd like that very much, Mr Drummond.'

'The captain of the guards will see that you're outfitted properly.' Drummond turned to Jenna. 'Where do these natives live? Have you got their village marked on the map you're preparing?'

'Village?' Jenna said. 'I've had problems enough mapping the site. We're surrounded by rain forest. There aren't any trails. You don't just go wandering around out there. You'll get lost or worse. Village? We haven't seen even one native, let alone a *village*.'

'And yet you're certain they're responsible?' Drummond turned to his assistant. 'Raymond, find them. Stop them.'

'Yes, sir.' Raymond opened the door.

'But Raymond . . .'

'Yes, sir?'

'Since this is their backyard, since they know it thoroughly, I want one native able to talk. Bring him to camp for questioning. Maybe he'll know where to find what we're looking for.'

As Raymond left the building, a man in a blue pilot's uniform appeared. He had a red logo, DRUMMOND INDUSTRIES, on his jacket pocket.

'Sir, there's a call for you on the helicopter radio.' He was slightly out of breath.

'Have it transferred to here. McIntyre, what frequency have you been using?'

McIntyre told the pilot, who hurried away.

Drummond gestured toward the map that Jenna had braced beneath her left arm. 'Let me see what you've accomplished.'

Jenna spread the map across a table.

'No, no, no,' Drummond said.

'What's wrong? I was thorough. I double-checked every—'

'That's exactly the problem. You were thorough. I told you specifically. I wanted a map that would look convincing to the Mexican authorities.' Drummond led her out the door,

221

gesturing toward the commotion of the site, workers clearing trees and stacking equipment.

Assaulted by harsh sunlight after the shadows of the room, Jenna shielded her eyes and directed her attention toward where Drummond pointed. As more and more trees were cut down and dragged away to be burned, as more bushes were plowed free, as what seemed to be hills became ever more distinctly pyramids, temples, and palaces, the legacy of the once-great Mayan empire, her heart pounded.

'Too much depends on this,' Drummond said. 'Your map can't—'

He was suddenly interrupted by a crackly, static-ridden voice on the radio.

'That's your call coming through,' McIntyre said.

'Is the scrambler functioning?'

McIntyre nodded. 'Just flick the switch.'

'Stay here. I won't be long.'

After Drummond entered the building and shut the door, leaving Jenna and McIntyre outside, Jenna shook her head, frustrated, puzzled, angry. 'That son of a bitch.'

'Keep your voice down,' McIntyre said. 'He might hear you.'

McIntyre was right, Jenna realized. Even with the noise from the vehicles and the workers, she was close enough to the door that her voice might carry.

But by that same logic . . .

The door fit the crude frame loosely. It had inched open after Drummond closed it. Jenna heard occasional raspy outbursts.

' . . . *Find the woman. If Delgado learns she isn't co-operating . . . ruined. Everything. Find her. Use every pressure. I don't care what you have to . . . Kill him if . . .*'

Then Jenna couldn't hear Drummond anymore, and at once she stepped farther from the door, joining McIntyre, feeling sick but trying to seem as if she were a good employee waiting patiently.

Drummond jerked the door open and stalked outside. A black pall appeared to surround him despite the sunlight that gleamed off his thick, white hair and his glasses. He was about to continue verbally assaulting Jenna when he noticed something to the left and looked briefly heartened.

Following his gaze, Jenna saw Raymond wearing outdoor clothes, carrying a rifle, entering the jungle. Even at a distance, his excitement was evident.

Then Drummond's brittle, forceful voice jerked her attention back to him.

'All of this,' he demanded, gesturing. 'You've been far too faithful on your map, far too diligent. The Mexican authorities can't be allowed to realize how massive and important a find this is. Your map has to make it seem minor, an insignificant site that doesn't merit undue attention, something that won't be an irreplaceable loss.' Drummond pointed toward the majestic temples, the hieroglyph-engraved palaces, and the great, terraced pyramid where gigantic snake heads guarded the bottom of the wide, high stairs that went up each side. 'Because ten days from now, I expect all of that to be leveled. Do you hear me, McIntyre?' He glared at the foreman. 'You knew the orders. You understood the schedule. Use bulldozers. Use sledge-hammers. Use dynamite. If you have to, use your fingernails. Ten days from now, I expect my equipment to be set up and all of this to be gone. Level it. Scatter the rubble. Truck it out. Dump it in sinkholes. Have the helicopters lift it out. I don't care how you do it. I want it gone!'

SIX

1

Alexandria, Virginia.

The safe site was on the third floor, yet another apartment in yet another sprawling complex into which Buchanan could easily blend. After he'd arrived in Washington from Florida, he'd used a pay phone to report to his controller, just as he'd reported at various stops along the Amtrak route. A man's voice told him to be waiting, seated, on the steps outside the Library of Congress at three p.m. Precisely at that time, a middle-aged man wearing a blue blazer and gray slacks stopped beside him and bent down to tie his right shoe. When the man departed, Buchanan concealed the small envelope that the man had slid toward him. After waiting five minutes longer, Buchanan then went into the Library of Congress, entered a men's room, and locked himself in a stall, where he opened the envelope, took out a key, and read a slip of paper that provided him with a name, some biographical information, an Alexandria address, and an apartment number. The paper and the envelope were far from ordinary. He dropped them into the water in the toilet and watched them dissolve. In the library's reference section, he used an area directory to tell him which major streets were near the Alexandria apartment, and shortly before six that evening, he got out of a

225

taxi a few blocks from his destination, walking the rest of the way, out of habit using evasion procedures in case he was being followed.

His name was now Don Colton, he'd been informed. He was supposed to be a writer for a travel magazine that he assumed was affiliated to his controllers. Posing as a travel writer was an excellent cover, Buchanan thought, inasmuch as a travel writer by definition was on the move a great deal and hence the neighbors wouldn't consider it unusual that they never saw him. However, because Buchanan's controllers would not have had sufficient time to tailor the cover specifically to him, he automatically assumed that this identity would be temporary, an all-purpose, one-size-fits-all persona that his controllers maintained for emergencies. As Don Colton, Buchanan was in a holding pattern and would soon be sent to God-knew-where as God-knew-who.

Avoiding the elevator, he used fire stairs to get to the third floor. After all, because most people preferred elevators, there was less chance of encountering anybody on the stairs. He reached a concrete corridor with fluorescent lights along the ceiling. As he had hoped, no one was in view, the tenants having already arrived home from work. Doors to apartments flanked each side. As he walked along green, heavy-duty carpeting, he heard music behind one door, voices behind another. Then he came to 327, used the key he'd been given, and entered the apartment.

He turned on the lights, scanned the combination living room-kitchen, locked the door, checked the closets, the bathroom, and the bedroom, all the while avoiding the windows, then turned off the lights, closed the draperies, and finally turned the lights back on, only then slumping on the sofa. He was safe. For now.

The apartment had a hotel-room feel to it, everything clean but utilitarian and impersonal. A corner of the living room had been converted into a mini-office with a desk, a word processor, a printer, and a modem. Several copies of the magazine he was supposed to work for were stacked on the coffee table, and when Buchanan examined their contents, he found articles under his pseudonym, another indication that Don Colton was an all-purpose identity. Obviously the magazines had been prepared well in advance, not just for him but for any operative who happened to need this type of cover. Don Colton — at least *this* Don Colton — wouldn't be in the neighborhood very long.

Nonetheless Buchanan still had to make his portrayal of Colton believable, and the first step was to familiarize himself with the articles he was supposed to have written. But halfway through the second essay — about Tahiti — he suddenly discovered that two hours had passed. He frowned. It shouldn't have taken him that long to read just a few pages. Had he fallen asleep? His headache — which had never gone away since he'd banged his skull in Cancun — worsened, and he surprised himself by no longer caring about his persona as a travel writer. Weary, he stood, went into the kitchen, which was separated from the living room only by a counter, and poured himself a drink from a bottle of bourbon that was next to the refrigerator along with bottles of gin and rum. After adding ice and water, he debated which to do first — to shower or to open one of the cans of chili he found in a cupboard. Tomorrow, he'd have to decide what to do about clean clothes. The ones he'd found in the bedroom closet were too small for him. But he couldn't leave the apartment without establishing a procedure with his employers so they'd know how to get in touch with him, and that was when the phone rang.

It startled him.

He pivoted toward the living room, staring toward the phone on a table next to the sofa. The phone rang a second time. He sipped from his bourbon, letting his nerves calm. The phone rang a third time. He *hated* phones. Squinting, he entered the living room and picked up the phone before it could ring a fourth time.

'Hello.' He tried to make his voice sound neutral.

'Don!' an exuberant male voice exclaimed. 'It's Alan! I wasn't sure you'd be back yet. How the hell are you?'

'Good,' Buchanan said. 'Fine.'

'The trip went okay?'

'The last part of it.'

'Yeah, your postcards mentioned you had a few problems at some earlier stops. Nothing you couldn't handle, though, right?'

'Right,' Buchanan echoed.

'That's really swell. Listen, buddy, I know it's getting late, but I haven't seen you in I can't remember when. What do you say? Have you eaten yet? Do you feel like getting together?'

'No,' Buchanan said, 'I haven't eaten yet.'

'Well, why don't I come over?'

'Yeah, why not?'

'Great, Don. Can't wait to see you. I'll be over in fifteen minutes. Think about where you want to eat.'

'Some place that's dark and not too crowded. Maybe with a piano player.'

'You're reading my mind, Don, reading my mind.'

'Be seeing you.' Buchanan set down the phone and massaged his aching temples. The man's reference to postcards and his own reference to a piano player had been the recognition sign and countersign that the note he'd destroyed at the Library of Congress had told him to use if he was contacted. His debriefing would soon begin.

Yet another.

His temples continued to ache. He thought about washing his face but first drank his glass of bourbon.

3

Fifteen minutes later, precisely on schedule, the doorbell rang. Buchanan peered through the door's security eye and saw a fortyish, short-haired, portly man in a brown-checkered sport coat. The voice on the phone had not been familiar, so Buchanan wasn't surprised that he'd never seen this man before, assuming that the voice on the phone belonged to this man. All the same, Buchanan had hoped that one of the controllers he'd dealt with previously would show up. He'd been through too many changes.

He opened the door warily. After all, he couldn't take for granted that the man was his contact. But the man immediately allayed his suspicions by using the same cheery tone that Buchanan had heard earlier. 'Don, you look fabulous. In your postcards, you didn't say you'd lost weight.'

'My diet didn't agree with me. Come on in, Alan. I've been thinking, maybe we shouldn't go out to eat. I'm not in the mood for a piano player.'

'Whatever.' The man who'd earlier identified himself as Alan, undoubtedly a pseudonym, carried a metal briefcase into the apartment and waited while Buchanan locked the door. Then the man's demeanor changed, as if he were an actor who'd stepped out of character when he walked off a stage. His manner became businesslike. 'The apartment was swept this afternoon. There aren't any bugs. How are you feeling?'

Buchanan shrugged. The truth was he felt exhausted, but he'd been trained not to indicate weakness.

'Is your wound healing properly?' the man asked.

229

'The infection's gone.'

'Good,' the man said flatly. 'What about your skull? I'm told you hit it on a—'

'Stupid accident,' Buchanan said.

'The report I received mentioned a concussion.'

Buchanan nodded.

'And a skull fracture,' the man said.

Buchanan nodded again, the movement intensifying his headache. 'A *depressed* skull fracture. A small section of bone on the inside was pushed against the brain. That's what caused the concussion. It's not like I've got a crack in the bone. It's not that serious. In Fort Lauderdale, I was kept in the hospital overnight for observation. Then the doctor let me go. He wouldn't have let me go if—'

The portly man who called himself Alan sat on the sofa but never took his gaze from Buchanan. 'That's what the report says. The report also says you'll need another checkup, another CAT-scan, to find out if the bruise on your brain has shrunk.'

'Would I be walking around if my brain was still swollen?'

'I don't know.' The man continued to assess Buchanan. 'Would you? Agents from Special Operations have a can-do attitude. Problems that would slow someone else down don't seem to bother you.'

'No. The mission comes first. If I think an injury impairs my ability to perform the mission, I say so.'

'Commendable. And if you thought you needed some time off, you'd say that, too?'

'Of course. Nobody turns down R and R.'

The man didn't say anything, just studied him.

To change the subject as much as to relieve his curiosity, Buchanan asked, 'What happened in Fort Lauderdale after I left? Was the situation dealt with to everyone's satisfaction? Were the photographs—?'

The man lowered his gaze, worked the combination locks on his briefcase, and opened it. 'I wouldn't know anything about that.' The man pulled out a folder. 'We have some paperwork to take care of.'

Uneasy, Buchanan sat across from him. His instincts troubled him. It might have been the consequence of fatigue, or perhaps it was due to the aftermath of stress. For whatever reason, there was something about the man's attitude that made Buchanan uncomfortable.

And it wasn't just that the man was brusque. In his eight years of working deep cover, Buchanan had dealt with controllers of various types, some of whom had a manner that would disqualify them from a popularity contest. But being personable wasn't a requirement for the job. Being thorough was, and sometimes there wasn't time to say things politely, and it wasn't smart to establish a relationship with someone whom the odds were you would never see again.

Buchanan had learned that the hard way over the years. In his numerous assumed identities, he'd occasionally found that he felt close to someone, to Jack and Cindy Doyle, for example. As much as he guarded against that happening, it nonetheless sometimes did, and it made Buchanan feel hollow after he moved on. Thus he could readily understand if this controller didn't want to conduct the debriefing on anything but an objective, unemotional basis.

That wasn't it, though. That wasn't what made Buchanan feel uncomfortable. It was something else, and the best he could do was attribute it to his experience with Bailey, to an instinct that warned him to be extra cautious.

'Here's my signed receipt,' the portly man who called himself Alan said. 'Now you can give me Victor Grant's ID.'

Buchanan made a snap decision then. He didn't trust this man. 'I don't have it.'

'What?' The man looked up from the receipt.

'I had to abandon the ID in the car when I drove it into the water in Fort Lauderdale . . . so the authorities would have a way to identify the driver after they couldn't find a body . . . so they'd decide Victor Grant was dead.'

'Everything? You left *everything?*'

'Driver's license. Credit card. Social security card. The works. I had to leave them in a jacket in a wallet so they wouldn't float away. And I had to leave *all* of them. The police would have thought it strange if all they found was a driver's license.'

'But the passport, Buchanan. I'm talking about the passport. You wouldn't have left the passport. You know that's the ID we care about. Anybody with a brain can arrange to get a fake driver's license. Who cares if the cops get their hands on it? But a fake passport, a first-class fake passport, hell, better than that because the passport blank came from the State Department. If the police had an expert study that passport, there'd be all kinds of questions that the people at State couldn't answer. And then maybe the questions would come in *our* direction.'

'I had to leave it,' Buchanan lied. The passport was in fact in the bedroom, in a small travel bag that he'd bought along with a toilet kit and a few spare clothes before leaving Florida. The travel bag also contained the handgun that Jack Doyle had given him. Buchanan wasn't about to tell this man about the handgun, either.

He continued, 'If the authorities did a thorough investigation of Victor Grant, they'd find out I'd been in Mexico. They'd find out I'd shown my passport down there. So they'd have to ask themselves, where is it now? They've got my wallet. They've got my suitcase – I left it in the trunk of the car. They've got all of Victor Grant's possessions. Except they don't have his body and they don't have his passport? No way. A good detective might decide that Victor Grant faked his death, then walked away with his passport, the only identification he'd need if he wanted to get out of the country. But since I left the passport in the jacket with my wallet, the authorities have one less detail to trouble them.'

'Smart, Buchanan,' the portly man said. 'There's just one problem.'

'Oh?'

'The police didn't find the passport.'

'What? Then it must have floated away.'

'But not the wallet?'

'Hey, the wallet was heavier. How do *I* know what happened? My orders were to make Victor Grant disappear. I did it the best way I knew how.'

The portly man stared at him.

'Has the missing passport made the cops think something's wrong?' Buchanan asked.

The portly man stared harder. 'You'll have to sign this document saying that you couldn't surrender the passport.'

'Whatever,' Buchanan said. He signed and returned the document, then watched the man who called himself Alan put it in his briefcase.

'The next order of business.' With an air of efficiency combined with distaste, the portly man opened and dumped the contents of a paper bag onto the coffee table.

Buchanan looked at the sprawl of magazines, catalogues, video-and-record-club solicitations, and various other forms of bulk mail. The items were addressed to several persons, Richard Dana, Robert Chambers, Craig Madden, and Brian MacDonald, the most recent pseudonyms that Buchanan had used before becoming Ed Potter in Mexico.

'House cleaning,' the portly man said.

Buchanan nodded. To appear believable in an assumed identity, he had to be equipped with more than just fake ID. Mail, for example. It wasn't natural for people never to get

233

mail. Bills had to be paid. Letters had to be received. Magazines . . . lots of people subscribed to magazines . . . if you said your name was Brian MacDonald and you got a magazine addressed to that name, the magazine became another bit of evidence that proved you were the person you claimed to be. So, under various names, Buchanan subscribed to magazines wherever he expected to live for an extended time. But just as he created individual characteristics for each person he pretended to be, so he had to make sure that the magazines matched each character's personality. Richard Dana subscribed to *Runner's World*. Robert Chambers liked *Gourmet*. Craig Madden was a movie fanatic and received *Premiere*. Brian MacDonald enjoyed *Car and Driver*. Because magazines often sold their subscription lists to catalogue companies, soon Buchanan's various characters would begin receiving catalogues about the subject in which they were supposedly interested, and this extra mail would help legitimize his characters.

Eventually, though, Buchanan would receive a new assignment and move on, discarding one identity, assuming another. In theory, the previous identity would no longer exist. Still, even though Buchanan had made arrangements to stop mail from coming to his former characters, a few items would inevitably arrive at places where his characters had used to live. To avoid arousing suspicion, he always left a forwarding address with the landlords at those places. That forwarding address was known in the trade as an accommodation address, a safe, convenient mail drop, usually a private mail service owned by, but not traceable to, Buchanan's controllers.

'Is there anything here that needs to be dealt with?' the portly man who called himself Alan asked. 'Some loose end that needs to be tied? We ought to know before we destroy this stuff.'

Buchanan sorted through the items. 'Nope. These

magazines can go. These catalogues. This circular is exactly what they call it – junk. This . . .'

He felt a chill as he lifted a postcard. 'It's addressed to Peter Lang. I haven't used that name in six years. How the hell did it get lost this long?'

'It didn't. Check the postmark. Someone mailed it from Baltimore . . . Last week.'

'Last week?' Buchanan felt cold. 'Who'd want to get in touch with Peter Lang after six years? Who'd remember him? Who'd care enough to . . . ?'

'That's what *we* want to know,' Alan said, his calculated gaze threatening. 'And why a postcard? Why not a letter? And what do you make of the message?'

Troubled, Buchanan studied it. The message was handwritten in black ink, the script small, the strokes thin, the lettering ornate yet precise.

A woman's handwriting. No name.

Five sentences, some of them incomplete. Seeming gibberish.

But not to Buchanan. He didn't need a signature to tell him who had sent the postcard. Because she would have taken for granted that several people, especially Buchanan's employers, would have read the message by now, he admired her indirection.

4

Here's the postcard I never thought I'd send. I hope you meant your promise. The last time and place. Counting on you. PLEASE.

Buchanan read the message several times, then glanced up at the portly man, who now was squinting.

'So?' The man squinted harder.

'It's a woman who knew me when I was Peter Lang. Someone I needed for window dressing.'

'That's all?'

Buchanan shrugged.

'Who was she, Buchanan?'

'It's been so long I don't even remember her name.'

'Don't tell me your famous memory is failing you.'

'I remember what's essential. She wasn't.'

'Why didn't she sign her name?'

'She was a flake. That much I recall. Maybe she thought it would be cute and mysterious if she sent an unsigned postcard.'

'And yet without a name on the card, a name you claim you can't remember, you know who sent the message.'

'She used to do this kind of stuff a lot. Unsigned, cryptic messages. I'd find them in my bathroom, in my pajamas, in my sock drawer. I told you she was a flake. But she sure was gorgeous, and I never read any handwriting as neat and elegant as this. She was proud of that – her handwriting.'

'But what does it mean?'

'Damned if I know. Maybe she was high on something when she wrote it. Or maybe she tried so hard to make the message cute that she didn't realize she was being incoherent.'

The portly man squinted even harder. 'Just like that, after six years, she decided to write to you.'

'Must be,' Buchanan said. 'Because that's what happened. She didn't even think to put a return address on it. That's how spur-of-the-moment she used to act.'

'What's this "last time and place" business?'

'Beats the hell out of me.'

The portly man didn't move. He just kept staring at Buchanan as if trying to make him uncomfortable enough to demonstrate a sign of weakness.

Buchanan returned his stare.

After thirty seconds, the portly man sighed and gestured for Buchanan to give back the postcard. He shoved it into the paper bag along with the magazines, catalogues, and circulars, then placed them in his metal briefcase and locked it. 'We'll talk again soon, Buchanan.' He stood.

'Wait a minute.'

'Is something wrong?' the man asked. 'Or maybe there's something you forgot to tell me?'

'Yeah. What about my new ID?'

'New ID?'

'The driver's license and credit card, all the documents for Don Colton.'

The man frowned. 'You must have gotten the wrong impression. You're not being issued new ID.'

'What?'

'You won't need any. The rent, the phone, and the other bills are paid through one of our cover organizations by mail. There's plenty of food here so you won't need a checkbook to go to the grocery store, and you won't need a credit card to go to a restaurant. And since we want you to stay close, you won't need ID to rent a car.'

'So what about clothes? I need a credit card to replace what I abandoned in Fort Lauderdale. What's in the closet here is too small.'

'There's a gray, cotton sweatsuit on the bedroom shelf. It's large enough to do for now. When I drive you to the hospital for your CAT-scan, I'll bring you a few more things.'

'That's *it*? You're leaving me without a way to prove my cover?'

'Buchanan, we don't *want* you to prove your cover. We don't want you to be in a position to *need* to prove your cover. We don't want Don Colton leaving this apartment. We don't want him wandering around the building or going to restaurants or to shopping malls and flashing ID. Don Colton's invisible. He's been living in this complex for years, and nobody knows him. He travels so much, you see. So as long as you stay in here, no one'll bother you, and for that matter, we don't want *you* bothering anybody, either. Do you get it?'

Buchanan narrowed his eyes. 'Yeah, I got it.'

'We don't want you even sending out for a pizza.'

'I said I got it. Anyway how *could* I order a pizza? I'm almost out of money.'

'Good.' The man lifted his briefcase and walked toward the door.

'I'm in limbo?'

The man kept walking. 'Until we've assessed the damage control on Cancun, Mérida, and Fort Lauderdale. A while ago, you told me you'd ask for time off if you thought you needed it. You said nobody turns down R and R.' The man reached the door, unlocked it, and glanced at Buchanan. 'Well, now you've got some. You've been in the field quite a while. Eight years. A *very* long while. It's time for a rest.'

'And what if I don't want a rest?'

The man gripped the doorknob. 'It's a funny thing, Buchanan.'

'What?'

'I was told you were a fanatic about assuming your identities.'

'That's right.'

'A real method actor. Invented a detailed history for each of your pseudonyms. Dressed, ate, and sometimes even walked the way you decided a particular character would. Gave each of them a distinct personality.'

'You're right again. Staying totally in character is what keeps me alive.'

'Sure. The thing is, I was also told that you'd practically bite off the head of any controller who called you by your real

238

name. But I just did, and in fact I've been doing it off and on since I came here. You should have been insisting that I call you Don Colton.'

'There's nothing strange about that. Until I get Don Colton's ID and background, I can't become him. I don't have any personality to assume.'

'Well, in that case, I'd expect you to have insisted that I call you Victor Grant.'

'How could I?'

'I don't understand.'

'Calling me Victor Grant is impossible. I wouldn't have responded.'

'Why?'

'Because Victor Grant is dead.' Abruptly Buchanan felt a further chill as he understood the significance of what he'd just said.

The man who called himself Alan understood the significance very well. 'As you said, you're in limbo.' He turned the knob and opened the door. 'Stay put. I'll be in touch.'

5

Buchanan leaned his back against the locked door and massaged the sides of his aching head. So much was wrong, he didn't know where to start analyzing.

Try starting with why you lied to him about the passport and why you didn't tell him you had a firearm.

I didn't want to lose them. I didn't trust him.

Well, you weren't wrong on that score. Whatever that conversation was, it sure wasn't a debriefing. He didn't ask you to talk about anything that you'd done. And he didn't give you new ID. He put you on ice. It was more like an

239

interrogation, except he didn't ask you any questions that weren't about . . .

The postcard.

Buchanan went to the counter in the kitchen and poured more bourbon and water into a glass. He took a long swallow, then felt his cheek muscles harden with tension.

The postcard.

Yeah, the passport wasn't the only thing you lied about . . . What's the big deal? Why didn't you tell him the truth?

Because he was too damned interested.

Hey, a postcard arrives last week for a man who hasn't existed, whom you haven't been, for the past six years. That's an attention-getter. Naturally they want to know what the hell's going on. Something from one of your pasts, some threat to the operation, catching up to you. Why didn't you tell him?

Because I'm not sure. If I did know what was going on, maybe I'd have told him.

Bullshit. The truth is you're scared.

No way.

Yes. Confused and scared. You haven't thought about her in all this time. You've *made* yourself not think about her. And now all of a sudden, bang, she's back in your head, and you don't know how to handle it. But this much is sure – you don't want *them* to have anything to do with her.

He stared at his glass of bourbon, his emotions powerful.

6

Here's the postcard I never thought I'd send.

She'd been furious the night she decided that she didn't want to see him anymore. She'd told him not to bother trying to get in touch with her again, that if she ever needed him,

240

she'd send him a Goddamned postcard.

I hope you meant your promise.

He'd told her that no matter how much time and distance was between them, all she had to do was ask, and he'd be there.

The last time and place.

He remembered the date of their breakup well because of what had been happening around them, the costumes, the music – October 31, Halloween. The time had been close to midnight, the place Café du Monde in New Orleans.

Counting on you. PLEASE.

In capital letters? She might as well have said that she was begging him.

That wasn't like her.

She was in trouble.

He continued staring at the glass of bourbon and imagined the tension she must have felt as she wrote the postcard. Maybe she had only seconds to write it, to condense it to its essentials and hope it was clear to him, even though she didn't sign her name.

She doesn't want anyone except me to know where she's going to be and when.

She's terrified.

7

The man who called himself Alan left Buchanan's apartment, heard the scrape of the lock, and proceeded along the green, heavy-duty carpet of the harshly lit, concrete hallway. He was pleased that no one happened to come out of another apartment and see him. Like Buchanan, he avoided the elevator and used the fire stairs — less chance of encountering anyone. But unlike Buchanan, who would have headed down to the street, the portly, short-haired man in the brown-checkered sport coat went up to the next landing, heard voices, waited in the stairwell until the voices were cut off by the sound of an elevator, and then walked briskly along the corridor until he reached the door to the apartment directly above Buchanan's. He knocked twice, paused, knocked twice more, heard a lock open, and was quickly admitted.

The apartment was dimly lit. He couldn't see who was present or how the unit was furnished. Nor could anyone who happened to be passing as he entered. But the moment the door was closed behind him, he heard the click of a switch, and at once the apartment's living room was filled with light. Thick, closed draperies prevented the light from being seen by anyone outside.

Five people were in the room. A tall, trim man with severe features and cropped, graying hair exuded the most authority. Although he wore a plain, blue, business suit, he stood with military bearing and in private was never referred to by his name but always as 'colonel'.

The next in charge was a younger man, in his forties, less tall, more muscular. He wore tan slacks, a brown blazer. Major Putnam.

Beside him was a blonde woman, in her thirties, gorgeous, her breasts bulging at her blouse. Captain Weller.

Finally there were two plain-clothed sentries, one of whom had admitted him and then relocked the door. The sentries had last seen him not long ago, just before he went down to Buchanan's apartment, so this time they didn't ask for identification. Indeed, they barely nodded to him before they redirected their attention toward the door.

The colonel, the captain, and the major didn't pay him much attention, either. After a confirming glance, they stared again at a bank of closed-circuit television screens and various black-and-white images of Buchanan's apartment. A long table supported a row of video-tape machines, each of which was in operation, recording everything that occurred in each room of Buchanan's apartment. On another table, several audio-tape machines were also in operation. Except for a sofa and two chairs shoved against a wall, the electronics were the room's only furnishings. It wasn't any wonder that the colonel had the lights dimmed when the hallway door was opened – he didn't want anyone to get a good look at what was in here.

The man who called himself Alan set his briefcase beside a box of donuts and a steaming coffee percolator on the counter between the kitchen and the living room. There weren't any ashtrays – the colonel refused to allow smoking. And there wasn't any clutter of crumpled napkins, stale food, and used styrofoam cups – the colonel insisted on an absolutely neat control room.

'What's he been doing since I left?' Alan asked. The question was directed to anyone who would bother to answer (they didn't always). As the only civilian in the apartment, he didn't feel obligated to use military titles. Indeed he was getting damned tired of sensing that these Special Operations types considered themselves superior to the Agency.

After a pause, the woman, Captain Weller, answered without looking at him, continuing to concentrate on the television screens. 'Leaned against the door. Rubbed his skull. Appears to have a headache. Went into the kitchen. Poured another drink.'

'Another?' Alan asked, disapproving.

His judgmental tone prompted the second-in-command, Major Putnam, to face him. 'It means nothing out of context.

Alcohol is one of his weapons. He uses it to disarm his contacts. If he doesn't maintain a tolerance for it, he's as open to attack as if he doesn't maintain his combat skills.'

'I've never heard *that* one before,' Alan said skeptically. 'If he was strictly mine, I'd be alarmed. But then, from the start, nothing about this unit was conventional, was it?'

Now the colonel turned. 'Don't condescend to us.'

'I wasn't. I was making a point about control.'

'The point is taken,' the colonel said. 'If he finishes this drink and makes another, I'll be concerned.'

'Right. It's not as if we haven't got plenty of other things to be concerned about. What's your analysis of my session with him?'

A movement on one of the monitors attracted everyone's attention. Again they stared at the screen.

Buchanan carried his drink from the kitchen.

On a separate black-and-white screen, he appeared in the living room and slumped on the sofa, placing his feet on the coffee table, leaning back, rubbing the moisture-beaded glass against his brow.

'Yeah, he sure seems to have a headache,' Alan said.

'Or maybe he's just tired from stress and traveling,' the woman said.

'A new CAT-scan will tell us what's going on in his head,' Alan said.

The woman turned. 'You mean, in his brain, of course. Not in his mind.'

'Exactly. That's what I meant. I asked you what's your analysis of my session with him.'

'His explanation about the passport was reasonable,' the major said. 'In his place, I might not have abandoned it, but perhaps that's why I'm not in his place. I don't have the talent for role-playing that he does. A water-destroyed passport, one that validated his identity without jeopardizing the passport's source, would have added credence to his character's death.'

'But,' Alan corrected, 'the passport was never found.'

'An accident of circumstance.'

'Our opinions differ. But we'll leave that subject for later,' Alan said. 'What about the postcard?'

'Again his explanation was reasonable,' the major said.

'This conversation sounds like an echo,' Alan said. 'I'm losing patience. If you wanted a whitewash, why did you need me here? I've got a wife and kids who wonder what I look like.'

'Whitewash?' the colonel intruded, his voice like steel against flint. '*I'm* losing patience with *you*. The person we're observing on these monitors, the person you had the privilege of interrogating, is without doubt the finest deep-cover operative I've ever had the honor of directing. He has survived longer, has assumed more identities, has endured greater dangers and accomplished more critical missions than any other deep-cover specialist I've ever heard about. He is one of a kind, and it is only with the greatest regret that I am forced to consider his termination.'

Ah, Alan thought, there it is. We're finally getting to it. He gestured toward the sentries. 'Are you sure you want to talk about something so serious in front of—?'

'They're loyal,' the colonel said.

'Just like Buchanan.'

'No one's questioning Buchanan's loyalty. It wasn't his fault that he was compromised. There was absolutely no way to predict that someone he knew in Kuwait and Iraq would walk into that restaurant in Cancun while he was making his pitch to those two drug dealers. The worst nightmare of a deep-cover specialist – one identity colliding with another. And there was no way to predict that Bailey would be so damned persistent, that he'd put together evidence showing Buchanan in three different identities. Jesus, the photographs. If only the son of a bitch hadn't started taking photographs.'

Especially of you and Buchanan together, Alan thought.

What the colonel said next seemed in response to the accusing look in Alan's eyes. 'I admit the mistake. That's why I sent you to interrogate him. I will never again allow myself to be in direct contact with him. But as it is, the damage is done, and *your* people made mistakes, too. If there'd been time in Fort Lauderdale, I'd have brought in one of my own surveillance teams. Instead I had to rely on . . . Your people assured me that they'd found Bailey's hotel room and confiscated all the photographs.'

'That was my information as well,' Alan said.

'The information was wrong. No photographs of Buchanan and myself were retrieved. And before Bailey could be interrogated, the bomb concealed in the picnic cooler was detonated.'

'Those were the orders,' Alan insisted. 'The location transmitter in the wall of the cooler would lead the team to Bailey when Buchanan delivered the money. Then the C-4 explosive that was also in the walls of the cooler would be detonated by remote-control. Bailey wouldn't be a problem anymore.'

'You're simplifying to excuse failure. The specific orders were to wait in case Bailey rendezvoused with the woman photographer who was helping him. The C-4 was chosen because it was a convenient means to take care of both of them.'

'*In case* they met,' Alan emphasized. 'But what if Bailey had already paid her off and wouldn't be seeing her again? Or what if Bailey took the money and abandoned the cooler?'

'Then you admit your people disobeyed orders by acting prematurely.'

Alan didn't reply.

'Well?' the colonel asked.

'The truth is, no one disobeyed. The bomb went off on its own.'

'*On its . . . ?*'

'The expert who assembled the bomb thought he'd set the remote-controlled detonator to a radio frequency that wasn't used in the area. In fact, it had to be triggered by two *different*, uncommon radio frequencies, one to arm it, one to set it off. All those boats at Fort Lauderdale. All those two-way radios. Apparently there *aren't* any uncommon frequencies down there.'

'Jesus,' the colonel said. 'The bomb could have gone off while Buchanan had it, before he gave the cooler to Bailey.'

'I don't know why *that* should bother you. You were just talking about the possibility of having Buchanan terminated.'

The colonel looked puzzled. Then abruptly he understood. 'Terminated *without* prejudice. What's the matter with you? Do you think I'd actually order the death of one of my men, an officer who served me faithfully for many years?'

'Whether he's faithful hasn't been proven.' Alan pointed toward one of the many television screens, toward the black-and-white image of Buchanan slumped on the sofa, his eyes closed, troubled, the moisture-beaded glass of bourbon and water held to his wrinkled brow. 'I'm not convinced he was truthful when I talked to him.'

'About the passport?'

'I wasn't referring to the passport. The postcard. *That's* what bothers me. I think he held back. I think he lied to me.'

'Why would he do that?'

'I'm not sure. But by your own admission, he'd been working under cover, in multiple identities, for an unusual amount of time. He endured a great deal of physical trauma in Mexico. His head obviously still hurts. Maybe he's about to fall apart. There are pictures of you and him that we can't locate. As well, there's a woman who saw Bailey with

Buchanan and *you* with Buchanan. A lot of loose ends. If Buchanan is compromised, if he does fall apart, well, we obviously don't need another Hasenfus on our hands.'

Alan was referring to an ex-Marine named Eugene Hasenfus who in 1986 was shot down while flying arms to U.S.-backed contra rebels in Marxist Nicaragua. When questioned by Nicaraguan authorities, Hasenfus implicated the CIA and caused a political scandal that revealed a secret, White-House-directed war in Nicaragua. Because intermediaries had been used to hire Hasenfus, the CIA could plausibly deny any connection to him. Nonetheless, Congressional and media attention directed toward the Agency had been potentially disastrous.

'Buchanan would never talk,' the colonel said. 'He'd never violate our security.'

'That's probably what someone said about Hasenfus when he was hired.'

'It'll never come to that,' the colonel said. 'I've made my decision. I'm putting Buchanan on inactive status. We'll ease him out slowly so he doesn't have culture shock. Or maybe he'll agree to become a trainer. But his days of deep cover are over.'

'Tomorrow, when he's taken for a new CAT-scan . . .'

'What are you getting at?' the colonel asked.

'I'd like to have sodium amytal administered to him and then have him questioned about that postcard,' Alan said.

'No.'

'But—'

'No,' the colonel repeated. 'He's *my* operative, and I know how he'd react if you used drug therapy to question him. He'd feel threatened, insulted, betrayed. Then we *would* have a problem. The fastest way to make a man disloyal is by *treating* him as if he's disloyal.'

'Then I insist on at least keeping him under surveillance,'

Alan said. 'There's something about him that bothers me. And I'm still bugged about that postcard.'

'Keeping him under surveillance?' The colonel shrugged and turned toward the television monitors, watching the black-and-white image of Buchanan slumped on the sofa, his eyes scrunched shut as if he had a headache, the glass of bourbon against his brow. 'I don't have a problem with that. After all, that's what we're already doing.'

8

Caught in limbo but not realizing it, Buchanan hadn't been conscious of being called by his real name when the portly man in the brown-checkered sport coat questioned him the previous night. But as soon as the man had drawn attention to what he'd been doing, as soon as Buchanan realized that he was suspended between identities, he became extremely self-conscious about his name. He was so thorough an impersonator that seldom in the past eight years had he thought of himself as Buchanan. To do so would have been incompatible with his various assumed identities. He didn't just pretend to be those people. He *was* those people. He had to be. The slightest weakness in his characterization could get him killed. For the most part, he'd so thoroughly expunged the name Buchanan from his awareness that if someone had attempted to test him by unexpectedly calling his name from behind him, he wouldn't have turned. Habit would not have controlled him. The name would have belonged to a stranger.

But now as the portly man who called himself Alan drove him to get his CAT-scan, Buchanan inwardly squirmed whenever his escort called him by his true name, something the escort did often, apparently by intention. Buchanan felt as he had the first time he'd asked a girl to dance or the first time he'd heard his voice on a tape recorder or the first time he'd made love. The doubt and wonder of those experiences had been positive, however, whereas the self-consciousness he endured at being called 'Buchanan' produced the negativity of fear. He felt exposed, vulnerable, threatened. Don't call me that. If certain people find out who I really am, it'll get me killed.

In Fairfax, Virginia, at a private medical clinic presumably overseen by Buchanan's controllers, he was again made nervous, inwardly squirming when the doctor assigned to him persistently called him by his real name.

How are you, Mr Buchanan? Does your head still hurt, Mr Buchanan? I have to do a few tests on you, Mr Buchanan. Excellent responses, Mr Buchanan. My nurse will take you downstairs for your CAT-scan, Mr Buchanan.

Christ, they didn't bother to give me even a minimal assumed identity, Buchanan thought. Not even just a John Doe cover name. I wouldn't have needed supporting documents. An arbitrary alias for purposes of the examination would have been fine. But my real name's on the medical file the doctor's holding. I can understand that they wanted to protect the Don Colton pseudonym. But I didn't have to use it. I could have called myself anything. This way, with my name associated with the CAT-scan, if anyone makes a comparison, I can be linked to *Victor Grant's* CAT-scan.

The doctor turned from examining the film. 'Good news. The bruise is considerably reduced, Mr Buchanan.'

If he calls me that one more time, I'll—

'And there's no indication of neurological damage. The shaking in your right hand has stopped. I attribute that previous symptom to trauma caused by the wound to your shoulder.'

'What about my headache?'

'After a concussion, a headache can persist for quite some time. It doesn't trouble me.'

'Well, you're not the one with the headache.'

The doctor didn't react to the attempt at humor. 'I can prescribe something for the pain, if you like.'

'Something with a label that says, "Do not drive or use heavy machinery while taking this medication"?'

'That's correct.'

'Thanks, but I'll stick to aspirin,' Buchanan said.

'As you wish. Come back in a week, let's make it November second, and I'll re-examine you. Meanwhile, be careful. Don't bang your head again. If you have any problems, let me know.'

Problems? Buchanan thought. The kind of problems I've got, you can't solve.

9

Here's the postcard I never thought I'd send.

10

'Do you want to tell me what's going on?' Buchanan asked as they drove along the Little River Turnpike from Fairfax back to Alexandria. The day was gray, a late October drizzle speckling the windshield.

The man who called himself Alan glanced at him, then peered forward again, concentrating on traffic. He turned on the windshield wipers. 'I'm not sure what you mean.'

'Why have I been exposed?'

As the drizzle changed to rain, the man turned on the windshield defroster. 'Exposed? What makes you think . . . ?'

Buchanan stared at him.

251

The man turned on the headlights.

'There's not much left,' Buchanan said, 'for you to toy with and avoid the question. What are you going to do next? Turn on the radio and keep switching stations, or pull over and start changing the oil?'

'What are you talking about, Buchanan?'

'That. My name. For the first time in eight years, people are using it openly. I'm deliberately being compromised. Why?'

'I told you last night. It's time for a rest.'

'That doesn't justify violating basic rules.'

'Hey, the doctor has a security clearance.'

'It was a needless violation,' Buchanan said. 'He certainly didn't need to know who I was in order to assess a CAT-scan. And he mentioned the wound in my shoulder, but he didn't get a look at that shoulder, and I didn't tell him about it. What else has he been told that he didn't need to know? How I got the wound?'

'Of course not.'

'Sure. I bet. This isn't just a rest. I'm not just in limbo. I'm being eased out. Am I right?'

The man steered into the passing lane.

'I asked you a question. Am I being eased out?'

'Nothing lasts forever, Buchanan.'

'Stop calling me that.'

'What *should* I call you? Who the hell do you think you are?'

Buchanan's skull throbbed. He didn't have an answer.

'An operative with your talent and experience could do a lot of good as a trainer,' Alan said.

Buchanan didn't respond.

'Did you expect to work under cover all your life?'

'I never thought about it.'

'Come on,' the man said. 'I fail to believe that.'

'I meant what I said. I literally never thought about it. I never thought beyond who I was during any given assignment.

252

If you start planning your retirement while you're working under cover, you start making mistakes. You forget who you're supposed to be. You fall out of character. That's a great way to insure you don't live long enough for the retirement you're not supposed to be planning.'

'Well, you'd better think about it now.'

Buchanan's skull ached more fiercely. 'Why is this being done to me? I didn't screw up. Nothing that happened was my fault. I compensated perfectly. The operation wasn't damaged.'

'Ah, but it could have been.'

'That still would not have been my fault,' Buchanan said.

'We're not discussing fault. We're discussing what did and didn't happen and what *almost* happened. Maybe you've become unlucky. The bottom line is you're thirty-two. In this game, that makes you a senior citizen. Eight years? Christ, it's amazing you're still alive. It's time to walk away.'

'The fact that I'm still alive proves how good I am. I don't deserve . . .'

The rain increased, drumming on the car's roof. The windshield wipers flapped harder.

'Did you ever see your file?'

Despite his pain, Buchanan shook his head.

'Would you like to?'

'No.'

'The psychological profile is very revealing.'

'I'm not interested.'

'You've got what's called a "dissociative personality." '

'I told you I'm not interested.'

The man changed lanes again, maintaining speed despite the rain. 'I'm not a psychologist, but the file made sense to me. You don't like yourself. You do everything you can to keep from looking inward. You split away. You identify with people and objects around you. You objectify. You . . . dissociate.'

Buchanan frowned ahead at the traffic obscured by the rain.

'In average society, that condition would be a liability,' the man continued. 'But your trainers realized what a prize they had when their computer responded to a survey by choosing your profile. In high school, you'd already demonstrated a talent – perhaps a better term is compulsion – for acting. At Benning and Bragg, your Special Ops commanders gave you glowing reports for your combat skills. Considering the unique slant of your personality, all that remained to qualify you was even *more* specialized training at the Farm.'

'I don't want to hear any more,' Buchanan said.

'You're an ideal undercover operative. It's no wonder you were able to assume multiple identities for eight years, and that your commanders thought you were capable of doing so without breaking down. Hell, yes. You'd already broken down. Working under cover was the way you healed. You hated yourself so much that you'd do anything, you'd suffer anything for the chance not to be yourself.'

Buchanan calmly reached out and grasped the man's right elbow.

'Hey,' the man said.

Buchanan's middle finger found the nerve he wanted.

'*Hey*,' the man repeated.

Buchanan squeezed.

The man screamed. Jerking from pain, he caused the car to swerve, its rear tires fishtailing on the wet, slick pavement. Behind and in the passing lane, other drivers swerved in startled response and blared their horns.

'Now the way this is going to work,' Buchanan said, 'is either you'll shut up or else you'll feel what it's like to lose control of a car doing fifty-five miles an hour.'

The man's face was the color of concrete. His mouth hung open in agony. Sweat beaded his brow as he struggled to keep control of the car.

He nodded.

'Good,' Buchanan said. 'I knew we could reach an understanding.' Releasing his grip, he sat rigidly straight and looked forward.

The man mumbled something.

'What?' Buchanan asked.

'Nothing,' the man answered.

'That's what I thought.'

But Buchanan knew what the man had said.

Because of your brother.

11

'What's he doing now?' the man who called himself Alan asked as he entered the apartment directly above Buchanan's.

'Nothing,' the muscular man, Major Putnam, said. He sipped from a styrofoam cup of coffee and watched the television monitors. Again he wore civilian clothes.

'Well, he must be doing *something*.' Alan glanced around the apartment. The colonel and Captain Weller weren't around.

'Nope,' Major Putnam said. 'Nothing. When he came in, I figured he'd pour himself a drink, go to the bathroom, read a magazine, watch television, do exercises, whatever. But all he did was go over to the sofa. There he is. That's what he's been doing since you left him. Nothing.'

Alan approached the row of television monitors. Massaging his right elbow where the nerve that Buchanan had pinched still troubled him, he frowned at a black-and-white image of Buchanan sitting on the sofa. 'Jesus.'

Buchanan sat bolt-straight, motionless, his expression rigid, his intense gaze focused on a chair across from him.

'Jesus,' Alan repeated. 'He's catatonic. Does the colonel know about this?'

255

'I phoned him.'

'And?'

'I'm supposed to keep watching. What did the two of you talk about? When he came in, he looked . . .'

'It's what we *didn't* talk about.'

'I don't understand.'

'His brother.'

'Christ,' the major said, 'you know that's an off-limits subject.'

'I wanted to test him.'

'Well, you certainly got a reaction.'

'Yeah, but it's not the one I wanted.'

12

Buchanan was reminded of an old story about a donkey between two bales of hay. The donkey stood exactly midpoint between the bales. Each bale was the same size and had the same fragrance. With no reason to choose one bale over the other, the donkey starved to death.

The story – which could never happen in the real world because the donkey could never be exactly at midpoint and the bales could never be exactly the same – was a theoretical way to illustrate the problem of free will. The ability to choose, which most people took for granted, depended on certain conditions, and without them, a person could be motiveless, just as Buchanan found that he was now.

His brother.

Buchanan had so thoroughly worked to obliterate the memory that for the past eight years he'd managed not to be conscious of the critical event that controlled his behavior. Not once had he thought about it. On rare occasions of weakness, late at night, weary, he might sense the nightmare lurking in the darkness of his subconscious, crouching, about to spring. Then he would muster all his strength of resolve to thrust up a mental wall of denial, of refusal to accept the unacceptable.

Even now, with his defenses taken from him, with his identity exposed, unshielded, he was repulsed sufficiently that the memory was able to catch him only partially, in principle but not in detail.

His brother.

His wonderful brother.

Twelve years old.

Sweet Tommy.

Was dead.

And he had killed him.

Buchanan felt as if he were trapped by ice. He couldn't move. He sat on the sofa, and his legs, his back, his arms were numb, his entire body cold, paralyzed. He kept staring toward the chair in front of him, not seeing it, barely aware of time.

Five o'clock.

Six o'clock.

Seven o'clock.

The room was in darkness. Buchanan kept staring, seeing nothing.

Tommy was dead.

And he had killed him.

Blood.

He'd clutched Tommy's stake-impaled body, trying to tug him free.

Tommy's cheeks had been terribly pale. His breathing had sounded like bubbles. His moan had been liquid, as if he were gargling. But what he gargled hadn't been salt water. It had been . . .

Blood.

'Hurts. Hurts so bad.'

'Tommy, oh, God, I'm sorry. I didn't mean to.'

Push him.

Just horsing around.

Didn't think Tommy would lose his balance and fall.

Didn't know anything was down in the pit.

A construction site. A summer evening. Two brothers on an adventure.

'Hurts so bad.'

'Tommy!'

'Doesn't hurt anymore.'

'*Tommy!*'

So much blood.

When Buchanan was fifteen.

Still catatonic, sitting bolt-straight on the sofa, staring at the darkness, Buchanan felt as if a portion of his mind were raising arms, trying to ward off the terrible memory. Although he was chilled, sweat beaded his brow. Too much, he thought. He hadn't remembered in such detail since the days and nights before Tommy's funeral and the unendurable summer that followed, the guilt-laden, seemingly endless season of grief that finally *had* ended when . . .

Buchanan's mind darted and burrowed, seeking any protection it could from the agonizing memory of Tommy's blood on his clothes, of the stake projecting from Tommy's chest.

'It's all my fault.'

'No, you didn't mean to do it,' Buchanan's mother had said.

'I killed him.'

'It was an accident,' Buchanan's mother had said.

But Buchanan hadn't believed her, and he was certain that he'd have gone insane if he hadn't found a means to protect himself from his mind. The answer turned out to be amazingly simple, wonderfully self-evident. Become someone else.

Dissociative personality. Buchanan imagined himself as his favorite sports and rock stars, as certain movie and television actors whom he idolized. He suddenly became a reader – of novels into which he could escape and become the hero with whom he so desperately wanted to identify. In high school that autumn, he discovered the drama club, subconsciously motivated by the urge to perfect the skills he would need to maintain his protective assumed identities, the personas that would allow him to escape from himself.

Then after high school, perhaps to prove himself, perhaps to punish himself, perhaps to court an early death, he'd joined the military, not just any branch, the Army, so he could enter Special Forces. The name said it all – to be special. He wanted to sacrifice himself, to atone. And one thing more – if he saw enough death, perhaps one death in particular would no longer haunt him.

As the man who called himself Alan had indicated, Buchanan's Special Operations trainers realized what a prize they had when their computer responded to a survey by choosing Buchanan's profile. A man who desperately needed to assume identities. An operative who wouldn't be wearied but on the contrary would flourish for long periods under deep cover.

Now they were stripping away his barriers, taking away his shields, exposing the guilt that had compelled him to be an operative and that he had managed to subdue.

Buchanan? Who the hell was Buchanan? Jim Crawford was a man he understood. So was Ed Potter. And Victor Grant. And all the others. He'd invented detailed personal backgrounds for each of them. Some of his characters were blessed (in Richard Dana's case literally, for Dana believed that he was the recipient of the grace of God as a born-again Christian). Others carried burdens (Ed Potter's wife had divorced him for a man who earned more money). Buchanan knew how each of them dressed (Robert Chambers was formal and always wore a suit and tie). He knew which kinds of music each liked (Peter

Sloane was crazy about country and western), and which foods (Jim Crawford hated cauliflower), and which types of women (Richard Dana liked brunettes), and which types of movies (Brian MacDonald could watch *Singin' in the Rain* every night of the week), and . . .

Who the hell was Buchanan? It was significant that Buchanan and his controllers always thought of him in terms of his last name. Impersonal. Objective. After eight years of having impersonated – correction, of having *been* – hundreds of people, Buchanan had no idea of how to impersonate himself. What were his speech mannerisms? Did he have a distinctive walk? Which types of clothes, food, music, et cetera, did he prefer? Was he religious? Did he have any hobbies? Favorite cities? What came naturally?

Christ, he hadn't been Buchanan in so long that he didn't know who Buchanan was. He *didn't want* to know who Buchanan was. The story of the donkey between the two bales of hay was his story. He was caught between the identity of Victor Grant, who was dead, and the identity of Don Colton, who wasn't formed. With no way to turn, with nothing to help him choose whom to be, he was paralyzed.

Self-defense made the difference – protective instincts. Sitting rigidly in the quiet, dark room, he heard a noise, the scrape of a key in the front door's lock. A portion of his mind jolted him. His body was no longer cold and numb. His lethargy drained, dispelled by adrenaline.

The doorknob creaked. As someone in the outside hallway slowly pushed the door open, the glare of fluorescent lights spilling in, Buchanan was already off the sofa. He darted to the left and disappeared into the darkness of the bedroom. He heard the flick of a switch and stepped back farther into the bedroom as light filled the living room. He heard a metallic scratch as someone removed the key from the lock. He heard a soft thunk as the door was gently shut. Cautious footsteps made a brushing sound as they inched across the carpet.

He tensed.

'Buchanan?' The voice was familiar. It belonged to the portly man who called himself Alan. But the voice sounded wary, troubled. 'Buchanan?'

Uneasy, Buchanan didn't want to respond to that name. Nonetheless he showed himself, careful to keep partially in the shadows of the bedroom.

Alan turned, his expression a mixture of concern and surprise.

'Don't you believe in knocking?' Buchanan asked.

'Well . . .' Alan rubbed his right hand against his brown-checkered sport coat, awkward. 'I thought you might be sleeping and . . .'

'So you decided to make yourself at home until I woke up?'

'No,' Alan said. 'Uh, not exactly.'

'Then *what* exactly?' The man was normally confident to the point of being brusque, but now he was behaving out of character. What was going on?

'I just thought I'd check on you to make sure you were all right.'

'Well, why wouldn't I be?'

'You, uh, you were upset in the car and . . .'

'Yes? And what?'

'Nothing. I just . . . I guess I made a mistake.'

Buchanan stepped completely from the darkness of the bedroom. Approaching, he noticed Alan direct his gaze furtively, nervously, toward a section of the ceiling in the far right corner.

Ah, Buchanan thought. So the place is wired – and not just with microphones.

With hidden cameras. Needle-nosed.

Yesterday when Buchanan had arrived, he'd felt relieved to have reached a haven: There'd been no reason for him to suspect the intentions of his controllers and hence no reason for him to check the apartment to see if it was bugged. Later, after last night's conversation with Alan, Buchanan had felt disturbed, preoccupied by the postcard, by the unexpected echo of one of his lives six years ago. It hadn't occurred to him to check the apartment. What would have been the point? Aside from the man who called himself Alan, there was no one to talk to and thus nothing for hidden microphones to overhear.

But video surveillance was a different matter. And far more serious, Buchanan thought. Something about me spooks them enough that they want to keep extremely close tabs on me.

But what? What would spook them?

For starters, being catatonic all afternoon and half the evening. I must have scared the hell out of whoever's watching me. They sent Alan down to see if I'd cracked up. The way Alan keeps pawing at his sport coat. After I bruised his arm this morning, he's probably deciding whether I'm disturbed enough that he'll have to draw his handgun.

Meanwhile the cameras are transmitting every move I make.

But Alan doesn't want me to know that.

Buchanan felt liberated. The sense of being on-stage gave him the motivation he needed to act the part of himself.

'I knocked,' Alan said. 'I guess you didn't hear me. Since you're not supposed to leave the apartment, I wondered if something had happened to you.' Alan seemed less nervous now that he'd come up with a believable cover story. He gestured with growing confidence. 'That injury to your head. Maybe you'd hurt it again. Maybe you'd slipped in the shower or something. So I decided to let myself in and check. I debrief operatives here a lot, so I always have a key.'

'I guess I ought to be flattered that you care.'

'Hey, you're not the easiest guy to get along with.' Alan

rubbed his right elbow. 'But I do my job and look after the people assigned to me.'

'Listen,' Buchanan said. 'About what happened in the car this morning . . . I'm sorry.'

Alan shrugged.

'A lot's been happening. I guess I'm having trouble getting used to not being under pressure.'

Again Alan shrugged. 'Understandable. Sometimes an operative still feels the pressure even when it's gone.'

'Speaking of which . . .'

'What?'

'Pressure.'

Buchanan felt it in his abdomen. He pointed toward the bathroom, went in, shut the door, and emptied his bladder.

He assumed that the bathroom, like the other rooms in the apartment, would have a needle-nosed camera concealed in a wall. But whether he was being observed while he urinated made no difference to him. Even if he *had* felt self-conscious, he would never have permitted himself to show it.

And even if his bladder hadn't insisted, he would still have gone into the bathroom.

As a diversion.

Because he needed time to be away from Alan. He needed time to think.

13

Here's the postcard I never thought I'd send. I hope you meant your promise. The last time and place. Counting on you. PLEASE.

Buchanan stepped from the bathroom, its toilet flushing. 'Last night you mentioned something about R and R.'

Alan squinted, suspicious. 'That's right.'

'Well, you call this being on R and R? Being caged in here?'

'I told you Don Colton's supposed to be invisible. If you start wandering in and out, the neighbors will think you're him, and when the next Don Colton shows up, they'll get suspicious.'

'But what if I'm out of here? Me. Buchanan. A furlough. I haven't had one in eight years. Who'd notice? Who'd care?'

'Furlough?'

'Under my own name. Might do me some good to be myself for a change.'

Alan cocked his head, squinting, nonetheless betraying his interest.

'Next week, I'm supposed to go back to that doctor,' Buchanan said. 'By then, maybe your people and the colonel will have decided what to do with me.'

'I don't have the authority to make that decision alone.'

'Talk with the colonel,' Buchanan said.

Alan continued to look interested. 'Where would you go? Since you don't have a passport, it can't be out of the country.'

'I wouldn't want to leave the country anyhow. Not that far. South. New Orleans. Two days from now is Halloween. A person can have a damned good time in New Orleans on Halloween.'

'I heard that,' Alan said. 'In fact, I heard that a person can have a damned good time in New Orleans *any*time.'

Buchanan nodded. His request would be granted.

But he wouldn't be going as himself.

No way, he thought.

He'd be stepping back six years.

He'd be reinventing himself to be the person he was *then*. A hundred lifetimes ago.

A once-happy man who liked jazz, mint juleps, and red beans with rice.

A charter pilot named Peter Lang who'd had the tragic love affair of his life.

14

Here's the postcard I never thought I'd send.

SEVEN

1

Pilots – especially when being a pilot is not their true occupation and they need to establish an assumed identity – ought to fly. Instead Buchanan-Lang took the train to New Orleans.

That method of travel had several advantages. One was that he found it relaxing. Another was that it was private inasmuch as he'd been able to get a sleeper compartment. Still another was that it took a while, filling the time. After all, he didn't have anything to do until Halloween the next evening. Certainly he could have spent the day sight-seeing in New Orleans. But the fact was, he was quite familiar with New Orleans, its docks, the French Quarter, the Garden District, Lake Pontchartrain, Antoine's restaurant, Preservation Hall, and most of all, the exotic cemeteries. Peter Lang had a fascination with exotic cemeteries. He visited them whenever he could. Buchanan didn't allow himself to analyze the implications.

However, the major reason for taking the train instead of flying was that there wasn't any metal detector and X-ray security at train stations. Thus he could bring the Beretta 9-millimeter pistol that Jack Doyle had given him in Fort Lauderdale. It was wedged between two shirts and two changes of underwear, along with Victor Grant's passport, next to the toilet kit in the small, canvas, travel bag that Buchanan had been carrying with him since Florida. As his confusion about his employers and about himself continued to aggravate him, he was grateful that he'd lied about the passport and that he hadn't told anyone about the handgun. The passport and the gun gave him options. They allowed him potential freedom. That he'd never before lied to a debriefer should perhaps have troubled him. It should perhaps have warned him that he was more disturbed than he realized, that the blow to his head had been more serious than he knew. But as he sat next to the window of his locked compartment, listening to the clack-clack-clack of the wheels on the rails, watching the brilliant autumn colors of the Virginia countryside, he persistently rubbed his aching head and was grateful that he hadn't tried to conceal the handgun somewhere in Don Colton's apartment. If he had, the cameras would have exposed him. As it was, his story had evidently been convincing. Otherwise his controllers wouldn't have given him money as well as ID in his real name and then have allowed him to take this brief trip.

He'd bought a paperback novel before boarding the train at Washington's Union Station, but he barely glanced at it while the train continued south. He just kept massaging his forehead, partially because of pain and partially because of concentration, while he stared out the window at intermittent towns and cities, hills and farmland.

Peter Lang. He had to remember everything about him. He had to *become* Peter Lang. Pretending to be a pilot wasn't a problem, for Buchanan *was* a pilot. It was one of several skills that he'd acquired while he was being trained. Almost without exception, the occupations he pretended to have were occupations with which his employers had arranged to give him some familiarity. In a few cases, he had genuine expertise.

But what *was* a problem was reacquiring Peter Lang's attitude, his mannerisms, his personality. Buchanan had never kept notes about his numerous characters. To document an impersonation was foolish. Such documents might eventually be used against him. On principle, a paper trail was never a good idea. So he'd been forced to rely on his memory, and there had been many assignments, especially those in which he was meeting various contacts and had to switch back-and-forth between identities several times during one day, when his ability to recall and adapt had been taxed to the maximum. He'd suffered the constant worry that he would switch characters unintentionally, that he would behave like character x in front of a contact when he was supposed to behave like character y.

Peter Lang.

2

Buchanan had been in New Orleans, posing as a charter pilot who worked for an oil-exploration company, supposedly flying technicians and equipment to various sites in Central America. His actual mission, however, had been to fly plainclothed Special Forces advisors to secret airfields in the jungles of Nicaragua, where they would train contra rebels to battle the Marxist regime. A year earlier, in 1986, when Eugene Hasenfus had been shot down over Nicaragua while attempting to drop munitions to the rebels, Hasenfus had told his captors that he assumed he had been working for the CIA. The trouble was that the United States Congress had specifically forbidden the CIA to have anything to do with Nicaragua. The resultant media exposure created a political scandal in which the CIA repeatedly denied any connection with Hasenfus. Since intermediaries had been used to hire him and since Hasenfus later repudiated his story, the CIA avoided blame, but Nicaragua continued to be a sensitive political subject, even though President Reagan had subsequently issued an executive order that overrode the congressional ban on U.S. aid to the contras. However, the resumption of aid was not supposed to include American soldiers on Nicaraguan soil attempting to topple the Nicaraguan government. Inasmuch as blatant military interference was potentially an act of war, the soldiers Buchanan flew to Nicaragua were, like Buchanan, dressed in civilian clothes. Also like Buchanan, they had false identities and could not be traced to the U.S. military.

Because New Orleans and Miami were the two cities most associated with covert aid to the contras, investigative journalists showed great interest in private firms that sent aircraft to Latin American countries. A plane scheduled to deliver legitimate merchandise to El Salvador, Honduras, or Costa Rica might make an unscheduled, illegal stop in Nicaragua, leaving men instead of equipment. Any journalist who could prove this unauthorized degree of U.S. military involvement would be a candidate for a Pulitzer prize. Thus Buchanan had to be especially careful about establishing his cover. One of his techniques had been to ask his employers to provide him with a wife, a woman who was in business with her husband, who liked to fly and could speak Spanish, who would ideally be Hispanic and who would thus not attract attention if she flew with her husband on his frequent trips to Latin America. Buchanan's intention was to deceive curious journalists into doubting that he had connections with Nicaragua. After all, they might think, who'd be callous enough to fly his wife into a war zone?

The wife his employers had supplied to him was indeed Hispanic. A spirited, attractive woman named Juana Mendez, she'd been twenty-five. Her parents were Mexicans who'd become U.S. citizens. A sergeant in Army Intelligence, she'd been raised in San Antonio, Texas, a city that Buchanan's persona, Peter Lang, claimed as his home town as well. Buchanan had spent several weeks in San Antonio prior to his assignment in order to familiarize himself with the city, lest someone test his cover story by trying to manipulate him into saying things about San Antonio that weren't accurate. Juana's constant presence with him would make it more difficult for anyone to question him about San Antonio. If he didn't know the answer, if he hesitated, Juana would answer for him.

Being Peter Lang had been one of Buchanan's longest assignments – four months. During that time, he and Juana had lived together in a small apartment on the second story of a quaint, clapboard building with ornate, wrought-iron railings and a pleasant, flower-filled courtyard on Dumaine Street in the French Quarter. Both he and Juana had known the dangers of becoming emotionally involved with an undercover partner. They had tried to make their public gestures of affection strictly professional. They had done their best not to be affected by their enforced private intimacy, eating together, combining laundry, using the same bathroom, sharing the same sleeping quarters. They didn't have intercourse. They weren't that undisciplined. But they might as well have, for the effect was the same. Sexual activity was only a part . . . and often a small part . . . and sometimes *no* part . . . of a successful marriage. In their four months together, Buchanan and Juana portrayed their roles so well that they finally admitted awkwardly to each other that they did feel married. In the night, while he'd listened to her softly exhale in sleep, he had felt intoxicated by her smell. It reminded him of cinnamon.

Shared stress is a powerful bonder. On one occasion, during a firefight with rebels in Nicaragua, Buchanan would never have been able to reach his plane and maneuver it for a take-off

271

from the primitive airstrip in the jungle if Juana hadn't used an assault rifle to give him covering fire. Through the canopy of his slowly turning aircraft, he had watched Juana run from the jungle toward the passenger door he had opened. She had whirled toward bushes, fired her M-16, then raced onward. Bullets from the jungle had torn up dirt ahead of her. She had whirled and fired again. Revving the engines, he had managed to get the plane in position and then had raised his own M-16 to shoot through the open hatch and give her covering fire. Bullets had struck the side of the plane. As she lunged toward the hatch, he'd released the brakes and started across the bumpy clearing. She'd scrambled in, braced herself at the open hatch, and fired repeatedly at the rebels in the jungle. When she'd emptied her weapon, she'd picked up his, emptying it as well. Then grabbing a seatbelt so she wouldn't fall out, she had laughed as the plane bounced twice and rose abruptly, skimming treetops.

To depend on someone for your life makes you feel close to that person. Buchanan had experienced that emotion in the company of men. But that four-month assignment had been the first time he had felt it with a woman, and in the end, he was a better actor than he wanted to be, for he fell in love with her.

He shouldn't have. He struggled desperately with himself to repress the feeling. Nonetheless, he failed. Even then, he didn't have sex with her. Despite powerful temptation, they didn't violate their professional ethics by getting physically involved. But they did break another rule, one that warned them not to confuse their roles with reality, although Buchanan didn't believe in that rule. His strength as an imposter was precisely that he *did* confuse his roles with reality. As long as he was portraying someone, that person *was* reality.

One night, while Buchanan was watching television, Juana

had come in from buying groceries. The troubled look on her face had made him frown.

'Are you all right?' Concerned, he'd walked toward her. 'Did something happen while you were out?'

Apparently oblivious to his question, she'd set down the bag of groceries and begun to unpack. But then he'd realized that she didn't care about the groceries. She was preoccupied by a jazz-concert handout that someone had given her on the street. She removed it from the bag, and when Buchanan saw the small X in the upper right corner, he'd understood why she looked disturbed. The person who'd given her the handout must have been their contact. The small X, made by a felt-tip pen, was their signal to dismantle the operation.

They were being reassigned.

At that moment, Buchanan had been terribly conscious of Juana's proximity, of her oval face, of her smooth, dark skin and the firm-looking outline of her breasts beneath her blouse. He'd wanted to hold her, but his discipline had been too strong.

Juana's usually cheerful voice had sounded tight with stress. 'I guess I knew we'd eventually be reassigned.' She'd swallowed. 'Nothing lasts forever, right?'

'Right,' he'd answered somberly.

'So . . . Do you think we'll be reassigned together?'

'I don't know.'

Juana had nodded, pensive.

'They almost never do.'

'Yes.' Juana had swallowed again.

The night before they left New Orleans, they'd taken a stroll through the French Quarter. It was Halloween, and the old part of the city had been more colorful and festive than usual. Revelers wore costumes, a great many of them depicting skeletons. The crowd danced, sang, and drank in the narrow streets. Jazz – some tunes melancholy, others joyous –

reverberated through open doors, merging, swelling past the wrought-iron railings above the crowd, echoing toward the reflection of the city's lights in the sky.

Oh when the saints . . .

Buchanan and Juana had ended their walk at Café du Monde near Jackson Square on Decatur Street. The famous, open-air restaurant specialized in café au lait as well as beignets, deep-fried French pastries covered with powdered sugar. The place had been extremely crowded, many costumed partygoers wanting caffeine and starch to offset the alcohol they'd consumed before they continued their revels. Regardless, Buchanan and Juana had stood in line. The October night had been balmy with the hint of rain, a pleasant breeze coming in from the Mississippi. Finally a waiter had guided them to a table and taken their order. They'd glanced around at the festive crowd, had felt out of place, uncomfortably subdued, and had finally discussed the subject that they'd been avoiding. Buchanan didn't recall who had raised the topic or how, but the gist had been, Is this the end, or do we continue seeing each other after this? And as Buchanan had faced the question directly, he'd suddenly realized how absurd it was. Tomorrow, Peter Lang wouldn't exist. So how could Peter Lang continue to have a relationship with his wife, who wouldn't exist tomorrow, either?

Softly, their conversation impossible to overhear in the din of the crowd, Buchanan had told her that their characters were at an end, and Juana had looked at him as if he were speaking gibberish.

'I'm not interested in who we were,' she had said. 'I'm talking about *us*.'

'So am I.'

'No,' she'd told him. 'Those people don't exist. *We* do.

Tomorrow, reality starts. The fantasy is over. What are we going to do?'

'I love you,' he'd said.

She'd exhaled, trembling slightly. 'I've been waiting for you to say that . . . Hoping . . . I don't know how it happened, but I feel the same. I love *you*.'

'I want you to know that you'll always be special to me,' Buchanan had said.

Juana had started to frown.

'I want you to know,' Buchanan had continued, 'that . . .'

Their waiter had interrupted, setting down a tray with their steaming coffee and hot, sugar-covered beignets.

As the aproned man left, Juana had leaned toward Buchanan, her voice low but tense with concern. 'What are you talking about?'

' . . . that you'll always be special to me. I'll always feel close to you. If you ever need help, if there's anything I can ever do . . .'

'Wait a minute.' Juana had frowned harder, her dark eyes reflecting a light in the ceiling. 'This sounds like goodbye.'

' . . . I'll be there. Any time. Any place. All you have to do is ask. There's nothing I wouldn't do for you.'

'You bastard,' she had said.

'What?'

'This isn't fair. I'm good enough to risk my life with you. I'm good enough to be used as a prop. But I'm not good enough for you to see after . . .'

'That's not what I meant,' Buchanan had said.

'Then what *does* it have to do with? You're in love with me, but you're giving me the brush-off?'

'I didn't mean to fall in love. I—'

'There aren't many reasons why a man walks away from a woman he claims he loves. And right now, the only one I can think of is, he doesn't believe she's good enough for him.'

'Listen to me . . .'

'It's because I'm Hispanic.'

'No. Not at all. That's crazy. Please. Just listen.'

'*You* listen. I could be the best thing that ever happened to you. Don't lose me.'

'But tomorrow I have to.'

'Have to? Why? Because of the people we work for? To hell with them. They expect me to sign up again. But I'm not planning to.'

'It's got nothing to do with them,' Buchanan had said. 'This is all about me. It's about what I do. We could never have a relationship after this, because I won't be the same. I'll be a stranger.'

'What?'

'I'll be different.'

She had stared at him, suddenly realizing the implications of what he was saying. 'You'd choose your work instead of—?'

'My work is all I have.'

'No,' Juana had said. 'You could have *me*.'

Buchanan studied her. Looked down. Looked up. Bit his lip. Slowly shook his head. 'You don't know me. You only know who I pretend to be.'

She looked shocked.

'I'll always be your friend,' Buchanan had said. 'Remember that. I swear to you. If you ever need help, if you're ever in trouble, all you have to do is ask, and no matter how long it's been, no matter how far away I am, I'll—'

Juana had stood, her chair scraping harshly on the concrete floor. People had stared.

'If I ever need you, I'll send you a Goddamned postcard.'

Hiding tears, she had hurried from the restaurant.

And that was the last time he had spoken to her. When he returned to their apartment, she had already packed and left. Hollow, he had stayed awake all night, sitting in the dark, staring at the wall across from the bed they had shared.

Just as he stared out at the darkness beyond the window of the compartment in the speeding train.

3

He had done it again, Buchanan realized.

He'd become catatonic. Rubbing at the pain in his skull, he had the sense of coming back from far away. The compartment was dark. The night beyond the window was broken only by occasional lights from farms. How long had—?

He glanced down at the luminous dial on his pilot's watch, Peter Lang's watch, disturbed to see that the time was eight minutes after ten. He'd left Washington shortly before noon. The train would long ago have left Virginia. It would be well into North Carolina by now, perhaps into Georgia. All afternoon and most of the evening? he thought in dismay. What's happening to me?

His head throbbing, he stood, turned on the lights in the locked compartment, felt exposed by his reflection in the window, and quickly closed the curtains. The reflected haggard face had looked unfamiliar. He opened his travel bag, took three aspirins from his toilet kit, and swallowed them with water from the tiny sink in the compartment's utility washroom. While he urinated, he felt his mind drifting again, going back six years, and he concentrated to pay attention to now.

He needed to get into character. He had to re-become Peter Lang. But he also had to be functional. He couldn't keep staring off into space. After all, the whole point of going to New Orleans, of finding out why Juana had sent the postcard, was to give himself a purpose, a sense of direction.

Juana. As much as he needed to focus on re-assuming the

character of Peter Lang, he had to focus on Juana. She'd be – what? – thirty-one now. He wondered if she'd kept in shape. She hadn't been tall, and she'd been thin, but her military-trained body had compensated. It had been hard and strong and magnificent. Would her thick, dark hair still be as short as when he'd known her? He had wanted to run his fingers through it, to clutch it, to tug it gently. Would her dark eyes still be fiery? Would her lips still have that sensuous contour? She'd had a habit, when she'd been concentrating, of pursing those lips and sticking them out slightly, and he had wanted to stroke them as much as he'd wanted to touch her hair.

What was his true motive for going back? he wondered. Was it really just to give himself mobility?

Or had the postcard awakened something in him? He'd repressed his memories of her, just as he'd repressed so much about himself. And now . . .

Maybe I shouldn't have let her go. Maybe I should have . . .

No, he thought. The past is a trap. Leave it alone. Obviously it's not doing you any good if it makes you catatonic. What you're feeling is a bush-league mistake. In your former lives, you left plenty of unfinished business, a lot of people whom you liked or at least whom your assumed identities liked. But you've never gone back before. Be careful.

But I didn't *love* those other people. Why did she send the postcard? What sort of trouble is she in?

Your controllers would have a fit if they knew what you were thinking.

The trouble is, I remember her so vividly.

Besides, I promised.

No, a warning voice told him. *You* didn't promise. Peter Lang did.

Exactly. And right now, that's who I am.

I meant what I said. I promised.

Welcoming the distraction of hunger, relieved to be in motion, Buchanan-Lang unlocked the compartment, checked the swaying corridor, saw no one, and was just about to leave when he decided that the simple lock on the compartment couldn't be trusted. He took his small travel bag – the passport and the handgun in it – with him, secured the compartment, and proceeded toward the dining car.

It was three cars away, and when he entered it, he discovered that it was almost deserted, a few passengers sipping coffee, waiters clearing dirty dishes from the tables. The overhead lights of the dining car gleamed off the windows and made the area seem extra bright, obscuring whatever was out in the darkness.

Buchanan rubbed his aching forehead and approached the nearest waiter.

The weary-looking man anticipated his question. 'Sorry, sir. We're closed. Breakfast starts at six in the morning.'

'I'm afraid I took a nap and overslept. I'm starved. Isn't there something you can give me so my stomach won't growl all night?' Buchanan discreetly held out a ten-dollar bill.

'Yes, sir. I understand your problem. I'll see what I can do. Perhaps a couple of cold roast-beef sandwiches to take with you.'

'Sounds good.'

'And maybe a soda.'

'A beer would be better.'

'Well,' a voice said behind Buchanan, 'I don't have the beer. But just in case, I did plan ahead and arranged for some sandwiches.'

Refusing to show that he was surprised, Buchanan made himself wait a moment before he slowly turned to face the woman whose voice he had heard. When he saw her, he was even *more* careful not to show his surprise. Because he definitely *was* surprised.

The woman had long, dramatic, flame-red hair. She was tall. In her late twenties. Athletic figure. Strong forehead. Excellent cheekbones. Fashion-model features.

He knew this woman. At least, he'd seen her before. The first time, she'd worn beige slacks and a yellow blouse. That had been in Mexico. She'd been taking photographs of him outside the jail in Mérida.

The second time, she'd worn jeans and a denim shirt. That had been near Pier 66 in Fort Lauderdale. She'd been taking photographs of him while he stopped his boat next to Big Bob Bailey in the channel.

This time, she wore brown, poplin slacks and a khaki, safari jacket, the type with plenty of pockets, several of which had objects in them. She looked like an ad from a Land's End catalogue. A camera bag was slung over her left shoulder. The camera itself dangled from a sling around her neck. The only detail that didn't fit the Land's End image was the bulging paper bag in her right hand.

With her left hand, she added ten dollars to the ten that Buchanan had already given the waiter. 'Thank you.' She smiled. 'I didn't think my friend would ever show up. I appreciate your patience.'

'No problem, ma'am.' The waiter pocketed the money. 'If there's anything else . . .'

'Nothing, thank you.'

As the waiter went back to clearing dirty dishes from a table, the woman redirected her attention toward Buchanan. 'I hope your heart wasn't set on those roast-beef sandwiches he mentioned. Mine are chicken salad.'

'I beg your pardon?' Buchanan asked.

'Chicken . . .'

'That's not what . . . Do we know each other?'

'You ask that after everything we've been through together?' The woman's emerald eyes twinkled.

'Lady, I'm not in the mood. I'm sure there are plenty of other guys on the train who . . .'

'Okay, if you insist, we'll play. Do we know each other?' She debated with herself. 'Yes. In a manner of speaking. You could say we're acquainted, although of course we've never met.' She looked amused.

'I don't want to be rude.'

'It doesn't matter to me. I'm used to it.'

'You've had too much to drink.'

'Not a drop. But I wish I *had* been drinking. I'm bored enough from waiting here so long. On second thought . . .' She turned to the waiter. 'A couple of beers sound good. Do you suppose we could still have them?'

'Certainly, ma'am. Anything else?'

'Make it *four* beers, and you may as well add those roast-beef sandwiches. I have a feeling this is going to be a long night.'

'Then maybe coffee . . . ?'

'No. The beers will be fine,' she said. As the waiter headed away from them, she turned again toward Buchanan. 'Unless you'd prefer coffee.'

'What I'd prefer is to know what the hell you think you're doing,' Buchanan said.

'Requesting an interview.'

'What?'

'I'm a reporter.'

'Congratulations. What's that got to do with me?'

'I'll make you a bet.'

Buchanan shook his head. 'This is absurd.' He started to leave.

'No, really. I'll bet I can guess your name.'

'A bet means you win or lose something. I can't see what I win or—'

'If I can't guess your name, I'll leave you alone.'

Buchanan thought about it. 'All right.' He sighed. 'Anything to get rid of you. What's my name?'

'Buchanan.'

'Wrong. It's Peter Lang.' Again he started to walk away.

'Prove it.'

'I don't have to prove anything. I'm out of patience.' Buchanan kept walking away.

She followed him. 'Look, I was hoping to do this in private, but if you want to make it difficult, that's up to you. Your name isn't Peter Lang any more than it's Jim Crawford, Ed Potter, Victor Grant, and Don Colton. You did use those names, of course. And many others. But your *given* name is Buchanan. First name: Brendan. Nickname: Bren.'

Muscles cramping, Buchanan stopped at the exit from the dining car. Not showing his tension, he turned, noted with relief that the tables at this end of the car were all empty. He pretended to be innocently exasperated. 'What do I have to do to get rid of you?'

'Get rid of me? That's a figure of speech, I hope.'

'I don't know what you're—'

She held up the bulging paper bag. 'I'm hungry. I couldn't find you on the train, so I kept waiting for you to come to the dining car. Then I worried that maybe you'd brought something with you to eat. Every half hour, I had to slip the waiter ten dollars so he'd let me keep my table without ordering. Another ten minutes, the place would have been empty, and he'd have made me leave. Thank God, you showed up.'

'Sure,' Buchanan said. 'Thank God.' He noticed the waiter come down the aisle toward them.

'Here are the sandwiches and the beer.' The waiter handed her another paper bag.

282

'Thanks. How much do I owe you?' She paid him, adding a further tip.

Then Buchanan and she were alone again.

'So what do you say?' The woman's emerald eyes continued to twinkle. 'At least you'll get something to eat. Since I couldn't find you in the coach seats, I assume you have a compartment. Why don't we . . . ?'

'If I really use all the names you claim I do, I must be involved in something very shady.'

'I try not to make judgments.'

'But what am I? In the mafia? A secret agent? Won't you be afraid to be alone with me?'

'Who says I'm alone? Surely you don't think I'd go on this assignment without help.'

'Don't tell me you're with those two guys who just finished their coffee at the other end of the car,' Buchanan said. 'They're leaving and not in this direction. It doesn't look to me like you're with anybody.'

'Whoever it is wouldn't let you see him.'

'Yeah, sure, right.'

'Just as I assume that anybody following you wouldn't be obvious, either.'

'Why would anybody follow *me*?' Buchanan suddenly wondered if he *was* being followed. 'This is certainly the weirdest . . . Okay. I'm hungry. I get the feeling you won't let me alone. Let's eat.'

He opened the door from the dining car. The clack-clack-clack of the wheels became louder. 'I'm warning you, though.'

'What?' She straightened.

'I'm not easy.'

'What a coincidence.' She followed.

Pretending not to notice her suspicion when he locked the door, Buchanan lifted the compartment's small table from the wall and secured its brace. Then he unpacked the paper bags and spread out their contents, making sure he took the roast-beef sandwiches since he didn't know what she might have put in the chicken-salad sandwiches while she waited for him. He twisted off the caps on two bottles of beer.

Throughout, she remained standing. In the narrow compartment, Buchanan felt very aware of being close to her.

He handed her an open bottle of beer, bit into a sandwich, and sat on one side of the table. 'You think you know my name. In fact, according to you, I've got several of them. What's yours?'

She sat across from him, brushing back a strand of red hair. Her lipstick was the same color. 'Holly McCoy.'

'And you say you're a reporter?' Buchanan drank from his beer, noting that she hadn't touched hers, thinking, Maybe she expects me to drink all four bottles and hopes the beer will make me less careful about what I'm saying. 'For what newspaper?'

'*The Washington Post.*'

'I read that paper a lot. But I don't think I've ever seen your name as a byline.'

'I'm new.'

'Ah.'

'This will be my first major story.'

'Ah.'

'For the *Post*. Before that, I worked as a feature writer for the *L.A. Times.*'

'Ah.' Buchanan swallowed part of a sandwich. The roast beef wasn't bad; a little dry, but the mayonnaise and lettuce compensated. He sipped more of his beer. 'I thought you were hungry. You're not eating.' As she made herself nibble at some chicken salad, he continued, 'Now what's this about an interview? And these names I'm supposed to have . . . I told you I'm Peter Lang.'

Buchanan regretted that. It had been a mistake. When the woman had confronted him in the dining car, he'd responded with the name of the role on which he was concentrating at the moment. His identities had become confused. He had no ID for Peter Lang. He had to correct the problem.

'I have a confession to make,' he said. 'I lied. You told me you'd leave me alone if you couldn't guess my name. So when you called me by my right name, I decided to pretend I was somebody else and hoped you'd go away.'

'I didn't,' she said.

'Then I might as well be honest.' He set down his bottle of beer and reached in his back pocket, bringing out his wallet, showing her his driver's license. 'My name *is* Buchanan. Brendan. Nickname: Bren. Although no one's called me "Bren" in quite a while. How did you know?'

'You're in the military.'

'Right again. And I repeat, how did you know? Not that it's any of your business, but I'm a captain with Special Forces. My home base is Fort Bragg. I'm on furlough, heading to New Orleans. So what?'

When in doubt, as long as it doesn't compromise an operation, the best deception is to tell the truth.

'You have a thing about soldiers?' he continued. 'Is that it?'

She tilted her head, a motion that emphasized her elegant neck. 'In a manner of speaking.'

'Well, as long as you're speaking, why don't you speak plainly?' Buchanan said. 'Enough is enough. You still haven't told me how you know my name. I've been a good sport. What's this about?'

'Humor me. I'd like to mention some code words to you,' she said.

'Code words? Of all the . . .' Buchanan gestured with exasperation.

'Tell me if they mean anything to you. Task Force One Hundred and Sixty. Seaspray. The Intelligence Support Activity. Yellow Fruit.'

Jesus Christ, Buchanan thought, not showing how startled he was. 'I've never heard of them.'

'Now why don't I believe you?'

'Look, lady—'

'Relax. Enjoy the sandwiches,' she said. 'I'll tell you a story.'

6

Operation Eagle Claw. On April 24, 1980, a U.S. military, counterterrorist unit known as Delta was sent into Iran to rescue fifty-two Americans who'd been held hostage in Tehran since November of 1979. Eight helicopters, three MC-130 troop planes, and three EC-130 fuel planes were scheduled to set down at a remote area, code-named Desert One. After refueling, the helicopters would then proceed to a landing site outside Tehran. The one-hundred-and-eighteen-man assault team, concealed by night, would enter the city and converge on the target zone.

From the outset, however, problems afflicted the mission. En route from the U.S. aircraft carrier *Nimitz* in the Persian Gulf, one of the helicopters had to turn back because of difficulties with its rotor blades. Soon, another had to return because of a failed navigational system. At Desert One, yet another helicopter malfunctioned, this time the victim of a hydraulic leak. Because no fewer than six helicopters were required for the mission, Operation Eagle Claw had to be aborted. But as the team pulled out, one of the remaining helicopters struck one of its companion, EC-130 fuel planes. The resulting explosion killed eight U.S. soldiers and critically burned five others. Flames prevented the bodies of the victims from being recovered. Secret papers and classified equipment had to be abandoned.

Humiliated and outraged, the Pentagon determined to find out what had gone wrong. Clearly, more than just mechanical failures were at fault. An exhaustive investigation concluded that various branches of the U.S. military had so competed with each other to be a part of the rescue that their efforts were dangerously counterproductive. Inefficiency, lack of preparedness, insufficient training, inadequate transportation, incomplete and unreliable information . . . the list of problems went on and on. It quickly became evident that if the United States were going to have an effective military antiterrorist group, that group would have to be capable of operating on its own, without needing help from outside sources, either military or civilian. Delta, the team of commandos who would have performed the hostage rescue, was assigned a permanent training base in a restricted section of Fort Bragg in North Carolina. A similar group, SEAL Team 6, was stationed at the Little Creek Naval Base in Virginia. The Joint Special Operations Command was created to supervise unconventional units in all branches of the U.S. military. A separate group, the Special Operations Division, was created to coordinate special operations exclusively within the Army.

7

As the woman talked, Buchanan finished one beer and opened another. He bunched up his sandwich wrappers, putting them in a paper bag. He stifled a yawn. 'This sounds more like a history lecture than a story. Remember, I'm assigned to Fort Bragg. I know all about the specifics of the failed hostage rescue and the establishment of Delta Force.'

'I'm sure you know much more than that,' Holly McCoy said. 'But let's take this one step at a time.'

Buchanan shrugged. As he listened to the clack-clack-clack of the swaying train, he gestured for her to continue.

'One of the first problems the Special Operations Division decided to deal with was transportation,' Holly said. 'It had taken Delta too long to get into Iran. The aircraft hadn't been adequate to the task. Too many channels in the military had needed to be informed about where and when Delta was going. Obviously some streamlining was in order. Delta needed to get to its targets as quickly and secretly as possible and with the best means. That's why Task Force One Hundred and Sixty and Seaspray were formed.'

Again Buchanan needed all his discipline not to show how startled he was by the mention of those code names. While his stomach muscles hardened, he pretended another yawn. 'Sorry. I don't want you to think you're boring me. Go ahead and finish your beer.'

Holly brushed back another strand of red hair, gave him an irritated look, and continued. 'Task Force One Hundred and Sixty was a classified Army unit that provided aviation for Delta as well as Special Forces and the Rangers. It had the big Chinook cargo helicopters as well as various utility choppers and gunships. Seaspray, though, was a totally off-the-books, covert, Army aviation unit that bought aircraft through civilian intermediaries, secretly modified the planes with state-of-the-art equipment . . . motor silencers, infrared radar, rocket launchers, that sort of thing . . . and used the planes for small-scale, secret missions. The civilian intermediaries that Seaspray used were provided by the CIA, and some of the work that Seaspray did was for another civilian agency, the

Drug Enforcement Administration. That's where the trouble started, I think. Civilians and the military working together but hiding that cooperation from the Pentagon and from Congress.'

Buchanan sipped more of his second beer and glanced at his watch. 'It's almost midnight. If there's a point to this, I suggest you get to it – before I fall asleep.'

'I doubt there's much risk of that,' Holly said. 'In fact, I think you're a lot more interested than you're pretending.'

'Interested in you. Except I prefer my dates to be less talkative.'

'Pay attention,' Holly said. 'The next problem for the Special Operations Division was obtaining intelligence. When the Shah fell from power in Iran in 1979, the CIA lost most of its assets there. During the Iran hostage crisis, the Agency wasn't able to furnish much reliable information about where the hostages were being held and how they were being guarded. Obviously Delta Force needed details about the situations it would have to face. But the intelligence it received had to have a military perspective to it. So the ISA was formed. The Intelligence Support Activity.'

Again Buchanan felt his muscles cramp. Jesus, he thought. Where the hell is this woman getting her information?

'ISA was another secret military unit,' Holly said. 'Its purpose was to send soldiers, who pretended to be civilians, into emergency situations in foreign countries – a terrorist crisis at an airport, for example. There, they conducted reconnaissance of possible Delta targets and not only provided intelligence but, if necessary, tactical support. This was something new. An operational military unit working under civilian cover and providing the sort of information that the CIA normally does. Commandos who were spies. The ISA was so unorthodox and hush-hush that most top officials in the

Pentagon didn't know anything about it. In theory, it didn't exist.'

Buchanan opened his third beer. He was going to close his eyes soon and pretend that the alcohol had put him to sleep.

'Pay attention,' Holly repeated.

'I am. I am.'

'You're going to like this part. The Special Operations Division discovered it had a problem. How was it going to keep all these secret units truly secret, even from the Pentagon, which has never been fond of unconventional tactics? The answer was to establish a security unit that itself was secret. Its code name was Yellow Fruit. Again military personnel used civilian cover. They dressed as civilians. They pretended to operate civilian businesses. But in reality they were providing security for Seaspray, the ISA, and several other covert military units. It was Yellow Fruit's job to make sure that everything stayed hidden.'

Holly studied him, waiting for a reaction.

Buchanan set down his beer bottle. He assumed his most judicious expression. 'Fascinating.'

'Is that all you've got to say?'

'Well, the operation certainly must have succeeded,' Buchanan said, 'assuming that what you just told me isn't a fantasy. The reason I know it succeeded is I've never heard of Yellow Fruit. Or the Intelligence Support Activity. Or Seaspray. Or Task Force One Hundred and Sixty.'

'You know, for the first time I think you might be telling the truth.'

'You're suggesting I'd lie to you?'

'In this case, maybe not. Those units were compartmentalized. Often members of one group didn't know about the other groups. For that matter, the ISA was compartmentalized within itself. Some members didn't know who their fellow members were. Plus, Seaspray and Yellow

Fruit were eventually exposed and disbanded. They don't exist anymore. By those names, at least. I know that Seaspray was later temporarily reformed, using the code name Quasar Talent.'

'Then if they don't exist . . .'

'Some of them,' Holly said. 'Others are still doing business as usual. And others have been newly created, much more secret, much more compartmentalized, much more ambitious. Scotch and Soda, for example.'

8

'Scotch and . . . ?' Buchanan felt the back of his neck turn cold.

'That's a code name for yet another undercover military group,' Holly said. 'It works with the Drug Enforcement Administration and the CIA to infiltrate the Central and South American drug networks and destroy them from within. But since those foreign governments haven't sanctioned the presence of plainclothed American soldiers, *armed* soldiers, using false names, on their soil, the operation is very much against the law.'

'Either you've got one hell of an imagination, or your sources must be in a mental ward,' Buchanan said. 'Whatever, it doesn't concern me. I don't know anything about this stuff, so why . . . ?'

'You used to work for the ISA, but six months ago you were transferred to Scotch and Soda.'

Buchanan stopped breathing.

'You're one of numerous Special Operations soldiers assigned to covert duty, wearing civilian clothes but armed and carrying forged identities who are in effect functioning as a military branch of the DEA and the CIA in foreign countries.'

Buchanan slowly straightened. 'All right, now I've had enough. That's it. What you're telling me . . . what you're accusing me of . . . is preposterous. If you said that kind of nonsense in front of the wrong people, some fool . . . a politician, for example . . . might actually believe you. And then I'd be in crap to my eyebrows. I'd be answering questions for the rest of my career. Because of a damned fantasy.'

'*Is* it a fantasy?' Holly reached in her camera bag and brought out a copy of the Cancun police sketch of him as well as copies of the photographs that Big Bob Bailey had shown Buchanan in Fort Lauderdale. 'These don't look like a fantasy.'

Buchanan's chest ached as he examined the police sketch and the pictures of him getting off a plane in Frankfurt, accompanied by Bailey, and of him in front of the jail in Mérida, accompanied by Garson Woodfield from the U.S. embassy. Some of the pictures were unfamiliar. They showed him on a power boat in the channel near Pier 66 in Fort Lauderdale, stopped next to another boat, talking to Bailey. The latter photograph had been taken from shore (Buchanan recalled turning and seeing Holly lower her camera), and the angle had been chosen so that it included a Fort Lauderdale sign in the background.

For God's sake, Buchanan thought, these photographs were supposed to have been destroyed. What happened in Fort Lauderdale after I left? Didn't the team do its job?

'So?' he asked, fighting not to reveal his tension. 'What are these supposed to mean?'

'You're really amazing.'

'What?'

'You sit there with a straight face and . . . You'd deny anything, no matter how strong the evidence was,' Holly said.

'These aren't evidence of anything. What are you talking about?'

'Come on. They show you posing as three different people.'

'They show three men who look a bit like me, and whatever they're doing, it certainly doesn't look like any secret agent stuff.'

'Jim Crawford. Ed Potter. Victor Grant.'

'Huey, Dewey, and Louie. Curly, Larry, and Moe. I don't know what you're talking about. And speaking of questions — which you're awfully good at coming up with but you don't seem to like to answer — *I'll ask you again*. How did you know my name? How did you know I'm a soldier? How the hell did you know I'd be on this train?'

Holly shook her head. 'Confidential.'

'And the junk you're accusing me of isn't? Look, there's a good way to prove that you're wrong about me. A simple way. It's very easy. You know my name is Buchanan. To prove I've got nothing to hide, I even showed you my driver's license. You know I'm stationed at Fort Bragg. So check on me. All you'll find is that I'm a captain whose specialty is field training. That's all. Nothing else. Nothing dark and mysterious. No cloak-and-dagger stuff.'

'I did check,' Holly said. 'And you're right about one thing. All I found out was what you just told me. There's plenty of paper work about you. But you travel around so much on these mythical training exercises that I couldn't find anyone who'd actually ever met you.'

'You asked the wrong people.'

'*Who?* Tell me who to ask. Not that it would make a difference. I take for granted that anyone you told me to ask would by definition be part of the conspiracy.'

'Lady, do you know what you sound like? The next thing you'll probably tell me I had something to do with the two Kennedy assassinations, not to mention Martin Luther King's.'

'Don't be condescending.'

'What I am is pissed off.'

'Or pretending to be. I've got a feeling you're all smoke and mirrors, layers within layers. Your name. Your ID. How can I be sure that "Buchanan" isn't just another pseudonym?'

'For God's sake . . .'

'Let's consider Delta Force, which is classified but everybody knows about it. It isn't nearly as covert and shadowy as ISA or Scotch and Soda. The members of Delta live off base. They have average, civilian apartments. They drive average, civilian cars. When they get up in the morning and go to work, it's just like they're going to any other job, except that *their* job is practicing how to blast their way into hijacked planes and rescue hostages. They wear civilian clothes. They carry civilian ID. *Fake* ID. Bogus names and backgrounds. No one who lives around them has any idea of who they really are or what they really do. In fact, most people at Fort Bragg don't have any idea, either. If members of Delta use that kind of cover, how deep would the cover be for someone who belonged to much more secret operations like ISA or Scotch and Soda?'

'You can't have it both ways, Holly. You say you want the truth, but apparently you don't intend to trust a single thing I say. What if I said I did belong to this Scotch and Soda thing? You'd probably say I was lying and actually belonged to something else.'

'You're very skilled. Honestly. My compliments.'

'Suppose you were right?' Buchanan asked. 'Isn't it foolish of you to accuse me of being some kind of spy? What if I felt threatened? I might have tried to keep you quiet.'

'I hardly think so,' Holly said. 'You wouldn't try to do anything to me unless you knew you could get away with it. I made sure I was protected.'

'You sound awfully confident.' Buchanan rubbed his aching forehead. 'Did you honestly think that I'd look at those photographs, lose control, and confess? Even if I did, I could deny it later. Your word against mine. Unless . . .'

Buchanan reached for her camera bag.

'Hey,' she said.

He tugged it away from where it hung on her shoulder. She tried to stop him, but he held her wrists together with his left hand while he used his right hand to open the bag. Inside there was a small tape recorder, a red light glowing, a slight hum as the recorder's wheels turned.

'My, my,' he said. 'I'm on candid camera. Only in this case it's candid audio. Naughty, naughty. It isn't nice to be deceptive.'

'Right. Coming from you.'

Buchanan pulled the machine out and traced a wire from it to a small microphone concealed in the latch on the outside of the bag. 'What were you using? An extra slow speed on the tape so you wouldn't have to worry about turning it over? And if you did have to turn it, you could always pretend to have to go to the bathroom?'

'You can't blame me for trying.'

Buchanan shut off the machine. 'For all the good it did you. I told you I've got nothing to do with this stuff you're talking about. That's all you have on the tape – my denial.'

Holly shrugged, looking less confident.

'No more games.' Buchanan stepped closer. 'Take off your clothes.'

She looked up sharply. '*What?*'

'Take off your clothes, or I'll take them off for you.'

'You can't be serious!'

'Lady, when you pick up men on trains, you have to expect they might want something more than conversation. *Take off your clothes.*' Buchanan banged his fist on the table.

'Get away from me!'

Outside the compartment, someone pounded on the door.

'Impressive,' Buchanan said. 'Quicker than I expected.'

Holly's expression was a combination of fright, relief, and bewilderment. 'What do you—? Quicker than—?'

Buchanan opened the door. A tall man in his thirties . . . square-jawed, broad-shouldered, heavy-chested, an ex-football-player type . . . was about to ram his shoulder against the door. He blinked in surprise at Buchanan's sudden appearance.

'And who are you?' Buchanan asked. 'The husband?'

The surly man looked past Buchanan to make sure that Holly was all right.

'Or the boyfriend? Come on,' Buchanan said. 'I'm running out of categories.'

'An interested party.'

'Then you might as well *join* the party.' Buchanan opened the door wider and gestured for the man to enter. 'There's no point in standing in the hall and waking the neighbors. I just hope we all fit in this tiny compartment.'

His rugged features contorted with suspicion, the man slowly entered.

Buchanan felt the man's wide shoulders press against him. He managed to close the door. 'It's a good thing you didn't bring company. We might run out of oxygen.'

'Shut up with the jokes,' the man said. 'Take off her clothes? What did you think you were—?'

'Inviting you,' Buchanan said.

The big man opened his mouth.

'That tape recorder's a little too obvious,' Buchanan said and turned to Holly. 'I figured you meant for me to find it. Then I'd feel safe to talk, nothing I couldn't deny later, your word against mine, but what I wouldn't know is that the good stuff would be transmitted by a microphone you were wearing to your partner in a nearby compartment. The only way I was going to find that microphone was by doing a strip search, so I thought I'd suggest the idea and see what happened.' He turned to the man. 'And here you are.'

'You . . .' Holly didn't finish the curse.

'Hey, I meant what I told you. I've got nothing to do with this secret agent stuff. But that doesn't mean I'm an idiot,' Buchanan said. 'Now is there anything else you want to ask me? Because it's late. I'm tired. I want to get some sleep.'

'You . . .'

'Yeah, I'm probably that, too,' Buchanan said.

'Come on, Holly,' her companion said.

Buchanan squeezed out of the way. With difficulty, he opened the door. 'Thanks for paying for the beer and sandwiches. You really know how to show a guy a good time.'

Holly's eyes narrowed. 'I'm staying.'

'Don't be crazy,' her companion said.

'I know what I'm doing,' she said.

'Look, this is all very interesting,' Buchanan said. 'But I mean it. I'm tired.'

'And *I* mean it. I'm staying.'

'Fine,' Buchanan said. 'Anything to convince you I'm telling the truth. You can satisfy yourself that I don't say anything incriminating in my sleep.'

'Holly, think about it,' her companion said.

'I'll be fine, Ted.'

'Yeah, Ted,' Buchanan said. 'She'll be fine. I promise I won't take off her clothes. Good night, Ted.' Buchanan guided him out the door. 'Stay tuned. I hope my snoring won't keep you awake.'

In the swaying corridor, a white-haired, elderly woman in a nightgown adjusted her spectacles and peered intensely at them from the compartment to the right.

'Sorry if we woke you, ma'am,' Buchanan said. He watched Ted walk along the corridor and enter the last compartment on the right. With a wave to both him and the elderly woman, Buchanan stepped back into his compartment and closed the door.

He locked it and studied Holly. 'So which position do you like? Top or bottom?'

'Don't get the wrong idea because I stayed. Ted's really very tough. If he thinks I'm not safe with you, he'll—'

'Bunks.'

'What?'

'I'm talking about bunks.' Buchanan reached up to grab a lever and pulled down the top one. He started to prepare the bottom one. 'I don't know what you expect to accomplish by this. But I suggest we flip a coin to see who uses the bathroom first.'

'Oh.'

'And if you don't happen to have a toothbrush, you can use mine.'

'On second thoughts . . .'

'You bet.' Buchanan unlocked and opened the door. 'Good night, Holly.'

'Good night.'

9

'*How did she know my real name? How did she know so many of my pseudonyms? How did she know where to find me?* I asked her those questions several times.' Buchanan was in a phone booth on Loyola Avenue not far from Union Passenger Terminal in New Orleans. The street was noisy. The October sky was hazy blue. The weather was warm and humid. But all Buchanan cared about was what he heard on the phone and whether he was being followed.

'We'll find out,' his deep-voiced contact officer said. 'Do

whatever you were going to do. Don't change your plans. We'll get back to you. But if anything new develops, call us immediately. Just remember, the evidence she claims to have – the photographs – they aren't conclusive.'

'But she's not supposed to have those photographs at all. What happened in Fort Lauderdale after I left?' Buchanan demanded. 'This problem was supposed to have been taken care of.'

'We thought the woman was merely a hired hand. Nobody guessed she'd be a reporter. When she didn't resurface, she didn't seem important.'

'For all I know, Bailey's involved in this, too.'

'No,' the voice said firmly. 'He isn't. Just stay calm. Enjoy your furlough. At the moment, the woman can't prove anything.'

'Tell the colonel he was in one of the photographs she showed me.'

'Don't worry. I'll be sure to tell him. Meanwhile, in case we need to get in touch with you, stick around your hotel room between six and eight tonight. After that, check the possible rendezvous sites we agreed on before you left.'

Tense, Buchanan hung up the phone, picked up his travel bag, opened the booth's door, and stepped out.

A redheaded woman and her male companion appeared from behind trees in a nearby park.

God, Buchanan thought.

He stalked toward them. 'Enough is enough. You're not going to ruin my furlough by following me.'

Holly McCoy looked disappointed that she'd been spotted. 'Who were you phoning? Your superior officers to tell them you'd been exposed?'

'An old friend who moved down here. Not that it's any of your business.'

'Prove it. Let's go visit him.'

299

'His girlfriend told me he had to go to Houston for an emergency sales conference.'

'Convenient. What's his name?'

'Lady, I'm annoyed that I won't get to see him, and you're not making things any better by—'

'Holly. Please, call me Holly. I mean, since we nearly spent the night together, we might as well use each other's first name.'

Buchanan turned to her male companion. 'Whatever you're being paid, it isn't enough. After listening to her all the time, don't you just want to put a noose around your neck and put an end to it all?'

He walked away toward the entrance to the nearby post office.

'Brendan!' Holly called.

Buchanan didn't respond.

'Bren!' she called.

Buchanan kept walking.

'Hey!' she called. 'What hotel are you using?'

It had been so long since anyone had used Buchanan's first name and his nickname that he didn't identify them with himself. Slowly they registered on him. He turned. 'Why should I make things easy for you? Damn it, find out for yourself.'

In front of the post office, a man got out of a taxi. Buchanan ducked in and gave directions to the driver. As the taxi sped into traffic, the last thing he heard Holly shout was, 'Hey!'

10

Brendan. Bren. As his first name and his nickname echoed in his consciousness, Buchanan became more aware of how long it had been since he had portrayed himself.

300

But this was different. Now he found himself confronted by the most complex assumption of identity that he had ever attempted. Not one identity but two. Simultaneously. Brendan Buchanan and Peter Lang. Not schizophrenia, for in that case, one identity would alternate with the other. No, *these* identities had to be multilayered, coexisting. Compatible, yet separate. Balanced within the same instant.

To fulfill his purpose for coming to New Orleans, to find out why Juana had sent the postcard, to learn the trouble she was in, he had to reconstruct Peter Lang. After all, Peter Lang had made the promise to help her. Peter Lang had been in love with her. Desperate not to be himself, Buchanan wanted very much to be Peter Lang.

But Peter Lang wasn't being followed by Holly McCoy. Peter Lang hadn't worked for the Intelligence Support Activity. He wasn't now assigned to Scotch and Soda. Oh, Peter Lang had worked for a clandestine branch of Special Operations. That was true. But not these particular ones. Peter Lang wasn't under investigation by *The Washington Post*. Brendan Buchanan was, and it was Brendan Buchanan who would have to deceive and discourage Holly McCoy.

Thus Peter Lang would pretend to be Brendan Buchanan. And Brendan Buchanan . . . Well, he had to do something while he was in New Orleans. He couldn't just sit in his hotel room and show Holly that she'd made him nervous. As a consequence, he would pretend to be Peter Lang and revisit the spots he had so admired when he'd lived here six years ago.

Peter Lang would have stayed at a place he knew in the French Quarter, but in theory, Brendan Buchanan had never been to New Orleans. He didn't know the secret good places. He would choose an easier-to-book, less quaint, but first-rate hotel, something near the French Quarter but also near the Riverwalk mall and the other downtown attractions. The Holiday Inn-Crowne Plaza, tall and gleaming, seemed ideal.

Having made a reservation for Brendan Buchanan, he checked in, was shown to his twelfth-floor room, waited until the bellhop had left, then locked the door, and transferred his handgun and Victor Grant's passport from his travel bag to his clothes. After all, the room might be searched. The passport fit within his lightweight, gray sportcoat. The gun fit underneath the sportcoat, behind his belt, at his spine. He didn't bother to check the view.

Two minutes after having been shown to his room, he left it, taking the fire stairs to the lobby. He scanned it to make sure that Holly McCoy wasn't in sight, then walked outside, and got in the taxi whose driver he had told to wait for him.

'Where you gwin to now, suh?' the elderly, silver-haired, resonant-voiced, black man asked.

'Metairie Cemetery.'

'Somebody die, suh?'

'All the time.'

'Ain't *that* the truth, suh.'

Buchanan's contact officer had told him to stay at the hotel from six to eight this evening in case he had to be given a message. But that was three hours from now, and Buchanan wanted to keep moving. More important, he wanted to do what Peter Lang would do. So he leaned back in the taxi, pretending to admire the sights as the driver headed down Tchoupitoulas Street, got on the 90 expressway, and merged with rushing traffic, speeding toward Metairie Road.

The huge cemetery, established in 1873, had once been a pre-Civil-War race track. Like the many other old cemeteries in New Orleans, it consisted of rows and rows of masonry tombs. Each tomb was one hundred feet long and four tiers high with niches into which coffins had been slid, the entrances sealed. The land was so flat and the Mississippi so close that in the previous century the city's moist soil had necessitated above-ground burial. Since then, modern drainage

302

systems had reduced the moisture problem. Nonetheless, tradition had been established, and most interments were still above ground.

Peter Lang had come here often. Among the old cemeteries he'd frequently visited, Metairie had been his favorite. His ostensible purpose for coming had been his taste for Gothic atmosphere and his interest in history, although the actual reason had been that the nooks and crannies of the decaying cemeteries had provided abundant locations for message dead drops (Buchanan-Lang's then control officer had had a morbid sense of humor). On rare occasions, a messenger had passed him a coded note by means of brush contact, the cemeteries so crowded with visitors and mourners that the skillful exchange would not have been detected.

Now Buchanan-Lang came for another reason. He associated the cemetery with Juana. She had often accompanied him on his visits, and her interest in the old tombs had eventually rivaled his. He particularly remembered her delight when she first came upon the miniature mausoleum built for Josie Arlington, a prominent madam in the city many years before. Josie had decided to have her tomb built from symbolic red stone and decorated with granite torches. As Buchanan-Lang reached the tomb, he could almost hear Juana's laughter. The haze in the sky had lifted. The sharp sun gleamed from deep blue, and in the sudden clarity that contrasted with the gloom of the crumbling cemetery, he imagined Juana standing next to him, her head tilted back, her smile bright, her hand on his shoulder. He wanted to hug her.

And tonight he would.

I should never have let you go. My life would have been so different.

I won't let you go a second time. I didn't know how much I needed you.

I meant what I said six years ago. I love you.

303

Or Peter Lang does.

But what about Buchanan-Lang? he wondered.

And what about *Buchanan*?

His skull wouldn't stop throbbing. He massaged his temples, but his headache continued to torture him.

11

Six p.m.

Back in his hotel room, he obeyed instructions and waited in case his superiors needed to contact him. He thought about ordering a meal from room service, but his appetite was gone. He thought about watching CNN, but he had no interest. Juana. He kept anticipating his reunion with her. He kept reliving their last night together six years ago. He kept regretting his failed opportunity.

He sat in a chair, and suddenly the room was in blackness. He'd left the draperies open to appreciate the sunset. A moment ago, it seemed, the sky had been crimson. Now abruptly it and the room were dark. Confused, uneasy, he glanced at the luminous dial on his watch.

Nine-sixteen?

No. That wasn't possible. The shadows must be playing tricks on him. He wasn't seeing the dial correctly. Leaning toward a table, he turned on a light and studied his watch, disturbed to discover that the time was indeed nine-sixteen, that three hours and sixteen minutes had passed without his being aware of them.

Dear God, he thought, that's the third time in the last three days. No. I'm wrong. It's the fourth. Jesus. Am I so preoccupied that I'm blotting out my surroundings?

He stood, went to the bathroom, then came back and paced, trying to regain his sense of motion. As he passed the telephone on the bureau near the closet, he was startled to notice that the tiny, red, message light was flashing.

But I didn't hear the phone ring.

Worried that his contact officer had tried to relay emergency instructions, he quickly picked up the phone and pressed 0.

After three buzzes, a woman answered. 'Hotel operator.'

He tried to sound calm. 'This is room twelve-fourteen. My message light is flashing.'

'Just a moment, sir, while I . . . Yes.'

Buchanan's heart pounded.

The operator said, 'Holly McCoy left a message at five forty-five. It says, "We're staying in the same hotel. Why don't we get together later?" I can call her room if you like, sir.'

'No, thank you. It won't be necessary.'

Buchanan set down the phone.

His emotions were mixed. He felt relieved that he hadn't missed an urgent message that his superiors had tried to give him. He felt equally relieved that the message he had received had been logged at five forty-five. *Before* he'd returned to his room. *Before* he'd sat down and lost over three hours. At least he wasn't losing touch so deeply that a phone call failed to rouse him.

But he also felt disturbed that Holly McCoy had managed to track him to this hotel. It wasn't just her annoying persistence that troubled him, her relentless pressure. It was something further. How had she found him? Was she so determined that she'd telephoned every one of the hundreds of hotels in the area and asked for . . . ?

When I made the reservation, I should have used a different name.

Hey, using different names is what got you into this. If Holly McCoy found out that you used an alias to register, then she'd *really* be suspicious. Besides, if you'd used an unauthorized false name to register, your superiors would have wondered what on earth you thought you were doing? You're supposed to be on R and R, not on a mission.

But that's exactly what Buchanan *was* on, a mission, and the rendezvous time was almost upon him. He had to get to Café du Monde by eleven o'clock. That was when he and Juana had arrived there six years ago.

Tonight. After making sure that his pistol was covered by his gray sport coat and securely braced behind his belt at his spine, he opened the door, checked the hallway, locked his room, and went quickly down the fire stairs.

12

The night was eerily similar to the one six years ago. For example, as Buchanan left the hotel, he noticed that the air was balmy with the hint of rain, a pleasant breeze coming in from the Mississippi. The same as before.

He took care to make sure that Holly McCoy wasn't in sight, but as he walked along Tchoupitoulas Street, restraining his pace so he wouldn't attract attention, another parallel between tonight and six years before became disconcertingly obvious. It was Halloween. Many pedestrians he passed wore costumes, and again similar to six years before, the most popular costume seemed to be a skeleton: a black, tight-fitting garment with the phosphorescent images of bones painted on it and a head mask highlighted with white representing a skull. With so many people resembling each other, he couldn't tell if he was being followed. More, all Holly McCoy needed to do to disguise her conspicuous red hair was to wear a head mask. By contrast, on *this* night, *he* looked conspicuous since he was one of the minority who weren't wearing a costume of some sort.

As he crossed Canal Street toward the French Quarter, he began to hear music, faint, then distinct, the increasing throb and wail of jazz. A while ago, he'd read in a newspaper that New Orleans had instituted a noise ordinance, but tonight no one seemed to care. Street bands competed with those in bars. Dixieland, the blues – these and many other styles pulsed along the French Quarter's narrow, crowded streets as costumed revelers danced, sang, and drank in celebration of the night of the dead.

> *. . . gone and left me.*
> *When the saints . . .*

Buchanan tried to lose himself in the crowd. He had less than an hour before he was supposed to be at Café du Monde, and he wanted to use that hour to guarantee that his meeting with Juana would not be observed.

As he headed up Bienville Street and then along Royal Street, then up Conti to Bourbon Street, he felt frustrated by the density of the crowd. It prevented him from moving as fast as he wanted, from taking advantage of opportunities to duck into a courtyard or down a side street. Every time he attempted an evasion tactic, a group would suddenly loom in front of him, and anyone who followed would not have trouble keeping up with him while blending with the festivities. He bought a devil's mask from a sidewalk vendor and immediately found that it restricted his vision so much that he bumped into people, making him feel vulnerable and selfconscious. He took it off, glanced at his watch, and was amazed to discover how much his concentration had compressed the time. It was almost eleven. He had to get to the rendezvous site.

Soon, he thought. Soon he would put his arms around Juana. Soon he'd be able to find out why she needed him. He'd help her. He'd show her how much he loved her. He'd correct the mistake he'd made six years ago.

Who had made?

Coming down Orleans Avenue, he reached the shadows of St Anthony's Garden. From there, he took Pirate's Alley down to Jackson Square. Its huge bronze statue of Andrew Jackson on horseback rose ghostlike from the darkness of the gardens in the locked, deserted park. Using one of the walkways that flanked the wrought-iron fence of the square, he at last reached Decatur Street and paused in the shadows next to the square while he studied his destination.

Where he stood was surprisingly free of the congestion and noise of the rest of the French Quarter. He felt apart from things, more vulnerable. Several glances behind him gave him the assurance of being alone.

And yet he felt threatened. Again he studied his destination. At last he stepped into view, felt as if he re-entered the world, crossed Decatur, and made his approach toward Café du Monde.

It was a large, concrete building whose distinctive feature was that its walls were composed of tall, wide archways that made the restaurant open-air. During heavy rains, the interior could be protected by lowering green-and-white striped canvas, but usually – and tonight was no exception – the only thing that separated people on the street from the restaurant's patrons were waist-high, iron railings. Tonight, the same as six years ago, the place was crowded more than usual. Because of the holiday. Because of Halloween. Expectant customers, many of them in costume, stood in a line on the sidewalk, waiting to be admitted.

Buchanan strained to catch a glimpse of Juana, hoping that the crowd would have made her decide to wait outside for him. He and Juana would be able to get away from the noise and confusion. He would lovingly put his arm around her and try to find a quiet place. He would get her to tell him what terrible urgency had made her send the postcard, allowing him a second chance.

There was an addition to the restaurant. Smaller than the main section, it had a green-and-white roof supported by widely separated, slender, white poles that made this part of the restaurant seem even more open-air. He stared past the low, metal railing toward the customers close together around small, circular tables. The place rippled with constant movement. Hundreds of conversations rushed over him.

Juana. He strained harder to see her. He shifted position to view the interior of the restaurant from a different angle. He scanned the line of waiting customers.

What if she's wearing a costume? he thought. What if she's afraid to the point that she put on a disguise? He wouldn't be able to recognize her. And she might not hurry to meet him. She might be so terrified that she had to assess everyone around him before she revealed herself.

Juana. Even if she *weren't* wearing a costume, how could he be certain he would recognize her? Six years had passed. She might have grown her hair long. She might have . . .

And what about him? How had *his* appearance, like his identities, changed in six years? Was his hair dyed the same color? Did he weigh the same? Should he have a mustache? He couldn't remember if Peter Lang had worn a mustache. Did—?

Juana. He brushed past waiting customers and entered the restaurant, determined to find her. She had to be here. The postcard couldn't have had any other meaning. She needed to see him. She wanted his help.

'Hey, buddy, wait your turn,' someone said.

'Sir, you'll have to go to the end of the line,' a waiter told him.

'You don't understand. I'm supposed to meet someone, and—'

'Please, sir. The end of the line.'

Juana. He backed away. His headache intensified as he scanned the crush of customers in the restaurant. Outside on the sidewalk, he rubbed his throbbing head. When a rush of people in costumes swept past him, he whirled to see if Juana might be one of them.

The knife slid into his side. Sharp. Cold. Tingly. Suddenly burning. It felt like a punch. It knocked him off balance. It made him groan. As he felt the wet heat of his gushing blood, someone screamed. People scrambled to get away from him. A man knocked against him. Fighting to stem the flow of his blood, he slipped. The iron railing appeared to rush toward him.

No! he mentally screamed. Not my head! Not again! I can't hurt my—!

EIGHT

1

Cuernavaca, Mexico.

The black limousine and its escort cars proceeded along Insurgentes Sur freeway, forced to maintain a frustrating, moderate speed as the caravan fought the congestion of holiday traffic heading south from the smog of Mexico City. After thirty-seven miles, the limousine and its escorts reached Cuernavaca, the capital's most popular but at the same time most exclusive retreat. It was easy to understand why the rich and powerful came here each weekend. Sheltered in an attractive, wooded valley, Cuernavaca had space, silence, pleasant weather, and most prized of all, clean air. Aztec rulers had built palaces here. So had Cortes. Emperor Maximilian had been especially fond of the area's gardens. These days, what important visitors from the capital valued were the luxurious hotels and the castlelike mansions.

The limousine proceeded along the stately streets of a quiet neighborhood and stopped at the large, iron gate of one of the mansions. Majestic shade trees projected above the high, stone wall that enclosed the spacious grounds. The uniformed driver stepped out of the limousine and approached an armed guard, who stood beyond the bars of the gate and scowled at the visitor. After a brief conversation in which the driver showed

311

the guard a document, the guard entered a wooden booth beside the gate and picked up a telephone, speaking to someone in the house. Thirty seconds later, he returned to the gate, opened it, and motioned for the driver to bring the limousine into the estate. As the escort cars attempted to follow, the guard raised his left hand to stop them. At the same time, another armed guard stepped into view to close and lock the gate.

The limousine proceeded along a shady, curved driveway, past trees, gardens, and fountains, toward the mansion. As it stopped before the stone steps at the entrance, one of the large double-doors opened, and a mustached, aristocratic-looking man came out. It was a measure of his need to seem respectful that he had not sent a servant to greet this particular visitor. His name was Esteban Delgado, and his surname – which meant 'thin' – was even more appropriate than when he'd met with the director of the National Institute of Archaeology and History in Acapulco a week earlier, for Delgado's body and features were now no longer merely rakishly slender but unhealthily gaunt. His aquiline face was pale, and he would almost have believed the rumors that he was seriously ill if he hadn't been acutely aware of the unbearable tension that he suffered.

At the bottom of the stairs, he forced himself to smile as the limousine's far, rear door opened and a well-dressed, fair-haired, pleasant-looking American in his middle thirties emerged from the car. The man gave the impression of exuding good-nature, but Delgado wasn't fooled, for the man's smile – on the rare occasions when he did smile, and this was not one of them – had no warmth. The man's name was Raymond, and the only time Delgado had seen him smile was during a cockfight.

Raymond ignored Delgado, assessed the estate's security, then came around the limousine and opened the other door.

An elderly man with thick glasses and dense white hair stepped out. He was in his eighties although, except for extremely wrinkled hands, he appeared to be in his sixties.

'Professor Drummond,' Delgado said with forced brightness. 'I had no idea that you planned to visit. If I had known, I would have arranged a reception in your honor.'

Drummond shook Delgado's hand with authority, fixed his gaze upon him, and waited a moment before he replied in Spanish, one of his seven languages. 'I happened to be in Mexico City on business and wanted to discuss something with you. Your office informed me that you were here. If you have an hour to spare . . .'

'Certainly.' Delgado led Drummond and his assistant up the stairs. 'It will be an honor to have you in my home.' Despite the shade trees, Delgado found that he was sweating. 'I'll have the servants bring some refreshments. Would you like a rum and Coke? Or perhaps . . .'

'I never drink alcoholic beverages. By all means, you have one if you wish.'

'I was going to send for some lemonade.'

They entered subdued light in the mansion and crossed the cool, echoing, marble vestibule. A colorfully dressed, teenage girl appeared at the top of the wide, curved staircase, seemed surprised that there were visitors, and abruptly obeyed Delgado's sharp gesture commanding her to go back to where she had been. At the end of a corridor, Delgado escorted Drummond and Raymond into a mahogany-paneled study that was furnished in leather and filled with hunting trophies as well as numerous rifles and shotguns in glass cabinets, many of the firearms antique. For once, Raymond's eyes displayed interest. Two servants immediately brought in refreshments and as quickly departed.

Neither Drummond nor Raymond picked up the lemonade. Instead Drummond leaned back in his chair, sitting imperiously straight, his long arms stretched out on the sides of the chair. His voice was brittle yet strong, his gaze direct. 'I suspect your associates have already told you, but we need to compare reactions.'

Delgado pretended to look confused.

'The woman, Minister. It will come as no surprise to you when I tell you that she has disappeared.'

'Ah.' Delgado's heart lurched, but he didn't show any reaction. 'Yes. The woman. I did receive information that led me to believe she had disappeared.'

'And?'

Delgado tried to make his voice stern. 'What do you intend to do about it?'

'What I *am* doing, what I *have* been doing, is using all my resources to locate her. Every element of her background, every conceivable place or person to whom she might run for shelter and help, is being investigated.'

'And yet after two weeks, you have no results.'

Drummond nodded in compliment. 'Your sources are excellent.'

'You still haven't answered my question. What do you intend to do about this?'

'Relative to you? Nothing,' Drummond answered. 'Our agreement remains the same.'

'I don't know why it should. You broke your part of the contract. You assured me you could control the woman. You were emphatic that she would solve my problem.'

'And she did.'

'Temporarily. But now that she's disappeared, the problem is the same as before.'

Drummond's aged eyes narrowed. 'I disagree. This disappearance cannot be traced to you.'

'*Unless she talks.*'

'But she won't,' Drummond said. 'Because if she planned to

314

talk, she *would* have by now. It's an obvious method by which she could try to save her life. She knows we would kill her in retribution. On principle. I believe that she remains silent out of fear and as a sign to us that if we leave her alone, she won't be a threat to us. I should say, a threat to *you*. After all, the problem is yours. I was merely doing you a favor by trying to correct it.'

Delgado's pulse increased with anger. 'Not a favor. A business agreement.'

'I won't quibble with terminology. I came to tell you that despite her disappearance, I expect to be allowed to conduct *my* business as you agreed.'

Delgado released his nervous energy by standing. 'That would be very difficult. The director of the National Institute of Archaeology and History has become furious about your control of the site in the Yucatán. He is mustering government support for a full investigation.'

'Discourage him,' Drummond said.

'He's very determined.'

Now it was Drummond's turn to rise. Despite his frail body, he dominated the study. 'I need only another few weeks. I'm too close. I won't be stopped.'

'Unless you fail.'

'I *never* fail.' Drummond bristled. 'I am an unforgiving partner. If *you* fail *me*, despite the woman's disappearance, I will take steps to make you regret it.'

'How? If you don't find the woman and she never talks.'

'She was necessary only to protect you. To expose you, all I need is this.' Drummond snapped his fingers.

In response, Raymond opened a briefcase, then handed Drummond a large envelope that contained a video tape.

Drummond gave the envelope to Delgado. 'It's a copy, of course. I've been saving it as a further negotiating tactic. Be careful. Don't leave it where your wife and daughter might wonder what was on it. Or the President. You wouldn't want *him* to see it. A political scandal of this sort would threaten his administration, and needless to say, it would destroy your chances of becoming his replacement.'

Delgado felt sweat trickle down his back as he clenched the video tape.

Abruptly the study's door was opened. Delgado whirled, his stomach cramping when he saw his wife step in. Intelligent, sophisticated, well-educated, she understood her role as a politician's spouse and always conducted herself perfectly. She tolerated Delgado's frequent absences and no doubt was aware of his frequent indiscretions. She was always there when he needed symbolic support at public functions. But then she had been raised in a family of politicians. From her youth onward, she had learned the rules. She was the sister of Delgado's best friend, the President of Mexico.

'I'm sorry to disturb you, dear. I didn't realize you had company. How are you, Mr Drummond?' she asked in perfect English. Her expensive clothes and jewelry enhanced her plain features.

'Excellent,' Drummond answered in Spanish. 'And yourself? I trust you are well, Señora.'

'Yes, I am fine. Would you care to stay for dinner?'

'Thank you, but I'm afraid I was just about to leave. Your husband and I needed to discuss some matters. I have to fly to Europe.'

'You're welcome any time,' she said. 'Esteban, I'll be in the garden.' She closed the door.

The room was uncomfortably silent for a moment.

'Think about it,' Drummond said. 'Don't be a fool and ruin everything you've worked so hard to achieve. Don't deny yourself the chance to achieve even greater things. Watch the tape, destroy it, and make the further arrangements we discussed.'

316

Delgado did not reveal the sudden anger that blazed inside him. You come to my home. You ignore my hospitality. You threaten me. You threaten my relationship with my wife and daughter. His jaw ached with fury. There will come a time when you do not have power over me.

And then I will destroy you.

'The director of the Institute of Archaeology and History,' Drummond said. 'When I told you to discourage him from interfering with what I'm doing at the site, I meant eliminate him. I want him replaced by someone who knows how to compromise, who won't make trouble, who values favors.'

2

New Orleans.
Buchanan squirmed.

'Welcome back. How are you feeling?'

He took a moment to understand what the woman asked him. He took another moment to answer.

' . . . Sore.'

'I bet.' The woman chuckled. It wasn't a chuckle of derision. It communicated sympathy. Its sound was soft yet deep.

He liked it.

He took another moment for the haze to clear enough that he realized he was in a hospital bed. He didn't know what pained him more, the throbbing in his head or the burning in his right side. His skull was wrapped with bandages. His side felt stiff from bandages as well. And stitches.

'You had me worried,' the woman said.

He focused on her, expecting to see a nurse leaning over the bed or possibly, blessedly, Juana, although this woman didn't have an Hispanic accent.

As he noticed her red hair, the significance of it alarmed him. He squirmed harder.

'Relax,' Holly McCoy said. 'You're all right. You're going to be fine.'

Like hell, he thought. Everything was wrong, *very* wrong, although his clouded thoughts prevented him from knowing precisely *how* wrong.

'Well,' a man said, 'I see you're coming around.'

A doctor. His white coat contrasted with his black skin. He entered the room and studied the medical chart attached to the foot of the bed, finally saying, 'The nurses on the night shift had to wake you periodically to test your neurological signs. Do you remember that?'

'. . . No.'

'Do you remember *me*?'

'. . . No.'

'Good. Because I didn't treat you last night when you were brought into the emergency ward. Answer my questions honestly. The first thing that comes into your mind. Understand?'

Buchanan nodded, wincing from the pain that the movement caused.

'Do you know why you're here?'

'. . . Stabbed.'

'Another good answer. Do you remember where?'

'. . . My side.'

The doctor smiled slightly. 'No. I mean where outside the hospital were you stabbed?'

'. . . French Quarter . . . Café du Monde.'

'Exactly. You were assaulted on the sidewalk outside the restaurant. As soon as you're up to it, the police will want a statement from you, although I gather your friend here has already provided most of the necessary details.'

Holly nodded.

My friend?

The police?

'If you're someone who likes company for his misery, you aren't alone,' the doctor continued. 'We had several mugging victims in the emergency ward last night, and some of them weren't as lucky as you. A few are in critical condition.'

'. . . Mugging?'

'I gave the police a description of the man who did it,' Holly said. 'Not that it helps. A pirate costume. Last night, a *lot* of people were wearing costumes.' She raised a plastic cup and placed a bent straw between his lips.

The water was cool.

'You're at the L.S.U. Medical Center,' the doctor said. 'Your wound required twenty stitches. But you were lucky. No major organs were injured. The blade didn't penetrate as much as it slashed.'

The police? Buchanan thought. Jesus, I was carrying a gun. What if they found it? They *must* have found it. And Victor Grant's forged passport. They'll wonder what—

'You struck your head when you fell,' the doctor said. 'You have a concussion.'

Another one?

'There doesn't appear to be any neurologic damage. Still, you might get tired of everybody asking you the same questions . . . Like, how many fingers am I holding up?'

'Three.'

'How old are you?'

'Thirty-two.'

'What's your name?'

. . .

'What's your name?' the doctor repeated.

He concentrated.

Of all the questions . . .

Come on. Come on. Who am I supposed to be?

319

'. . . Peter Lang.' He exhaled.

'Nope. Wrong answer. Your wallet — which the mugger didn't manage to get, by the way — indicates that your name is . . .'

'Brendan Buchanan.'

'Better,' the doctor said. 'Much better. So let's be clear. What's your name?'

'. . . Brendan Buchanan.'

'Then why did you say your name was Peter Lang?'

'. . . A friend of mine. Have to tell him what happened to me.'

'Ms McCoy can make your phone calls for you. You had me worried for a moment. I was afraid the concussion was more severe than your CAT-scan indicated.'

Didn't get my wallet? To know that, the police must have searched me. They *must* have found the gun.

And the passport, too! Maybe this doctor expected me to call myself Victor Grant.

A nurse had been taking his blood pressure. 'One-fifteen over seventy-five.'

The doctor nodded with approval. 'Try to open your eyes as wide as you can. I need to shine this light at your pupils. Good. Now follow the movement of my hand. Bear with me while I tap at your joints. I have to draw the end of this hammer along the bottoms of your feet. Fine. Your reflexes don't seem impaired. Your lungs sound normal. Your heartbeat is strong and regular. I'm encouraged. Try to rest. I'll be back this afternoon.'

'I'll keep him company.' Holly gave Buchanan another sip of water.

'As long as he rests. I don't want him talking a lot. On the other hand, I don't want him sleeping a lot, either. Not until I'm sure he's out of danger.'

'I understand. I'll just be here to reassure him,' Holly said.

'TLC never hurts.' The doctor started to leave, then looked back. 'You've certainly been having your share of injuries, Mr Buchanan. What caused the wound to your shoulder?'

' . . . Uh. It . . .'

'A boating accident,' Holly said. 'The edge of a propeller.'

'It's a good thing you've got medical insurance,' the doctor said.

3

Tense, Buchanan waited for the doctor and the nurse to leave, then slowly turned his head and stared at Holly.

She smiled engagingly. 'You want more water?'

' . . . What's going on?'

'You know, when I was a little girl, I couldn't decide whether to be a nurse or a reporter. Now I'm getting to be both.'

Buchanan breathed with effort, his voice a gravelly whisper. 'What happened? How did . . . ?'

'Save your strength. Last night, I followed you from the hotel.'

'How did you know where I was staying?'

'That's confidential. Rest, I told you. I'll do the talking. I figured you had to leave the hotel sometime, so I waited across the street. There's no back exit, except for service doors. But I didn't think you'd draw attention to yourself by making the staff wonder why you'd use a service door, so it seemed to me the best bet was the front. Mind you, I did have Ted . . . you remember Ted, from the train . . . watching the back. He and I were linked by two-way radios. When you came out, I was just one of several people wearing costumes. Otherwise, this red hair would have been a giveaway. You didn't notice when I followed you.'

Buchanan breathed. 'Ought to dye it.'

'What?'

'Your hair. For following people. Change the color to something bland.'

'Never. But I guess you've changed the color of *your* hair often enough.'

He didn't respond.

Holly gave him another sip of water. 'By the way, was my answer right? When the doctor asked how you got the wound to your shoulder? A boating accident? When you were Victor Grant, isn't that what you told the Mexican police?'

'I don't know what you're talking about.'

'Sure.'

His eyelids felt heavy.

Where does she get her information? he thought.

'Confidential,' she said.

'What?'

'You asked where I got my information. That's confidential.'

I did? I asked her that out loud?

He couldn't keep his eyes open.

4

The doctor pointed at the uneaten tuna sandwich. 'Your lack of appetite worries me.'

'Hospital food. I never liked it. I can smell all the other meals that were on the cart.'

'Mr Lang . . .'

'Buchanan.'

'Right. Mr Buchanan. I just wanted to be sure. If you want to get out of here, you're going to have to satisfy my slightest concern about your concussion. If I were you, I'd eat that meal, and then I'd ask the nurse to get me another.'

Buchanan mustered the strength to reach for the sandwich.

'Here, I'll give you a hand,' Holly said.

'I think the doctor wants to see if I can do it by myself.'

'You're a student of human nature,' the doctor said. 'After you've enjoyed your meal, I want you out of bed and walking around a little. To the bathroom, for example. I need to be satisfied that your legs and the rest of you are all in working order.'

'Did anyone ever tell you you're a slave driver?'

The black doctor raised his eyebrows. 'You're getting better if you can make jokes. I'll be back to examine you later.'

The moment the doctor left, Buchanan set down the tuna sandwich. He glanced at Holly. 'I don't suppose you'd eat this for me. Or dump it somewhere and make it look as if I finished everything.'

'Do the manly thing and eat it yourself if you want to get out of here.' Holly's emerald eyes gleamed with mischievousness.

'How do you get your eyes that color? Tinted contact lenses?'

'French eye drops. A lot of movie stars use them. The drops emphasize the color of their eyes. It's a trick I learned when I was working in Los Angeles. Come to think of it, you'd find the trick handy. For when you're altering your appearance. You wouldn't have to fool around with those tinted contact lenses, you mentioned.'

'Why would I want to alter my appearance?'

She sounded exasperated. 'You don't give up.'

'Neither do you. Last night. What happened? You didn't finish telling me.'

'I followed you through the French Quarter and over to Café du Monde. By then, it was eleven o'clock. You seemed to be looking for somebody. In fact, you were looking pretty hard.'

'An old friend I'd arranged to meet. The only reason I didn't want you following me was that I was getting tired of your questions.'

'And here you are, listening to more of them.'

'Café du Monde.'

'I was watching from across the street, so I didn't see everything perfectly. You came out of the restaurant. There was a commotion, a group of costumed people going by. They acted as if they'd been drinking. Then one of them, a man dressed as a pirate, bumped into you. All of a sudden you grabbed your side and spun. A woman screamed. People were scrambling to get out of your way. You tripped over somebody. You hit your head on an iron railing. I ran toward you, but not before I noticed the guy in the pirate costume shove a knife back into his belt as he disappeared into the crowd down the street. I stayed with you, trying to stop the blood while one of the waiters in the restaurant phoned for an ambulance.'

'Blood doesn't make you squeamish?'

'Hey, I can't write the end of my story if you die on me.'

'And all along, I thought it was my personality that attracted you.'

'Which one?'

'What?'

'Which personality? You've had so many.'

Buchanan set down a remnant of the tuna sandwich. 'I give up. I can't think of any way to convince you that . . .'

'You're right. There *isn't* any way to convince me. And last night made me more sure than ever. The man in the pirate costume didn't try to mug you. I just told that to the police so they wouldn't wonder about you. No, that wasn't an attempted mugging. That was an attempted *murder*.' She sat straighter. 'Why? Who were you meeting? What's—?'

'Holly.'

' —going on that—?'

'I've got a question of my own,' Buchanan said. 'I had something with me. If anyone found it, I'm sure the police would have—'

'Sure,' Holly said.

'—given it back or—'

'Wanted to have a very deep heart-to-heart with you about it.' Holly opened her purse. 'Is this what you lost?'

Inside the purse, Buchanan saw his Beretta 9-millimeter semiautomatic pistol. His eyes narrowed.

'You didn't drop it,' Holly said. 'I felt it while I was trying to stop you from bleeding. Before the police and the ambulance arrived, I managed to get it off you without being noticed.'

'No big deal. I carry it for protection.'

'Sure. Like when you're meeting an old friend. I don't know what the gun-concealment laws are in this state, but it's my guess you need a permit to carry this. And for certain, if you're legitimate, I know the Army wouldn't approve of you walking around armed while you're on furlough.'

'Hey, a lot of people carry guns these days,' Buchanan said. 'That attempted mugging last night proves why.'

'An attempted murder, not a mugging.'

'That proves my point. Some nut gets drunk, maybe cranked up on drugs. He's wearing a pirate costume. Suddenly he thinks he's a real pirate. So he stabs somebody. The equivalent of a drive-by shooting. Only this is a walk-by stabbing.'

'You expect me to believe that?'

'Look, I have no idea why he stabbed me. It's as good a theory as any,' Buchanan said.

'But would the cops buy it if they'd also found the other thing you lost?'

Other . . . ? Buchanan felt suddenly cold.

'I've been waiting for you to ask me about it.' After glancing at the door to make sure no one was looking in, Holly reached under the pistol and removed a passport from her purse. 'The ambulance attendants had to get your jacket off so they could check the wound. I told them I was your girlfriend and hung on to the jacket. A good thing I did. For your sake.' She opened the passport. 'Victor Grant. My, my.'

Buchanan felt even more chilled.

'Not a bad picture of you. Your hair was a little shorter. Yep, the gun along with a passport that didn't match the ID in your wallet would definitely have made the police wonder what was going on,' Holly said. 'For starters, they'd have suspected you were running drugs. Actually, that's not so far from the truth, given your involvement with covert operations like Scotch and Soda.'

Buchanan stopped breathing.

'So?' Holly put the passport back under the gun in her purse. 'You've always got so many reasonable explanations for your unusual behavior. What's your story this time?'

Buchanan pulled his salad toward him.

'Suddenly hungry? Trying to fill the time while you come up with a reason for the fake passport?'

'Holly, I . . .'

He picked up his fork.

'Can't think of one, can you?' she asked.

He put down the fork and sighed. 'You don't want to mess around with this. Do yourself a favor and bow out quietly. Forget you ever saw that passport.'

'Can't. I've always wanted a Pulitzer. I think this'll get me one.'

'Pay attention. Let's assume for the moment that you're right.' Buchanan held up a hand. 'I'm not admitting anything, but let's assume. The people you'd be up against don't play by any rules you know about or can imagine. What you might get instead of a Pulitzer is a coffin.'

'Is that a threat?'

'It's a hypothetical, well-intentioned warning.'

'Don't you think I've protected myself? I've made copies of my research. They're with five different people I trust.'

'Sure. Like your lawyer. Your editor. Your best friend.'

'You've got the idea.'

'All predictable,' Buchanan said. 'A good black-bag man could find where the research was hidden. But it's probable that no one would even bother looking. If your research was so wonderful, the story would have been published by now. You've got nothing but suspicions. All deniable. But if anybody feels threatened by that research, they might not know or care that you've left copies of the research with other people. They might just decide to get rid of you.'

'What about you?' Holly asked.

'You mean, would *I* think about getting rid of you? Don't be absurd. I've got nothing to do with any of this. I was only giving advice.'

'No. What about *you*? Don't *you* feel threatened?'

'Why on earth would I . . . ?'

'If you were on a sanctioned mission, you wouldn't be traveling under your own identity, not while you carried a passport under someone else's name. Your controllers won't like that. After what happened to you in Mexico and Florida, they'll think they've got a loose cannon. They'll wonder what in God's name you were doing with a gun and a passport that you weren't supposed to have. You've got other problems besides me. You and your controllers must have established a schedule for staying in touch. If you've missed any part of that schedule, they'll be very nervous. You'd better call them.'

'If I'm who you say I am, do you honestly think I'd call them in front of you? On an unsecured phone?'

'You'd better do something. They'll be getting impatient. And don't forget this – the longer you're out of touch with

327

them, the more suspicious they'll be about your ability to do your work.'

Buchanan felt pressure behind his ears.

'I see your appetite improved,' the doctor said, coming back into the room.

'Yeah, I'm almost done with my salad.'

'Well, finish your Jell-O, Mr Lang.'

'Buchanan.'

'Then take your walk to the bathroom. After that, I might be encouraged enough to think about releasing you.'

5

Wearing sneakers, jeans, and a short-sleeved, blue shirt that he'd asked Holly to buy for him to replace his blood-stained shoes and clothing, Buchanan felt trapped in the wheelchair that a nurse insisted he keep sitting in while she wheeled him from the elevator and through the hospital's crowded lobby to the main doors.

'I told you I can walk,' Buchanan said.

'Until you trip and fall and sue the hospital. Once you're out those doors, you're on your own. Meanwhile you're my responsibility.'

Through the doors, amid the din of street noises, Buchanan was forced to raise a hand to his eyes, the bright sun making him squint painfully.

The nurse helped him out of the wheelchair. 'You said somebody was going to meet you?'

'Right,' Buchanan lied. He hadn't seen Holly for quite a while and had no idea what had happened to her. Normally he would have felt reprieved from being pestered by her questions, but at the moment, he felt nervous. Worried. The gun and the passport. *He had to get them back.* 'I'll just sit over on that bench. My friend ought to be here any minute.'

'Enjoy your day, Mr Buchanan.'

'Lang.'

The nurse looked strangely at him as she took the chair away.

He wondered why.

Then he realized.

His skin prickled.

What's happening to me?

The moment the nurse disappeared into the hospital, he stood. The reason he hadn't wanted to be brought down in a wheelchair was that he didn't want to leave the hospital before he had a chance to get to a pay phone.

Managing not to waver, he re-entered the lobby and crossed toward a bank of telephones. His hand shook as he put coins in a slot. Thirty seconds later, he was talking to a contact officer.

'Where have you been?' the gruff voice demanded.

Keeping his own voice low, relieved that the phone on either side of him wasn't being used, taking care that he wouldn't be overheard, Buchanan answered, 'I've been in a hospital.'

'*What?*'

'A guy tried to mug me,' he lied. 'I didn't see him coming. I got stabbed from behind.'

'Good God. When you didn't show up at the various rendezvous points this morning, we got worried. We've had a team waiting in case you're in trouble.'

'I got lucky. The wound isn't serious. Mostly they kept me in the hospital for observation. With so many nurses coming in and out, I didn't want to risk phoning this number, especially since the hospital would automatically have a record of the number. This is the first chance I've had to call in.'

'You had us sweating, buddy.'

'The emergency's over. If you had people at the rendezvous

329

sites, that means you had something you wanted me to know about. What is it?'

'About the woman reporter you met on the train . . . Is your phone secure?'

'Yes.'

'Then this is the message. Continue your furlough. Don't worry about the reporter. We're taking steps to guarantee that she's discouraged.'

Buchanan's grip tightened on the phone.

'Check in at the rendezvous sites on schedule. We'll let you know if anything else develops.'

'Roger,' Buchanan said. Swallowing dryly, he set down the phone.

But he didn't turn away. He just kept staring at the phone.

Taking steps to guarantee that she's discouraged? What the hell did that mean?

It wasn't considered professional for him to ask to have a deliberately vague term clarified. His superiors never said more or less than they intended to. Their use of language, even when vague, was precise. 'Discouraged' could mean anything from seeing that Holly lost her job . . . to attempting to bribe her . . . to discrediting her research . . . to trying to scare her off, or . . .

Buchanan didn't want to consider the possibility that Holly might be the target of ultimate discouragement.

No, he thought. They wouldn't assassinate a reporter, especially one from *The Washington Post*. That would enflame the story rather than smother it.

But reporters *have* been assassinated from time to time, he thought.

And it wouldn't look like an assassination.

As he turned from the phone, he touched the bandage on his right side, the stitches under it.

Holly – wearing a brown, paisley dress that enhanced the

red of her hair and the green of her eyes — was in a chair twenty feet away.

Buchanan didn't show his surprise.

She came over. 'Checking in with your superiors?'

'Calling another friend.'

'Why don't I believe you?'

'Listen, I want you to stay away from me,' Buchanan said.

'And end a beautiful relationship? Now you're trying to hurt my feelings.'

'I'm serious. You don't want to be around me. You don't want to attract attention.'

'What are you talking about?'

Buchanan crossed the lobby, heading toward the hospital's gift shop.

'Hey, you're not going to get rid of me that easily.' Her high heels made muffled sounds on the lobby's carpet.

'I'm trying to do you a favor,' Buchanan said. 'Take the strong hint. Stay clear of me.'

In the gift shop, he paid for a box of super-strength Tylenol. His head wouldn't stop aching. He'd been tempted to ask the doctor to give him a prescription for something to stop the pain, but he'd known that the doctor would have been troubled enough as a consequence to want to keep him in the hospital longer. The only consolation was that the headache distracted Buchanan from the pain in his side.

Holly followed him from the gift shop. 'I've got a few things to show you.'

'Not interested.' He stopped at a water fountain, swallowed three Tylenol, wiped water from his mouth, and headed toward the exit. 'What *does* interest me is getting my belongings back.'

'Not a chance.'

'Holly.' He pivoted sharply toward her. 'Let's pretend I *am* the kind of person you think I am. What do you suppose would

331

happen to you if I told the people I work for that you had a false passport with my picture in it? How long do you think you'd get to walk around with it?'

Her emerald eyes became more intense. 'Then you didn't tell them.'

'What do you mean?'

'I wondered if you would. I doubted it. You don't want your superiors knowing you had that passport – and lost it. What did you want it for in the first place?'

'Isn't it obvious? So I'd be able to leave the country.'

'Is there something wrong with using your own passport?'

'Yeah.' Buchanan scanned the people near the exit. 'I don't have one. I've never been issued one.'

They reached the noisy street. Again the glare of the sun stabbed his eyes. 'Where's your friend? Ted. The guy on the train. It's my guess you don't go anywhere without him.'

'He's nearby, looking out for my welfare.'

'Using a two-way radio? I won't keep talking with you unless you prove to me this conversation isn't being recorded.'

She opened her purse. 'See? No radio.'

'And my belongings aren't in there, either. Where'd you put them?'

'They're safe.'

In front of the hospital, a man and a woman got out of a taxi. Buchanan hurried to get in after they walked toward the lobby.

Holly scrambled in after him.

'This isn't a good idea,' Buchanan said.

'Where to?' the driver asked.

'Holiday Inn-Crowne Plaza.'

As the taxi pulled from the curb, Buchanan turned to Holly. 'This is not the game you seem to think it is. I want my belongings returned to me. Give me the key to your room. I'll get what's mine, pack your things, and check you out.'

'What makes you think I want to leave the hotel?'

Buchanan leaned close. 'Because you do not want to be seen near me. Don't ask me to be more explicit. This is as plain as I can make it.'

'You're trying to scare me again.'

'You bet, and lady, I hope I'm succeeding.'

6

'Close enough,' Buchanan told the driver.

'But we got another two blocks, suh.'

'This is fine. Take the lady for a drive. Be back on this corner in thirty minutes.' Buchanan stared at Holly. 'The key to your room.' He held out his hand.

'You're really serious.'

'The key.'

Holly gave it to him. 'Lighten up. Your belongings, as you call them, aren't in my room anyhow.'

'Where are they? In *Ted's* room?'

She didn't answer.

'I mean it, Holly. Neither you nor your friend wants to be found with my things in their possession. It wouldn't be healthy for you.'

Her face changed color slightly, paling, as if he were finally getting his message across. 'What do I get in return?'

'Peace of mind.'

'Not good enough,' Holly said.

'What do you want?'

'The chance to keep talking with you.'

'I told you I'll be back in half an hour.'

Holly studied him. 'Yes. All right. They're in Ted's room.'

'I don't suppose you have a key to it.'

'As a matter of fact.' She handed it to him. 'In case I needed to get your belongings and Ted wasn't around.'

'You just did a very smart thing.' Buchanan got out of the taxi.

'Be careful when you pack my underwear. They're expensive. I don't want the lace torn.'

Buchanan stared at her and shut the door.

7

The two blocks felt like two miles. Along the way, Buchanan unwrapped the bandage from around his skull and shoved it into a trash can. By the time he reached the Crowne Plaza, he felt lightheaded, his brow filmed with sweat. His only consolation was that as he entered the softly lit lobby, escaping the hammer force of the sun, his headache felt slightly less severe.

Rather than go directly up to Ted's room and then Holly's, he decided he'd first better learn if he had any messages. He checked the lobby to see if anybody showed any interest in him.

There. In the corner on the right next to the entrance. A man, late twenties, in a blue seersucker suit. Sitting in a lounge chair. Reading a newspaper.

The well-built man was in a perfect position to see people coming into the lobby before they had a chance to notice him. The man's glance in Buchanan's direction was ever so brief but ever so intense. And like a good operative, the man gave no sign that he recognized Buchanan.

So they staked out the hotel, Buchanan thought.

But it isn't me they're looking for.

No. The person they're looking for is Holly.

Showing no indication that the man in the corner interested him, Buchanan went over to the front desk, waited while a clerk took care of a guest, and then stepped forward.

'Yes, sir?'

'Are there any messages for me? My room number's . . .'

The clerk smiled, waiting.

'My room number's . . .'

'Yes?'

' . . . Damn.' Buchanan's pulse raced. 'I can't remember what it is. I left my key here at the desk when I went out, so I'm afraid I can't tell you the number on it.'

'No problem, sir. All you have to do is give me your name. The computer will match the name with your room number.'

'Victor Grant,' Buchanan said automatically.

The clerk tapped some letters on a computer keyboard, hummed, and studied the screen. He began to frown. 'Sorry, sir. No one by that name is registered here.'

'Victor Grant. There must be.'

'No, sir.'

Jesus, Buchanan suddenly realized. 'Brendan Buchanan. I gave you the wrong name.'

'Wrong name? What do you mean, sir?'

'I'm an actor. We're making a movie in town. My character's name is Victor Grant. I'm so used to responding to that name I . . . If I'm into my character *that* much, I ought to win an Oscar.'

'What kind of movie is it, sir?'

'Did you ever see *The Big Easy?*'

'Of course, sir. I see all the films made in New Orleans.'

'Well, this is the sequel.'

'I have it now, sir. Brendan Buchanan. Room twelve-fourteen. And no, there aren't any messages.'

'Could I have my key, please?'

The clerk complied. 'What other movies have you been in?'

'None. Until now, I've worked on the stage. This is my big break. Thanks.'

Buchanan walked toward the elevator. He pressed the button

and gazed straight ahead, waiting for the doors to open, certain that the clerk was staring toward him. Don't look back. Don't look back.

Victor Grant? You're losing it, buddy. When you left the hospital, you made the same mistake. You told the nurse you were . . .

No. That was a *different* mistake. You told the nurse you were *Peter Lang*. Now you say you're . . .

You can't even keep the names consistent.

His head ached. It wouldn't stop aching.

The doors at last opened. Inside, alone, as the elevator rose, Buchanan sagged against a wall, wiping sweat from his forehead, wondering if he were going to be sick.

Can't. I have to keep moving.

He had no intention of going to his room. The only reason he'd lied and told the clerk that he'd left his key at the desk before going out was that he needed an explanation for his not being able to say what his room number was. What had really happened to his key was that it had fallen out of his jacket while it was being removed from him after he was wounded. He was so preoccupied that he truly couldn't recall the number of his room. The lapse scared him.

Two floors above his own, he got off the elevator and used the key that Holly had given him to open Ted's door. It took him less than five minutes to find the gun and Victor Grant's passport where Ted had hidden them under the mattress.

Victor Grant. Buchanan stared at the photograph in the passport. He was tempted to tear the document to pieces and burn it in the sink. That would solve one problem. There'd be one less piece of evidence linking him to a past identity. But what he'd told Holly was true. He'd hung on to the passport in case he needed to get out of the country. And the way things were developing, he might still have a need to do that.

Victor Grant.

Peter Lang.

Brendan Buchanan.

Pick one, damn it. Be consistent.

What are you here for?

Juana.

Where was she last night? Why did somebody stab me? Was somebody trying to stop me from helping . . . ?

Pay attention. What are you going to do?

Hell, who am I going to be?

Holly. He still had to deal with . . .

He looked in a closet and found a brown sport coat that Ted had left. Although Ted had broader shoulders, the garment fit Buchanan better than he expected. He shoved the passport into one of its pockets and the gun behind his belt at the spine, making sure that the jacket covered it. When he left the room, no one noticed.

Now for Holly's room.

It was two doors down, and as Buchanan approached it, he kept thinking about the man in the seersucker suit in the lobby. If they staked out the hotel, isn't it logical that they'd put someone in Holly's room to grab her when she came in? Maybe I ought to stay out of this. Maybe the smart thing to do is keep walking toward the elevator. Let Holly check herself out of the hotel, or let Ted do it for her. Now that I've got the gun and the passport, why should I care about . . . ?

Buchanan slowed, thinking, The longer Holly waits, the greater the odds that someone *will* be in her room when she comes back.

So what? That still isn't your concern. If something happened to her, it'd be one less thing for you to worry about. One less . . .

He pivoted, knocked on her door, announced, 'Hotel housekeeping,' knocked again, and unlocked the door.

The room was empty. It took him even less time to pack her

things than it had for him to find the gun and the passport in Ted's room. He took care only when he put her underwear into her suitcase. What Holly had said was true. It was expensive, and it did have lace. He liked the feel of it.

She would have been required to leave a credit card number when she checked in. He found an early-check-out form on the counter beside the television, filled it out, and left it on the bed, pleased that she hadn't brought much luggage as he carried the two bags down the fire stairs and out a service exit, all the while thinking of the lace on the underwear he'd packed. It had been a long time since he'd felt intimate with a woman. Not had sex with but felt intimate with. As long as six years ago.

And Juana.

8

Exertion, combined with the glaring sun, squeezed sweat from him. The stitches in his right side, the tenderness of his wound, required him to carry one bag in his left hand, the other wedged under his left arm. Exhaust fumes from passing cars aggravated his headache and made him nauseous.

At least, the taxi was waiting as promised. When the driver saw that Buchanan was having trouble with the bags, he got out. 'Here, let me help, suh.'

'Thanks.' Buchanan gave him ten dollars, then turned his attention toward Holly and someone else sitting in the back seat.

He frowned.

While the driver carried the bags toward the trunk, Buchanan got in the back seat next to a square-faced man who was built like a college football player gone to seed. 'Well, Ted, long time no see.'

From the opposite side, Holly leaned forward. 'I figured he might as well travel with us instead of keep following in another taxi. We picked him up while you were gone.'

'Ted, I appreciate the help with the bags.'

'What help?'

'My point exactly.'

'You should have asked.'

'I shouldn't have needed to.'

'Just like *you* didn't feel you needed to ask my permission to go into my room. I don't like the idea of someone rummaging through my stuff. And that's my jacket you're wearing.'

'Very observant. So what do you think, Ted? Doesn't fit me too bad, huh? Here's your key back.'

Holly tried to distract them. 'Did you find what you were looking for?'

'Right away. Ted isn't very good at this.'

'Hey,' Ted said.

'All right, I can understand why you're angry,' Holly said. 'When I saw you coming, *I* should have helped with the bags. I knew you'd just been released from the hospital. I'd have gotten out to help a friend.'

'Well, this guy isn't a friend,' Ted said.

'Ted,' Holly said in warning. She turned to Buchanan. 'Look, I'm sorry. Remember, it was your idea to check me out of that hotel. If you want to go in for melodramatic gestures to try to scare me, you can't expect me to cooperate in the tactic.'

'Then maybe we ought to go back so I can introduce you to the fellow waiting for you in the lobby.'

Holly's eyes narrowed. 'That's a joke, right?'

'He didn't look like he had a sense of humor.'

'This is all bullshit,' Ted said.

'Right, Ted. Bullshit,' Buchanan said. 'I don't care what happens to you, but until Holly and I get some issues settled, I'd just as soon she stayed in good health.'

'Quit trying to scare me,' Holly said.

'Where to, suh?' The driver had gotten back into the taxi and was waiting.

'That errand wore me out.' Buchanan rubbed his sweaty forehead. 'I came here to enjoy the sights. I think a river cruise would relax me. Why don't you take us over to Toulouse Street Wharf? It's almost two-thirty. Maybe we've still got time to get on the *Natchez*.'

As the taxi pulled into traffic, Holly said, 'For a man who claims he was never in New Orleans before, you certainly know a lot about the tourist attractions.'

'I studied them in a guide book.'

'Right. When was that? When you were unconscious?'

9

As its calliope whistled 'Way Down South in Dixie,' the colorfully trimmed paddlewheeler eased away from the wharf and began its tour along the Mississippi. Hundreds of passengers crowded the railings on the three decks, enjoying the breeze off the river, studying the docks they passed, warehouses, a refinery, a War-of-1812 battlefield, and a pre-Civil-War plantation mansion.

While the passengers seemed to enjoy the strength of the sun, Buchanan's eyes were still sufficiently sensitive that he stayed in the shadow of a canopy at the stern. Holly sat next to him. Since most passengers were at the railing, there was little chance that their conversation would be overheard.

Holly shook her head. 'I don't understand. Why a steamboat cruise?'

'Process of elimination.' Buchanan sipped from one of the Cokes that he'd bought for Holly and himself when they came aboard. 'I need time to think, a *place* to think.' After swallowing two more Tylenol, he shut his eyes and tilted his head back.

'You should have stayed in the hospital longer.'

'Too much to do,' Buchanan said.

'Yeah, like watching the muddy Mississippi. Ted didn't like it when you made him stay behind with my bags.'

'You said you wanted to talk. The thing is, I don't want company while we're doing it. This way, he can't follow. And pretty soon we'll be far enough that those two-way radios you mentioned won't be able to communicate with each other. By the way, where are you hiding yours? In your purse? Or maybe . . . ?' Buchanan gestured toward the open neckline of her dress.

'Okay.' Sounding discouraged, she reached inside her dress, unhooked a tiny microphone and miniature transmitter from her bra strap, and handed it to him. 'You win.'

'Too easy.' Buchanan shut the transmitter off, feeling her body heat on the metal. 'How do I know there aren't others?'

'There's only one way to be sure. But if I wouldn't let you search me in your train compartment, I'm certainly not . . .'

'What did you want to talk about?'

'For starters, who do you think tried to kill you? And please, don't give me that guff about a walk-by, random stabbing.'

'Who? Yes, that's the big question, isn't it?'

'One of them.'

The issue had been preoccupying Buchanan since he'd wakened in the hospital. If he addressed it out loud, he'd also be distracting Holly from his role in Scotch and Soda. 'Open your purse.'

She did.

He didn't find a tape recorder.

'Okay, I'll tell you this much. I wasn't lying when I said I came to New Orleans to see a friend.' He debated whether to continue. 'A woman.' He thought about it. 'None of this is

341

classified. I don't see any reason not to . . . It's been six years since I heard from her, but recently she sent me a message that she needed help. My friend is very independent. She's definitely not the type to ask for help unless the problem's serious.'

'This friend, was she your lover?'

'Are you a reporter or a gossip columnist? I ought to tell you that's none of your business.'

Holly waited.

Buchanan bit his lower lip. 'Could have been my lover. Maybe should have been. Maybe we'd have gotten married.'

'But . . . ?'

'Well, let's just say I was having some problems figuring out who I was.' Past tense? Buchanan asked himself. At the moment . . . 'Anyway, I was supposed to meet her last night, eleven o'clock, at Café du Monde. She didn't show up. But that guy did with his knife.' Leaning back in the deck chair, feeling his handgun behind his belt and against his spine, Buchanan suddenly realized that the only reason his wound hadn't been more serious was that the gun had deflected the blade. As he appreciated how close he'd come to dying, he started sweating again.

In contrast, his mouth became dry. Disturbed, he swallowed more Coke. 'Is it a coincidence that the man happened to show up and pick me as a victim while I was looking for my friend, who happened *not* to show up? I try to keep an open mind. I do my best to have healthy skepticism. But the coincidence is too hard to ignore. I have to believe that my friend and the man with the knife are connected.'

'And he was trying to stop you from helping your friend?'

'Unless you can think of a better explanation.'

'Well, one part of your logic troubles me. Since she didn't show up, you wouldn't have been able to know what she wanted, so it wouldn't have been necessary for you to be stopped.'

'Or maybe—'

Buchanan's heartbeat matched the thump-thump-thump of the paddlewheeler's engine.

'Maybe someone was afraid that when she didn't show up, I'd become so upset that I wouldn't stop until I found out where she was and why she needed me.' Buchanan's voice hardened. 'If so, they were right to be afraid. Because that's exactly what's going to happen.'

10

The steamboat rounded a bend.

'At the hospital, you said you had something for me to look at.'

Holly straightened. 'Yes. But you wouldn't give me a chance.'

'Because I wanted my belongings back. Now I've got them.' Despite his headache, Buchanan mustered strength. He had to keep playing the game. 'I'll look at whatever it is you want me to see. Anything it takes to settle your suspicions. I need to help my friend. But I can't do it if you keep interfering. Ask the rest of your questions. I want to be done with this.'

Holly opened her purse, studied him as if doubtful about something, then pulled three folded newspaper clippings from an envelope.

Puzzled, Buchanan took them and glanced at the date at the top of the first one. 'Six days ago.' He frowned.

He frowned harder when he saw that the story was datelined Fort Lauderdale.

EXPLOSION KILLS THREE

FT LAUDERDALE – *A powerful explosion shortly*

before midnight last night destroyed a car in the parking lot of Paul's-on-the-River restaurant, killing its occupant, identified by a remnant of his driver's license as Robert Bailey, 48, a native of Oklahoma. The explosion also killed two customers leaving the restaurant. Numerous other cars were destroyed or damaged. Charred fragments of a substantial amount of money found at the scene prompted authorities to theorize that the explosion may have been the consequence of a recent, escalating war among drug smugglers.

His heart now pounding faster than the thump-thump-thump of the paddlewheeler's engine, Buchanan lowered the clipping and turned to Holly. No matter what, he couldn't let her detect his reaction. His head ached even more fiercely. 'All those people killed. A terrible thing. But what does this have to do with me? Why did you show it to—?'

'Are you denying that you knew Robert Bailey?'

'I don't know anything about this.'

And that was certainly the truth, Buchanan thought.

He strained to look calm as dismay flooded through him.

Holly squinted. 'Mostly he called himself "Big Bob" Bailey. Maybe that refreshes your memory.'

'Never heard of him.'

'Jesus, Buchanan, you are making me impatient. You and I both know he bumped into you in Cancun. I was *there*.'

Buchanan felt as if he'd been jolted by electricity.

'I was watching from a corner of the restaurant,' Holly said. 'Club Internacional. I saw it happen. That's when all your trouble started. When Bailey stumbled into one of your lives.'

Buchanan came close to revealing his shock.

'Those two drug dealers became suspicious when Bailey

called you "Crawford" instead of "Potter". They took you down to the beach. Bailey went after you. He told me later that he interrupted a fight. You shot the two drug dealers and their bodyguard. Then you ran along the beach into the night, and the police arrested Bailey, thinking he was responsible.'

'You're not a reporter. You're a fiction writer. When was this supposed to have happened? I've never been to Cancun. I've never . . .'

'Not as Brendan Buchanan you haven't, but you sure as hell were there as Ed Potter. I told you I was in the *restaurant*. I saw it happen!'

How? Buchanan thought. *How did she get there? How did she know I'd be there? How did—?*

'You saw me taking pictures of you outside the jail in Mérida,' Holly said. 'Of course, that doesn't prove you knew Bailey, even though I saw the police bring him in to see you at the jail. But later, near Pier 66 in Fort Lauderdale, you saw me photographing you and Bailey talking to each other in the channel. I already showed you the pictures I took.'

'You showed me photographs, yes, and I admit one of the men did have some resemblance to me. He *wasn't* me,' Buchanan said. 'But he did resemble me. The thing is, I've never been to Fort Lauderdale, either.'

'I believe you.'

'Good.'

'As Brendan Buchanan. But as Victor Grant, you very definitely have been to Fort Lauderdale.'

Buchanan shook his head as if disappointed that she persisted in her delusion. 'And one of the men in the photographs you showed me is Bailey?'

Holly looked exasperated.

'I don't get it,' Buchanan said. 'Did you know this Bailey? Were you following him? Why are you so interested in . . . ?'

'I wasn't following him. I was following *you*. And why am I interested in Bailey? *Because he worked for me.*'

Buchanan felt his stomach cramp.

Two children ran by, clampering down stairs to a lower deck. Their mother hurried after them, shouting for them to be careful. Buchanan was grateful for the interruption.

'Oh, he wasn't working for me when he bumped into you in Cancun,' Holly said. 'But I made sure he was working for me after that. What's the word you people use? I recruited him. A thousand dollars, plus expenses. Bailey was really down on his luck. He didn't think twice before he accepted.'

'That's still a lot of money for a reporter to be able . . .'

'Big story. Big expense account.'

'Your editor won't be happy when your story doesn't hang together.'

Holly looked furious. 'Are you on another planet? Do they teach you people to deny everything no matter how obviously true it is? Or are you so out of touch with reality that you can honestly convince yourself that none of this happened, because it happened to someone else, even though that someone else is you?'

'I'm sorry about what happened to Bailey,' Buchanan said. 'I meant what I told you. It's a terrible thing. But you have to believe me – I had nothing to do with it.'

Who did, though? Buchanan thought. How did—?

The answer was suddenly obvious.

They had plastic explosive in the walls of the cooler I gave him. When he got in his car, he must have opened the cooler to look at the money and . . .

That's all he had to do to detonate it. Open the cooler.

But what if he'd opened the cooler while I was with him?

'What's the matter?' Holly asked.

' . . . Excuse me?'

'You turned pale again.'

'It's just this headache.'

346

'I thought perhaps it was because you'd glanced at the second clipping.'

'Second . . . ?' Buchanan lowered his gaze toward the second of the three clippings in his hand.

MURDER-SUICIDE

FT LAUDERDALE – *Responding to a telephone call from a frightened neighbor, police early this morning investigated gunshots at 233 Glade Street in Plantation and discovered the bodies of Jack Doyle (34) and his wife, Cindy (30), both dead from bullet wounds. It is believed that Mr Doyle, despondent about his wife's cancer, shot her with a .38-caliber, snub-nosed revolver while she slept in their bedroom, then used the same weapon on himself.*

Buchanan reread the story. He read it again. And then again. He stopped being aware of the motion of the steamboat, of its thumping engines, of the splashing paddlewheel. He was oblivious to the crowd at the railings, the trees along the river, and the humid breeze on his face.

He just kept staring at the piece of newspaper.

'I'm sorry,' Holly said.

Buchanan took a while before he realized that she had said something. He didn't respond. He just kept staring at the clipping.

'Are you going to deny you knew him? If you're tempted to, don't,' Holly said. 'I took photographs of you and Jack Doyle together, just as I did of you and Bailey.'

'No,' Buchanan said. With tremendous effort, he lowered the clipping and turned, concentrating on Holly. His mind reeled from the implications of what he'd just read. For the first time in his long career as a deep-cover operative, he did the unthinkable.

347

He broke cover. 'No.' His unsteadiness, combined with the motion of the steamboat, made him feel as if he were about to fall from his chair. 'I won't deny it. I knew Jack Doyle. And Cindy. His wife. I knew her, too. I liked her. I liked her a lot.'

Holly's eyes became more intense. 'Earlier, you were talking about coincidence, about how sometimes it has to be more than that, like your friend not showing up at Café du Monde but a man showing up to stab you. Well, that's how I feel about what you just read. You knew Bailey. He's dead. You also knew Jack Doyle and his wife. They're dead, too. And it all happened on the same night. What's . . . ? I just realized something.'

'What?'

'The look on your face. You're a hell of a good actor. But nobody's *that* good. You really didn't know anything about Bailey and the Doyles being killed.'

'That's right.' Buchanan's throat was so dry that he could hardly speak. 'I *didn't* know.' His eyes ached as he reached for his Coke can and swallowed.

For an instant, he stubbornly suspected that he'd been tricked, that these newspaper clippings weren't genuine. But he couldn't maintain his suspicion. By hindsight, what had happened to Bailey and the Doyles felt so operationally right, so tactically logical that he didn't doubt the truth of what had happened. He'd been tricked, yes. But not by Holly.

'Or maybe there is a coincidence,' she said. 'Maybe Jack Doyle did just happen to kill his wife the same night Bailey died in an explosion.'

'No.'

'You think it was a double murder?'

'It can't be anything else.'

'How can you be sure?'

Buchanan pointed at the newspaper article. ' " . . . shot her with a thirty-eight-caliber, snub-nosed revolver." No way.'

'I'm missing something. What's wrong with using a thirty-eight-caliber . . . ?'

'Snub-nosed revolver? This,' Buchanan said. 'Jack Doyle was an ex-SEAL.'

'Yes. A Navy commando. I still don't . . .'

'Weapons were his business. To him, a thirty-eight-caliber, snub-nosed revolver was a toy. Oh, he did have one in his house. For his wife. In case Cindy had to protect herself while he was away. But Jack had a lot of other handguns there as well, and for him, the weapon of choice was a nine-millimeter, semiautomatic pistol. He loved his wife so much that I envied him. Her cancer was serious. It wasn't responding to treatment. She was probably going to die from it. But it hadn't yet reached the point where her suffering was greater than her dignity could bear. When that day came, though, if Jack decided . . . with Cindy's permission . . . to free her from her suffering, he sure as hell would not have used a weapon that he didn't respect.'

'Your world's a whole lot different than mine,' Holly said. 'Ethics about which weapon to use for a murder-suicide.'

'Jack wasn't any nut. Don't think for a minute that . . .'

'No,' Holly said. 'That isn't what I meant. What I did mean was exactly what I said. Your world's very different than mine. No value judgment intended. My father was an attorney. He didn't approve of guns. The first time I saw one, aside from in movies, was when I was reporting on a gang war in Los Angeles.'

Buchanan waited.

'So,' Holly said. 'If it was a double murder, who did it? The same people who killed Bob Bailey?' Holly asked.

Temples throbbing, Buchanan sipped his Coke, then stared at the label. 'I had nothing to do with any of it.'

'You still haven't read the third newspaper clipping.'

Buchanan lowered his gaze, apprehensive about what he would see.

349

ACCIDENT VICTIM STILL NOT FOUND

FT LAUDERDALE — Divers continue to search for the body of Victor Grant, the presumed occupant of a rental car that last night crashed through a barrier and sank within a section of the Intracoastal Waterway south of Oakland Park Boulevard. Numerous empty beer cans in the vehicle lead authorities to suspect that Grant was intoxicated when he lost control of his car. A suitcase and a windbreaker containing a wallet with Victor Grant's identification were recovered from the car. Police suspect that the victim's body floated from an open window and became wedged between one of the numerous docks in the area.

Buchanan felt as if he plummeted and would never hit bottom.

'The reason I didn't kick and fight when you wanted your Victor Grant passport back,' Holly said, 'is I've taken photographs of every page. I've got photographs of you in Fort Lauderdale. I can link you to Bailey. I can link you to Doyle. This newspaper article proves that somebody named Victor Grant was in Fort Lauderdale and disappeared the same night Bailey and Doyle were killed. You said my editor would be disappointed because my story didn't hang together. Well, it seems to me that the story hangs together beautifully.'

Buchanan felt a jolt as if he *had* struck bottom.

'I'm waiting for a reaction,' Holly said. 'What do you think about my story now?'

'The real question is, What do I feel?'

'I don't understand.'

Buchanan rubbed his aching forehead. 'Why does ambition make people so stupid? Holly, the answer to the question, What do I feel?, is I feel terrified. And so should you. I'm a fortune teller, did you know that? I really have a gift for predicting the future. And given what you've just told me, I can guarantee that if you go any farther with this story, you'll be dead by this time tomorrow.'

Holly blinked.

'And,' Buchanan said, his voice hoarse, 'if I don't give the best performance of my life, so will I. Because the same people who killed Jack Doyle and Bob Bailey will make sure of it. Is that plain enough for you? Is that what you wanted me to say? That would make a good quote. It's too bad you can't use it.'

'Of course I can use it. I don't care if you deny it or—'

'You're not listening!'

Buchanan spoke so loudly that several people standing along the railing of the steamboat swung and stared at him.

He leaned close to Holly, his voice a raw whisper. 'In your world, people are afraid of getting caught breaking the law. In *my* world, people make their own laws. If they feel threatened, they'll shoot you or drop you from a building or hit you with a car and then have a good dinner, feeling justified because they've protected themselves. You will absolutely, positively, be dead by this time tomorrow if we don't find a way to convince my people that you are not a threat to them. If *I* feel terrified, you're a fool if *you* don't.'

Holly studied him. 'This is another act. You're just trying to trick me into backing off.'

'I give up,' Buchanan said. 'Look out for yourself. Believe me, I intend to look after *my*self.'

11

Buchanan walked into the Crowne Plaza's lobby. While he waited for the elevator, he glanced around and noticed that the man in the seersucker suit had been replaced by a man in a jogging suit. He, too, was pretending to read a newspaper.

After all, there wasn't much to do that seemed natural while sitting in a lobby and watching for someone. This second man was a clone of the first: late twenties, well-built, short hair, intense eyes.

Military, Buchanan thought. The same as the first man. Civilian intelligence agencies had access to surveillance personnel of various appearances. In contrast, military surveillance operatives tended to resemble each other in terms of sex, age, body type, and hairstyle. More, they had a collected, disciplined, single-minded look about them.

Holly, he thought. They're still looking for her.

He got into the elevator, went up to the twelfth floor, and took out his key. Holly's revelations on the steamboat, combined with the pain in his side and the ache in his head, had exhausted him. Fear had exerted its effect. He needed to rest. He needed to think.

When he opened the door . . .

Three people were waiting for him. They sat in plain view, obviously not wanting to startle him and provoke a defensive reaction.

Buchanan knew each of them.

Alan, the portly man who a few days before had been Buchanan's debriefer at the apartment complex in Alexandria, Virginia, sat on the bed. In Alexandria, he'd habitually worn a brown-checkered sport coat. Here, his sport coat was again checkered, but this time the color was blue.

On the sofa, a muscular man – Major Putnam – sat next to an attractive, blonde woman – Captain Weller. Buchanan had met them on the yacht in Fort Lauderdale. Each wore civilian clothes: in the major's case, a beige suit; in the captain's, a white, silk blouse and blue skirt, both of which were tight and were no doubt intended to attract public attention away from the two men.

Buchanan glanced toward the right, toward the bathroom, to

352

make sure that no one else was waiting. The closet was open, unoccupied.

He took his key from the lock, closed the door, locked it, and walked toward them. Late-afternoon sunlight filled the room.

'Captain,' the major said.

Buchanan nodded and stopped five feet away.

'You don't seem surprised to see us,' the major said.

'At the Farm, I had an Agency trainer who used to say, "The only thing you ought to expect is the *un*expected." '

'Good advice,' the woman said. 'I understand a mugger stabbed you.'

'That I certainly *didn't* expect.'

'How's the wound?'

'Healing. Where's the colonel?'

'I'm afraid he couldn't make it,' Alan said.

'Well, I hope you haven't been waiting long.'

'Aren't you curious how we got in?'

Buchanan shook his head.

'Captain' – the major looked displeased – 'you were seen in the hotel lobby at one-forty-five. Supposedly you were going to your room. Now you've come back, but no one saw you leave in the interim. Where have you been for the past three hours?'

'Taking a steamboat ride.'

'Is that before or after you checked the reporter out of her room?'

'So you know about that? After. In fact, the reporter went with me on the steamboat ride.'

'*What?*' Captain Weller leaned forward, her blouse tightening against her breasts. 'Weren't you informed that we were looking for her?'

'I was told you intended to discourage her. But she kept hounding me, so I decided to do some discouraging of my own. I scared her away from the story.'

'You . . . ? How did . . . ?'

353

'By using her arguments against her. She showed me these.'
Buchanan pulled the newspaper clippings from a jacket pocket
and set them on the coffee table. As the major grabbed and
read them, Buchanan continued, 'About Bob Bailey dying in
an explosion. About Jack Doyle killing his wife and then
himself. Alan' – Buchanan turned to him – 'you left out a few
things when you told me what happened in Fort Lauderdale
after I disappeared from there. Did you know about Bailey and
the Doyles?'

'It didn't seem necessary to tell you.'

'Why?'

'The less you knew about Bailey, the better. If you were
interrogated, your confusion would be genuine. As far as the
Doyles are concerned, well, we didn't want to burden you with
the knowledge that a man you had worked with had killed his
wife and then himself shortly after you left them.'

'I convinced the reporter that what happened to the Doyles
was actually a double murder.'

'You what? Oh, Jesus,' the major said.

'I asked her to consider a hypothetical situation,' Buchanan
said. 'If Bailey was killed because he was blackmailing me, and
if the Doyles were killed because they knew too much and
might be linked to me when the divers couldn't find my body,
what did that say about the further lengths certain people
would go in order to keep Scotch and Soda – she mentioned it
first – a secret? I don't think there's anything paler than a
redhead when the blood drains from her face. She suddenly
realized how much danger she was in, that writing a front-page
story wasn't worth losing her life for. She's in a taxi on her way
to the airport, where she'll catch the first plane back to
Washington. There won't be any story.'

'You actually believe her?'

'Yes. I told her I'd kill her if she ever wrote the story. I
believe her because I know *she* believed *me*.'

The room became silent.

'She's out of it,' Buchanan said.

The major and the captain looked at each other.

Come on, Buchanan thought. *Take the bait.*

'We'd want all the photographs and the negatives.' Alan shifted his weight on the bed.

The major and the captain turned in his direction, as if they hadn't been aware of him until now, surprised that he'd spoken.

'That's not a problem,' Buchanan said. 'She's already agreed to give them to me. As a gesture of good faith' — he pulled some photographs from an inside pocket of his jacket — 'these are the ones she had on her.'

'You honestly think she'll stick to her bargain?' the major asked.

'She's too afraid not to.'

'You certainly must have been convincing.'

'That's my specialty. Being convincing.'

But have I convinced *you?* Buchanan thought.

'She could make copies of the photographs and create new negatives,' the major said.

'Or hold some back,' the captain added. 'The only way to be sure is to get rid of her.'

Alan squirmed again, then stood from the bed. 'I don't know.' He shook his head, troubled. 'Would that really solve anything? Even if she were terminated, we'd still have to worry that she had copies of her research hidden with friends. There'd be no guarantee that we could find it all. Fear can be an effective motivator. If Buchanan thinks he managed to neutralize the situation without the need for violence, maybe we ought to go along with his suggestion. After all, no matter how much we made her death seem like an accident, there would still be repercussions. Suspicions. Killing her might cause more problems than it solves.'

Inwardly Buchanan sighed. I've got him. He's agreeing. Now all I have to do is . . .

The major frowned. 'I'll have to talk with the colonel.'

'Of course,' Alan said sarcastically. 'The colonel has the final word. The Agency doesn't count in this. Only you people.'

The major responded flatly, 'We have as much authority as you. The colonel has to be consulted.'

Shit, Buchanan thought. I only got a postponement.

He quickly tried another approach.

'I have something else for you to tell the colonel.'

'Oh?'

' . . . I'm resigning.'

They stared.

'You were already planning to take me out of operations and use me as an instructor. Why do things halfway? Accept my resignation. If I'm out of the military, I won't be a threat to you.'

'Threat? What do you mean?' the major asked.

'I think that's obvious enough. The real problem here is me.'

The room seemed to shrink.

'I repeat, Captain. What do you mean?' the major asked.

'We wouldn't be in this situation if it hadn't been for what happened to me in Cancun and then in Fort Lauderdale. The operation wouldn't be threatened if I were out of the way. That wasn't a mugger who stabbed me last night. It was someone working for you.'

'That's absurd,' the captain said.

'Using a street weapon so it wouldn't look like a professional hit. Because of the knife, I didn't figure it out right away. No reputable assassin would ever use a blade. Compared to a bullet, it's too uncertain. For that matter, too risky, because you have to get right next to your target. But then I realized that what looked like an amateur killing would be a perfect cover for a professional one. Bailey, the Doyles, me. We'd all be dead. A suspicious coincidence, yes. But each of the deaths would be explainable without any need to drag in a conspiracy

356

theory. And if the reporter had a car accident . . .'

Everyone became very still.

'All because of the photographs,' Buchanan said. 'The ones that showed you, Major, and you, Captain, and more important, the colonel with me on the yacht in Fort Lauderdale. For me to be exposed wasn't a problem. You knew I'd never implicate anyone. But for you two to have your photograph on the front page of *The Washington Post*, and in particular for the colonel to be on the front page, that's a different matter. That would lead to the exposure of all sorts of things. You don't have to worry about any of that now. The reporter isn't going to write her story. And even if I hadn't scared her off, the photograph of me with the two of you and the colonel doesn't mean anything if I can't be linked to Scotch and Soda. You don't need to go to the trouble of killing me. I'll do you all a favor and disappear.'

The group seemed frozen.

Finally the major cleared his throat, then looked awkwardly at the woman and finally Alan.

'Come on,' Buchanan said. 'We've got a problem. Let's discuss it.'

'Captain, do you realize what you sound like?' the major asked, uneasy.

'Direct.'

'Try "paranoid".'

'Fine,' Buchanan said. 'Nobody ordered my termination. We'll pretend it was the random act of violence you wanted it to resemble. However you want to play this. It makes no difference to me. Just so you get the point. I'll disappear. That way you've got double protection. Holly McCoy won't write her story. I won't be around to be questioned.'

'To hear you talk like this.' The major frowned. 'I'm glad we did decide to observe you. You've definitely been undercover too long.'

'I think you'd better get some rest,' Alan said. 'You've just been released from the hospital. You've got to be tired.'

The woman added, 'Being stabbed. Injuring your head again. In your place, I'd—'

'How'd you know I hurt my head again? I didn't mention it to anybody.'

'I just assumed.'

'Or you heard it from the man you sent to kill me.'

'Captain, you're obviously distressed. I want you — in fact, I order you — to stay in this room, to try to relax and get some sleep. We'll be back here at nine hundred hours tomorrow morning to continue this conversation. Hopefully, you'll feel less disturbed by then.'

'I honestly don't blame you for trying to protect the mission,' Buchanan said. 'But let's not talk around the problem. Get it out in the open. Now that I've given you a better solution, you don't have to kill me.'

Alan studied Buchanan with concern, then followed the major and the captain somberly out the door.

12

Buchanan's legs felt unsteady as he crossed the room and secured the lock. The strain of the conversation had intensified his headache. He shoved three Tylenol caplets into his mouth and went into the bathroom to drink a glass of water. His mouth was so dry that he drank a second glass. His reflection in the mirror showed dark patches under his eyes. I'm losing it, he thought.

In the bedroom, he awkwardly closed the draperies. His side hurt when he stretched out on the bed. The darkness was soothing.

But his mind wouldn't stop working.

Did I pull it off?

Were they convinced?

He didn't understand why he was so concerned about Holly's safety. He'd met her only a few days ago. In theory, they were antagonists. Most of his troubles were due to her interference. In fact, it could be argued that Jack and Cindy Doyle were dead because of her. But the truth was that Holly McCoy hadn't killed the Doyles. His own people had. Just as they'd killed Bailey. And they'd have killed me, too, if I'd been around when Bailey opened the cooler to look at his money.

So they waited for another chance to get me, a way that wouldn't look suspicious even to a reporter.

Holly McCoy.

Have I grown attracted to her? he wondered. There had been a time when he could have justified anything − the murder of a reporter, anything − for the sake of maintaining an operation's security. Now . . .

Yes?

Maybe I don't care about the operation any longer. Or maybe . . .

What?

Maybe I'm becoming a human being.

Yeah, but *which* human being?

13

'One more time,' Alan said. 'I want to be sure about this.' He drove a rented Pontiac from the Crowne Plaza hotel. Major Putnam sat next to him. Captain Weller leaned forward from the back. 'Do any of you know anything about an order to terminate Buchanan?'

'Absolutely not,' the captain said.

'I received no such instructions,' the major said.

'And *I* didn't,' Alan said.

'What's this about Jack and Cindy Doyle?' the major asked. 'I thought their deaths were a murder-suicide.'

'So did I,' the captain said. 'Buchanan caught me totally off-balance when he said they were a double murder. I don't know anything about orders to terminate *them*.'

'Who tried to kill Buchanan?' Alan asked.

'An attempted mugging is still the most logical explanation,' the major said.

'In the middle of a crowd outside a restaurant?' Alan gripped the steering wheel harder. 'A pickpocket, sure. But I never heard of a pickpocket who drew attention to himself by stabbing the guy he was trying to lift a wallet from.'

'How about some weirdo who gets his kicks out of stabbing people in public?' the captain asked.

'That makes more sense.' Alan turned onto Canal Street, squinting at headlights. 'It's crazy, but it makes sense.'

'The thing is, Buchanan believes *we* did it,' the major said. 'And that's just as crazy.'

'But do you think he *really* believes it?' the captain asked. 'He's an actor. He says things for effect. He can be very convincing.'

'He certainly convinced me,' Alan said.

'But why would he lie?' the major asked.

'To create a smoke screen. To confuse us and divert our attention from the reporter.'

'Why?' the major repeated.

'Buchanan might be right that killing the reporter would cause more problems than it solves,' Alan said. 'If she's genuinely intimidated and she doesn't write the story, we've accomplished our purpose.'

'If. I keep hearing a lot of ifs.'

'I agree with Buchanan,' the captain said. 'I think it's better if we do nothing at this point and just sweat it out.'

'On that score, the colonel's opinion is the only one that matters,' the major said.

They drove in silence.

'We still haven't . . .' Alan scowled at the bright lights of traffic.

'What?' the captain asked.

'*Did* someone try to kill Buchanan? Not a whacko but a professional following orders. And if we didn't give the orders, who did?'

14

The rule was, if a contact didn't show up at an agreed place on schedule and if no arrangements had been made for an alternate time and place for a meeting, you returned to the rendezvous site twenty-four hours later. With luck, whatever had prevented the contact from coming to the meeting would no longer be an obstacle. But if the contact didn't show up the second time . . .

Buchanan didn't want to think about it. He made his way through the French Quarter. Crowded, narrow streets. Dixieland. The blues. Dancing on the sidewalk. Commotion. But no costumes. This time, with no masks to hide people's faces, Buchanan would have a much better chance to learn if he was being followed. Last time, he'd been conspicuous because he hadn't been wearing a costume. Now, just one of many people in street clothes, he would have a much better chance of blending with a crowd, slipping down an alley, and evading anyone who did try to follow.

With a sense of déjà vu that made him wince from the memory of when the knife had entered his side, he passed the shadows of Jackson Square, studied Decatur Street, and once more crossed toward Café du Monde. Again, the restaurant was busy, although not as much as on Halloween. To make sure that the crowd didn't prevent him from entering, he'd taken care to arrive early, at ten-fifteen rather than the scheduled time of eleven when he had last been here with Juana six years ago.

He festered with impatience. Never showing it, he waited his turn and was escorted by a waiter past pillars through the noise of the crowd to a seat at a small, circular, white-topped table surrounded by similar, busy tables at the back in a corner. By chance, the table was in exactly the spot he would have chosen to give him an effective view of the entrance.

But he wasn't satisfied. He needed something more, another way to be sure, a further guarantee, and when he saw his chance, he stood to claim a suddenly empty table near the center of the restaurant. It was here, he remembered, that he and Juana had sat six years earlier. Not this same table. He could never be positive of that. But the position was close enough, and when Juana came in, she would have no trouble finding him. Her gaze would scan the congested room, settle on the area that she associated with him, and there he would be, rising, smiling, walking toward her, eager to hold her.

He glanced at his watch. Ten-forty. Soon, he thought. Soon.

His headache made him sick again. When the waiter came to take his order, he asked for the specialty: café au lait and beignets. He also asked for water. That was what he really wanted. Water. The coffee and the beignets were just so he'd be allowed to sit here. The water was so he could swallow more Tylenol.

Soon.

Juana.

'*I love you,*' he had told her. '*I want you to know that you'll always be special to me. I want you to know that I'll always feel close to you. I swear to you. If you ever need help, if you're ever in trouble, all you have to do is ask, and no matter how long it's been,*' *no matter how far away I am, I'll—'*

Buchanan blinked, realizing that the waiter was setting down the water, the coffee, and the beignets. After he swallowed the Tylenol, he was startled when he glanced at his watch. Fifteen minutes had passed like fifteen seconds. It was almost eleven o'clock.

He kept staring toward the entrance.

Here's the postcard I never thought I'd send. I hope you meant your promise. The last time and place. Counting on you. PLEASE.

'Is something wrong, sir?'

'Excuse me?'

'You've been sitting here for half an hour and you haven't touched your coffee or the beignets.'

'Half an hour?'

'Other people would like a chance to sit down.'

'I'm waiting for someone.'

'Even so, other people would like—'

'Bring me another round. Here's ten dollars for your trouble.'

'Thank you, sir.'

Buchanan stared at the entrance.

Midnight.

One o'clock. People frowned toward him, whispering.

By two o'clock, he knew that she wouldn't be coming.

What in God's name had happened to her? She needed his help. Why hadn't she let him prove he loved her?

15

He packed his bag and dropped a signed check-out form on the bed. At three a.m., no one saw him leave the hotel through a service exit. Stepping out of shadows onto Lafayette Street, he hailed a taxi.

'Where to, suh?' The driver looked wary, as if a man carrying a suitcase at three a.m. might be a threat.

'An all-night car-rental agency.'

The driver debated briefly. 'Hop in. It's kinda late to be takin' a trip.'

'Isn't it, though.'

He slumped in the back seat, thinking. It would have been easier to fly to where he needed to go. But he didn't want to wait until morning and catch the first plane to his destination. For one thing, the major, the captain, and Alan might arrive earlier than they'd said they would and intercept him. For another, because he didn't have enough cash to buy an airplane ticket, he'd need to use a credit card. But the only credit card he had was in Brendan Buchanan's name. That would leave a paper trail for the major, the captain, and Alan to follow.

This way, while he'd still have to use a credit card to rent a car, there'd be no record of where he was planning to drive. The paper trail would end right here in New Orleans. And with luck, the major, the captain, and Alan would accept that he'd decided to do what he'd told them and disappear. In a perfect world, they would consider this a reassuring gesture and not a threat. To direct their thinking, he'd written a note about his determination to disappear, had sealed the note in an envelope addressed to Alan, and had left it on the bed in the hotel room beside the signed check-out form.

'Here we are, suh.'

'What?' He roused himself and looked out the taxi's side window, seeing a brightly lit car-rental office next to a gas station.

'If I was you, suh, I'd take it easy drivin'. You look beat.'

'Thanks. I'll be fine.'

But I'd better look more alert when I rent the car, he thought.

He paid the driver and didn't show the effort needed to carry his bag into the office, where the bright lights hurt his eyes.

A weary-looking, spectacled man shoved a rental agreement across the counter. 'I'll need to see your credit card and your driver's license. Initial about the insurance. Sign at the bottom.'

He had to look at the credit card he'd set on the counter to see which name he was using. 'Buchanan. Brendan Buchanan.'

If only this headache would ease off.

Juana.

He had to find Juana.

And there was only one place he could think to start.

16

'It's been taken care of,' Raymond said.

Seated at the rear of the passenger compartment of his private jet, Alistair Drummond peered up from a report he was reading. The fuselage vibrated softly as the jet streaked through the sky. 'Specifics,' he said.

'According to a radio message I just received,' Raymond said, 'last night, the director of Mexico's National Institute of Archaeology and History was killed in a car accident near the National Palace in Mexico City.'

'Tragic,' Drummond said. Despite his age, he didn't show the strain of having flown to a business meeting in Moscow, then to another in Riyadh in Saudi Arabia before his present trans-Atlantic flight back to Mexico's Yucatán peninsula, all within forty-eight hours. 'Do we have evidence that Delgado was responsible?'

'The man Delgado ordered to do it is on our payroll. He'll implicate Delgado if we ask him, provided we guarantee he won't be punished.'

'We?' Drummond asked.

'I meant "you".'

'Your confusion of pronouns troubles me, Raymond. I'd hate to think that you consider me an equal.'

'No, sir, I don't. I won't make the mistake again.'

'Has his successor been chosen?'

Raymond nodded.

'An executive favorable to our cause?'

Raymond nodded again. 'And money will make him more so.'

'Good,' Drummond said, his voice brittle, one of the few signs of his age. 'We no longer need the woman, even if we find her. The leverage she provided against Delgado isn't necessary any longer now that we have another way to put pressure on him. In all probability, Delgado will be Mexico's next president, but not if we reveal his crimes. Let him know we have proof that he ordered the death of the Institute's director, that his political future continues to depend on me.'

'Yes, sir.'

'Then, when he becomes president, I'll have even more influence.'

'All the influence you need.'

'Never,' Drummond corrected him.

'Perhaps then you do need the woman.'

The old man scowled, his wrinkles deepening so much that his true age began to show. 'I almost lost everything because of her. When your operatives find her . . .'

'Yes, sir?'

'Make certain they kill her on sight.'

NINE

1

San Antonio, Texas.

Buchanan arrived by nightfall. He'd driven west on Route 10 from New Orleans to Baton Rouge, past numerous small towns into Texas, toward Beaumont and Houston and finally . . .

His headache, combined with the pain in his side, had forced him to rest several times along the way. At Beaumont, he'd rented a hotel room in mid-morning so that he could shave and shower and sleep for a couple of hours. The hotel clerk had looked puzzled when he checked out at noon. That was no good, attracting attention like that. It wasn't any good, either, that his scarcity of cash forced him to use his credit card to rent the room. Now there was a further paper trail, although by the time Alan, the major, and the captain traced him to the hotel, he'd be long gone, and they still wouldn't know his destination. Sure, if they checked the records of his past assignments, they might guess it, but he'd had a great many assignments in the six years since he'd known Juana, and it would take them quite a while to make the connection between her, New Orleans, and San Antonio. By then, he'd be somewhere else.

He ate take-out food while he drove, hamburgers, french

fries, po'boys, tacos, anything to give him fuel, washing it down with plenty of Coca Cola, relying on the soft drink's calories and caffeine to maintain his energy. Three times, he pulled off the busy highway and napped at a rest stop. He parked the rented Taurus near the toilet facilities so that the noisy coming and going of vehicles and travelers would prevent him from sleeping too deeply, for he knew that if he did truly sleep, he wouldn't waken until the next day.

He had to keep moving. He had to get to San Antonio and begin the urgent process of finding out what had happened to Juana. Why had she failed to meet him? What trouble had caught up to her? Despite his pain and confusion, he had sufficient presence of mind to ask himself if he were overreacting. A promise made six years ago to a woman whom he hadn't seen since then. A plea for help in the form of a cryptic postcard.

Maybe the postcard didn't mean what he thought. Did it make sense for Juana to contact him after so long a time? And why him? Wasn't there anyone else whom she could ask for help?

What made *him* the logical choice?

He didn't have answers. But this much he knew for certain. Something had happened to him.

Something terrifying.

He tried to establish when it had begun. Perhaps when he'd been shot in Cancun, or when he'd injured his head while he made his escape, swimming across the channel. Perhaps when he'd been tortured in Mérida and had struck his head on the concrete floor. Or possibly later when he'd been stabbed and had *again* struck his head.

The more he considered those possibilities, the less he thought that they were the source of his fear, however. No doubt they were contributing factors. But as he analyzed the past weeks, as he replayed his various traumas, one incident disturbed him more than any.

The trauma had not been physical. It had been mental.

It threatened his sense of identity.

Or rather multiple identities. During the past eight years, he had been more than two hundred people. On some days, he had impersonated as many as six different people while attempting to recruit a series of contacts. During the past two weeks, he'd been confused with Jim Crawford and had identified with Peter Lang while he'd impersonated Ed Potter and Victor Grant and Don Colton and . . .

Brendan Buchanan.

That was the trouble. After disposing of Victor Grant, he'd expected to be given yet another identity. But at the Alexandria apartment, Alan had told him that there wouldn't be a new identity, that he was being transferred from field operations, that he would have to be . . .

Himself.

But who the hell was that? He hadn't been Brendan Buchanan for so long that he didn't know who on earth Brendan Buchanan was. On a superficial level, he didn't know such basics as how he liked to dress or what he liked to eat. On the deepest level, he was totally out of touch with himself. He was an actor who'd so immersed himself in his roles that when his roles were taken away from him he became a vacuum.

His profession wasn't only what he did. It defined what he *was*. He was nothing without a role to play, and he realized now how brutally the realization had struck him that he couldn't be Brendan Buchanan for the rest of his life. Thus, to escape being Brendan Buchanan, he would become Peter Lang. He would hunt for the most important person in Peter Lang's world. And possibly in his own world, for the more he thought about it, the more he wondered how positively his life would have changed if he had stayed with Juana.

I *liked* Peter Lang, he thought.

And Peter Lang had been in love with Juana.

2

Past Houston, he used a pay phone outside a truck stop. It fascinated and disturbed him that the only person he cared about from Brendan Buchanan's world was Holly McCoy. He'd known her only a few days. She was a threat to him. And yet he had an irresistible urge to protect her, to insure that she escaped the danger she had created for herself because she'd investigated him. He thought he had convinced the major, the captain, and Alan of her intention not to pursue the story. There was a strong chance they would leave her alone. But what about the colonel? Would the colonel agree with their recommendation?

Buchanan hadn't been lying when he'd told them that Holly had flown back to Washington, and he hadn't been lying when he'd said that he'd made Holly frightened enough not to pursue the story. Still he had to reinforce her resolve. Assuming that her phones would be tapped, he'd told her that he would use the name Mike Hamilton if he needed to leave a message on her answering machine or with someone at *The Washington Post*. As it happened, she was at the newspaper when he called there.

'How are you?'

'Wondering if I made a mistake,' Holly answered.

'It wasn't a mistake, believe me.'

'What about your negotiations? Did they work?'

'I don't know yet'

'Oh.'

'Yes. Oh. Did you send them what you promised?'

' . . . Not yet.'

'Do it.'

'It's just that . . . It's such good material. I hate to . . .'

'Do it,' Buchanan repeated. 'Don't make them angry.'

'But giving up the story makes me feel like a coward.'

'There were plenty of times when I did things rather than think of myself as a coward. Now those things don't seem worth it. I have to keep on the move. The best advice I can give you is . . .' He wanted to say something reassuring but couldn't think of anything. 'Stop worrying about bravery and cowardice. Follow your common sense.'

He hung up, left the pay phone, got quickly into the rented Taurus, and returned to the busy highway, squinting from the painful sunlight that now was low in the west ahead of him. Even the Ray-Bans he'd bought at noon in Beaumont didn't keep the sun's glare from feeling as if a red-hot spike had been driven through each eye and into his skull.

Follow your common sense?

You're good at giving advice. You don't seem to want to take it, though.

3

Shortly after nine p.m., he drove from the low, grassy, often wooded, rolling plains of eastern Texas and entered the lights of San Antonio. Six years ago, when he'd been researching the character of Peter Lang, he'd spent several weeks here so he wouldn't be ignorant about his fictional character's home town. He'd done the usual touristy things like visiting the Alamo (its name was a Spanish word, he learned, which meant 'cottonwood tree') as well as the restored Spanish Governor's Palace, the San Jose Mission, and *La Villita* or The Little Village, a reconstructed section of the original, eighteenth-century Spanish settlement. He spent a lot of time at Riverwalk, the Spanish-motif shopping area along the landscaped banks of the San Antonio River.

But he'd also spent a lot of time in the suburbs, in one of which – Castle Hills – Juana's parents had lived. Juana had used a cover name so that an enemy could not have found out who her parents were and gone to San Antonio to question them about her supposed husband. There'd been no need and in fact it would have been disruptive for Buchanan to meet her parents. He knew where they lived, however, and he headed straight toward their home, making a few mistakes in direction but surprising himself by how much he remembered from his previous visit there.

Juana's parents had a two-story brick and shingled house fronted by a well-tended lawn that had sheltering oak trees. When Buchanan parked the rented Taurus at the curb, he saw that lights were on in what he gathered was the living room. He got out of the car, locked it, and studied his reflection that a street light cast on the driver's side window. His rugged face looked tired, but after he combed his hair and straightened his clothes, he at least appeared neat and respectable. He was still wearing the brown sport coat that he had taken from Ted's room back in New Orleans. Slightly too large for him although not unbecomingly so, it had the advantage of concealing the handgun that he'd tucked behind his belt at his spine before he got out of the Taurus.

He glanced both ways along the street, out of habit watching the shadows for any sign that the house was under surveillance. If Juana were in trouble as the postcard and her failure to meet him suggested, if she were on the run – which would explain why she hadn't shown up at Café du Monde – there was a possibility that her enemies would watch her parents in case she contacted them in person or telephoned and inadvertently revealed where she was. The Juana who'd been in the military would never have let anyone know the name and location of her parents. But a great deal could have happened in the intervening six years. She might have foolishly trusted someone enough to give that person information that was now being used against her, although being foolish had never been one of Juana's characteristics.

Except maybe for falling in love with Peter Lang.

The street suggested no threat. There weren't any vehicles parked on this block. No one was loitering at a corner, pretending to wait for a bus. Lights in the other houses revealed what appeared to be normal family activity. Someone might have been hiding in bushes, of course, although in this neighborhood where everybody seemed to take pride, a prowler on long-term surveillance wouldn't be able to hide easily, especially from the German shepherd that a man was walking on a leash along the opposite sidewalk. Still, that was assuming the man with the dog was not himself on surveillance.

Buchanan took just a few seconds to register all this. From someone else's point of view, he would have seemed merely a visitor who'd paused to comb his hair before walking up to the house. The night was mild, with the fallen-leaf fragrance of autumn. As he stopped on the brick porch and pushed a button, he heard not only the doorbell but the muted sound of a laughtrack on a television sitcom. Then he heard footsteps on a hardwood floor, and a shadow appeared at the window of the front door.

A light came on above him. He saw an Hispanic woman — in her late fifties, with shoulder-length, black hair and an appealing oval face — peer out at him. Her intense, dark eyes suggested intelligence and perception. They reminded him of Juana, although he didn't know for sure that this woman was Juana's mother. He had never met her parents. There was no name on the mailbox or beneath the doorbell. Juana's parents might have moved during the past six years. They might even have died. When he arrived in San Antonio, Buchanan had been tempted to check a phone book to see if they still lived at this address, but by then he was so anxious to reach the house that he hadn't wanted to waste even a minute. He would know soon enough, he'd told himself.

· An amateur might have phoned from New Orleans, and if he managed to contact Juana's parents, that amateur might have tried to elicit information from them about whether Juana was in trouble. If so, he would have failed, or the information he received would have been suspect. Most people were gullible, but even a fool tended to hold back when confronted by personal questions from a stranger using a telephone, no matter how good that stranger's cover story was. A telephone was a lazy operative's way of doing research. Whenever possible, face-to-face contact was the best method of obtaining information, and when the military had transferred Buchanan for training at the CIA's Farm in Virginia, Buchanan had quickly acquired a reputation as being skilled at, what was called in the trade, elicitation. His instructor's favorite assignment had been to send his students into various local bars during Happy Hour. The students were to strike up conversations with strangers, and in the course of an hour, they had to gain the trust of those strangers to such a degree that each stranger would reveal the day, month, and year of his birth as well as his social-security number. Experience had proved to the instructor that such personal information was almost impossible to learn in a first-time encounter. How could you invent a casual question that would prompt someone you'd never met to blurt out his social-security number? More than likely, your question would result in suspicion rather than information. All of the students in the class had failed. Except for Buchanan.

The Hispanic woman unlocked the door and opened it, although she didn't release the security chain. Speaking through the five-inch gap in the door, she looked puzzled. 'Yes?'

'*Señora Mendez?*'

'*Si.*'

'*Perdone*. I know it's late. My name's Jeff Walker, and I'm a friend of your daughter.' Buchanan used the Spanish he'd learned at the Defense Language Institute in Monterey, California when he'd been preparing for his mission into Mexico. 'I haven't seen her in several years, and I don't know where she lives. I'm visiting town for a couple of days, and . . . Well, I hoped that she was around. Can you tell me where to find her?'

Juana's mother studied him with suspicion. However, her suspicion seemed tempered by an appreciation that he was using Spanish. Juana had told him that while her parents were bilingual, they much preferred speaking Spanish and they felt slighted when whites whom they knew spoke Spanish forced them to speak English.

'*Conoce a mi hija?*'

'*Si,*' Buchanan continued in Spanish. 'I know your Juana. We were in the military together. I knew her when she was stationed here at Fort Sam Houston.' That had been one of Juana's cover assignments. Although she had worked with Army Intelligence and was affiliated with Special Forces at Fort Bragg, her ostensible assignment had been with the 5th Army headquarters here in San Antonio. 'We got along real well. Several times we went out together. I guess you could say . . . Well, we were close. I wish I'd kept in touch with her. But I was overseas for a while and . . . I'd sure like the chance to say hello.'

Juana's mother continued to study him with suspicion. Buchanan was certain that if he hadn't been speaking Spanish and if he hadn't mentioned Fort Sam Houston, she wouldn't have listened to him this long. He needed something else to establish his credibility. 'Do you still have that dog? The golden retriever? What was his name? Pepe. Yeah. Juana sure loved that dog. When she wasn't talking about baseball, she was talking about him. Said she liked to take Pepe out for a run along the river when she wasn't on duty.'

The mother's suspicion began to dissolve. 'No.'

'I beg your pardon?'

'The dog. Pepe. He died last year.'

'Oh. I'm sorry to hear that, Señora Mendez. Losing a pet can be like . . . Juana must have taken it hard.'

'You say your name is Jeff Walker?'

'That's right.' Buchanan made sure to stand straight, as if his character retained habits of bearing from when he'd been in the military.

'I don't remember her mentioning you.'

'Well, six years is a while ago. Juana certainly told me a lot about you. The way I hear it, you make the best chicken fajitas in town.'

The mother smiled slightly. 'Those were always Juana's favorite.' The smile became a frown. 'I would remember you if I'd met you before. Why didn't Juana ever bring you to the house?'

I've got another 'why', Buchanan thought with growing concern. Why so many questions? What the hell's going on?

4

Two blocks along the street, a small, gray van was parked in front of a house with a FOR SALE sign on the lawn. The van had been parked there for several days, but the neighbors had not been troubled by its presence. On the contrary, they felt reassured because the van's driver, a private detective, had paid a visit to everyone who lived on that block and had explained that recent vandalism in the neighborhood had prompted a security firm with clients in the area to dispatch a guard to keep a watch on several homes in the district, particularly the vacant house, which seemed a natural target for vandals. If the neighbors had telephoned the number on the business card that they were given, a professional-sounding secretary would have told them that what the private detective had said was correct. The man did work for the firm. What the secretary would not have said, of course, was that she was speaking from an almost empty, one-room, downtown office, and that the security firm had not existed two weeks ago.

The private detective's name was Duncan Bradley. He was twenty-eight years old. Tall and slim, he almost always wore sneakers and a cotton sweat suit as if he expected at any moment to play basketball, his favorite leisure activity. He preferred so informal an outfit because it was comfortable during lengthy stakeouts, and this particular stakeout – already lengthy – promised to become even longer.

He and his partner were working twelve-hour shifts, which meant that the van, the windows of which were shielded so that no one could see in, had to be equipped with cooking facilities (a microwave) and toilet facilities (a porta-potty). The cramped working conditions also meant that the van had needed to be customized in order to comfortably accommodate Duncan Bradley's six-foot-eight-inch frame. Thus all the seats had been removed from the back and replaced by an extra-long mattress clamped to a plank and tilted upward on a fifteen-degree angle so that Duncan, who constantly lay upon it, didn't need to strain his neck by his persistent need to keep looking up.

What he looked at was the monitor for a miniature television camera that projected from the van's roof and was hidden by the cowling of a fake air-vent. This camera, a version of the type used in assault helicopters, had considerable magnification ability so that it was able to show the license plate of a car parked two blocks farther along the street, a blue Ford Taurus with Louisiana license plates. This camera also had state-of-the-art, night-vision capability, and thus, although the street was for the most part in shadow, Duncan had no trouble seeing the green-tinted image of a man who got out of the Taurus, combed his hair, glanced at the neighborhood as if admiring it, and then walked toward the house. The man was Caucasian, about five-foot-eleven, in his middle thirties. He was well-built but not dramatically muscular. He was dressed casually, unremarkably. His hair was of moderate length, neither long nor short. His features were rugged but not severe, just as he was good-looking, handsome but not in a way that attracted attention.

'This is November second,' Duncan said into a tape recorder. 'It's nine-thirty at night. I'm still in my surveillance vehicle down the street from the target area. A man just showed up at the house.' Duncan proceeded to describe the car and its driver, including the Louisiana license number. 'He's not too tall, not too short. A little of this, a little of that, not too much of one thing or another. Could be something, could be nothing. I'm monitoring audio surveillance.'

Duncan lowered the tape recorder and turned up the volume on an audio receiver, then adjusted the ear phones he was wearing. The receiver corresponded with several miniature microphone-transmitter units that Duncan had hidden in the phones and light switches of every room in the target house. The units were tapped into the house's electrical system and thus had a permanent source of power. They were programmed to transmit on an FM band that wasn't used in San Antonio, and hence the transmission wouldn't interfere with television or radio reception in the house and possibly make the occupants suspicious.

The day he'd been given this assignment, Duncan had

waited until the targets were both out of the house. They'd made things easy for him by doing so after supper when the neighborhood was dark. Followed by Duncan's partner, the targets had driven to a shopping mall, and if they'd decided to return sooner than anticipated, Duncan's partner had a cellular phone with which he could have transmitted a warning beep to the pager that Duncan wore. Of course, Duncan had not depended on the good fortune that the targets had left the house unattended while it was dark. If necessary, he could have entered the unoccupied house during the daylight by posing as an employee of the lawn-care company that the targets hired to maintain their property. No neighbor would have thought it unusual for a man wearing a lawn-care uniform and carrying an insect-spray cannister the size of a fire extinguisher to check the bushes at the side of the house and then to proceed intently around to the back. Duncan had invaded the house through a patio door, picking its lock in fifteen seconds, installing all the microphones within forty minutes.

In the van, dials on the receiver's console allowed him to adjust the sound level from each transmitter. The equipment also permitted Duncan to record the sound from each transmitter onto separate tapes. He hadn't been doing much recording, however. In the two weeks since he'd had this assignment, he'd heard nothing but what seemed to be normal household conversation. If the occupants were using a private code to communicate secret information, Duncan had detected no indication of it. Phone calls had been the usual neighborhood chit-chat. Dinner talk had mostly been about the husband's extremely successful car-repair business. At night, the couple watched a lot of television. They hadn't had sex as long as Duncan had been listening.

For most of this evening, Duncan had been listening to the laughtrack on a string of TV situation comedies. Now, when he heard the doorbell and the husband telling the wife to answer it, he activated a bank of tape recorders and lowered the volume of the transmitter in the living room, at the same time raising the volume of the transmitter in the front hallway.

Duncan understood Spanish. It was one of the reasons that he'd been assigned to this house, and right from the start of the conversation, he felt charged. Because right from the start, the stranger, who said his name was Jeff Walker, asked about Juana Mendez, and baby, we are in business now, Duncan thought. We are finally getting some action. While he eagerly listened and adjusted dials and made sure that the tape machines were recording every word, he simultaneously pushed a button on his cellular telephone. The number he needed to call had been programmed into the phone.

'You know my daughter?' Mrs Mendez was saying in Spanish.

The man who called himself Jeff Walker was explaining that he'd known Juana in the military, at Fort Sam Houston.

With the cellular phone pressed against his left ear, Duncan heard it buzz.

The man who called himself Jeff Walker was talking about a dog that Juana Mendez had owned. Whoever this guy was, he certainly seemed to know her.

The cellular phone buzzed a second time.

Now Jeff Walker was carrying on about how Juana had bragged about her mother's chicken fajitas.

You're laying it on a bit thick, aren't you, buddy? Duncan thought.

Abruptly someone answered the phone, a smooth male voice absorbing the cellular static. 'Tucker here.'

'This is Bradley. I think we've got ignition.'

380

'Why didn't Juana bring me to the house?' Continuing to use Spanish, Buchanan repeated the question that Juana's mother had asked him. 'You know, I wondered that myself. I think it was because she wasn't sure if you and your husband would approve.'

Buchanan was taking a big chance here, but he had to do something to distract her from her suspicion. Something was wrong, and he didn't know what, but he thought if he put her on the defensive about *one* thing, she might open up about *other* things.

'Why wouldn't we approve?' Juana's mother asked. Her dark eyes flashed with barely controlled indignation. 'Because you're white? That's crazy. Half my husband's employees are white. Many of Juana's high-school friends were white. Juana knows we're not prejudiced.'

'I'm sorry. That isn't what I meant. I didn't intend to insult you. Juana told me – in fact she emphasized – that you didn't have any objection if she dated someone who wasn't Hispanic.'

'Then why wouldn't we have approved of you?' Juana's mother's dark eyes flashed again.

'Because I'm not Catholic.'

' . . . Oh.' The woman's voice dropped.

'Juana said you'd told her many times that was one thing you expected of her . . . that if she got serious about a man, he would have to be a Catholic . . . because you wanted to be certain that your grandchildren would be raised in the Church.'

'Yes.' Juana's mother swallowed. 'That is true. I told her that often. Apparently you do know her well.'

In the background, a man's gruff voice interrupted. 'Anita, who are you talking to? What's taking you so long?'

Juana's mother glanced down the hallway toward the

entrance to the living room. 'Wait here,' she told Buchanan and closed the door.

Feeling exposed, Buchanan heard muffled words.

Juana's mother returned. 'Please, come in.'

She didn't sound happy about the invitation, though, and she didn't *look* happy as she locked the door behind them and escorted Buchanan into the living room.

It was connected via an archway to the kitchen, and immediately Buchanan smelled the lingering fragrance of oil, spices, onions, and peppers from dinner. The room had too much furniture, mostly padded chairs and various wooden tables. A crucifix hung on the wall. A short, heavy-chested, fiftyish man with pitch-black hair and darker eyes than his wife sat in an Easy-Boy recliner. His face was round but craggy. He wore work shoes and a blue coverall that had a patch – MENDEZ MECHANICS. Buchanan remembered that Juana had told him about the six garages her father owned throughout the city. The man was smoking a cigar and holding a bottle of Corona beer.

'Who are you?' It was difficult to hear him because of the laughter from the television.

'As I told your wife, my name is . . .'

'Yes. Jeff Walker. Who *are* you?'

Buchanan frowned. 'I'm sorry. I don't understand.'

Juana's mother fidgeted.

'I'm a friend of your daughter,' Buchanan said.

'So you claim.' The man looked nervous. 'When is her birthday?'

'Why on earth would . . . ?'

'Just answer the question. If you're as good a friend as you say, you'll know when she has her birthday.'

. . .

'Well?'

'As I recall, it's in May. The tenth.' Buchanan remembered

it because six years previously he and Juana had started working together in May. Under the pretense of being husband and wife in New Orleans, they'd made a big deal about her birthday on the tenth.

'Anybody could look that up in a file. Does she have any allergies?'

'Señor Mendez, what's this about? I haven't seen her in several years. It's very hard to remember if . . .'

'That's what I thought.'

'But I recall she had a problem with cilantro. That always surprised me, her being allergic to a herb that's used so often in Hispanic cooking.'

'Birth marks?'

'This is . . .'

'Answer the question.'

'There's a scar on the back of her right leg, up high, near her hip. She said she got it when she was a kid, climbing over a barbed-wire fence. What's next? Are you going to ask me how I saw the scar? I think I made a mistake. I think I shouldn't have come here. I think I should have gone to some of Juana's friends to see if *they* knew where I could find her.'

As Buchanan turned toward the door, Juana's mother said sharply, 'Pedro.'

'Wait,' the father said. 'Please. If you're truly a friend of my daughter, stay.'

Buchanan studied him, then nodded.

'I asked you those question because . . .' Pedro seemed in turmoil. 'You're the fourth friend of Juana to ask where she is in the past two weeks.'

Buchanan didn't show his surprise. 'The fourth . . . ?'

'Is she in trouble?' Anita's voice was taut with anxiety.

'Like you, each of them was white,' Pedro said. 'Each was male. Each hadn't seen her in several years. But unlike you, they didn't have any personal knowledge about her. One of them claimed that he'd served with her at Fort Bragg. But Juana was *never* assigned to Fort Bragg.'

That was wrong, Buchanan knew. Although Juana's cover military assignment had been at Fort Sam Houston, her actual assignment had been through Fort Bragg. But her parents would never have known that because Juana would never have broken cover to tell them. So they naturally thought that the man who claimed to be Juana's friend was lying when he claimed that he'd known Juana at Bragg. Quite the contrary: the man was telling a version of the truth. Whoever he was, he knew Juana's background in detail. But he had made a mistake in assuming that her parents would also know it.

Juana's father continued, 'Another supposed friend claimed that he had known Juana at college here in San Antonio. When I asked which one, he looked confused. He didn't seem to know that she had transferred from Our Lady of the Lake University to St Mary's University. Anyone who knew her well would have known that information.'

Buchanan mentally agreed. Somebody had fucked up and skimmed through her file instead of reading it in detail.

'The third supposed friend,' Pedro said, 'claimed that, like you, he had dated her when they worked together here at Fort Sam Houston, but when we asked why we had never met him since Juana brought most of her boyfriends to see us, he didn't have an explanation. At least, *you* did, just as you actually seem to know personal things about her. So I will ask you again . . . Jeff Walker . . . is our daughter in trouble?'

Juana's mother waited, clutching the sides of her dress.

Buchanan had a difficult, quick decision to make. Pedro was inviting him into their confidence. Or maybe Pedro was offering bait. If Buchanan admitted his true intentions, Pedro might very well suspect that Buchanan was yet another impersonator sent by Juana's enemies to find her.

He decided to take the gamble. 'I think so.'

Pedro exhaled as if he were finally hearing what he wanted, even though the knowledge dismayed him.

'I knew it,' Juana's mother said. 'What kind of trouble? Tell us. We've been worried to death about . . .'

'Anita, please, no talk about death.' Pedro squinted toward Buchanan and repeated the question that his wife had asked. 'What kind of trouble?'

'If I knew, I wouldn't be here,' Buchanan said. 'Last week, I received a message that she needed to see me. The message was vague, as if she didn't want anyone else to read it and figure out what she was telling me. But *I* could figure it out. She desperately needed help. There's a place in New Orleans that was special to us. Without mentioning it, she asked me . . . begged me, really . . . to meet her there at the same time and date we'd last been there. That would have been at eleven p.m. on Halloween. But she didn't show up that night or the night after. Obviously something's wrong. That's why I came here. Because you were the only people I could think of to try to establish contact with her. I figured that you of all people would have some idea what was going on.'

Neither Pedro nor Anita said anything.

Buchanan gave them time.

'No,' Anita said.

Buchanan gave them more time.

'We don't know anything,' Anita said. 'Except that we've been worried because she hasn't been behaving normally.'

'How?'

'We haven't heard from her in nine months. Usually, even when she's on the road, she phones at least once a week. She did say she'd be away for a while. But nine months?'

'What does she do for a living?'

Pedro and Anita looked uncertain.

'You don't know?'

'It's something to do with security,' Pedro said.

'*National* security?'

'Private security. She has her own business here in San Antonio. But that's as much as Juana told us. She never discussed specifics. She said that it wouldn't be fair to her clients. She couldn't violate their confidence.'

Good, Buchanan thought. She stayed a pro.

'All right,' he said, 'so she hasn't been in touch in nine months. And suddenly several men who claim to be old friends of hers show up to ask if you know where they can find her. What else isn't—?'

Abruptly Buchanan noticed that Juana's parents were looking at him differently. Their gaze was harder, more wary, their need to confess their concerns about their daughter now tempered by renewed suspicion about him. The risk he'd taken had finally caught up to him. His remark about the other men who'd come looking for her had prompted Juana's parents to associate him with those men.

But he was troubled by something else. The intensity of his headache had made him temporarily relax his guard. If an enemy were trying to find Juana and if that enemy were impatient enough to send three different men to ask Juana's parents about where she could be found, might not that enemy have gone farther in an effort to learn what the parents knew? Might not that enemy have . . . ?

'Excuse me. May I use your bathroom?'

Pedro's suspicion made him look surly. He nodded grudgingly. 'It's down the hall. The first door on the left.'

'Thank you.'

Buchanan stood, feigning self-consciousness, and went along the hallway. In the bathroom, which was bright, white, and extremely ordered, he locked the door, strained to get some urine from his bladder, flushed the toilet, and turned on the sink to wash his hands.

He left the water running, silently opened the medicine

cabinet, found a nail file, and used it to unscrew the wall plate to the light switch. Taking care not to touch the wires, he unscrewed the switch from its cavity in the wall and pulled it out to study what was behind.

His discovery increased the nausea that his headache caused. A miniature microphone-transmitter was attached to the wires. Because most people felt that a bathroom gave them privacy, that was the room they'd least likely suspect had a bug, hence the first room that Buchanan always checked. And because Mrs Mendez kept this bathroom scrupulously clean, about the only place in the room where she wouldn't find a bug was behind the light switch, a spot favored by professional eavesdroppers. The phones were probably miked as well.

Okay, Buchanan thought. Here we go.

He shut off the water, the sound of which he had hoped would conceal the noise he'd made when he unscrewed the wall plate. Now he unlocked the bathroom door and went back to the living room, where it was obvious that Juana's parents had been whispering about him.

'Pedro, I apologize,' Buchanan said.

'For what?'

'When I was washing my hands in the bathroom, I must have pulled the sink-plug lever too hard. It looks like I broke it. I can't get the sink to drain. I'm sorry. I . . .'

Pedro stood, scowling, and strode toward the bathroom, his chest stuck out, his short legs moving powerfully.

Buchanan got ahead of him in the hallway and put a finger over his own lips to indicate that he wanted Pedro not to say anything. But when Pedro didn't get the message and opened his mouth to ask what was going on, Buchanan had to put his hand firmly over Pedro's mouth and shake his head strongly from side to side, mouthing in Spanish the quiet message, *Shut up*. Pedro looked startled. *The house is bugged*, Buchanan continued mouthing.

387

Pedro didn't seem to understand. He struggled to remove Buchanan's hand from his mouth. Buchanan responded by pressing his left hand against the back of Pedro's head while at the same time he continued to keep his right hand over Pedro's mouth. He forced Pedro into the bathroom and bent his head down so that Pedro could see behind the light switch that Buchanan had pulled from the wall. Pedro owned a string of car-repair shops. He had to be familiar with wiring. Surely Pedro would know enough about other types of wiring to realize that the small gadget behind the light switch shouldn't be there, that the gadget was a miniature microphone-transmitter.

Pedro's eyes widened.

Comprende? Buchanan mouthed.

Pedro nodded forcefully.

Buchanan released his grip on Pedro's head and mouth.

Pedro wiped his mouth, which showed the strong impression of Buchanan's hand, glared at Buchanan, and rattled the plug-lever on the sink. 'There. You see, it was nothing. You merely hadn't pulled the lever far enough. The water's gone now.'

'At least I didn't break it,' Buchanan said.

Pedro had several pens and a note pad in the top pocket of his coveralls. Quickly Buchanan removed the pad and one of the pens. He wrote, *We can't talk in the house. Where and when can we meet? Soon.*

Pedro read the message, frowned, and wrote, *7 a.m. My shop at 1217 Loma Avenue.*

'I do not trust you,' Pedro said abruptly.

'What?' The effect was so convincing that Buchanan took a moment before he realized that Pedro was acting.

'I want you out of my house.'

'But—'

'Get out.' Pedro grabbed Buchanan's arm and tugged him

along the hallway. 'How much plainer can I make it? Out of my house.'

'Pedro!' Anita hurried from the living room into the hallway. 'What are you doing? Maybe he can help us.'

'Out!' Pedro shoved Buchanan toward the front door.

Buchanan pretended to resist. 'Why? I don't understand. What did I do? A couple of minutes ago, we were talking about how to help Juana. Now all of a sudden . . .'

'There is something not right about you,' Pedro said. 'There is something too convenient about you. I think that you are with the other men who came to look for Juana. I think that you are her enemy, not her friend. I think that I should never have spoken to you. Get out. Now. Before I call the police.'

Pedro unlocked the door and yanked it open.

'You've made a mistake,' Buchanan said.

'No, *you* did. And you will make a greater mistake if you ever come near my home again.'

'Damn it, if you don't want my help . . .'

'I want you out!' Pedro shoved Buchanan.

Buchanan lurched outside, feeling exposed by the porch light above him. 'Don't touch me again.'

'Pedro!' Anita said.

'I don't know where my daughter is, but if I did, I would never tell you!' Pedro told Buchanan.

'Then go to hell.'

6

'You'd better get here pronto,' Duncan Bradley said into his cellular phone while he listened to the transmissions from the house. 'Something about the guy who showed up definitely rubbed Mendez against the grain. Mendez thinks the guy's with us. They're yelling at each other. Mendez is kicking him out.'

'Almost there. Just two blocks away,' Duncan's partner said through the cellular phone.

'You might as well be two *miles* away.' Duncan stared at the green, magnified, night-vision image on his closed-circuit television screen. 'I can see the dude coming off the lawn toward his car. He'll be gone before you get here.'

'I told you I'm close. Can you see my headlights?'

Duncan glanced at another screen that showed the murky area behind his van. 'Affirmative.'

'Perfect. When he pulls away, I'll be just another car on the road,' Tucker said. 'He won't think anything when he sees my lights behind him.'

'He's getting in his car,' Duncan emphasized.

'No problem. The license number you gave me.'

'What about it?'

'I accessed the Louisiana motor-vehicles computer. The Taurus belongs to a New Orleans car-rental agency.'

'That doesn't tell us much,' Duncan said.

'There's more. I phoned the agency. Pretended to be a state trooper. Said there'd been an accident. Wanted to know who'd rented the car.'

'And?'

'Brendan Buchanan. That's the name on the rental agreement.'

Tucker's headlights loomed larger on the rearview television screen.

On the frontview screen, two blocks away, the Taurus's lights came on. The car pulled away.

With a flash, Tucker's Jeep Cherokee passed the van. Duncan pivoted his gaze from the night-vision television image and smiled toward the front windshield and the swiftly receding taillights of Tucker's jeep.

'See, I told you,' Tucker said through the cellular phone. 'No sweat. I'm on him. No headlights pulling away from the curb behind him. Nothing to make him suspicious.'

'Brendan Buchanan?' Duncan wondered. 'Who the hell is Brendan Buchanan? And what's his connection with the woman?'

'The head office is checking on him.' Tucker's taillights diminished to red specks as he followed the even more minute specks of the Taurus. 'Meantime, I'll find out where he's staying. We'll pay him a visit. We'll find out all we need to know about Brendan Buchanan.'

7

A microphone-transmitter required something to receive its broadcast. Depending on the strength of the transmitter, the receiver might be as far away as a mile. But practical considerations – static-producing electrical equipment in the area, for example – usually required that the receiver be much closer to the source. As well, it was useful for the person monitoring the reception to maintain visual surveillance on the target area. Thus the odds were, Buchanan concluded, that the receiver was in the neighborhood . . . possibly in a building, although in this respectable, single-family-dwelling area it would have been difficult for a surveillance team to take over a house . . . more likely in a vehicle of some sort. But there weren't any other cars parked on the street in this block. Buchanan had noticed that when he'd arrived, and he checked again as he crossed the lawn toward his rented car.

He turned to glare at Pedro Mendez, who continued to stand on his front porch, scowling at Buchanan.

Damned good, Pedro, Buchanan thought. You missed your calling. You could have been an actor.

Pretending to be furious, Buchanan spun toward his Taurus. As he rounded it to unlock the driver's side, he glanced both ways along the street, and there it was, some kind of vehicle parked two blocks away. He hadn't noticed it before because the vehicle, small down there, was in shadows between widely spaced street lights. The only reason he noticed it now was that the headlights of an approaching car exposed it.

I think it's time to pay somebody a visit, Buchanan thought as he started the Taurus, turned on its lights, and drove away. The headlights of the approaching car came up behind him, aggravating his headache.

Somebody wants to find Juana badly enough that they bug the house. But they still can't be sure Juana didn't get a message to her parents in a way that the microphones couldn't detect, so whoever wants to find Juana becomes impatient and sends somebody around to the house to pretend they know Juana and ask where she is. No success. They send somebody else. Nothing. So they send yet another . . .

Does that make sense? Buchanan wondered. They must have realized that three old friends coming around in two weeks would make Juana's parents suspicious. Then why would—?

Yes, Buchanan thought. If Juana *is* in touch with her parents, whoever is after her wants her to know that her parents are being watched. They want to make Juana nervous about her parents. They want to threaten her by implying a threat against her parents. They hope that'll force her to come out of hiding.

And now that I showed up, now that the surveillance unit knows there's a wild card, they might get nervous enough to stop being patient and have a long, forceful chat with Juana's parents. I have to let Pedro and Anita know they're in danger.

And what about me? Buchanan thought as he steered around a corner. Whoever's after Juana will want to talk to a stranger who suddenly shows up and asks the same questions they did.

Buchanan steered around another corner.

The headlights behind him kept following.

My, my, Buchanan thought.

8

Falls Church, Virginia.

The colonel had chosen a motel on the edge of town, using a pay phone to reserve a room under a pseudonym. At eleven p.m., after he'd used an electronic scanner to make sure that the room was free of microphones, his three associates arrived, their clothes speckled with water from the dank November rain that had greeted them at Washington National Airport following their flight from New Orleans.

All of them looked tired, even Captain Weller who normally exuded sexual vitality. Her blonde hair looked stringy, her blouse wrinkled. She took off her jacket, slumped on the motel room's sofa, and toed off her high-heeled shoes. Major Putnam and Alan had haggard, red cheeks, presumably from fatigue combined with the dehydration that occurs on aircraft and the further dehydrating effect of alcohol.

'Can we get some coffee?' Captain Weller asked.

'Over there,' the colonel said flatly. 'The carafe on the tray beside the phone.' In contrast with his visitors, the colonel looked fit and alert, standing as straight and attentively as ever. He'd shaved and showered before he'd arrived, partly to keep himself fresh, partly to appear more energized than his companions. His clothes, too, were fresh: shined Bally loafers, pressed gray slacks, a starched white shirt, a newly purchased, red-striped tie, and a double-breasted, blue blazer. The effect was to make his tall, trim body suggest the military, even though he did not wear military clothing.

'Oh.' Captain Weller glanced toward the carafe on the tray

393

beside the phone. She and Major Putnam, who slumped on a chair beside the television, did not wear military clothing either. 'Right. I didn't notice it when I came in.'

The colonel's eyes narrowed as if to imply that she had been failing to notice a lot of things.

Alan, the only civilian in the room, loosened his rumpled tie, unbuttoned the top of his wrinkled shirt, and walked over to the coffee, pouring a cup. Everyone in the room looked surprised when he carried the cup over to Captain Weller and then returned to pour another cup, blowing steam from it, sipping. 'What are we doing here? Couldn't this have waited until the morning? I'm dead on my feet, not to mention I've got a wife and kids who haven't seen me in—'

The colonel's flint-and-steel voice interrupted, 'I want a thorough update. No more of your hints and guesses that you don't feel comfortable talking about because you don't trust the security of the phones.'

'Hey,' Alan said, 'if we'd been given portable scramblers, I'd talk on phones all you wanted, but once burned, twice shy, Colonel. In this case, we need extra-tight security.'

'I couldn't agree more.' The colonel stood straighter. Rain pelted against the window, making the dismal room even less agreeable. 'That's why I ordered you to be here right now instead of at home in bed with your wife.'

Alan's expression hardened. 'Ordered, Colonel?'

'Somebody tell me what's going on.' The colonel's voice became more flinty. 'Major, you've been unusually silent so far.'

'A lot of it you already know.' The major rubbed the back of his neck. 'In New Orleans, we went to meet Buchanan at his hotel room. The arrangement was to be there at nine-hundred hours. He didn't respond when we knocked. After we tried several times, we asked a maid to unlock the door. The day before, he'd been released from the hospital. Maybe he'd fainted or something. What we found was his room key, a signed check-out form . . . obviously he didn't want the hotel to start a search for him . . . and this note addressed to Alan.'

The colonel took the note and scanned it.

'So he says he's going to do us a favor by dropping out of sight. That way, he's an invisible man, and the reporter from the *Post* can't verify her story if she pursues it.'

'That seems to be the idea,' the major said.

'And how do you feel about this?' The colonel scowled.

'Hell, I don't know,' the major said. 'This is all out of hand. Everything's so confused. Maybe he's right.'

'Damn it, have you forgotten that you're an officer in the United States Army?'

The major straightened with controlled indignation. 'No, sir, I definitely have not.'

'Then why must I remind you that Captain Buchanan is absent without permission? *A deserter*. Our operatives can't just decide to quit and go off on their own, especially when they know as much as Buchanan does. We'd have chaos, a security nightmare. I can see I haven't been supervising you closely enough. What this assignment requires is more discipline, more—'

It was Alan's turn to interrupt, 'No, what this assignment needs is for *everybody* to remember who's an officer in the United States Army.' He set down his coffee cup with such force that liquid splashed over the side. 'That's where this assignment went wrong in the first place, with military personnel doing work that's supposed to be done by civilians. You've been impersonating civilians so long you don't know the difference.'

'By "civilians," you mean the Agency.'

'Obviously.'

'Well, if the Agency had been doing its job, it wouldn't have needed to call on *us*, would it?' the colonel said. 'During the eighties, your people got so stuck on gadgets and satellites you forgot it took operatives on site to get the truly useful information. So after you screwed up enough times . . . Iran, Iraq, the old USSR . . . even the Soviet collapse caught you by surprise . . . you decided you needed a team of on-line, can-do personnel to pull your asses out of the fire. Us.'

'Not *my* ass,' Alan said. 'I've never been a fan of gadgets. It wasn't my fault that—'

'The truth is,' the colonel said, 'when the Cold War ended, your people realized you'd be out of a job if you didn't find something else to do. But the trouble is, all the jobs that needed to be done, like stomping out Third-World drug lords, required more risks than you wanted to take. So you asked *us* to take the risk. After all, the reason there hasn't been more success against the drug lords is you've been using the top men as informants in exchange for giving them immunity. It's kind of tough to go after people you've been chummy with. So you ask *us* to go after them and do it in such a way that they don't realize *you're* the ones who turned against them.'

'Hey,' Alan said, 'it's not one of *my* people who suddenly thinks he's a free spirit and drops out of sight.'

'Captain Buchanan wouldn't have been able to drop out of sight,' the colonel said, 'if *your* people had kept proper surveillance on the hotel.'

'It wasn't *my* people who were put in charge of watching that hotel,' Alan said. 'If this had been turned over to me . . . This is a military screwup all the way. Soldiers don't have any business doing—'

'That's enough,' the colonel said. 'Your opinion is no longer *required*.'

'But—'

'That is all.' The colonel swung toward the major and the captain, who looked shocked by the sudden argument they'd witnessed. 'What do we do about Buchanan?'

Captain Weller cleared her throat. 'I phoned his credit-card company and claimed that he was my husband, that his card had been stolen. I expected that maybe he'd have bought a plane ticket. I was wrong. The credit-card company told me someone using his name had rented a car in New Orleans.'

'And?' the colonel demanded.

'The next thing, someone using his card rented a motel room in Beaumont, Texas.'

'I'm impressed, Captain. I assume our people are in Beaumont now.'

'Yes. But Buchanan isn't there.'

'Isn't . . . ?'

'It turns out he only stayed a couple of hours. He left at noon.'

'*What*?'

'Obviously he wants to keep on the move,' Captain Weller said.

'To where?'

She shook her head. 'He seems to be heading west. The credit-card company promised to keep me informed.'

'There's only one problem,' Alan said.

They looked at him.

'The next time Buchanan surfaces with that card, the company won't only shut off his credit. It'll send the police after him. That'll be dandy, won't it? To have the police involved.'

'Shit,' Captain Weller said.

'And if you get your hands on him first,' Alan said, 'what are you going to do with him? Put him in solitary confinement? Don't you see how out of control this could get? Why don't you just let the man alone to disappear as he promised?'

Rain pelted against the window.

'Last night, you reported that he was convinced we were trying to assassinate him,' the colonel said.

'Correct.'

'Well, his suspicions are absurd. He's paranoid if he thinks we've turned against him. What does that say about his ability to disappear as he promised? Maybe he'll keep coming back to haunt us. And what about the reporter? She surrendered her research. But did she keep copies? Will she kill the story as she promised?'

'Whatever we decide, let's do it fast,' the major said. 'I've got two dozen undercover personnel in Latin America who expect me to make sure they have backup. Every minute I spend worrying about Buchanan, I run the risk that something else will go wrong. If only Buchanan had cooperated. All he had to do was stick to his cover story and become a trainer. What's wrong with being a trainer?'

'Because that isn't what he is,' Alan said.

They stared at him.

'And I'm not sure Buchanan is who he is, either,' Alan said.

9

The man following Buchanan became less conspicuous as they drove toward downtown San Antonio. When they reached better-lighted streets, Buchanan was able to see that the man used a Jeep Cherokee, gray, a good, unobtrusive color for a surveillance vehicle, especially at night. The man took care to stay back among other cars when he had the chance. It was only the first two minutes that had given him away.

It had been enough.

Buchanan pulled into a gas station, filled the tank, and went into the office to pay. When he came out, he noticed that the Jeep Cherokee was parked down the street from the gas station.

A little farther along the road, Buchanan stopped at a mini-mall and went into a Tex-Mex, quick-service restaurant, where he ate a beef-and-bean burrito and drank a Coke while he carefully glanced out the window toward where the Jeep Cherokee was parked in the shadows at the edge of the mall. Behind the steering wheel, the driver was talking into a car phone.

The spices in the burrito made Buchanan's face warm. Or maybe he was feverish from fatigue. He didn't know. His injured side ached. I've got to get some rest, he thought and swallowed three more Tylenol caplets.

The restaurant had an exit near the rest rooms in back. Buchanan stepped out behind the mini-mall and hurried along a shadowy alley in the direction of where the Jeep Cherokee was parked.

The man behind the steering wheel was too busy talking on the phone and watching the entrance to the restaurant to notice when Buchanan came up behind him on the passenger side. The moment the man – in his late twenties, wearing a Houston Oilers' jacket – set down the phone, Buchanan opened the passenger door, got in, and rammed his pistol into the man's beefy ribs.

The man groaned, his surprise aggravating his pain.

'What's your name?' Buchanan asked.

The man was too afraid to answer.

Buchanan pressed the gun harder against the man's ribs. 'Your *name*.'

'Frank . . . Frank Tucker.'

'Well, let's take a drive, Frank.'

The man seemed paralyzed with shock.

'Drive, Frank, or I'll kill you.' The threat was starkly matter-of-fact.

The man obeyed.

'That's right,' Buchanan said. 'Nice and easy into traffic. Keep both hands on the steering wheel.'

They passed Buchanan's car. He'd parked it along with

several other cars in front of the Tex-Mex restaurant, where it wouldn't be conspicuous until the lot was otherwise empty at closing time.

'What do you want?' The man's voice trembled.

'Well, for starters . . .' Buchanan used his free hand to grope beneath Frank's windbreaker. He found a holster but no weapon. 'Where's the piece, Frank?'

The man's nervous gaze indicated the glove compartment.

Buchanan opened it and found a Smith and Wesson .357 Magnum revolver. 'So where are the others?'

'I don't *have* any others.'

'Maybe, Frank. I'll soon find out. But if you're lying, I'll blow off your right kneecap. You'll be a cripple for the rest of your life, which might be a whole lot shorter than you'd hoped. Turn into this convenience store. Swing around. Go back the way we came.'

'Listen, I don't know what this is about, but I'll give you all the money I have, and—'

'Spare me the line, Frank. Careful. I told you, both hands on the steering wheel.' Buchanan cocked his pistol and shoved it harder against Frank's ribs.

'Come on, man! If I hit a bump, that thing might go off.'

'Then don't hit a bump,' Buchanan said. 'What are you? Official or private?'

'I don't know what you—'

'Who do you work for?'

'I don't work for anybody.'

'Right, Frank. You just decided to amuse yourself by following me.'

'I wasn't following you. I've never seen you before.'

'Of course, Frank. We're just two strangers who bumped into each other and happen to be carrying guns. A coincidence. A sign of the times.' Buchanan studied him. 'You're not a cop. If you were, you'd have been covered by a backup team. You could be with the mob, but an Oilers' jacket and a Jeep Cherokee aren't exactly their style. What are you?'

No answer.

'Frank, I'm getting bored talking to myself. If I find a PI license on you, I'll shoot *both* your kneecaps.' Buchanan reached for the man's wallet.

'All right, all right.' Sweat beaded Frank's trembling upper lip. 'I'm a PI.'

'Finally we're getting to know each other. Tell me, Frank. Where'd you get your training? Come on. Keep up the conversation. Your training. Where did you—?'

'I learned on the job.'

'That's what it looks like. On the job and from movies. Here's a tip. When there isn't much traffic, follow your target from one block over. Stay parallel to him. If you keep the same speed, you'll see him at every intersection. But the odds are, he won't notice you. Only when you *don't* see him do you go over to the street he's on. That's where you made your first mistake – by staying behind me. Your second mistake was failing to lock your doors. It should have been harder for me to get at you. Third mistake: I don't care how uncomfortable it feels on a lengthy stakeout, keep your gun in your holster where you can reach it in a hurry. It's useless in the glove compartment if somebody's climbing into your car and pointing a gun at you.'

The phone rang.

'No, Frank. Keep your hands on the steering wheel.'

The phone rang a second time.

'Whoever it is can wait to talk to you,' Buchanan said. 'In fact, why don't we talk to him in person? Let's go back to Castle Hills.'

On his tilted mattress in the rear of the van, Duncan Bradley kept watch on the television screen that showed the magnified area in front of the Mendez house two blocks away. Simultaneously he listened to his earphones, although the audio transmissions from the target area had stopped thirty minutes ago, shortly after the man who called himself Jeff Walker had been forced from the Mendez house. The wife had argued with the husband about what he had done, about how the stranger might have been able to help find their daughter. The husband had told her to shut up, that the stranger was obviously no different than the other imposters who had asked about Juana. They'd gone to bed in sullen silence.

While he listened, Duncan kept trying to telephone his partner. Twice now, he'd let the phone ring ten times before canceling the attempted call. Tucker's failure to answer troubled him. Granted, there might be a reasonable, non-threatening explanation. Tucker might have followed Jeff Walker into a hotel, for example. But Duncan's unease prompted him to pick up the cellular phone yet again and press the button that would automatically dial Tucker's number.

He never had a chance to press the number, however, because movement attracted his gaze toward the second television and green-tinted, night-vision images of what was going on behind the van. The movement he'd seen was Tucker's Jeep Cherokee stopping behind him. The jeep's headlights went off. Duncan exhaled. Something must have gone wrong with Tucker's car phone. That was why he'd come back to tell him in person what he'd learned about Jeff Walker.

As the monitor showed Tucker getting out of his jeep and approaching the rear door of the van, Duncan raised himself off the mattress, crawled on his hands and knees toward the back, heard Tucker's knock, and opened the door.

'What happened to your phone? I've been trying to—' Duncan's throat clamped shut. His mouth hung open in stunned surprise as he saw a man next to Tucker. The man must have been hiding in the jeep. The man was Jeff Walker.

The man had a gun.

Oh, shit, Duncan thought.

11

The persistent ringing of the doorbell made Pedro Mendez angry.

For a lot of reasons. Worry about his daughter, confusion about Jeff Walker, and apprehension about the microphone in the bathroom's light-switch socket had made him so restless that it seemed he would never get to sleep. What was Jeff Walker going to tell him when they met at the garage tomorrow morning? Tense, Pedro had squirmed beneath the covers until at last, impossibly, mercifully, he'd somehow managed to doze, and now somebody was pushing that damned doorbell.

'Anita, stay in bed,' he ordered as he fumbled to his feet, put on a housecoat and slippers, grabbed a baseball bat from the closet, and stormed downstairs. Through the front door's window, he saw the shadow of a man on the murky porch. By God, if this was someone else looking for his daughter, Pedro intended to make very sure that the man explained what was going on.

But when Pedro turned on the porch light, his determination wavered when he saw that the man was Jeff Walker, who gestured impatiently for Pedro to unlock and open the door.

Pedro obeyed to a certain extent, making sure that when he

inched the door open, he didn't release the security chain. 'What do you—?'

'Hurry. I have to show you something.' Jeff Walker pointed urgently toward the street.

Staring past him toward the darkness, Pedro noticed a small van at the curb. 'What are you doing here at—?'

'Please,' Jeff Walker said. 'It's about Juana. It's important.'

Pedro hesitated. But only for a moment. There was something about Jeff Walker that insisted on being trusted. Compelled, Pedro stifled his misgivings and opened the door.

Jeff Walker was already off the porch, moving quickly toward the van.

Pedro ran to catch up to him. 'What do you want to show me? Whose van is—?'

For the third time, Pedro was interrupted, this time because Jeff Walker opened the back of the van and turned on a flashlight.

Two men . . . naked, their hands tied behind them by their shirt sleeves, their ankles tied by their pant legs, their mouths stuffed with their underwear . . . lay on the floor of the van. They were lashed together by their belts. When the light revealed them, they squirmed.

'I know it's hard to be sure under these conditions,' Jeff Walker said, 'but are these two of the men who came to your house and asked about Juana?'

Pedro took the flashlight and stepped closer, aiming the beam from one face to the other. 'Yes. How did—?'

'They've been watching your house,' Jeff Walker said.

Pedro aimed the flashlight beam toward shelves of electronic equipment along the right side of the van. A television monitor showed a green-tinted, magnified image of the area in front of his house. Several tape recorders were linked to audio receivers. So it wasn't only *one* microphone that had been planted in the house, Pedro thought in dismay. The whole house must be . . . His knees felt weak. The pavement seemed to tilt.

Jeff Walker removed the gag from one of the men. 'Who else was working with you? Where do I find him?'

The man had trouble speaking, his mouth dry from the absorbent cloth that had been taken from his mouth.

Pedro flinched as Jeff Walker shoved a pistol against the man's testicles and asked, 'Who was the third man who came to Pedro's house?'

But as unnerved as Pedro felt, he leaned closer, desperate to learn everything he could.

'Somebody . . . somebody working for us part-time. We only used him one day. He went back to . . .' The man seemed to realize he was saying too much and shut up.

'Back to where?' Jeff Walker asked. When he didn't get an answer, he sighed. 'I don't believe you are taking me seriously.' He shoved the underwear back into the man's mouth, took a pair of pliers from an open tool case, and yanked out a clump of pubic hair.

The man screamed silently, tears welling from his eyes.

Pedro was shocked. At the same time, he was so afraid for Juana that a part of him wanted impatiently to grab the prisoner's head and bang it against the van's floor, anything to get answers.

Jeff Walker pivoted toward the second man, removed the underwear that gagged him, and sounded very reasonable when he said, 'Now I'm sure you wouldn't want that to happen to you. After I plucked every inch of your hair, I'd use some of Pedro's matches to singe the stubble. By the time I was through, your groin would look like the neck on a well-done turkey. But I've never liked the neck. I always . . .' He made a cutting motion as if he had a knife.

The first man continued to thrash in pain.

'Where did your part-time employee go back to?' Jeff Walker

asked. 'Your accent isn't Texan. Where's home base for you?'

Jeff Walker brought the pliers toward the man's groin.

'Philadelphia,' the man blurted.

'You're watching this house to find Juana Mendez. Why?'

Yes, Pedro thought. *Why?*

The man didn't answer.

'Pedro, go get your matches.'

Pedro's angry resolve surprised him. He turned toward the house.

'Wait,' the man blurted. 'I don't know. That's the truth. I really don't. We were told to watch for her, to learn where she was.'

'And if you saw her? If you found out where she was?' Jeff Walker demanded.

Pedro listened intently.

The man gave no response.

'You're disappointing me,' Jeff Walker said. 'You need a reminder.' He leaned toward the first man and used the pliers to yank out more pubic hair.

Pedro suddenly began to appreciate Jeff Walker's tactic, realizing that the pain Jeff Walker inflicted on these men wasn't physical but psychological.

The first man thrashed, his tear-streaked face contorted by another silent scream. Since the two men were lashed together, every time the first man jerked, the second man was jolted.

'Care to try again?' Jeff Walker asked the second man, whose eyes bulged with fear. 'What were you supposed to do if you saw Juana or found out where she was?'

'Phone the people who hired us.'

'Who are they?'

'I don't know.'

'You don't know why they want her. You don't know who they are. It seems to me there's an awful lot you don't know.

And it's making me angry.' Jeff Walker pinched his pliers into the skin of the second man's groin.

'No,' the second man pleaded.

'Who hired you?'

'They used an intermediary. I never had a name.'

'But you know how to get in touch with them.'

'On the phone.'

'What's the number?'

'It's programmed into . . .' The second man pointed his chin toward a cellular telephone on the floor of the van. 'All I had to do was press the recall button, number eight, and send.'

'Do they know I came to the house?'

'Yes.'

'What's your check-in code.'

'Yellow Rose.'

Jeff Walker picked up the phone. 'I hope for your sake that you're telling the truth.' He pressed the three buttons as instructed, placed the phone against his ear, and waited for someone to answer.

It took less than half a ring. Pedro was close enough to the phone to hear a seductive male voice say, 'Brotherly Love Escort Service.'

What Pedro heard next astonished him. Jeff Walker mimicked the second man's voice.

12

'This is Yellow Rose,' Buchanan said into the phone. 'That guy who came to the Mendez house tonight still worries me. Have you got anything more on him?'

The male voice lost its smoothness. 'Just what I told you. His name isn't Jeff Walker. It's Brendan Buchanan. He rented the Taurus in New Orleans, and . . . Wait a minute.

Something's coming in on another line.' The connection was interrupted.

Buchanan waited, disturbed that these people had been able to learn his real name so fast.

The connection abruptly resumed, the voice strained. 'It's a good thing you called. Be careful. Our computer man found out that Brendan Buchanan is a captain in Army Special Operations, an instructor at Fort Bragg.'

Damn it, Buchanan thought.

'So I was right to be worried,' Buchanan said. 'Thanks for the warning. We'll be careful.'

Troubled, Buchanan pressed the END button. Throughout the call, the number he'd contacted had been shown on a display at the top of the phone. Now he took a pad and pencil from the floor of the van, printed the number, tore off the sheet of paper, and put it in a shirt pocket.

He studied the second man, deciding what further questions to ask, when suddenly he heard approaching footsteps. Whirling, he saw Anita Mendez crossing the lawn toward the van. She wore a housecoat. Her face was contorted with worry, puzzlement, and fear.

'Anita,' Pedro said, 'go back in the house.'

'I will not. This is about Juana. I'm sure of it. I want to know what it is.'

As she rounded the back of the van, she stopped abruptly, startled to see the naked, bound men. '*Madre de Dios*.'

'These men can help us find Juana,' Pedro said. 'This is necessary. Go back to the house.'

Anita glared. 'I'm staying.'

Fatigue made Buchanan's headache worsen. 'Does Juana have an office here in town?'

The interruption made Anita and Pedro look at him.

'Yes,' Anita said. 'At her home. Although she is seldom there.'

408

'I don't have time to wait until morning,' Buchanan said. 'Can you take me there now?'

Pedro frowned. 'You think she is at her home? You think she is hurt and . . .'

'No,' Buchanan said. 'But maybe her office records can tell me why someone in Philadelphia wants to find her.'

Anita started toward the house. 'I'll get dressed and take you.'

'We both will,' Pedro said, hurrying after her.

At once Buchanan turned to the second man where he lay bound on the floor of the van. 'If Juana's home is in town, you must have other sentries watching the place.'

The man didn't answer.

'The easy way or the hard way.' Buchanan showed him the pliers.

'Yes, another team,' the man said.

'How many men?'

'Two. The same as here.'

'They alternate shifts?'

'Yes.'

The tactic was flawed, Buchanan knew. Thorough surveillance wasn't possible if only one man at a time watched a target site. Suppose Juana showed up. The spotter would phone for help. But how could the spotter be sure that a team would arrive in time to trap her?

As Buchanan brooded, the shadow of a long object secured horizontally to the van's left wall attracted his attention. He shifted the flashlight's beam to see what it was.

His stomach felt cold. Seeing the object made him realize that the surveillance tactic did make sense. In an efficient, deadly way.

The object on the wall was a sniper's rifle equipped with a state-of-the-art, night-vision, telescopic sight. The intent of the surveillance wasn't to capture Juana. It was to kill her the minute she was spotted.

13

Juana's home was in the hills south of the city, along the western bank of the San Antonio River. They took forty-five minutes to get there, Pedro driving the van while Buchanan sat in back and guarded the captives, Anita following in the Jeep Cherokee. En route, Buchanan used the pliers again, forcing the first man to give him the telephone number that would put him in touch with the sniper who watched Juana's home.

The telephone barely made a noise before a man's gravelly voice answered, 'Yellow Rose Two.'

'It's Frank,' Buchanan said. Trained to mimic voices, he made himself sound like the first man. 'Anything doing?'

'Quiet as hell. No sign of movement here for the past two weeks. I think we're wasting our time.'

'But at least we're being paid to waste it,' Buchanan said. 'I'm going to stay with Duncan and watch the Mendez place. Meantime, I thought I'd better tell you I'm sending a guy out there in my jeep. That's how you'll know he belongs. He's going to pick the front lock and go in to check a few things we're beginning to think we missed, especially some stuff in her files.'

'I'm not sure that's a good idea. If she's watching the house, debating whether to go in, she'll get spooked if she sees anybody.'

'I agree. The thing is, it's not like I have a choice. This wasn't *my* idea. These are orders.'

'Fucking typical,' the sniper said. 'They pay us to do a job, but they won't let us do it properly.'

'Just let the guy I'm sending do *his* job when he shows up,' Buchanan said.

'No sweat. Be seeing you.'

Sooner than you expect, Buchanan thought as he broke the connection.

14

A little after one in the morning, Pedro warned Buchanan that they were about a mile from Juana's home.

'Close enough. Stop right here,' Buchanan said.

After Anita pulled up behind them, he got out of the van, told Anita to wait with Pedro, and drove Tucker's Jeep Cherokee over a murky rise, proceeding the rest of the way along a winding, partially wooded road. His headlights revealed mist drifting in from the river. They also showed new streets and the start of construction on houses for a new subdivision.

Juana won't like that.

What you mean is, you pray to God that she's still alive so she'll be *able* not to like it.

Pedro and Anita had described the house, which for the present was one of a very few along the river, so Buchanan had no trouble finding it. Wooden and single-story, on stilts in case of flooding, it reminded him more of a cabin than a house as he passed a cottonwood tree and stopped in the gravel driveway. Quaint, rustic. If Juana's dog had still been alive, Buchanan imagined how much Juana would have enjoyed running with it along the river.

. . . had still been alive.

Man, you sure are thinking about death a lot.

You bet, with a sniper watching me from God knows where.

Buchanan's back felt tense as he opened the screened porch and approached the main door. With the mist coming in from the river, the sniper might not have been able to recognize the

411

car whose headlights had veered toward the house. What if he came down to investigate?

Play the scenario you described to him, Buchanan thought.

He picked the two dead-bolt locks and entered, smelling the must of a building that had not been occupied for quite a while. Feeling vulnerable even in the darkness, he shut the door, locked it, felt along the wall, and found a light switch. A lamp came on, revealing a living room that had a bookshelf, a television, a VCR, and stereo equipment, but very little furniture, just a leather sofa, a coffee table, and a rocking chair. Obviously Juana hadn't spent much time here. Otherwise, she would have paid more attention to its furnishings. Also, few furnishings suggested that she seldom had company.

Buchanan proceeded across the room, noting the dust on the sofa and the coffee table, further evidence that Juana hadn't been here in some time. He glanced into the kitchen, turned on its light, and assessed its neat appearance, its minimum of appliances. Remote, austere, the place gave Buchanan a sense of loneliness. It made him feel sorry for her.

Down a hallway, the first door he came to − on the left, facing the river − was an office. When Buchanan turned on the overhead light, he saw that here, too, everything was kept to a minimum: a metal filing cabinet, a swivel chair, a wooden table upon which sat a computer, a laser printer, a modem, a telephone, a goose-neck lamp, a yellow note pad, and a jar filled with pencils and pens. Otherwise, the room was bare. No rug. No pictures. Impersonal.

He wondered what the sniper would be thinking in the misty darkness outside. How would the man react as he watched various lights come on in the house? Despite the instructions that the man had been given, would he come down to investigate?

Buchanan opened the top drawer of the filing cabinet, and immediately two things became important to him. The first was that each file had a stiff folder with hooks on each side that suspended the file rigidly on metal tracks along each side at the top of the drawer. The second was that the files were arranged alphabetically but that the files in A to the middle of D were bunched together, separated by a slight gap from the rest of the files that continued D through to L. The rigid hooks on each side of the neighboring files prevented them from expanding to fill the gap. Obviously, one of the D files had been removed. Possibly Juana had done it. Possibly an intruder who'd been searching as Buchanan was. No way to tell.

Buchanan opened the second drawer, found the files marked M through to Z, and noticed a slight gap where a T file appeared to have been removed. D and T. Those were the only two apparent omissions. Buchanan thought about it as he opened the bottom drawer and discovered a Browning 9-millimeter semiautomatic pistol. The basic necessities, he thought.

What did Juana do for a living? Her parents had said that she was involved in private security. That kind of work would be a logical progression from what Juana had done in military intelligence. But private security could mean anything from doing risk assessments to installing intrusion detectors to providing physical protection. She might be a freelance or work for a major corporation.

He shut the bottom drawer, reopened the top one, and began to read some of the files. A pattern became obvious. Juana's principal activity had been to act as a protective escort for business women, female politicians and entertainers, or the wives of their male equivalents, primarily when they traveled to Spanish-speaking countries or to cities in America that had a sizeable Hispanic population. The logic was clear. A protector had to blend with the local population. Because Juana was Hispanic, she would lose considerable effectiveness in an environment in which her Latin facial characteristics and skin color attracted attention. There wasn't any point in her working in Africa, the Orient, the Mideast or northern Europe, for example. For that matter, even some of the northern United States. But Spain and Latin America were ideal for her. With that kind of travel, it wasn't any wonder that she stayed away from home for months at a time. Possibly her absence could be easily explained. Possibly she was merely on an assignment.

Then why the postcard? Why did she need my help?

Something to do with a job she was on? She might have wanted to hire me.

The notion that her interest in him would have been professional and not personal made Buchanan feel hollow. But only for a moment. He quickly reminded himself that a request for professional help would not have required so unusual and secretive a means of contacting him.

And snipers wouldn't be lying in wait to kill her.

No. Juana was in trouble, and even if she'd been away on a lengthy assignment, she wouldn't have neglected to phone her parents, certainly not for nine months in a row. Not willingly.

Something was stopping her. Either she wasn't physically capable of doing it, or else she didn't want to risk involving her parents in what had happened to her.

At the back of each file, Buchanan found itemized statements, copies of bills submitted and checks received. He learned that Juana's business had been quite successful. She'd been earning fees that ranged from five thousand dollars for consultations to ten thousand dollars for two-week escort jobs to a hundred thousand dollars for a two-month protective assignment in Argentina. A note in the file indicated that there had evidently been some shooting in the latter case. Protection was a demanding, sophisticated occupation for those who knew what it truly entailed. The best operatives were paid accordingly. Even so, Juana had been unusually successful.

Buchanan made a rough estimate that she'd been earning close to a half-million dollars a year.

And living this simply, paradoxically without security devices? What had she been doing with the money? Had she been saving it, investing it, planning to retire in her mid-thirties? Again, Buchanan had no way to tell. He searched the office but didn't find a bank book, a statement from a brokerage firm, or any other sign of where she might have placed her money. Now that he thought about it, there hadn't been any mail outside or on the coffee table. Juana must have told the post office to hold it for her. Or else her parents had been picking it up. Before they'd come out here tonight, Anita had mentioned that she and Pedro sometimes drove out to inspect the place. Buchanan made a mental note to ask them about her mail, about whether she ever received statements from financial institutions.

At once the room appeared to sway, although actually it was his legs that caused the effect. They were wobbly. Exhausted, he sat in the tilt-back chair and rubbed his throbbing temples. The last time he'd slept through the night had been forty-eight hours ago, but that had been in the hospital, and even then, his sleep had not been continuous, the nurses waking him intermittently to check his vital signs. Since then, he'd slept for a few hours at the motel in Beaumont, Texas, and had a few naps at freeway rest stops en route to San Antonio. The knife wound in his side ached, its stitches making him itchy. The almost-healed bullet wound in his shoulder ached as well. His eyes were gritty from lack of sleep.

The files, he thought. Whoever was concerned enough to want to find Juana and kill her would have searched her home in hopes of discovering a clue about where she was hiding. If they wanted to kill her because she knew too much about them, they would have searched for and removed any evidence that linked her with them.

A name that begins with D. Another that begins with T. Those had been the two files that were obviously missing. Of course, the files might not be missing at all. Juana might have caused the gap in the sequence of the files when she replaced two files, scrunching a group of other files together in order to make room, leaving a space where her fingers had been.

But I've got to start somewhere, Buchanan thought. I have to assume that two files *are* missing and that they're important. He leaned back in the chair, hearing it creak, thinking that the pages in the files looked like computer printouts, wondering if the files might be in the computer.

And realized that the creak he had heard had not been from the chair but from the hallway.

15

Slowly Buchanan turned his head.

A man stood in the doorway. Mid-thirties. Five-foot-ten. A hundred and fifty pounds. His hair was sandy and extremely short. His face, like his build, was thin, but not unhealthily so; something about him suggested he was a jogger. He wore cowboy boots, jeans, a saddle-shaped belt buckle, a faded denim shirt, and a jeans jacket. The latter was slightly too large for him and emphasized his thinness.

'Find what you're looking for?' The man's flat, mid-Atlantic accent contrasted with his cowboy clothes.

'Not yet.' Buchanan lowered his hands from where he'd been massaging his temples. 'I've still got a few places to check.'

I locked the door after I came in, he thought. I didn't hear anybody follow me. How did—?

This son of a bitch hasn't been watching from outside. He's been hiding somewhere in the house.

416

'Such as?' The man's hands stayed by his side. 'What places haven't you checked?'

'The computer records.'

'Well, don't let me hold you up.' The man's cheeks were dark with beard stubble.

'Right.' Buchanan pressed the computer's ON button.

As the computer's fan began to whir, the man said, 'You look like hell, buddy.'

'I've had a couple of hard days. Mostly I need sleep.'

'I'm not having any picnic, hanging around here, either. Nothing to do but wait. Where I bunked.' The man pointed toward the next room down the hall. 'Weird. No wonder the woman had it locked. Probably didn't want her parents to see what she had in there. At first, I thought it was body parts.'

'Body parts?' Buchanan frowned.

'The stuff in that room. Belongs in a horror movie. Fucking bizarre. You mean you weren't told?'

What in God's name is he talking about? Buchanan wondered. 'I guess they didn't figure I needed to know.'

'Seems strange.'

'The stuff in that room?'

'No. That you weren't told,' the man said. 'If they sent you out here to take another look for something to tell us where the target is, the first thing they'd have done was prepare you for weird shit.'

'All they mentioned were the files.'

'The computer's waiting.'

'Right.' Buchanan didn't want to take his gaze away from the assassin, but he wasn't being given a choice. If Buchanan didn't seem to care about business, the man would become more suspicious than he already seemed.

Or maybe the man's suspicion was only something that Buchanan imagined.

417

On the computer screen, the cursor flashed where a symbol asked the user what program was to be activated.

'What's your name?' the killer asked.

'Brian MacDonald.' Buchanan immediately reverted to that identity, the one he'd assumed prior to becoming ex-DEA operative Ed Potter and going to Cancun, where all his recent troubles had started.

Brian MacDonald was supposed to have been a computer programmer, and in support of that identity, Buchanan had received instruction in that subject.

'Having trouble getting into the computer?' the killer asked. 'It didn't give *me* any trouble when they ordered *me* to erase a couple of files. You know about that, right? They told you I erased a couple of files?'

'Yes, but those files aren't what interest me.'

The cursor kept flashing next to the program-prompt sign. Juana's printed-out files had not been in a spreadsheet format but rather in standard prose paragraphs.

A word-processing program. But which one?

Buchanan-MacDonald typed DIR. At once the disc drive made clicking sounds, and a list of the symbols for the computer's programs appeared on the screen.

One of those symbols was WS, the abbreviation for a word-processing program known as WordStar.

Buchanan-MacDonald exited the list of the computer's programs and typed WS after the symbol that asked him what program he wanted. The computer's hard-disc drive made more clicking sounds. A list of other files appeared on the screen.

DIRECTORY OF DRIVE C:
A \ B \ C \ D \ E \ F \ G \ H \ I \
J \ K \ L \ M \ N \ O \ P \ Q \ R \
S \ T \ U \ V \ W \ X \ Y \ Z \

Buchanan-MacDonald knew that AUTOEXEC.BAK was a precautionary backup for AUTOEXEC.BAT, a program that allowed the computer's user to switch from one file to another. The designation '.1k' merely indicated the small amount of memory space that this program used. As for the alphabetical series, Juana had evidently subdivided her clients' files into subdirectories governed by the first letter of each client's last name.

Or so Buchanan guessed. At the moment, he was intensely preoccupied by the presence of the man in the doorway. The killer's breathing seemed to have become loud, strident, as if he were disturbed by something.

'Having problems?' the killer asked. 'Don't you know what to do next? Do I have to show you?'

'No,' Buchanan said. If he'd been alone, he would have accessed the subdirectories for D and T. But he didn't dare. If the killer had erased files in those subdirectories as he'd earlier mentioned, the man would wonder why Buchanan was interested in those same groups of names.

'But what I *want* to do next,' Buchanan said, 'is get something for this damned headache.' Slowly he stood, using his left hand to massage the back of his neck. 'Does the woman have any aspirin around here?'

The killer stepped slightly backward. He still kept both hands at his sides, not yet fully alarmed. But Buchanan, his heart pounding, had a sense that a crisis was about to explode.

Or it might have been that the man wasn't stepping backward defensively but rather to let Buchanan go past him and into the bathroom.

It was extremely hard to know.

'Bufferin,' the killer said. 'The medicine cabinet. Top shelf.'

'Great.'

But the man stepped out of the way yet again as Buchanan approached him, and obviously this time he was making sure that Buchanan didn't come within an arm's length of him.

The bathroom – across from the computer room – was dusty. White walls. White floor. White shower curtain. Simple. Basic.

Buchanan had no choice except to pretend to look for the aspirins, even though his headache was the last thing he now cared about. He opened the medicine cabinet, found the aspirin, swallowed two and returned to the computer room. It was empty.

He heard a buzz. Surprised, he stared down at the cellular phone that he had taken from the van and attached to the left side of his belt. He'd taken that phone instead of the one in the jeep because the jeep's phone wasn't portable. This way, if Pedro and Anita needed to get in touch with Buchanan, they could use a second phone, a nonportable one, that was part of the surveillance van's instrument panel. Now Pedro or Anita was evidently calling him to warn him about something.

Or maybe the call was from the surveillance team's controllers in Philadelphia.

Buchanan couldn't just let it keep ringing. That would arouse even more suspicion.

But as he reached to unhook the phone from his belt, he saw motion in the hallway. The killer appeared, and now he, too, had a cellular phone. He must have gotten it from the room where he'd been hiding.

He didn't look happy.

'Funny thing,' the killer said. 'I never heard of Brian MacDonald. I just called Duncan's van to make sure everything about you is on the up and up, and damned if *your* phone doesn't respond to his number, which tends to suggest that your phone is actually Duncan's phone, which makes me wonder why in hell—'

While the killer talked, keeping his left hand around the cellular phone, he moved his right hand beneath his jeans jacket. As Buchanan had noticed, the jacket was slightly too large, a logical reason for which would be that the killer had a holstered handgun beneath it.

'A coincidence,' Buchanan said. 'You're calling Duncan while somebody else is calling me. I'll show you.' He used his left hand to reach for the phone.

The killer's eyes focused on that gesture.

Simultaneously Buchanan shoved his right hand back beneath his sport coat, drawing his pistol from behind his belt at his spine.

The killer's eyes widened as he yanked his own pistol from beneath his jeans jacket.

Buchanan shot.

The bullet hit the man's chest.

Although the man was jolted backward, he still kept raising his weapon.

Buchanan's second bullet hit the man's throat.

Blood flew.

The man was jolted farther backward.

But his reflexes made his gunhand keep rising.

Buchanan's third bullet hit the man's forehead.

The impact knocked the man over. His gunhand jerked toward the ceiling. His spastic finger pulled the trigger. The pistol discharged, blowing a hole in the hallway ceiling. Plaster fell.

The man struck the hardwood floor in the computer room. He shuddered, wheezed, and stopped moving. Blood pooled around him.

Buchanan hurried toward the fallen man, aimed his pistol toward the man's head, kicked his gun away, and checked for life signs.

The man's eyes were open. The pupils were dilated. They

didn't respond when Buchanan shoved his fingers toward them.

Quickly, Buchanan searched the man's clothes. All he found were a comb, coins, a handkerchief, and a wallet. He set the wallet on the table and hurried to get a small rug that he'd seen in the living room. After rolling the body onto the rug, he pulled the rug along the hallway, through the living room, and toward a back door in the kitchen.

The oppressive night concealed him. Shivering, his skin prickling from the river's dampness, Buchanan tugged the body across a screened porch, down three steps, and toward this deserted section of the river. He eased down the bank, found a log, hunched the body over it, shoved the log into the current, and watched as the body slipped off as soon as the current grabbed the log. The two objects drifted away, at once out of sight in the darkness. Buchanan threw the rug as far as he could into the river. He took out the man's gun, which he'd put beneath his belt, and threw it out into the river as well, obeying the rule of never keeping a weapon whose history you don't know. Finally he took out the killer's cellular phone along with the three empty shell casings from Buchanan's semiautomatic – he'd picked them up as he left the house – and threw them toward where the gun had splashed. He stared toward nothing, took several deep breaths to calm himself, and hurried back to the house.

16

His ears rang from the roar of the gunshots. His nostrils widened from the stench of cordite and blood. Drawing his weapon had pulled the stitches in his side and strained the muscles in his injured shoulder. Tugging the body had further strained his side and shoulder. His head continued to feel as if a spike had been driven through it.

He locked the back door behind him, found another rug, took it into the computer room, and set it over the pool of blood. Then he opened a window to clear the smells of violence. Next, he searched the man's wallet, found close to three hundred dollars in various denominations, a driver's license for Charles Duffy of Philadelphia and a credit card for that name. Charles Duffy might be an alias. It probably was. It didn't matter. If these credentials had been good enough for the killer, they were good enough for Buchanan. He shoved the wallet into his pocket. He now had a new identity. On the unlikely chance that anybody in this remote area had heard the shots and came to investigate, everything looked normal, except for the finger-sized hole in the hallway ceiling, which by itself wouldn't arouse suspicion, although the pieces of plaster on the floor would. Buchanan picked them up and shoved them into a pocket.

With haste, he sat before the computer, glanced at the file directory on the screen, A B C D . . . , moved the flashing cursor from A to D, and pressed RETURN.

The disc drive made a clicking sound. A new list of files appeared on the screen, a subdirectory for all the headings under D.

..		\ DARNELL	3k	DARNELL.BAK	3k
DAYTON	2k	DAYTON.BAK	2k	DIAZ	4k
DIAZ.BAK	4k	DIEGO	5k	DIEGO.BAK	5k
DOMINGUEZ	4k	DOMINGUEZ.BAK	4k	DRUMMER	5k
DRUMMOND.BAK	5k	DURAN	3k	DURAN.BAK	3k
DURANGO	5k	DURANGO.BAK	5k		

Quickly, Buchanan opened the top drawer of the filing cabinet and took out the printed documents for D. The only

423

way he could think of to learn whether someone had removed any of the files was to compare the names on the files with those in the computer's subdirectory. Even so, he didn't have much hope. The man who'd been hiding here to kill Juana had said that he'd erased some files in the computer, presumably to stop an investigator from doing what Buchanan was trying to do. Almost certainly the computer's list would match the names on the printed files. He wouldn't be able to tell which documents were missing.

Each computer file had a companion file marked BAK, the short form for BACKUP, signifying that the computer's memory retained the previous version of a newly updated file. DARNELL. DARNELL.BAK. Comparing, Buchanan found a printed file for that name.

He continued. DAYTON. DAYTON.BAK. Check. DIAZ. DIAZ.BAK. Check. DIEGO. DIEGO.BAK. Check. He was finding printed files for every name on the computer screen. DOMINGUEZ. DOMINGUEZ.BAK. DRUM-MER. DRUMMER.BAK. DURAN. DURAN.BAK. DURANGO. DURANGO.BAK. Every name was accounted for.

He leaned back, exhausted. He'd wasted his time. There'd been no point in risking his life to come here. All he'd learned was that someone was determined to kill Juana, which he'd known already.

And for that, he himself had nearly been killed.

He rubbed his swollen eyelids, glanced at the computer screen, reached to turn off the computer, but at the final instant, stopped his trembling hand, telling himself that no matter how hopeless, he had to keep trying. Even though the subdirectory for the files that began with T would probably be as uninformative as the subdirectory for D, he couldn't ignore it.

He shifted his hand from the OFF button to the keyboard, about to switch subdirectories, when something about the image on the screen made him feel cold. He'd been aware that a detail had been troubling the edge of his consciousness, but he'd attributed his unease to apprehension and the disturbing aftermath of violence.

Now he realized what had been troubling him. His eyes had played a trick on him. DRUMMER. DRUMMER.BAK. Like hell. Drummer didn't have a backup file. The backup file was for DRUMMOND. Buchanan was certain that he hadn't seen a file for Drummond, but by now exhaustion so controlled him that he couldn't trust what he thought he was sure of. His hands shook as he sorted through the printed files. DRUMMER. DURAN. DURANGO. No Drummond.

Christ, he thought. When the killer erased the Drummond file, he hadn't thought to erase the backup file, or maybe he'd considered doing so but had been stopped because his eyes played the same trick on him that Buchanan's eyes had played, creating the impression that DRUMMOND.BAK was actually DRUMMER.BAK. The names looked so much alike.

Drummond.

Buchanan didn't know what the name signified, and when he accessed the DRUMMOND.BAK file, he found to his dismay that it was empty. Either Juana had created the file but never put information into it, or else the assassin had erased it from the inside.

Buchanan accessed the subdirectory for T, and now that he knew what to look for, he checked the backup files rather than the primary ones, comparing the names to those on the printed T documents that he took from the filing cabinet. TAYLOR.BAK. TAMAYO.BAK. TANBERG.BAK. TERRAZA.BAK. TOLSA.BAK. He was becoming more aware of the considerable number of Hispanic names. TOMEZ.BAK. Buchanan's pulse increased.

There wasn't any Tomez in the printed files or in the primary files of the computer's subdirectory for T. Again, Buchanan entered the file, and again he found nothing. Cursing, he wondered if Juana herself had erased the contents of the file. All Buchanan had was two last names, and if the assassin hadn't made the mistake of not deleting the backup titles, Buchanan wouldn't even have learned those names.

Frustrated, he debated what else to do, reluctantly shut off the computer, and decided to make a quick search of the house, even though he was sure that whoever wanted to kill Juana had sanitized the place.

That was when a chill swept through him as he remembered something odd that the killer had said. '*Where I bunked. Weird. No wonder the woman had it locked. Probably didn't want her parents to see what she had in there. At first, I thought it was body parts.*'

17

Body parts?

There'd been so much to do that until now Buchanan hadn't had the time to find out what the killer referred to. Apprehensive, he stood, left the computer room, and walked along the short hallway toward the next room on the left. The door was open, but the light was off, so that Buchanan couldn't see what was in there. When the killer had gone in to get his cellular phone, he evidently had known exactly where to find it and hadn't needed to turn on a light. Now Buchanan braced himself, noticed that the door had a dead-bolt lock, unusual for an indoor room, and groped along the inside wall to find a light switch.

When the overhead light gleamed, he blinked, not only from the sudden illumination but as well because of what he saw.

The room was startling.

Body parts? Yes, Buchanan could understand why the killer had first thought that body parts were what he was looking at.

Everywhere, except for a corner where the killer had placed a mattress for himself, there were tables upon which objects that resembled noses, ears, chins, cheeks, teeth, and foreheads were laid out in front of mirrors that had lights around them. One table had nothing but hair – different colors, different styles. Wigs, Buchanan realized. And what seemed to be body parts were prosthetic devices similar to what plastic surgeons used to reconstruct damaged faces. Another table was devoted exclusively to several makeup kits.

As Buchanan entered the room, staring to the right and then the left, then straight ahead, studying each table and the various array of eerily realistic imitations of human features, he understood that in her security business Juana had become a version of what *he* was. But whereas his own specialty was creating new personalities, hers was creating new appearances.

He'd never been confident with disguises. On occasion, he would grow a mustache or a beard, or else he would put on well-made facsimiles. A few times, he had used non-corrective contact lenses that changed the color of his eyes. A few other times, he had altered the length, style, and color of his hair. As well, he always tried to make each of his identities dress differently from the others, preferring particular watches, belts, shoes, shirts, sunglasses, even ballpoint pens, anything to make each character distinctive, just as each character had a favorite food, favorite music, favorite writer, favorite . . .

But Juana had become the ultimate impersonator. If Buchanan's suspicion was correct, she hadn't only been altering her personality with each job — she had been totally altering her physical appearance, not just her clothes but her facial characteristics, her weight, her height. Buchanan found padding that would have increased Juana's bust size. He found other padding that would have made her look pregnant. He found cleverly designed sneakers that had lifts that would have made her seem taller. He found makeup cream that would even have lightened the color of her skin.

A part of him was filled with professional amazement. But another part was horrified, realizing that at Café du Monde in New Orleans, she could have been sitting right next to him while he waited for her to enter the restaurant, and he would never have known how close she was. During his quest, he might have bumped into her or even spoken to her and never have been aware.

What had happened to her in the past six years? Where had she learned this stuff? Who was he looking for? She could be anybody. She could *look* like anybody. He remembered the last conversation they'd had. 'You don't know me,' he'd said to justify his inability to commit to her. 'You only know who I pretend to be.'

Well, she had outdone him, becoming the ultimate pretender. As he'd gone through the house, he'd thought it frustrating and strange that he'd found no photographs of her. He'd wanted so much to be reminded of her brown eyes, her shiny black hair, her hauntingly lovely face. Then he'd suspected that her hunters had taken the photographs so they'd be better able to memorize what she looked like. But if so, he now understood, the photographs wouldn't do

428

them any good because there wasn't any definitive image of her. It may have been that Juana herself had removed the photographs because she no longer identified with any individual version of her appearance. Buchanan suddenly had the terrible sense that the woman he (or Peter Lang or whoever the hell he was) had fallen in love with was as insubstantial as a ghost. As himself. He felt sick. But he still had to find her.

18

He closed the window in the computer room, then used a handkerchief to wipe his fingerprints off everything he had touched. He shut off lights as he left each room, reconfirmed that he had done everything he had to, and finally shut the front door behind him, using his picks to relock the two dead-bolts. When the killer's partner arrived to begin his shift, the partner would take a while to figure out what had happened. The two rugs that had been moved (and one of which was missing), the bullet hole in the hallway ceiling, the blood beneath the rug that Buchanan had put in the computer room – each individually would not be obvious, but together they would eventually tell the story. The killer's partner would then waste time looking for the body. His report to his bosses would be confused, adding to the further confusion that the two snipers watching the Mendez house couldn't be found, either. The only certainty was that the people who were hunting Juana knew that a man named Brendan Buchanan had visited Juana's parents, and that made it equally certain that they would associate Brendan Buchanan with everything that had happened tonight. By morning, they'll be hunting me, he thought. No. They'll be hunting Brendan Buchanan.

With luck, it'll take them a while to realize that tonight I became Charles Duffy.

Patting the wallet that he'd taken from the dead man and put in his jacket, Buchanan got into the Jeep Cherokee and backed from the driveway. His hands shook. His wounds hurt. His head throbbed. He'd come to the limit of his endurance. But he had to keep going.

A mile down the murky road, at the bottom of a misty hollow, he came to the van. Getting out of the jeep, he kept his right hand behind his back so that he could quickly draw his weapon if there had been trouble while he was away. He saw movement in the mist, tensed, then relaxed somewhat as Anita came toward him, telling him in Spanish that Pedro was in back with the bound and gagged sentries.

'The phone kept ringing.'

'I know,' Buchanan said.

'We thought it might be you, but it didn't ring twice, stop, and then ring again as you said it would if it was you. We didn't answer.'

'You did the right thing.'

Buchanan studied her. She seemed nervous, yes, but not in a way that suggested she knew that someone was hiding and aiming a weapon at her. Nonetheless he didn't fully relax until he made sure that the prisoners were as they had been and that nothing had happened to Pedro.

'Did you find Juana?' Pedro asked.

'No.'

'Did you find any sign of her?'

'No,' Buchanan lied.

'Then this was pointless. What are we going to do?'

'Leave me alone with these men for a minute. Sit with your wife in the jeep,' Buchanan said.

'Why?' Pedro looked suspicious. 'If you're going to question them about Juana, I want to hear.'

'No.'

'What do you mean? I told you if this is about my daughter, I want to hear.'

'Sometimes it's better to be ignorant.'

'I don't understand,' Pedro said.

'You will. Just leave me alone with these men.'

Pedro hesitated, then somberly got out of the van.

Buchanan watched to make sure that Pedro got into the jeep with Anita. Only then did he close the van's rear doors. The back of the van smelled from when Buchanan had allowed each man to use the porta-potty before he drove to Juana's house. They were still naked and looked chilled.

He aimed a flashlight at one man and then the other. 'You should have told me the sentry was in the house.'

Terror made their eyes wide, their faces gaunt.

'Now he's dead,' Buchanan said.

Their fearful expressions intensified.

'That puts the two of you in an awkward position,' Buchanan said. He took out his gun and used his other hand to ungag the first man.

'I figured,' the man said. 'That's why you sent the man and woman away. You didn't want them to see you kill us.'

Buchanan picked up a blanket from a corner of the van.

'Sure,' the man said in despair. 'A blanket can make a not-bad silencer.'

Buchanan pulled the blanket over the man and his partner. 'I wouldn't want you to get pneumonia.'

'What?' The man looked surprised.

'If our positions were reversed,' Buchanan said, 'what would *you* do to *me*?'

The man didn't answer.

'We're alike, yet we're not,' Buchanan said. 'Both of us have killed. The difference is, I'm not a killer.'

'I don't know what you're talking about.'

'Is the distinction too subtle for you to grasp? I'll make it plain. I'm not going to kill you.'

The man looked simultaneously troubled and bewildered, as if mercy were not a familiar concept.

'Provided you follow the ground rules,' Buchanan said.

'What kind of . . . ?'

'First of all, you're going to stay tied up until sunset,' Buchanan said. 'You'll be fed, given water, and allowed to use the toilet. But you'll remain in the van. Is that clear?'

The man frowned and nodded.

'Second, when you're released, you will not harm Pedro and Anita Mendez. They know nothing about me. They know nothing about their daughter. They're totally ignorant about any of this. If you torture them or use any other means to interrogate them, I'll get angry. You do not want me to be angry. If anything happens to them, I'll make your worst fears seem an understatement. You can hide. You can switch identities. It won't do you any good. I make a specialty of finding people. For the rest of your life, you'll keep looking behind you. Clear?'

The man swallowed. 'Yes.'

Buchanan got out of the van, left the doors open, and gestured for Pedro and Anita to come over.

Pedro started to say something in Spanish.

Buchanan stopped him. 'No. We have to speak English. I want to make sure that these men understand every word.'

Pedro looked confused.

'You're going to have a busy day watching them,' Buchanan said. 'I want you to find a place where this van won't be conspicuous. Maybe in back of one of your garages.' He explained his conversation with the prisoners. 'Let them go at sunset.'

'But . . .'

'Don't worry,' Buchanan said. 'They won't bother you. In

fact, they'll be leaving town. Won't you?' he asked the first man.

The first man swallowed again and nodded.

'Exactly. Now all I need is for you to tell me if you have a check-in schedule,' Buchanan said. 'Is there anybody you have to phone at a specific time to let your employer know there hasn't been trouble?'

'No,' the man said.

'You're sure? You're negotiating for your life. Be very careful.'

'We're supposed to phone only if we have a question or something to report,' the man said.

'Then let's wrap this up.' Buchanan's legs were rubbery from pain and fatigue. He turned to Pedro and Anita. 'I need something to eat. I need a place to sleep.'

'We'd be honored to have you as a guest,' Anita said.

'Thanks, but I'd prefer that you don't have any idea where I am.'

'We'd never tell.'

'Of course not,' Buchanan said, not bothering to correct her, knowing that Pedro and his wife didn't have the faintest idea of how vulnerable they would be to torture. 'The less you know about any of this, the better, though. As long as these men realize you can't tell them anything, you're safe. Just keep the bargain I made. Release them at sunset. Meanwhile, on our way into town, I need to pick up my car. My bag's in the trunk.'

'What happens later? After you rest?' Pedro asked.

'I'm leaving San Antonio.'

'To where?'

Buchanan didn't answer.

'Are you going to Philadelphia? To find the people who hired these men? The people you spoke to on the phone?'

Buchanan still didn't answer.

'What happened at Juana's house?'

'Nothing,' Buchanan said. 'Pedro, drive the van while I stay in back and watch these men. Anita, follow in the jeep.'

'But what about Juana?'

'You have my word. I'll never give up.'

19

The Yucatán peninsula.

McIntyre, the sunburned, leathery foreman of the demolition crew, lay feverish and helpless on a cot in the log building that his men had constructed when they'd first arrived at the site. Dense trees and shrubs had still covered the ruins back then. The ruins themselves had still been here. Sanity had still prevailed.

Now, as it took all of McIntyre's strength for him to use his good arm to wipe sweat from his brow, he wished from the depths of his soul that he had never agreed to his damnable contract with Alistair Drummond. The considerable fee – a greater sum than he'd ever received for any assignment – had been irresistible, as had the equally considerable bonus that Alistair Drummond had promised if the project were successfully completed. McIntyre had worked all over the world. In the course of his career, his nomadic existence had resulted in two divorces, in his being alienated from two women he loved and two sets of children he adored. All because of McIntyre's urge to conquer the wilderness, to put order where there was chaos. But *this* assignment had required him to destroy order and create chaos, and now he was being punished.

The earth itself seemed infuriated by the obscenity that McIntyre and his crew had caused to happen here. Or maybe it was the gods in whose honor the ruins had been constructed. An odd thought for him, McIntyre realized. After all, he had never been religious. Nonetheless, as his death approached, he found that he was increasingly thinking about ultimates. What he would once have called superstition now seemed to make perfect sense. The gods were angry because their temples and shrines had been desecrated.

Destroy the ruins, Drummond had commanded. Scatter them. His word be done. And with each dynamite blast, with each crunch of a bulldozer, with each hieroglyph-covered block of stone dumped into a sinkhole, the earth and the gods beneath had protested. Periodic tremors had shaken the camp. Their duration had lengthened. And with the increased tremors had come a further horror, myriad snakes escaping from holes and fissures in the ground, a pestilence of them, only to be controlled by spraying kerosene and scorching the earth, further despoiling it. A pall of smoke hung over the devastated ruins.

For a time, the snakes had seemed everywhere, but as the tremors had stopped, the snakes had simultaneously vanished. No longer disturbed, they'd returned to their underground nests.

Not in time, however. At least for McIntyre. The previous day, just before sunset, he had reached into a tool box to get a wrench and felt a sharp, burning pain just above his right wrist. Compelled by fear, rushing toward the medical tent, he barely had a glimpse of the tiny snake that slithered from the tool box and into a hole. The camp physician, an unshaven man who always seemed to have a cigarette in his mouth and whiskey on his breath, had injected McIntyre with antivenom and disinfected the puncture wounds, all the while assuring McIntyre that he'd been very lucky inasmuch as the fangs had missed the major blood vessels in his arm.

But as McIntyre had shivered from fear and shock, he hadn't felt lucky at all. For one thing, different snake toxins required different types of antivenom, but McIntyre hadn't been able to get a good enough look at the snake that had bitten him in order to identify it. For another, even if he had been given the correct antivenom, he still desperately needed emergency care in a hospital. But the nearest major hospital was in Campeche, a hundred and fifty miles away. A road had not yet been built through the jungle to allow a vehicle to leave the ruins. The only way McIntyre could be taken to Campeche in time for the medical treatment he urgently needed was by helicopter. But two of the camp's helicopters were much farther away, in Vera Cruz getting supplies, and weren't expected back for twelve hours. The third helicopter was in camp but disabled. That was why McIntyre had been reaching into the tool box when the snake hidden there bit him — he'd been helping a mechanic to fix the chopper's hydraulic system.

As he lay on a bunk in a corner of the camp's office, his mind seemed to float while death spread slowly through his body. Death felt suffocatingly hot, squeezing moisture from his body, soaking his clothes. At the same time, death felt unbearably cold, racking him with chills, making him wish fervently for more blankets.

McIntyre's vision clouded. Sounds were muffled. The roar of bulldozers, the blast of explosions, the din of jackhammers seemed to come from far away instead of from the remnants of the ruins outside his office. But the one thing he listened for, the one sound he knew he couldn't fail to hear no matter how far away, was the rapid whump-whump-whump of a helicopter, and to his despair, he still had not detected it. If the chopper in camp weren't soon fixed, if the other choppers didn't soon return, he would die, and it occurred to him, making him furious despite how

436

weak he was, that adequate medical care in camp was one of the conditions that Alistair Drummond had guaranteed. Since Drummond had failed to make good on that promise, perhaps none of the other promises would have been fulfilled either. The bonus, for example. Or the fee for the job. Maybe Drummond would have all kinds of reasons for not being able to complete the terms of the contract.

This suspicion had obviously not occurred to any of the surviving workers. They were so eager to get out of here that they attacked the job with relentless fury. Their impatience filled them with greater anticipation of the reward they'd been guaranteed. Nothing discouraged their greed, not the tremors, not the snakes, certainly not McIntyre's impending death. They had persisted despite efforts by Indians in the area to scare them away. Those natives, descendents of the original Maya who had built these monuments, had been so outraged by the obliteration of the ruins that they had sabotaged equipment, poisoned the camp's water, set boobytraps, attacked sentries, and in effect waged war. Responding, calling it self-defense, the workers had hunted and killed any native they found, dumping the corpses into wells in unconscious imitation of the human sacrifice once practised by the Maya. In this region untouched by civilization, the struggle had reminded McIntyre of what had happened four hundred years earlier when the Spaniards had invaded the region. The area was sealed. No outsider would ever know what had happened here. Certainly no outsider would be able to prove it. When the job was finished, all that would matter would be the results.

Delirious, McIntyre heard the office door come open. From outside, bulldozers crunched past. Then the door was closed, and footsteps crossed the earthen floor toward this area of the office.

A gentle hand touched his brow. 'You're still feverish.' A woman's voice. Jenna's. 'Do you feel any better?'

'No.' McIntyre shivered as more sweat oozed from his body.

'Drink this water.'

'Can't.' He struggled to breathe. 'I'll throw it up.'

'Just hang on. The mechanics are working as fast as they can to fix the chopper.'

'Not fast enough.'

Jenna knelt beside his cot and held his left hand. McIntyre remembered how surprised he had been to learn that the camp's surveyor-cartographer was female. He'd insisted that this was no place for a woman, but she'd soon overcome his chauvinistic attitudes, proving that she could adapt to the jungle as well as any man. She was in her forties, the same as McIntyre. She had honey-colored hair, firm-looking breasts, an appealing smile, and in the three months they'd been working together, McIntyre had fallen in love with her. He had never told her. He'd been too afraid of being rejected. If she did reject him, their working relationship would have been intolerable. But as soon as the job was completed, he had intended to . . .

Stroking his left hand, Jenna leaned close, her voice interrupting his thoughts. 'But I'm betting there'll be a chopper here quicker than we can repair the one we've got.'

'I . . .' McIntyre's mouth was parched. 'I don't know what . . .'

'Drummond will be here soon. We'll put you in his chopper to get you to a hospital.'

'Drummond?'

'Don't you remember?' Jenna wiped a damp cloth across his forehead. 'We talked about this when I used the radio a half hour ago.'

'Radio? Half hour ago?'

'We found what Drummond wants.' Jenna spoke quickly, her voice taut with excitement. 'It was here all along. Right under our noses. We had the instructions from Drummond's translation, but we were too clever. We made the search too hard. We thought the instructions were using figures of speech, but all along, the text was meant to be taken literally. The god of darkness. The god of the underworld. The god of the pyramid. It was so damned easy, Mac. Once your men leveled the pyramid, it was so obvious why the Maya built it where they did. We found what Drummond wants.'

TEN

1

Washington, D.C.

One-thirty in the afternoon. As soon as Buchanan got off the TWA flight from San Antonio, he headed toward the first row of pay phones he saw in the terminal at National Airport. He'd managed to get some sleep during the five-hour, several-stop trip. The naps, combined with the additional four hours of sleep he'd gotten the night before at a motel near San Antonio's airport, had given him back some energy, as had a carbohydrate-rich breakfast at the airport and another on the plane. His wounds still hurt. His head still ached. But he felt more alert than he had in days, adrenaline pushing him. He was traveling as Charles Duffy. He felt in control again.

A man answered Holly's phone at *The Washington Post*, explained that she was on another line, and asked who was calling.

'Mike Hamilton.'

That was the name Buchanan had told Holly he would be using to contact her. He had to assume that the colonel and Alan would have her under surveillance, watching for any sign that she didn't intend to keep her agreement with them. If she seemed intent on pursuing the story, if she gave indications that she had not surrendered all of her research, there was a strong chance they would move against her. For certain, if the colonel and Alan found out that Buchanan remained in contact with her, that would be enough to arouse their suspicions to a deadly level. Even if Holly weren't in danger, Buchanan couldn't afford to use his real name. The colonel and Alan would be searching for him.

That thought made Buchanan uneasy as he waited for Holly to come on the line. His nervousness wasn't caused by concern about his safety. Rather he was nervous because he wondered about his motives. What did he think he was doing? You didn't just leave a top-secret, undercover, military operation as if you were quitting a job at Domino's Pizza. For eight years as a deep-cover operative and for three years prior to that, Buchanan had followed every order. He was a soldier. It was his job to be obedient. He'd been proud of that. Now suddenly his discipline had snapped. He'd walked away, not even toward the future but into the past, not as himself but as one of his characters.

Hey, buddy, he told himself, it's not too late. You'd better get back in line and with the program. Phone the colonel. Tell him you made a mistake but you're better now. Tell him you'll do whatever he wants. You'll be an instructor. You'll stay out of sight. Anything.

But a stronger thought insisted.

Have to find Juana.

He must have said that out loud because a woman's voice was suddenly speaking to him on the telephone. 'What? I didn't hear what you said. Mike? Is that you?'

The throaty, sensuous voice belonged to Holly.

Buchanan straightened. 'Yeah, it's me.' Before leaving San Antonio this morning, he'd called Holly's apartment to make certain she was in Washington, to insure he didn't make the trip for nothing. Six-thirty in Texas had been seven-thirty along the Potomac. She'd been awake and about to go to work

442

when she'd picked up the phone rather than let her answering machine take the message. Assuming that her phone was tapped, he'd used the name Mike Hamilton and made tentative arrangements to meet her.

'Is our late lunch still on?' she now asked.

'If your schedule's free.'

'Hey, for you, it's always free. I'll meet you in McPherson Square.'

'Give me forty minutes.'

'No rush.'

'See you.' Buchanan put the phone back on its hook. The conversation had gone perfectly. Sounding natural, it had nonetheless contained the words 'no rush,' the code they'd chosen in New Orleans to indicate that Holly did not sense a threat. 'See you' was Buchanan's equivalent message.

He picked up his small bag, turned from the phone, and joined a mass of passengers that had just gotten off another flight. Both National and Dulles airports were under constant surveillance from various government agencies. Some of the surveillance was a throwback to the Cold War. Some of it was due to a practical need to know which travelers of importance were showing up unexpectedly in the nation's capital. A lot of it had to do with the increasing conviction that Mideastern terrorists were poised to make their long-postponed assault on the United States.

Buchanan had no reason to suspect that the colonel would have operatives watching the airport in case he passed through. After all, logic suggested that Washington would be one of the places Buchanan wanted most to avoid. Besides, his paper trail would have led the colonel's operatives to San Antonio by now. Before leaving Texas, Buchanan had left his car at an office of the company from which he'd rented it. That would be the dead end of the paper trail. The colonel's people would assume that Buchanan had flown out of San Antonio since the

443

car-rental office was near the airport. But they would have no way of knowing that Buchanan had used Charles Duffy's name and credit card to rent the motel room and buy a plane ticket to Washington.

The only risk Buchanan took in the airport was that someone would notice him by accident, but that would happen only if he drew attention to himself, and he wasn't about to get that careless. Buchanan-Lang-Duffy-Hamilton blended skillfully with fellow travelers, exited into a drab, damp afternoon, got into a taxi, and headed toward downtown Washington. The terminal had not been a threat.

But McPherson Square would be another matter.

2

In New Orleans, before Holly had gone back to Washington, Buchanan had explained to her that if he phoned and suggested they get together, she was to choose a public place in the area. The place had to be part of her routine. ('Do nothing conspicuous.') It had to have numerous entrances. ('So we don't get trapped.') And it had to be dependable in terms of not being closed at unpredictable hours. ('I was once told to meet a man at a restaurant that had burned down the day before. Nobody on the team advising me had checked the location to make sure the rendezvous site was viable.')

In terms of those criteria, McPherson Square was ideal. The park was hardly likely to have burned down. It was as public as a restaurant but far more open, and it was only a few blocks from Holly's office, hence a natural place for her to meet someone.

Buchanan managed to reach the rendezvous area before the forty-minute deadline. Watching the newspaper building from a crowded bus stop farther along L Street, he saw Holly come out of *The Washington Post* and head down 15th Street, but at the moment, he wasn't so much interested in her as he was in anyone who might be following her. He waited until she was out of his sight, waited another fifteen seconds, then strolled with other pedestrians toward the corner. There, while waiting for a traffic light, he glanced in Holly's direction down 15th Street toward her destination on K Street.

She wore a London Fog raincoat, tan, an excellent neutral color when you didn't want to stand out in a crowd. A matching cap had the extra merit of concealing Holly's red hair, which she'd tucked up beneath it. The only thing conspicuous about her was the camera bag that she carried in lieu of a purse.

It was enough for Buchanan to distinguish her from other tan raincoats in the crowd. He followed slowly, glancing unobtrusively at store windows and cars, subtly scanning the area to see if Holly had anyone observing her.

Yes. A man in a brown leather jacket on the opposite side of the street.

As the man walked, he never took his gaze away from Holly. On occasion, he adjusted something in his left ear and lowered his chin toward his right chest, moving his lips.

Buchanan studied the street more intently and saw a man on the corner ahead of Holly. The man wore a business suit, held an umbrella, and glanced at his watch a couple of times as if waiting for someone. But he too adjusted something in his ear and did so at the same time that the first man was lowering his chin and moving his lips. Hearing-aid-style audio receivers. Lapel-button miniature microphones.

But which group – the colonel's or Alan's – was tailing Holly? Were they military or civilian, from special operations or the Agency? As Holly reached K Street and crossed toward the park, Buchanan got a look at the backs of the men who went after her. They had narrow hips, their torsos veering upward toward broad shoulders, a distinctive build for special-operations personnel. Their training was designed to make them limber while giving them considerable upper-body strength. Too much muscle in their legs and hips would slow them down. But muscle in the upper body didn't interfere with anything, creating only advantages. Buchanan himself had once possessed that body build, but since it would identify his background to anyone who understood these matters, he'd cut back on building up his arms and shoulders, going instead for activities that gave him stamina and agility.

Now that he had a distinctive silhouette to look for, he noticed two other men dressed in civilian clothes and with a special-operations build. The colonel must certainly be apprehensive about her, or else he wouldn't have so many men on her, Buchanan thought. The two men he'd just noticed were ahead of Holly, staking out the park. The only way they could have known to get to the park ahead of her was if they had her phones tapped and knew where and when she had arranged to meet someone named Mike Hamilton. He'd been right to be cautious.

Instead of following Holly into the park, Buchanan hung back, turned right on K Street, and went around the next block. His approach returned him to 15th Street but this time farther south, where 15th intersected with I Street. From a busy entrance to the Veterans Administration Building, he looked across to the leafless trees in the park and glimpsed Holly sitting on a bench near the statue of General McPherson in the middle of the square. Pedestrians came and went, but the four broad-shouldered men had spread out through the park and were now immobile, on occasion touching an ear or lowering a chin, concentrating on Holly, then switching their attention to anyone who seemed to be approaching her.

How do I get a message to her? Buchanan thought.

Continuing along I Street, he came to a black man who held

a small sign that said I'LL WORK FOR FOOD. The man needed a hair cut but had shaved. He wore plain, clean clothes. His leather shoes looked freshly shined but were worn down at the heels.

'Can you spare the price of a hamburger?' the man asked. His eyes showed subdued bitterness. Shame struggled with anger as he tried to maintain his dignity even though he was begging.

'I think I can do better than the price of a hamburger,' Buchanan said.

The man's eyebrows narrowed. His expression became puzzled, with a trace of wariness.

'You want to work?' Buchanan asked.

'Look, I don't know what's on your mind, but I hope it isn't trouble. The last guy stopped told me if I wanted to work, why the hell didn't I get a job? He called me a lazy bastard and walked away. Get a job? No shit. I wouldn't be out here beggin', lettin' people call me names if I could find a job.'

'How does this sound?' Buchanan asked. 'Five minutes work for a hundred dollars?'

'A hundred dollars? For that much money, I'd . . . Wait a minute. If this is about drugs or . . .'

3

At a safe-site apartment five blocks north of *The Washington Post*, the phone barely rang before the colonel stopped pacing and grabbed it off its hook. 'Home Video Service.'

'Looks like it's a no-show,' a man's voice said. 'Whoever this Mike Hamilton is, he was supposed to meet her at twenty after two. But now it's quarter to three, the drizzle's turning to rain, and she's making moves as if that park bench she's sitting on is awfully cold.'

'Keep watching until she goes back to work and our man in her department can take over watching her,' the colonel said.

'Maybe that's what she's doing now. Working,' the man's voice said. 'Just because the guy at the desk next to hers never heard her talk about anybody named Mike Hamilton, that doesn't mean Hamilton still can't be a source for a story she's working on. Hell, for that matter, he might be a friend she knew when she worked in California.'

'Might be, Major? I don't like my officers to make assumptions. The tapes of the conversations don't mention California or anything else. She and Hamilton talk as if they've got some kind of relationship. But what? It's all smoke.'

'Well, most people don't review their life history when they phone somebody for lunch.'

'Are you being sarcastic, Major?'

'No, sir. Definitely not. I'm just trying to think out loud and analyze the problem. I'm guessing that if this meeting with Hamilton has anything to do with us, she wouldn't be doing it in plain sight. Besides, we checked our computer records. No one named Hamilton was ever associated with our operations.'

'No one named Hamilton?' the colonel said. 'Doesn't it seem relevant to you that one of our specialties is pseudonyms? Damn it, what if Hamilton isn't his real name?'

The line became silent for a moment. 'Yes, sir, I get your point.'

'Since she came back from New Orleans, everything she's done has been routine. Now, for the first time, she's doing something that can't be fully explained. For her sake, I hope it doesn't involve us. I want to believe what she told Buchanan, that she's given up the story. But I also want to know who the hell Mike Hamilton is.'

'Colonel, you can depend on me to . . . Hold it. I'm getting a report from the surveillance team . . . Somebody's approaching the woman.'

448

The colonel stopped moving, stopped blinking, stopped breathing. He stared at the opposite wall.

'False alarm, sir,' the voice said. 'It's a black guy with a sign about needing a job. He's trying to beg from everybody in the park.'

The colonel exhaled and seemed to come out of a trance. 'Maintain surveillance. Keep me informed. I want to know what that woman's doing every second.' With force, he terminated the connection.

From a chair in the corner of the room, Alan studied him. 'Why don't you give it a rest? Whatever happens will happen regardless if you're staring at the phone.'

'You don't seem to take this seriously.'

'Oh, I take it very seriously,' Alan said. 'To me, this is a sign of how out of control this operation has become. Instead of taking care of business, you're wasting all your resources worrying about Buchanan and this reporter.'

'Wasting?'

'As far as I'm concerned, both problems are solved. Let Buchanan keep digging a hole to bury himself. He's gone, and I say fine. He'll act his way into oblivion. About the reporter – hey, without Buchanan she doesn't have a story. It's as simple as that. If she breaks her agreement, we'll deny everything she says, accuse her of putting her career ahead of the truth, and challenge her to produce this mysterious man she claims was God knows how many people.'

'Maybe she can.'

'What are you talking about?' Alan asked.

'She's the reason Buchanan walked away from us,' the colonel said. 'But maybe it's not just professional. He tried to protect her, after all. Maybe there's something personal between them.'

Alan frowned.

'One of Buchanan's talents is changing his voice, imitating

other people,' the colonel said. 'Hasn't it occurred to you that no matter what this guy sounds like on tape, Mike Hamilton could be Buchanan?'

4

Before Holly had returned to Washington from New Orleans, there hadn't been time for Buchanan to explain all the basics of how to behave if she thought she were being watched. The most important thing, he'd emphasized, was not to become so self-conscious that she exaggerated her movements as if putting on a show for someone. 'Never do something that you wouldn't normally do. Never fail to do something that you *would* normally do.'

At the moment, what Holly would normally have done would have been to stop sitting on a goddamned park bench when the drizzle turned to rain. She'd been on the bench since twenty after two, the rendezvous time she'd established with Buchanan. Now he was twenty-five minutes late, and in New Orleans he had told her that thirty minutes was the maximum time she should ever wait for him to show up. Otherwise, if she were under surveillance, she would make her observers wonder why she was lingering. That she was lingering now became even more conspicuous given the recent turn in the weather.

Holly strongly suspected that she should do the natural thing and leave right now. Buchanan had told her that if he ever failed to show up, she should return to the rendezvous area twenty-four hours later, provided he didn't get a message to her in the meantime. Returning tomorrow would be conspicuous, yes, but it was a lot less conspicuous than seeming not to have the brains to get out of the rain. There weren't many people in the park any more; most had headed toward the shelter of buildings. She felt as if she were center stage and hoped that she seemed natural when she looked around. When she made up her mind and stood, she abruptly noticed movement to her left.

The movement had been there for about a minute. She just hadn't paid attention to it. It was so common that she took it dismally for granted. But now, turning, she saw a black man with a cardboard sign that said I'LL WORK FOR FOOD approach a woman who was hurrying through the park. The black man said something to her. The woman shook her head with force and kept hurrying. The black man continued through the park. The rain had begun to streak the inked letters on his sign so that now it said I ORK OR OOD.

Holly felt a pang of sympathy as the black man approached another hurrying pedestrian, a man this time, who strode quickly on as if the beggar were invisible. Now the black man's sign began to droop.

Oh, hell, at least one good thing will come out of this, Holly thought. She reached in her camera bag, took a dollar from her wallet, and handed it to the man as he reached her. She felt so dejected that she would have given him more, just to heighten her spirits, but she kept remembering Buchanan's instruction not to do anything unusual. A dollar at least was better than a quarter.

'Thank you, ma'am.' What he said next startled her. 'Mike Hamilton says you're being watched.'

Holly's pulse faltered. 'What?'

'You're to go over to the Fourteenth Street entrance to the Metro. Take the train to . . . Metro Center. Go out the east doors. Walk toward the . . . yes . . . the National Portrait Gallery. He'll be in touch.'

Pocketing the dollar Holly had given him, the black man moved on.

Holly's instinct was to rush after him, to ask for a more

detailed explanation, to question him about how Buchanan had known she was being watched.

But her instinct was totally wrong, she knew, and she fiercely repressed it, ignoring the black man's retreat, acting as if he were an inconvenient interruption, glancing around as if still in hope that the person she waited for would arrive. She didn't dare act immediately after speaking to the man. If so, whoever was watching her might suspect that she'd been given a message.

She waited. Five seconds. Ten seconds. Fifteen. Drops of water fell from the brim of her hat. What was the most natural thing to do? To check all around her one more time, then shake her head with annoyance, and walk away.

She headed back toward work, then stopped as if she had a better thought, and changed direction, moving in the opposite direction toward the 14th Street entrance to the Metro. Certainly the conflict she acted out was true to what she was feeling. Two days ago, Buchanan had scared her during their talk on the paddlewheeler in New Orleans. He had made the potential threat to her seem disturbingly vivid. Because of the story she was researching. The story about *him*. Seeing the deadly conviction in his eyes had made Holly feel cold. This man had killed. The men he worked with had killed. They didn't operate by any rules that Holly understood. A Pulitzer Prize wouldn't be any consolation to her in the grave.

But what about journalistic responsibility? What about the courage of being a professional? Holly had dodged those issues by postponing her decisions, by telling herself that if she waited for further developments, the story might get even better. She hadn't walked away from the story; she was merely letting it cook. Sure. Then why was she so terrified because Buchanan had gotten in touch with her? What did he want? If she were the reporter she'd always believed she was, she ought to be eager. Instead she had the feeling a nightmare was starting.

452

Ten minutes later, amid the echoing rumble of trains behind her, she climbed the congested stairs from Metro Center, exited onto noisy, traffic-glutted G Street, and walked through the rain toward the huge Greek-Revival quadrangle that housed the National Portrait Gallery. Despite the weather, the sidewalk was crowded, people hurrying. And here too there were indigents, wearing tattered, rain-soaked clothes, asking for quarters, food, work, whatever, or sometimes holding signs that announced their need.

One of them had a sign identical to that of the black man in the park. I'LL WORK FOR FOOD. She started to pass.

'Wait, Holly. Give me a quarter,' the indigent said.

To hear him call her by name shocked her as if she'd touched an exposed electrical wire. Overwhelmed, she stopped, managed to make herself turn, and saw that the stooped man in the tattered clothes and droopy hat with grime on his face was Buchanan.

'Jesus,' she said.

'Don't talk, Holly. Just give me a quarter.'

She fumbled for her wallet in her camera case, obeying, liking the way he said her name.

Buchanan kept his voice low. 'Drummond. Tomez. That's all I have. No first names. The sort of people who'd need protection. Find out everything you can about possible candidates. Pretend to make a pay-phone call at the gallery. Meet me at eight tonight. The Ritz-Carlton. Ask the hotel operator to connect you with Mike Hamilton's room. Keep moving.'

All the while, Buchanan held out his hand, waiting for Holly to give him the quarter. He took it, saying louder, 'Thanks, ma'am. God bless you,' turning to an approaching man, saying, 'Can you spare a quarter, just a quarter?'

Holly kept moving as Buchanan had instructed, proceeding toward the National Portrait Gallery, hoping that she looked

453

natural. But if she managed to keep her pace steady, her mind swirled from fear and confusion.

5

The large, blue helicopter cast a streaking shadow over the dense Yucatán jungle below. In the rear compartment, Alistair Drummond's scowl became so severe that its wrinkles added years, making him look the eightysomething that he was. He'd been sitting rigidly straight, but now, with each piece of information that Raymond told him, Drummond sat even straighter. His brittle voice managed to be forceful despite the whump-whump-whumping roar of the aircraft's engine. '*Brendan Buchanan?*'

'An instructor for Army Special Forces, assigned to Fort Bragg. He rented a car in New Orleans and drove to San Antonio to visit the woman's parents. Our sentry there called to say that Buchanan used the name Jeff Walker when he claimed he was a friend of their daughter and asked if they knew where she was.'

'*Is* he a friend?' Drummond squinted through his thick glasses. 'Why would he use an alias? Obviously he's hiding something. But what? What does he want with the woman?'

'We don't know,' Raymond said. 'But the two men assigned to watch the Mendez house are missing now. So is one of the men assigned to the target's house outside San Antonio. His partner found recent blood beneath a carpet and a bullet hole in the ceiling. It would be foolish not to make the connection between Buchanan's appearance and their *dis*appearance. If he shows up again, I've given orders to have him killed.'

Drummond's ancient frame trembled. 'No. Cancel that order. Find him. Follow him. Maybe he'll lead us to her. Did they work together at Fort Bragg? Learn his connection with

454

her. He might know places to look that we haven't imagined.'

6

While flying from San Antonio to Washington National, Buchanan had used an in-flight phone and Charles Duffy's telephone credit card to call several hotels in Washington, needing to make a reservation for the night. As he'd expected, the task was frustrating. Most of the good hotels in Washington were always full. He'd started at the middle of the price scale but finally decided to try the high end, reasoning that the recession's effect might have made extremely expensive hotels less popular. As it happened, Buchanan got lucky with the Ritz-Carlton. The early morning checkout of a Venezuelan group due to a political emergency at home had caused several rooms to be available. If Buchanan-Duffy had called a half hour later, the hotel clerk assured him, the rooms would have been spoken for. Buchanan was able to reserve two.

The Ritz-Carlton was among the most fashionable hotels in Washington. Filled with an amber warmth, designed to seem like an English club, it had numerous European furnishings as well as British paintings from the eighteenth and nineteenth centuries, most of the artwork depicting dogs and horses. After Buchanan's brief contact with Holly near the National Portrait Gallery, he had noticed that Holly continued to be followed but that none of her surveillance team appeared to be interested in him. Even so, he had needed to be sure and used extensive evasion techniques involving the subway, buses, and taxis to determine if he was followed. Those techniques took two hours, and Buchanan assumed that if the surveillance team had been interested in him and had managed to stay with him, they'd have picked him up by then. So he felt reasonably protected when he checked in at the Ritz-Carlton shortly after five p.m. He showered, applied new dressing and bandages to the stitches in his knife wound, changed into dry clothes from his travel bag, ate a room-service hamburger, and lay on the bed, trying to muster his energy as well as focus his thoughts.

The latter was difficult. The last two days of constant travel had wearied him as had his activities throughout the afternoon. Eight years earlier or even last year, he wouldn't have been this tired. But then last year he hadn't been nursing two wounds. And he hadn't been suffering from a persistent, torturous headache. He'd been forced to buy another package of Tylenol, and he wasn't a fool – he knew that the headache could no longer be treated as a temporary problem, that it had to be related to the several injuries to his skull, that he needed medical attention. All the same, he didn't have time to worry about himself. If he went to a doctor, he'd probably end up spending the next week under hospital observation. Not only would a stay in the hospital be a threat to him, keeping him in one place while his hunters tracked him down, but it would increase the danger for someone else.

Juana. He couldn't waste time caring about himself. He'd done too much of that for too long. He needed to care about someone else. Juana. He had to find her. Had to help her.

7

The telephone rang at eight in the evening. Precisely on time. Good. Buchanan sat up in bed and reached for the phone, answering with a neutral voice. 'Hello.'

'Mike?' The deep, sensuous female voice was unmistakably Holly's.

'Yes. Where are you?'

'I'm using a house phone in the lobby. Do you want me to

come up? What's your room number?'

'At the moment, it's three-twenty-two. But I want you to go to five-twelve. And Holly, you have to do it in a certain way. Take the elevator to the third floor. Then use the stairs to go up to the fifth. Anybody watching the numbers above the elevator in the lobby will assume that you didn't go any farther than the third floor.'

'On my way.' Tension strained her voice.

Buchanan broke the connection and pressed the button for the hotel operator, telling her, 'Please, don't put through any phone calls until eight tomorrow morning.'

He left the light on, picked up his travel bag, walked out of the room, put a DO NOT DISTURB sign on the door, made sure that the door was locked behind him, and headed toward the fire stairs. As he started toward the fifth floor, he heard the elevator stop behind him on the third.

Holly arrived at room 512 a minute after he did. The room was registered to Charles Duffy. It and Mike Hamilton's room had been rented using Charles Duffy's credit card. Buchanan had told the check-in clerk that Mike Hamilton would be arriving soon. After showering and changing, he'd gone back down to the lobby, waited until the clerk who'd checked him in was off on an errand, and then had checked in again with a different clerk, this time as Mike Hamilton.

When Buchanan turned from letting Holly in and relocking the door, she surprised him, dropping her camera bag and a briefcase onto a chair, putting her arms around him, holding him tightly.

She was trembling.

Buchanan wondered if she were putting on an act, trying to seem more distraught than she actually was.

'How do you stand living this way?' She spoke against his shoulder.

'What way? This is normal.' He responded to her embrace.

'Normal.' Her voice dropped.

'It's just stage fright.' He smelled her perfume.

She stepped away, looking depressed. 'Sure.' As rain pelted against the window behind the closed draperies, she took off her wet London Fog hat and overcoat, then listlessly shook her hair free.

Buchanan had forgotten how red her hair was, how green her eyes.

She wore a sand-colored, linen pant suit, a scooped, white T-shirt, and a brown belt. The outfit complimented her height and figure, the flow of her hips and breasts.

He felt attracted to her, remembered how her breasts had felt against him, and forced himself to concentrate on business.

'I wanted a room where we wouldn't be disturbed if the men following you decided to barge in,' he explained. 'This way, if they talk to the desk clerk, they'll think they know where you are and who you're seeing.'

'That part I understand.' Holly slumped on the Victorian sofa. 'But what I *don't* understand is why you told me to pretend to make a call from a pay phone at the National Portrait Gallery. Who was I supposed to be talking to?'

'Mike Hamilton.'

Holly ran her fingers through her hair and didn't seem to follow his logic.

'Otherwise how were you supposed to know Mike Hamilton wanted to meet you here?'

'But . . .' She frowned. 'But you'd already told me as I came out of the metro station.'

'The people following you didn't know that. Holly, you have to remember: in this business, everything's an act. You want your audience to know only what's necessary for you to maintain an illusion. Suppose I'd just let you go back to work and then had phoned you and told you to meet me here. Your phones are tapped. This hotel would have been staked out fifteen minutes after I completed the call. They'd have found out who Mike Hamilton was. Regardless of the switch in the rooms, you and I would be being questioned right now.'

'Nothing you do is uncalculated.'

'That's how I stay alive.'

'Then how do I know I'm really being followed? How do I know that this business in the park and at the Metro station isn't just a charade to frighten me into cooperating with you and staying away from the story?'

'You don't. And I can't prove it to you. Correction. That's wrong. I *can* prove it to you. But the proof might get you killed.'

'There. You're doing it again,' Holly said. 'Trying to frighten me.' She crossed her arms and rubbed them as if she were cold.

'Have you eaten?' Buchanan asked.

'No.'

'I'll order you something from room service.'

'I don't have any appetite.'

'You've got to eat something.'

'Hey, fear's good for losing weight.'

'How about some coffee? Or tea?'

'How about telling me what the names you gave me have to do with my story?'

'They don't,' Buchanan said.

'*What?* Then why did you get in touch with me? Why did you put me through all this, being followed and passing secret messages and—?'

'Because I didn't have any choice. I need your help.'

Holly jerked her head up. 'You need my help? What could possibly—?'

'Drummond and Tomez. People important enough to need protection. What did you find out about them?'

'Why do you need to know?'

'It's better if you don't know anything about—'

'Bullshit,' Holly said. 'Since I met you on the train to New Orleans, you've been playing games with my mind. Everything has to be your way, and you're damned good at manipulating people into doing it. Well, this is one time that isn't going to happen. If you need my help, there has to be something in it for me. If it isn't about the story I was working on, what *is* it about? Maybe I can use *that* as a story. Quid pro quo, buddy. If I have to give up something, I want to get something in return.'

Buchanan studied her, then feigned reluctance. 'Maybe you're right.'

'Jesus, you are really something. You never stop acting. I get the impression you meant to tell me all along, but this way it looks like *you're* doing *me* a favor instead of the other way around.'

Buchanan slowly grinned. 'I guess you're too smart for me. How about that coffee?'

'Tea. And if you're going to tell me a story, I think I feel my appetite coming back.'

8

'It concerns the woman I told you about in New Orleans,' Buchanan said after ordering food. 'The friend who sent me a message asking for help. The one I was supposed to meet at Café du Monde. Except she didn't show up.'

Holly nodded. 'Your former lover.'

'No. I told you we were never lovers.' Buchanan brooded. 'In fact, I think that's when a lot of my problems started. Because I didn't commit to her.' He remembered how much he had wanted to, how much he had denied himself for the sake of duty.

Holly's face didn't change expression. But her eyes did, narrowing, assessing him.

'One of the last things I told her,' Buchanan said, 'was that she couldn't be in love with me because she didn't know me – she only knew who I pretended to be.'

Holly's eyes narrowed more. 'It certainly seems you never stop acting. For example, right now. I can't tell if this is the truth or more manipulation.'

'Oh, it's the truth. Even if you don't believe it, it's the truth. This is one of the most honest things you'll ever hear from me. I want to help her because I want to be the person I was when I knew her. I want to choose to be somebody and to stay that somebody. I want to stop changing. I want to be consistent.'

'Because of all the people you impersonated?'

'I told you I don't know anything about—'

'Don't act so defensive. I'm not trying to get you to admit to anything. You want to stop changing? Why make it so complicated? Why be somebody else? Why not be yourself?'

Buchanan didn't answer.

'You don't like yourself?'

Buchanan still didn't answer.

'This woman, what was her name?'

Buchanan hesitated. All his instincts and training warned against revealing information. He prepared to lie.

Instead he told the truth. 'Juana Mendez.'

'When you knew her, I'm assuming you were on an assignment together.'

'You know what you can do with your assumptions.'

'No need to get touchy.'

'Since the first time I spoke to you, I have never revealed confidential information. Everything I've said about my background has been hypothetical, a "what if" scenario. As far as you're concerned, I'm an instructor in military special operations. That's all I've ever admitted to. This has nothing

461

to do with the story you abandoned. I want that understood.'

'As I said, no need to get touchy.'

'After you left New Orleans . . .' He told her about his drive to San Antonio, his discovery that both Juana's and her parents' homes were under surveillance, and his search of Juana's records. He omitted all reference to the man he'd killed. 'Drummond and Tomez. The files for those names were the only ones that seemed to be missing. Juana was a security specialist. I have to assume those people were clients.'

'Important enough to need protecting.' Pensive, Holly walked toward the briefcase she'd set on a chair and opened it. 'I used the reference system at the *Post*.'

'That's why I had to get in touch with you. I didn't have access to anyone else who could get the information I needed as quickly as you could.'

'You know . . .' Holly studied him. 'Sometimes you might consider trying to impersonate somebody with tact.'

'What?'

'I don't delude myself that you'd go to all this trouble if you didn't have something to gain. All the same, it wouldn't have hurt you if you'd also left the impression that you found me interesting.'

'Oh . . . I'm sorry.'

'Apology accepted. But if you were this charming with Juana Mendez, it's no wonder things didn't work out.'

'Look, I'm trying to make up for mistakes.'

Holly didn't speak for a moment. 'Let's see if this helps. Drummond and Tomez. I had my suspicions, but I wanted to check thoroughly before I made any conclusions.'

'Drummond is *Alistair* Drummond,' Buchanan said. 'I more or less figured that already. The last name brings him immediately to mind. He's rich, famous, and powerful enough to fit the profile.'

'Agreed. I kept checking, but he's the only Drummond I

think we should consider.' Holly pulled a book and several pages in a file folder out of the briefcase. 'Bedtime reading. His biography and some printouts of recent stories about him. I'd have given you his *auto*biography, but it's such a public-relations whitewash that for dependable information it's useless. Certainly it doesn't show any skeletons in closets, and in Drummond's case, skeletons in closets might not be a figure of speech.'

'What about Tomez?' Buchanan asked.

'That was harder. I'm a Frank Sinatra fan myself.'

'What's he got to do with . . . ?'

'Jazz. Big bands. Tony Bennett. Billie Holiday. Ella Fitzgerald.'

'I still don't see what . . .'

'Listened to much Puccini lately?'

Buchanan looked blank.

'Verdi? Rossini? Donizetti? Not ringing any bells? How about titles? *La Boheme. La Traviata. Lucia di Lammermoor. Carmen.*'

'Operas,' Buchanan said.

'Give the man a cigar. Operas. I guess you're not a devotee.'

'Well, my taste in music . . .' Buchanan hesitated. 'I don't *have* any taste in music.'

'Come on, everybody likes *some* kind of music.'

'My characters do.'

'What?'

'The people I . . . Heavy metal. Country and western. Blue grass. It's just that I never got around to impersonating anybody who liked opera.'

'Buchanan, you're scaring me again.'

'For the past week, I've been thinking of myself as a man named Peter Lang. *He* likes Barbra Streisand.'

'You really are scaring me.'

'I told you I'm changeable.' Buchanan-Lang smiled oddly.

'But no one I've ever been had an interest in opera. If he had, believe me I'd be expert enough on the subject to give you a lecture. What does opera have to do with the name "Tomez"?'

'*Maria* Tomez,' Holly said. 'The name occurred to me immediately but not as strongly as Alistair Drummond. I wanted to make sure there weren't any famous or rich or powerful people named Tomez whom I didn't know about.' Holly took another book and file from the briefcase. 'And indeed there *are* some, but they're not pertinent here. Maria Tomez — to quote from her press releases — is the most controversial, charismatic, and compelling mezzo soprano in the opera world today. As far as I'm concerned, she's the only candidate for your attention.'

'What makes you so sure?'

'Because for the past nine months Alistair Drummond and Maria Tomez have, despite the difference in their ages, been an item.' Holly paused for effect. 'And Maria Tomez disappeared two weeks ago.'

9

Buchanan leaned forward. '*Disappeared?*'

'That's what her ex-husband claims. Don't you read the newspapers?' Holly asked.

'The past few days, I haven't exactly had time.'

'Well, this morning the ex-husband went to the New York City police department and insisted that she'd been missing for at least the past two weeks. To make sure he wasn't treated as a crank, he brought along a couple dozen newspaper and television reporters. It turned into quite a circus.'

Buchanan shook his head. 'But why would he think he'd be treated as a crank?'

'Because he and Maria Tomez had a very public and very nasty divorce. He's been badmouthing her ever since. He recently filed a lawsuit against her, claiming she lied about her financial assets when they divided their property during the divorce. He insists he has a right to ten million dollars. Naturally the police might think she dropped out of sight to avoid him. But the ex-husband swears he honestly believes something has happened to her.'

Holly gave Buchanan a page from the previous day's *Washington Post* and a photocopy of a profile in the *Post*'s Sunday magazine from five years earlier. Buchanan scanned the newspaper story and the profile. The ex-husband, Frederick Maltin, had been an agent who discovered Maria Tomez when she was twenty-two, starring in a production of *Tosca* in Mexico City. While a few male Hispanics, Placido Domingo, for example, had achieved significant careers in opera, no Hispanic female had ever had similar success. Until Maria Tomez. Indeed, despite her talent and fiery stage presence, the fact that she was Mexican had worked against her, relegating her to regional operas, mostly in South America. Traditionally, female opera stars got their training in Europe and America. For Tomez to have been trained in Mexico meant that she was combating a professional prejudice when she auditioned for major opera companies in the United States and Italy.

But Frederick Maltin, who had been on vacation in Mexico, had been enchanted from the moment he first heard Maria Tomez sing. He had sent flowers to her dressing room after the performance, along with his business card and his Mexico City telephone number. When he received a call the next morning, he considered it significant that the call had come so early and that it was Maria herself who had called, not her representative. Which tended to suggest that she either didn't *have* a representative or else didn't have confidence that the

465

representative would contact him at her request. Professionally speaking, she was available.

Maltin invited her to lunch. They continued their conversation after an afternoon rehearsal and later, at dinner, after an evening performance of a different opera, *Rigoletto*. As Maltin repeatedly emphasized, in those days Maria's schedule had been brutal, and he had sworn to her that if she agreed to let him represent her, he would change all that. He would make her a worldwide opera phenomenon. He would arrange it so that she performed only where and when she wanted to. Two years later, he had achieved his promise.

They married in the interim, and working relentlessly on her behalf, advising her about her clothes, her hairstyle, and her makeup, insisting that she lose weight, hiring a physical trainer to give her body definition, calling in every favor owed to him by anyone of influence in the opera world, Maltin promoted Maria Tomez as a singer in the passionate tradition of Maria Callas and Teresa Stratas. The former was Italian, the latter Greek, and Maltin's genius was in making his client's weakness her strength, in making audiences associate Maria Tomez with those divas because of a common denominator they shared, their ethnic origins. For Maria Tomez at least, it suddenly became fashionable to be Hispanic. Out of curiosity, European audiences came to hear her sing. Impressed, they stayed. Enthusiastic, they kept attending her other performances. After Frederick Maltin finished creating her public image, Maria Tomez never had any performance that wasn't a sell-out.

Buchanan rubbed his throbbing forehead. 'This guy Maltin sounds like a cross between Svengali and Professor Henry Higgins.'

'That's why the marriage failed,' Holly said. 'He wouldn't stop controlling her. He supervised everything she did. He dominated so much that she felt smothered. She endured it for

466

as long as she could. Then fifteen years after she met him, she abruptly left him. It's almost as if something inside her snapped. She retired from performing. She went into seclusion, making occasional public appearances, mostly keeping to herself.'

'This started . . .' Buchanan picked up the newspaper article to jog his memory. 'She divorced him six months ago, a few months after she took up with Alistair Drummond. But why would a comparatively young woman – what is she? thirty-seven now? – choose a man in his eighties?'

'Maybe Drummond makes no demands. I know that seems out of character for him. But maybe he just wants to shelter her in exchange for the pleasure of her company.'

'So she went into seclusion, and now her ex-husband claims she's disappeared altogether.' Buchanan frowned. 'He could be wrong, or he could be lying. He's an expert in publicity, after all. He could be trying to attract so much attention that to get any peace, she'll have to deal with his claims about the property settlement.'

'Or maybe something really happened to her.'

'But what?' Buchanan became impatient. 'And what does that have to do with Juana? Was Juana protecting her? Are they both hiding somewhere? Are they . . . ?' He was about to say 'dead,' but the word stuck in his throat, making him feel choked.

Someone knocked on the door. Buchanan spun.

'Room service,' a man's voice said from the hallway.

Buchanan breathed out. 'Okay.' He glanced toward Holly and lowered his voice. 'In case this is trouble, take your camera bag and the briefcase. Hide in the closet.'

Holly's brow knotted with worry.

'I think everything will be fine. It's only a precaution,' Buchanan said. 'Here, don't forget your coat and hat.'

'I asked you before. How do you stand living this way?'

After shutting the closet, Buchanan approached the room's entrance, peering through the small lens in the door, seeing the distorted image of a man in a hotel uniform next to a room-service cart in the hallway.

Buchanan no longer had his handgun. Having traveled with it from Fort Lauderdale to Washington to New Orleans to San Antonio, he'd finally been forced to throw it down a storm drain. His trainers had emphasized – never keep a weapon that links you to a crime. Plus, the urgency of his self-imposed deadline had required him to use a commercial airline to get back to Washington, and he wasn't about to risk getting caught with a handgun in an airport.

With no other weapon but his body, Buchanan concealed his tension and opened the door. 'Sorry I took so long.'

'No problem.' The man from room service wheeled in the cart. A minute later, he'd turned the cart into a table and set out the food.

Wary about having to compromise his hands, Buchanan signed the bill and added a fifteen percent tip.

'Thanks, Mr Duffy.'

'Don't mention it.'

Buchanan locked the door behind the waiter. Slowly he relaxed and exhaled.

Holly emerged from the closet, her features strained. 'I guess in your line of work you have to distrust everybody.'

'I was taught early – a person's either on the team or not.'

'And if not?'

'There aren't any innocent bystanders.'

'Cynical.'

'Practical.'

'And what about me?'

Buchanan took a long time answering. 'You're not a bystander.'

468

10

Buchanan had ordered pasta primavera for both of them. Now, instead of eating, he glanced at his watch, saw that it was ten o'clock, and went to the phone. Before leaving San Antonio, he and Pedro Mendez had chosen a pay phone near where Pedro worked. Buchanan had instructed Pedro to be waiting next to the phone at nine – ten o'clock in Washington. An enemy could not have anticipated that location and eavesdropped on the line when Buchanan called to make certain that there hadn't been any trouble after the prisoners were released.

Pedro had been told to use English if he was being pressured. To Buchanan's relief, he used Spanish.

'Any problems?'

'The men followed the agreement,' Pedro said. 'When I let them go, they did not harm us.'

Buchanan imagined the courage that Pedro and Anita had required in order to go through with their part of the bargain.

'But I do not think they are far away,' Pedro said. 'I have to believe that they are nearby, watching us.'

'I think so, too,' Buchanan said. 'I never believed them when they said they'd leave town. Don't remove the microphones from your house. Do everything as usual. The two things protecting you are that they believe you don't know anything about your daughter's whereabouts, and that they need you alive and well in case Juana tries to get in touch with you. If they harm you, they're destroying a potential link with her. Pedro, I need to ask you a question. It might have something to do with Juana, but I want you to think carefully before you let me ask it. Because if it helps explain why Juana disappeared, you'll be putting yourself in danger. You'll have exactly the kind of information that whoever's trying to find Juana needs to know.'

The line was silent for a moment.

'I don't have a choice,' Pedro said. 'If this is about my daughter, if it might help her, I must do my best to answer your question.'

Buchanan's respect for Pedro kept increasing. 'Does the name "Maria Tomez" mean anything to you? Did Juana ever mention her? Does Maria Tomez have anything to do with—?'

'Of course,' Pedro said. 'The singer. I don't know anything about opera, but I saw her perform. A year ago, she came to San Antonio to sing at HemisFair.' Pedro referred to one of San Antonio's main attractions. The site of the 1968 world's fair, it had been converted into a cultural-athletic complex, linked to the city by a canal. 'I remember because that was one of the few times Juana told us anything about her work. She was hired to do the security for the performance. In fact, she gave us front-row seats. I didn't want to go, but Anita made me, and I was surprised that I liked it. I don't remember the name of the opera. It was about students living in slums. Maria Tomez played somebody who was dying from a disease. The words were in Italian, but Spanish is close enough to Italian that I understood. Maria Tomez sang like an angel. I was stunned. But what does this have to do with Juana and what happened to her? How would an opera singer who came here a year ago . . . ?'

'I don't know yet. Listen carefully, Pedro. From time to time, I'll phone your office to make sure no one's bothering you. I'll use the name "Ben Clark". Can you remember that? Ben Clark. I'll ask about a Ford you're supposed to be repairing. If you tell me it'll cost a lot of money to fix, I'll know you're in trouble, and I'll get there as soon as I can to help you.'

' . . . Ben Clark.'

'Right. Take care, Pedro.'

'Jeff Walker, whoever you are, thank you.'

Exactly, Buchanan thought as he set down the phone. Whoever I am.

When he turned, he saw Holly watching him.

'What's the matter? Why are you looking at me like that?'

'Ben Clark? A Ford? In this room, you're Charles Duffy. Downstairs, you're Mike Hamilton. You mentioned something about Peter Lang. That doesn't include . . . How the hell do you keep it all straight?'

'Sometimes I wonder.' To avoid the topic, he sat down and started eating, not realizing how ravenous he was until the first bite of food hit his stomach. During his phone call, the pasta had gotten cold. It didn't matter. He couldn't get enough of it.

Holly set down her fork. 'You've been constantly on the go since you left the hospital.'

Buchanan kept eating, trying to ignore his headache.

'Don't you think it's time you slowed down?'

'Can't. As soon as we finish eating, I'll get you out of the hotel. Then I have to take a trip.'

'Where?'

'It's better if you don't know.'

'You don't trust me? After I proved I want to help? You said I was on the team.'

'It's not a matter of trust. What you don't know won't hurt you – and it won't hurt me if . . .'

'What you're trying not to say is if I'm questioned, I can't give away your next move.'

Buchanan swallowed a piece of bread and stared at her. 'The men watching you have nothing to do with what happened to Juana. But if they see us together, they'll assume you're back on the story about *them*, and they'll do everything they can to protect themselves.'

'Now you've done it.' Holly shuddered.

'What?'

471

'Scared me again. Just when I get to feeling normal, you remind me . . .'

'Nothing is ever normal.'

'Right. I keep forgetting.'

11

Buchanan went with her down the fire stairs to the third-floor landing. Her instructions were to take the elevator from that floor down to the lobby. That way, to anyone watching the numbers above the elevator in the lobby, it would seem that Holly had been in Mike Hamilton's third-floor room all evening. 'If anybody stops you, tell them to leave you alone or you'll call a cop. But if it gets serious, tell them a version of the truth. You're doing a story on the Maria Tomez disappearance and whether there's some connection between Tomez and Drummond. If they pressure you about Mike Hamilton, tell them he's a confidential source who works for Drummond. Tell them the man contacted you, using a false name. He's a disgruntled employee. He wants to make trouble for Drummond, but he doesn't want the trouble to be traced to him. So far he hasn't been much use.'

At the third-floor fire stairs, Buchanan motioned for Holly to wait while he checked that the corridor was safe. After peering cautiously out the door, he stepped back, his expression concerned enough to make Holly frown.

He motioned for her to follow. 'We have to hurry. Two men are outside Mike Hamilton's room.'

Before leaving 512, Buchanan had packed, made sure that the books and research files were in his travel bag, and filled out an early check-out form, putting it on the bed. A note explained that Mike Hamilton was checking out, too, but that as agreed all expenses were to be on Charles Duffy's credit card. 'I don't want any more people looking for me than necessary. Quickly. Let's go.'

He hurried with Holly down the fire stairs to the exit for the lobby. 'Wait until some people get off the elevator. Go out behind them. Where do you live?'

She told him.

'I'll leave a minute after you. I'll take a taxi, and if I'm not followed, I'll have the driver go past your place. By then, your own taxi should have brought you home. Leave a light on behind an open window in front. If I see that a window's open, I'll know you're okay.'

'Taxi? I brought my car.'

'Then you'll get home faster. The elevator's opening. Now.'

She touched his cheek. ' . . . Be careful.'

Buchanan felt the impression of her fingers for quite a while after she was gone.

12

'Buchanan!'

It must have been the result of fatigue.

'Buchanan!'

Or else it resulted from his conversation with Holly. Although he'd come to Washington thinking of himself as Peter Lang impersonating Charles Duffy and Mike Hamilton, he'd been distracted into talking to Holly as the core identity he'd been trying to avoid.

'Buchanan!'

So when he heard a man call his name as he walked along the rain-misted street away from the hotel, Buchanan almost turned reflexively to see who wanted him.

It was a mistake, he instantly realized, and he caught himself before he fully turned, but he did twist his head partially, and that was all the indication his hunter needed.

'Yeah, you! Buchanan!'

Buchanan kept walking, not changing his pace, not appearing to feel pressured, although he did feel pressured. A lot. Nerves quickening, he heard rapid footsteps behind him on the wet sidewalk. One person, it sounded like, but Buchanan didn't dare look to see if he was right.

The time was nearly ten-thirty. Traffic was sparse, sporadic headlights gleaming through the beads of moisture in the gloomy air. Buchanan had glanced casually from side to side when he'd left the hotel, a natural thing to do, one that allowed him to check for any sign that Holly had been detained or that anyone was outside watching him. Seeing no problem, he had turned off Massachusetts Avenue, heading south on 21st Street.

Now, heart pounding, he realized that 21st was a one-way street and that the traffic was headed in a southern direction just as he was which meant that all the cars approached from behind him. Unless he looked over his shoulder, he had no way to tell if a vehicle would be veering toward him. But if he did look, he would reinforce his pursuer's suspicion. Plural. Other urgent footsteps had joined the first.

'God damn it, Buchanan!' a different voice yelled.

The voice was directly behind him, close enough to attack.

With no other viable option, Buchanan whirled, seeing a well-built, short-haired man in his mid-twenties lurch to a sudden, defensive stop.

But not quickly enough. Buchanan struck the man's chest with the palm of his right hand. The blow was hard but controlled, calculated to knock the man off balance but not to break his ribs.

The man was jolted backward. He exhaled forcefully, a practiced reaction that helped him absorb the impact. That reaction and the resistance the man's solid chest provided told

474

Buchanan that this wasn't a civilian. The man was military: trim hips, broad shoulders for upper-body strength. While the man briefly lost his balance, Buchanan swung his right leg hard, twisting it so that his shin bone struck along the outside of the man's left thigh. A major, sensitive nerve ran down each leg in that area. If the nerve were traumatized, the victim suffered not only intense pain but temporary paralysis in the leg.

As Buchanan anticipated, before the man could retaliate from the blow to his chest, he grunted, grasped his leg, and toppled sharply. That left a second man rushing toward Buchanan, cursing, reaching beneath his windbreaker. Buchanan threw his travel bag toward him, forcing the man to zigzag while raising a hand to deflect the bag. Before the man could recover from this distraction and draw the handgun he was reaching for, Buchanan came in close, rammed the palm of his hand sharply against the bottom of the man's nose, and felt cartilage snap. The man's vision would blur. The pain would be intense. That gave Buchanan enough time to jab an elbow into the man's solar plexus and yank the man's pistol away as he doubled over.

Immediately Buchanan whirled, grabbed the first man struggling to stand, and walloped him against a lamp post. The man's head made a whunking sound. Then Buchanan whirled yet again, back to the second man, who lay sprawled on the sidewalk, fighting to breathe through his broken nose, spewing blood.

If this had been combat, Buchanan would have killed them. As it was, he didn't want to make the incident even more serious than it was. If he eliminated the colonel's men, the next time their orders would be to do the same to him instead of to detain him. Or perhaps these men *had* been ordered to kill him. Otherwise, why would the second man have been drawing a weapon?

From where Buchanan had come, at the corner of Massachusetts Avenue and 21st Street, a well-dressed, elderly man and woman gaped in Buchanan's direction. The woman pointed a trembling arm, her outcry shrill.

Buchanan grabbed his travel bag and ran. His reaction wasn't caused only by fear that a police car would soon arrive. What sent adrenaline surging through him in even greater quantity, with greater urgency, were the two men who'd scurried around the corner in response to the woman's cry. Seeing Buchanan, they charged, and their chests were as muscled, their shoulders as broad as the men on the sidewalk.

Buchanan ran harder, the stitches in his knife wound threatening to tear open. He didn't care. He had to keep straining. Because when the second two men had seen him and raced toward him, both had reached beneath windbreakers, pulling out handguns, and there was no question now. This wasn't just a surveillance team. It was a hit team.

What had they done to Holly?

But he couldn't let himself think about that. He had to concentrate on staying alive. The first priority was to get off this damned one-way street, where the direction of traffic left him vulnerable from behind. Approaching P Street, he risked wasting time to look behind him on his left, saw an opening between two approaching cars, and darted between them, hoping that the cars would shield him, having noticed that the men were raising their weapons. A horn blared. Brakes squealed. He scrambled onto the opposite sidewalk and skidded on a slippery puddle but kept his balance, then bolted around the corner as the cars stopped shielding him and two gunshots roared, bullets shattering a window across from him.

Tightening his grip on the pistol he'd taken from the man whose nose he'd broken, Buchanan raced in a greater frenzy. The misty rain seemed thicker, the night darker. There wasn't any traffic. The rain discouraged pedestrians. Ahead, opposite, on the right, a murky street light revealed a lane that headed south, bisecting the block between 21st and 20th. Buchanan lunged toward it, his travel bag slowing his momentum, but he couldn't ditch the bag. He couldn't give up the books and files that were in it.

Behind him, he heard curses, strident breathing, rapid footsteps. The sign for the lane said Hopkins. Sprinting from P Street onto it, he flinched as bullets struck the corner he passed. At once, he whirled, crouched, and aimed one-handed with his elbow propped on his bent knee, controlling his trembling arm. Sweat merged with beads of mist on his brow. Leaning out from the corner, he wasn't able to see clearly enough to line up the front and rear sights of the pistol. But if he couldn't, his pursuers couldn't aim clearly, either. Judging as best as he could, he squeezed the trigger rapidly, firing three times, the shots echoing in the narrow street, assaulting his eardrums.

Nonetheless he heard the clink of ejected cartridges striking the pavement and a groan as if he'd hit one of the men, although he had no way of knowing if any of his bullets had connected because both men dove flat on the pavement and shot in his direction, their gun muzzles flashing. A bullet blew a chunk off the corner of the building, nearly hitting Buchanan's eyes. He flinched and shot three more times toward the men, who now rolled in opposite directions, seeking cover behind parked cars.

Buchanan wasn't about to get caught outnumbered in a stationary gun battle. The moment he lost sight of the men, he ducked backward, rose, and charged toward the end of the narrow street. The gunshots had caused lights to come on in upstairs apartments. People foolishly showed their silhouettes at windows. Buchanan kept racing. He heard a distant siren grow louder. He heard a window open. He heard a shout above him. But the rapid, echoing footsteps behind him were the only sounds he cared about.

Spinning, seeing the two men appear at the entrance to the narrow street, Buchanan fired twice more. The men separated and lunged into doorways.

Buchanan zigzagged, trying to confuse their aim. A bullet tugged at his left sleeve; another forced tickling air past his right ear. But this time, he didn't hear gunshots, only eerie muffled sounds as if hands were striking pillows. The men had put sound-suppressors on their weapons, making the noise of Buchanan's own weapon seem even more explosive when he spun again and fired. More lights came on in upper apartment windows. The siren sped closer, louder. Another joined it.

Buchanan sprinted from the narrow street, racing through the misty rain across O Street, charging to the left toward 20th Street. Relieved to be temporarily out of the line of fire, he suddenly tensed as headlights blazed behind him. In the middle of the street, not knowing which way to dive, he had to spin, and the headlights streaked directly toward him. Brakes squealed. But the car wouldn't be able to stop soon enough. Buchanan had to leap forward, onto the hood of the car, sliding along it to absorb the impact, his face pressing against the windshield, stunned to see the unmistakable red hair of Holly McCoy behind the steering wheel.

Holly's face was contorted in a shocked, silent scream. Then a flapping windshield wiper struck the side of Buchanan's face, and he snapped his head up, peering over the top of the skidding car, seeing the two gunmen appear at the exit from the narrow street. Breathing rapidly, Buchanan raised his weapon and fired along the roof of the car, unable to aim effectively but shooting four times, often enough to send the men scurrying back into the cover of the narrow street.

'Drive, Holly! Don't stop! Drive!'

The car quit skidding and increased speed. Sliding,

Buchanan banged his face against the windshield. He glanced frantically over his shoulder, seeing that they'd reached 20th Street. A one-way heading north, it forced Holly to veer left into a break in sparse traffic. But the momentum caused Buchanan to slide sideways on his stomach, to his left, across the car's wet hood. With a travel bag in his left hand and a pistol in his right, he couldn't grab for anything. But even if his hands had been free, there wasn't anything on the slick hood to grab.

The car kept veering. He kept sliding. He anticipated his impact on the pavement. Tuck in your elbows. Roll. Keep your head up, he mentally shouted to himself. He couldn't afford another trauma to his head. And then he was slipping off the left side of the hood. Heart pounding, seeing the sideview mirror, he hooked his right elbow around it, bent his legs up under him, felt a jolt, and dangled. The sideview mirror sagged from his weight. He kept his elbow crooked around it, dangling lower, his shoes inches above the pavement. The car skidded. His shoes touched the pavement. The car slowed. When the sideview mirror snapped off, Buchanan landed hard, rolling in a puddle, the wind knocked out of him, but not before the car had stopped, its momentum throwing him forward.

He lurched to his feet. More headlights blazed toward him. He heard sirens. He thought he heard racing footsteps. Then he definitely heard Holly shout from inside the car. She pressed a button that unlocked the doors.

But instead of opening the passenger door in front, Buchanan yanked open the door in back and dove in, slamming the door behind him. Sprawling out of sight, he yelled, 'Go, Holly! Move!'

She obeyed, squinting ahead past the flapping windshield wipers, darting her gaze toward her rearview mirror, straining to see if the sirens belonged to police cars chasing her. But the headlights behind her remained steady, and no men appeared on the sidewalk to shoot at her, and the sirens became farther away, less intimidating.

'What happened?' she asked in dismay.

As she turned right onto Massachusetts Avenue, steered a quarter of the way around Dupont Circle, and then headed south on Connecticut Avenue, Buchanan quickly explained, all the while remaining low on the back seat, out of sight. Even though their hunters knew what type of car Holly drove, they'd be looking for a man and a woman, not a woman alone.

Holly's hands were sweaty on the steering wheel. 'Are you hurt?'

'I pulled some stitches.' His voice was taut. 'If that's the worst, I'll be fine.'

'Until the next time.'

'Thank God you just happened to be driving along that street.'

'There was nothing "just happened" about it.'

'What do you—?'

'When you started down Twenty-First Street and they chased you, you ran from the sidewalk and darted between two passing cars.'

'Right, but how did you know about—?'

'The second car, the one that beeped at you, was mine. After the hotel's parking attendant brought it to me, I decided to drive around the block to see if I was being followed.'

'Sounds like you're learning.'

'And I also wanted to see if you got out of the hotel okay. I was driving toward you when I saw the fight, but you ran in front of me before I could get your attention. Then you disappeared along P Street. I was past that intersection, so I figured if I turned left onto O, I might get a glimpse of you coming from Hopkins or Twentieth Street.'

'But what if I'd stayed on P Street?'

'You don't strike me as the type to run in a straight line.'

'You really *are* learning,' Buchanan said.

'Evasion and escape.' Holly exhaled. 'I missed that course when I was in journalism school.'

'I didn't mean to get you involved. It was the farthest thing from my mind. I'm sorry, Holly.'

'It's done. But I helped make it happen. I didn't need to agree to meet you. I could have kept my distance. I'm a big girl. I stopped letting people control me a long time ago. Do you want the truth? I thought you wanted to meet me to tell me something that would put me back on the story. I got foolish and greedy. Now I'm paying the price.'

'Then you understand.' Staying low in the back seat, Buchanan spoke reluctantly. 'You realize that because they caught us together, they think we're both a threat to them. It was a possibility before, but now your life really is in danger.'

Holly tried to control her breathing. 'I had another reason for agreeing to meet you. An even more foolish reason. It had nothing to do with the story. Deep down, I wanted to see you again. Dumb, huh?'

Except for the flapping of the windshield wipers and the drone of the engine, the car became quiet.

Holly waited.

She finally said, 'Don't respond. Just let what I said hang there. Make me feel like a jerk.'

'No. I . . .'

'What?'

'I'm flattered.'

'You'd better say something more positive than that, or

481

so help me, I'll stop this car and . . .'

'What I'm trying to explain is, I'm not very good at this. I'm not used to anybody caring about me.' Buchanan's disembodied voice came from the darkness of the back seat. 'I've never been in one place long enough to establish a relationship.'

'Once.'

'Yes. With Juana. That's right. Once.'

'And now I'm risking my life to help you find another woman. Wonderful. Great.'

'It's more complicated than that,' Buchanan said.

'I don't see how . . .'

'It's not just that I was never in one place long enough to establish a relationship. I was never one *person* long enough. It isn't me who wants to find Juana. It's Peter Lang.'

'Peter Lang? Didn't you say he was one of your pseudonyms?'

'Identities.'

'I think I'm going to scream.'

'Don't. Later. Not now. Get us out of town.'

'In which direction?'

'North. Toward Manhattan.'

'And what's in—?'

'Frederick Maltin. The ex-husband of Maria Tomez. There's one other thing we have to do.'

'Get you a shrink.'

'Don't make jokes.'

'That wasn't a joke.'

'Stop at a pay phone.'

'I'm beginning to think *I'm* the one who needs a shrink.'

14

At one a.m., between Washington and Baltimore, Holly parked at a truck stop on I-95. Buchanan got out and used a pay phone.

A man answered, 'Potomac Catering.'

'This is Proteus. I need to speak to the colonel.'

'He isn't here right now, but I'll take a message.'

'Tell him *I* got the message. Tell him there won't be any trouble. Tell him I could have killed those four men tonight. Tell him to leave me alone. Tell him to leave Holly McCoy alone. Tell him I want to disappear. Tell him my business with Holly has nothing to do with him. Tell him Holly doesn't know or care about him.'

'You sure have a lot to tell him.'

'Just make certain *you* do.'

Buchanan hung up, knowing that the number of the pay phone would automatically have shown itself on a screen on the catering service's automatic-trace phone. If the colonel wouldn't accept Buchanan's attempt at a truce, a team of men would soon converge on this area.

Buchanan hurried back into the car, this time in the front. 'I did my best. Let's go.'

As she pulled out into traffic, he reached for his travel bag. The effort made him wince.

He took off his pants.

'Hey, what do you think you're doing?' Holly asked.

His legs were bare.

'Changing my clothes. I'm soaked.' In the flash of passing headlights, he squinted at the waist of his pants. 'And bleeding. I was right. Some stitches did open up.' He took a tube of antibiotic cream and a roll of bandages from his travel bag, then started to work on his side. 'You know what I could use?'

'A normal life?'

'Some coffee and sandwiches.'

'Sure. A picnic.'

15

The colonel frowned and set down the phone. In the safe-site apartment five blocks north of *The Washington Post*, Alan – who'd been watching the colonel while listening on an extension – set down his phone as well.

The only sound was the faint drone of a car that went by outside.

'Do you want my advice?' Alan asked.

'No.' The colonel's narrow face looked haggard from strain and fatigue.

'Well, I'll give it to you anyhow.' Alan's portly cheeks were emphasized by whisker shadow. 'Buchanan's waving you off. He's asking for a truce. Agree to it. You've got nothing to win and everything to lose.'

'That's your opinion, is it?' the colonel asked dryly. 'I'm not used to taking advice from civilians, especially when they don't understand the serious nature of Buchanan's offense. A soldier can't be allowed to just walk away from his unit, certainly not Buchanan. He knows too much. I told you before, his behavior makes him a security risk. We're talking about chaos.'

'And gun battles in the street aren't chaos? This has nothing to do with principle or security. It's about pride. I was afraid of what would happen when the military became involved in civilian intelligence operations. You don't like taking advice from civilians? Well, maybe you ought to read the Constitution. Because taking advice is exactly what you're supposed to do. Without the Agency's oversight on this, you'd be autonomous. You'd love that, wouldn't you? Your own private army to do with as you want. Your own private wars.'

'Get out of here,' the colonel said. 'You're always grumbling about never seeing your wife and kids. Go home.'

'And give you control? No damned way. I'm staying with you until this issue is resolved,' Alan said.

'Then you're in for a long, hard ride.'

'It doesn't need to be. All you have to do is leave Buchanan alone.'

'I can't! Not as long as he's with that reporter.'

'But Buchanan says that his business with the reporter has nothing to do with you.'

'*And you believe that?*'

'He's not a fool. I was talking about gains and losses. He has nothing to gain if he turns against you, and everything to lose. But if you hunt him, he'll turn against you out of spite, and frankly, Colonel, he's the last person I'd want to be my enemy.'

ELEVEN

1

Buchanan woke to a throbbing headache aggravated by banging metal and a roaring engine. He roused himself and blinked through the windshield at where a sanitation crew was emptying cans and throwing bags of refuse into the back of a garbage truck. He glanced at his watch – 8 a.m. Holly was driving north on Madison Avenue in New York City.

'You should have wakened me.' Buchanan shielded his eyes from the hazy sunshine.

'So you could keep me company? No. You obviously needed the rest. Besides, I didn't mind the quiet. It gave me a chance to think.'

'About what?'

'I realized I can't go back. Not until we find a way to convince them this has nothing to do with them. I have to keep moving forward.'

'But there's only so far you can keep going until you drop. I'm not the only one who needed rest.'

'I took your advice,' Holly said.

'I don't remember giving . . .'

'Last night, I asked you how you'd managed to drive all the way from New Orleans to San Antonio, as tired as you must have been after having been wounded. You said you'd napped at rest stops along the way. So whenever I had to stop to go to the bathroom, I locked the car doors and closed my eyes. You're right. People make so much noise, slamming their car doors, it's hard to sleep more than a few minutes.'

'You certainly don't look like you've been up most of the night.'

'The miracle of cosmetics. Thanks to sinks and mirrors at rest stops. If we're going to pull this off, by the way, you need a shave.'

Buchanan rubbed his jaw, reached into his travel bag, pulled a safety razor from a pouch, and began to scrape it along his beard-stubbled cheeks.

'Ouch,' Holly said. 'Doesn't that hurt?'

'You get used to it. A lot of times on assignments, this was the only way to try to keep clean.'

He waited uneasily, hoping that she wouldn't take advantage of the reference and ask him questions about those assignments.

Instead she passed the test and merely concentrated on her driving.

'Have we got any coffee left?' he asked.

'We drank it all. But now that you mention it . . .'

She pulled over to a curb, parked with the motor running, ran into a coffee shop, and returned in a minute with two styrofoam cups of coffee and four Danish.

'You're a good provider.'

'And you'd better keep being a good teacher,' Holly said. 'The Sherry-Netherland's one block over on Fifth. It was mentioned in yesterday's article in the *Post*. How do you want to do this?'

'First, we find a parking garage that has space.'

'Easier said than done.'

'Then we look for somebody watching Frederick Maltin's apartment.'

'Why would someone be watching—?'

'To tie up an unfortunate loose end. I don't think he was expected to be as big a problem as he's become, going to reporters, drawing attention to Maria Tomez's disappearance. My guess is, whoever's responsible will want to take care of that.'

2

The Sherry-Netherland was diagonally across from the Plaza Hotel on Fifth Avenue. Immediately across from it were the Grand Army Plaza and an entrance to Central Park. Despite the upscale address, so many people came and went, lounged and loitered in the area that it wasn't difficult for Buchanan and Holly to portray a convincing version of two tourists when they arrived an hour later. It was cool but pleasant for early November. They strolled around the block, admired buildings, checked out the entrance to the park, and effectively scouted the busy area.

'Somebody could be watching from neighboring buildings, of course,' Buchanan said as he took a photograph of a skyscraper, using Holly's camera. 'But it doesn't look like anybody in the crowd is doing that.'

They sat on a bench near the gold-gilded statue of William Tecumseh Sherman.

'What now?' Holly asked.

'Time for you to do some role-playing. But I'm afraid it's a tough one.'

'Oh?'

'You're going to have to impersonate a reporter.'

She jammed her elbow into his ribs.

'Hey, Jesus, watch it,' Buchanan said. 'That came close to where I was stabbed.'

'I might stab you myself if you keep acting that way.'

Buchanan laughed. 'You brought your reporter's ID, I hope.'

'Always. It's in my camera bag.'

'Well, I just became your assistant. Call me . . . who was that guy who tagged along with you in New Orleans?'

'Ted.'

'Right. Call me Ted. We're about to pay a professional visit to Mr Maltin. You'd better let your assistant carry the camera bag.'

'You know, you don't do that often enough.'

'Carry your bag?'

'No. A moment ago, you were smiling.'

They waited for the light, crossed at 59th Street, and headed north along crowded Fifth Avenue toward the canopied entrance to the Sherry-Netherland. Nodding to the uniformed doorman who was getting a taxi for a well-dressed, elderly woman, Buchanan pushed the revolving door and entered ahead of Holly to check out the lobby.

Gentle lights gave it a golden hue. Colorful flowers stood in a vase on a side table. Ahead, on the right, a short corridor led to elevators. On the left, across from the corridor, the reception counter was next to a newspaper-magazine shop. A uniformed clerk stood in the lobby, another behind the counter. A middle-aged, spectacled woman straightened things next to the cash register at the magazine shop.

No sign of a threat, Buchanan decided as he waited for Holly to come out of the revolving door and join him.

'Yes, sir?' The clerk in the lobby stepped forward.

Typically the clerk singled out the male of a couple. But because Buchanan was supposed to be Holly's assistant, he straightened the camera bag around his shoulder and turned to her, his eyebrows raised, waiting for her to answer.

Holly immediately assumed her role. 'I'm a reporter.' She held out her press ID.

The clerk glanced at the card, his inspection cursory, probably paying attention to the newspaper's name and little else, Buchanan hoped. Holly hadn't volunteered her own name, and with luck, the clerk wouldn't have noticed it on the card.

'I'm here to see Mr Maltin.' Holly put the press card away.

'Did you have an appointment?'

'No. But if he's free, I'd appreciate ten minutes of his time.'

'One moment.' The clerk walked over to the counter and picked up a phone, pressing numbers. 'Mr Maltin, there's a reporter from *The Washington Post* to see you. A lady with a photographer . . . Yes, sir, I'll tell them.' The clerk set down the phone. 'Mr Maltin doesn't wish to be disturbed.'

'But yesterday, he couldn't get enough of reporters.'

'All I know is he doesn't wish to be disturbed.'

'Please, call him back.'

'I'm afraid I—'

'Really, it's important. I have information about his missing wife.'

The clerk hesitated.

'He'll be very unhappy if he finds out you didn't give him the message.'

The clerk's gaze darkened. 'One moment.' He walked back to the desk, picked up the phone, pressed numbers, and this time spoke with his back turned so that Holly and Buchanan couldn't hear what he said. When the clerk pivoted in their direction and set down the phone, he looked irritated. 'Mr Maltin will see you. Come with me.'

They followed the clerk toward a row of elevators, and after they got in, the clerk stared straight ahead, pressing the button for the thirtieth floor. Sure, Buchanan thought. This way he guarantees that we get off where we're supposed to be going.

At the thirtieth floor, the clerk waited until Holly rang the bell for Frederick Maltin's apartment. Only when Maltin opened the door, glowered at Holly and Buchanan, and gestured grudgingly for them to enter, did the clerk step back into the elevator.

Buchanan and Holly walked past Maltin, who shut the apartment door impatiently and strode toward the middle of a spacious room.

Spacious was an understatement. The high, rectangular room was large enough to hold at least four standard rooms. The wall to the left and the long one directly ahead were a panorama of windows that began at thigh-level and went all the way to the ceiling, continuing around the room, giving a spectacular view of Fifth Avenue to the south and Central Park directly across. The furniture, tastefully arranged, was antique. Buchanan had the impression of polished wood and crystal, of expensive fabrics and Oriental rugs, of authentic-looking Cubist paintings. A gleaming grand piano stood in a corner, next to a display of what appeared to be museum-quality ceramics. It wasn't any wonder that Frederick Maltin had complained about the financial terms of his divorce from Maria Tomez. He was obviously used to luxury.

'I don't know what information you think you have about my ex-wife, but it isn't pertinent any longer because I just heard from her.'

Buchanan needed all his discipline not to start asking questions. The scenario made this Holly's show. She had to carry it.

She did. 'Then you must be relieved.'

'Of course. Very much.' Frederick Maltin was a man of medium height and weight, in his middle forties, with a moderate amount of hair with a moderate amount of gray in it. As for the rest of his characteristics, there was nothing medium or moderate about him. His dainty, thin-soled, polished, black shoes and meticulously pressed, blended-wool, double-breasted, blue suit were obviously foreign, custom-designed, and hand-sewn. His brilliant, white shirt and subtle, striped tie had contrasting textures of premium silk. It was impossible for Buchanan not to pay attention to Maltin's diamond cufflinks as the man made a show of impatience by checking the time on his diamond-studded Cartier watch. He had a sapphire ring on the small finger of his left hand. All told, it probably cost him twenty thousand dollars to get dressed in the morning.

'The hotel clerk said you needed ten minutes with me, but I can't spare even that much time,' Maltin continued. His voice was reedy, imperious.

'But surely you're eager to tell the press the good news,' Holly said. 'Yesterday, there was so much commotion about your insistence that something had happened to her. You'll want everyone to know it was a false alarm.'

'Well, yes,' Maltin said, 'of course. I hadn't . . . You're right. It's important for you and other reporters to inform her fans that she hasn't been harmed.'

Holly sounded puzzled. 'The way you say that . . . It's as if you haven't called the media yet.'

'I . . . The news just reached me. I'm still adjusting. I'm so relieved, you see.' Maltin removed a burgundy, silk handkerchief from the breast pocket of his suit and wiped his brow.

Yeah, you look relieved all to hell, Buchanan thought.

'I haven't had time to compose myself. To make plans.'

'What did your ex-wife tell you?' Holly asked. 'Where has she been for the past two weeks?'

Maltin looked blank. 'Away. She told me where, but she doesn't want me to reveal the precise location. She wants to stay away a while longer. To rest. After this misunderstanding, reporters will swarm all over her if they get the opportunity.'

'Well, can't you give us a general idea of where she is?'

'France. But that's all I intend to reveal.'

'Did she explain why she dropped out of sight?'

'She wanted to take a trip. In my impatience about these unfortunate legal matters, I made the mistake of assuming that because I couldn't contact her, something disastrous must have happened to her.'

As Buchanan surveyed the room again, he smelled the faint odor of cigarette smoke, but there weren't any ashtrays in this fastidiously maintained room. Nor was there any odor of cigarette smoke on Maltin's clothes. Buchanan was always amazed that smokers didn't realize how pervasive the odor of their habit was. In this case, cigarette smoke from a distant area of the spacious apartment drifted in this direction. And Buchanan had the strong conviction that Frederick Maltin not only didn't smoke but also didn't approve of anyone smoking in his presence, certainly not in his apartment.

'I'll make a confession,' Maltin said. 'I overreacted because Maria wouldn't respond to my telephone calls. When she sold her apartment a few weeks ago and seemed to vanish, I was outraged that she'd ignored me, that she hadn't consulted with me. She used to consult with me about everything. I couldn't imagine she'd be that independent, even though we were divorced. So my pride insisted she must have been the victim of foul play. Ridiculous of me.'

'Yes,' Buchanan said, the first time he'd spoken. 'Do you mind if I use your bathroom?'

'Indeed I do. Very much.'

'But this is an emergency. I have to go.'

Buchanan walked across the room, heading toward a door at the far end.

'Wait. What do you think you're doing?' Maltin exclaimed in outrage. 'You can't . . . Stop right there. You stop where you are!'

'But I told you I need a bathroom.' Buchanan opened the

494

door, entering a tastefully, expensively decorated hallway.

Maltin charged after him. 'If you don't stop, I'll call the police!'

Buchanan kept on. The cigarette smoke was stronger. It seemed to come from . . .

He opened a door on his left, revealing an oak-furnished study from which cigarette smoke drifted. A surprised man straightened from where he'd been leaning his hips against a large, polished desk. He was in his middle thirties, wore an average suit, had hair in slight need of a trim, needed a touch-up on his shoes, held a cigarette, and generally looked like the sort of person whom Frederick Maltin would prefer to avoid.

'Sorry,' Buchanan said. 'I thought this was the bathroom.'

'No problem,' the man said.

A handgun, butt forward, bulged beneath the left side of the man's suit. To draw the weapon, he would have to use his right hand, but his right hand held the cigarette. The man leaned forward as if to flick ashes into a waste can. What he did instead was drop the cigarette into the waste can and grab for his weapon.

Not soon enough. Buchanan didn't want gunshots to alarm anyone in the building. Clutching the strap of the camera bag, he turned as if to leave. And kept turning. Gaining momentum, he swung the bag hard and fast. The bag collided with the side of the man's jaw. It hit with a loud, sharp whack. The man arched sideways. His eyes rolled up in his head. Blood flew out of his mouth. With a groan, he landed on an Oriental carpet, skidded, and slammed his skull against the bottom of a shelf of leatherbound books. He breathed but otherwise didn't move.

'Jesus Christ.' Frederick Maltin had rushed along the hallway and now gaped in shock at the man on the floor. 'Jesus Christ, what have you done?'

'I think he didn't want me to use the bathroom.'

'Oh, Jesus Christ.'

'Yeah, I get the idea. But Jesus isn't going to help you.'

Buchanan drew his own gun, which made Maltin gasp and Holly, behind him, flinch. Approaching the man on the floor, Buchanan aimed the weapon at the man's head while he took the man's .357 revolver away. Then he checked the man's pulse, turned the man's head so that he wouldn't choke from the blood in his mouth, and straightened, shaking his head. 'Sorry about the blood on the carpet, Fred. You ought to be careful about the people you hang around with or rather . . .' Buchanan noticed a satchel on the desk and opened it. 'Or rather the people you do business with. How much money is in this satchel? It sure is a lot of hundred-dollar bills. Banded in five-thousand-dollar units.' Buchanan took them out and made stacks. 'What would you estimate? Let's see. One hundred thousand. Two hundred thousand. Hard to squeeze all of it in there, and heavy to lug around, but yeah, I'd say that what we've got here, all told, is a million dollars.'

Maltin's mouth hung open. His face had turned pale.

Behind him, in the corridor, Holly looked stunned, not only by the money but by what she was witnessing.

'Fred, get down on your knees.'

Maltin trembled. 'Why?'

'Just do it. Here.' Buchanan went past Maltin, over to Holly, and gave her the revolver. 'If Fred tries to stand up, shoot him.' With a baleful stare toward Maltin, Buchanan went into the corridor.

'But where are you going?' Holly asked.

'To make sure we're alone.'

3

Working cautiously, ready with his pistol, Buchanan proceeded from room to room, searching everywhere. Just because he'd found one man, that didn't mean there wouldn't be others hiding in other sections of the apartment.

But he found no one. Relieved, he walked back into the study, again examined the man on the floor, satisfied himself that the man's life signs were steady, tied his hands with his belt, and turned to Maltin, whose face was beading with sweat that he couldn't wipe away fast enough. Indeed Maltin's burgundy handkerchief was soaked.

'Sit down, Fred. You look as if you're going to faint. Is there anything we can get you? A glass of water? Some brandy? Make yourself at home.'

Maltin's face was the color of concrete. Sweating more profusely, he nodded with a trace of desperation. 'Over there. In the top desk drawer.'

Buchanan opened the drawer and made a 'tsking' sound. 'Fred, I'm disappointed in you. You mean to tell me you're a candy sniffer? Naughty, naughty, Fred. Haven't you ever heard of just saying no?'

Buchanan took a vial of white powder from the drawer and set it on the desk. 'But hey, the privacy of your home, an informed adult, blah, blah. Help yourself.'

Maltin glared at him, then pulled the top from the vial, and inhaled cocaine up one nostril, then the other.

'You got a little on your lip there, Fred.'

Maltin wiped it off and licked his finger.

'That's it. Don't be wasteful. Now are you comfy, Fred? Are you ready for some conversation?'

'You son of a bitch.'

Buchanan slapped him so hard that Maltin didn't have time to blink before his head was snapped sideways and specks of white powder flew out of his nose. The slap filled the room like the crack of a whip. It left a raw, red, welting handprint on Maltin's cheek.

Holly raised a startled hand to her mouth.

Buchanan slapped Maltin's other cheek, using even more force, snapping Maltin's head in the other direction.

Maltin wept uncontrollably. 'Please, don't kill me.' He wailed, his eyes scrunched pathetically, tears welling out of them. 'Please.'

'You're not paying attention,' Buchanan said. 'I want conversation. This satchel. This money, Fred. No one carries around this much cash for anything that's legal. What is it? A payoff? Were you already thinking about how to get it to an offshore bank so you wouldn't have to pay taxes on it? I mean, paying taxes on a payoff, that doesn't seem reasonable, does it? So what were you being paid off for, Fred? It had to do with your ex-wife, right? You drew attention to her, and somebody didn't like that. So you were told to shut up, and the inducement was . . . Well, you had a choice. A bullet in the brain, or a million bucks in the bank. But you're no dummy. Hell, for a million bucks, you'd sell out anybody. It doesn't matter if Maria Tomez is in trouble. She divorced you, so let the bitch take care of herself. Right, Fred? Pay attention, Fred. Tell me I'm right, or I'll slap you till your head's turned around.'

Buchanan raised his hand as if to swing, and Maltin cringed. 'Please, no, don't, no, please.'

'Don't mumble. Fred. The money's a payoff, and we got here while it was happening. The deal was you were supposed to call off the media, and since we were insisting, you decided to interrupt the proceedings and handle us. Except you hadn't worked out your routine yet. But by noon, when you called the reporters you spoke to yesterday, your act would have been perfect. Right, Fred? *Right?*' Buchanan feinted his hand at him.

Maltin swallowed tears, blubbered, and nodded.

'Now just so this isn't a one-way conversation, I've got a question for you, Fred? Are you ready?'

Maltin struggled to breathe.

'Who paid you off?'

Maltin didn't answer.

'Fred, I'm talking to you.'

Maltin bit his lip and didn't answer.

Buchanan sighed, telling Holly, 'I'm afraid you'd better leave us alone. You don't want to see this.'

'Drummond,' Maltin whimpered.

'What, Fred? You're mumbling again. Speak up.'

'Alistair Drummond.'

'My, my,' Buchanan said. 'Your ex-wife's new companion. And why would Alistair Drummond pay you a million dollars to keep you from telling the media you can't find her?'

'I . . .'

'You can tell me, Fred.'

'I don't know.'

'Come on, don't disappoint me, Fred. You were doing so well. Why would Drummond pay you off? Think about it. Make a wild guess.'

'I tell you I don't know!'

'Have you ever had any bones broken, Fred?' Buchanan reached for the little finger on Maltin's right hand.

'No! I'm telling the truth!' Maltin yanked his hand away. 'Don't touch me, you bastard! Leave me alone! I mean it! I'm telling the truth! I don't know *anything!*'

'For the last time, Fred, I'm asking you to make a wild guess.'

'*Nothing* about Maria has made any sense since she left me and went on that cruise with Drummond nine months ago.'

'Cruise, Fred? Exactly what cruise are we talking about?'

'Off Acapulco. Drummond has a two-hundred-foot yacht.

He told her she could relax on board while the divorce was being settled. She may have hated me as a husband, but she relied on me as a manager. After that cruise, though, she wouldn't speak to me about anything. She canceled business meetings with me. She wouldn't take my telephone calls. The few times I saw her in public, at the Met or at charity events, Drummond's bodyguards wouldn't let me near her. Damn it, by not dealing with me, she's costing me money! A lot of money!'

'Relax, Fred. The million dollars you were paid to stop bothering her will keep you in cocaine for a while. But do you want some advice? If I were you, I'd use the money to travel. Light and fast and far away. Because I have a very strong feeling that when this is over, whatever it's about, Alistair Drummond intends to guarantee that you keep quiet, to make sure you don't come back for more money, to give you a jolt of cocaine that'll take you right out of this world, if you get my meaning. In fact, I'm surprised he didn't do it already. My guess is he didn't want it to happen so soon after you were making speeches in front of those reporters. Too coincidental. Too suspicious. But it *will* happen, Fred. So I suggest you liquidate, haul ass, change your name, and dig a deep hole. Bury yourself. Because they'll be coming.'

Maltin's face contorted.

'Be seeing you, Fred.'

'But . . . ?' Maltin gestured toward the unconscious man on the floor. 'What about . . . ?'

'The way I see it, you have two options. Think up a good story, or be gone by the time he wakes up. Got to run, Fred.'

'Lord, I've never seen anything like that,' Holly said.

They had emerged from the Sherry-Netherland, turned right off Fifth Avenue, and were walking along Central Park South. Traffic blared while tourists waited to get on horse-drawn carriages.

'Keep a slower pace,' Buchanan said. The sunlight aggravated his headache. 'We don't want to look as if we're running away from anything.'

'And we're not?' Holly whispered nervously. 'You broke a man's jaw. You assaulted Maltin. He'll have called the police the second we left his apartment.'

'No,' Buchanan said. 'He'll be packing.'

'How can you be sure? Every time I hear a police siren—'

'Because if *you've* never seen anything like what just happened, Maltin hadn't, either. If he called the police, he would also have called hotel security, but no one tried to stop us when we left.' Buchanan guided Holly into the Seventh Avenue entrance to Central Park. A cool November breeze tugged at his hair.

'Why are we going into—?'

'Backtracking. We'll turn right at this path up ahead and head back the way we came. To find out if we're being followed by anyone connected with the guy in Maltin's apartment. Besides, there aren't many people in the park. We can talk without being overheard. Maltin was terrified.'

'No kidding. I felt terrified myself. I got the feeling you were out of control. Jesus, you were going to break his fingers.'

'No. I knew I wouldn't have to. But you and Maltin believed I would. The performance was successful.'

'Don't you do anything without calculation?'

'Would you have preferred that I *did* break his fingers?

Come on, Holly. What I did back there was the equivalent of doing an interview.'

'Not like any interview *I* ever conducted.'

Buchanan glanced behind him, then scanned the trees and bushes on either side of them.

'I don't mean just the threats,' Holly said. 'Why didn't you keep questioning him? How do you know he was telling the truth?'

'His eyes,' Buchanan said.

'*Your* eyes looked as if you were a maniac.'

'I'm good with them. I practice with them a lot. They're the key to being an operative. If somebody believes my eyes, they'll believe everything else.'

'Then how can you be so sure about *Maltin's* eyes? Maybe *he* was pretending.'

'No. It takes one to know one. Maltin's a single-role person. A shit who crumbles as soon as his power is taken away. It's no wonder Maria Tomez divorced him. He told me everything I needed to hear. I could have cross-examined him, but that would have wasted time. I already know what we have to do next.'

'What?'

They left the park and entered the din of traffic at the Avenue of the Americas exit.

'Be practical. Check into a hotel,' Buchanan said. 'Get some food and rest. Do some research.'

'And after that?'

'Find Alistair Drummond's yacht.'

5

After using a subway and three taxis to make sure that they weren't being followed, they ended in the general area where they had started, managing to find a vacancy at the Dorset, a softly carpeted, darkly paneled hotel on 54th Street between the Avenue of the Americas and Fifth Avenue. There they brought Holly's car from the parking garage and left it with the hotel's attendant, then registered as Mr and Mrs Charles Duffy and went to their room on the twenty-first floor. Buchanan felt reassured that the room was near the elevators and the fire stairs. They were in so public an area that it was unlikely anything threatening would happen. More, the location gave Buchanan and Holly access to several close escape routes.

They ordered room service: coffee, tea, salads, steaks, baked potatoes, French bread, plenty of vegetables, ice cream. While waiting for the food, Holly showered. Then Buchanan did. When he came out of the bathroom, wearing a white robe supplied by the hotel, Holly – also wearing a robe – was using a hotel hair dryer.

She turned it off. 'Sit down. Pull your robe down to your waist.'

'What?'

'I want to check your stitches.'

His back tingled as her fingers touched his skin.

She circled the almost healed bullet wound in his right shoulder, then moved her fingers lower, inspecting the knife wound. 'You did pull a few stitches. Here.' She took antibiotic cream and bandages from his travel bag. 'There doesn't seem to be any infection. Hold still while I . . .'

'Ouch.'

'Some tough guy you are.' She laughed.

'How do you know I'm not acting? How do you know I'm not trying to get your sympathy?'

'You test people by checking their eyes. I have other ways.'

'Oh?'

She ran her fingers up to his shoulders, turned him, and kissed him.

The kiss was long. Gentle. A slight parting of the lips. A tentative probing of the tongue. Subtle. Sensual.

Buchanan hesitated.

Despite his protective instincts, he put his hands behind her, holding her, feeling her well-toned back beneath her robe.

Her breath was sweet as she exhaled with pleasure and pulled slowly away. 'Yep. You definitely want sympathy.'

Now it was Buchanan's turn to laugh.

He reached to kiss her again.

And was interrupted by a knock on the door.

'Room service,' a man said from outside in the corridor.

'You're corrupting me,' Holly said.

'What do you mean?'

'I'm beginning to think your habits are normal. Here.' She reached beneath the pillow. 'Doesn't everybody need this when room service arrives? Tuck this into the pocket of your robe.' She handed him his pistol.

6

It was sunset when Buchanan wakened, dusk thickening behind the closed draperies. He stretched, and enjoyed the feeling of having had a good meal, of having slept naked beneath smooth sheets, of having Holly's body next to him. She wore her robe. He'd discarded his own after making love. Exhaustion had been like a narcotic that made them stretch out and doze. She attracted him: her humor, her sensuous features, her tall, slender, athletic grace. But he had always made a point of never allowing his personal life to interfere with his work, of never becoming physically and emotionally involved with anyone on an assignment. It clouded your judgment. It . . .

Hell, you never had any personal life. There wasn't any 'you' to have it. All you had were the identities you assumed.

And that's why you're here right now. That's what brought you this far. Because you kept that rule of being uninvolved when you worked with Juana, no matter how much you wanted her, and now you're searching for her, trying to make amends.

Are you going to make the same mistake again, this time with Holly?

What's wrong with me? he thought. Searching for one woman while I'm becoming attracted to another?

Get your mind straight.

He got out of bed, put on his robe, and walked over to a chair next to which he stacked the books and files that Holly had given him. Setting a lamp on the floor where it wouldn't cast much light and wake Holly, he leaned back in the chair and began to read.

Two hours later, Holly raised her head, rubbed her eyes, and looked over at him.

'Hi.' She smiled, lovely even after having just wakened.

'Hi.'

'How are you?'

'Feeling as if I've just seen a ghost.'

'I don't understand.'

'This material you gave me. I think I know what's going on. I don't spook easily, but this makes me cold.'

Holly sat up straight. 'What are you talking about?'

'The photographs in these books. There's something about . . .'

Holly got out of bed, tied her robe, and came quickly over. 'Show me.' She pulled a chair next to his, then peered at the book in his lap. 'What photographs?'

'This biography of Maria Tomez. I still have a lot to read, but one thing that's clear is that Frederick Maltin didn't just discover her and manage her. In a very real sense, he created her.'

Holly looked curious, waiting for him to continue.

'I've never seen her perform,' Buchanan said, 'but from what I gather, Maria Tomez sings not just well but passionately. That's her reputation, a fiery, passionate diva. An opera critic wouldn't ever go this far, but to put it bluntly, Maria Tomez is . . .'

'Sexy,' Holly said.

'That's the word. But look at these early photographs.' Buchanan turned pages in the book. 'This is Maria Tomez at the beginning of her career. Before Frederick Maltin. When she was singing in Mexico and South America, and none of the major critics was paying attention to her.'

Buchanan placed his index finger on a photograph of a young, short, overweight, dark-skinned woman with an insecure look in her eyes, a broad nose, an unbecoming hairstyle, pudgy cheeks, and slightly crooked teeth.

'All that hair piled on top of her head,' Holly said. 'And the way her oversized costume hung on her, as if trying to hide the weight.'

'The early reviews are unanimous about the quality of her voice, but it's obvious that the critics are holding back, trying to be kind, talking about her awkward stage presence,' Buchanan said. 'What they're really saying is she's too frumpy to be treated seriously as a stage performer.'

'Sexist but true,' Holly said. 'The big money goes to the woman with a great voice *and* magnetism.'

'The night Maltin saw her performing *Tosca* in Mexico City, Maria Tomez wasn't even scheduled. She was the understudy who had to step in when the production's star got sick.'

'I wonder what Maltin saw in her.'

'Someone to dominate. Someone to sculpt and shape. If Maltin had heard her perform under other circumstances, he wouldn't have associated her with a sexy role like Tosca. But once he did, he took advantage of the possibilities. According to this biography, no one had ever shown so much interest in her. Her career was going nowhere. What did she have to lose? She turned herself over to him. She gave him absolute obedience.'

'And?'

'Look at these next few photographs. What do you notice?'

'Well, she's progressively thinner. And her costumes take advantage of that.' Holly picked up the book to examine the photographs more closely. 'Obviously her hairstyle's been changed. Instead of being piled on top of her head, it's now swept back. It's long and thick. It's loose and curled. There's a kind of wild abandon to it.'

'As if a breeze is blowing it,' Buchanan said. 'As if she's on a cliff and the sea is crashing below her. What's the word? Tempestuous? That's what I noticed, too. The hairstyle has a passionate look to it. Now check *this* photograph.'

Holly did and shook her head. 'I don't know what . . .' At once Holly pointed. 'Her nose. It's been narrowed and straightened.'

'And check *this* photograph taken three months later.'

'This time I really don't get it,' Holly said.

'She's smiling.'

'Right.'

'Is she smiling in the previous one?'

'No.'

'And in the one before that?'

'She's not smiling there either, but in this first picture, she is, and . . . Oh, my God,' Holly said, 'the teeth. They aren't the same. They're crooked at the start, and now . . . She's had them straightened and capped.'

'Or Frederick Maltin did,' Buchanan said. 'He promised her that within two years he'd have her career turned around. What none of the publicity mentions is how much physical

507

alteration was necessary. In the next photograph, three months further along, her eyebrows are different. In the photograph after that, it looks as if something chemical or surgical has been done to her hair to raise the scalp line, to give her more forehead, to help proportion the rest of the face.'

'And all the while, she's been losing weight,' Holly said with excitement. 'Her wardrobe's been getting more stylish. The designs make her look taller. She's wearing expensive necklaces and earrings that glint and look good to the camera. *Those* changes attract the most attention, so the other, gradual, one-by-one changes become less noticeable. They're subtle and equally important, but done over a long enough period, they don't make anybody realize the degree to which she's been reconstructed.'

'Her fame was still growing,' Buchanan said. 'She wasn't under the same close scrutiny then that she would be in her prime, so a lot of the changes wouldn't have been noticed as she moved from opera house to opera house in various countries. Still, look at these later photographs, after she'd become a sensation. The changes continued. Here. Am I wrong, or has she had cosmetic surgery around her eyes, to make them seem more intense? In *this* photograph, have her earlobes been shortened? There's something about them that's different and makes her face look more proportioned.'

'Not only that, but her breasts seem higher,' Holly said. 'Possibly some kind of surgery there as well. Her waist seems longer. This is amazing. At first, it just seems that she's maturing and glowing from her success. But I think you're right. She was being sculpted and shaped. Frederick Maltin created her.'

'Once her body matched the passionate roles that Maltin wanted her to play, the critics paid more attention to her voice,' Buchanan said. 'She became an overnight sensation that took two years and who knows how many visits to dentists and surgeons. And all of a sudden she wasn't awkward on stage – because she wasn't selfconscious about her appearance anymore. She'd been made beautiful, and she loved being adored. The more her audiences applauded, the better she improved her stage technique to encourage their applause. Her voice blossomed. She became rich. Or rather she and Maltin became rich. Part of the deal was that she'd marry him. Not that I think Maltin cared about having sex with her. My guess is, he wanted to control her finances, and he could do that better as her husband in addition to being her manager. For fifteen years, he controlled her. Maybe he threatened to reveal the true story behind her success, to release before-and-after pictures, that sort of thing. Then one day at the start of this year, it became too much. She finally left him. She and Drummond met at a charity benefit in Monaco. They struck up a friendship. Drummond became her escort. Maybe he seemed safe to her. After all, he was old enough to be her grandfather. He was thousands of times richer than her. He probably didn't want sex. In fact, on the surface, there wasn't anything she could give him that he needed or didn't already have. So she kept seeing him, but the gossip photographers wouldn't leave them alone, and Drummond offered her a chance to get away from the public eye, to relax and regroup, to keep her picture out of the magazines, not to mention to be out of touch with the jerk she was divorcing. Drummond flew her to his yacht off the western coast of Mexico. A vacation in her home country. She stayed on board three weeks, flew back to New York, bought an apartment, retired from singing, and in effect, like Garbo, told the world that she wanted to be left alone.'

'Now, months later, she disappears.' Holly frowned. 'And your friend who sometimes provided security for her disappears as well. What happened two weeks ago? What's going on?'

509

'I don't think it happened two weeks ago.'

Holly didn't move for a moment. Then she straightened.

'I think it happened on the yacht,' Buchanan said.

'*What* happened? I still don't—'

'The photocopies of the recent articles you gave me don't reproduce the pictures very well. But this page from yesterday's *Washington Post* has clear photographs. A shot of Maltin at his news conference. A recent shot of Maria Tomez during one of her infrequent public appearances. Dark glasses. Concealing hat.'

'Tell me what you're getting at.'

'It looks like Maria Tomez had some work done on her jaw line. It's just a little different. And the ridges on her collar bone are a little different,' Buchanan said.

'A nose job's one thing,' Holly said. 'But changing a jaw line? Altering ridges on a collar bone? That's major reconstructive work.'

'Exactly,' Buchanan said. 'This last photograph. I don't think it's Maria Tomez. The more I look at it . . . the more I'm sure it's Juana impersonating her.'

7

'*But how is such a thing possible?*' Sounding frustrated, Holly drove rapidly along the busy expressway. Headlights blazed in the opposite lanes. 'Sure, Montgomery had a double in the Second World War. Movie stars use doubles all the time. These days, theatrical makeup is so realistic that actors can believably change their appearance. But Montgomery wasn't showing up at society charity benefits. As far as the movies go, cameras can play a lot of tricks. This is different. We're talking about a critically acclaimed opera singer. I don't care how good the makeup was, no one could

510

imitate that once-in-a-generation voice.'

'But Juana didn't have to,' Buchanan said, still frozen by the implications of what he'd discovered.

Holly steered quickly around a truck and drove faster.

'The newspaper articles are emphatic,' Buchanan said. 'Maria Tomez retired from performing after she finished the cruise on Drummond's yacht. She went into seclusion in New York, except for brief public appearances, none of which involved singing. In some of these articles, she complains about having had pneumonia, about recurring laryngitis. The reporters note that her voice was hoarse. Since that's the one thing Juana couldn't have faked, she removed the problem by pretending to have problems with her voice. Otherwise, both women are Hispanics, with the same general build and facial characteristics. Maria Tomez kept changing her appearance in gradual ways, after all, so if Juana didn't look absolutely like her, it wouldn't have attracted attention. It would have been just another case of how Maria Tomez continued to change. As long as Juana's special makeup guaranteed that the similarities far outnumbered the differences. How many people know Maria Tomez intimately? Her ex-husband, whom she refused to see. Her other business contacts, whom she shut out after she retired. Her entourage, which she apparently changed after the cruise. Alistair Drummond, who continued to see her after the cruise and accepted her as Maria Tomez. We're talking about a woman who guarded her privacy to begin with. All Juana had to do was take a few phone calls from time to time, complain about a cold, appear briefly in public, get her picture in the paper, and no one would suspect that she wasn't the person she pretended to be.'

'Except you.' Holly steered around another vehicle, squinting from the glare of headlights. '*You* suspected.'

'Because I had a reason to suspect. Because I'd seen the makeup room in Juana's house. Because I became more struck by Juana's resemblance to Maria Tomez as I looked at the photographs. Juana was on my mind, so I made the connection. What she did was brilliant. I can't get over what a genius she was at impersonating. I could never have done the equivalent.'

'The question is, why?' Holly said. 'Why did Juana impersonate her?'

'One common denominator is Alistair Drummond. The retirement, the need for seclusion, came after the cruise on Drummond's yacht. Drummond accepted Juana as Maria Tomez, and it was someone working for Drummond who paid Frederick Maltin to stop talking to reporters about his ex-wife. The disappearance . . . I think I understand,' Buchanan said quickly.

The tone in his voice made Holly shiver. 'What?'

'There were *two* disappearances.'

'*Two?*'

'It wasn't Maria Tomez but Juana who disappeared a few weeks ago. Drummond's doing his damnedest to find her. *Why?* Because if I'm right, nine months ago Maria Tomez never got off Drummond's yacht. That was Juana, and Drummond doesn't want anyone to know about the switch.'

Holly clenched the steering wheel. 'What in God's name happened on that yacht?'

8

LaGuardia Airport. To get there, they'd used Holly's car rather than a taxi because after checking out of the Dorset, they didn't want to attract attention by leaving her car in the hotel's garage for an indefinite period. At the airport's parking ramp, however, it wasn't unusual for cars to be left for quite a while.

They'd been forced to rush. They had needed luck with reservations and traffic. Nonetheless they'd managed to get two tickets on the last flight out of LaGuardia for Miami, and although they got to the boarding gate with only seconds to spare, that didn't matter. The point was, they were on the plane.

During the flight, both were too tense to sleep. They had no appetite. Still, they ate the lasagne the airline served, needing to maintain their strength.

'Your itinerary. Cancun, Mérida, and Fort Lauderdale,' Holly said.

'I've never admitted to being in any of those places,' Buchanan told her.

'But the rest aren't in doubt. Washington, New Orleans, San Antonio, Washington again, New York, now Miami and points south. All in two weeks. Hanging around with you could be exhausting. And this is normal for you.'

'Better get used to it.'

'I think I'd like that.'

Back at the Dorset, Buchanan had wondered if the home port for Drummond's yacht would be the same as the city where Drummond's corporate headquarters were located. Knowing that all large vessels were required to file a float plan indicating the length and itinerary of an intended voyage, he had phoned the coast guard in San Francisco. However, the officer on duty told him that the yacht was based somewhere else – they didn't have a float plan for it. Buchanan had then phoned the National Association of Insurance Underwriters at its main offices in Long Beach, California. Eight p.m. east-coast time had been five p.m. west-coast time. He made contact just before the office closed.

'My name's Albert Drake.' He pretended to be agitated. 'My brother, Rick, works on . . . God, I can't remember . . . The *Poseidon*. That's it.' Buchanan knew the name from the

513

research Holly had given him. 'Alistair Drummond owns it. A two-hundred-foot yacht. But Rick didn't leave an itinerary. Our mother's had a stroke. I have to get in touch with him, but I don't know how else . . . The coast guard suggested . . .'

Large vessels require such large amounts of insurance that the underwriters for the insurance companies insist on knowing where those vessels are at all times. As soon as Drummond's yacht reached a new berth, its captain was obligated to report his location to the insurance officials.

9

Key West.
After arriving in Miami past midnight, Buchanan and Holly used Charles Duffy's credit card to rent a car and began the 150-mile drive south along the Florida keys. During the trip, they stopped for take-out coffee and alternated driving while the other dozed, mercury-vapor lights along the extensive forty-two bridges of the Overseas Highway hurting their eyes and adding to their fatigue.

It was just before dawn when they arrived at their destination, the southernmost community in the continental United States. Key West, only four miles long and one-and-a-half miles wide, had a permanent population of almost thirty thousand. One of the last bastions of the counterculture in America, the sand-and-coral island remained synonymous with the unorthodox life style of Hemingway, who had once lived there and whose home – with its numerous cats supposedly descended from the novelist's original pets – was a national historic landmark. The town's atmosphere and architecture were an exotic blend of Bahamian, West Indian, and Cuban influences. It was known for its deep-sea fishing and its tropical foods. There was a U.S. naval air station. John James

Audubon once had been in residence, also Harry Truman. The singer-novelist Jimmy Buffet was its most famous current spokesman.

But there was only one thing in Key West that Buchanan cared about, and after he and Holly caught a few more hours of sleep at a cheap motel that accepted cash in advance (he was getting nervous about using Charles Duffy's credit card), they cleaned up, ate, then got to business. An hour's stroll around the crowded harbor, where they bought sandals, short-sleeved pullovers, and cut-off jeans so they wouldn't be conspicuous, gave Buchanan ample chance to pose seemingly casual questions to vendors and fishermen. Soon he and Holly were able to stand on the wharf, lean forward against the railing, breathe the humid, tangy, salt air, and study their target.

Drummond's yacht, gleaming white against the green-blue of the Gulf of Mexico, was anchored a hundred yards off shore. Two hundred feet long, with three decks and a helicopter pad on the top (the chopper had taken off yesterday, heading south, Buchanan had been told by a fisherman), the yacht should have inspired awe but instead made Buchanan feel cold despite the eighty-five-degree temperature. The sleekly styled profile seemed threatening, like the curved tip of a massive hunting knife. The large sunning area at the stern, with windows providing a view from the upper decks, made Buchanan think of voyeurs and exhibitionists. Regardless of its resplendent white exterior, the yacht appeared cloaked in a black pall of gloom.

'Sometimes,' Holly said, 'when you're deep in thought, your eyes and face change. You look like a stranger.'

'How?'

'Solemn. Troubled.'

'Just so we understand each other, this has nothing to do with Maria Tomez,' Buchanan said. 'I want to know what happened to her, yes. But more than anything, I want to know what happened to Juana.' He turned his attention from the yacht and focused on Holly, who concentrated on his gaze, confused. 'A lot of this doesn't make sense to me. What I feel about you, for example. But I have to settle old accounts before I start new ones. After this is over, you and I can talk about what we have.'

Her red hair blowing in the wind, Holly thought about what he had said and nodded. 'I never assumed there were any guarantees. I never planned this. I got swept along. Fine. We understand each other. First things first. So now that we've found the yacht, what do we do?'

'You noticed the way I spoke to the fishermen and vendors in the area? A little conversation combined with a few well-chosen questions. The technique is called elicitation. It's the equivalent of what you'd call doing an interview. But the difference is that *your* subjects almost always know they're being interviewed whereas *my* subjects must never know. Sometimes, if they realize they're being pumped for information, their reaction can be lethal.'

Holly listened attentively.

'I thought you might be offended because I'm telling you how to do an interview,' Buchanan said.

'This whole thing's been a learning experience. Why should it stop now?'

'Good,' Buchanan said. 'Okay, elicitation.' He told her about his training, how he'd been required to practise by going into bars and striking up conversations with strangers, getting them to reveal such intimate data as their social security numbers and their birth dates, not only month but year.

'How did you manage that?' Holly asked. 'I'd have thought you were snooping.'

'I'd sit next to my target, have a few drinks, make small talk, comment on the television program that was showing above the bar, and at one point say that I'd learned something

516

interesting today. The response, of course, would be "What?" I'd pull out my wallet and show him my forged social-security card. "These numbers all mean something," I'd say. "I thought they were assigned sequentially, but if you break down each group, you see that the numbers tell all kinds of things like when and where I was born. See, this number means I came from Pittsburgh, and this group of numbers was assigned to whoever was born in nineteen-sixty, and this number here tells which month, and . . . Here, I'll show you. What's your number? I'll bet you a dollar I can tell you where and when you were born." '

Holly shook her head in amazement. 'Is that really true?'

'That I was trained that way?'

'No. About the social security number.'

'What's yours? Let's see if I can tell you when and where you were born.'

Holly laughed. 'It works. You make up a place and date, and to show how wrong you are, the person you're interviewing tells you the information you want. Slick.'

'Elicitation,' Buchanan repeated. 'The art of extracting information without allowing your target to realize that you're extracting it. It's a standard method used by operatives trying to obtain military, political, and industrial secrets. It usually happens in bars, and the targets are usually assistants, secretaries, officers of lower rank, the kind of people who might feel frustrated in their positions and don't mind talking about their problems at work, provided they're stimulated with proper subtlety. A few drinks. A show of interest. One piece of information leads to another. It usually takes time, several meetings, but sometimes it can be done quickly, and in this case, it has to be because I have to find out what's happened to Juana. If she's still alive . . .' Buchanan's voice tightened. 'If she's still alive, I have to get the pressure off her.'

Holly studied him. 'What do we do?'

517

'What *you* have to do is be just what you are: sexy and desirable.'

Holly looked puzzled.

'While we've been talking, a launch from Drummond's yacht has been coming toward shore. Three crew members are on board.'

Squinting from sunlight off the water, Holly followed Buchanan's gaze.

'We'll watch where they go,' Buchanan said. 'Maybe they're in town on an errand. But maybe this is their day off. If they go into a bar, I'll . . .'

10

'Damn it, I didn't want to drive all this way in the first place,' Buchanan said. 'What's in it for me? Every time I turn around, you're winking at some young stud with a bulge in his shorts.'

'Keep your voice down,' Holly said.

'Harry warned me about you. He said to watch you every second. He said you'd screw any male old enough to get an erection, the younger the better.'

'Keep your voice down,' Holly said more strongly.

'I notice you don't deny it. You just don't want anybody to know the truth.'

'Stop it,' Holly warned. 'You're embarrassing me.'

They were in the Coral Reef Bar, sitting in a corner that had fishing nets on one wall and a stuffed marlin on the other. The small circular table had a cloth with wavy lines and numbers that made it look like a nautical chart. The ceiling lights were chandeliers that resembled the rudder wheel on a ship.

Buchanan slumped in a captain's chair and swallowed half a glass of beer. 'Keep my voice down. That's all you say. I'll make you a deal. I'll keep my voice down if you keep your pants on. Waiter, two more beers.'

'I'm not thirsty,' Holly said.

'Did I say I was ordering for you? Waiter! I've changed my mind. Make it a bourbon on the rocks.'

'You already had two at the other place. Two beers here and . . . Dave, it's only noon, for God's sake.'

'Just shut up, okay?' Buchanan slammed the table. 'I'll drink when I want to. If you'd stop jumping into bed with every—'

'Sir,' a voice said, 'you're disturbing the other customers.'

'Tough shit.'

'Sir,' the man said, a *big* man, blond, with a brush cut and muscles straining at his T-shirt, 'if you don't keep your voice down, I'm going to have to ask you to leave.'

'Ask all you want, pal, but I'm staying right here.' Buchanan swallowed the rest of his beer and yelled to the waiter, 'Where's that bourbon?'

People were staring.

'Dave,' Holly said.

Buchanan slammed the table again. 'I told you, shut the fuck up!'

'Okay,' the big man said. 'Let's go, buddy.'

'Hey!' Buchanan objected as the big man grabbed him. 'What the—?' Jerked to his feet, pretending to stagger, Buchanan fell against the table, upsetting glasses. 'Jesus, watch my arm. You're breaking it.'

'I'd like to, buddy.'

As the big man twisted Buchanan's arm behind his back and guided him toward the exit, Buchanan glared backward toward Holly. 'What are you waiting for? Let's go.'

Holly didn't answer.

'I said let's go!'

Holly still didn't answer. She flinched as Buchanan kept shouting from outside the bar. Slowly she raised her beer glass to her lips, sipped, squinted at her trembling hand, lowered the glass, and wiped at her eyes.

'Are you all right?'

Holly looked up at a good-looking, tanned, slender man in his twenties who wore a white uniform.

She didn't answer.

'Hey, I really don't mean to bother you,' the man said. 'You've had enough of that already. But you do look a little shook up. If there's anything I can do . . . Can I buy you another drink?'

Holly wiped at her eyes again, straightening, trying to look dignified. She directed her gaze, frightened, toward the door. 'Please.'

'Another beer for the lady.'

'And . . .'

'What?'

'I'm . . . I'd really appreciate it if you could make sure he doesn't hurt me when I leave.'

11

Buchanan leaned against the railing on the dock. Surrounded by the activity of tourists and fishermen, he wouldn't be noticed as he watched the launch cutting through the green-blue water, passing cabin cruisers and fishing boats, returning to the three-decked, two-hundred-foot-long, gleaming, white yacht that was anchored beyond the other vessels, a hundred yards off shore. The overhead sun was now behind him so that he didn't have to squint from the reflection of sunlight off the Gulf of Mexico. He had no trouble seeing that among the three crew members returning to the yacht, a gorgeous, red-headed woman was chatting agreeably with them, one of the crew members allowing her to put her hand on the wheel of the launch's controls.

As they boarded the yacht, Buchanan nodded, glanced around to make sure he wasn't being watched, and strolled away. Or seemed to. The fact is that as he wandered along the Key West dock, he persistently, subtly studied the yacht, pretending to take pictures of the town, using the telephoto lens on Holly's camera as a telescope. After all, Holly might get in trouble over there, although she'd been adamant that she was able to take care of herself. Even so, if she came out onto one of the decks and looked agitated, he had told her he would get to her as fast as he could.

Near five o'clock, the launch left the yacht again, coming toward shore: the same three crew members and Holly. She got out on the dock, kissed one of the men on the cheek, ruffled another's hair, hugged the third, and walked with apparent contentment into town.

Buchanan reached their small, shadowy, motel room a minute before she did. Worry made the time seem longer.

'How did it go?' he asked with concern as she came in.

She took off her sandals and sat on the bed, looking exhausted. 'They sure had trouble keeping their hands to themselves. I had to stay on the move. I feel like I've been running a marathon.'

'Do you want a drink of water? How about some of this fruit I bought?'

'Yeah, some fruit would be nice. An orange or . . . Great.' She sipped from the Perrier he brought her. 'Is this what you call a debriefing?'

'Yes. If this were business.'

'Isn't it? You make the agent you've recruited feel comfortable and wanted. Then you . . .'

'Hey, not everything I do is calculated.'

'Oh?' Holly studied him for a moment. 'Good. In that case, the yacht. There are fifteen crew members. They take turns coming ashore. They think Drummond's – to quote one of the

521

crew members – a domineering asshole. He scares them. While he's aboard. But when the cat's away, the mice play, sometimes bringing women aboard. To show off the yacht and get even with Drummond for the way he abuses them.'

Buchanan set a pencil and a notepad on the dingy table. 'Draw a diagram for the layout of each room on each deck. I need to know where everything is, where and when the crew eat and sleep, every detail you can think of. I know you're tired, Holly. I'm sorry, but this is going to take a while.'

12

It wasn't difficult getting a wetsuit. There were plenty of dive shops in Key West. The water was warm enough that Buchanan normally wouldn't have needed to rent the insulating suit, but the stitches in his side made this an abnormal situation. He needed to protect the healing knife wound. He wanted to minimize the amount of blood that would dissolve from the scabs around the stitches and disperse through the water. As in Cancun, when he'd escaped the police by swimming across the channel from the island to the mainland, he worried about sharks and barracuda. Back then, of course, it had been blood from a bullet wound that had worried him, but the difference was the same. At least, this time he'd been able to prepare, although another element from the Cancun swim continued to trouble him – his headache.

His skull wouldn't stop throbbing. He felt as if his nerves were leather cords being stretched to the snapping point. But he couldn't let the pain distract him. He had to keep going, swimming through the three a.m. water, his black wetsuit blending with the night. He kept his arms loose at his sides, moving his feet gently, stroking with his fins, trying anxiously not to make noise or create whitecaps in the water. He kept his face down as much as possible, even though he had blackened it before leaving shore so that it wouldn't contrast with the dark water. The stars glistened. A quarter moon was beginning to rise. That would be enough light for him as he eased closer to the yacht.

Then he touched the anchor chain. Peering up, he heard no footsteps or voices. Although the wetsuit made the water feel even warmer than it was, he shivered involuntarily, his testicles receding toward his groin. He squinted back toward the lights of Key West, thought of Holly waiting for him, mustered his resolve, took off his mask and flippers, tied them to the chain, and began to climb. The effort strained his shoulder and his side. But he had to keep moving. Slowly, soundlessly, he pulled himself up the chain until he reached where it went into the hull. The hole was too small for him to enter, but it and the bulky chain gave him places to wedge his mesh-rubber slippers while he fought for balance, reached up, and grasped the edge of the bow. Drawing himself up, he peered over the edge, saw no one, looked for intrusion detectors, saw no evidence of them either, and squirmed over the railing onto the softly lit deck.

As he scurried for cover beneath an exterior stairway, he knew he left a trail of water, but that couldn't be avoided. Fortunately most of the water had drained from his wetsuit while he'd climbed. Soon the remainder would stop trickling out. Until then, he had to take advantage of the time he had.

A few windows were lit on the decks that loomed above him. The stairways, corridors, and walkways had lights as well. But they glowed, separate enough and weakly enough that there were abundant shadows into which Buchanan could creep. The mesh-rubber slippers that he'd worn beneath his fins had ridges along the soles that gave them traction. He left almost no water as he made his way softly along a walkway, into a corridor, and up a stairwell.

He followed Holly's instructions. Her description of the yacht's layout had been detailed. So had her assessment of the crew, who evidently were unmotivated when the master wasn't there to intimidate them. Buchanan listened intently, heard no one, emerged from the stairwell, and crept along a corridor on the middle deck, passing doors on each side. Only one door attracted him – at the end on the right. Holly had said that was the one area the crew hadn't shown her.

'Off limits,' they'd told her.

'Why?' she had asked.

'We don't know. It's always locked,' had been the answer.

The door was situated between the door to Drummond's sleeping quarters on the right and the door to the yacht's reception area, a large, luxuriously appointed room that occupied a third of this level and had windows that looked down on the sun deck at the stern.

'Well, you must have *some* idea what's in there,' Holly had said to the crew members.

'None. We were told we'd lose our jobs if we ever tried to get in.'

The door had two double-bolt locks. Buchanan removed two short metal prongs from a pocket of the wetsuit. He'd finished picking the first lock when he heard footsteps on the stairway at the opposite end of the corridor. Fighting to keep his hands steady, he worked the pins in the second lock.

The footsteps came lower, closer.

Buchanan didn't dare look in that direction. He had to keep concentrating on the lock, manipulating the metal prongs.

The footsteps were almost to the bottom.

Buchanan turned the knob, slipped into the murky room, and closed the door. He held his breath, pressed an ear against the bulkhead, and listened. After thirty seconds, still not having heard any sound from the corridor, he found a light switch, flicked it, and blinked from the sudden illumination.

What he saw made him frown. In this narrow room, which was connected by a locked door to Alistair Drummond's sleeping quarters, there were several rows of television monitors and video tape recorders.

Buchanan turned down the sound controls, then activated the monitors. In a moment, the glowing screens revealed numerous rooms and sections of decks. On one screen, he watched two crew men in the control room. On another screen, he saw two other crew members watching television. On a third screen, he saw a half-dozen crew members sleeping on bunks. On a fourth, he saw a man – presumably the captain – sleeping in a room that he had to himself. On other screens, Buchanan saw numerous empty bedrooms. Those dark rooms and the others in which people slept appeared with a green tint, an indication that a night-vision lens was being used on the hidden cameras that monitored those areas. The monitors that showed exterior sections of the yacht were also tinted green. Presumably the cameras would automatically convert to a normal lens when the indoor lights were on or during daylight.

So Alistair Drummond likes to eavesdrop on his guests, Buchanan thought. The old man goes into his bedroom, locks his door, unlocks the door to this adjacent room, and comes in here to see what his crew is doing when he isn't around, more important to see what his guests are up to – undressing, relieving themselves, fucking, doing drugs, whatever. And all of it can be recorded for repeated viewing enjoyment.

Buchanan directed his attention to a locked metal cabinet. After picking its lock, he opened the cabinet and found row upon row of labeled video tapes. August 5, 1988. October 10, 1989. February 18, 1990. Buchanan glanced quickly over them, noting that they were arranged sequentially. At least a hundred. Alistair Drummond's greatest hits.

The cruise Buchanan wanted to know about had occurred

during February. He found a tape for that month, put it into a player, and pressed the 'on' button, making sure that the sound was off. The video quality was remarkably clear, even when the images had a greenish tint. The cruise had been well attended. Various shots of various locations showed guests in their most intimate, revealing, compromising positions. Oral sex and sodomy were especially popular. Buchanan eventually counted thirteen men and twelve women. The men – in middle age – had an overbearing manner, as if addicted to wielding power. The women were attractive, well dressed, and treated as if they were hookers. All the men and women were Hispanic.

Buchanan noticed an ear plug and inserted it into the television monitor. After adjusting the sound, he was able to hear what was on the tape. As he concentrated to translate the Spanish voices, he realized from comments they made that the women were indeed hookers and that the men were high-ranking members of the Mexican government. At once he realized something else. These tapes weren't intended merely for Drummond's voyeuristic pleasure.

Blackmail crossed Buchanan's mind at the same time as he reacted with shock to the sight of Maria Tomez on the screen. At least, he believed it was Maria Tomez. Thinking about doubles, he couldn't be sure. He needed to study the image carefully before he was convinced that it was definitely Maria Tomez and not Juana impersonating her. The night-vision lens tinted the image green. It showed what appeared to be the sun deck at the rear of the yacht. The angle was from above, downward, as if the camera had been hidden in an upper wall or beneath an elevated walkway. A digital display indicated that the time the tape had been made was 1:37 in the morning. The sound track was somewhat crackly. Nonetheless Buchanan was able to hear distant party music, a woman laughing faintly.

Maria Tomez, wearing an elegant, low-cut, evening gown, leaned against the stern's railing, her back to the camera, apparently watching the wake of the ship. A man spoke to her in Spanish, and she turned. A tall, slender, thin-faced, hawk-nosed, Hispanic male, wearing a dinner jacket, stepped into view. He spoke again. This time, Maria Tomez answered. The quality of the sound became better, presumably because Drummond had used a remote control to adjust the directional microphone hidden on the sun deck. 'No, I'm not cold,' Maria Tomez said in Spanish.

The camera zoomed in as the man approached her.

13

'My God,' Holly said. She watched the tape and felt sick. 'Jesus.'

Dismayed, Buchanan had sealed the tape in a plastic bag that he'd found in the room. Muscles rigid from tension, he had made a copy of the tape but otherwise left everything the way he had found it. Then he had locked the door behind him and crept down to the main deck. His head continued to ache all the while he'd climbed down the anchor chain, retrieved his mask and fins from where he'd tied them, and swam back to shore, this time on his back, keeping the tape above water.

The tape ended, and Holly continued to stare at the screen in disgust. 'God damn him to hell.'

What she had seen on a video player that Buchanan had rented when he returned to the motel was the rape and murder of Maria Tomez. Or possibly the sequence was in the reverse – murder and then rape, if it was possible to rape, as opposed to violate, a corpse. 'Rape' implied overcoming someone's will whereas a corpse couldn't object to anything, and perhaps the latter was what the tall, slender, hawk-nosed man had liked, an absolute lack of resistance.

The man had approached Maria Tomez, asking again if she felt cold. He'd put his arm around her with the pretense of warming her. Maria Tomez had taken his arm away. The man had persisted, and Maria Tomez had begun to struggle. 'Now, now,' the man had said drunkenly, 'you must not be cold to *me*. I forbid it.' He had chuckled, pinning her with his arms, kissing her face and neck, trying to kiss the tops of her breasts all the while she squirmed and twisted her face from side to side and tried to push him away. 'Be warm,' he had said in Spanish. 'Be warm. *I* am warm. Can you feel it?' He had chuckled again. When she shoved at him, he had laughed and shaken her. When she slapped his face, he had punched her. She had spat at him. '*Puta*,' he had said and struck her with an uppercut that jolted her up, then back, then down. As she toppled, he grabbed for her, his fingers catching the top of her gown, ripping, exposing her breasts. As the back of her skull hit the deck, he lunged and kept ripping, exposing her stomach, her groin, her thighs, her knees. He tore off her lacy underwear. For a moment, he paused. The camera showed Maria Tomez motionless, naked on her back on the deck, her dress spread out on either side like broken wings. The man's paralysis lasted another second. Abruptly he opened his belt, dropped his pants, and fell upon her. His breathing was rapid and hoarse. His buttocks kept pumping. Then he moaned and slumped and chuckled. 'Now do you feel warm?' She didn't answer. He nudged her. She didn't move. He slapped her again. When she still didn't move, he groped to his knees, grasped her face, squeezed her cheeks, twisted her head from side to side, and breathed more hoarsely. Urgently he stood, buckled his pants, glanced furtively around, lifted Maria Tomez to her feet.

And with an expression that combined fear with disgust, threw her overboard.

As Holly continued to stare in dismay at the static-filled

screen, Buchanan stepped past her to shut off the VCR and the television. Only then did Holly move. She lowered her gaze and shook her head. Buchanan slumped in a chair.

'Was she dead?' Holly asked quietly. 'When he dropped her into the water?'

'I don't know.' Buchanan hesitated. 'He might have broken her neck when he hit her. She might have suffered a fatal concussion when her skull struck the deck. He might have smothered her while he was on top of her. But she might also have been in shock, catatonic, still alive when he threw her into the water. The son of a bitch didn't even take the trouble to make sure. He didn't care if she was alive. All he cared about was himself. He'd used her. Then he threw her away. Like a sack of garbage.'

The room was dark. They sat in silence for quite a while.

'So what happened next?' Holly asked bitterly. 'What do you figure?'

'The man who killed her probably thought he could convince people that she fell off the yacht. He was drunk, of course, and that would have affected his judgment in several ways. Either he would have had the false confidence to report having seen her fall. Or else a part of his mind would have warned him to go to his cabin, sober up, and seem as confused as everybody else when Maria Tomez was reported missing. Then he could have plausibly suggested that perhaps she'd been drinking, had lost her balance and fallen over the railing.'

'Except that Alistair Drummond knew the truth,' Holly said.

Buchanan nodded. 'He'd watched everything on the monitor in his private video-surveillance room. And a tape of a rape-homicide is so much more useful than oral sex, sodomy, and drug use when you want to blackmail a member of the Mexican government. Drummond must have been delighted. I imagine him going to her murderer, revealing what's on the

529

tape, and arranging a coverup in exchange for certain favors. The initial stage wouldn't have been difficult. All Drummond needed to do was order his pilot to fly the yacht's helicopter to the mainland. Then Drummond could have told his guests that Maria Tomez had left the cruise early. They'd have no reason to suspect differently.'

'After that, though,' Holly said.

'Yes, after that,' Buchanan said. 'Drummond must have felt inspired when he thought of Juana. Perhaps Maria Tomez had told him about the clever way she had of avoiding tedious social events by using Juana to double for her. Perhaps Drummond found out another way. For certain, though, he did find out. He needn't have told Juana anything incriminating. All he had to do was explain that Maria Tomez wanted absolute privacy and offer Juana an irresistible amount of money to impersonate Maria Tomez for an extended period of time.'

'So complicated and yet so simple,' Holly said. 'If I weren't so disgusted, I'd call it brilliant.'

'But what does Drummond want from the person he's blackmailing?' Buchanan said. 'Obviously not money. Drummond's so rich it's hard to imagine that money alone would motivate him, especially the comparatively small amount that even a wealthy Mexican politician could give him. You're a reporter. Do you recognize the man on the tape?'

Holly shook her head. 'Mexico isn't my specialty. I wouldn't know one of its politicians from another.'

'But we can find out.' Buchanan stood.

'How?'

'We're going back to Miami.' His voice was like flint against steel. 'Then we're flying to Mexico City.'

'This is Buttercup.' Clutching the phone, speaking urgently, the husky-voiced woman used the code name she'd been assigned.

On the other end of the line, a man's sleep-thickened voice was tinged with annoyance. 'What time is . . . ? Lord, it's almost five in the morning. I got to bed only an hour ago.'

'I'm sorry. This was the first chance I had to call.'

'They've been looking everywhere for you.' The man had said his name was Alan, although he was probably using a pseudonym.

'That's what I was afraid of. Is it safe to talk?'

'This call is being relayed from another phone,' Alan said. 'The two phones are linked by scramblers. Why are you calling me? I told you it had to be an emergency.'

'I'm with Leprechaun.' The woman used the code name they'd agreed upon.

'Yes. I assumed.'

'You have to understand. He's been telling the truth. What he's doing has no involvement with . . .' She tactfully didn't mention Scotch and Soda.

'I assumed that as well. I believe he genuinely wants out. It's his superiors who need reassurance.'

'But *how?*'

'It's a little late to ask that,' Alan said. 'You're part of the problem, after all. If you'd stayed away from him . . .'

'But in Washington, he came to *me*.'

'Same difference. You're together. Guilt by association. His superiors believe that the two of you reneged on your bargain not to publicize their activities.'

'This has nothing to do with their activities. How do I get that across to . . . ? Should I phone them? Give me a number to call and . . .'

'No,' Alan said sharply. 'You'll only make things worse. They can instantly trace any call you make. You'd be guiding them to you.'

'*Then what do I do?*'

'Sever ties with Leprechaun,' Alan said. 'Go to ground. Wait until I tell you it's safe to reappear.'

'But that could take *months*.'

'True.'

'Damn it, I wish I'd never listened to you. When you approached me, I should have told you I wasn't interested.'

'Ah, but you couldn't,' Alan said. 'The story was too good to ignore.'

'And now it might get me killed.'

'Not if you're careful. Not if you stop making mistakes. There's still a way to salvage things.'

'You son of a bitch,' she said. 'You're still thinking of the story.'

'I'm thinking of approaching another journalist, who might be interested in telling *your* story. That would draw so much attention to you that they wouldn't dare make a move to have you eliminated. I could bring you in. The two of us could still get what we want.'

'What *you* want. All *I* want is a normal life. Whatever that is. Lord, I'm not sure anymore.'

'You should have thought of that before you accepted my information,' Alan said. 'But I repeat, if you're careful, if you do what I tell you, I think I can eventually bring you in safely. For now, go to ground. Assume another identity.'

'And what about Leprechaun?'

Alan didn't answer.

'I asked you, what about Leprechaun?' Holly said.

'Sometimes we can't get everything we want.'

'What are you talking about?'

'I never wanted this to happen. Really. I'd hoped that . . .

He's a soldier. He'd understand more than you. Sometimes there are . . .'

'What?'

'Casualties.'

As Holly turned from staring at the phone in the booth down the lane from her room in the Key West motel, she saw a man's shadow next to ferns in the pre-dawn gray. In the numerous palm trees, birds began to chirp.

'I can't talk anymore,' Holly said into the phone.

'Trouble?' Alan asked.

'Let's just say I didn't win the Publisher's Clearing-House Sweepstakes.'

Holly set down the phone.

Buchanan stepped out of the shadows. Despite a pre-dawn breeze off the ocean, the air was humid.

'I thought you were taking back the wetsuit gear,' Holly said.

'I was. I paid the motel clerk to return it for me when the dive shop opens.' Buchanan stopped before her. 'Who were you calling?'

She glanced away from him.

'At least, you're not trying to lie,' Buchanan said. 'And at least, you had brains enough not to make the call from the motel room where there'd be a record on the bill. Not that it matters. The area's so small that automatic tracing equipment will tell our hunters we're in Key West.'

'No,' Holly said. 'The number I called is private. Your people wouldn't know about it.'

'So *you* say. In my business, I don't take anything for granted unless I do it myself. *All* phones are suspect. It must have been really important for you to make the call.'

'I did it for us.'

'Oh?'

'I was trying to get us out of at least part of the mess we're in,' Holly said.

'What part is that? Right now, it seems we've got plenty of mess to go around.'

Holly bit her lip. 'Shouldn't we talk about this when we're back in our room?'

'And give you time to think up believable answers? No, I think we ought to keep talking.' Buchanan grasped her arm. 'Exactly what part of the mess were you trying to get us out of?'

He guided her along the lane. The sky was less gray. The breeze was stronger. Birds scattered into the sky.

'All right, I've been wanting to tell you since we were in New York,' Holly said. 'God, I'm so relieved to . . . At the start, the reason I knew you were in Cancun, the reason I was able to get to Club Internacional ahead of time and watch you talk to those two . . .' She almost said 'drug distributors,' then looked around the shadowy lane and chose other language, wary of being too specific before she reached their room. '. . . businessmen. The reason I . . .'

'Someone in my unit set me up.' Buchanan opened the squeaky door to their room.

Holly spun in surprise. 'You knew that?'

'It was the only explanation that made sense. Someone on the inside. No one else could have known where I'd be. The same person who told you about Yellow Fruit, Seaspray, the Intelligence Support Activity, and Scotch and Soda. That information could have come only from one of my superiors.'

Still grasping Holly's arm, Buchanan led her into the room, turned on the light, closed the door, locked it, and guided her to the bed. He set her down firmly. 'Who?' he asked.

Holly fidgeted.

'*Who?*'

'What will you do? Beat it out of me?'

'No.' Buchanan studied her. 'Cut my losses.' He put his toilet kit into his travel bag, glanced around the room to make sure that he hadn't forgotten anything, and walked toward the door. 'There are buses that'll take you back to Miami.'

'Wait.'

Buchanan kept walking.

'Wait. I don't know his real name. I only know him as Alan.'

Buchanan paused. 'Medium height. Chubby face. Short, brown hair. Early forties.'

'Yes. That's him.'

'I know him. He was my controller a while ago. He's with the . . .'

The hesitation seemed to be a test for Holly. She decided to fill in the gap. 'The Agency.'

Buchanan seemed reassured by her candor. He walked toward the bed. 'Keep talking.'

'He was very straightforward about what he wanted. He doesn't approve of the military's involvement in civilian intelligence operations. American servicemen, armed, in civilian clothes, using false ID, conducting Agency operations in foreign countries. It's bad enough to have a civilian caught as a spy. But a member of Army Special Forces? On active duty? Pretending to be a civilian? On a strike team intended to topple unfriendly foreign governments or engage in an unsanctioned private war against major drug dealers? If the public realized how out of control the relationship between the CIA and the military had become, Congress would be forced into a major investigation of American intelligence tactics. The Agency is under enough pressure, as it is. One more controversy, and it might be replaced by an intelligence bureau with stricter limits. That's what Alan's afraid of. So he came to me and gave me certain information, insisting that he never be named, that he be cited only as a reliable government source. To make my story look less like a setup, he didn't tell me everything. He gave me just enough hints that my work in checking them out and linking them would provide me with

535

evidence to maintain the fiction that I'd come up with the story on my own . . . Why are you looking at me like that?'

'It doesn't make sense. If Alan was afraid that exposing the Agency's use of unauthorized military action would threaten the Agency, why the hell would he give you the story? It's exactly what he doesn't want.'

'No.' Holly shook her head. 'He was very specific about that, and I agreed. You and *only* you were to be the object lesson.'

'Oh, Christ,' Buchanan said.

'The idea was that I'd expose you as a single example of the dangerous use of the military in civilian intelligence operations. The government wouldn't have any more information than what was in my story. I'd testify that I didn't know anything further. The congressional investigation would eventually end. But the message would be clear. If the CIA was using military strike teams, it had better stop, or else the Agency and certain Special Operations units would be severely limited, if not disbanded. Careers would be destroyed.'

'Sure.' Buchanan's voice was strained. 'And in the meantime, you'd be a journalist celebrity. And Alan would have the shop back in his control.'

'That was the idea,' Holly said.

'Politics.' Buchanan made the word sound like a curse.

'But it's not the idea any longer.'

'What are you talking about?'

'That's why I phoned Alan,' Holly said. 'To cancel my agreement with him. I told him I wanted out. I told him I wanted to talk to your superiors, to assure them that what we're doing isn't related to them, that you aren't a risk to them and neither am I.'

'You honestly expected he'd go along? No hard feelings? Nice try? We can't win 'em all? That sort of thing? Jesus.'

'Alan told me he was sorry things got out of hand.'

'I bet.'

'We're still being hunted. He suggested I distance myself from you while he figures out a way to bring me in.'

'Damned good advice.' Buchanan squinted. 'Distance yourself.'

'No,' Holly said. 'I won't let you go.'

'Just how the hell do you think you're going to stop me?'

'Follow.'

'Lots of luck. What is it with you? You still think I'm a front-page story?'

No answer.

'Then maybe you figure it's safer to stay with me and run from them than to try to do it by yourself.'

Still no answer.

'Look, I don't have time to guess what you're thinking. I've got to get out of Key West before your phone call brings a hit team down here.'

'You.'

'What?' Buchanan frowned.

'You,' Holly said. 'That's why I want to go with you.'

'Make sense.'

'I can't make it any plainer. I want to be with you. It's not just because I feel safe with you, although I do. It's . . . I didn't expect you to be what you are. I didn't expect to feel attracted to you. I didn't expect that I'd get so used to being with you that my stomach cramps at the thought of your going away.'

'Now who's playing a role?'

'I'm telling the truth! I got *used* to you. And as long as we're spreading blame around, don't forget you're the one who came to me the second time. I wouldn't be in danger if you hadn't decided to use me. Hell, in Washington I saved your life. That ought to prove something.'

'Yeah, and I'm so wonderful that you fell in love with me.'

She started to say something.

'Save your energy,' Buchanan said. 'You're going to get your wish.'

Holly's eyes widened in surprise.

'I can't leave you behind,' Buchanan said. 'I just realized I made a mistake. I told you where I was going.'

'Yes. Mexico City,' Holly said.

'Because of Juana, I can't change my plans. I swore I'd help her if she ever needed me, and I intend to keep that promise. Which means I can't let you wander around until you're caught and you tell them where I've gone and what I'm doing. Pack. I want to get off this island before they get here.'

Holly breathed out. 'Thanks.'

'Don't thank me. This isn't a favor. As soon as I think you're no longer a risk to me, I'm cutting you loose. But in the meantime, Holly, pay attention. Take this advice. Do not force me to treat you as an enemy.'

15

The Yucatán peninsula.

A pall of smoke clung to the massive clearing. As construction proceeded, the crackle of gunshots punctuated the roar of bulldozers, cranes, and other heavy machinery. So did the crackle of flames, the source of the smoke that filled the area. Trees were being burned back, the clearing widened, anything to reduce the cover from which natives − descendants of the original Maya − persisted in their attacks on the construction crew and the equipment. The scattered stones of the leveled ruins of once-magnificent, towering pyramids and temples still lay among the towers that had replaced them, these made of steel. Occasionally the earth tremored, but the workers and guards no longer paid attention. As with the snakes, the smoke, and the gunshots, those who labored here had become used to anything. The job mattered. Completing it. Being paid. Escaping.

Alistair Drummond did that to a person, Jenna thought as she obeyed his orders, completing the archaeological survey map that would show that the ruins were not as impressive as photographs from space had led scholars to expect. A few minor structures. Numerous scattered stones, the result of earthquakes. Pathetic remnants of a formerly great culture. With one exception. The Mayan ball court. For reasons unexplained – perhaps because one intact structure might lend credence to his story – Drummond had insisted that the ball court, a distance from the area of demolition and construction, be spared. There, on its grassy, rectangular surface flanked by stone terraces upon which royal spectators had nodded approval, teams of men wearing leather armor had played a game in which they attempted to throw a punishing globe the size and weight of a medicine ball through a vertical hoop on either side of the court. The stakes of the game had been ultimate. Life or death. Perhaps that was why Drummond had spared it – because the ball court represented his cruelty, his pursuit of a goal at any cost.

He and Raymond had arrived yesterday afternoon, brazenly, in Drummond Enterprises' large, blue helicopter, as if he had nothing to hide as he took charge of the final stages of the operation. 'You've done well,' he'd told Jenna. 'You'll get an extra bonus.'

Jenna had muttered acquiescence, mentally screaming, All I want is to get out of here with my sanity. Her co-worker, her friend, her potential lover, the project's foreman, McIntyre, had died yesterday, from snakebite, a half hour before Drummond's helicopter had arrived. Jenna had prayed for the helicopter to arrive sooner so that Mac could be flown to a hospital, but the moment she had seen Drummond's determined, wizened face as the old man strode toward her through the smoke, she had realized that Drummond would never have agreed to waste the resources of the helicopter to take a dying man from the camp. 'He'll be dead before he gets to the hospital. We don't have time. Make him as comfortable as possible,' Drummond would have said. As it was, what he did say was, 'Bury him where the natives can't get to him. No, I've changed my mind. Burn him. Burn them all.'

'All' were the natives who'd been exterminated in their attempts to stop the desecration of their sacred land. Jenna had been certain she was going insane when she realized that a massacre had taken place. She'd known of tribes that were exterminated in South America, in the depths of the Amazon rain forest. But it had never occurred to her that portions of Mexico were equally remote and that communication with the outside could be so minimal that no one 'in the world' would have any idea of what was happening here. By the time word leaked out, there'd be no evidence of the atrocity. And who was going to talk? The workers? By acquiescing to the slaughter, by accepting obscenely huge bonuses, they were implicated. Only a fool would break the silence.

Now, standing in the camp's log-walled office, remembering how Mac had writhed feverishly on a cot in the corner not twenty-four hours ago, she listened numbly to final commands from Drummond about the charts she had prepared.

'Above all' – Drummond's aged voice was filled with phlegm – 'the extent of the true discovery must be made to dwarf the archaeological ones. There'll be photographs, of course. But your charts will be given primary attention.'

At that moment, the door opened, and Raymond came in, wearing jungle clothing, holding a rifle, his face sooted from smoke, his shirt crimson with blood. 'If there are more, *I* can't find them.'

'But a different kind of enemy might be coming here. I think he's hunting us,' Drummond said, dismissing Jenna, who left the hut.

Raymond straightened, challenged. 'Who?'

'A dead man.'

Raymond furrowed his brow.

'Charles Duffy,' Drummond said. 'Do you recognize the—?'

'Yes, he was hired to watch the target's home in San Antonio. To deal with her if she arrived. He disappeared from the house three nights ago.'

'He's no longer missing,' Drummond said. 'His body washed up on a bank of the San Antonio River. He'd been shot. The authorities say he had no identification. One of the men you hired was able to get a look at the body in the morgue, however, and has no doubt that it's Duffy. But Mr Duffy is remarkable,' Drummond continued. 'While dead, he used his credit card to fly from San Antonio to Washington, D.C. He stayed at the Ritz-Carlton. For a portion of the next day, he stayed at the Dorset Hotel in Manhattan. After that, he and a companion flew to Miami where they rented a car.'

Raymond brooded. 'I don't understand the Washington connection, but the Dorset isn't far from the target's apartment in Manhattan.'

'And from the ex-husband. He was paid a visit by a man and a woman the day before yesterday. They interrupted the agreed-upon payment to him.'

'Maltin knows nothing,' Raymond said. 'All you paid him for was to stop attracting attention to the target's disappearance.'

'Nothing?' Drummond looked furious. 'Maltin knew it was I who paid him. That's what the man and woman learned from him. The woman so far hasn't been identified, although she has red hair and she claimed to work for *The Washington Post*, but the man's description matches that of the same man who interfered with surveillance on the home of the target's parents.'

'Buchanan?' Raymond scowled.

'Yes. Buchanan. Now think. What's the Miami connection?' Drummond snapped.

'The yacht. It's south of there. In Key West.'

'Exactly,' Drummond said. 'The captain reports that three crew members brought a woman aboard yesterday afternoon. A woman with red hair.'

'She must have been helping Buchanan. Checking ways to sneak aboard.'

Drummond nodded. 'I have to assume he knows something about the tape. And I have to assume that he'll keep coming closer. Intercept him. Kill him.'

'But where would I find him?'

'Isn't it obvious? What's the next link in the chain?'

'Delgado.'

'Yes. Mexico City. I just received word from my contacts at Miami International Airport that a man calling himself Charles Duffy bought two airline tickets to Mexico City. The helicopter will have you there by this afternoon.'

TWELVE

1

Mexico City.

The unregulated exhaust from countless smoke-belching factories and ill-maintained automobiles burning leaded fuel was trapped by a thermal inversion above the mountain-surrounded metropolis and made the air in the largest and fastest-growing city in the world virtually unbreathable. Buchanan's throat felt scratchy. He began to cough as soon as he and Holly got tourist cards and left Juarez International Airport. His eyes burned from the haze, so dense that if not for its acrid smell and biting taste it might have been thought to be mist. The air conditioner in the taxi they hired wasn't working. Nonetheless he and Holly closed their windows. Better to swelter inside the cab than to breathe the noxious atmosphere outside.

It was nine-fifteen. They'd managed to drive from Key West to Miami in time to catch an eight a.m. United flight to Mexico City. Because of a time-zone change backward, the duration of the flight had actually been two hours and fifteen minutes, and after eating a cheese-and-onion omelet supplied by the airline, Buchanan had been able to doze. For too long now, his schedule had been erratic. His exhaustion worsened. His headache continued to torture him.

So did the bitterness he felt toward Holly. Against his instincts, he had actually begun to trust her. As she'd pointed out to him, she *had* saved his life, and in other ways, she'd been of considerable help. But he needed to keep reminding himself that she was a reporter. In the stress of his search for Juana, he'd already indirectly revealed too much about his past. More, it made him angry to think that this woman whom he had allowed to get close to him had been sent by Alan to destroy him.

For her part, Holly remained silent, as if understanding that anything she said would be misinterpreted, as if knowing that her presence would be tolerated only if she didn't draw his attention to her.

'The National Palace,' Buchanan told the cab driver in Spanish, and the words were similar enough to English that Holly understood, although she didn't ask why they were going to a palace instead of to a hotel. Or maybe the National Palace *was* a hotel. She didn't know. She'd never been to Mexico City before. As it turned out, their destination was neither a hotel nor a palace but Mexico's center of government.

Even in the dense haze of pollution, the site was impressive. Amid congested traffic, an immense square was flanked by massive buildings, two of which were cathedrals. The National Palace itself was renowned for its arches, pillars, and patios.

After leaving the taxi, Buchanan and Holly passed through a crowd and entered the Palace's vestibule, where large, colorful murals lined the main staircase and the first-floor corridors. The murals, by Diego Rivera, conveyed the sprawling history of Mexico from the era of the Aztecs and Maya, to the invasion by the Spaniards, to the mixture of races, the numerous revolutions, and ultimately an idealized future in which Mexican peasants worked happily and coexisted gloriously with nature. Given the pollution outside, that idealized future was obviously a long way off.

Buchanan stopped only a moment to assess the murals. He'd become more intense, more driven, as if he were controlled by a terrible premonition and he didn't dare waste even a second. In a noisy, echoing corridor, he spoke to a guide and was directed toward a door down the hall. There, in a gift shop, Buchanan ignored books and artifacts on sale, scanning the walls, seeing photographs of what were obviously government officials, some in groups, others alone. He studied several of the photographs, as did Holly, although she risked a sideways glance toward him that revealed his alarmingly rigid cheek muscles and a strong, furious pulse in his neck and temple. His dark eyes seemed to blaze. He pointed at a photograph, the image catching Holly's attention as well: a tall, slender, thin-faced, hawk-nosed, Hispanic male in his early forties. The man had a mustache, wore an expensive suit, and exuded arrogance.

'Yes,' Holly said.

Buchanan turned to a young, female clerk and pointed toward the photograph. '*Este hombre. Como se llama, por favor?*'

'*Quien? Ah, si. Esteban Delgado. El Ministro de Asuntos Interiores.*'

'*Gracias,*' Buchanan said. As he bought a book, he asked the clerk more questions, and five minutes later, when he and Holly left the gift shop, Buchanan had learned that the man who'd raped and murdered Maria Tomez was 'not just the Minister of the Interior. He's the second most powerful man in Mexico. Next in line to be president. According to the clerk, that's common knowledge,' Buchanan said. 'In Mexico, when the outgoing president chooses his replacement, the election is mostly a formality.'

Surprised that he'd broken his silence toward her, Holly took advantage of the opportunity, hoping that his anger toward her had softened. 'Unless somebody's got a videotape of him that's so disgusting it would totally destroy his career, not to mention put him in prison.'

'Or get him executed.' Buchanan rubbed his pained forehead. 'A man like Delgado would give anything not to have that tape made public. The question is what, though? What does Drummond want?'

'And what happened to Juana Mendez?'

Buchanan's gaze was intense. 'Yes. That's finally what this is about. Juana.'

The word stung, as did its implication: not you.

'Don't just tolerate me,' Holly said. 'Don't just keep me along because you're afraid I'll turn against you. I'm not your enemy. Please. Use me. Let me help.'

2

'My name is Ted Riley,' Buchanan said in Spanish. With Holly, he stood in a carpeted, paneled office, the door of which was labeled *Ministro de Asuntos Interiores*. Minister of the Interior. A bespectacled, gray-haired secretary nodded and waited.

'I'm the interpreter for Señorita McCoy.' Buchanan gestured toward Holly. 'As you can see from her credentials, she is a reporter for *The Washington Post*. She is in Mexico City for a limited time doing interviews with important government officials – to learn their opinions about how America could improve its relations with your country. If at all possible, could Señor Delgado spare a few moments to speak with her? It would be greatly appreciated.'

The secretary looked sympathetic, spreading her hands in a gesture of regret. 'Señor Delgado is not expected in the office for the rest of the week.'

Buchanan sighed in frustration. 'Perhaps he would meet us if we travel to where he is. Señorita McCoy's newspaper considers his opinions to be of particular importance. It is widely known that he is likely to be the next president.'

The secretary looked pleased by Buchanan's recognition that she was associated with future greatness.

Buchanan continued, 'And I am certain that Señor Delgado would benefit from complimentary remarks about him in the newspaper that the president of the United States reads every morning. It would be a fine opportunity for the minister to make some constructive comments that would prepare the American government for his views when he becomes president.'

The secretary debated, assessed Holly, and nodded. 'One moment, please.'

She entered another office, shut the door, and left Buchanan and Holly to glance at each other. Numerous footsteps clattered past in the hallway. In rows of offices, voices murmured.

The secretary returned. 'Señor Delgado is at his home in Cuernavaca, an hour's drive south of here. I will give you directions. He invites you to be his guests for lunch.'

3

'Can I ask you something?'

Holly waited for a reply, but Buchanan ignored her, staring straight ahead as he drove their rented car south along the Insurgentes freeway.

'Sure, what did I expect?' Holly said. 'You haven't been communicative since . . . Never mind. We'll skip that topic. What I want to ask is, how do you do it?'

Again, Buchanan didn't reply.

'At Delgado's office,' Holly said. 'That secretary could just as easily have told us to get lost. Somehow you manipulated her into phoning Delgado. I've been trying to figure out how. It wasn't what you said exactly. It . . .'

'I get in someone else's mind.'

Holly frowned at him. 'And the CIA taught you how to do this?'

Buchanan's voice hardened. 'Now you're being a reporter again.'

'Will you stop being so defensive? How many times do I have to tell you? I'm on *your* side. I'm not out to destroy you. I . . .'

'Let's just say I had training along the line.' Buchanan clutched the steering wheel and continued to stare at the busy highway. 'Being a deep-cover operative isn't just having false documents and a believable cover story. To assume an identity, I have to transmit the absolute conviction that I am who I claim to be. That means believing it absolutely myself. When I spoke to that secretary, I *was* Ted Riley, and something in me went out to her. Went into her mind. Stroked her into believing in me. Remember we talked about elicitation? It isn't merely asking subtle questions. It's enveloping someone in an attitude and emotionally drawing them toward you.'

'It sounds like hypnotism.'

'That's how I made my mistake with you.' Buchanan's tone changed, becoming bitter.

Holly tensed.

'I stopped concentrating on controlling you,' Buchanan said.

'I still don't understand.'

'I stopped acting,' Buchanan said. 'For a while with you, I had an unusual experience. I stopped impersonating. Without realizing it, I became somebody I'd forgotten about. Myself. I related to you as . . . me.' He sounded more bitter.

'Maybe that's why I became attracted to you,' Holly said.

Buchanan scoffed. 'I've been plenty of people better than

myself. In fact, I'm the only identity I don't like.'

'So now you're avoiding yourself by being . . . who did you say you once were? Peter Lang? . . . searching for Juana?'

'No,' Buchanan said. 'Since I met you, Peter Lang has become less and less important. Juana matters to me because . . . In Key West, I told you I couldn't decide anything about my future until I settled my past.' He finally looked at her. 'I'm not a fool. I know I can't go back six years and God knows how many identities and start up where I left off with her. It's like . . . For a very long time I've been pretending, acting, switching from role to role, and I've known people I couldn't allow myself to care about in those roles. A lot of those people needed help that I couldn't go back and give them. A lot of those people died, but I couldn't go back and mourn for them. Most of my life's been a series of boxes unrelated to each other. I've got to connect them. I want to become . . .'

Holly waited.

'A human being,' Buchanan said. 'That's why I'm pissed at you. Because I let my guard down, and you betrayed me.'

'No,' Holly said, touching his right hand on the steering wheel. 'Not anymore. I swear to God – I'm not a threat.'

4

After the noise and pollution of Mexico City, Cuernavaca's peace and clean air were especially welcome. The sky was clear, the sun bright, making the valley resplendent. In an exclusive subdivision, Buchanan followed the directions he'd been given and found the street he wanted, coming to a high, stone wall within which a large, iron gate provided a glimpse of gardens, shade trees, and a Spanish-style mansion. A roof of red tile glinted in the sun.

Buchanan kept driving.

'But isn't that where we're supposed to go?' Holly asked.

'Yes.'

'Then why . . . ?'

'I haven't decided about a couple of things.'

'Such as?'

'Maybe it's time to cut you loose.'

Holly looked startled.

'Anything might happen. I don't want you involved,' Buchanan said.

'I *am* involved.'

'Don't you think you're going to extremes to get a story?'

'The only extreme I care about is what I have to do to prove myself to you. Delgado's expecting a female reporter. Without me, you won't get in. Hey, you established a cover. You claim you're my interpreter. Be consistent.'

'Be consistent?' Buchanan tapped his fingers on the steering wheel. 'Yeah. For a change.'

He turned the car around.

An armed guard stood behind the bars of the gate.

Buchanan got out of the car, approached the man, showed Holly's press card, and explained in Spanish that he and Señorita McCoy were expected. With a scowl, the guard stepped into a wooden booth to the right of the gate and spoke into a telephone. Meanwhile, another armed guard watched Buchanan intently. The first guard returned, his expression as surly as before. Buchanan's muscles compacted. He wondered if something had gone wrong. But the guard unlocked the gate, opened it, and motioned for Buchanan to get back in his car.

Buchanan drove along a shady, curved driveway, past trees, gardens, and fountains, toward the three-story mansion. Simultaneously he glanced in his rearview mirror, noting that the guard relocked the gate. He noted as well that other armed guards patrolled the interior of the wall.

'I feel a lot more nervous than when I went on Drummond's yacht,' Holly said. 'Don't *you* ever feel—?'

'Each time.'

'Then why on earth do you keep doing it?'

'I don't have a choice.'

'In this case, maybe. But other times . . .'

'No choice,' Buchanan repeated. 'When you're in the military, you follow orders.'

'Not now, you're not. Besides, you didn't have to join the military.'

'Wrong,' Buchanan said, thinking of the need he'd felt to punish himself for killing his brother. He urgently crushed the thought, disturbed that he'd allowed himself to be distracted. Juana. He had to pay attention. Instead of Tommy, he had to keep thinking of Juana.

'In fact, I don't think I've *ever* felt this nervous,' Holly said.

'Stage fright. Try to relax. This is just a walk-through,' Buchanan said. 'I need to check Delgado's security. Your performance shouldn't be difficult. Just conduct an interview. You're perfectly safe. Which is a hell of a lot more than Delgado will be when I figure out how to get to him.'

Concealing his intensity, Buchanan parked in front of the mansion. When he got out of the car, he noticed other guards, not to mention groundskeepers who seemed more interested in visitors than in their duties. There were closed-circuit television cameras, wires in the panes of the windows, metal boxes among the shrubbery – intrusion detectors.

I might have to find another place, Buchanan thought.

Subduing his emotions, he introduced Holly and himself to a servant, who came out to greet them and escort them into a cool, shadowy, echoing, marble vestibule. They passed a wide, curved staircase and proceeded along a hallway to a mahogany-paneled study that smelled of wax and polish. Furnished in leather, it was filled with hunting trophies as well as numerous rifles and shotguns in glinting, glass cabinets.

Although Buchanan had never met him, Delgado was instantly recognizable as he stood from behind his desk, more hawk-nosed and more arrogant-looking than he appeared on the videotape and in photographs. But he also seemed pale and thinner, his cheeks gaunt as if he might be ill.

'Welcome,' he said.

Buchanan vividly remembered the images that showed Delgado raping and murdering Maria Tomez. As soon as he had the information he needed, Buchanan planned to kill him.

Delgado came closer, his English impressive, although his syntax was somewhat stilted. 'It is always a pleasure to speak with members of the American press, especially when they work for so distinguished a periodical as *The Washington Post*. Señorita . . . ? Forgive me. I have forgotten the name that my secretary . . .'

'Holly McCoy. And this is my interpreter, Ted Riley.'

Delgado shook hands with them. 'Good.' He ignored Buchanan and kept his attention on Holly, obviously intrigued by her beauty. 'Since I speak English, we will not need your interpreter.'

'I'm also the photographer,' Buchanan said.

Delgado gestured dismissively. 'There will be an opportunity for photographs later. Señorita McCoy, may I offer you a drink before lunch? Perhaps wine?'

'Thank you, but it's a little too early for . . .'

'Sure,' Buchanan said. 'Wine would be nice.' There hadn't been time to teach Holly not to turn down an offer to drink with a target. Refusing alcohol stifled the target's urge to be companionable. It made the target suspect that you had a reason not to want to relax your inhibitions.

'On second thought, yes,' Holly said. 'Since we're having lunch.'

'White or red?'

'White, please.'

'Chardonnay?'

'Fine.'

'The same for me,' Buchanan said.

Delgado continued ignoring him and turned to the servant, who had remained at the door. *'Lo haga, Carlos.* Do it.'

'Si, Señor Delgado.'

The white-coated servant stepped back and disappeared along the hallway.

'Sit down, please.' Delgado led Holly toward one of the padded leather chairs.

Buchanan followed, noticing a man on a patio beyond the glass doors that led to the study. The man was an American in his middle thirties, well-dressed, fair-haired, pleasant-looking.

Noticing Buchanan's interest in him, the man nodded and smiled, his expression boyish.

Delgado was saying, 'I know Americans like to keep to a busy schedule, so if you have a few questions you would like to ask before lunch, by all means do so.'

The man came in from the patio.

'Ah, Raymond,' Delgado said. 'Have you finished your stroll? Come in. I have some guests I would like you to meet. Señorita McCoy from *The Washington Post.*'

Raymond nodded with respect and went over to Holly. 'My pleasure.' He shook hands with her.

Something about the handshake made her frown.

Raymond turned and approached Buchanan. 'How do you do? Mister . . . ?'

'Riley. Ted.'

They shook hands.

At once Buchanan felt a stinging sensation in his right palm. It burned.

His hand went numb.

553

Alarmed, he looked over at Holly, who was staring in dismay at *her* right palm.

'How long does it take?' Delgado asked.

'It's what we call a two-stepper,' Raymond said. As he took off a ring and placed it in a small jeweler's box, he smiled again, his blue eyes bottomless and cold.

Holly sank to her knees.

Buchanan's right arm lost all sensation.

Holly toppled to the floor.

Buchanan's chest felt tight. His heart pounded. He sprawled.

Desperate, he fought to stand.

Couldn't.

Couldn't do anything.

His body felt numb. His limbs wouldn't move. From head to foot, he was powerless.

Staring above him, frantic, helpless, he saw Delgado smirk.

The blue-eyed American peered down, his empty smile chilling. 'The drug comes from the Yucatán Peninsula. It's the Mayan equivalent of curare. Hundreds of years ago, the natives used it to paralyze their victims so they wouldn't struggle when their hearts were cut out.'

Unable to turn his head, unable to get a glimpse of Holly, Buchanan heard her gasp, trying to breathe.

'Don't *you* try to struggle,' Raymond said. 'Your lungs might not bear the strain.'

5

The helicopter thundered across the sky. Its whump-whump-whumping roar vibrated through the fuselage. Not that Buchanan could feel the rumble. His body continued to have absolutely no sensation. The cabin's presumably hard floor

554

might as well have been a feathered mattress. Neither hard nor soft, hot nor cold, sharp nor blunt had any significance. All was the same: numb.

In compensation, his senses of hearing and sight intensified tremendously. Every sound in the cabin, especially Holly's agonized wheezing, was amplified. Beyond a window of the cabin, the sky was an almost unbearably brilliant turquoise. He feared that he would have gone blind from the radiance if not for merciful flicks of his eyelids, which – like his heart and lungs – weren't part of the system controlled by the drug.

Indeed his heart was nauseatingly stimulated, pounding wildly, no doubt at least in part from fear. But if he vomited (assuming that his stomach, too, wasn't paralyzed), he would surely gag and die. He had to concentrate on controlling his fear. He didn't dare lose his discipline. The faster his heart pounded, the more his lungs wanted air. But his chest muscles wouldn't cooperate, and the panic of involuntary, smothering hyperventilation almost overcame him.

Concentrate, he thought. Concentrate.

He struggled to fill his mind with a calming mantra. He strove for a single, all-consuming thought that gave him purpose. Juana, he thought. Juana. Juana. Have to survive to help her. Have to survive to find her. Have to survive to save her. Have to . . .

His frenzied heart kept speeding. His panicked lungs kept insisting. No. The mantra wasn't working. Juana? She was a distant memory, years away – in Buchanan's case, literally lifetimes away. He'd been so many people in the meanwhile. Searching for her, as determined as he'd been to find her, he'd really been searching for himself, and as a new, all-consuming, all-purposeful thought filled his mind –

—it was unwilled, spontaneous—

—Holly—

—listening to her struggle to breathe—

—need to help Holly, need to save Holly—

– he suddenly knew that he finally had a purpose. Not for Peter Lang. Not for any of his other assumed identities. But for Brendan Buchanan. And that realization gave him an urge to look forward rather than behind, something he hadn't felt since he'd killed his brother so long ago. Brendan Buchanan had a purpose, and it had nothing to do with himself. It was simply, absolutely, to do everything in his power to make sure that Holly survived this. Not because he wanted her to be with him. But because he wanted her to live. Trapped in himself, he had found himself.

While his heart continued to speed, he sensed – from a change in pressure behind his ears – that the helicopter was descending. He couldn't move his head to notice where Delgado sat next to Raymond, but he could hear them talking.

'I don't see why it was necessary for me to come along.'

'It was an order that Mr Drummond radioed to me as I was flying to Cuernavaca. He wants you to see the progress at the site.'

'Risky,' Delgado said. 'I might be associated with the project.'

'I suspect that was Mr Drummond's idea. It's time for you to pay off your debt.'

'That ruthless son of a bitch.'

'Mr Drummond would consider it a compliment to be called ruthless. Look down there. You can see it now.'

'My God.'

The helicopter continued descending, the pressure behind Buchanan's ears more painful.

Painful? Buchanan suddenly realized that he was feeling something. He had never expected to welcome pain, but now he did – joyously. His feet tingled. His hands seemed pricked by needles. The stitches in his knife wound began to itch. His nearly healed bullet wound throbbed. His skull felt swollen, his excruciating headache returning. These sensations didn't occur all at one time. They came separately, gradually. Each gave him hope. He knew that if he tried to move, he'd be able to, but he didn't dare. He had to keep still. He had to make sure that his limbs were fully functional. He had to wait for the ideal moment to . . .

'Just about now, the drug should be wearing off,' Raymond said.

A strong grip seized Buchanan's left wrist and snapped a handcuff onto it. Then the left wrist was tugged behind Buchanan's back, and with force, a handcuff was snapped onto his right wrist.

'Comfortable?' Raymond's tone suggested that he might have been speaking to a lover.

Buchanan didn't answer, continuing to pretend that he couldn't move. Meanwhile the clink and scrape of metal told him that Holly was being handcuffed as well.

The helicopter's roar diminished, the pitch of its rotor blades changing, as it settled onto the ground. The pilot shut off the controls, the blades spinning with less velocity, the turbine's roar turning into a whine.

When the hatch was opened, Buchanan expected his eyes to be assaulted by a blaze of sunlight. Instead a shadow blanketed him. A haze. He'd noticed that the sky had become less brilliantly blue as the helicopter descended, but with so much else to think about, he hadn't paid the lack of clarity much attention. Now the haze swirled into the cabin, and the odor was so acrid that he coughed reflexively. Smoke! Nearby something was on fire.

Buchanan kept coughing.

'The drug temporarily stops your saliva glands from working,' Raymond said, dragging Buchanan from the cabin, dumping him onto the ground. 'That makes your throat dry. In fact, your throat'll feel irritated for quite some time.'

Raymond's tone suggested that he enjoyed the thought of Buchanan's discomfort.

Holly coughed as well, then groaned as Raymond dragged her from the cabin and dumped her next to Buchanan. Smoke drifted past them.

'Why are you burning so many trees?' Delgado sounded alarmed.

'To make as wide a perimeter as possible. To keep the natives away.'

'But won't the flames ignite the—?'

'Mr Drummond knows what he's doing. Everything's been calculated.'

Raymond kicked Buchanan's side.

Buchanan gasped, making himself sound more in pain than he was, thankful that Raymond hadn't kicked him in the side where he'd been stabbed.

'Get up,' Raymond said. 'Our men have better things to do than carry you. I know you can do it. If you don't, I'll kick you all the way to the office.'

To prove his point, Raymond kicked Buchanan again, this time harder.

Buchanan struggled to his knees, wavered, and managed to stand. His mind swirled, imitating the smoke that forced him to cough once more.

Holly staggered upright, almost falling, then gaining her balance. She looked at Buchanan in terror. He tried to communicate an expression of reassurance.

It didn't work. Raymond shoved both of them, nearly knocking them down before their momentum jerked them upright and forward. They were being herded toward a wide log building that was partially obscured by smoke.

But what captured Buchanan's attention was the welter of activity around him, workmen rushing, bulldozers and trucks laboring past, cranes lifting girders and pipes. Amid the din of machinery, Buchanan thought he heard a shot, and then he saw stone blocks scattered before him, hieroglyphs on them, obviously from ruins. Here and there, he saw the stunted remains of ancient temples. At once, as the smoke cleared temporarily, he had a brief view of a pyramid. But the pyramid wasn't ancient, and it wasn't composed of stone blocks.

This one, tall and wide, was built of steel. Buchanan had never seen anything like it. The structure was like a gigantic tripod, its legs splayed, unfamiliar reinforcements linking them. Though he'd never seen anything like it, he knew intuitively what it was, what it resembled. An oil derrick. Is that what Drummond wants down here? he wondered. But why does the derrick have such an unusual design?

At the smoke-hazed, log building, Raymond shoved the door, then thrust Buchanan and Holly through the opening.

Buchanan almost fell into the shadowy, musty interior, his eyes needing time to adjust to the dim, generator-powered, overhead light bulbs. He staggered to a halt, straightened, felt Holly stumble next to him, and found himself blinking upward at Alistair Drummond.

6

None of the photographs in the biography and the newspaper stories Buchanan had read communicated how fiercely Drummond dominated a room. Behind thick spectacles, the old man's eyes were deep in their sockets and radiated an unnerving, penetrating gaze. Even the age in his voice worked to his advantage, powerful despite its brittleness.

'Mr Buchanan,' Drummond said.

The reference was startling. How did he find out my name? Buchanan thought.

Drummond squinted, then turned his attention to Holly.

'Ms McCoy, I trust that Raymond made you comfortable on the flight. Señor Delgado, I'm pleased that you could join me.'

'The way it was put to me, I didn't feel I had a choice.'

'Of course, you have a choice,' Drummond said. 'You can go to jail or become the next president of Mexico. Which would you prefer?'

Raymond had shut the door after they entered. Now it was bumped open, the cacophony of the construction equipment intruding. A woman in dusty jeans and a sweaty work shirt came in, holding long tubes of thick paper that Buchanan thought might have been charts.

'Not now, God damn it,' Drummond said.

The woman looked startled. Smoke drifted behind her as she backed awkwardly from the building and shut the door.

Drummond returned his attention to Delgado. 'We're much farther along than I anticipated. By tomorrow morning, we ought to be able to start pumping. When you get back to Mexico City, I want you to make the necessary arrangements. Tell your people that everything's in place. I don't want any trouble. The payments have been made. I expect everyone to cooperate.'

'You brought me here to tell me what I already knew?'

'I brought you here to see what you sold your soul for,' Drummond said. 'It's not good to keep a distance from the price of your sins. Otherwise you might be tempted to forget the bargain you made. To remind you, I want you to see what happens to my two guests.' With a fluid motion amazing for his age, he turned toward Buchanan and Holly. 'How much do you know?'

'I found this in their camera bag,' Raymond said. He placed a video tape on a table.

'My, my,' Drummond said.

'I played it at Delgado's.'

'And?'

560

'The copy's a little grainy, but Delgado's performance is as enthralling as ever. It holds my attention every time,' Raymond said.

'Then you know more than you should,' Drummond told Buchanan and Holly.

'Look, this isn't any of our business,' Buchanan said.

'You're right about that.'

'I'm not interested in oil, and I don't care about whatever you're doing to punish Delgado,' Buchanan said. 'All I'm trying to do is find Juana Mendez.'

Drummond raised his dense, white eyebrows. 'Well, in that you're not alone.'

They stared at each other, and Buchanan suddenly realized what must have happened. Juana had agreed to work for Drummond and impersonate Maria Tomez. But after several months, Juana had felt either trapped or threatened, or possibly she'd just been disgusted by Drummond. Whatever her motive, she'd broken her agreement and fled. Along the way, unable to risk a phone call to Buchanan's superiors, needing to contact Buchanan but without allowing any outsider to understand her message, she'd mailed the cryptic postcard that only Buchanan could decipher. Meanwhile, Drummond's people had frantically searched for her, staking out her home and her parents' home and anywhere else they suspected she might go. They had to guarantee her silence. If the truth about Maria Tomez were revealed, Drummond would no longer have control of Delgado. Without Delgado, Drummond wouldn't have the political means to sustain this project. The oil industry in Mexico had been nationalized back in the thirties. Foreigners weren't allowed to have the influence in it that Drummond evidently wanted. That this was an archaeological site made the political problem all the more enormous, although from the looks of things, Drummond had solved the archaeological problem simply and obscenely by destroying the ruins. When Delgado became president of Mexico, he could use his power with appropriate politicians. A back-door arrangement could be made with Drummond. For discovering and developing the site, Drummond would secretly be paid the huge profits that foreign oil companies used to earn before the days of nationalization. But that wasn't all of it, Buchanan sensed. There was something more, a further implication, although he was too preoccupied with saving his life to analyze what it was.

'Do you know where Juana Mendez is?' Drummond asked.

'For all I know, she's working on that oil rig out there.'

Drummond chuckled. 'Such bravado. You're a credit to Special Forces.'

The reference surprised Buchanan. Then it didn't. 'The car I rented in New Orleans and drove to San Antonio.'

Drummond nodded. 'You used your own credit card to rent it.'

'I didn't have an alternative. It was the only card I had.'

'But it gave me a slight advantage,' Drummond said. 'When my people saw you arrive at the Mendez house in San Antonio, they were able to use the car's license number to find out who had rented the car and then to research your identity.'

Identity, Buchanan thought. After so many years of surviving as other people, I'm probably going to die because of my own identity. He felt totally exhausted. His wounds ached. His skull throbbed with greater ferocity. He didn't have any more resources.

Then he looked at Holly, at the terror in her eyes, and the mantra again filled his mind. Have to survive to help Holly. Have to save Holly.

'You're an instructor in tactical maneuvers,' Drummond said.

Buchanan tensed. Instructor? Then Drummond hadn't penetrated his cover.

Drummond continued, 'Did you know Juana Mendez at Fort Bragg?'

Desperate, Buchanan tried to find a role to play, an angle with which to defend himself. 'Yes.'

'How? She was in Army Intelligence. What does that have to do with—?'

Abruptly a role came to mind. Buchanan decided to play the most daring part of his life. Himself.

'Look, I'm not a field instructor, and Juana's Army-Intelligence status was only a cover.'

Drummond looked surprised.

'I'm looking for Juana Mendez because she sent me a postcard, telling me in code that she was in trouble. It had to be in code because I'm not supposed to exist. Juana used to belong and I still do belong to a special-operations unit that's so covert it might as well be run by ghosts. We look after our own: past members as well as present. When I got the SOS, my unit sent me to find out what was going on. I've been reporting on a regular basis. My unit still has no idea where Juana Mendez is. But they know I was in Cuernavaca. They know I was headed toward Delgado, and after him, they know I was headed toward you. They won't be able to track me here, not right away, not without questioning Delgado. But they will question him, and they will come to you, and believe me, these men care only about sacrifice and loyalty. If they do not find me, they will destroy you. Take my word – at the moment, Holly McCoy and I are your most valuable assets.'

Drummond sighed. From outside the building, amid the muffled roar of the construction equipment, Buchanan thought he heard another gunshot.

'For something you invented on the spur of the moment, that's an excellent negotiating posture,' Drummond said. 'I'm a collector, did you know that? That's how I came to be here. Journalists' – he nodded toward Holly – 'have always wondered what motivates me. What do *you* think, Ms McCoy?'

Despite her evident fear, Holly managed to say, 'Power.'

'Partially correct. But only in a simplistic way. What keeps me going, what gives me drive, is the desire to be unique. To own unique things, to be in unique situations, to control unique people. I became interested in the Yucatán because of my collection. Three years ago, an individual came to me with an object of great price. The ancient Maya had their own version of books. They were long strips of thin bark that were folded again and again until they resembled small accordions. Historians call them codices. When the Spaniards invaded this area in the fifteen-hundreds, they were determined to destroy the native culture and replace it with their own. In their zeal, they set fire to the Mayan libraries. Only three authenticated codices are known to have survived. A fourth may be a forgery. But a fifth exists. It is authentic, and I own it. It is absolutely unique because unlike the others, which are lists, mine has substantial information. Of course, I didn't know that at the time. I bought it because I had the means to and because I didn't want anyone else to own it. Naturally I wanted to know what the hieroglyphs signified, so I hired the world's greatest experts in Mayan symbols. You might say I owned those experts. And I eventually discovered that the text described the presence of a massive oil field in this area. The Maya called it the god of darkness, the god of black water, the god that seeps from the ground. At first, I thought they were using metaphors. Then it came to me that they were being literally descriptive. The text emphasized that the god was held in control by temples and a great pyramid, but the location described in the text didn't match any known ruins. Early this year, *these* ruins were discovered thanks to photographs taken from a space shuttle. Because I controlled Delgado, I was able to control this site, to bring in my own people, to seal off the area, to search.'

'And in the process, destroy the ruins,' Buchanan said.

'An unavoidable necessity.' Drummond raised his shoulders. 'Besides, *I'd* seen the ruins. Why should I care if anyone else does? I didn't want to start drilling until I was certain. It turned out that the oil seepage was exactly where the text said it would be. Beneath the pyramid. The pyramid rested on it, capped it, kept the god in control. But the uniqueness doesn't end there. Oil in the Yucatán means nothing if you can't get to it. This area is so unstable that conventional equipment is useless here. That's why no one else took the trouble to explore for oil in this region. Periodic earthquakes would have destroyed their derricks. But *my* equipment is one of a kind. It's designed to be flexible, to withstand quakes. Because of it, from now on geologists can look for oil in areas that they previously ignored because there wasn't any way to develop the site. Of course, they'll have to pay a considerable amount to get permission to use my equipment. I doubt they'll ever find an oil field as immense as this one is, however. It's of Kuwaiti proportions, far beyond my expectations. And that's what finally makes this situation truly unique. When the field is fully developed, the oil will not be used.'

Buchanan must have looked surprised, for in response, Drummond's eyes gleamed. 'Yes. It won't be used. To put so much oil on the market would cause the price of oil to plummet. It would be an economic disaster to the oil-producing nations. When Delgado becomes president, he'll allow me to negotiate with the other oil-producing nations for them to pay Mexico *not* to put its oil on the market. And there's no limit to what they will pay us. As a consequence, less oil will be used. In that sense, you could say I'm a humanitarian.' Drummond smirked.

'Or maybe you just want to collect the world,' Buchanan said.

'What we're discussing is whether your argument is persuasive enough to make me want to collect *you*.' Drummond squinted toward Raymond. 'Find out if he's lying about this covert special-operations group.'

7

The sun was low, adding to the gloom of the acrid smoke that drifted across the area. Buchanan coughed again as he and Holly were shoved through the haze toward the only part of the ruins that Drummond had allowed to remain intact.

'The ball court,' Drummond said.

The haze lifted enough for Buchanan to see a flat, stone, playing surface one hundred feet long and twenty-five feet wide. On each side was a wall, fifteen feet high, the top of which was a terrace from which spectators could watch. Drummond climbed steps to the terrace, followed by Delgado, a guard and Holly. She looked sick from fear. Her handcuffs had been removed. She nervously rubbed her wrists.

Another guard removed Buchanan's handcuffs, then followed the others to the terrace. Buchanan too rubbed his wrists, trying to increase the flow of blood to his numb hands. Anxiety surged through him as he studied the walls of the court, noting the hieroglyphs and the drawings engraved on the stone.

'The acoustics of the ball court are amazing.' Drummond spoke from the terrace, peering down at Buchanan. 'I'm using a normal voice, and yet it sounds as if I have a microphone.'

Despite the roar of construction equipment in the background, despite the closer crackle of flames and the occasional bark of a gunshot, Buchanan heard Drummond with remarkable clarity. The crusty voice seemed to echo from and be amplified by all points of the court.

'The game was called *pok-a-tok*,' Drummond said. 'If you study the engravings on the stone wall below me, you can see images of the ancient Maya playing the game. They used a latex rubber ball roughly the size and weight of a medicine ball. The intention was to hurl the ball through the vertical stone circle projecting from the middle of this side of the court. A second stone circle projects from the other side of the court. Presumably that was the goal for the opposite team. The ancient Maya considered *pok-a-tok* more than mere recreation. To them, it had enormous political and religious significance. In their mythology, the two gods who founded their race did so by winning this game in a contest with other gods. There is evidence that commoners were never allowed to witness the game. Only nobles, priests, and royalty. There is further evidence that the game was a prelude to human sacrifice and that it was played most often with warriors captured from other tribes.'

'The stakes were life and death.' Raymond's voice came suddenly from behind Buchanan, making him whirl.

8

What Buchanan saw stunned him. Threw his mind off balance. Assaulted his sanity. For a moment, he told himself that he had to be hallucinating, that fatigue combined with his concussion had distorted his perceptions.

But as Raymond stepped through the haze of smoke, tinted crimson by the lowering sun, Buchanan forced himself to accept that what confronted him, however grotesque, was definitely, dismayingly real.

Raymond was partially naked. He wore thick, leather pads around his waist and groin. Similar armor was strapped to his shoulders, elbows, and knees. Otherwise his body was bare, his

567

nipples showing. His exposed muscles displayed the strength and tone that could have come only from hours of daily exercise.

Buchanan, who had been in excellent condition before he began his assignment in Mexico, had been on the move for so long and been so wearied by his various injuries that he hadn't had time for exercise and wasn't in peak condition.

Raymond's leather armor looked grotesque enough. But what added to the dismaying sense of surreality was a helmet he wore, from which long feathers of numerous brilliant colors were swept back, creating the illusion that a Mayan warrior had stepped not only through smoke but through time. In addition, he carried a large ball that he dropped to the stone court. As it struck and rolled, it caused a thunking echo that communicated how solid and heavy it was. He threw leather pads at Buchanan's feet. 'Undress and put them on.'

'Like hell,' Buchanan said.

Raymond picked up the ball and hurled it at Buchanan, who dodged but not soon enough, the drug still affecting him. The glancing impact of the ball against his left arm was startlingly painful.

'Undress and put on the armor, or you won't last thirty seconds in the game,' Raymond said.

Buchanan slowly complied, gaining time, calculating. Above him, Holly looked even more terrified. Buchanan strained to think of a way for the two of them to escape, but no plan was adequate against the guard next to Holly and the automatic weapon in his hands. The guard would shoot before Buchanan could climb the wall and get to them.

As Buchanan's naked skin felt prickly cold despite the sweat dripping from him, he strapped on the rough, thick, leather armor.

'I designed these myself,' Raymond said, 'based on the drawings on these walls.' He pointed to Buchanan's left, just

568

below the vertical stone hoop that projected from the top of the wall. 'That engraving, in particular, interests me.'

Buchanan frowned in that direction, and for a moment, the image – a warrior in armor, with a feathered headdress – looked disturbingly like Raymond.

'When I first stepped onto this ball court,' Raymond said, 'I felt as if I'd come home. I felt as if I'd been here, as if I'd played here. Long, long ago.'

Buchanan kept staring at the image. Appalled, he realized that the warrior was clutching a severed human head, blood dripping from the neck as the warrior raised the skull by its hair.

'That's what I meant about life and death,' Raymond said. 'You see, the penalty for the losers was execution. And the winner? He not only got to stay alive. He got to be the executioner.'

'What are we talking about here?' Buchanan demanded. 'Are you telling me that if I win, I go free?'

Except for the din of construction equipment in the background, the ball court became silent.

'That's what I thought,' Buchanan said. 'For me, it's a no-win situation.'

'It may have been for the ancient Maya as well,' Drummond interrupted, his voice filled with phlegm.

'What's that supposed to mean?'

'There's a theory among a few historians of Mayan culture that it wasn't the losers who were executed but rather the winners.'

'That's absurd,' Buchanan said. 'Who on earth would want to play?'

'Raymond agrees with you,' the old man said. 'But the theory is that winning was such an honor it put you on a level with the gods. The next logical step was for you to be sacrificed so that you could take your place among the gods.'

'It sounds to me like the only true winners were those who watched.'

'Yes,' Drummond said. 'As I told you, I pursue the unique. I'm about to be privileged to witness a rarity. For the first time in five hundred years, a game of *pok-a-tok* is going to be played. For me.'

'And how is this supposed to prove whether I'm telling the truth about the special-ops unit that'll come here looking for me? Am I supposed to confess so I won't have my head cut off?'

'Oh, I think as the game progresses, you'll have many painful inducements to tell the truth,' Drummond said. 'But it's not you I'm concerned about. My interest is in Ms McCoy. I suspect that what she sees will make her more than willing to tell the truth. In exchange for ending what's being done to you.'

'It won't do you any good,' Buchanan said. 'She doesn't know anything about my unit.'

'Perhaps. I'll soon find out. Raymond, if you're ready.'

9

The ball struck Buchanan's back with such force that he was knocked to the stone floor, his chin scraping on one of the slabs. If not for the padded leather armor, he suspected that the ball would have broken some of his ribs. Gasping, ignoring his pain, he scrambled to his feet and charged toward the ball. Raymond got there at the same time he did.

Buchanan rammed his padded elbow against the side of Raymond's head, knocking him sideways. Before Raymond could recover, Buchanan lifted the ball, its weight surprising him, and hurled it at Raymond, who grunted and lurched back as the ball struck his thigh and bounced off his leather armor, thudding onto the court.

'No, no, no,' Drummond said from the platform. 'This won't do at all. The point of the game is to throw the ball through the stone hoop, not at your opponent.'

'Why didn't you tell that to Raymond when he threw it at me to begin with? What the hell was he doing?'

'Getting your attention,' Raymond said.

'How many points does it take to win?'

'Well, that's a problem.'

'Yeah, I thought so.'

'No, you don't understand,' Drummond said. 'You see, *no one* knows how many points are required in order to win. That information hasn't survived the centuries. We'll have to improvise.'

'Ten.' Raymond smiled.

'Ten what?' Buchanan asked in fury. 'Do you mean I have to win by ten points? For Christ's sake, what are you saying?'

'The best of ten. Whoever gets to ten first.'

'And then what?'

'It depends on the answers I receive from you and Ms McCoy,' Drummond said.

Without warning, Buchanan dodged toward the ball, picked it up, and lunged toward the vertical hoop. As he aimed to throw, Raymond battered his padded shoulder against Buchanan's arm, jolting him sideways, slamming him against the stone wall.

Buchanan groaned, spun, and struck Raymond's chest with the ball. Continuing to grip the ball, Buchanan kept spinning as Raymond stumbled backward. Braced beneath the stone hoop, Buchanan hurled the ball and felt his heartbeat surge when he saw the ball arc through the vertical circle.

Raymond's hands struck Buchanan's back, knocking him

forward and down, Buchanan's chin again scraping on the court.

Jesus, Buchanan said. Not my head. I can't let anything happen to my head. Another concussion would . . .

He scrambled to his feet, wiped blood from his chin, and glared at Raymond.

'*No, no, no,*' Drummond repeated. '*You're not playing by the rules.*'

'Tell that to Raymond!' Buchanan shouted. '*I'm* the one who got the ball through the hoop.'

'But you didn't get the ball through legally!'

'*What are you talking about?*'

'You're not allowed to use your hands!'

'Not allowed to—?'

'We don't know much about the game.' Drummond gestured forcefully. 'But we do know this. Presumably except for picking up the ball, you were not allowed to use your hands. The ball was kept in motion by thrusting it with your forearms, your shoulders, your hips, your knees, and your head.'

The idea of hitting the ball with his head made Buchanan inwardly flinch. It would probably kill him.

'For breaking the rules, you have to be given a penalty. One point demerit. Now you have to score eleven while Raymond needs only ten. Unless of course he breaks a rule.'

'Sure. But somehow I get the feeling he'll make up the rules as he goes along and I'll keep breaking rules that haven't been invented yet.'

'Just play the game,' Raymond said.

Before Buchanan could react, Raymond scurried toward the ball, picked it up with his hands, threw it into the air, caught it with his forearms, and hurled it toward the hoop, the ball flying neatly through.

Thunking, the ball landed at Buchanan's feet.

'Raymond, I get the feeling you've been practising.'

'Good sport,' Drummond said. 'I like a man who loses a point graciously.'

'But I'll bet you like winners more,' Buchanan said.

'Then make me like you better,' Drummond said. 'Win.'

Buchanan managed to grab the ball. At once he felt his legs kicked out from under him as Raymond leapt, hitting with his feet.

Buchanan fell backward, the weight of the ball against his chest. He struck the court hard, grateful for the leather armor on his shoulders. Even so, his impact sent a spasm through the shoulder that was still healing from where he'd been shot in Cancun. The weight of the ball took his breath away.

Raymond jerked the ball from his hands, threw it into the air again, caught it with his forearms again, and hurled it toward the vertical hoop, scoring another point.

'Yes, you've definitely been practising.' As Buchanan came to his feet, he felt his body begin to stiffen.

'This isn't amusing at all. You're going to have to try harder,' Drummond said.

Sooner than anticipated, Buchanan scooped up the ball, grasped it with his forearms, pretended to lunge toward the hoop, but actually watched for Raymond to attack, and as Raymond darted to slam against him, Buchanan spun. Clutching the ball to his chest, avoiding Raymond, Buchanan jabbed with his elbow as Raymond went past, and Raymond lurched, doubling over, holding his side from the pain in his left kidney. Instantly Buchanan ran toward the hoop, stood with his back to it, cautiously watched Raymond, then risked a glance upward, judged his distance from the hoop, and threw the ball up behind him with his forearms, exhaling with satisfaction when the ball hurtled through.

'Excellent coordination,' Drummond said. 'You look like you've had experience with basketball. But this game has aspects of volleyball and soccer as well. How were you at those?'

Distracted, Buchanan felt the wind knocked out of him as Raymond attacked head first, plowing his skull into Buchanan's stomach, knocking him over.

Buchanan writhed, struggling to breathe. Meanwhile Raymond scooped up the ball and scored another point.

'What's the name of your special-operations unit?' Drummond asked. 'This mythical unit that's supposed to come and rescue you or else punish me if I harm you.'

Buchanan wavered upright, wiped blood from his chin, and squinted toward Raymond.

'I asked you a question,' Drummond demanded. 'What is the name of your unit?'

Buchanan pretended to dart toward the ball. Raymond lunged to intercept him. Buchanan zigzagged, coming toward Raymond from the opposite side, once more ramming his padded elbow into Raymond's left kidney.

The repeated damage to the area made Raymond groan, faltering with his hands on the ball. Buchanan yanked it away, wedged it between his forearms, and started to throw. Pain blurred his vision as Raymond tackled him from behind at his midsection.

Falling, Buchanan was terribly conscious of the ball beneath him, of Raymond's weight on top of him. When he hit the court, he felt as if the ball were a wedge against which the top and bottom of his body were being split in opposite directions. Raymond's plummeting body shoved the ball against Buchanan's stomach. For a terrifying moment, Buchanan couldn't breathe. He felt smothered.

Then Raymond scrambled free, and Buchanan rolled off the ball, gasping, knowing that his abdomen had been bruised, worse, that the stitches in his knife wound had been torn open beneath the leather armor that girded his right side.

Raymond picked up the ball with his forearms and, without any visible strain, threw it, scoring another point.

The court echoed with the powerful thunk of the ball as it landed. Construction equipment kept roaring in the background. The fires kept crackling. A gunshot reverberated from the forest. Smoke, tinted crimson by the sunset, drifted over the court.

Drummond coughed.

He kept coughing. Phlegm rattled in his throat. He spat and finally managed to say, 'You'll have to try harder. *What is the name of your special-operations unit?*'

Stiff, weary, in pain, Buchanan stood. If he and Holly were going to get out of this alive, he had to convince Drummond that the old man couldn't afford the consequence of killing his hostages.

'Name, rank, and serial number,' Buchanan said. 'But I'll go to hell before I give you classified information.'

'You don't know what hell can be,' Drummond said. '*What is the name of your special-operations unit?*'

Buchanan grabbed for the ball. Although his movements were an excruciating effort, he had to keep trying. He had to ignore the sticky wetness beneath the leather pad on his right side. He had to overcome his pain.

Raymond sprinted to intercept him, stooping to grab the ball.

Buchanan increased speed, getting to Raymond much sooner than expected, kicking, his right shin striking the unprotected area between Raymond's shoulders and his abdomen.

Bent over, Raymond took the kick so hard that he was lifted off the court. He tilted in midair, landed on his side, rolled onto his back, kept rolling, came to his feet, and whacked his forearm across Buchanan's face so hard that Buchanan's teeth snapped together.

For a moment, Buchanan was blind, jolted backward.

575

Raymond struck him again, knocking him farther backward. Blood flew. Dazed, Buchanan prepared for a third blow, shielding his face, ducking to the left, unable to see clearly.

'*What is the name of your unit?*' Drummond demanded.

Raymond struck again, smashing Buchanan's lips.

Then suddenly Buchanan had nowhere to go. He was thrust against the wall of the court. Through blurred vision, he saw Raymond drawing back his arm to strike yet again.

'*The name of your unit?*' Drummond shouted.

'Yellow Fruit!' Holly blurted.

'Yellow . . . ?' Drummond sounded confused.

'You want the unit's name! That's it!' Holly's voice was unsteady from terror. 'Stop. My God, look at the blood. Can't you see how hurt he is?'

'That's the general idea.' Raymond struck Buchanan again.

Buchanan slumped to his knees.

Keep going, Holly. Buchanan strained to clear his vision. Damn it, keep on. Hook them.

Yellow Fruit! She hadn't told Drummond about Scotch and Soda. Instead she'd used the name for a unit that was no longer operative. She was following what Buchanan had taught her during their search. When you're absolutely stuck, tell the truth, but only that portion of the truth that's useful. Never expose your core identity.

'And what exactly is Yellow Fruit?' Drummond demanded.

'It's a covert Army unit that supplies security and intelligence to special-operations units.' Holly's voice continued to shake.

'And how do you know this? A while ago, Buchanan assured me that your knowledge was limited.'

'Because of a story I've been working on. I've tracked down leads for a year. Buchanan's one of them. I wouldn't be here if I hadn't tried to get close to him and hope he'd say more than he meant to.'

'Did he?'

'Not enough to satisfy you. Damn it, I've got nothing to do with this. I want out of this. Jesus, tell him what he wants, Buchanan. Maybe he'll let us go.'

'Yes,' Drummond said, 'take her advice and tell me everything I want.'

Buchanan was kneeling, his head bowed. Wiping blood from his mouth, he nodded. Abruptly he struck Raymond in his solar plexus, doubling Raymond over, striking again, this time with an uppercut that made Raymond's eyes cross and sent him reeling back, collapsing on the court. Raymond's feathered helmet rolled away.

Buchanan struggled to his feet. If he'd been allowed to use his Special-Forces, hand-to-hand-combat skills, he would not have had so much trouble dealing with Raymond. But winning in hand-to-hand combat wasn't the point. Winning the game was. Otherwise, Drummond might become so outraged that he'd order Buchanan and Holly to be executed. And Buchanan doubted that the rules of *pok-a-tok* included karate.

As it was, the damage that he had inflicted on Raymond was sufficient to leave Raymond sprawled on the court. Wavering, Buchanan picked up the ball between his forearms. He studied the vertical hoop, tried to clear his blurred vision, and threw the ball underhanded. His stomach turned cold when the ball struck the edge of the ring and thunked back toward him.

Shit, he thought. He wiped sweat from his eyes, whirled to make certain that Raymond was still on his back, then glared up at Holly.

'You bitch!' he shouted. 'You were just leading me on! All I meant to you was a story!'

'Damned right!' she shouted back. 'Did you figure you were so wonderful I'd fall hopelessly in love with you? Get real, and look in the mirror! I don't intend to get killed because of you! For God's sake, tell him what he wants!'

Buchanan turned toward the ring, threw the ball with his forearms again, and this time the ball went through.

'Tell him what he wants?' Buchanan glared harder. 'I'll tell him, bitch. Just enough to save my life. *You're* the threat to him, not me. You're the damned reporter! I'm a soldier! I can be trusted to keep my mouth shut!'

Buchanan threw the ball yet again. It arced through the ring. 'And I'll win this fucking game.'

'Just enough to save *your* life?' Holly turned paler than she already was. 'Hey, we're in this together!'

'Wrong.'

Buchanan threw the ball.

And cursed when it struck the edge of the ring.

'And *you're* wrong as well,' Raymond said unexpectedly.

Buchanan turned to look behind him.

Raymond had stood. Blood streamed from his mouth, dripping onto his leather armor. 'You're not going to win, after all.'

Raymond scrambled toward the ball.

Buchanan lunged after him.

And slipped.

He'd been standing too long in one place. The blood from the opened stitches in his side had seeped from beneath his armor. It had trickled down his leg and formed a slippery pool where he stood.

Although he didn't fall, the strenuous effort of regaining his balance lost him sufficient time that Raymond was able to throw the ball through the ring.

Without pause, Raymond darted toward it again. But as he scooped it up, Buchanan swept his right forearm beneath the ball, freeing it from Raymond's grip. Using his other forearm, Buchanan thrust the ball against Raymond's left shoulder. The ball's impact made Raymond groan. It rebounded, and as Raymond staggered back, Buchanan caught the ball with

578

upraised forearms. Hurling it, seeing it touch the ring, he felt elated.

Then his chest cramped. The ball did not go through. It bounced off the edge and fell back. Jesus. Running forward, Buchanan leapt. But he didn't get there soon enough. He didn't raise his arms quickly enough. In midair, he had to strike the ball with his padded left shoulder. It flew back toward the ring.

And bounced yet again. But this time, Buchanan was ready. As he completed his leap and landed on the court, he raised his forearms, caught the ball, threw, and scored a point.

'Bravo,' Drummond yelled. 'Yes, that's how the game is played! Shoulders! Angles! Rebounds!'

'Bitch, watch me win!' Buchanan yelled at Holly. 'You're the one who's going to lose! You're the one who's going to die! You'll wish you'd never met me! You'll wish you'd never led me on!'

At once Buchanan felt his breath taken away as hands slammed his back, propelling him against the side of the court. In a daze, Buchanan raised his padded forearms to cushion the impact against the stone wall. He spun and was slammed again, this time by Raymond's right padded shoulder, a full blow to the chest. Then Buchanan's back struck the wall, and a sharp pain made him fear that one of his ribs had been broken.

'Argue with her later,' Raymond said. *'How do you contact your unit?'*

'Exactly,' Drummond said. He coughed again, violently. More smoke swirled over him. The construction equipment continued roaring. Increasing gunshots reverberated, closer.

'Not until we have a deal!' Buchanan winced from the pain in his chest. Another pool of blood formed at his feet. He felt lightheaded and fought to concentrate. He had to keep Holly and him alive. Play your role, Holly. Play your role.

'What kind of deal?' Drummond asked.

'I tell you what you need, and I get to walk away,' Buchanan said. 'In exchange for calling off my unit, I stay alive. But this bitch gets what she deserves.'

'You'd believe any bargain I made with you?' Drummond asked.

'Hey, your problem hasn't changed! If anything happens to me, my unit comes after you!' Buchanan held his chest, the sharp pain restricting his breath.

'And what about Juana Mendez? Do you expect me to believe you won't stop looking for her? Or maybe *she* no longer matters to you, either.'

'No.' Buchanan sweated. 'She's the reason I'm in this. I'll keep looking. I'll convince her this is none of her business. I want her left alone. The same as me.'

'She must be very special to you.'

'Years ago, I should have married her.'

'Buchanan, don't do this to me,' Holly said. 'Don't sell me out.'

'Shut up. Anybody who uses me the way you did *deserves* to be sold out.'

'All right,' Drummond said. 'Deal with the woman as you like. How do you contact your unit?'

Buchanan told them a radio frequency. 'If you're using a telephone, the number is . . .' He told them that as well.

'That's a lie,' Holly said.

Good, Buchanan thought. Keep going, Holly. Take my cue. Play the role. Buy us time.

'A lie?' Drummond asked.

'I don't know about the radio frequency, but the telephone number isn't the one I saw him use several times when he reported in. *That* number was . . .' She gave a different one.

'Ah,' Drummond said. 'It seems you haven't been perfectly honest,' he told Buchanan.

'*She's* the one who's lying,' Buchanan said. 'I have to call my

580

people by midnight. Let me use your radio and—'

'This is bullshit,' Raymond said.

He picked up the ball and hurled it through the ring.

He did so again.

And again.

'You're stalling,' Raymond said. 'The two of you are pretending to fight with each other until you hope we're so confused that we'll keep you alive a little longer.'

Raymond threw the ball and scored another point. 'That's nine.' He stared at Buchanan. 'I don't believe either of you. One more point, and you're dead.'

As Raymond prepared to throw the ball a final time, Buchanan lunged. He felt a tremor. The court seemed to ripple. His legs became wobbly.

Nonetheless he kept charging. When Raymond threw, the ball struck the side of the rim. Buchanan intercepted it in midair, bounced it off his padded forearms, and knocked it through the ring.

But as he landed, his legs buckled. He was suddenly aware that the roar of the construction equipment had stopped. By contrast, the crackle of flames and the rattle of gunshots became louder. Men screamed.

He wavered.

'One more,' Raymond said.

He picked up the ball. 'One more.'

He glared at Buchanan. 'And the loser pays the penalty.'

He threw the ball.

Buchanan didn't even bother to see if it went through the ring. He was too busy struggling to remain upright, preparing to defend himself.

Above him, he heard a commotion. Scuffling. A shout. Someone falling.

'Buchanan!' Holly screamed. 'Behind you!'

Risking the distraction, he glanced quickly backward and

saw that the guard had fallen from the terrace.

No! he realized. He was wrong. The guard hadn't fallen. He'd been pushed! By Holly.

The fifteen-foot drop had dazed the man. He lay, holding his leg as if it might be broken. The man had lost his grip on his automatic weapon.

Buchanan scurried off balance toward it and was knocked to the side by the startling, heavy impact of the ball against his back.

My head! It almost hit my head! I'll die if it hits my head!

Buchanan heard more gunshots, more screams, but all he cared about was Raymond stalking toward him.

'You lost,' Raymond said. His blue eyes glinted with anticipation. His boyish smile was stiff and cruel. It made him look devoid of all sanity. 'I'm going to kill you with this.' He picked up the weighty ball. 'It's going to take a long time. Finally I'm going to use the ball to smash your head like an eggshell.'

Dizzy, Buchanan stumbled unwillingly back. He slipped on his blood. His brain felt swollen, his skull in terrible pain. He feinted toward the right, then dove toward the left, grabbing the fallen guard's automatic weapon.

Raymond stood over him, swaying, the ball raised over his head, preparing to hurl it down with all his strength.

Buchanan aimed the Uzi and pulled the trigger.

But nothing happened.

The weapon had jammed.

Buchanan's bowels felt as if they were suddenly filled with boiling water.

With a laugh, Raymond compacted his muscles to propel the ball down toward Buchanan's face.

And froze, his body eerily motionless. His blue eyes seemed more empty than ever, glassy. His grotesque smile seemed even more rigid.

At once the ball fell from his hands, dropping behind him, thunking on the court.

But his arms remained upstretched.

Blood trickled from his mouth.

He toppled forward, Buchanan scrambling to get out of the way.

As Raymond's face struck the court, Buchanan saw a mass of arrows embedded in Raymond's back.

He stared forward, in the direction from which the arrows must have come, but all he saw was smoke. Hearing a noise to his right, he spun. The guard, having adjusted to the shock of his fall from the terrace, was drawing a pistol. Buchanan pulled back the arming lever on his Uzi, freed the shell that had jammed, chambered a fresh round, and pulled the trigger, hitting the guard with a short, controlled burst that jolted him backward and down, blood flying.

'Holly!' Buchanan yelled. The terrace above him was deserted. 'Holly! Where—?'

'Up here!'

He still couldn't see her.

'On my stomach!'

'Are you all right?'

'Scared!'

'Can you climb down? Where are Drummond and—?'

'Ran!' She raised her head. 'When they saw . . . My God.' She pointed past Buchanan.

Whirling, crouching, aiming the Uzi, Buchanan squinted toward the smoke at the end of the court. Any moment, he feared that more arrows would be launched.

He saw movement.

He tightened his finger on the trigger.

Shadows, then figures, emerged from the smoke.

Buchanan felt a chill surge through him. Earlier, when Raymond had arrived with his leather armor and his feathered helmet, Buchanan had experienced an uncanny sense that Raymond was stepping not only through smoke but time.

Now Buchanan had that skin-prickling sensation again, but in this case, the figures striding toward him from the smoke were indeed Maya, short and thin, with straight black hair, dark brown skin, round heads, wide faces, and almond-shaped eyes. Like Raymond, they wore leather armor and feathered helmets, and for a dismaying instant, his mind swirling, Buchanan felt as if he'd been sucked back a thousand years.

The Maya carried spears, machetes, bows and arrows. A dozen men. Their leader kept his stern gaze on Buchanan all the while he approached, and Buchanan slowly lowered the Uzi, holding it with his left hand parallel to his leg, pointing the weapon down toward the ball court.

The Maya stopped before him, their leader assessing Buchanan. In the background, only the crackle of flames could be heard. The gunshots had stopped, and Buchanan thought he knew why – this wasn't the only group of Maya who, outraged by the desecration of their ancestors' temples, had finally rebelled instead of allowing themselves to be hunted.

The Mayan chieftain narrowed his gaze with fierce emotion and raised his machete.

Buchanan didn't know if he was being tested. It took all his control not to raise the Uzi and fire.

The chieftain whirled toward Raymond's body, striking with the machete, chopping off Raymond's head.

With contempt, the chieftain raised the head by its hair.

As blood drained from the neck, Buchanan couldn't help being reminded of the engraving on the wall of the ball court that Raymond had singled out at the start of the game.

The chieftain pivoted and hurled the skull toward the stone ring. It whunked against the rim, spun, then hurtled through, and landed on the court, spattering blood, rolling, making the sound of an overripe pumpkin.

Raymond, you were wrong, Buchanan thought. It wasn't the loser but the winner who got sacrificed.

The chieftain scowled toward Buchanan and raised his machete a second time. Buchanan needed all of his discipline not to defend himself. He didn't flinch. He didn't blink. The chieftain nodded, made a forward gesture with the machete, and led his companions past Buchanan, as if he didn't exist, as if he and not they were a ghost.

Buchanan felt paralyzed for a moment, watching them stride forward into the smoke, disappearing as if they had never been, and then his legs felt wobbly. He glanced down, appalled by the amount of blood at his feet, *his* blood, the blood from his reopened knife wound.

'Holly!'

'Next to you.'

He spun. Her features strained with fright, she seemed to have appeared from nowhere.

'Lie down,' she said.

'No. Can't. Help me. This won't be over' – he swallowed, his mouth dry – 'until we find Drummond and Delgado.'

Ahead, through the smoke, men shrieked.

Dizzy, Buchanan put his arm around Holly and stumbled forward, ready with his Uzi. They entered the smoke. Briefly, nothing could be seen. Then they emerged into what seemed a different world. The ball court had been left behind. So had hundreds of years. They faced the obscene, pyramid-shaped oil rig that stood where a pyramid of stone, a temple, a holy place, had once stood, focusing the energy of the universe.

Except for the crackle of flames, the place was unnervingly

silent. The bodies of construction workers lay all around.

'Dear God,' Holly murmured.

Abruptly Buchanan heard a metallic whine. An increasing whump-whump-whump. An engine's roar.

The helicopter, Buchanan realized. Drummond and Delgado had reached it. He strained to peer up, squinting in pain past the flames that whooshed up from trees ahead of him. There. He saw the blue helicopter rising.

But something was wrong. It wobbled. It had trouble gaining altitude. As Buchanan struggled to clear his vision, he saw the cluster of men that clung to its landing skids, desperate to be carried away. Inside the crowded chopper, someone had opened a hatch, kicking at the men, trying to knock them off the struts.

The helicopter wavered, fought for altitude.

And plummeted into the blazing trees. An instant later, a walloping explosion burst from the flames, scattering bodies and wreckage in all directions. The blast reverberated across the site and into the jungle.

Buchanan and Holly were jolted back, horrified, smoke drifting over them. Coughing, wiping sweat and grime from their faces, they surveyed the wreckage. The steel pyramid had been struck by a huge, spinning chunk from the helicopter. A support beam had been severed. The derrick listed, drooped, and toppled, metal screeching. Construction equipment was buried by twisted metal. Only the remnants of once great monuments, the ruins of the ruins that Drummond had allowed to remain, seemed permanent.

A man groaned, 'Help.'

Buchanan glanced around, hobbling, following the voice through the smoke.

'Here. Oh, God, please help.'

Buchanan recognized the voice before he saw him. Delgado.

The man lay on his back, a spear projecting from his chest. His face was ashen.

'Help.' He gestured weakly toward the spear. 'Can't move. Pull it out.'

'Out? Are you sure?'

'Yes.'

'If that's what you want,' Buchanan said. Knowing what would happen, he gripped the spear and tugged.

Delgado screamed. At once his scream became a gurgle as the force of the spear's removal caused him to hemorrhage internally. Blood erupted from his mouth.

'For what you did to Maria Tomez,' Buchanan said, 'you deserve a whole lot worse.'

Holly clung to him, just as *he* clung to Holly. The sun was setting. The crimson-tinted, smoke-obscured area seemed completely deserted.

'Dear Christ,' Holly said, 'did *all* of them die? Everybody?'

'The Maya. I don't see them,' Buchanan said. 'Where are they?'

The bump of a falling log disturbed the illusion. Buchanan stared toward the right.

And bristled, finding another survivor.

Alistair Drummond staggered from a leaning, smoking remnant of the log building that had been the camp's office.

At last he showed his age. Even more than his age. Stooped, shriveled, his cheeks gaunt, his eyes sunken, he seemed the oldest man Buchanan had ever seen.

Noticing Buchanan, the old man shuddered, then hobbled to try to get away.

Weakness forced Buchanan to hobble in imitation. Several times, Drummond fell. So did Buchanan. But relentless, Buchanan persisted, passing hieroglyph-covered blocks of stone that stood next to fallen clumps of twisted girders.

Drummond faltered from something before him. Turning,

he tried to stand proudly, failing miserably, as Buchanan stumbled up to him.

'I thought you died on the helicopter,' Buchanan said.

'They wouldn't let me on.' Drummond's white hair had been singed by flames. His scalp had been seared. He was almost bald. 'Can you believe it?' Drummond's voice wavered. 'They were all so eager to escape that they wouldn't let me on.'

'Tell me,' Buchanan said. 'What made you ever think you could get away with this?'

'Think? I *know*. As old as I am, as powerful as I am, what can anybody do to punish me? Never forget I'm so very rich.'

'What you are is a bastard.'

Buchanan reached out and pushed him with his right index finger. The minuscule force was enough to throw the old man off balance. His gangly arms flailed. He listed. He screamed. He fell.

What had stopped him from continuing to hobble away from Buchanan was a deep, wide pit above which the ancient Maya had built their stone pyramid to hide and control the god of darkness, the god of black water, the god that seeped from the earth. The steel pyramid with which Drummond had replaced the original pyramid had collapsed into the pit, and at the bottom, oil rippled thickly, its petroleum smell nauseating.

Drummond struck the surface of the oil.

And was swallowed.

'He wanted that oil so damned bad. Now he's got it,' Buchanan said.

He sank to the ground. His mind swirled.

11

Holly's blurred face hovered over him.

The Mayan chieftain, who'd confronted him in the ball

court, seemed to hover next to her, the colorful feathers of his headdress radiant in the crimson sunset. Other warriors appeared, gripping blood-covered spears and machetes. Holly seemed not to realize her danger.

Buchanan tried to raise a hand to point and warn her. He couldn't move the hand. He tried to open his mouth and tell her. His mouth wouldn't move. The words wouldn't come. He felt as if the earth spun beneath him, tugging him into a vortex.

The Mayan chieftain stooped, his broad, round face distorting the closer it came to Buchanan.

In his delirium, Buchanan felt himself being lifted and placed upon a litter. He had a floating sensation. Although his eyelids were closed, he saw images. A towering pyramid. Statues that depicted gigantic snake heads. Evocative hieroglyphics. Magnificent palaces and temples.

Then the jungle rose before him, and he was carried through a clearing in the trees and bushes, a clearing that went on and on, his litter bearers proceeding along a wide pathway made of gray stone, higher than the forest floor. It seemed to him that everywhere, except on the pathway, snakes made the ground ripple.

Night settled over them. Nonetheless they continued, Holly staying close to his litter, the Mayan chieftain guided by moonlight, leading the way.

This is how it was a thousand years ago, Buchanan thought.

They came to a village, where through a gate, beyond a head-high wooden stockade, torches flickered, revealing huts. The walls of the huts were made from woven saplings, the roofs from palm fronds. Pigs and chickens, wakened by the procession, scattered noisily. Villagers waited, short, round-faced, dark-haired, almond-eyed, the women wearing ghostly, white dresses.

Buchanan was taken into one of the huts. He was placed on a

hammock — so the snakes can't get at me, he thought. Women undressed him. In the light from a fire, the chieftain peered at his wounds.

Holly shrieked and tried to stop him, but the villagers restrained her, and after the chieftain sewed Buchanan's knife wound shut, after he applied a compress to Buchanan's almost-healed bullet wound, after he put salve on Buchanan's cuts and bruises, he examined Buchanan's bulging eyes, and used a knife to shave the hair from one side of Buchanan's head.

And raised a pulley-driven wooden drill to Buchanan's aching skull.

The sharp point was excruciating.

As if a huge boil had been lanced, Buchanan fainted from the ecstasy of tremendous release.

12

'How long have I been unconscious?' Buchanan managed to ask. His mind was clouded. His body felt unrelated to him. Words were like stones in his mouth.

'Two weeks.'

That so surprised him his thoughts were jolted, forced to be less murky. He raised his right hand toward the bandage around his skull.

'Don't touch it,' Holly said.

'What happened to my—? How did—?'

Holly didn't answer. She soaked a clean cloth in rain water that she'd collected in half a hollowed-out coconut shell. While Buchanan lay partially naked on a hammock outside a hut, the late afternoon sunlight comfortably warm against his wounds, she bathed him.

'Tell me.' He licked his dry, swollen lips.

'You almost died. You'd lost a lot of blood, but the medicine man was able to stop it.'

'My head. What about my—?'

'You were raving. Convulsing. Your eyes were so huge I was afraid they'd pop out of your head. Obviously there was pressure behind them. He operated.'

'What?'

'On your head. He drilled a hole in your skull. Blood spurted across the hut as if . . .'

Buchanan's strength waned. His eyelids drooped. He licked again at his dry lips.

Holly raised another hollowed-out half of a coconut and gave him rain water to drink.

It dribbled down his chin, but he kept trying and was able to swallow most of it, luxuriating in its cool sweetness.

'Drilled a hole in . . .' he murmured.

'Primitive surgery. From a thousand years ago. It's like this place is suspended in time. No electricity. Everything they need they get from the forest. Their clothes are hand-made. Their soap is . . . They burn corncobs to boil water. Then they put the ashes from corncobs into the water and use it to scour dirty clothes. Then they take the clothes out and rinse the ashes from the clothes in other boiling pots. The clothes are incredibly clean. Then they pour the water on their crops so the corncob ashes can be a fertilizer.'

Buchanan had trouble concentrating. His eyelids kept drooping.

'Primitive surgery,' he said in muted dismay.

That was two days later, the next time he wakened.

Holly told him that she'd managed to get him to swallow liquids – water and chicken broth – while he was unconscious, but although he was hydrated, he'd lost an alarming amount of weight and would have to try to eat soon, regardless if his stomach might not feel up to it.

591

'I'm ready,' Buchanan said.

She dipped a wooden spoon into a clay bowl, tested the squash soup to make sure it wasn't too hot, and placed it into his mouth.

'Delicious.'

'Don't give me credit. I didn't make it. There's a woman who comes with food. She gestures to tell me what to do about you.'

'And the medicine man?'

'He comes twice a day to give you a spoonful of a thick, sweet-smelling syrup. It might be the reason you didn't get an infection. I wish I understood their language. I tried the little Spanish I know, but they don't seem to recognize it. We communicate with sign language.'

'Why did they go to so much trouble?' Buchanan wondered. 'Why did they let us live?'

'I don't know,' Holly said. 'They treat you as if you're a hero. I don't understand.'

'Something to do with the game,' Buchanan said. 'Fighting against Raymond. Being obvious enemies with Drummond. The natives decided we're on their side.' Buchanan brooded. 'I lost the game, and yet . . . In the old days, it could be the Maya felt so sorry for the loser that they took care of him.'

'Why would they feel sorry for him?'

'Because the winner was sacrificed and got to be with the gods.'

'Raymond isn't with the gods.'

'No. Nor is Drummond. He's in hell where he deserves to be,' Buchanan said. 'He reminds me of the colonel.'

'The colonel?'

Buchanan hesitated. 'What happened at the drilling site is yours. Write about it. Just leave me out of it. But what I'm going to tell you now is off the record.'

'Hey, if you don't know enough to trust me by now . . .'

Buchanan hesitated again, then made a decision. 'Maybe trust is another part of what it means to be human. I certainly trusted you back there in the ball court. You were convincing, and yet I believed you were acting when you said that you'd stayed with me just because of the story.'

'And I trusted you, even when you told Drummond that you didn't care if I died. All I did was believe you were acting and follow your lead, but I didn't know where we were going. What did you hope to accomplish?'

'Raymond had part of it right. I wanted them to be so confused that they'd have to keep us alive until they figured out which one of us was telling the truth. Eventually they'd have been tempted to try those telephone numbers we gave them, and the automatic trace would have led the colonel's hit team in this direction. With luck, we'd have still been alive.'

'Chancy.'

'No kidding. In that kind of situation, there aren't any long-term plans. But you and I sure made a good team.'

'Well, I had a good teacher,' Holly said.

'I was telling you about my commanding officer. The colonel and Drummond are very much alike. The colonel has a goal, and nothing matters except achieving it.'

'But that's standard military discipline.'

'No. The military has ethics. Politicians don't. It's politicians who give soldiers immoral goals. But sometimes a soldier like the colonel comes along and . . .' Buchanan's fragile strength waned. Only his angry thoughts kept him going. 'I'm beginning to think that it was the colonel who had Jack and Cindy Doyle killed. And Big Bob Bailey. Because of the photographs you took of me with the colonel. Because he was afraid he'd be identified as the director of Scotch and Soda, and his career would be ruined. Also, I think it was the colonel who arranged to have me knifed in New Orleans. So you wouldn't have anybody to question. So the story would die with me. He turned against his own to protect himself. Maybe he's getting kickbacks from the drug deals that Scotch and Soda is making in Latin America. Who the hell knows? But one day I'll find out. And one day the colonel will have to justify himself to me.'

'What about Juana?'

'Drummond's men will stop looking for her now that he's dead and they're not being paid. Knowing how skilled she became at disguising her appearance, I don't think I can ever find her.'

'But do you intend to keep trying?'

'You mean, does she still matter to me?'

Holly nodded.

'Yes,' Buchanan said.

Holly lowered her eyes.

'But not the way *you* matter,' Buchanan said.

Holly looked up.

'She's a friend who needed help, and for too long in my life, I wasn't able to help friends I'd known under other identities. I need to find out that she's safe. My guess is, once she learns that Drummond and Delgado are dead, she'll gradually come into the open. I look forward to seeing her again.' Buchanan touched her arm. 'But I swear to you. She's not your rival.'

Holly felt overwhelmed by emotion. 'What happens to us now?'

'One thing's certain. The colonel will never find us here.'

'True. That's certainly looking on the bright side.'

'Is it so bad here?'

'With you. No,' Holly said. 'Strange. As beat up as you look, there's something about . . . Your eyes. Even though you're angry about the colonel, you seem at peace.'

'I'm myself.'

Holly frowned in confusion.

'Something's missing from me,' Buchanan said. 'Maybe it's

594

because of everything we've been through. Or maybe it's because of you. Or . . . When the medicine man drilled into my skull, I think he took out more than blood. I think he took out whatever was in my head that tortured me for so long. I've come to terms with the past. I want to move on. With you. What matters now isn't the past but the present.' Buchanan squeezed Holly's hand. 'And the future. No more trying to run from myself. No more assumed identities.'

'It'll be a pleasure getting to know you,' Holly said.

'I'm kind of curious about it myself.'

'Yes.' Holly kissed him. 'It's what I've been waiting for.'

Extreme Denial

This book is for Richard Schoegler and Elizabeth Gutierrez, who introduced my wife and me to the City Different.

How do I love thee? Let me count the ways.
Elizabeth Barrett Browning

Denial is not a river in Egypt.
Bumper Sticker

ONE

1

Decker told the Italian immigration official that he had come on business.

'What type?'

'Corporate real estate.'

'The length of your visit?'

'Two weeks.'

The official stamped Decker's passport.

'*Grazie*,' Decker said.

He carried his suitcase from Leonardo da Vinci Airport, and although it would have been simple to make arrangements for someone to meet him, he preferred to travel the twenty-six kilometers into Rome by bus. When the bus became mired in predictably dense mid-city traffic, he asked the driver to let him off, then waited for the bus to proceed, satisfying himself that no one had gotten off after him. He went into the underground, chose a train at random, rode to the next stop, returned to the streets, and hailed a taxi. Ten minutes later, he left the taxi and went back to the underground, took a train to the next stop, and hailed another taxi, this time telling the driver to take him to the Pantheon. His actual destination was a hotel five blocks from there. The precautions were possibly needless, but Decker was convinced that he had stayed alive as long as he had by virtue of being indirect.

The trouble was that the effort was wearing him down.

3

Staying alive wasn't the same as living, he had decided. Tomorrow, Saturday, would be his fortieth birthday, and of late, he had become uncomfortably aware of the passing time. Wife, children, a home – he had none of these. He traveled a lot, but he always felt apart from wherever he was. He had few friends and seldom saw them. What his life came down to was his profession. That wasn't good enough anymore.

As soon as he checked into his hotel, which had pillars and plush carpets, he fought jet lag by showering and putting on fresh clothes. Sneakers, jeans, a denim shirt, and a blue blazer were appropriate for a mild June day in Rome. They were also what a lot of other American male tourists his age were wearing, and would keep him from attracting attention. He left the hotel, blended with pedestrians, and walked along busy streets for half an hour, doing his best to make certain that he wasn't being followed. He reached the most congested area of Rome, the Piazza Venezia, where the main streets of the city came together. The din of a traffic jam provided background noise as he used a public telephone.

'Hello,' a male voice answered.

'Is this Anatole?' Decker asked in Italian.

'Never heard of him.'

'But he told me he'd be at this number.' Decker gave a number that was different from the one he had used.

'The last two digits are wrong. This is five seven.' The connection was broken.

Decker replaced the phone, checked that no one was watching him, and melded with the crowd. So far no problem. By mentioning specific numbers, the voice was telling Decker to come ahead. But if the voice had told him, 'You're wrong,' the message would have been to stay away because *everything* was wrong.

4

2

The apartment, near Via Salaria, was three flights up, not too fancy, not too plain.

'How was the flight?' the occupant asked. His voice, with a slight New England accent, sounded the same as the one on the phone.

Decker shrugged and glanced around at the modest furniture. 'You know the old joke. The best kind is the kind you walk away from.' He completed the recognition code. 'I slept through most of it.'

'So you don't feel jet lag.'

Decker shook his head.

'You don't need a nap.'

Decker inwardly came to attention. Why is this guy making an issue of jet lag? A nap? Is there a reason he doesn't want me with him for the rest of the day?

The man he was speaking to was someone with whom he had not worked before: Brian McKittrick, thirty years old, six feet one inches tall, heavy set. He had short blond hair, beefy shoulders, and the kind of square jaw that Decker associated with college football players. Indeed, there was a lot about McKittrick that reminded Decker of college football players – the sense of pent-up energy, of eagerness to get into action.

'No nap,' Decker said. 'What I want is to catch up on a few things.' He glanced at the lamps and the wall plugs, deciding not to take anything for granted. 'How do you like staying here? Some of these old apartments have trouble with roaches.'

'Not here. I check every day for bugs. I checked just before you came over.'

'Good.' Satisfied that the room was free of electronic surveillance, Decker continued, 'Your reports indicate that you've made progress.'

'Oh, I found the bastards, all right.'

'You mean your contacts did.'

'That's right. That's what I meant.'

'How?' Decker asked. 'The rest of our people have been searching everywhere.'

'It's in my reports.'

'Remind me.'

'Semtex.' McKittrick referred to a sophisticated plastic explosive. 'My contacts spread word in the kind of hangouts these bastards like to use that Semtex was available to anyone willing to pay enough.'

'And how did you find your contacts?'

'A similar way. I spread the word that I'd be generous to anyone who supplied the information I needed.'

'Italians.'

'Hell, yes. Isn't that the point? Cutouts. Plausible deniability. An American like me has to start the ball rolling, but after a while, the team has to be nationals of the country where we're working. The operation can't be traced back to us.'

'That's what it says in the text books.'

'But what do *you* say?'

'The nationals have to be dependable.'

'You're suggesting my contacts might not be?' McKittrick sounded testy.

'Let's just say the money might make them eager to please.'

'For God sake, we're hunting terrorists,' McKittrick said. 'Do you expect me to get informants to cooperate by appealing to their civic duty?'

Decker allowed himself to smile. 'No, I believe in the old-fashioned way – appealing to their weaknesses.'

'Then there you are.'

'But I'd like to meet them,' Decker said.

McKittrick looked uncomfortable.

'Just to get a sense of what we're dealing with,' Decker added.

'But it's all in my reports.'

'Which make for fascinating reading. The thing is, I've always been a hands-on kind of guy. How soon can you arrange a meeting?'

McKittrick hesitated. 'Eleven tonight.'

'Where?'

'I'll have to let you know.'

Decker handed McKittrick a piece of paper. 'Memorize this phone number. Got it? Fine.' Decker took the specially treated paper into the kitchen, poured water on it, and watched it disintegrate, dissolving down the drain. 'To confirm the meeting, call that number at eight tonight, or every half hour after that, up to ten. But after ten, don't bother. I'll assume you couldn't get your contacts together. In which case, try for tomorrow night, or the night after that. Each night, the same schedule for calling. Ask for Baldwin. My response will be Edward.'

'The phone's at your hotel?'

Decker assessed him. 'You're beginning to worry me. No, the phone isn't at my hotel. And when you call that number, make sure you don't do it from here.'

'I know the drill.'

'Call from a payphone you've never used before.'

'I said I know the drill.'

'All the same, it never hurts to be reminded.'

'Look, I know what you're thinking,' McKittrick said.

'Really?'

'This is the first time I'm running an operation. You want to make sure I'm up to the job.'

'You're right, you do know what I'm thinking,' Decker said.

'Well, you don't need to worry.'

'Oh?' Decker asked skeptically.

'I can handle myself.'

3

Decker left the apartment building, crossed the busy street, noticed a passing taxi, and motioned for the driver to meet him around the next corner. There, out of sight from where McKittrick might be watching from his apartment, Decker apologized to the taxi driver, saying that he had changed his mind and wanted to walk a little more. As the driver muttered and pulled away, Decker went back to the corner but didn't show himself. The cafe on the corner had windows that faced the main street and the side street. From the side street, staying out of view as much as possible, Decker could look through the side window and then the front window, providing himself with a view of McKittrick's apartment building. Sunlight reflecting off the front window would help to make Decker unobtrusive.

Sooner than Decker expected, McKittrick emerged from the apartment building. The stocky man drew a hand through his short blond hair, looked nervously both ways along the street, saw an empty taxi, eagerly hailed it, and got in.

While waiting, Decker had needed something to do so he wouldn't appear to be loitering. From a lamp post, he had unchained a motorbike that he had rented. He had unlocked the storage compartment, folded his navy blazer into it, taken out a brown leather jacket and a helmet with a dark concealing visor, and put them on. With his appearance sufficiently changed that McKittrick would not recognize him if he checked for surveillance, Decker started the motorbike and followed.

He wasn't encouraged by the meeting. The problems that he had sensed in McKittrick's reports now seemed more manifest and troubling. It wasn't merely that this was the first time McKittrick had been given a position of authority. After all, if the man was going to have a career, there *had* to be a first time, just as there had been a first time for Decker. Instead, the source of Decker's unease was that McKittrick was too damned sure of himself, obviously not fully skilled at tradecraft and yet not humble enough to know his limitations. Before flying to Rome, Decker had already recommended to his superiors that McKittrick be assigned to another, less sensitive operation, but the son of a legend in the profession (OSS, charter member of the CIA, former Deputy Director of Operations) evidently couldn't be shuffled around without the legend demanding to know why his son wasn't being given opportunities for advancement.

So Decker had been sent to have a look, to make sure that everything was as it should be. To be a nursemaid, Decker thought. He followed the taxi through congested traffic, eventually stopping as McKittrick got out near the Spanish Steps. Decker quickly chained the motorbike to a lamp post and went after him. There were so many tourists that McKittrick should have been able to blend with them, but his blond hair, which ought to have been dyed a dark, non-dramatic color, made him conspicuous. Another lapse in tradecraft, Decker thought.

Squinting from the bright afternoon sun, he followed McKittrick past the Church of the Trinita dei Monti, down the Spanish Steps to Spanish Square. Once famous for its flower sellers, the area was now occupied by street merchants with their jewelry, ceramics, and paintings spread out before them. Ignoring the distractions, Decker kept after McKittrick, turning right past Bernini's Boat Fountain, shifting through the crowd, passing the house where Keats had died in 1821, finally seeing his quarry enter a cafe.

Yet another mistake in tradecraft, Decker thought. It was foolish to seek refuge in a place with so many people outside: someone watching would be difficult to notice. Choosing a spot that was partially sheltered, Decker prepared himself for a wait but again McKittrick came out sooner than expected. He had a woman with him. She was Italian, in her early twenties, tall and slim, sensuous, with an oval face framed by short dark hair and sunglasses tilted on top of her head. She wore cowboy boots, tight jeans, and a red T-shirt that emphasized her breasts. Even from thirty yards away, Decker could tell she wasn't wearing a bra. McKittrick had his arm around her shoulders. She in turn had an arm around his hips, her thumb hooked into a back pocket of his slacks. They proceeded down Via dei Condotti, took a shadowy side street on the right, paused on the steps of a building, kissed hungrily, then entered the building.

4

The phone call came through at nine p.m. Decker had told McKittrick that the number didn't connect with Decker's hotel. The number did connect, however, with a payphone in a hotel down the street, in the lobby of which Decker could wait, reading a newspaper, without attracting attention.

Every half-hour, starting at eight, he had strolled to the phone, waited five minutes, then returned to his comfortable chair. At nine, when the phone rang, he had been in place to pick it up. 'Hello?'

'Baldwin?' McKittrick's vague New England accent was recognizable.

'Edward?'

'It's on for tonight at eleven.'

'Where?'

McKittrick told him.

The location made Decker frown. 'See you.' Uneasy, he hung up the phone and left the hotel. Despite what he had told McKittrick, he did have jet lag and would have preferred not to work that night, especially since he had been busy for the remainder of the afternoon, going to the international real-estate consulting agency for which he ostensibly worked, reporting in, establishing his cover. His contact at the agency had been keeping a package, about the size of a hardback novel, that had arrived for Decker. After returning to his hotel room, Decker had opened the package and made sure that the pistol he removed, a Walther .380 semi-automatic pistol, was functional. He could have chosen a more powerful weapon, but he preferred the Walther's compactness. Only slightly larger than the size of his hand, it came with a holster that clipped inside the waist of his jeans, at his spine. The weapon didn't make a bulge against his unbuttoned blazer. All the same, it didn't reassure him.

5

There were five of them – the tall attractive woman whom Decker had seen with McKittrick, and four men, all Italian, from early to late twenties, thin, with slicked-back hair. Their appearance suggested that they thought of themselves as a club – cowboy boots, jeans, Old West belt buckles, denim jackets. They even smoked the same brand of cigarettes – Marlboros. But a stronger factor linked them. The facial resemblance was obvious. They were four brothers and a sister.

The group sat in a private room above a cafe near the Piazza Colonna, one of Rome's busiest shopping areas, and the site for the meeting troubled Decker. Not only was it in far too public an area, but with short notice, McKittrick shouldn't have been able to reserve a room in what was obviously a popular night spot. The numerous empty wine and beer bottles on the table made clear that the group had been in the room for quite some time before Decker arrived.

While McKittrick watched from a corner of the room, Decker established rapport, then got to the point. 'The people we're after are extremely dangerous,' he said in Italian. 'I don't want you to do anything that puts you at risk. If you have even the slightest suspicion that you've attracted their attention, ease off. Report to my friend.' He gestured toward McKittrick. 'Then disappear.'

'Would we still get the bonus we were promised?' one of the brothers asked.

'Of course.'

'Can't ask for anything fairer than that.' The young man finished a glass of beer.

Decker's throat was beginning to feel scratchy from the dense cigarette smoke in the room. It didn't help the headache that his jet lag had begun to give him. 'What makes you confident you've found the people we want?'

One of the brothers snickered.

'Did I say something amusing?' Decker asked.

'Not you. Them. The group we were asked to look for. We knew immediately who it was. We went to university with them. They were always talking crazy.'

'Italy for Italians,' their sister said.

Decker looked at her. Until now, she hadn't said much. Since the afternoon, she'd changed her T-shirt. Now it was blue. Even with a denim jacket partially covering it, she obviously still wasn't wearing a bra.

'That's all they talked about. Italy for Italians.' The sister had been introduced as Renata. Her sunglasses remained tilted up onto her dark, boyishly short hair. 'They couldn't stop complaining about the European Community. They kept insisting that lowering national barriers was just a way for Italy to be contaminated by outsiders. They blamed the United States for backing the unified-Europe movement, for trying to create a vast new market for American goods. If the rest of Europe wanted to be corrupted, that was fine, but Italy had to fight to keep the United States from dominating it economically and culturally. So when American diplomats began being killed in explosions, the first people we thought of were this group, especially when they made those phone calls to the police, calling themselves the Children of Mussolini. Mussolini was one of their heroes.'

'If you suspected them, why didn't you go to the police?' Decker asked.

Renata exhaled smoke from a cigarette and shrugged. 'Why? These people used to be our friends. They weren't hurting *us*. But they *would* hurt us after they were released from jail because of insufficient evidence against them.'

'Maybe the authorities could have found sufficient evidence.'

Renata scoffed. The movement of her slim, sensuous body made her breasts move under the T-shirt. 'I assure you these people are not fools. They wouldn't leave proof of what they had done.'

'Then I'll ask you again. Without proof, what makes you sure you've found the people we want?'

'Because after Brian started paying us –' she gestured toward McKittrick, alarming Decker that McKittrick had given her his real name – 'we kept a close watch on our friends. We followed them one night. They were in a car a half block behind the limousine when the explosion killed your ambassador as he was being driven back to the embassy after attending the opera. They must have used a remote detonator.'

Decker concealed the tense emotion that made him briefly silent. The assassination of Ambassador Robbins had been the outrage that caused extremely powerful figures in Washington to lose their customary caution and demand that something be done to stop these monsters – one way or another. The covert pressure on Decker's superiors was the reason McKittrick had attracted so much favorable attention among them. If McKittrick's contacts could positively identify the terrorists responsible for the assassination, half the problem would be solved. The other half would be what to do with the information.

'Maybe they just happened to be in the area,' Decker said.

'They drove away laughing.'

Decker's throat felt constricted. 'Do you know where they live?'

'Renata gave me that information,' McKittrick interrupted. 'But obviously they won't stay at the addresses forever.' He gestured for emphasis. 'They have to be dealt with soon.'

Yet another lapse in tradecraft, Decker noted with concern. Contacts should never know what a handler is thinking. And what did McKittrick mean by 'dealt with'?

'Renata tells me they have a club they like to go to,' McKittrick said. 'If we can get them all together...'

6

'What the hell were you doing in there?' Decker asked as he walked angrily with McKittrick after the meeting was over.

'I don't know what you're talking about.'

Decker glanced tensely around. Squinting from the glare of numerous passing headlights, he noticed an alley and gripped McKittrick's left arm to guide him away from the area's clamorous nightlife.

'You compromised the assignment,' Decker whispered hoarsely as soon as he was away from pedestrians. 'You gave them your *real name*.'

McKittrick looked awkward and didn't respond.

'You're sleeping with that woman,' Decker said. 'Didn't your trainers explain to you that you never, never, never become personally involved with your contacts?'

'What makes you think I'm sleeping with—'

'Your imitation of stand-up mouth-to-mouth resuscitation this afternoon.'

'You *followed* me?'

'It wasn't very damned hard. You're breaking so many rules I can't keep up with . . . From the smell of alcohol on you, I have to assume you were partying with them before I arrived.'

'I was trying to get them to feel comfortable with me.'

'*Money*,' Decker said. 'That's what makes them comfortable. Not your winning personality. This is business, not a social club. And what did you mean by "dealt with"?'

' "Dealt with"? I don't remember saying—'

'It sounded to me as if you were actually suggesting, in front of outsiders, that the people we're after are going to be . . .' In spite of his low tone and the relative secrecy of the alley, Decker couldn't bring himself to say the incriminating words.

'Extreme denial,' McKittrick said.

'What?'

'Isn't that the new euphemism? It used to be "terminate with extreme prejudice". Now it's "extreme denial".'

'Where the hell did you hear—'

'Isn't that what this operation's about? Those bastards will keep killing until somebody stops them permanently.'

Decker pivoted, staring from the darkness of the alley toward the pedestrians on the brightly lit street, afraid that someone might have overheard. 'Have you gone insane? Have you told anyone else what you just told me?'

McKittrick hesitated.

'The woman?' Decker demanded. 'You told the woman?'

'Well, I had to introduce the idea to her. How else was I going to get them to do it?'

'Jesus,' Decker muttered.

'Plausible deniability. I've invented a rival network. *They* take out the first group, then phone the police, and call themselves the Enemies of Mussolini.'

'Keep your voice down, damn it.'

'No one can prove we're involved.'

'The *woman* can,' Decker said.

'Not when I disappear and she doesn't have physical evidence.'

'She knows your *name*.'

'My *first* name only,' McKittrick said. 'She loves me. She'll do anything for me.'

'You—' Decker leaned close in the darkness, wanting to make certain that only McKittrick heard his fierce whisper. 'Listen to me carefully. The United States government is not in the business of assassination. It does not track down and kill terrorists. It accumulates evidence and lets the courts decide the appropriate punishment.'

'Yeah, sure, right. Just like the Israelis didn't send a hit team after the terrorists who killed eleven Jewish athletes at the 1972 Munich Olympics.'

'What the Israelis did has nothing to do with *us*. *That* operation was canceled because one of the men they killed was innocent. That's why *we're* not in the assassination business.'

'Fine. Now *you* listen to me,' McKittrick said. 'If we let those bastards get away because we don't have the guts to do what's right, both of us will be out of a job.'

'Noon tomorrow.'

'What?'

'Go to your apartment and stay there,' Decker said. 'Don't do anything. Don't contact the woman. Don't go out for a newspaper. Don't do *anything*. I will knock on your door at noon sharp. I will tell you what our superiors have decided to do about you. If I were you, I'd have my bags packed.'

7

Happy fortieth birthday, Decker told himself. In his bathroom mirror, the haggard expression on his face confirmed how poorly he had slept because of his preoccupation with McKittrick. His headache from jet lag and the choking haze of cigarette smoke he had been forced to breathe persisted. A late-night room-service meal of fetuccini and Chicken Marsala sat heavily in his stomach. He seemed to have gained a few more lines of character in his rugged features, the start of crows' feet around his watchful aquamarine eyes. As if all of that wasn't enough, he found a strand of gray in his slightly long, wavy, sandy hair. Muttering, he jerked it out.

Saturday morning. The start of the weekend for most people, Decker thought, but not in *my* line of work. He couldn't remember the last time he had felt the sense of leisure that he associated with a true weekend. For no reason that he immediately understood, he remembered following McKittrick down the Spanish Steps and past the house where Keats had died. He imagined Keats coughing his life away, the TB filling him up, choking him. So young, but already having achieved greatness.

I need some time off.

Decker put on jogging clothes, tried to ignore the hazy automobile exhaust and the crowded sidewalks, and ran to the international real-estate consulting firm that he had reported to the day before, satisfied that his erratic route would keep anyone from following him. After showing his identification, he was admitted to an office that had a scrambler attached to its phone. Five minutes later, he was talking to his supervisor at a similar international real-estate consulting firm in Alexandria, Virginia. The supervisor had a scrambler calibrated to the same frequency as Decker's.

The conversation lasted fifteen minutes and made Decker

even more frustrated. He learned that McKittrick's father had been informed of Decker's intentions, probably by means of a phone call that McKittrick had made to his father late the night before (Decker could only hope that McKittrick had used a payphone and spoken with discretion). The father, not just a legend in the intelligence community but a former chairman of the National Security Council who still retained considerable political influence, had questioned Decker's own professionalism and accused Decker of attempting to have McKittrick transferred so that Decker could take the credit for McKittrick's achievement in finding the terrorists. While Decker's superior claimed that he privately sided with Decker over McKittrick, the fact was that prudence and his pension forced him to ignore Decker's warnings and to keep McKittrick in place. 'Babysit him,' the superior said. 'Prevent him from making mistakes. Verify the rest of the information in his reports. We'll pass the information to the Italian authorities and pull both of you out. I promise you'll never have to work with him again.'

'It's right now I'm worried about.'

Decker's run back to his hotel did nothing to ease his frustration. He placed towels on the floor of his room and did 150 push-ups, then the same amount of sit-ups, sweat dripping from his strong shoulders, narrow hips, and sinewy legs. He practiced several martial arts moves, then showered and put on fresh jeans as well as a clean blue Oxford-cloth shirt. His brown leather jacket covered his pistol. His stomach continued to bother him.

8

It was noon exactly when, as scheduled, Decker knocked on McKittrick's door.

No one answered.

Decker knocked again, waited, frowned, knocked a third time, waited, frowned harder, glanced to each side along the corridor, then used the lock-pick tools concealed in the collar of his jacket. Ten seconds later, he was in the apartment, securing it behind him, his weapon already drawn. Had McKittrick stood him up, or had something happened to him? With painstaking caution, Decker started searching.

The living room was deserted. So were the bathroom, the kitchen, and the bedroom, including the closets. Decker hated closets – he never knew what might be crouching in them. His chest tight, he completed the search, sat on a padded chair in the living room, and analyzed the possibilities. Nothing in the apartment seemed out of place, but that proved nothing. McKittrick could be in trouble somewhere else. Or it could be, Decker thought for the second time, that the son of a bitch stood me up.

Decker waited, in the process conducting another search of McKittrick's apartment, this time in detail. In, under, and behind every drawer. Under the mattress and the bed. Under the chairs and sofa. In the light fixtures. In and behind the toilet tank.

What he found appalled him. Not only had McKittrick failed to destroy his notes after sending in his report, but as well, he had hidden the notes in a place not hard to predict – beneath shelfpaper in the kitchen. Next to the names of the members of the group Decker had met the previous night, he found addresses, one of which was for the apartment building into which McKittrick had gone with Renata. Decker also found the address of something called the Tiber Club.

Decker memorized the information. He put the notes on a saucer, burned them, crumbled the ashes into powder, peered out the kitchen's small window, saw the brick wall of an alley, and let a breeze scatter the ashes. Hunger fought with the discomfort in his stomach. He cut a slice from a loaf of bread, returned to the living room, and slowly ate, all the while frowning at the front door.

By then, it was three in the afternoon. Decker's misgivings strengthened. But what should he do about them? he wondered. He could go back to the international real-estate consulting firm and make an emergency telephone call to warn his supervisor that McKittrick had failed to be present at an appointment. But what would *that* accomplish, aside from creating the impression that Decker was determined to find fault with McKittrick? The guy's tradecraft was sloppy – Decker had already made an issue of that. So wasn't it likely that McKittrick had either forgotten or deliberately ignored the appointment? Maybe he was in bed with Renata right now.

If that's the case, he might be smarter than *I* am, Decker thought. When was the last time *I* was in bed with anybody? He couldn't remember. Because he traveled so much, he had few close female friends, all of them in his line of work. Casual pickups were out of the question – even before the spread of AIDS, Decker had avoided one-night stands on the theory that intimacy equaled vulnerability, that it didn't make sense to let down his guard with someone he knew nothing about.

This damned job, Decker thought. It not only makes you paranoid; it makes you a monk.

He glanced around the depressing living room. His nostrils felt irritated by the smell of must. His stomach continued to bother him.

Happy fortieth birthday, he told himself.

9

Decker had finished all the bread in the apartment by the time a key scraped in the lock. It was almost nine p.m. McKittrick rushed in, breathless, and froze when he saw Decker.

'Shut the door,' Decker said.

'What are you—'

'We had an appointment, remember. Shut the door.'

McKittrick obeyed. 'Weren't you told? Didn't my father—'

'He relayed a message to me, all right. But that didn't seem a reason to cancel our chat.' Decker stood. 'Where the hell have you been?'

'You don't *know*?'

'What are you talking about?'

'You haven't been *watching*?'

'Make sense.'

McKittrick hurried to the television set and turned it on. 'Three different television crews were there. Surely one of the channels is still broadcasting from—' His hand shook as he kept switching stations. '*There*.'

At first, Decker didn't understand what he was seeing. Abruptly the loud confusing images sent a wave of apprehension through him. Thick black smoke choked the sky. Flames burst from windows. Amid a section of wall that had toppled, firemen struggled with hoses, spewing water toward a large, blazing building. Fire trucks wailed to a stop among the chaos of other emergency vehicles, police cars, ambulances, more fire trucks. Appalled, Decker realized that some of the wailing came not from sirens but from burn victims being lifted onto stretchers, their faces charred, twisted with pain, not recognizably human. Unmoving bodies lay under blankets as policemen forced a crowd back.

'What is it? What in God's name happened?'

Before McKittrick could answer, a television reporter was talking about terrorists, about the Children of Mussolini, about the worst incident yet of anti-American violence, about twenty-three American tourists killed and another forty-three injured in a massive explosion, members of a Salt Lake City tour group that had been enjoying a banquet at the Tiber Club in honor of their final night in Rome.

'*The Tiber Club?*' Decker remembered the name from the list he had memorized.

'That's where Renata told me the terrorists like to go.' McKittrick's skin was ashen. 'She told me the plan was foolproof. Nothing could screw it up. It wasn't supposed to happen like this! Renata swore to me that—'

'Quit babbling.' Decker gripped McKittrick's shoulders. 'Talk to me. *What did you do?*'

'Last night.' McKittrick stopped to take several quick breaths. 'After the meeting, after we argued.' McKittrick's chest heaved. 'I knew I didn't have much time before you took the operation away from me and stole the credit for it.'

'You actually believe that bullshit you told your father? You think I'm *jealous* of you?'

'I had to do something. I couldn't be sure that my phone call to my father would solve the problem. There was a plan that Renata and I had been talking about. A perfect plan. After I left you, I went back to the cafe. Renata and the others were still in the upstairs room. We decided to put the plan into motion.'

'Without authorization.' Decker was appalled.

'Who was I going to get it from? *You?* You'd have told me not to. You'd have done your best to have me reassigned. You'd have used the same plan yourself.'

'I am trying very hard to keep my patience,' Decker said. On the television, flames shot from doorways, forcing firemen to stumble back as another section of wall fell. The wail of sirens intensified. Smoke-shrouded attendants loaded bodies into ambulances. 'This plan. Tell me about this perfect plan.'

'It was simple to the point of brilliance.'

'Oh, I'm sure it was.'

'Renata and her group would wait until the terrorists came together in one place – an apartment maybe, or the Tiber Club. Then someone from Renata's group would hide a satchel filled with plastic explosive near where the terrorists would have to pass when they came out. As soon as they appeared, Renata would press a remote control that detonated the explosive. It would look as if the terrorists had been carrying the explosive with them and the bomb went off by mistake.'

Decker listened with absolute astonishment. The room seemed to tilt. His face became numb. He questioned his sanity. This couldn't be happening, he told himself. He couldn't possibly be hearing this.

'Simple? Brilliant?' Decker rubbed his aching forehead. 'Didn't it occur to you that you might blow up the wrong people?'

'I'm absolutely positive that Renata's group has found the terrorists.'

'Didn't it also occur to you that you might blow up a lot of innocent people with them?'

'I warned Renata not to take chances. If there was the slightest doubt that someone else would be in the blast area, she was to wait.'

'*She?*' Decker wanted to shake McKittrick. 'Where's your common sense? Most people wouldn't be capable of detonating the explosion. Why would *she?*'

'Because I asked her.'

'What?'

'She loves me.'

'I must be asleep. This must be a nightmare,' Decker said. 'In a little while, I'll wake up. None of this will have happened.'

'She'd do *anything* for me.'

'Including murder?'

'It isn't murder to kill terrorists.'

'What the hell do *you* call it?'

'An execution.'

'You're amazing,' Decker said. 'Last night you called it "extreme denial". Call it whatever you want. It's still killing, and when someone agrees to do it, you've got to ask yourself what makes them capable of doing it. And in this case, I don't think it's love.'

'I can't believe she's doing this only for the money.'

'Where was the plastic explosive supposed to come from?'

'Me.'

Decker felt as if he'd been slapped. '*You* supplied it?'

'I'd been given Semtex at the start of the operation – so Renata's group could try to infiltrate the terrorist group by offering them Semtex as a sign of good faith.'

'*You* supplied the . . . ?' With greater horror, Decker stared toward the sirens wailing on the television, toward the smoke, flames, and wreckage, toward the bodies. '*You're* responsible for—'

'No! It was a mistake! Somehow the satchel went off at the wrong time! Somehow the club was filled with Americans! Somehow the— I . . . Renata must have . . . mistake.' McKittrick ran out of words, his broad mouth open, his lips moving, no sounds coming out.

'You weren't given enough Semtex to cause that much damage,' Decker said flatly.

McKittrick blinked at him, uncomprehending.

'You had only a sample,' Decker said. 'Enough to tempt the terrorists and make them think they'd get more. Renata had to have access to a lot more of it in order to destroy that entire building.'

'What are you saying?'

'Use your common sense! You didn't recruit a group of students to help you find the terrorists! You idiot, you recruited the *terrorists themselves*!'

McKittrick's eyes went blank with shock. He shook his head fiercely. 'No. That's impossible.'

'They've been staring you in the face! It's a wonder they kept themselves from *laughing* in your face. Classic entrapment. All the time you've been screwing Renata, she's been asking you questions, and you've been telling her our plans, everything we've been doing to try to catch them.'

McKittrick's face became more ashen.

'I'm right, aren't I?' Decker asked. 'You've been telling her *everything*.'

'Jesus.'

'Last night, when you warned them you might be reassigned, they decided the game was over. It was time for them to go back to work. Did *you* suggest implementing the plan and moving against the terrorists, or did Renata?'

'She . . .' McKittrick swallowed. '*She* did.'

'To help you in your career.'

'Yes.'

'Because she loved you.'

'Yes.'

'Was the plan *her* idea in the first place?'

'Yes.'

'And now she's used the sample of Semtex you gave her. I'll bet they've got photographs and tape recordings that document your participation. She put the sample with some of her own, and she blew up a tour group of Americans. You wanted to promote your career? Well, buddy, your career is over.'

10

'What a mess.' In the international real-estate consulting firm, Decker listened to his superior's weary voice on the scrambler-protected telephone. 'All those people killed. Terrible. Sickening. Thank God it's not my responsibility anymore.'

Decker took a moment before the implication struck him. He sat straighter, clutching the phone harder. 'Not your responsibility? Whose is it? *Mine?* You're dumping this on *me*?'

'Let me explain.'

'I had nothing to do with it. You sent me in at the last minute. I reported back that I thought the operation was in trouble. You ignored my advice, and—'

'*I'm* not the one who ignored your advice,' Decker's superior said. 'McKittrick's father took over. *He's* in charge now.'

'*What?*'

'The operation is *his* responsibility. As soon as he got his son's phone call, he started badgering everyone who owed him favors. Right now he's on his way to Rome. He ought to be arriving at . . .'

11

The Astra Galaxy eight-seat corporate jet, ostensibly privately owned, set down at Leonardo da Vinci Airport just after midnight. Decker waited beyond customs and immigration while a tall, white-haired, patrician-looking man dealt with the officials. As near as Decker could tell, there were no other passengers on the jet. The man was seventy-two but in amazing shape, broad-shouldered, tan, with craggy handsome features. He wore a three-piece, blended-wool, gray suit that showed no effects of the long, hastily scheduled flight any more than did Jason McKittrick himself.

Decker had met the legend three times before and received a curt nod of recognition as McKittrick approached him.

'Did you have a good flight? Let me take your suitcase,' Decker said.

But McKittrick kept a grip on the suitcase and walked past Decker, proceeding toward the airport's exit. Decker caught up to him, their footsteps echoing in the cavernous facility. Few people were present at so late an hour.

Decker had rented a car, a Fiat. In the parking area, McKittrick watched him scan the vehicle to make sure that no eavesdropping devices had been planted while Decker was in the airport. Only after McKittrick was inside the Fiat and Decker was driving through a gloomy drizzle toward the city did the great man finally speak.

'Where's my son?'

'At a hotel,' Decker said. 'He used the passport for his alternate identity. After what happened . . . I assume you were told en route?'

'About the explosion?' McKittrick nodded somberly.

Decker stared ahead past the flapping windshield wipers. 'After the explosion, I didn't think it was safe for your son to stay at his apartment. The terrorists know where he lives.'

'You suspect they might attack him?'

'No.' Decker glanced at numerous headlights in his rearview mirror. In the dark and the rain, it was difficult to determine if he was being followed. 'But I have to assume they'll release information and evidence about him to the police. I take for granted that was the point – to connect an American intelligence operative to a terrorist attack against Americans.'

McKittrick's expression hardened.

'As soon as I've assured myself that we're not being followed, I'll drive you to him,' Decker said.

'You seem to have thought of everything.'

'I'm doing my best.'

'So have you thought about who's going to be blamed for this?' McKittrick asked.

'Excuse me?'

Rain pattered on the car's roof.

'You, for instance?' McKittrick asked.

'There is no way I am going to take the blame for—'

'Then think of someone else. Because if there is one thing you can be confident of, it is that my son is *not* going to take the blame.'

12

The modest hotel was on a modest street – nothing about it attracted attention. After nodding to the night porter and showing one of the hotel's keys to prove he belonged there, Decker escorted McKittrick across the small lobby, past the elevator, up carpeted stairs. The son's room was only a few floors above them, and whenever possible, Decker avoided the potential trap of elevators.

McKittrick seemed to take the precaution for granted. Even carrying his suitcase, the tall, elderly man displayed no sign of exertion.

They came to room 312. Decker knocked four times, a code to let McKittrick's son know who was coming in, then used his key to unlock the door. The room's darkness made him frown. He flicked a light switch and frowned more severely when he saw that the bed had not been slept in. 'Shit.'

'Where is he?' McKittrick demanded.

Knowing that the effort was futile, Decker peered into the bathroom and the sitting room. 'Your son has a bad habit of not following orders. This is twice today that he didn't stay put when I told him to.'

'He must have had an excellent reason.'

'That would be a change. He left his suitcase. Presumably that means he's planning to come back.' Decker noticed an envelope on the bedside table. 'Here. This is addressed to you.'

McKittrick looked uneasy. 'You told him I was coming?'

'Of course. Why? What's the matter?'

'Perhaps that wasn't the wisest thing.'

'What's wrong with telling him that his father was coming?'

But McKittrick had already opened the note. His aged eyes narrowed. Otherwise, he showed no reaction to what he was reading.

At last, he lowered the note and exhaled.

'So?' Decker asked.

McKittrick didn't answer.

'What is it?'

McKittrick still didn't answer.

'Tell me.'

'I'm not certain.' McKittrick sounded hoarse. 'Perhaps it's a suicide note.'

'Suicide? What the—' Decker took the note from him. It was handwritten, its salutation giving Decker an image of an Ivy-Leaguer who had never grown up.

Pops –

I guess I screwed up again. Sorry. I seem to say that a lot, don't I? Sorry. I want you to know that this time I really tried. Honestly, I thought I had it all figured out. The bases covered. The game in the bag. Talk about being wrong, huh? I don't know which is worse – embarrassing you, or not becoming you. But I swear to you, this time I won't run away from my mistake. The responsibility is mine. And the punishment. When I've done what needs to be done, you won't be ashamed of me any longer.

Bry

McKittrick cleared his throat as if he was having difficulty speaking. 'That was my nickname for Brian. Bry.'

Decker reread the note. ' *"The responsibility is mine. And the punishment."* What's he saying?'

'I'm very much afraid that he intends to kill himself,' McKittrick said.

'And that's going to stop you from being ashamed of him? You think that's what his last sentence means?' Decker shook his head. 'Suicide might wipe out *his* shame, but it wouldn't stop *yours*. Your son isn't talking about killing himself. That wouldn't be dramatic enough.'

'I don't know what you're—'

'He's a grandstander. "I won't run away from my mistake. The responsibility is mine. And the punishment." He's not talking about suicide. He's talking about getting even. He's going after them.'

13

As Decker swerved the rented Fiat onto the side street off Via dei Condotti, his headlights pierced the persistent rain, revealing two police cars, their roof lights flashing. Two policemen in rain slickers stood in the illuminated entrance to an apartment building, talking to several distressed-looking people in the vestibule, all of whom wore pajamas or night robes. Lights were on in many windows.

'Damn it, I hoped I'd be wrong.'

'What *is* this place?' McKittrick asked.

'I followed your son and a woman here on Friday,' Decker said. 'Her first name's Renata. I wasn't given her last. Probably an alias. She's the leader of the group your son recruited, which means she's the leader of the group that blew up the Tiber Club. In other words, the terrorists.'

'That's an assumption. You can't be certain that the two groups are the same,' McKittrick said.

'Your son keeps using a phrase that I'd say you're in – extreme denial.'

Decker slowed, easing past the police cars on the narrow street. As tires splashed through puddles, the policemen looked toward the Fiat, then resumed talking to the people in the vestibule.

'And you can't be certain that those policemen have anything to do with Brian,' McKittrick said.

'You know as well as I do – we can't accept coincidence. If I were Brian, this is the logical place that *I'd* go first. To try to get even with the woman who betrayed him. There's one way to find out. You want me to stop so you can go back and talk to the police?'

'Lord, no. Keep driving. Because I'm an American, they'd want to know why I was interested. They'd ask so many questions, I'd be forced to show my credentials.'

'Right. And if Brian can be linked to whatever happened at that apartment building, you'd be linked to *him* and to what happened at the Tiber Club, assuming the terrorists sent the police evidence about his involvement in the explosion. Wouldn't that be a pretty mess?'

'Do you suppose Brian found the woman?' McKittrick's voice deepened with concern.

'I doubt it. There wasn't an ambulance.' Decker sped onto another street.

'You're worried that he was furious enough to have killed her?'

'No. What worries me is the reverse.'

'I don't understand.'

'*Her* killing *him*,' Decker said. 'Your son's out of his depth. What's worse, he isn't humble enough to know it. These people

31

are expert killers. They don't just do their work well. They love it. It gave them a kick to toy with Brian, but if they ever thought he was a serious threat, he'd be dead in an instant. There might not be enough of him left to send home for a funeral.'

McKittrick sat tensely straighter. 'How can we stop him?'

Decker squinted toward the rain past the flapping windshield wipers. 'Your son likes to leave documents around his apartment – a list of his contacts and their addresses, for example.'

'Dear God, are you telling me his tradecraft is that faulty?'

'I get the feeling you haven't been listening to me. Twenty-three people are dead, forty-three injured. That's how faulty his tradecraft is.'

'The list,' McKittrick said, agitated. 'Why did you mention the list?'

'Before I burned it, I memorized it,' Decker said. 'Renata's name and address were at the top. It's logical for him to have gone there first. I think it's also logical that he'll go to every other address until he finds her.'

'But if they're really the terrorists, they won't be at those addresses.'

'Exactly.' Decker swerved around another corner. 'They're professionals. They wouldn't have given Brian their real addresses. Renata probably used that apartment back there as an accommodation, part of the scam. But it doesn't look like Brian figured that out. He's too furious. He wants to get even. The people he terrorizes at those addresses won't have the vaguest idea what's going on. Maybe Renata counted on him to do this. Maybe it's her final joke.'

McKittrick's tone was urgent. 'Where's the closest address on the list?'

'Across the river. But I don't see any point in going there. He's got too big a head start.' Decker increased speed, his tires hissing on the wet pavement. 'He might be at the third or fourth address by now. I'm going to skip to the farthest, then the second farthest, go at them in reverse order, and hope our paths cross.'

14

The rain increased. The only thing in our favor, Decker thought, is that it's the middle of the night. There aren't any traffic jams to slow us down.

All the same, he had to concentrate to drive swiftly and yet safely on the slick pavement. His troubled sleep the previous night had not been sufficient to overcome his jet lag. Now his sense of sleep deprivation intensified, his eyes feeling scratchy, his forehead aching. He felt pressure behind his ears.

Amazingly, especially given his age, McKittrick showed no signs of jet lag at all, his tall frame erect. He pointed. 'What are those large buildings ahead?'

'City University.' After pausing to check a map, Decker took a side street, then another, each more gloomy and narrow, trying to see the numbers on buildings squeezed together. He stopped before a doorway. 'This is the address.'

McKittrick stared through the windows. 'Everything's quiet. No lights on. No police.'

'Looks like he hasn't been here.' A noise in the car made Decker whirl.

McKittrick had his hand on the door latch. He was getting out, standing on the curb, only partially visible in the night and the rain.

'What are you—'

'It's been quite a few years,' McKittrick said with dignity. 'But I still remember how to conduct surveillance. Leave me here. Go to the next address.'

'But—'

'Perhaps my son is already here, or perhaps he's on his way. Perhaps we'll pass him without knowing it if we go to the next address. But this way, if I remain, at least *this* address is secure.'

'I don't think splitting up is a good idea,' Decker said.

'If I were a man your age, would you argue about what I'm doing?'

'. . . No.'

'Then there you have it.' McKittrick started to close the door.

'Wait,' Decker said.

'I won't let you talk me out of this.'

'That's not what I wanted. Here. You'd better take this. When I heard you were flying in, I had a package delivered to the office. I've been waiting to see if it was necessary to give it to you.'

'A pistol?' McKittrick reacted with astonishment. 'Do you honestly think I need a *pistol* to confront my son?'

'I have a very bad feeling about what's happening tonight.'

'I refuse to—'

'Take it, or I'm not leaving you here.'

McKittrick studied him. His dark eyes intense, he accepted the weapon.

'I'll be back as soon as I can,' Decker said. 'How will I find you?'

'Drive slowly through this area. *I'll* find *you*.' McKittrick shut the door, shoved the pistol beneath his suit coat, and walked away into the darkness. Only when the elderly man's rain-haloed figure was no longer visible in the Fiat's headlights did Decker drive onward.

15

It took Decker eight minutes to reach the next-to-last address on the list. Along the way, he debated what to do if there was no indication that Brian had been there. Stay, or go on to another address?

What happened next settled the matter. Even from blocks away, Decker heard sirens wailing in the darkness. He saw a crimson glow above rain-obscured buildings. His stomach hard with apprehension, he steered the Fiat onto the street he wanted and braked immediately before the glaring lights of rumbling fire trucks and other emergency vehicles. Flames licked from the windows of an apartment building. Smoke billowed. As firemen aimed hoses toward the blaze, ambulance attendants ministered to survivors, draping blankets around them, giving them oxygen.

Appalled, Decker got out of the Fiat, came close enough to determine that the fiery building was in fact the one he had come to check, then hurried through a gathering crowd back to the car, reversed direction, and sped away into the rain.

His heart pounded. What the hell is happening? he thought. Was Brian trying to get even by setting fire to the buildings, hoping to trap the terrorists inside? Surely even someone so out of control as Brian would have realized that other people besides the terrorists would be injured – if the terrorists were injured at all, if they had been foolish enough to remain at the addresses they had given Brian.

He has only one more address to go, Decker thought. Where I left his father. Driving urgently through the rain-filled night, Decker skidded and regained control of the Fiat. Near the university, he again took a side street, then another, feeling trapped in the narrow confines. The address where he had left McKittrick's father was only a half block farther when Decker stomped his brake pedal, swerving, nearly hitting a tall burly figure who suddenly appeared in the glare of his headlights. The figure was drenched, his face raised to the storm clouds; he was shaking his fists, screaming.

The figure was Brian. Decker's windows were closed. Only when he scrambled out of the Fiat, racing through puddles to restrain Brian did he hear what Brian screamed.

'*Liars! Bastards!*'

Decker had left his headlights on, their illumination reflecting off the rain streaming down Brian's face.

'*Cowards!*'

Lights came on in windows.

'We have to get you off the street,' Decker said.

'*Fight me!*' Brian screamed inexplicably toward the darkness.

More lights came on.

'FIGHT ME!'

Cold rain soaked Decker's hair and chilled his neck. 'The police will be looking for you. You can't stay here. I have to get you out of here.' He tugged Brian toward the car.

Brian resisted. More windows became illuminated.

'For God's sake, come on,' Decker said. 'Have you seen your father? I left him here.'

'*Bastards!*'

'Brian, listen to me. Have you seen your father?'

Brian wrenched himself free of Decker's grasp and once more shook his fists toward the sky. '*You're afraid!*'

'What's going on down there?' a man yelled in Italian from an upper apartment.

Decker grabbed Brian. 'With the commotion you're making, your father couldn't help but know you're here. He should have joined us by now. Pay attention. I need to know if you've seen him.'

At once a premonition chilled Decker. 'Oh, Jesus, no. Brian. Your father. Has something happened to him?'

When Brian didn't respond, Decker slapped him, twisting his head, sending rain drops flying from Brian's face.

Brian looked shocked. The Fiat's headlights reflected off his wild eyes.

'Tell me where your father is!'

Brian stumbled away.

Apprehensive, Decker followed, seeing where Brian led him – to the address that Brian's father had intended to watch. Even in the rainy gloom, Decker could see that the door was open.

Trying to restrain his too-quick breathing, Decker withdrew his pistol from beneath his leather jacket. As Brian entered, Decker pushed him to a crouch and stooped to hurry after him, his eyes adjusting enough to the darkness to make him aware he was in a courtyard. He saw a wooden crate to his right and shoved Brian toward it. Kneeling on wet cobblestones, Decker aimed over the crate, scanning indistinguishable objects, peering up toward the barely detectable railings of balconies to the right and left and straight ahead.

'Brian, show me,' Decker whispered.

For a moment, he wasn't certain that Brian had heard. Then Brian shifted position, and Decker realized that Brian was pointing. As Decker's vision adjusted even more to the darkness, he saw a disturbing patch of white in the far-right corner.

'Stay here,' he told Brian, and darted toward another crate. Aiming, he checked nervously around him, then hurried forward again, this time to what might have been an ancient well. His wet clothes clung to him, constricting his muscles. He was close enough to determine that the patch of white he had seen was hair – Jason McKittrick's hair. The elderly man lay with his back propped against a wall, his arms at his sides, his chin on his chest.

Decker glanced once more around him, then ran through the rain, reaching McKittrick, crouching beside him, feeling for a pulse. Despite the gloom, it was obvious that an area on the right breast of his gray suit coat was darker than the rain would have caused. Blood. Decker kept checking for a pulse, feeling McKittrick's wrist, his neck, his chest.

Inhaling with triumph, he found one.

He whirled to aim at a sudden approaching figure.

It was Brian, scrambling across the courtyard and collapsing next to his father, pressing his face against his father's head. 'Didn't mean to.'

'Help me,' Decker said. 'We have to get him to the car.'

'Didn't know who he was.'

'What are you talking about?'

'Didn't realize.'

'*What?*'

'Thought he was one of *them*.' Brian sobbed.

'*You* did this?' Decker grabbed Brian, finding that he had a revolver in his jacket pocket.

'I couldn't help myself. He came out of the darkness.'

'Jesus.'

'I had to shoot.'

'God help—'

'I didn't mean to kill him.'

'You didn't.'

'I'm telling you I—'

'He isn't dead!'

In the darkness, Brian's stunned look was barely discernible.

'We have to get him to the car. We have to take him to the hospital. Grab his feet.'

As Decker reached for McKittrick's shoulder, a bumble bee seemed to buzz down past Decker's head. A projectile whacked against the wall behind him.

Flinching, Decker scurried toward the protection of a crate. The shot – from a sound-suppressed weapon – had come from above him. He aimed fiercely upward, blinking from the rain, unable to see a target in the darkness.

'They won't let you,' Brian said.

'*They?*'

'They're here.'

Decker's heart felt squeezed as he realized why Brian had been yelling in the street. Not at the sky or God or the Furies.

He'd been screaming at the terrorists.

Brian remained in the open, beside his father.

'Get over here,' Decker told him.

'I'm safe.'

'For God's sake, get over here behind this crate.'

'They won't shoot me.'

'Don't talk crazy.'

'Before you got here, Renata showed herself to me. She told me the best way to hurt me is to let me live.'

'What?'

'So I can suffer for the rest of my life, knowing I killed my father.'

'But your shot didn't kill him! He isn't dead!'

'*He might as well be.* Renata will never let us take him out of here. She hates me too much.' Brian pulled his revolver from his pocket. In the gloom, it seemed that he pointed it at himself.

'Brian! No!'

But instead of shooting himself, Brian surged to his feet, cursed, and disappeared into the darkness at the back of the courtyard.

Amid the pelting rain, Decker – shocked – heard Brian's footsteps charging up an exterior wooden staircase.

'Brian, I warned you!' a woman shouted from above. The husky voice was Renata's. 'Don't come after me!'

Brian's footsteps charged higher.

Lights came on in balcony windows.

'I gave you a chance!' Renata shouted. 'Stay away, or I'll do what I did at the other apartment buildings!'

'You're going to pay for making a fool of me!'

Renata laughed. 'You did it to yourself!'

'You're going to pay for my father!'

'You did *that* yourself!'

Brian's footsteps pounded higher.

'Don't be an idiot!' Renata shouted. 'The explosives have been set! I'll press the detonator!'

Brian's urgent footsteps kept pounding on the stairs.

Their rumble was overwhelmed by thunder, not from the storm but from an explosion whose blinding flash erupted out of an apartment on the fourth balcony at the back. The ear-stunning roar knocked Decker backward. As wreckage cascaded, the ferocity of the flames illuminated the courtyard.

A movement to Decker's left made him turn. A thin, dark-haired man in his early twenties, one of the brothers whom Decker had met at the cafe the night before, rose from behind garbage cans.

Decker stiffened. They must be all around me, but in the dark, I didn't know it!

The young man hadn't been prepared for Renata to detonate the bomb. Although he had a pistol, his attention was totally distracted by a scream on the other side of the courtyard. With wide-eyed dismay, the young man saw one of his brothers swatting at flames on his clothes and in his hair that had been ignited by the falling, burning wreckage. The rain didn't seem to affect the flames. The second brother kept screaming.

Decker shot twice at the first brother, hitting his chest and head. As the gunman toppled, Decker pivoted and shot twice at the man in flames, dropping him, also. The gunshots were almost obscured by the crackle and roar of the fire as it spread from the fourth balcony.

More wreckage fell. Crouching behind the crate, Decker scanned the area in search of more targets. Brian. *Where was Brian?* Decker's peripheral vision detected motion in the far-left corner of the courtyard, near the door that he and Brian had come through.

But the movement wasn't Brian. The tall, slim, sensuous figure that emerged from the shadows of another stairway was Renata. Holding a pistol equipped with a sound-suppressor, she shot repeatedly toward the courtyard, all the while running toward the open doorway. The muffled shots, normally no louder than a fist against a pillow, were totally silent because of the roaring chaos of the blaze.

Behind the crate, Decker sprawled on the wet cobblestones and squirmed forward on his elbows and knees. He reached the side of the crate, caught a glimpse of Renata nearing the exit, aimed through the rain, and shot twice more. His first bullet struck the wall behind her. His second hit her in the throat. She clutched her windpipe, blood spewing. Her throat would squeeze shut. Death from asphyxiation would occur in less than three minutes.

Despite the din of the flames, Decker heard a scream of anguish. One of Renata's brothers showed himself, racing from the open stairway, shooting toward the courtyard, grabbing Renata where she had fallen, dragging her closer to the open doorway. At once he shot again – not at Decker, but instead toward the stairwell at the back of the courtyard, as if protecting himself from bullets that came from that direction. As Decker aimed, the last brother appeared, shot repeatedly in Decker's direction, and helped to get his sister out of view into the street. Decker emptied his pistol, hastily ejected its magazine, and inserted a full one. By then, the terrorists were gone.

Sweat mixed with rain on his face. He shuddered, spun in case there were other targets, and saw Brian jump down the last few steps of the open stairway at the back of the courtyard.

Brian clutched his revolver, his hand shaking.

'We have to get out of here!' Decker yelled.

No more than a minute had passed since the explosion. People wearing pajamas and sometimes less were charging onto the balconies and down outdoor stairways to get away from the fire.

Decker avoided a chunk of flaming wreckage and rushed to Brian, who had an arm around his father, lifting him.

'I can feel him breathe!' Brian said.

'Give me his legs.'

Decker heard people rushing in panic down the stairs as he and Brian carried McKittrick across the courtyard toward the open doorway.

'Wait,' Decker said. He set down McKittrick's legs and aimed cautiously out toward the street. He saw a car speed away from the curb, its red taillights becoming rapidly smaller, the vehicle skidding through puddles, around a corner, disappearing.

Decker was far enough from the roaring flames to hear the pulsing wail of approaching sirens. One of the terrorists might have stayed, hiding behind a car, hoping to create an ambush. But Decker was betting that the sirens were as worrisome to the terrorists as to himself.

He decided to take the chance. 'Let's go!' he told Brian.

As people crowded behind them, he and Brian hurried to carry McKittrick toward the Fiat and set him in the back seat. Brian stayed in back with his father while Decker slid behind the steering wheel and sped away, narrowly missing people in the street. At the same time, numerous sirens wailed louder behind the Fiat. Pressing his foot on the accelerator, Decker glanced nervously at the rearview mirror and saw the flashing lights of emergency vehicles appear on the rainy street behind him.

But what about up ahead? he wondered, his hands tense on the steering wheel. The street was so narrow that if fire trucks or police cars sped around a corner, heading in Decker's direction, there'd be no way around them. The Fiat would be trapped.

A rain-slick corner loomed. Decker swerved, finding himself

on a street that was wider. No approaching lights flashed in the darkness ahead. The sirens were farther behind him.

'I think we got away,' Decker said. 'How's your father?'

'He's still alive. That's the best I can say.'

Decker tried to breathe less quickly. 'What did Renata mean about threatening to do what she did at the other apartment buildings?'

'She told me she rigged explosives at some of them. After I showed up, looking for her and the others . . .' Brian had trouble speaking.

'As soon as you were out of the area, she set off the charges?'

'Yes.'

'You'd made such a commotion, barging into the apartments, that the other people in the building would have come out to learn what was going on? They'd associate you with the explosions?'

'Yes.'

'Renata wanted an American to be blamed?'

'Yes.'

'Damn it, you let her use you again,' Decker said.

'But I got even.'

'Even?'

'You saw what I did. I shot her.'

'*You* . . . ?' Decker couldn't believe what he was hearing. He felt as if the road wavered. '*You* didn't shoot her.'

'In the throat,' Brian said.

'No.'

'You're trying to claim *you* did?' Brian demanded.

My God, he truly is crazy, Decker thought. 'There's nothing to brag about here, Brian. If you had shot her, it wouldn't make me think less of myself or more of you. If anything, I'd feel sorry for you. It's a terrible thing, living with the memory of—'

'*Sorry for me?* What the hell are you talking about? You think

43

you're better than I am? What gives you the right to feel so superior?'

'Forget it, Brian.'

'Sorry for me? Are you trying to claim *you* did what *I* did?'

'Just calm down,' Decker said.

'You hate me so much, the next thing you'll be claiming *I* was the one who shot my father.'

Decker's sense of reality was so threatened that he felt momentarily dizzy. 'Whatever you say, Brian. All I want to do is get him to a hospital.'

'Damned right.'

Decker heard a pulsing siren. The flashing lights of a police car raced toward him. His palms sweated on the steering wheel. At once the police car rushed past, heading in the direction from which Decker had come.

'Give me your revolver, Brian.'

'Get serious.'

'I mean it. Hand me your revolver.'

'You've got to be—'

'Just once, for Christ's sake, listen to me. There'll be other police cars. Someone will tell the police a Fiat sped away. There's a chance we'll be stopped. It's bad enough we have a wounded man in the car. But if the police find our handguns—'

'What are you going to do with my revolver? You think you can use ballistics from it to prove I shot my father? You're afraid I'll try to get rid of it?'

'No, *I'm* going to get rid of it.'

Brian cocked his head in surprise.

'As much as I don't want to.' Decker stopped at the side of the murky street and turned to stare at Brian. 'Give . . . me . . . your . . . revolver.'

Squinting, Brian studied him. Slowly, he reached in his

jacket pocket and pulled out the weapon.

Decker pulled out his own weapon.

Only when Brian offered the revolver, butt first, did Decker allow himself to relax a little. In the courtyard, before he had helped to lift McKittrick's father, he had picked up the elderly man's pistol. Now he took that pistol, his own, and Brian's. He got out of the Fiat into the chilling rain, scanned the darkness to see if anyone was watching, went around to the curb, knelt as if to check the pressure on one of his tires, and inconspicuously dropped the three handguns down a sewer drain.

Immediately he got back into the Fiat and drove away.

'So that takes care of that, huh?' Brian said.

'Yes,' Decker answered bitterly. 'That takes care of that.'

16

'He has lost a great deal of blood,' the emergency-room doctor said in Italian. 'His pulse is weak and erratic. His blood pressure is low. I do not wish to be pessimistic, but I am afraid that you must prepare yourself for any eventuality.'

'I understand,' Decker said. 'This man's son and I appreciate anything you can do for him.'

The doctor nodded gravely and went back into the emergency room.

Decker turned to two weary-looking hospital officials, who stood respectfully in a corner of the waiting room. 'I'm grateful for your cooperation in this matter,' Decker told them. 'My superiors will be even more grateful. Of course, a suitable gesture of gratitude will be made to everyone involved.'

'Your superiors have always been most generous.' One of the officials took off his spectacles. 'We will do our best to make certain that the authorities are not informed about the true cause of the patient's injury.'

'I have total confidence in your discretion.' Decker shook hands with them. The money he slipped into their palms disappeared into their pockets. '*Grazie.*'

As soon as the officials left, Decker sat beside Brian. 'Good. You kept your mouth shut.'

'We have an understanding with this hospital?'

Decker nodded.

'Is this place first rate?' Brian asked. 'It seems awfully small.'

'It's the best.'

'We'll see.'

'Prayer wouldn't hurt.'

Brian frowned. 'You mean you're religious?'

'I like to keep my options open.' Decker peered down at his wet clothes, which were clinging to him. 'What they're doing for your father is going to take a while. I think we'd better go back to your hotel and put on dry clothes.'

'But what if something happens while we're gone?'

'You mean, if he dies?' Decker asked.

'Yes.'

'It won't make any difference whether we're in this room or not.'

'This is all your fault.'

'What?' Decker felt sudden pressure behind his ears. '*My* fault?'

'You got us into this mess. If it wasn't for you, none of this would have happened.'

'How the hell do you figure that?'

'If you hadn't shown up on Friday and rushed me, I could have handled Renata and her group just fine.'

'Why don't we talk about this on the way to your hotel?'

17

'He claims that as soon as you got him out of the hospital, you shoved him into an alley and beat him up,' Decker's superior said.

'He can claim anything he wants.' It was Monday. Again, Decker was in an office at the international real-estate consulting firm, but this time, he was speaking to his superior in person rather than on a scrambler-protected telephone.

The gray-haired superior, whose sagging cheeks were florid from tension, leaned forward across the table. 'You deny the accusation?'

'Brian was injured in the incident at the apartment building. I have no idea where this fantasy about my beating him comes from.'

'He says you're jealous of him.'

'Right.'

'That you're angry because he found the terrorists.'

'Sure.'

'That you're trying to get even with him by claiming that he accidentally shot his father.'

'Imagine.'

'And that you're trying to take credit for shooting the terrorists whom *he* in fact shot.'

'Look,' Decker said, 'I know you need to protect your pension. I know there's a lot of political pressure, and you need to cover your ass. But why are you dignifying that jerk's ridiculous accusations by repeating them to me?'

'What makes you think they're ridiculous?'

'Ask Brian's father. He's awfully weak. It's a miracle he pulled through. But he'll be able to—'

'I already *have* asked him.'

Decker didn't like his superior's solemn tone. 'And?'

'Jason McKittrick verifies everything Brian claims,' the superior said. 'Terrorists shot him, but not before he saw his son shoot three of the terrorists. Of course, ballistic tests might have corroborated what Jason McKittrick says, but *you* saw fit to dispose of all the weapons that were used that night.'

Decker's gaze was as steady as his superior's. 'So that's how it's going to be.'

'What do you mean?'

'Jason McKittrick warned me from the start – his son wasn't going to take the blame. I liked the old man enough that I stopped treating the warning seriously. I should have been more careful. The enemy wasn't out there. He was next to me.'

'Jason McKittrick's character isn't in question here.'

'Of course not. Because nobody wants Jason McKittrick as an enemy. And nobody wants to accept the responsibility for allowing his incompetent son to ruin a major operation. But *somebody's* got to be at fault, right?'

The superior didn't answer.

'How did you manage to hide Brian's involvement in this?' Decker asked. 'Didn't the terrorists send incriminating evidence about him to the police?'

'When you phoned to warn me about that possibility, I alerted our contacts in the police department. A package did arrive. Our contacts diverted it.'

'What about the media? No package was sent to them?'

'A television station, the same station the terrorists had earlier been sending messages to. We intercepted that package, also. The crisis is over.'

'Except for twenty-three dead Americans,' Decker said.

'Do you wish to make any change in your report?'

'Yes. I did beat the hell out of that jerk. I wish I'd beaten him more.'

'Any other change?'

'Something I should have added,' Decker said.

'Oh? What's that?'

'Saturday was my fortieth birthday.'

The superior shook his head. 'I'm afraid I don't see the relevance of that remark.'

'If you'll wait a moment, I'll type up my resignation.'

'Your— But we're not asking you to go *that* far. What on earth do you think resigning will get you?'

'A life.'

TWO

1

Decker lay on the bed in his New York hotel room. Using his right hand, he sipped from a glass of Jack Daniels. Using his left hand, he aimed the television's remote control and restlessly switched channels. Where do you go when you've been everywhere? he asked himself.

New York had always been good for him, a place to which he'd automatically headed when he had a rare free weekend. Broadway, the Metropolitan Opera, the Museum of Modern Art – these had always beckoned like old friends. Days, he had used to enjoy a soothing ritual of jogging through Central Park, of lunching at the Carnegie deli, of browsing through the Strand book store, of watching the sidewalk artists in Washington Square. Nights, he had liked to check out who was singing at the Algonquin Room. Radio City Music Hall. Madison Square Garden. There had always been plenty to do.

But this trip, to his surprise, he wanted to do none of it. Mel Torme was at Michael's Pub. Normally Decker would have been the first in line to get a seat. Not this time. Maynard Ferguson, Decker's favorite trumpeter, was at the Blue Note, but Decker didn't have the energy to clean himself up and go out. All he did have energy for was to pour more bourbon into his glass and keep pressing the channel changer on the TV's remote control.

After flying back from Rome, he hadn't considered returning to his small apartment in Alexandria, Virginia. He had no attachment to the small bedroom, living room, kitchenette, and bath. They weren't his home. They were merely a place for storing his clothes and sleeping between assignments. The dust that greeted him whenever he returned made his nose itch and gave him a headache. There was no way he could allow himself to break security and hire a cleaning lady to spruce the place up for his arrival. The thought of a stranger going through his things made his skin prickle – not that he would ever have left anything revealing in his apartment.

He hadn't let his superior – correction: his *former* superior – know where he was going after he submitted his resignation. New York would have been on the list of predictables, of course, and it would have been a routine matter for someone following him to confirm the destination of the flight Decker had boarded. He had used evasion procedures when he arrived in New York. He had stayed in a hotel, the St Regis, that was new to him. Nonetheless, ten minutes after he had checked in and been shown to his room, the telephone had rung, and of course, it had been his superior – correction again: damn it, *former* superior – asking Decker to reconsider.

'Really, Steve,' the weary-sounding man had said, 'I appreciate grand gestures as much as the next person, but now that you've done it, now that it's out of your system, let's let bygones be bygones. Climb back aboard. I agree, this Rome business is a mess from every angle, an out-and-out disaster, but resigning isn't going to change things. You're not making anything better. Surely you understand the futility of what you've done.'

'You're afraid I'm angry enough to tell the wrong people about what happened, is that it?' Decker had asked.

'Of course not. Everybody knows you're rock solid. You wouldn't do anything unprofessional. You wouldn't let us down.'

'Then you don't have anything to worry about.'

'You're too good a man to lose, Steve.'

'With guys like Brian McKittrick, you'll never know I'm gone.' Decker had set the phone on its receptacle.

A minute later, the phone had rung again, and this time, it had been his former superior's superior. 'If it's an increase in salary you want—'

'I never had a chance to spend what you paid me,' Decker said.

'Perhaps more time off.'

'To do what?'

'Travel.'

'Right. See the world. Rome, for instance. I fly so much I think there's something wrong with a bed if it isn't shaped like an airline seat.'

'Look, Steve, everybody gets burned out. It's part of the job. That's why we keep a team of experts who know how to relieve the symptoms of stress. Honestly, I think it would do you a world of good if you took a shuttle down to Washington right now and had a talk with them.'

'Didn't you listen? I told you I'm sick of flying.'

'Then use the train.'

Again Decker set the phone on its receptacle. He had no doubt that if he tried to go outside, he would be intercepted by two men waiting for him in the lobby. They would identify themselves, explain that his friends were worried about his reaction to what had happened in Rome, and suggest driving him to a quiet bar, where they could discuss what was bothering him.

To hell with that, Decker thought. I can have a drink in my room. By myself. Besides, the ride they gave me wouldn't be to a bar. That was when Decker picked up the phone, ordered a bottle of Jack Daniels and plenty of ice from room service, unplugged the phone, turned on the television, and began switching channels. Two hours later, as darkness thickened beyond his closed drapes, he was a third of the way through the bottle and still switching channels. The staccato images on the screen were the test pattern of his mind.

Where to go? What to do? he asked himself. Money wasn't an immediate problem. For the ten years he had worked as an operative, a considerable portion of his salary had gone into mutual funds. Added to that sum was the sizeable amount of accumulated parachute pay, scuba pay, demolitions pay, combat pay, and specialty pay that he had previously earned as a member of a classified military counterterrorist unit. Like many of the military's highest trained soldiers, he had been recruited into intelligence work after he had reached an age when his body could no longer function as efficiently as his special-operations duties required – in Decker's case, when he was thirty, after a broken leg, three broken ribs, and two bullet wounds suffered in various classified missions. Of course, even though Decker was no longer physically superior enough to belong to his counterterrorist unit, he was still in better condition than most civilians.

His investments had increased to the point that his net worth was three hundred thousand dollars. In addition, he planned to withdraw the fifty thousand dollars that he had contributed to his civilian government pension. But despite his relative financial freedom, he felt trapped in other ways. With the whole world to choose from, he had narrowed his choices to this hotel room. If his parents had still been alive (and briefly he fantasized that they were), he would have paid them a long-postponed visit. As things were, his mother had died in a car accident three years earlier and his father from a heart attack a few months afterward, both while he was on assignment. The last time he had seen his father alive was at his mother's funeral.

Decker had no brothers or sisters. He had never married,

partly because he had refused to inflict his spartan way of life on someone he loved, partly because that way of life prevented him from finding anyone with whom he felt free to fall in love. His only friends were fellow operatives, and now that he had resigned from intelligence work, the controversial circumstances behind that resignation would prompt those friends to feel inhibited around him, not certain about which topics would be safe to discuss.

Maybe I made a mistake, Decker thought, sipping more bourbon. Maybe I shouldn't have resigned, he brooded, switching channels. Being an operative gave me a direction. It gave me an anchor.

It was killing you, Decker reminded himself, and it ruined for you every country where you ever had an assignment. The Greek islands, the Swiss Alps, the French Riviera, the Spanish Mediterranean – these were but a few of the glamorous areas where Decker had worked. But they were tainted by Decker's experiences there, and he had no wish to go back and be reminded. In fact, now that he thought about it, he was struck by the irony that, just as most people thought of those places as glamorous, so Decker's former profession was often portrayed in fiction as being heroic, whereas Decker thought of it as no more than a wearying, stultifying, dangerous job. Hunting drug lords and terrorists might be noble, but the slime of the quarry rubbed off on the hunter. It certainly rubbed off on me, Decker thought. And as I found out, some of the bureaucrats I worked for weren't all that slime-free, either.

What to do? Decker repeated to himself. Made sleepy by the bourbon, he peered through drooping eyelids at the television set and found himself frowning at something that he had just seen. Not understanding what it had been, oddly curious to find out, he roused himself and reversed channels, going back to one that he had just flicked past. As soon as he found the image that had intrigued him, he didn't understand *why* it had intrigued him. All he knew was that something in it had subconsciously spoken to him.

He was looking at a documentary about a team of construction workers renovating an old house. The house was unusual, reminiscent of earthen, pueblo-style dwellings he had come across in Mexico. But as he turned up the sound on the television, he learned that the house, astonishingly elegant regardless of its simple design, was in the United States, in *New* Mexico. It was made from adobe, the construction foreman explained, adding that 'adobe' referred to large bricks made of straw and mud. These bricks, which resulted in an exceptionally solid, sound-proofed wall, were covered with a clay-colored stucco. The foreman went on to explain that an adobe house was flat-roofed, the roof slanted slightly so that water could drain off through spouts called *canales*. An adobe house had no sharp edges; every corner was rounded. Its entrance often had a column-supported overhang called a *portal*. The windows were recessed into thick walls.

Leaving the distinctive dwelling whose sandy texture and clay color blended wonderfully with the orange, red, and yellow of its high-desert surroundings, the announcer made some concluding comments about craft and heritage while the camera panned across the neighborhood. Amid mountain foothills, surrounded by junipers and piñon trees, there were adobe houses in every direction, each with an eccentric variation so that the impression was one of amazing variety. But as the announcer explained, in a sense adobe houses *were* unusual in New Mexico, because they were present in force in only one city.

Decker found that he was leaning forward to hear the name of that city. He was told that it was one of the oldest settlements in the United States, dating back to the fifteen hundreds and the Spanish conquest, still retaining its Spanish character: the city whose name meant holy faith, these days nicknamed the City Different, Santa Fe.

2

Decker was right to be suspicious – two men were waiting for him in the lobby. The time was just after eight a.m. He turned from the checkout counter, saw them, and knew that there wasn't any point in trying to avoid them. They smiled as he crossed the busy lobby toward them. At least, the right men had been chosen for the assignment, Decker thought. Their controllers obviously hoped that he would let his guard down since he knew both of them, having served with them in military special operations.

'Steve, long time. How you been?' one of the men asked. He and his partner were close to Decker's height and weight – six feet tall, a hundred and ninety pounds. They were also around Decker's age – forty. Because they had gone through the same physical training, they had a similar body type – narrow hips and a torso that broadened toward solid shoulders designed to provide the upper-body strength essential in special operations. But there, the resemblance with Decker ended. While Decker's hair was sandy and slightly wavy, the man who had spoken had red hair cut close to his scalp. The other man had brown hair combed straight back. Both men had hard features and wary eyes that didn't go with their smiles and their business suits.

'I'm fine, Ben,' Decker told the red-haired man. 'And you?'

'Can't complain.'

'How about *you*, Hal?' Decker asked the other man.

'Can't complain, either.'

No one offered to shake hands.

'I hope the two of you didn't have to keep watch all night.'

'Only came on at seven. Easy duty,' Hal said. 'Checking out?' He pointed toward Decker's suitcase.

'Yeah, a last-minute change of plan.'

'Where you headed?'

'La Guardia,' Decker said.

'Why don't we drive you?'

Decker tensed. 'I wouldn't want you to go to any trouble. I'll catch a taxi.'

'No trouble at all,' Hal said. 'What kind of buddies would we be if after all these years of not seeing you, we didn't put ourselves out for you. This won't be a minute.' Hal reached into his suit coat, pulled out a thin cellular phone, and pressed numbers. 'You'll never guess who we just bumped into,' he said into the telephone. 'Yeah, we're talking to him right now in the lobby. Good, we'll be waiting.'

Hal broke the transmission and put the phone away. 'Need help with your suitcase?'

'I can manage.'

'Then why don't we go outside and wait for the car?'

Outside, traffic was already dense, car horns blaring.

'See,' Ben said. 'You might not have been able to get a taxi.' He noticed a uniformed doorman coming toward them. 'Everything's under control,' he told the man, motioning him away. He glanced toward the overcast sky. 'Feels like it might rain.'

'It was forecast,' Hal said.

'The twinge in my left elbow is all the forecast I need. Here's the car,' Ben said.

A gray Pontiac, whose driver wasn't familiar to Decker, pulled up in front of the hotel. The car's back seat had tinted windows that made it difficult to see in.

'What did I tell you?' Ben said. 'Only a minute.' He opened the passenger door and gestured for Decker to get in.

Heart pounding, Decker glanced from Ben to Hal and didn't move.

'Is there a problem?' Hal asked. 'Don't you think you'd better get in? You've got a plane to catch.'

'I was just wondering what to do about my suitcase.'

'We'll put it in the trunk. Press the button that opens the trunk, will you?' Ben told the driver. A moment later, the back latch made a thunking sound. Ben took Decker's suitcase, lifted the back lid, set the suitcase inside the trunk, and closed the lid. 'There, that takes care of that. Ready?'

Decker hesitated another moment. His pulse racing faster, he nodded and got in the back of the Pontiac. His stomach felt cold.

Ben got in beside him while Hal took the passenger seat in front, turning to look back at Decker.

'Buckle up,' the thick-necked driver said.

'Yeah, safety first,' Ben said.

Metal clinked against metal as Decker secured his seatbelt, the others doing the same.

The driver pressed a button that caused another thunking sound and locked all the doors. The Pontiac's engine rumbling, he steered into traffic.

3

'A mutual acquaintance told me you said on the phone last night you were tired of flying,' Ben said.

'That's right.' Decker glanced out the tinted windows toward pedestrians carrying briefcases, purses, rolled-up umbrellas, whatever, walking briskly to work. They seemed very far away.

'So why are you catching a plane?' Hal asked.

'A spur of the moment decision.'

'Like your resignation.'

'That wasn't spur of the moment.'

'Our mutual acquaintance said it sure seemed like it.'

'He doesn't know me very well.'

'He's beginning to wonder if *anybody* does.'

Decker shrugged. 'What else is he wondering?'

'Why you unplugged your phone.'

'I didn't want to be disturbed.'

'And why you didn't answer your door when one of the guys on the team knocked on it last night.'

'But I *did* answer the door. I just didn't open it. I asked who it was. On the other side of the door, a man said "Housekeeping". He told me he was there to turn down my bed. I told him I had turned down the bed myself. He told me he had fresh towels. I told him I didn't need fresh towels. He told me he had mints for the bedside table. I told him to shove the mints up his ass.'

'That wasn't very sociable.'

'I needed time alone to think.'

Ben took over the questioning. 'To think about what?'

As the Pontiac stopped at a light, Decker glanced to the left toward the red-haired man. 'Life.'

'Big subject. Did you figure it out?'

'I decided that it's the essence of life for things to change.'

'*That's* what this is all about? You're going through a change of life?' Hal asked.

Decker glanced ahead toward the brown-haired man in the front passenger seat. The Pontiac had resumed motion, proceeding through the intersection.

'That's right,' Decker said. 'A change of life.'

'And that's why you're taking this trip?'

'Right again.'

'To where exactly?'

'Santa Fe, New Mexico.'

'Never been there. What's it like?'

'I'm not sure. It looks nice, though.'

'*Looks* nice?'

'Last night, I watched a TV show about some construction workers fixing up an adobe house there.'

The Pontiac headed through another intersection.

'And that made you decide to go there?' Ben interrupted.

Decker turned to him in the back seat. 'Yep.'

'Just like that?'

'Just like that. In fact, I'm thinking about settling there.'

'Just like that. You know, that's what has our mutual acquaintance concerned, these sudden changes. How do you suppose he's going to react when we tell him that on the spur of the moment you decided to move to Santa Fe, New Mexico, because you saw an old house there being fixed up on television?'

'An adobe house.'

'Right. How do you suppose that'll make him think about the maturity with which you made other snap decisions?'

Decker's muscles hardened. 'I told you, my resignation wasn't a snap decision. I've been thinking about it for quite a while.'

'You never mentioned it to anybody.'

'I didn't figure it was anybody's business.'

'It was a lot of people's business. So what made the difference? What pushed you into making the decision? This incident in Rome?'

Decker didn't answer.

Raindrops beaded the windshield.

'See, I told you it was going to rain,' Ben said.

The rain fell heavier, causing a hollow, pelting sound on the Pontiac's roof. Pedestrians put up umbrellas or ran for doorways. The tinted back-seat windows made the darkening streets seem even darker.

'Talk to us about Rome,' Ben said.

'I don't intend to talk to *anybody* about Rome.' Decker strained to keep his breathing steady. 'I assume that's the point of this conversation. You can go back and assure our mutual acquaintance that I'm not indignant enough to share my indignation with anybody – I'm just damned tired. I'm not interested in exposés and causing a commotion. The opposite – all I want is peace and quiet.'

'In Santa Fe, a place you've never been.'

Again Decker didn't answer.

'You know,' Hal said, 'when you mentioned Santa Fe, the first thought that popped into my mind was, there are a lot of top-secret installations in the area – the Sandia weapons testing lab in Albuquerque, the nuclear lab at Los Alamos. The second thought that popped into my head was Edward Lee Howard.'

Decker felt a weight in his chest. Howard had been a CIA operative who sold top-level details about the agency's Moscow operation to the Soviets. After a failed lie-detector test aroused the agency's suspicions, he had been fired. While the FBI investigated him, he had moved to New Mexico, had eluded his surveillance teams, and had managed to escape to the Soviet Union. The city where he had been living was Santa Fe.

'You're suggesting a parallel?' Decker sat straighter. 'You're suggesting I'd do something to hurt my country?' This time, Decker didn't bother trying to control his breathing. 'You tell our mutual acquaintance to reread my file and try to find anything that suggests I suddenly forgot the meaning of honor.'

'People go through changes, as you've been pointing out.'

'And these days most people go through at least three careers.'

'I'm having trouble following you again, Decker.'

'I had my military career. I had my government career. Now it's time for my third.'

'And what's it going to be?'

'I don't know yet. I wouldn't want to make any spur of the moment decisions. Where are you taking me?'

Hal didn't answer.

'I asked you a question,' Decker said.

Hal still didn't answer.

'It better not be the agency's rehabilitation clinic in Virginia,' Decker said.

'Who said anything about Virginia?' Hal seemed to make a choice. 'We're taking you where you *wanted* us to take you – La Guardia.'

4

Decker bought a one-way ticket. During the six-hour flight, which included a stopover in Chicago, he had plenty of time to think about what he was doing. His behavior was bizarre enough that he could understand why his former superiors were troubled. Hell, he himself was troubled by his behavior. His entire professional life had been based on control, but now he had surrendered to whimsy.

Santa Fe's airport was too small for large passenger jets. The nearest major airport was in Albuquerque, and as the American Airlines MD-80 circled for a landing, Decker was appalled by the bleak sunbaked yellow landscape below him, sand and rocks stretching off toward barren mountains. What else did you expect? he told himself. New Mexico's a *desert*.

At least, Albuquerque's compact four-level terminal had charm, its interior decorated with colorful Native American designs. The airport was also remarkably efficient. In a quick ten minutes, Decker had his suitcase and was standing at the Avis counter, renting a Dodge Intrepid. The car's name appealed to him.

'What's the best way to get to Santa Fe?' he asked the young woman behind the counter.

She was Hispanic and had a bright smile that enhanced the expressiveness of her dark eyes. 'That depends on whether you want the quick route or the scenic route.'

'Is the scenic route worth it?'

'Absolutely. If you've got the time.'

'I've got nothing *but* time.'

'Then you've got the right attitude for a New Mexican vacation. Follow this map,' she said. 'Go north a couple of miles on Route 25. Turn east on Interstate 40. After about twenty miles, turn north on the Turquoise Trail.' The clerk used a felt-tip pen to highlight the map. 'Do you like margaritas?'

'Love them.'

'Stop in a town called Madrid.' She emphasized the first syllable as if distinguishing it from the way the capital of Spain was pronounced. 'Thirty years ago, it was almost a ghost town. Now it's an artists' colony. There's a beat-up old place called the Mineshaft Tavern that brags it has the best margaritas in the world.'

'And are they?'

The woman merely flashed her engaging smile and handed him the car keys.

As Decker drove past a metal silhouette of two racehorses outside the airport and followed the clerk's directions, he noticed that Albuquerque's buildings seemed no different from those in any other part of the country. Now and then, he saw a flat-roofed stuccoed structure that looked something like the adobe he had seen on television, but mostly he saw peaked roofs and brick or wood siding. It worried him that the television program might have exaggerated, that Santa Fe would turn out to be like everywhere else.

Interstate 40 led him past a hulking jagged line of mountains.

Then he turned north onto the Turquoise Trail, and things began to change. Isolated log cabins and A-frames now seemed the architectural norm. In a while, there weren't any buildings at all. There was more vegetation – junipers and piñon trees, various types of low-growing cacti, and a sagebrush-like shrub that grew as high as six feet. The narrow road wound around the back side of the mountains that he had seen from Albuquerque. It angled upward, and Decker recalled that a flight attendant on the MD-80 had made a comment to him about Albuquerque's being a mile-high city, five thousand feet above sea level, the same as Denver was, but that Santa Fe was even higher, seven thousand feet, so it was a climb to get there. For the first few days, visitors might feel slow and out of breath, the flight attendant had told him. She had joked that a passenger once asked her if Santa Fe was seven thousand feet above sea level all year round.

Decker didn't notice any physical reaction to the altitude, but that was to be expected. After all, he had been trained to think nothing of high-altitude low-opening parachute jumps that began at twenty thousand feet. What he did notice was how remarkably clear the air had become, how blue the sky, how bright the sun, and he understood why a poster at the airport had called New Mexico the land of the dancing sun. He reached a plateau, and his breath was taken away as he peered to the left and saw a rolling desert vista that seemed to go on for hundreds of miles to the north and south, the western view bordered by far-away mountains that looked higher and broader than those near Albuquerque. The road's gradual climb took him to further sharp curves, at many of which the vistas were even more spectacular. Decker felt as if he was on top of the world.

Madrid, which Decker had to keep reminding himself was pronounced with an accent on the first syllable, was a village of shacks and frame houses, most of which were occupied by what appeared to be survivors of the counterculture in the sixties. The community stretched along a narrow wooded hollow bordered on the right by a slope covered with coal, the reason the town had been founded at the turn of the century. The Mineshaft Tavern, a rickety two-story wooden structure in need of paint, was about the largest building in town and easy to find, directly to the right at the bottom of the curving slope into town.

Decker parked and locked the Intrepid. He studied a group of leather-jacketed motorcyclists going by. They stopped at a house down the road, unstrapped folded-down easels and half-completed paintings on canvases, and carried them into the house. With a grin, Decker climbed the steps to the tavern's enclosed porch. His footsteps caused a hollow rumbling sound beneath him as he opened a squeaky screen door that led him into a miniature version of a turn-of-the-century saloon complete with a stage. Currency from all over the world was tacked to the wall behind the bar.

The shadowy place was half-full and noisy with spirited conversation. Sitting at an empty table, Decker gathered the impression of cowboy hats, tattoos, and beaded necklaces. In contrast with the efficiency of the Albuquerque airport, it took a long time before a ponytailed man wearing an apron and holding a tray ambled over. Don't be impatient, Decker told himself. Think of this as a kind of decompression chamber.

The knees of the waiter's jeans were ripped out.

'Someone told me you've got the best margaritas in the world,' Decker said. 'Surely that isn't true.'

'There's a way to find out.'

'Bring me one.'

'Anything to eat?

'What do you recommend?'

'At noon, the chicken fajitas. But in the middle of the afternoon? Try the nachos.'

'Done.'

The nachos had Monterey Jack cheese, green salsa, pinto beans, lettuce, tomatoes, and jalapeño peppers. The peppers made Decker's eyes water. He felt in heaven and realized that if he'd eaten this same food two days earlier, his stomach would have been in agony.

The margarita truly was the best he had ever tasted.

'What's the secret?' he asked the waiter.

'An ounce and a quarter of the best tequila, which is one hundred percent blue agave. Three quarters of an ounce of Cointreau. One and a half ounces of freshly squeezed lemon juice. A fresh wedge of lime.'

The drink made Decker's mouth pucker with joy. Salt from the rim of the glass stuck to his lips. He licked it off and ordered another. When he finished that, he would have ordered yet another, except that he didn't know how the alcohol would hit him at this altitude. Driving, he didn't want to injure anyone. Plus, he wanted to be able to find Santa Fe.

After giving the waiter a twenty-five percent tip, Decker went outside, feeling as mellow as he had felt in years. He squinted at the lowering sun, glanced at his diver's watch – almost four-thirty – put on his Ray-Bans, and got into the Intrepid. If anything the air seemed even clearer, the sky bluer, the sun more brilliant. As he drove from town, following the narrow winding road past more juniper and piñon trees and that sagebrush-like plant that he meant to learn the name of, he noticed that the color of the land had changed so that red, orange, and brown joined what had been a predominance of yellow. The vegetation became greener. He reached a high curve that angled down to the left, giving him a view for miles ahead. Before him, distant, at a higher elevation, looking like miniatures in a child's play village, were tiny buildings nestled among foothills behind which rose stunningly beautiful mountains that Decker's map called the Sangre de Cristo range, the Blood of Christ. The sun made the buildings seem golden, as if enchanted; Decker remembered noticing that the motto on New Mexico's license plates was 'the land of enchantment'. The vista, encircled by the green of piñon trees, beckoned, and Decker had no doubt that was where he was headed.

5

Within the city limits (SANTA FE. POPULATION 62,424), he followed a sign that said HISTORIC PLAZA. The busy downtown streets seemed to become more narrow, their pattern like a maze, as if the four-hundred-year-old city had developed haphazardly. Adobe buildings were everywhere, none the same, as if each of them had also been added to haphazardly. While most of the buildings were low, a few were three stories high, their pueblo design reminding him of cliff dwellings – he discovered they were hotels. Even the city's downtown parking garage had a pueblo design. He locked the Intrepid, then strolled up a street that had a long portal above it. At the far end, he saw a cathedral that reminded him of churches in Spain. But before he reached it, the Plaza appeared on the left – rectangular, the size of a small city block, with a lawn, white metal benches, tall sheltering trees, and a Civil War memorial at its center. He noticed a diner called the Plaza Cafe and a restaurant called the Ore House, bunches of dried red peppers dangling from its balcony. In front of a long low ancient-looking adobe building called the Palace of the Governors, native Americans sat against a wall beneath a portal, blankets spread before them on the sidewalk, silver and turquoise jewelry arranged for sale on the blankets.

As Decker slumped on a bench in the Plaza, the mellowing

effect of the margaritas began to wear off. He felt a pang of misgiving and wondered how big a mistake he had made. For the past twenty years, in the military and then working as an intelligence operative, he had been taken care of, his life structured by others. Now, insecurely, he was on his own.

You wanted a new beginning, a part of him said.

But what am I going to do?

A good first step would be to get a room.

And after that?

Try reinventing yourself.

To his annoyance, his professional training insisted – he couldn't help checking for surveillance as he crossed the Plaza toward a hotel called La Fonda. Its decades-old Hispanic-influenced lobby had warm dark soothing tones, but his instincts distracted him, nagging at him to ignore his surroundings and concentrate on the people around him. After getting a room, he again checked for surveillance as he walked back to the city's parking garage.

This has got to stop, he told himself. I don't have to live this way anymore.

A man with a salt-and-pepper beard, wearing khakis and a blue summer sweater oversized enough to conceal a handgun, followed him into the parking ramp. Decker paused next to the Intrepid, took out his car keys, and prepared to use them as a weapon, exhaling as the man got in a Range Rover and drove away.

This has got to stop, Decker repeated to himself.

He purposefully didn't check behind him as he drove to the La Fonda's parking garage and carried his suitcase up to his room. He deliberately ate dinner with his back to the dining-room entrance. He resolutely took a random night-time stroll through the downtown area, choosing rather than avoiding poorly lit areas.

In a wooded minipark next to a deep concrete channel through which a stream flowed, a figure emerged from shadows. 'Give me your wallet.'

Decker was dumbfounded.

'I've got a gun. I said, give me your fucking wallet.'

Decker stared at the street kid, who was barely visible. Then he couldn't help himself. He started laughing.

'What's so fucking funny?'

'You're holding me up? You've got to be kidding me. After all I've been through, after I force myself to be careless.'

'You won't think it's so fucking funny when I put a fucking bullet through you.'

'Okay, okay, I deserve this.' Decker pulled out his wallet and reached inside it. 'Here's all the money I've got.'

'I said I wanted your fucking wallet, not just your money.'

'Don't push your luck. I can spare the money, but I need my driver's license and my credit card.'

'Tough fucking shit. *Give it to me.*'

Decker broke both his arms, pocketed the gun, and threw the kid over the channel's rim. Hearing branches snap as if the kid had landed in bushes next to the stream, Decker leaned over the edge and heard him groan in the darkness below. 'You swear too much.'

He made a mental note of the nearest street names, found a payphone, told the 911 dispatcher where to send an ambulance, dropped the pistol into a sewer, and walked back to the La Fonda. At the hotel's bar, he sipped cognac as a countermeasure to adrenaline. A sign on the wall caught his attention.

'Is that a joke?' he asked the bartender. 'It's against the law to wear firearms in here?'

'A bar is about the only place where firearms *can't* be worn in New Mexico,' the bartender answered. 'You can walk down the street with one, as long as it's in plain sight.'

'Well, I'll be damned.'

72

'Of course, a lot of people don't follow the law. I just assume they're carrying a concealed weapon.'

'I'll be double damned,' Decker said.

'And everybody I know keeps one in their car.'

Decker stared at him as dumbfounded as when the kid in the minipark had tried to hold him up. 'Looks like there's something to be said for taking precautions.'

6

'The Frontiersman is a Christian gun shop,' the clerk said.

The statement caught Decker by surprise. 'Really,' was all he managed to say.

'We believe that Jesus expects us to be responsible for our own safety.'

'I think Jesus is right.' Decker glanced around at the racks of shotguns and rifles. His gaze settled on pistols in a locked glass counter. The store smelled sweetly of gun oil. 'I had in mind a Walther .380.'

'Can't do it. All out of stock.'

'Then how about a Sig-Sauer .928?'

'An excellent firearm,' the clerk said. He wore sneakers, jeans, a red plaid work shirt, and a Colt .45 semiautomatic on his belt. Stocky, in his mid-thirties, he had a sunburn. 'When the US military adopted the Beretta 9mm as its standard sidearm, the brass decided a smaller sidearm would be useful as a concealed weapon for intelligence personnel.'

'Really,' Decker said again.

The clerk unlocked the glass case, opened the lid, and took out a pistol the size of Decker's hand. 'It takes the same ammunition the Beretta does, 9mm. Holds a little less, thirteen in the magazine, one in the chamber. Double action, so you

73

don't have to cock it to shoot it – all you have to do is pull the trigger. But if the hammer *is* cocked and you decide not to fire, you can lower the hammer safely with this decocking lever on the side. Extremely well made. A first-rate weapon.'

The clerk removed the magazine and pulled back the slide on top, demonstrating that the pistol was empty. Only then did he hand it to Decker, who put the empty magazine back into the grip and pretended to aim at a poster of Saddam Hussein.

'You've certainly sold me,' Decker said.

'List price is nine hundred and fifty. I'll let you have it for eight hundred.'

Decker put his credit card on the counter.

'I'm sorry about this,' the clerk said, 'but Big Brother is watching. You can't have the pistol until you fill out this form and the police check you out to make sure you're not a terrorist or public enemy number one. More paperwork, thanks to the federal government. Costs you ten dollars.'

Decker looked at the form, which asked him if he was an illegal alien, a drug addict, and/or a felon. Did whoever designed the form actually believe that anyone would answer 'yes' to those questions? he wondered.

'How soon can I pick up the pistol?'

'The law says five days. Here's a reprint of a George Will article about the right to bear arms.'

Stapled to the article was a quotation from scripture, and that's when Decker realized how truly different the City Different was.

Outside, he basked in the morning sunlight, admiring the Sangre de Cristo mountains that rose dramatically just outside the eastern side of town. He still had trouble believing that he had come to Santa Fe. In his entire life, he had never been this impetuous.

As he drove away, he reviewed his active morning and the various arrangements he had made: opening a bank account, transferring money from the institution he had used in Virginia, contacting the local branch of the national stock-brokerage firm he used, phoning his landlord in Alexandria and agreeing to pay a penalty for breaking his lease in exchange for the landlord's agreeing to pack up and forward Decker's modest belongings. His numerous decisions had exhausted him and made the reality of his presence in Santa Fe increasingly vivid. The more arrangements he made, the more he committed himself to staying. And there were so many other decisions to make. He needed to turn in his rental car and buy a vehicle. He needed to find a place to live. He needed to figure out a way to employ himself.

On the car radio, he heard a report on public broadcasting's 'Morning Edition' about a trend among middle-aged mid-level corporate executives to abandon their high-pressure jobs (before their corporations downsized and eliminated their positions) and move to the western mountain states, where they started their own businesses and survived by their wits, finding that the adventure of working for themselves was exciting and fulfilling. The announcer called them 'lone eagles'.

At the moment, Decker felt alone, all right. The next thing I'd better do is find an alternative to a hotel room, he told himself. Rent an apartment? Buy a condo? How committed *am* I? What's a good deal? Do I simply check the listings in the newspaper? In confusion, he noticed a realtor's sign in front of one of the adobe houses on the wooded street he was driving along, and he suddenly knew he had an answer to more than just the question of where to set up housekeeping.

7

'A fixer-upper,' the woman said. She was in her late fifties, with short gray hair, a narrow sunwrinkled face, and plentiful turquoise jewelry. Her name was Edna Freed, and she was the owner of the agency whose sign Decker had noticed. This was the fourth property she had shown him. 'It's been on the market for over a year. An estate sale. Nobody lives here. The taxes, insurance, and maintenance fees are a nuisance to the estate. I'm authorized to say they're willing to accept less than their asking price.'

'What *is* the asking price?' Decker asked.

'Six hundred and thirty-five thousand.'

Decker raised his eyebrows. 'You weren't kidding when you told me this was a pricy market.'

'And getting pricier each year.' Edna explained that what was happening to Santa Fe had happened to Aspen, Colorado, twenty years earlier. Well-to-do tourists had gone to Aspen, fallen in love with that picturesque mountain community, and decided to buy property there, driving up values, squeezing out locals who had to move to housing they could afford only in other towns. Santa Fe was becoming equally expensive, mostly because of affluent newcomers from New York, Texas, and California.

'A house I sold last year for three hundred thousand came on the market again nine months later and went for three hundred and sixty,' Edna said. She wore a Stetson and wraparound sunglasses. 'As Santa Fe houses go, it was ordinary. It wasn't even adobe construction. All the contractor did was fix up a frame house and apply new stucco.'

'And this *is* adobe?'

'You bet.' Edna led him from her BMW, following a gravel lane to a high metal gate between equally high stuccoed walls. The gate had silhouettes of Indian petroglyphs. Beyond it were a courtyard and a portal. 'The place is incredibly solid. Knock on this wall next to the front door.'

Decker did. The impact of his knuckles made him feel as if

he tapped stone. He studied the house's exterior. 'I see some dry rot in the columns that support this portal.'

'You've got a good eye.'

'The courtyard's overgrown. Its inside wall needs restuccoing. But those repairs don't seem to justify your calling this a fixer-upper,' Decker said. 'What's the real problem? The place is on two acres in what you tell me is a desirable area, the museum district. It has views in every direction. It's attractive. Why hasn't it sold?'

Edna hesitated. 'Because it isn't one big house. It's two small houses joined by a common wall.'

'What?'

'To get from one structure to the other, you have to go outside and in through another door.'

'Who the hell would want that inconvenience?'

Edna didn't have an answer.

'Let's see the rest of it.'

'Despite the layout, you mean you might still be interested?'

'I have to check something out first. Show me the laundry room.'

Puzzled, Edna took him inside. The laundry room was off the garage. A hatch led to a crawlspace under the house. When Decker emerged from below, he swatted dust from his clothes, feeling satisfied. 'The electrical system looks about ten years old, the copper pipes a little more recent, both in good shape.'

'You *do* have a good eye,' Edna said. 'And you know where to look first.'

'There's no point in redesigning the place if the infrastructure needs work, too.'

'Redesigning?' Now Edna was even more baffled.

'The way the property is laid out, the garage is between the adjoining houses. But it's possible to convert the garage into a room, put a corridor in the back of that room, and knock out part of the common wall, so the corridor leads into the other house, unifying both halves.'

'Well, I'll be . . .' Edna glanced at the garage. 'I never noticed.'

Decker debated with himself. He hadn't planned on a house this expensive. He thought about his three hundred thousand dollars in savings, about the down payment and the mortgage payments and whether he wanted to be house poor. At the same time, the investment possibilities intrigued him. 'I'll offer six hundred thousand.'

'Less than the asking price? For this valuable property?'

'For what I believe you called a fixer-upper. Or did my suggestion suddenly make the house more appealing?'

'To the right kind of buyer.' Edna took a good look at him. 'Why do I get the idea you've done a lot of negotiating for property?'

'I used to be an international real-estate investment consultant.' Decker gave her a business card that the CIA had supplied him. 'The Rawley-Hackman Agency, based in Alexandria, Virginia. They're not Sotheby's International, but they handle a lot of special properties. My expertise was finding properties that had more value than they appeared to have.'

'Such as *this* one,' Edna said.

Decker shrugged. 'My problem is, six hundred thousand is absolutely as much as I can afford.'

'I'll make that point to my client.'

'Emphasize it, please. The standard twenty percent down payment is a hundred and twenty thousand. At the current rate of eight percent, a thirty-year mortgage on the remainder is . . .'

'I'll have to get my rate book from the car.'

'No need. I can do the math.' Decker scribbled on a notepad. 'About thirty-five hundred a month. A little more than forty-two thousand a year.'

'I've never seen anybody that quick with numbers.'

Decker shrugged again. 'One other problem – I can't afford the house if I don't have a job.'

'Such as selling real estate?' Edna burst out laughing. 'You've been trying to sell *me*.'

'Maybe a little.'

'I like your style.' Edna grinned. 'If you can sell me, you can sell anybody. You want a job, you've got one. The thing is, how are you going to afford the renovation?'

'That's easy. Cheap labor.'

'Where on earth do you hope to find that?'

Decker held out his hands. 'Right here.'

8

While serving in military special operations and later as a civilian intelligence operative, Decker had experienced fear on numerous occasions – missions that had gone wrong, threats that could not have been anticipated – but nothing matched the terror with which he woke in the middle of the ensuing night. His heart pounded sickeningly. Sweat stuck his T-shirt and boxer shorts to him. For a moment, he was disoriented, the darkness smothering. This wasn't his room in the La Fonda. Immediately he reminded himself that he had moved to a rental unit that Edna was managing. It was even smaller than the apartment he had given up in Alexandria, but at least it was cheaper than the La Fonda, and economizing was an urgent priority.

His mouth was dry. He couldn't find a light switch. He bumped his hip against a table as he groped his way to the sink in the tiny bathroom. He needed several glasses of water to satisfy his demanding thirst. He felt his way toward the single room's window and opened the twig shutters. Instead of a majestic view, he saw moonlight gleaming on cars in a parking lot.

What the hell have I done? he asked himself, beginning to sweat again. I've never owned anything big in my life. And I just signed papers committing myself to buying a six-hundred-thousand-dollar house that's going to cost me a hundred and twenty thousand down and forty-two thousand a year in mortgage payments. *Have I gone crazy?* What's the agency going to think when they hear I'm investing in serious real estate? They're going to wonder what makes me believe I can afford it. The truth is, I *can't* afford it, but *they* won't know that.

Decker couldn't help thinking of a recent scandal that involved an operative named Aldrich Ames who had passed secrets about the agency's Moscow network to the Russians in exchange for two and a half million dollars. The results had been disastrous – operations destroyed, agents executed. It had taken years before the agency's counterintelligence unit suspected a double agent and finally focused its attention on Ames. To the agency's horror, the counterintelligence team discovered that, as a part of a standard review, Ames had nearly failed two lie detector tests but that the results had been described as ambiguous and a judgment made in his favor. Further, the team learned that Ames had made extraordinary investments in real estate – several vacation homes and a ten-thousand-acre ranch in South America – and that he had hundreds of thousands of dollars in various bank accounts. Where on earth had the money come from? Not long afterward, Ames and his wife had been arrested for espionage. The agency, which had become lax about keeping an eye on the personal lives of its operatives, adopted new stringent security measures.

And I'm going to be the target of some of those measures, Decker warned himself. I'm already being watched because of my attitude when I quit. The papers I signed today are going to set off alarms. I have to call Langley first thing in the morning. I have to explain what I'm doing.

That'll be a trick. Just what *am* I doing? Decker touched a chair behind him and sank into it. The darkness pressed harder against him. The purchase agreement I signed has an escape clause, he reminded himself. When the house is inspected tomorrow, I'll use a flaw the inspector comes up with as an excuse to back out.

Right. I was too ambitious. Caution – that's the ticket. Slow and careful. Avoid doing anything out of the ordinary. Put the brakes on. Have numerous back-up plans. Don't be dramatic. I mustn't let my emotions get control of me.

For God's sake, he told himself, that's the way I've been living for the past ten years. I just described my life as an operative. He slammed his hand against the side of the chair. I dealt with fear before. What have I got to lose?

The chance to live.

Three weeks later, he took possession of the house.

9

Santa Fe was Julian's, El Nido, the Zia Diner, Pasqual's, Tomasita's, and countless other wonderful restaurants. It was margaritas, nachos, and red and green salsa. It was spectacular mornings, brilliant afternoons, and gorgeous evenings. It was ever-changing sunlight and constantly shifting high-desert colors. It was mountains in every direction. It was air so clean that there were views for hundreds of miles. It was landscapes that looked like Georgia O'Keefe paintings. It was the Plaza. It was the art galleries on Canyon Road. It was Spanish Market and Indian Market. It was Fiesta. It was watching the aspen turn autumn yellow in the ski basin. It was snow that made the city look like a Christmas card. It was candles stuck in sand in paper bags, lining the Plaza to illuminate it on Christmas Eve. It was glorious wild flowers in the spring. It was more hummingbirds than he had ever seen. It was the gentle rain that fell late every afternoon in July. It was the feel of the sun on his back, of sweat and the healthy ache of his muscles as he worked on his house.

It was peace.

THREE

1

'Steve, you're on floor duty today, right?' Edna asked.

In his office, Decker looked up from a buyer's offer that he was preparing for one of his clients. 'Until noon.' All the brokers in the agency were normally so busy showing properties that they seldom came into the office, but Edna insisted that someone always be available for walk-in clients and telephone inquiries, so each broker was required to spend a half-day every two weeks on 'floor duty'.

'Well, someone's in the lobby, looking for an agent,' Edna said. 'I'd handle it, but I have to get over to Santa Fe Abstract for a closing in fifteen minutes.'

'No problem. I'll take care of it.' Decker put the buyer's offer into a folder, stood, and headed toward the lobby. It was July, thirteen months after he had come to Santa Fe, and any doubts that he'd had about his ability to support himself had quickly vanished. Although some of Santa Fe's realtors failed and dropped out each year, he himself had done well. Techniques of elicitation that he had used to gain the confidence of operatives he was debriefing turned out to have application to making clients feel at ease. He was now up to four million dollars in sales, which provided a six percent commission of two hundred and forty thousand dollars. Of course, he had to split half of that with Edna, who provided office facilities, advertisements, and the nuisance details of running a business, not to mention an organization for Decker to disappear into. Even so, one hundred and twenty thousand was more than he had ever earned in one year in his life.

He came around a corner, approached the front desk, and saw a woman standing next to it, looking at a color brochure of available homes. With her head bowed, Decker couldn't see her features, but as he approached, he took in her lush auburn hair, tanned skin, and slim figure. She was taller than most women, about five foot seven, in excellent shape. Her outfit was distinctly East Coast: a nicely fitted, dark-navy Calvin Klein suit; smartly cut, low-heeled Joan & David shoes; pearl earrings; and a woven, Italian-leather black bag.

'May I help you?' Decker asked. 'You'd like to speak to an agent?'

The woman glanced up from the brochure. 'Yes.'

She smiled, and Decker felt something shift inside him. He didn't have time to analyze the sensation, except to compare it to the sudden change in heart rhythm, almost a lurch, that came during moments of fear. In this case, though, the sensation was definitely the opposite of fear.

The woman – in her early thirties – was gorgeous. Her skin glowed with health. Her blue-gray eyes glinted with intelligence and something else that was hard to identify, something appealingly enigmatic. She had a symmetrical face that was a perfect combination of a sculpted jaw, high cheekbones, and a model's forehead. Her smile was radiant.

Although Decker's lungs didn't want to work, he managed to introduce himself. 'Steve Decker. I'm an associate broker with the firm.'

The woman shook hands with him. 'Beth Dwyer.'

Her fingers felt so wonderfully smooth that Decker didn't want to release her hand. 'My office is just around the corner.'

As he led the way, he had a chance to try to adjust to the

pleasant tightness in his chest. There are certainly worse ways to earn a living, he thought.

The offices in the agency were spacious cubicles, their six-foot-high partitions constructed to look like adobe walls. Beth cast a curious gaze toward the tops of the partitions, which were decorated with gleaming black pottery and intricately patterned baskets from the local Indian pueblos.

'Those window seats that look like plaster benches – what are they called? *Bancos?*' Her voice was deep and resonant.

'That's right. *Bancos,*' Decker said. 'Most of the architectural terms here are Spanish. Can I get you anything? Coffee? Mineral water?'

'No, thanks.'

Beth peered around with interest at a Native American rug and other Southwestern decorations. She paid particular attention to some New Mexican landscape prints, walking over, leaning close to them. 'Beautiful.'

'The one that shows the white-water rapids in the Rio Grande gorge is my favorite,' Decker said. 'But just about any outdoor scene around here is beautiful.'

'I like the one *you* like.' Behind her attempt at good humor lurked a puzzling hint of melancholy. 'Even in a print, the delicacy of the brush strokes is obvious.'

'Oh? Then you know about painting?'

'I've spent most of my life trying to learn, but I'm not sure I ever will.'

'Well, if you're an artist, Santa Fe is a good place to be.'

'I could tell there was something about the light the moment I got here.' Beth shook her head in self-deprecation. 'But I don't think of myself as an artist. "Working painter" would be a more accurate description.'

'When did you get here?'

'Yesterday.'

'Since you want to buy property, I assume you've been here before, though.'

'Never.'

Decker felt as if a spark had struck him. He tried not to show a reaction, but reminded of his own experience in coming here, he found himself sitting straighter. 'And after a day, you've decided you like the area enough that you're interested in buying property here?'

'More than interested. Crazy, huh?'

'I wouldn't call it that.' Decker glanced down at his hands. 'I've known a few other people who decided to live here on the spur of the moment.' He looked at her again and smiled. 'Santa Fe makes people do unusual things.'

'That's why I want to live here.'

'Believe me, I understand. Even so, I wouldn't feel I was doing my job if I didn't caution you to take things slowly. Look at some properties, but give yourself a breathing space before you sign any documents.'

Beth crinkled her eyes, curious. 'I never expected to hear a real estate broker tell me *not* to buy something.'

'I'd be glad to sell you a house,' Decker said, 'but since this is your first time here, it might be better if you rented something first, to make certain Santa Fe is really the place for you. Some people move here from Los Angeles, and they can't stand the leisurely pace. They want to change the town so it matches their nervous energy.'

'Well, I'm not from Los Angeles,' Beth said, 'and the way my life has been going lately, a leisurely pace sounds mighty tempting.'

Decker assessed what she had just revealed about herself. He decided to wait before trying to learn anything else.

'A soft-sell realtor,' Beth said. 'I like that.'

'I call myself a facilitator. I'm not trying to sell property as much as I'm trying to make my client happy. A year down the road, I want you to have no regrets about whatever you decide to do, whether it's buying or not buying.'

'Then I'm in good hands.' Her blue-gray eyes – Decker had never seen eyes that color – brightened. 'I'd like to start looking as soon as possible.'

'I have appointments until two. Is that soon enough?'

'No instant gratification?' She laughed a little. The sound reminded Decker of wind chimes, although he sensed a pensiveness behind it. 'I guess two o'clock it will have to be.'

'In the meantime, if you can give me an idea of your price range— How do you like to be called? Mrs Dwyer? Or Beth? Or . . . ?' Decker glanced at her left hand. He didn't see a wedding ring. But that didn't always mean anything.

'I'm not married.'

Decker nodded.

'Call me by my first name.'

Decker nodded again. 'Fine, Beth.' His throat felt tight.

'And my price range is between six and eight hundred thousand.'

Decker inwardly came to attention, not having expected so high a figure. Normally, when potential clients came in to discuss houses in the upper six figures, they brought an attitude with them, as if they were doing Decker a big favor. In contrast, Beth was refreshingly natural, unassuming.

'Several first-rate properties are available in that price range,' Decker said. 'Between now and two, why don't you study these listings? There are prices and descriptions.' He decided to fish for more information about her. 'You'll probably want to discuss them with anyone who came to town with you. If you like, when we go out looking, bring a friend along.'

'No. It'll be just the two of us.'

Decker nodded. 'Either way is fine.'

Beth hesitated. 'I'm by myself.'

'Well, Santa Fe is a good town to be alone in without being lonely.'

Beth seemed to look at something far away. 'That's what I'm counting on.'

2

After Decker escorted Beth to the exit from the building, he remained at the open door and watched her stroll along the portal-roofed sidewalk. She had a grace that reminded him of the way female athletes moved when they weren't exerting themselves. Before she reached the corner, he made sure to step back inside the building in case she looked his way as she shifted direction. After all, he didn't want her to know that he was staring at her. In response to a question, he had told her that a good place to eat lunch was La Casa Sena, a restaurant that had outdoor tables beneath majestic shade trees in the gardened courtyard of a two-story Hispanic estate that dated back to the 1860s. She would enjoy the birds, the flowers, and the fountain, he had said, and now he wished that he was going there with her instead of heading off to deliver the buyer's offer that he had been working on when Beth arrived.

Normally, the chance to make another sale would have totally occupied Decker's thoughts, giving him a high. But today, business didn't seem that important. After presenting the offer and being told, as expected, that the seller needed the time allowed in the offer to consider it, Decker had a further appointment – lunch with a member of Santa Fe's Historic Design Review Board. Barely tasting his chicken fajitas, he managed to keep up his end of the conversation, but really, he was thinking of Beth Dwyer, their appointment at two, and how slowly the time was going.

Why, I'm missing her, he thought in surprise.

At last, after paying for lunch, he returned to the agency, only to feel his emotions drop when he found that Beth wasn't waiting for him.

'The woman who came in to see me this morning,' he told the receptionist. 'Thick auburn hair. Slightly tall. Attractive. Has she been back?'

'Sorry, Steve.'

Disappointed, he went down the corridor. Maybe she came in when the receptionist wasn't looking, he thought. Maybe she's waiting for me in my office.

But she wasn't. His emotions dropping farther as he sank into the chair behind his desk, he asked himself, What's the matter with me? Why am I letting myself feel this way?

Movement attracted his attention. Beth was standing at the entrance to his office. 'Hi.' Her smile made him feel that she had missed *him*.

Decker's heart seemed to shrink. So much like fear, he thought again, yet so much the opposite.

'I hope I'm not late,' she said.

'Right on time.' Decker hoped that he sounded natural. 'Did you have a good lunch?'

'It was even better than you led me to expect. The courtyard made me think I was in another country.'

'That's what Santa Fe does to people.'

'Northern Spain or a lush part of Mexico,' Beth said. 'But different from either.'

Decker nodded. 'When I first came here, I met someone who worked in the reservation department at one of the hotels. He said he often had people from the East Coast telephone him to ask what the customs restrictions were, the limit on duty-free goods that they could take back home, that sort of thing. He said he had a hard time convincing them that if they were Americans, there weren't any customs regulations here, that New Mexico was part of the United States.'

This time, Beth's laughter made him think of champagne. 'You're serious? They literally believed that this was a foreign country?'

'Cross my heart. It's a good argument for the need to teach geography in high school. So did you have a chance to study the listings I gave you?'

'When I wasn't devouring the best enchiladas I've ever tasted. I can't tell which I like better – the green or the red salsa. Finally I combined them.'

'The locals call that combination "Christmas".' Decker put on his leather jacket and crossed the room toward her. He loved the subtle fragrance of the sandalwood soap she used. 'Shall we go? My car is in the back.'

It was a Jeep Cherokee, its four-wheel-drive essential in winter or when exploring the mountains. Decker's color preference had been white, but when he'd bought the car a year earlier, his long experience as an intelligence operative had taken control of him, reminding him that a dark color was inconspicuous, compelling him to choose forest green. A part of him had wanted to be contrary and choose white anyhow, but old habits had been difficult to put away.

As he and Beth drove north along Bishop's Lodge Road, he pointed to the right past low shrubs and sunbathed adobe houses toward the looming Sangre de Cristo mountains. 'The first thing you have to know is, real estate values here are based in large part on the quality of the mountain views. Some of the most expensive houses tend to be in this area, the east, near the Sangres. This section also gives you a good view of the Jemez mountains to the west. At night, you can see the lights of Los Alamos.'

Beth gazed toward the foothills. 'I bet the views from there are wonderful.'

'This will make me sound like a New Ager, I'm afraid, but I don't think houses belong up there,' Decker said. 'They interfere with the beauty of the mountains. The people who live up there get a good view at the expense of everyone else's view.'

Intrigued, Beth switched her gaze toward Decker. 'You mean you actually discourage clients from buying houses on ridges?'

Decker shrugged.

'Even if it costs you a sale?'

Decker shrugged again.

' . . . I'm beginning to like you better and better.'

Decker drove her to houses she had found appealing in the listings he had shown her: one near Bishop's Lodge, two on the road to the ski basin, two along Acequia Madre. 'The name means Mother Ditch,' he explained. 'It refers to this stream that runs along the side of the road. It's part of an irrigation system that was dug several hundred years ago.'

'That's why the trees are so tall.' Beth looked around, enthused. 'The area's beautiful. What's the catch, though? Nothing's perfect. What's the downside of living around here?'

'Small lots and historic regulations. Plenty of traffic.'

'Oh.' Her enthusiasm faded. 'In that case, I guess we'd better keep looking.'

'It's almost five. Are you sure you're not tired? Do you want to call it a day?'

'I'm not tired if you're not.'

Hell, Decker thought, I'll drive around with you until midnight if you want me to.

He took her to a different area. 'This one's out near where I live. On the eastern edge of town, near that line of foothills. The nearest big hills are called Sun and Moon. You ought to hear the coyotes howl on them at night.'

'I'd like that.'

'This is *my* street.'

Beth pointed toward a sign on the corner. 'Camino Lindo. What's the translation?'

' "Beautiful road".'

'It certainly is. The houses blend with the landscape. Big lots.'

'That's my place coming up on the right.'

Beth leaned forward, turning her head as they passed it.

'I'm impressed.'

'Thanks.'

'And envious. Too bad *your* house isn't for sale.'

'Well, I put a lot of work into it. Mind you, the house just beyond mine *is* for sale.'

3

They walked along a gravel driveway past the chest-high sagebrush-like plants that Decker had been intrigued by when he first came to Santa Fe, and that he had learned were called chamisa. The attractive house was similar to Decker's – a sprawling, one-story adobe with a wall-enclosed courtyard.

'How much is it?' Beth asked.

'Near your upper limit. Seven hundred thousand.' Decker didn't get a reaction. 'It's had a lot of improvements. Sub-floor radiant heating. Solar-gain windows in back.'

Beth nodded absently as if the price didn't need to be justified. 'How big is the lot?'

'The same as mine. Two acres.'

She glanced to one side and then the other. 'I can't even see the neighbors.'

'Which in this case would be me.'

She looked at him strangely.

'What's the matter?' Decker asked.

'I think I'd enjoy living next to you.'

Decker felt his face turn red.

'Do you think the owner would mind being interrupted at this hour?'

'Not at all. The old gentleman who lived here had a heart attack. He moved back to Boston where he has relatives. He wants a quick sale.'

Decker showed her the front courtyard, its desert flowers and shrubs looking stressed from the July heat. He unlocked the carved front door, entered a cool vestibule, and gestured toward a hallway that led straight ahead toward spacious rooms. 'The house is still furnished. Tile floors. Vigas and latillas in all the ceilings.'

'Vigas and . . . ?'

'Large beams and small intersecting ones. It's the preferred type of ceiling in Santa Fe. Plenty of *bancos* and kiva fireplaces. Colorful Mexican wall tiles in the three bathrooms. A spacious kitchen. Food-prep island with a sink. Convection oven. Skylights and—' Decker stopped when he realized that Beth wasn't listening. She seemed spellbound by the mountain view from the living-room windows. 'Why don't I spare you the list? Take your time and look around.'

Beth walked slowly forward, glancing this way and that, assessing each room, nodding. As Decker followed, he felt selfconscious again – not awkward, not uneasy about himself, but literally conscious of himself, of the feel of his jeans and leather jacket, of the air against his hands and cheeks. He was conscious that he occupied space, that Beth was near him, that they were alone.

At once he realized that Beth was talking to him. 'What? I'm sorry. I didn't catch that,' Decker said. 'My mind drifted for a moment.'

'Does the purchase price include the furniture?'

'Yes.'
'I'll take it.'

4

Decker clicked glasses with her.

'It's such a wonderful house. I can't believe the owner accepted my offer so fast.' Beth took a celebratory swallow from her margarita. When she lowered the globe-shaped glass, some foam and salt remained on her upper lip. She licked them away. 'It's as if I'm dreaming.'

They were at a window table in a second-floor Hispanic restaurant called Garduño's. The place was decorated to look like a Spanish hacienda. In the background, a mariachi band strolled the floor, serenading enthusiastic customers. Beth didn't seem to know where to look first, out the window toward one of Santa Fe's scenic streets, at the band, at her drink, or at Decker. She took another sip. 'Dreaming.'

In the background, customers applauded for the guitarists and trumpeters. Beth smiled and glanced out the window. When she looked back at Decker, she wasn't smiling any longer. Her expression was somber. 'Thank you.'

'I didn't do much. All I did was take you around and—'

'You made me feel comfortable. You made it easy.' Beth surprised him by reaching across the table and touching his hand. 'You have no idea how much courage it took to do this.'

He loved the smoothness of her hand. 'Courage?'

'You must have wondered where I got seven hundred thousand dollars to pay for the house.'

'I don't pry. As long as I'm confident that the client can afford it . . .' He let his sentence dangle.

'I told you I was an artist, and I do make a living at it.

But— I also told you I wasn't married.'

Decker tensed.

'I used to be.'

Decker listened in confusion.

'I'm buying the house with . . .'

Money from a divorce settlement? he wondered.

' . . . a life insurance policy,' Beth said. 'My husband died six and a half months ago.'

Decker set down his glass and studied her, his feelings of attraction replaced by those of pity. 'I'm sorry.'

'That's about the only response that means anything.'

'What happened?'

'Cancer.' Beth seemed to have trouble making her voice work. She took another sip from her drink and stared at the glass. 'Ray had a mole on the back of his neck.'

Decker waited.

'Last summer, it changed shape and color, but he wouldn't go to the doctor. Then it started to bleed. Turned out to be the worst kind of skin cancer. Melanoma.'

Decker kept waiting.

Beth's voice became strained. 'Even though Ray had the mole cut out, he didn't do it soon enough to stop the cancer from spreading . . . Radiation and chemotherapy didn't work . . . He died in January.'

The mariachi band approached Decker's table, the music so loud that he could barely hear what Beth said. Urgent, he waved them away. When they saw the fierce expression in his eyes, they complied.

'So,' Beth said, 'I was lost. Still am. We had a house outside New York, in Westchester County. I couldn't stand living there any longer. Everything around me reminded me of Ray, of what I'd lost. People I thought were my friends felt awkward dealing with my grief and stayed away. I didn't think I could get more lonely.' She glanced down at her hands. 'A few days ago, I was at my psychiatrist's office when I came across a travel magazine in the waiting room. I think it was *Condé Nast Traveler*. It said that Santa Fe was one of the most popular tourist destinations in the world. I liked the photographs and the description of the city. On the spur of the moment . . .' Her voice trailed off.

A colorfully dressed waitress stopped at their table. 'Are you ready to order now?'

'No,' Beth said. 'I'm afraid I've lost my appetite.'

'We need more time,' Decker said.

He waited until the waitress was out of earshot. 'I've made some spur of the moment decisions myself. As a matter of fact, coming to Santa Fe was one of them.'

'And did it work out?'

'Even better than I hoped.'

'God, I hope I'll be able to say the same for me.' Beth traced a finger along the base of her glass.

'What did your psychiatrist say about your sudden decision?'

'I never told him. I never kept the appointment. I just set down the travel magazine and went home to pack. I bought a one-way ticket to Santa Fe.'

Decker tried not to stare, struck by how parallel their experiences were.

'No regrets,' Beth said firmly. 'The future can't possibly be any worse than the last year.'

5

Decker parked his Jeep Cherokee in a carport at the rear of his house. He got out, almost turned on a light so he could see to unlock his back door, but decided instead to lean against the metal railing and look up at the stars. The streets in this part of town didn't have lights. Most people in the area went to sleep early. With almost no light pollution, he was able to gaze up past the piñon trees toward unbelievably brilliant constellations. A three-quarter moon had begun to rise. The air was sweet and cool. What a beautiful night, he thought.

In the foothills, coyotes howled, reminding him that he had earlier mentioned them to Beth, making him wish that she were next to him listening to them. He could still feel her hand on his. During their dinner, they had managed to avoid further depressing topics. Beth had made a deliberate attempt to be festive as he walked her the short distance to the Inn of the Anasazi. At the entrance, they had shaken hands.

Now, as Decker continued to gaze up at the stars, he imagined what it would have been like to drive her from the restaurant, past the darkened art galleries on Canyon Road, past the garden walls of the homes along Camino del Monte Sol, finally arriving at Camino Lindo and the house next to his.

His chest felt hollow. You certainly are messed up, he told himself.

Well, I haven't fallen in love for a very long time. He searched his memory and was amazed to realize that the last time he had felt this way had been in his late teens before he entered the military. As he'd often told himself, military special operations and his subsequent career as an intelligence operative hadn't encouraged serious romantic involvement. Since coming to Santa Fe, he had met several women whom he had dated — nothing serious, just casual enjoyable evenings. With one of the women, he had had sexual relations. Nothing permanent had come out of it, however. As much as he liked the woman, he realized that he didn't want to spend the rest of his life with her. The feeling had evidently been mutual. The woman, a realtor for another agency, was now seeing someone else.

But Decker's present emotions were so different from what

he had felt toward that other woman that they unsettled him. He recalled having read that ancient philosophers considered love to be an illness, an unbalancing of mind and emotions. It sure is, he thought. But how on earth can it happen so fast? I always believed that love at first sight was a myth. He recalled having read about a subtle sexual chemical signal that animals and humans gave off, called pheromones. You couldn't smell them. They were detected biologically rather than consciously. The right person could give off pheromones that drove a person wild. In this case, Decker thought, the right person is absolutely beautiful, and she definitely has my kind of pheromones.

So what are you going to do? he asked himself. Obviously, there are problems. She's recently widowed. If you start behaving romantically toward her, she'll find you threatening. She'll resent you for trying to make her disloyal to the memory of her dead husband. Then it won't matter if she lives next door – she'll treat you as if she's living in the next state. Take it one day at a time, he told himself. You can't go wrong if you act truly as her friend.

6

'Steve, there's someone to see you,' the office receptionist said on the intercom.

'I'll be right out.'

'No need,' another voice said on the intercom, surprising him – a woman's voice whose sensuous resonance Decker instantly identified. 'I know the way.'

Heart beating faster, Decker stood. A few seconds later, Beth entered the office. In contrast with the dark suit she had worn yesterday, she now wore linen slacks and a matching tan jacket that brought out the color of her auburn hair. She looked even more gorgeous.

'How are you?' Decker asked.

'Excited. It's moving day.'

Decker didn't know what she meant.

'Last night, I decided I couldn't wait to move in,' Beth said. 'The house is already furnished. It seems a shame to leave it empty. So I telephoned the owner and asked if I could rent the house until the paperwork was done and I could buy it.'

'And he agreed?'

'He couldn't have been nicer. He said I could get the key from you.'

'You most certainly can. In fact, I'll drive you there.'

On the busy street outside his office, Decker opened his Cherokee's passenger door for her.

'I tossed and turned all night, wondering if I was doing the right thing,' Beth said.

'Sounds like me when *I* first came to town.'

'And how did you get over it?'

'I asked myself what my alternative was.'

'And?'

'I didn't have one,' Decker said. 'At least one that didn't mean the same as surrendering to what was wearing me down.'

Beth searched his eyes. 'I know what you mean.'

As Decker got in the car, he glanced across the street and felt something tighten inside him. A stationary man among a crowd of strolling tourists made Decker's protective instincts come to attention. What aroused his suspicion was that the man, who had been staring at Decker, turned immediately away as Decker noticed him. The man now stood with his back to the street, pretending to be interested in a window display of Southwestern jewelry, but his gaze was forward rather than downturned, indicating that what he was really doing was studying the reflection in the window. Decker checked his rearview mirror and saw the man turn to look in Decker's direction as Decker

101

drove away. Common-length hair, average height and weight, mid-thirties, undistinguished features, unremarkable clothes, muted colors. In Decker's experience, that kind of anonymity didn't happen by accident. The man's only distinguishing characteristic was the bulk of his shoulders, which his loose-fitting shirt didn't manage to conceal. He wasn't a tourist.

Decker frowned. So is it review time? he asked himself. Have they decided to watch me to see how I'm behaving, whether I've been naughty or nice, whether I'm any threat?

Beth was saying something about the opera.

Decker tried to catch up. 'Yes?'

'I like it very much.'

'I'm a jazz fanatic myself.'

'Then you don't want to go? I hear the Santa Fe Opera is one of the best.'

Decker finally realized what she was talking about. 'You're asking me to go to the opera with you?'

Beth chuckled. 'You weren't this slow yesterday.'

'What opera is it?'

'*Tosca.*'

'Well, in that case,' Decker said. 'Since it's Puccini. If it was Wagner, I wouldn't go.'

'Smart guy.'

Decker made himself look amused while he turned a corner and checked his rearview mirror to see if he was being followed. He didn't notice anything out of the ordinary. Maybe I'm wrong about that man watching me.

Like hell.

7

The opera house was a five-minute drive north of town, to the left, off the highway to Taos. Decker followed a string of cars along an upward winding road, their lights on as sunset began to fade.

'What a beautiful setting.' Beth glanced at the low shadowy piñon-covered hills on both sides of the car. She was even more impressed after they reached the top of a bluff, parked the car in twilight, and strolled to the amphitheater built down into the far side of the bluff. She was intrigued by the appearance of the people around her. 'I can't tell if I'm underdressed or overdressed.' She herself wore a lace shawl over a thin-strapped black dress that was highlighted by a pearl necklace. 'Some of these people are wearing tuxedos and evening gowns. But some of them look like they're on a camping expedition. They've got hiking boots, jeans, wool shirts. That woman over there is carrying a knapsack and a parka. I'm having a reality problem. Are we all going to the same place?'

Decker, who wore a sports coat and slacks, chuckled. 'The amphitheater has open sides as well as an open roof. Once the sun is down, the desert gets cool, sometimes as low as forty-five. If a wind picks up, that lady in the evening dress is going to wish she had the parka you mentioned. During intermission, there'll be a lot of people buying blankets from the concession booth. That's why I brought this lap-robe I've got tucked under my arm. We might need it.'

They surrendered their tickets, crossed a welcoming open courtyard, and followed the ticket-taker's directions, mingling with a crowd that went up stairs to a row of wide wooden doors that led to various sections of the upper tier of seats.

'This door is ours,' Decker said. He gestured for Beth to go ahead of him, and as she did, he took advantage of that natural-seeming moment to glance back over his shoulder, scanning the courtyard below to discover if he was still under surveillance. It was a reversion to old habits, he realized with some bitterness.

Why did he allow himself to care? The surveillance was pointless. What possible compromising activity would his former employer think he was up to at the opera? His precaution told him nothing; there was no evidence of anyone below who showed more interest in him than in getting into the opera house.

Careful not to reveal his preoccupation, Decker sat with Beth to the right on an upper tier. They didn't have the best seats in the house, he noted, but they certainly couldn't complain. For one thing, their section of the amphitheater wasn't open to the sky, so while they had a partial view of the stars through the open space above the middle seats, their seats in the back didn't expose them as much to the cool night air.

'That opening in the middle of the roof,' Beth said. 'What happens when it rains? Does the performance stop?'

'No. The singers are protected.'

'But what about the audience in the middle seats?'

'They get wet.'

'Stranger and stranger.'

'There's more. Next year, you'll have to go to the opening of the opera season in early July. The audience has a tailgate party in the parking lot.'

'Tailgate party? You mean like at football games?'

'Except in this case, they drink champagne and wear tuxedos.'

Beth burst out laughing. Her amusement was contagious. Decker was pleased to discover that the surveillance on him was forgotten, that he was laughing with her.

The lights dimmed. *Tosca* began. It was a good performance. The first act – about a political prisoner hiding in a church – was appropriately threatening and moody, and if no one could equal Maria Callas's legendary performances of the title role, the evening's soprano gave it an excellent try. When the first act ended, Decker applauded enthusiastically.

But as he glanced toward the lower level, toward a

refreshment area to the left of the middle seats, he suddenly froze.

'What's the matter?' Beth asked.

Decker didn't respond. He kept peering toward the refreshment area.

'Steve?'

Feeling pressure behind his ears, Decker finally answered. 'What makes you think something's the matter?'

'The look on your face. It's like you saw a ghost.'

'Not a ghost. A business associate who broke an agreement.' Decker had seen the man who had been watching him earlier in the day. The man, wearing a nondescript sports coat, stood near the refreshment area down there, ignoring the activity around him, staring up in Decker's direction. He wants to see if I remain up here or go back through those doors and outside, Decker thought. If I leave, he's probably got a lapel mike that allows him to tell a partner with an earphone that I'm headed in the other man's direction. 'Forget him. I won't let him spoil our evening,' Decker said. 'Come on, would you like some hot chocolate?'

They went back to the doors through which they had entered, walked along a balcony, and descended stairs to the crowded courtyard. Surrounded by people, Decker couldn't determine who else might be watching him as he guided her around the left side of the opera house toward the refreshment area where he had seen the man.

But the man wasn't there any longer.

8

Throughout the intermission, Decker managed to make small talk, finally escorting Beth back to their seats. She gave no indication that she suspected his tension. When *Tosca*'s second act began, the burden of not spoiling Beth's evening was temporarily removed from him, and he could concentrate his full attention on what the hell was happening.

From one point of view, the situation made sense, he thought – the agency was still concerned about his outraged reaction to the disastrous Rome operation, and they wanted to make sure he hadn't vented his emotions by finding a way to betray them, selling information about secret operations. One indication of whether he was being paid for information would be how hard he worked as a real-estate broker and whether he spent more money than was commensurate with his income level.

Fine, Decker thought. I expected a review. But surely they would have done it sooner, and surely they could have done it from a distance simply by monitoring my real-estate transactions, my stock and bond accounts, and what I've got in the bank. Why, after more than a year, are they watching me so closely? At the opera, for God's sake.

In the dark, Decker squinted toward the intricately decorated 1800 Italian set, so absorbed in his thoughts that he barely heard Puccini's brooding music. Unable to resist the impulse, Decker turned his head and focused on the shadowy refreshment area to the left of the middle seats, where he had last seen the man who was watching him.

His back muscles became rigid. The man was down in that area again, and there wasn't any way to misinterpret the man's intentions, not when he ignored the opera and peered up in Decker's direction. Evidently the man assumed that he had not been spotted and that the shadows he stood among were sufficient protection for him to continue to keep from being seen. The man didn't realize that the lights from the stage spilled in his direction.

What Decker next reacted to sent a shock of alarm through

his nervous system. Not a ghost, but it might as well have been, so startling was another man's appearance, so unexpected, so impossible. The second man had emerged from shadows and stopped next to the first man, discussing something with him. Decker told himself that he had to be mistaken, that it was merely an illusion created by the distance. Just because the man seemed to be in his early thirties, had short blond hair, and was somewhat overweight with beefy shoulders and rugged square features didn't mean anything. Lots of men looked like that. Decker had met any number of former college football players who—

The blond man gestured forcefully with his right hand to emphasize something he said to the other man, and Decker's stomach contracted as he became absolutely convinced that his suspicion was correct. The blond man down there was the same man who had been responsible for the deaths of twenty-three Americans in Rome, who had been the reason Decker resigned from the agency. The operative in charge of putting Decker under surveillance was Brian McKittrick.

'Excuse me,' Decker told Beth. 'I need to use the rest room.' He edged past a man and woman sitting next to him. Then he was out of the row, up the stairs, through the doors in back.

On the deserted balcony, he immediately broke into a run. At the same time, he studied the moonlit area below him, but if a member of the surveillance team was in the courtyard, Decker didn't see him. There wasn't time to be thorough. Decker was too busy scrambling down the stairs and charging toward the dimly lit left side of the opera house, the direction in which he had seen McKittrick disappear.

The anger he had felt in Rome again flooded through him. He wanted to get his hands on McKittrick, to slam him against a wall and demand to know what was going on. As he raced along the side of the opera house, anguished music throbbed into the high desert night. Decker hoped that it obscured the scrape of his hurried footsteps on concrete steps. At once caution controlled him. Wary, he slowed, staying close to the wall, stalking past the rest rooms, studying the shadows near the refreshment stand, the last place he had seen McKittrick.

No one was there. How could I have missed them? he thought. If they came along the side of the opera house, we would have bumped into each other. Unless they had seats in the amphitheater, Decker told himself. Or unless they heard me coming and hid. Where? In a rest room? Behind the refreshment stand? Behind the wall that separates this area from the desert?

Despite the music swelling from the amphitheater, he heard the sound of movement behind night-obscured piñon trees on the opposite side of the wall. Are McKittrick and the other man watching me from out there? For the first time, Decker felt vulnerable. He crouched so that the low wall gave him cover.

He thought about vaulting the wall to pursue the noises. As quickly, he told himself that in the greater darkness behind the wall, he'd be putting himself at a tactical disadvantage, the noise of his own footsteps warning McKittrick that he was coming. The only other course of action was to race back along the sidewalk next to the amphitheater and wait in front for McKittrick and his partner to come out from the desert. Or maybe they'll just go to the parking lot and drive to town. Or maybe those noises you heard were just a wild dog's paws on the ground. And maybe, damn it, I ought to quit asking myself questions and demand that somebody give me some answers.

9

'Decker, have you any idea what time it is?' his former superior complained. The man's voice was thick from having been

wakened. 'Couldn't this have waited until the morning instead
of—'

'Answer me,' Decker insisted. He was using a payphone in a
shadowy corner of the deserted courtyard in front of the opera
house. 'Why am I under surveillance?'

'I don't know what you're talking about.'

'*Why are your people watching me?*' Decker clutched the
phone so hard that his knuckles ached. Intense music swelled
from the theater and echoed toward him.

'Whatever's going on, it has nothing to do with me.' His
former superior's name was Edward. Decker remembered the
sixty-three-year-old man's sagging cheeks that always turned
red when he was under tension. 'Where are you?'

'You know exactly where I am.'

'Still in Santa Fe? Well, if you are in fact being watched—'

'Do you think I could possibly make a mistake about
something like that?' Despite the emotion in his words, Decker
strained to keep his voice from projecting across the courtyard,
hoping that a crescendo of angry singing concealed his own
anger.

'You're overreacting,' Edward said wearily over the phone.
'It's probably only a routine follow-up.'

'Routine?' Decker studied the deserted courtyard to make
sure no one was coming toward him. 'You think it's routine that
the jerk I worked with thirteen months ago is in charge of the
surveillance team?'

'Thirteen months ago? You're talking about—'

'Are you going to make me be specific over the phone?'
Decker asked. 'I told you then, and I'm telling you now – I will
not leak information.'

'The man you worked with before you resigned – *he's* the one
watching you?'

'You actually sound surprised.'

'Listen to me.' Edward's aging, raspy voice became louder, as if he was speaking closer to the phone. 'You have to understand something. I don't work there anymore.'

'What?' Now it was Decker's turn to sound surprised.

'I took early retirement six months ago.'

Decker's forehead throbbed.

'My heart condition got worse. I'm out of the loop,' Edward said.

Decker straightened as he saw movement on the theater's balcony. His chest tight, he watched someone walk along it and stop at the steps down to the courtyard.

'I'm being absolutely candid with you,' Edward said on the phone. 'If the man you worked with last year is watching you, I don't know who ordered him to do it or why.'

'Tell them I want it stopped,' Decker said. On the balcony, the person – it was Beth – frowned in his direction. Hugging her shawl, she descended the stairs. The music intensified.

'I don't have any influence with them anymore,' Edward said.

Beth reached the bottom of the courtyard and began to cross toward him.

'*Just make sure you tell them to stop.*'

Decker broke the connection as Beth reached him.

'I got worried about you.' A cool breeze tugged at Beth's hair and made her shiver. She tightened her shawl around her. 'When you didn't come back—'

'I'm sorry. It was business. The last thing I wanted was to leave you alone up there.'

Beth studied him, puzzled.

From the theater, the singing reached a peak of anguish and desperation. Beth turned toward it. 'I think that's where Scarpia promises Tosca that if she sleeps with him, her lover won't be executed.'

Decker's mouth felt dry, as if he had tasted ashes, because he

110

had lied. 'Or maybe it's where Tosca stabs Scarpia to death.'

'So do you want to stay and hear the rest, or go home?' Beth sounded sad.

'Go home? God, no. I came to enjoy myself with you.'

'Good,' Beth said. 'I'm glad.'

As they started back toward the theater, the music reached an absolute peak. Abrupt silence was broken by applause. Doors opened. The audience started coming out for another intermission.

'Would you like more hot chocolate?' Decker asked.

'Actually, right now I could use some wine.'

'I'll join you.'

10

Decker escorted Beth through her shadowy gate, into the flower-filled courtyard, pausing beneath the portal and the light that Beth had left on above her front door. She continued to hug her shawl tightly around her. Decker couldn't tell if that was from nervousness.

'You weren't kidding about how cool it can get at night, even in July.' Beth inhaled deeply, savoring something. 'What's that scent in the air? It smells almost like sage.'

'It's probably from the chamisa bushes that line your driveway. They're related to sagebrush.'

Beth nodded, and Decker was certain now that she was indeed nervous. 'Well.' She held out her hand. 'Thank you for a wonderful evening.'

'My pleasure.' Decker shook hands with her. 'And again, I apologize for leaving you alone.'

Beth shrugged. 'I wasn't offended. Actually, I'm used to it. It's the sort of thing my husband did. He was always interrupting social evenings to take business calls or make them.'

'I'm sorry if I brought back painful memories.'

'It's not your fault. Don't worry about it.' Beth glanced down, then up. 'This was a big step for me. Last night and tonight are the first times since Ray died—' She hesitated. ' . . . that I've gone out with another man.'

'I understand.'

'I often wondered if I'd be able to make myself go through with it,' Beth said. 'Not just the awkwardness of dating again after having been married for ten years, but even more—' She hesitated again. 'The fear that I'd be disloyal to Ray.'

'Even though he's gone,' Decker said.

Beth nodded.

'Emotional ghosts,' Decker said.

'Exactly.'

'And?' Decker asked. 'How do you feel now?'

'You mean, aside from having flashbacks to being a nervous teenager on the doorstep saying good night to her first date?' Beth chuckled. 'I think—' She sobered. 'It's complicated.'

'I'm sure it is.'

'I'm glad I did it.' Beth took a long breath. 'No regrets. I meant what I said. Thank you for a wonderful evening.' She looked pleased with herself. 'Hey, I was even adult enough to do the asking, to invite *you* to go out with *me*.'

Decker laughed. 'I enjoyed being asked. If you'd let me, I'd like to return the favor.'

'Yes,' Beth said. 'Soon.'

'Soon,' Decker echoed, knowing that she meant she needed a little distance.

Beth pulled a key from a small purse and put it into the lock. In the foothills, coyotes howled. 'Good night.'

'Good night.'

11

Wary, Decker checked for surveillance as he went home. Nothing seemed out of the ordinary. In the days to come, he remained vigilant in his search for anyone watching him, but his efforts achieved no results. McKittrick and his team were no longer in evidence. Perhaps Edward had relayed Decker's message. The surveillance had been called off.

FOUR

1

It seemed to happen slowly, but in retrospect, there was an inevitability about it that made Decker think time was hurrying them. He saw Beth often in the days to come, giving her advice about the mundane matters of where the best grocery stores were and how to find the nearest post office and whether there were real-life reasonably priced stores away from the touristy expensive boutiques near the Plaza.

Decker took Beth hiking up the arroyo next to St John's College, past the Wilderness Gate subdivision, to the top of Atalaya Mountain. It was a measure of how good her physical condition was that she was able to complete the three-hour hike, even though her body had not yet fully adjusted to the high altitude. Decker took her to the massive flea market that occurred on weekends on a field below the opera house. They went to the Indian cliff-dwelling ruins at Bandelier National Monument. They played tennis at the Sangre de Cristo Racquet Club. When they got tired of New Mexican food, they ate turkey meatloaf and gravy at Harry's Roadhouse. Often they just barbecued chicken at Beth's place or Decker's. They went to foreign movies at the Jean Cocteau Cinema and Coffee House. They went to Indian Market and the related auction at the Wheelwright Museum, only a short walk from Camino Lindo. They went to the horse races and the Pojoaque Pueblo casino. Then on Thursday, September 1, at eleven in the morning, Beth met Decker at the Santa Fe Abstract and Title Company, signed documents, handed over a check, and gained ownership of her house.

2

'Let's celebrate,' Beth said.

'You're going to hate me for saying I've got several appointments I absolutely have to keep.'

'I didn't mean right now.' Beth nudged him. 'I might be stealing all your time, but I do admit, once in a while you have to make a living. I meant tonight. I'm sick of eating fat-free white meat all the time. Let's be sinful and barbecue two juicy T-bones. I'll bake some potatoes and make a salad.'

'That's your idea of a celebration – not going out?'

'Hey, this will be my first night as a Santa Fe property owner. I want to stay home and admire what I bought.'

'I'll bring the red wine.'

'And champagne,' Beth added. 'I feel as if I should crack a bottle of champagne against the front gate, sort of like launching a ship.'

'Would Dom Perignon be good enough?'

3

When Decker arrived at six as they had agreed, he was surprised to see an unfamiliar car in Beth's driveway. Assuming that a maintenance person would have used a truck or a car with a business name on it, wondering who would be visiting at this hour, he parked beside the unmarked car, got out, and noted that the blue Chevrolet Cavalier had an Avis rental-car folder on its front passenger seat. As he walked along the gravel driveway toward the front gate, the carved door beyond it came open and Beth appeared beneath the portal with a man whom Decker had never seen before.

The man was slender and wore a business suit. Of medium height, with soft features, he had thinning, partially gray hair and looked to be in his early fifties. His suit was blue, decently cut, but not expensive. His shirt was white and emphasized the pallor of his skin. Not that the man looked sick. It was just that his suit and his lack of a tan were a good indication that he wasn't from Santa Fe. In the year and a quarter that Decker had been living in the area, he hadn't seen more than a dozen men wearing suits, and half of them had been on business from out of town.

The man stopped talking in the middle of a sentence, ' . . . would cost too much for—' and turned toward Decker, raising his narrow eyebrows in curiosity as Decker opened the front gate and approached them beneath the portal.

'Steve.' Buoyant, Beth kissed him on the cheek. 'This is Dale Hawkins. He works for the gallery that sells my paintings in New York. Dale, this is the good friend I told you about – Steve Decker.'

Hawkins smiled. 'To hear Beth tell it, she couldn't have survived here without you. Hi.' He held out his hand. 'How are you?'

'If Beth's been saying good things about me, I'm definitely in an excellent mood.'

Hawkins chuckled, and Decker shook hands with him.

'Dale was supposed to be here yesterday, but some business in New York held him up,' Beth said. 'In all the excitement about closing the deal on the house, I forgot to tell you he was coming.'

'I've never been here before,' Hawkins said. 'But already I

realize that the visit is long overdue. The play of sunlight is amazing. The mountains must have changed color a half-dozen times while I was driving up from Albuquerque.'

Beth looked terribly pleased. 'Dale came with good news. He managed to sell three of my paintings.'

'To the same buyer,' Hawkins said. 'The client is very enthusiastic about Beth's work. He wants to have a first look at anything new she does.'

'And he paid five thousand dollars for the first-look privilege,' Beth said excitedly, 'not to mention a hundred thousand for the group of three paintings.'

'A hundred ... thousand?' Decker grinned. 'But that's fantastic.' Impulsively, he hugged her.

Beth's eyes glistened. 'First the house, now this.' She returned Decker's hug. 'I have plenty to celebrate.'

Hawkins looked as if he felt out of place. 'Well.' He cleared his throat. 'I ought to be going. Beth, I'll see you tomorrow morning at nine.'

'Yes, at Pasqual's for breakfast. You remember my instructions how to get there?'

'If I forget, I'll ask someone at the hotel.'

'Then I'll show you around the galleries,' Beth said. 'I hope you like walking. There are over two hundred of them.'

Decker felt obligated to make the offer. 'Would you like to stay and have dinner with us?'

Hawkins raised his hands in amusement. 'Lord, no. I can tell when I'm in the way.'

'If you're sure.'

'Positive.'

'I'll go out with you to your car,' Beth said.

Decker waited under the portal while Beth went and spoke briefly to Hawkins in the driveway. Hawkins got in his car, waved, and drove away.

Beth made a little skipping motion, beaming as she returned to Decker. She pointed toward the paper bag he was holding. 'Is that what I think it is?'

'The red wine and the Dom Perignon. The champagne's been chilling all afternoon.'

'I can't wait to open it.'

4

Beth twitched her nose as champagne bubbles tickled it. 'Would you like to see a surprise?'

'*Another* one?' The Dom Perignon trickled brightly over Decker's tongue. 'This is turning into quite a day.'

'I'm a little nervous about showing you, though.'

Decker wasn't sure what she meant. 'Nervous?'

'It's very private.'

Now Decker *really* didn't know what she meant. 'If you want to show me.'

Beth seemed to make a decision, nodding firmly. 'I do. Follow me.'

They left the handsomely tiled kitchen, crossed a colorful cotton dhurry rug in the living room, and went down a skylit corridor at the front of the house. It led past a door to the laundry room and took them to another door. *That* door was closed. Whenever Decker had visited Beth, she had kept what was in there a secret.

Now she hesitated, looked deeply into Decker's aquamarine eyes, and let out a long deep breath. 'Here goes.'

When she opened the door, Decker's first impression was of color. Splotches of red and green, blue and yellow. A brilliant rainbow seemed to have burst, its myriad parts spread before him. His second impression was of shape, of images and

121

textures that blended together as if they shared a common life force.

Decker was silent a moment, so impressed that he couldn't move.

Beth studied him more intensely. 'What do you think?'

' "Think" isn't the word. It's what I *feel*. I'm overwhelmed.'

'Really?'

'They're beautiful.' Decker stepped forward, glancing all around the room at paintings on easels, paintings leaning against the walls, other paintings hanging above them. 'Stunning.'

'I'm so relieved.'

'But there must be . . .' Decker did a quick count. ' . . . over a dozen. And they're all about New Mexico. When did you—'

'Every day since the day I moved in, whenever I wasn't with you.'

'But you didn't tell me a word about them.'

'I was too nervous. What if you hadn't liked them? What if you had said they were like every other local artist's work?'

'But they're not. They're very definitely not.' Decker walked slowly from one to another, taking in their images, admiring them.

One, in particular, attracted his attention. It showed a dry creek bed with a juniper tree and red wild flowers on the rim. It appeared simple and unpretentious. But Decker couldn't help feeling that there was something beneath the surface.

'What's your opinion?' Beth asked.

'I'm afraid I'm more comfortable looking at paintings than talking about them.'

'It's not so hard. What do you notice first? What dominates?'

'The red wild flowers.'

'Yes,' Beth said. 'I got interested in them the moment I found out what they were called: "Indian paintbrush".'

'You know, they do look like artist's brushes,' Decker said. 'Straight and slender with red bristles on top.' He thought a moment. 'A painting about flowers called paintbrushes.'

'You're getting it,' Beth said. 'Art critics describe this sort of thing as "self-referential", a painting about painting.'

'Then that might explain something else I'm noticing,' Decker said. 'Your swirling brushstrokes. The way everything blends together. What's the technique called? Impressionism? It reminds me of Cezanne and Monet.'

'Not to mention Renoir, Degas, and *especially* Van Gogh,' Beth said. 'Van Gogh was a genius at depicting sunlight, so I figured I could make the painting more self-referential if I used Van Gogh's techniques to depict the uniqueness of New Mexico.'

' "The Land of the Dancing Sun".'

'You're very quick. I'm trying to catch the peculiar quality of Santa Fe's light. But if you look closely, you can also see symbols hidden in the landscape.'

' . . . well, I'll be damned.'

'Circles, ripples, sunburst patterns. The symbols the Navajo and other Southwestern Indians use to represent nature.'

'References within references,' Decker said.

'All intended to make the viewer sense that even an apparently simple creek bed rimmed by a juniper tree and red wild flowers can be complicated.'

'Beautiful.'

'I was so nervous that you wouldn't like them.'

'What did your art dealer say about them?' Decker asked.

'Dale? He was certain he could sell them all.'

'Then what does *my* opinion matter?'

'It matters, believe me.'

Decker turned to stare at her. Pulse racing, he couldn't stop himself. '*You're* beautiful.'

She blinked, startled. 'What?'

The words rushed out of him. 'I think about you all the time. I can't get you out of my mind.'

Beth's tan turned pale.

'I'm sure this is the biggest mistake I ever made,' Decker said. 'You need to feel free. You need space and— You'll probably avoid me from now on. But I have to say it. I love you.'

5

Beth studied him for what seemed the longest while.

I've really messed this up, Decker thought. Why couldn't I have kept my mouth shut?

Beth's gaze was intense.

'Bad timing, I guess,' Decker said.

Beth didn't answer.

'Can we go back?' Decker asked. 'Can we pretend this never happened?'

'You can never go back.'

'That's what I was afraid of.'

'And it *did* happen.'

'It certainly did.'

'You'll regret it,' Beth said.

'Do you want me to leave?'

'Hell, no. I want you to kiss me.'

The next thing Decker realized, he had his arms around her. The back of his neck tingled from the touch of her hands. When they kissed, he felt as if his breath had been taken away. At first, her lips were closed, their pressure against his tentative. Then her lips parted. Her tongue met his, and he had never felt so powerfully intimate a touch. The kiss lengthened and deepened. Decker began to tremble. He couldn't control the reaction. He had risked his life countless times as a member of military special operations and as an intelligence operative. He had encountered fear in its most powerful forms. What he was feeling now had all the symptoms of fear, but the emotion was quite the opposite. It was ecstasy. His fingertips became numb. His heart pounded with chest-swelling speed. When he lowered his hands to cup her hips, he trembled harder. He pressed his lips against her neck, aroused by the lingering scent of delicate soap and of the deeper primal smell of salt and musk, earth and heat and sky. It filled his nostrils. It made him feel that he was suffocating. He unbuttoned her blouse and slid his hands beneath her brassiere, touching her breasts, her nipples growing, hardening to his touch. His legs would no longer support him. He sank to his knees, kissing the silken skin of her stomach. With a shudder, she sank lower, drawing him to the floor. They embraced and rolled, kissing more deeply. He seemed to float, feeling as if he had been taken out of his body. Simultaneously he was conscious *only* of his body, of *Beth's* body. He wanted to go on kissing and touching her forever, to touch more and more of her. Hurrying, needing, they undressed each other. When he entered her, he felt transported. He couldn't get far enough within her. He wanted to be totally one with her. When they came, he felt suspended in a moment between frenzied heartbeats that lengthened and swelled and erupted.

6

Decker opened his eyes, peering up at the vigas and latillas that beamed the flat ceiling. The evening sun cast a crimson glow through a window. Silent, Beth lay next to him. In fact, she had not spoken for several minutes, since the moment she had climaxed. But as the silence persisted, Decker became uneasy, worried that she was in the throes of regret, second thoughts, guilt that she had been unfaithful to her dead husband. Slowly, she moved, turning to him, touching his cheek.

So it was going to be all right, he thought.

Naked, Beth rose to a sitting position. Her breasts were firm, the size of Decker's cupped palms. He recalled the exquisite hardness of her nipples.

She glanced down at the brick floor she sat upon. They were still in the room where she kept her paintings, the glorious color of which surrounded them. 'Passion is wonderful. But sometimes there's a price to pay.' She chuckled again. 'These bricks. I bet I've got bruises on my spine.'

'My knees and elbows have the top layer of skin scraped off,' Decker said.

'Let me see. Ouch,' Beth said. 'If we'd got any wilder, we'd have to go to the emergency ward.'

Decker started laughing. He couldn't stop himself. It kept coming and coming. Tears welled from his eyes.

Beth laughed, as well: a soul-releasing expression of joy. She leaned toward him and kissed him again, but this time the kiss communicated tenderness and affection. She touched his strong chin. 'What you said before we— Did you mean it?'

'Completely and totally. The words seem inadequate. I love you,' Decker said. 'So much so that I feel as if I didn't know anything about myself until this moment, that I've never been truly alive until now.'

'You didn't say you're a poet as well as an art critic.'

'There's a lot you don't know about me,' Decker said.

'I can't wait to learn it all.' Beth kissed him again and stood.

Decker felt a tightness in his throat as he admired her nakedness. It pleased him that she was comfortable with his admiration. She stood before him, her hands next to her hips, her nude body angled slightly sideways, one foot before the other and positioned at a right angle, suggestive of a dancer's pose, natural, without any trace of embarrassment. Her navel formed a tiny hollow in her flat stomach. Her dark pubic hair was soft and tufted. Her body had the contoured, supple tone of an athlete. Decker was reminded of the sensuous way in which ancient Greek sculptors portrayed nude women.

'What's that on your left side?' Beth asked.

'My side?'

'That scar.'

Decker looked down at it. The jagged indentation was the size of the tip of a finger. 'Oh, that's just—'

'You have another one on your right thigh.' Frowning, Beth knelt to examine them. 'If I didn't know better, I'd say—'

Decker couldn't think of a way to avoid the subject. 'They're from bullet wounds.'

'Bullet wounds? How on earth did—'

'I didn't know enough to duck.'

'What are you talking about?'

'I was with the US Rangers that invaded Grenada back in '83.' Again it grieved Decker to have to lie to her. 'When the shooting broke out, I didn't hit the ground fast enough.'

'Did they give you a medal?'

'For stupidity?' Decker chuckled. 'I did get a Purple Heart.'

'They look painful.'

'Not at all.'

'Can I touch them?'

'Be my guest.'

Gently, she placed a finger into the dimple on his side and then into the one on his thigh. 'You're sure they don't hurt?'

'Sometimes on damp winter nights.'

'When that happens, tell me. I know how to make them feel better.' Beth leaned down to kiss one, then the other. Decker felt her breasts slide along his abdomen toward his thigh. 'How does that work for you?' she asked.

'Everything's working just fine. Too bad they didn't have nurses like you when I was taken to a military hospital.'

'You wouldn't have gotten any sleep.' Beth snuggled next to him.

'Sleep isn't everything,' Decker said.

It was enough to lie close to her, enjoying her warmth. Neither of them moved or spoke for several minutes. Through the window, the crimson of the sunset deepened.

'I think it's time for a shower,' Beth said. 'You can use the one off the guest room, or . . .'

'Yes?'

'We can share mine.'

The gleaming white shower was spacious, doubling as a steam area. It had a built-in tiled bench and jets on each side. After lathering and sponging each other as the spray of hot water streamed over them, after kissing and touching, stroking, caressing, and exploring as steam billowed around them, their slippery bodies sliding against each other, they sank to the bench and made trembling, heart-pounding love again.

7

The evening was the most special of Decker's life. He had never felt such emotional commitment to physical passion, such regard – and indeed awe -- for the person with whom he was sharing that passion. After he and Beth had made love for the second time, after they had finished showering and dressed, he became aware of other unfamiliar feelings, his sense of completeness, of belonging. It was as if their two physical unions had produced another kind of union, intangible, mystical. As long as he was near Beth, he felt that she was within him and he within her. He didn't have to be close enough to touch her. It was enough merely to see her. He felt whole.

As he sipped Dos Equis beer while he barbecued the T-bones Beth had requested, he glanced toward stars beginning to appear in the sky, its evening color remarkably like that of Beth's eyes. He gazed down the wooded slope behind Beth's house toward the lights of Santa Fe spread out below him. Feeling a contentment he had never before known, he peered through the screen door into the glow of the kitchen and watched Beth preparing a salad. She was humming to herself.

She noticed him. 'What are you looking at?'

'You.'

She smiled with pleasure.

'I love you,' Decker said again.

Beth came toward him, opened the door, leaned out, and kissed him. A spark seemed to jump from her to him. 'You're the most important person in the world to me.'

At that moment, it occurred to Decker that the hollowness he had suffered for many years had finally been filled. He thought back a year and a quarter to Rome and his fortieth birthday, the ennui he had endured, the personal vacuum. He had wanted a wife, a family, a home, and now he would have all of them.

8

'I'm afraid I'm going to have to leave town for a couple of days,' Beth said.

'Oh?' Driving along the narrow piñon-rimmed curves of Tano Road, north of town, Decker looked over at her, confused. It was Friday, September 9, the end of the tourist season, the first evening of Fiesta. He and Beth had been lovers for eight days. 'Is it something sudden? You didn't mention it before.'

'Sudden? Yes and no,' Beth said, gazing over sunset-bathed low hills toward the Jemez mountains to the west. 'Finding out that I had to take the trip the day after tomorrow is sudden. But I knew I'd have to do it eventually. I need to go back to Westchester County. Meetings with lawyers – that sort of thing. It's about my late husband's estate.'

The reference to Beth's late husband made Decker uncomfortable. Whenever possible, he had avoided the subject, concerned that Beth's memories of the man would make her ambivalent about her relationship with Decker. Are you jealous of a dead man? he wondered.

'A couple of days? When do you expect to be back?' Decker asked.

'Actually, maybe longer. Possibly a week. It's crass and petty, but it *is* important. My husband had partners, and they're being difficult about how much his share of the business is worth.'

'I see,' Decker said, wanting to ask all sorts of questions but trying not to pry. If Beth wanted to share her past with him, she would. He was determined not to make her feel crowded. Besides, this was supposed to be a joyous evening. They were on their way to a Fiesta party at the home of a film producer for whom Decker had acted as realtor. Beth obviously didn't want to talk about her legal problems, so why make her do it? 'I'll miss you.'

'Same here,' Beth said. 'It'll be a long week.'

9

' . . . died young.'

Decker heard the fragment of conversation from a group of women behind him as he sipped a margarita and listened to a jazz trio positioned in a corner of the spacious living room. The tuxedoed pianist was doing a nice job on a Henry Mancini medley, emphasizing *Moon River*.

'From tuberculosis,' Decker heard behind him. 'Only twenty-five. Didn't start writing until he was twenty-one. It's amazing how much he accomplished in so little time.'

Decker turned from listening to the piano player and studied the two hundred guests that his client, the film producer, had invited to the Fiesta party. While uniformed caterers brought cocktails and hors d'oeuvres, the partygoers went from room to room, admiring the luxurious home. Famous local residents mixed freely. But the only person in the room who occupied Decker's attention was Beth.

When Decker had first met her, she had worn only East Coast clothing. But gradually that had changed. Tonight, she wore a festive Hispanic-influenced Southwestern outfit. Her skirt and top were velvet, their midnight blue complementing her blue-gray eyes and auburn hair. She had tucked back her hair in a ponytail, securing it with a silver barrette whose glint matched that of her silver squash-blossom necklace. She was sitting with a group of women around a coffee table made from black-smithed iron that supported a two-hundred-year-old door. She looked comfortable, at ease, as if she had been living in Santa Fe for twenty years.

'I haven't read him since I was at UCLA,' one of the women was saying.

'Whatever made you get interested in poetry?' another woman asked, as if the thought appalled her.

'And why Keats?' a third woman asked.

Decker mentally came to attention. Until that moment, he hadn't known which writer the group was discussing. The reference, through a complex chain of association, sparked his memory, taking him back to Rome. He repressed a frown as he vividly recalled following Brian McKittrick down the Spanish

Steps and past the house where Keats had died.

'For fun, I'm taking a course at St John's College,' a fourth woman said. 'It's called "The Great Romantic Poets".'

'Ah,' the second woman said. 'I can guess which word in the title appealed to you.'

'It's not what you're thinking,' the fourth woman said. 'It's not like those romances you like to read, and I confess I do, too. This is different. Keats did write about men and women and passion, but that's not what he's about.'

The repetition of Keats's name made Decker think not only of McKittrick but of twenty-three dead Americans. It troubled him that a poet synonymous with truth and beauty could be irrevocably associated in his mind with a restaurant full of charred corpses.

'He wrote about emotion,' the fourth woman said. 'About beauty that *feels* like passion. About . . . It's hard to explain.'

Darkling I listen; and, for many a time / I have been half in love with easeful death. Keats's dirge-like lines occurred spontaneously to Decker. Before he realized what he was doing, he joined the conversation. 'About beautiful things that seem even more heartachingly beautiful when seen through the eyes of someone very young and about to die.'

The group looked up at him in surprise, except for Beth who had been watching him with covert affection throughout the conversation.

'Steve, I didn't realize you knew anything about poetry,' the fourth woman said. 'Don't tell me when you're not helping people find beautiful houses like this, *you* take courses at St John's, also.'

'No. Keats is just a memory from college,' Decker lied.

'Now you've got me interested,' one of the women said. 'Was Keats really in his early twenties and dying from TB when he wrote those great poems?'

Decker nodded, thinking of shots being fired in the dark in a rainy courtyard.

'When he was twenty-five,' the fourth woman repeated. 'He's buried in Venice.'

'No, in Rome,' Decker said.

'Are you sure?'

'The house where he died is near Bernini's Boat Fountain, to the right as you go down the Spanish Steps.'

'You sound as if you've been there.'

Decker shrugged.

'Sometimes I think you've been everywhere,' an attractive woman said. 'One of these days, I'm going to get you to tell me the fascinating story of your life before you came to Santa Fe.'

'I sold real estate other places. It wasn't very interesting, I'm afraid.'

As if sensing that Decker wanted to move on, Beth mercifully stood and took his arm. 'If anybody's going to hear the story of Steve's life, it's going to be me.'

Grateful to be relieved from talking about his mood, Decker strolled with Beth outside onto an extensive brick patio. In the cool night air, they peered toward the star-filled sky.

Beth put an arm around his waist. Smelling her perfume, Decker kissed her cheek. His throat felt pleasantly tight.

Leading her off the patio, away from the lights and the crowd, concealed by shadowy piñon trees, Decker kissed her with passion. When Beth reached up, linking her fingers around his neck, returning the kiss, he felt as if the ground rippled. Her lips were soft yet firm, exciting. Through her blouse, her nipples pressed against him. He was breathless.

'So go ahead – tell me the fascinating story of your life.'

'Some time.' Decker kissed her neck, inhaling her fragrance. 'Right now, there are better things to do.'

But he couldn't stop thinking of Rome, of McKittrick, of

what had happened in the courtyard. The dark nightmare haunted him. He had hoped to put everything that McKittrick represented behind him. Now, as he had two months ago, he couldn't help wondering why in God's name McKittrick had shown up in Santa Fe to watch him.

10

'It arrived?'

'This afternoon,' Decker said. 'I didn't have a chance to show you.' After the party, they were driving back along shadowy Camino Lindo.

'Show me now.'

'You're sure you're not tired?'

'Hey, if I get tired, I can always stay at your place and use it,' Beth said.

The 'it' they referred to was a bed that Decker had commissioned from a local artist, John Massey, whose specialty was working with metal. Using a forge, a hammer, and an anvil, Massey had shaped the iron bedposts into intricate designs that resembled carved wood.

'It's wonderful,' Beth said after Decker parked the Cherokee in the carport and they went inside. 'Even more striking than you described.' She touched the metal's smooth black finish. 'And those figures cut out of the headboard – or headmetal – or whatever you call it when it's made out of iron. These figures look like they're based on a Navajo design, but they also look like Egyptian hieroglyphs, their feet out one way, their hands out another. Actually, they look like they're drunk.'

'John has a sense of humor. They're not based on anything. He makes them up.'

'Well, I sure like them,' Beth said. 'They make me smile.'

Decker and Beth admired it from various angles.

'Certainly looks solid,' Decker said.

Beth pressed a hand on the mattress. She raised her eyebrows, mischievous. 'Want to try it out?'

'You bet,' Decker said. 'If we break it, I'll make John give me my money back.'

He turned off the light. Slowly, amid lingering kisses, they undressed each other. The bedroom door was open. Moonlight streamed through the high, wide, solar-gain windows in the corridor outside the bedroom. The glow on her breasts made Decker think of ivory. Kneeling, worshipping, he brought his lips down.

11

They must have come over the back wall. That was at seven minutes after three in the morning. Decker was able to be specific about the time because he had an old-fashioned alarm clock with hands, and when he checked it later, he discovered that was when the hands had stopped moving.

Unable to sleep, he lay on his side, admiring Beth's face in the moonlight, imagining that she had already returned from her business trip, that their separation was over. In the distance, he heard the muted pop-pop-pop of firecrackers being set off at private parties that continued the Fiesta celebrations. There were going to be a lot of hangovers tomorrow morning, he thought. And sleepy neighbors kept up by parties next to them. The police will be busy, responding to complaints. How late is it? he wondered, and turned toward the clock.

He couldn't see its illumination. Suspecting that he had put some of Beth's clothing in front of it, he reached to remove the obstacle but instead touched the clock itself. Puzzlement made him frown. Why would the clock's light be off? The pop-pop-pop of distant firecrackers persisted. But the noise wasn't intrusive enough to prevent him from hearing something else – the faint scrape of metal against metal.

Troubled, Decker sat up. The noise came from beyond the foot of his bed, from the solar-gain corridor outside his bedroom, from the door on the right at the end of the corridor. That door led outside to a small flower garden and patio. Faintly, metal continued to scrape against metal.

In a rush, he put a hand over Beth's mouth. The moonlight revealed the shock with which her eyes opened. As she struggled against his hand on her mouth, he pressed his head against her left ear, his voice a tense whisper. 'Don't try to say anything. Listen to me. Someone's trying to break into the house.'

The metal scraped.

'Get out of bed. Into the closet. Hurry.'

Naked, Beth scrambled out of bed and dashed into the closet on the right side of the room. The closet was large, a walk-in, ten by twelve feet. It had no windows. Its darkness was greater than that of the bedroom.

Decker yanked open the bottom drawer on his bedside table and removed the Sig-Sauer .928 pistol that he had bought when he first arrived in Santa Fe. He crouched next to the bed, using it for cover while he grabbed the bedside telephone, but as he put the phone to his ear, he knew that there wasn't any point in pressing 911 – he didn't hear a dial tone.

Abrupt silence aggravated Decker's tension. The sound of metal scraping against metal had stopped. Decker lunged into the walk-in closet, couldn't see Beth, and took cover next to a small dresser. As he aimed toward the corridor beyond his open bedroom door, he shivered from stress, his nude body feeling cold although he was sweating. The back door on the right, which he had been intending to oil, squeaked open.

Who the hell would be breaking in? he asked himself. A burglar? Possibly. But suspicions from his former life took possession of him. He couldn't put away the icy thought that unfinished business had caught up to him.

Immediately the intrusion detector made a rhythmic beeping sound: the brief alert the system provided before the full ear-torturing blare of the alarm. Not that the alarm would do any good – because the telephone line had been cut, the alarm's signal couldn't be transmitted to the security company. If the intrusion detector hadn't been rigged to a battery in case of a power failure, the warning beep wouldn't even be sounding now.

At once the beeps became a constant wail. Shadows rushed into the bedroom. Rapid flashes pierced the darkness, the staccato roar of automatic weapons assaulting Decker's eardrums. The flashes illuminated the impact of countless bullets against the bed sheets, pillow feathers flying, mattress stuffing erupting.

Before the gunmen had a chance to realize their mistake, Decker fired, squeezing the trigger repeatedly. Two of the gunmen lurched and fell. A third man scrambled from the bedroom. Decker shot at him and missed, the bullet shattering a solar-gain window as the man disappeared into the corridor.

Decker's palms were moist, making him grateful that his pistol had a checkered non-slick grip. His bare skin exuded more sweat. Traumatized by the roar of the shots, his eardrums rang painfully. He could barely hear the security system's wail. He wouldn't be able to detect any sound the gunman made trying to sneak up on him. For that matter, Decker didn't know if the three gunmen were the only intruders in the house, and he couldn't tell how seriously he had injured the two men he had shot. Would they still be capable of firing at him if he tried to leave the closet?

He waited anxiously for his night vision to return after the glare of the muzzle flashes. It worried him that he didn't know where Beth was. Somewhere in the spacious closet, yes. But had she found cover, perhaps behind the cedar chest? He couldn't risk glancing behind him in hopes of detecting her murky shadow in the darkness. He had to keep his attention directed toward the bedroom, prepared to react if someone attacked across it. At the same time, he felt a cold spot on his spine, terribly aware that the closet had another entrance, a door behind him that led into the laundry room. If the gunman snuck around and attacked from that direction . . .

I can't guard two directions at once, Decker thought. Maybe whoever else is out there ran away.

Would *you* have run away?

Maybe.

Like hell.

Apprehension made him rigid. The middle of the night, the phone and the electricity cut off, no way to call for help, no way for the alarm to be transmitted to the police – all the gunman had to worry about was a neighbor being wakened by the shots or by the alarm. But could those noises be heard from outside the thick adobe house? The nearest house was several hundred yards away. The noise would be muted by the distance. The gunshots might sound like the distant firecrackers Decker had heard. The intruder might think he had a little more time.

The attack didn't come from the laundry room. Instead an automatic weapon roared from the entrance to the bedroom, the muzzle flashes brilliant, bullets tearing up each side of the closet's doorjamb, strafing the open space between them, hitting the wall beyond, shredding clothes on hangers, bursting shoe boxes and garment bags, sending chunks of fabric, wood, and cardboard flying, fragments striking Decker's bare back. The acrid stench of cordite filled the area.

As suddenly as it began, the din of the automatic weapon

stopped, the only sound the blare of the security system. Decker didn't dare shoot at where the muzzle flashes had been. The gunman would likely have shifted position and be waiting to aim at the flash from Decker's pistol if he returned fire.

Immediately Decker became aware of movement in the closet. Beth's naked figure darted from a shadowy corner. She knew the house. She knew about the door to the laundry room. As she twisted the knob and pushed at the door, the submachine gun roared, its bullets chasing her. Decker thought he heard her moan. There was so much noise he couldn't tell, but as she vanished into the darkness of the laundry room, she clutched her right shoulder. Decker's urge was to rush to her, but he didn't dare give in to that suicidal impulse. The gunman was counting on him to lose control, to show himself. Instead Decker pressed himself closer to the small dresser, ready with his pistol, hoping that the gunman himself would lose patience.

Please, Decker thought. Dear God, *please*. Don't let Beth be hurt.

He strained to watch the entrance to the bedroom. He wished that he could hear if the gunman was moving around out there, but his ears rang even more painfully. That could work the other way around, he realized. Since *his* hearing was compromised, whoever was trying to kill him probably wouldn't be hearing well, either. There might be a way to turn their mutual affliction to his advantage. Next to the dresser that shielded him was a waist-high metal stepladder that he used for reaching items on the top shelf. It was about the width of a man's shoulders. Grabbing a shirt that he had left on the dresser, Decker draped it over the low stepladder. In the darkness, the silhouette looked like someone crouching. He pushed the stepladder ahead of him, praying that the gunman's hearing was indeed compromised, that the wail of the security system would keep him from hearing the scraping sounds the stepladder made on the floor. With force, he shoved the stepladder from the closet, sending it skittering upright across the bedroom toward where he had last seen the gunman.

An explosion of gunfire tore the shirt apart, knocking the ladder over. Simultaneously Decker fired several times at the muzzle flashes in the hallway. The flashes jerked toward the tile floor, illuminating a man who was bent over in pain, his submachine gun blasting holes in the tile floor. As the man fell, the roaring flashes stopped.

Afraid that his own flashes would have made him a target, Decker rolled. He came to a crouch on the opposite side of the closet's entrance, fired again toward the man he had just hit, then toward each of the men he had previously shot, and quickly retreated into the darkness of the laundry room.

Beth. He had to find Beth. He had to make sure Beth wasn't injured. He had to keep her from running again and revealing herself until he knew for certain there was no one else in the house. In the laundry room, the sweet smell of detergent emphasized the bitterness of cordite. Sensing movement between the hot-water tank and the water softener, he inched toward it and found Beth, only to be startled by a fiery blast from a shotgun as the closed door to the laundry room blew inward, stunning him with its concussion. He and Beth dropped to the floor.

His night vision already impaired by the close flash from the shotgun, Decker was further blinded by a second flash, another shotgun blast. The bulky shadow of a man charged inside, firing a third time, as Decker aimed high, shooting upward from where he lay on his stomach.

Hot liquid streamed over Decker. *Blood?* But the liquid wasn't just hot; it was almost scalding. And it didn't just stream; it cascaded. The water tank must have been hit, Decker thought in desperation, straining to ignore his pain from the high temperature of the liquid sloshing over him while he concentrated on the darkness across from him where seconds earlier muzzle flashes had revealed the man with the shotgun. He felt Beth's panicked breathing next to him. He smelled blood, its coppery odor unmistakable. A *strong* odor. But not just from the direction of the man with the shotgun. It also seemed to come from next to him. The terrible thought kept insisting, *Had Beth been hit?*

As his night vision improved after the assault of the muzzle flashes, he detected the murky outline of a body on the floor at the entrance to the laundry room. Beth trembled beside him. Feeling the spasms of her terror, Decker calculated how many times he had fired and struggled against a terror of his own when he realized that he had only one round left.

Drenched by the painfully hot water, he pressed a finger to Beth's lips, silently urging her to be quiet. Then he squirmed across the laundry room's wet floor toward the entrance. Moonlight through the hallway's skylight helped him to see the shotgun that had fallen beside the corpse.

Or at least Decker hoped it was a corpse. Prepared to fire his last bullet, he checked for a pulse. Finding none, he relaxed only slightly as he searched beneath the corpse's windbreaker, his left hand touching a revolver. Immediately he shoved the shotgun into the laundry room, returned to Beth in the darkness, felt for and raised the trapdoor to the crawlspace that led under the house, and guided Beth toward it. Most homes in Santa Fe were built on concrete slabs and didn't have basements; a few, like Decker's, had a four-foot-high service tunnel under the floor.

Rigid, Beth resisted descending the wooden stairs. An odor of dust rose from the gloom. Then she seemed to accept the crawlspace as a sanctuary, trembling, hurriedly descending, hot water pouring down with her. Decker squeezed her right arm in what he hoped she accepted as a gesture of reassurance, then closed the hatch.

The blare from the security system continued to unnerve him as he crept toward the darkness of the far corner, positioning himself beside the furnace. From there, he had a line of fire toward each entrance to the laundry room. He had the gunman's revolver in his left hand, his own pistol in his right, and as a last resort the gunman's shotgun, which he had pulled next to him, hoping that the gunman had not used all its ammunition.

But something else unnerved him, giving him a terrible sense of urgency. He knew that patience was the key to survival. If he tried to investigate the house, he might show himself to anyone who was hiding out there. The prudent thing to do was to stay in place and let *someone else* show himself. But Decker couldn't restrain his need to hurry things. He imagined Beth's growing sense of claustrophobia as she hunkered naked in the musty darkness of the crawlspace. He imagined her increasing pain. When he had touched her right arm to try to give her reassurance, his fingers had come away smeared with a liquid that was thicker than water. The liquid was warm and smelled of blood. Beth had been hit.

I need to get her to a doctor, Decker thought. I can't wait any longer. He crept from behind the furnace, approached the entrance to the hallway, prepared to rush out, to aim one way and then the other, but instead froze as a flashlight beam settled on the corpse before him.

He pressed himself against the inside wall. Sweat mixed with the water that slicked him as he concentrated on that exit from the laundry room, then glanced nervously across to the door that led into the closet. Why would they use a flashlight? It didn't make sense to reveal themselves. The flashlight must be a trick, he thought, an attempt to distract me while someone comes from the opposite direction, from the darkness of the closet.

Surprising him, the flashlight moved away, heading back toward the front door. That didn't make sense, either. Unless . . . Did he dare trust what he was thinking? A neighbor might have decided that the muffled staccato blasts he was hearing definitely didn't come from firecrackers. The neighbor might have called 911. The flashlight might belong to a policeman. That was how a lone policeman would behave – as soon as he saw the body, not knowing what he was involved in, possibly a gunfight, he would retreat and radio for help.

Decker's already sickeningly rapid heartbeat pounded even faster. Under other circumstances, he wouldn't have dared to take the risk of revealing his position. But Beth had been shot. God alone knew how serious the wound was. If he hesitated any longer, she might bleed to death in the crawlspace. He had to do *something*.

'Wait!' Decker shouted. 'I'm in the laundry room! I need help!'

The flashlight beam stopped going away, glared back along the hallway, and focused on the entrance to the laundry room. Decker immediately realized the further risk he had taken. His ears were ringing so painfully that he couldn't tell if anyone shouted back to him. If he didn't answer or if what he shouted didn't logically connect with what the policeman shouted (assuming this in fact *was* a policeman), he would make the policeman suspicious.

'I live here!' Decker shouted. 'Some men broke in! I don't know who you are! I'm afraid to come out!'

The flashlight beam shifted position, as if whoever held it was finding cover in a doorway.

'I can't hear you! There was shooting! My eardrums are messed up!' Decker shouted. 'If you're a policeman, slide your badge down the hall so I can see it from this doorway!'

Decker waited, glancing nervously from the doorway toward

the opposite door that led into the closet, apprehensive that he was leaving himself open to an attack. He had to take the chance. Beth, he kept thinking. I have to help Beth.

'Please!' Decker shouted. 'If you're a policeman, slide your badge down!'

Because he couldn't hear it skittering, he was surprised by the sudden appearance of the badge on the brick floor of the corridor. The badge was stopped by the body of the gunman.

'Okay!' Decker's throat was sore. He swallowed with difficulty. 'I'm sure you're trying to figure out what happened! You're as nervous as *I* am! When I come out, I'll have my hands up! I'll show them first!'

He set the handguns onto a laundry counter to his right where he could scramble back and grab them if he had misjudged the situation. 'I'm coming out now! Slowly! I'll show my hands first!' The moment he stepped free of the doorway, his hands high over his head, the flashlight beam shifted swiftly toward his eyes, nearly blinding him, making him feel more helpless.

It seemed as if time was suspended. The flashlight beam kept glaring at him. The policeman, if that was who this was (and despite the badge on the floor, Decker was suddenly having powerful doubts), didn't move, just kept studying him.

Or was it a gunman aiming at him?

Decker's eyes felt stabbed by the flashlight beam fixed on them, and he wanted to lower a hand to shield his vision, but he didn't dare move, didn't dare unnerve whoever was studying him. The flashlight beam dropped down to his nakedness, then returned to his eyes.

At once time began again.

The flashlight beam moved, approaching. Decker's mouth was terribly dry, his vision so impaired that he couldn't see the dark looming figure, couldn't see how the man was dressed, couldn't identify him.

Then the flashlight and the figure were close, but Decker still couldn't tell who confronted him. His raised hands felt numb. He had the sense that the figure was talking to him, but he couldn't hear.

Unexpectedly the figure leaned close, and Decker was able to make out dimly what the figure shouted.

'*You can't hear?*'

The peripheral glow of the flashlight showed that the figure, a stocky Hispanic man, wore a uniform.

'I'm almost deaf!' The din of the alarm and the ringing in his ears were excruciating.

'*. . . are you?*'

'*What?*' Decker's voice seemed to come from far outside himself.

'*Who are you?*'

'Stephen Decker! I own this house! Can I put my hands down?'

'*Yes. Where are your clothes?*'

'I was sleeping when they broke in! I don't have time to explain! My friend's in the crawlspace!'

'*What?*' The policeman's tone expressed less confusion than astonishment.

'The crawlspace! I have to get her out of there!' Decker swung toward the laundry room, the flashlight beam swinging with him. His hands trembled as he grabbed the metal ring recessed into the trapdoor. He pulled the hatch fiercely upward and groped down the wooden steps into the darkness, smelling earth and dampness and the disconcerting odor of blood.

'Beth!'

He couldn't see her.

'Beth!'

From above him, the flashlight beam filled the pit, and he saw Beth huddled naked, trembling, in a corner. He rushed to her, almost out of the flashlight's range but not so far that he didn't notice how pale her face was. Her right shoulder and breast were smeared with blood.

'*Beth!*'

He knelt, holding her, ignoring the dirt and cobwebs that clung to him. He felt her sobbing.

'It's all right. You're safe.'

If she responded, he didn't know. He couldn't hear, and he was too busy guiding her toward the steps from the crawlspace and up toward the flashlight, the policeman helping her up, startled by her nakedness. Decker covered her with a dirty shirt from a hamper in the laundry room. She stumbled weakly, and he had to hold her up as they made their way along the corridor toward the front door.

Decker had the sense that the policeman was shouting to him, but he still couldn't hear. 'The alarm pad's near the front door! Let me turn it off!'

He reached the pad on the wall at the exit from the corridor and briefly wondered why it was illuminated when the electricity was off, then remembered that the alarm system had a battery that supplied back-up power. He pressed numbers and felt his shoulders sag in relief when the alarm stopped.

'Thank God,' he murmured, having to contend now only with the ringing in his ears. He was still holding Beth up. In dismay, he felt her vomit. 'She needs an ambulance.'

'*Where's a phone?*' the policeman shouted.

'They aren't working! The power's off! The phone's are down!' Decker's ears felt less tortured. He was hearing slightly better.

'*What happened here?*'

Dismayingly, Beth slumped.

Decker held her, lowering her to the brick floor in the vestibule. He felt a cool breeze from the open front door. 'Get help! I'll stay with her!'

'I'll use the radio in my patrol car!' The policeman rushed from the house.

Glancing in that direction, Decker saw two stationary headlights gleaming beyond the courtyard gate. The policeman disappeared behind them. Then all Decker paid attention to was Beth.

He knelt beside her, stroking her forehead. 'Hang on. You'll be all right. We're getting an ambulance.'

The next thing he knew, the policeman had returned and was stooping beside him, saying something that Decker couldn't hear.

'The ambulance will come in no time,' Decker told Beth. Her forehead felt clammy, chilled. 'You're going to be fine.' I need to cover her, Decker was thinking. I need to get her warm. He yanked open a closet behind him, grabbed an overcoat, and spread it over her.

The policeman leaned closer to him, speaking louder. Now Decker could hear. 'The front door was open when I arrived! *What happened? You said someone broke in?*'

'Yes.' Decker kept stroking Beth's hair, wishing the policeman would leave him alone. 'They must have broken in the front as well as the back.'

'*They?*'

'The man in the hallway. Others.'

'*Others?*'

'In my bedroom.'

'*What?*'

'Three. Maybe four. I shot them all.'

'Jesus,' the policeman said.

FIVE

1

A chaos of crisscrossing headlights gleamed in the spacious pebbled driveway outside Decker's house. Engines rumbled. Radios crackled. The eerily illuminated silhouettes of vehicles seemed everywhere, patrol cars, vans, a huge utility truck from Public Service of New Mexico, an ambulance speeding away.

Naked beneath an overcoat that didn't cover his bare knees, Decker leaned, shivering, against the stucco wall next to the open courtyard gate, staring frantically toward the receding lights of the ambulance speeding into the night. He ignored the policemen searching the area around the house, their flashlights wavering, while a forensics crew carried their equipment past him.

'I'm sorry,' one of the policemen said, the stocky Hispanic who had been the first to arrive and who had eventually introduced himself as Officer Sanchez. 'I know how much you want to go with your friend to the hospital, but we need you here to answer more questions.'

Decker didn't reply, just kept staring toward the lights of the ambulance, which kept getting smaller in the darkness.

'The ambulance attendants said they thought she'd be okay,' Sanchez continued. 'The bullet went through her right arm. It didn't seem to hit bone. They've stopped the bleeding.'

'Shock,' Decker said. 'My friend's in shock.'

The policeman looked uncomfortable, not sure what to say. 'That's right. Shock.'

'And shock can kill.'

The ambulance lights disappeared. As Decker turned, he noticed confused movement between the headlights of a van and the hulking Public Service of New Mexico utility truck. He tensed, seeing two harried civilians caught between policemen, the indistinct group coming swiftly in his direction. Had the police captured someone associated with the attack? Angry, Decker stepped closer to the open gate, ignoring Sanchez, focusing his attention on the figures being brought toward him.

A man and a woman, Decker saw as the nearest headlights starkly revealed their faces, and immediately his anger lessened.

The two policemen flanking them had a look of determination as they reached the gate. 'We found them on the road. They claim they're neighbors.'

'Yes. They live across the street.' The harsh ringing persisted in Decker's ears, although not as severely. 'These are Mr and Mrs Hanson.'

'We heard shots,' Hanson, a short, bearded man, said.

'And your alarm,' Hanson's gray-haired wife said. She and her husband wore rumpled casual clothes and looked as if they had dressed quickly. 'At first, we thought we had to be wrong. There couldn't be shots at your house. We couldn't believe it.'

'But we couldn't stop worrying,' Hanson said. 'We phoned the police.'

'A damned good thing you did,' Decker said. 'Thank you.'

'Are you all right?'

'I think so.' Decker's body ached from tension. 'I'm not sure.'

'What *happened*?'

'That's exactly the question *I* want to ask,' a voice intruded.

Bewildered, Decker looked beyond the gate toward where a man had appeared, approaching between headlights. He was tall, sinewy, wearing a leather cowboy hat, a denim shirt, faded blue jeans, and dusty cowboy boots. As Officer Sanchez shone his flashlight toward the man, Decker was able to tell that the man was Hispanic. He had a narrow handsome face, brooding eyes, and dark hair that hung to his shoulders. He seemed to be in his middle thirties.

'Luis.' The man nodded in greeting to Officer Sanchez.

'Frederico.' Sanchez nodded back.

The newcomer directed his attention toward Decker. 'I'm Detective Sergeant Esperanza.' His Hispanic accent gave a rolling sound to the 'r's.

For a fleeting moment, Decker was reminded that 'Esperanza' was the Spanish word for 'hope'.

'I know this has been a terrible ordeal, Mr . . . ?'

'Decker. Stephen Decker.'

'You must be frightened. You're confused. You're worried about your friend. Her name is . . . ?'

'Beth Dwyer.'

'Does she live here with you?'

'No,' Decker said. 'She's my next-door neighbor.'

Esperanza thought about it, seeming to make the logical conclusion. 'Well, the sooner I can sort out what happened, the sooner you can visit your friend in the hospital. So if you bear with me while I ask you some questions . . .'

Abruptly the light above the front door, a motion detector, came on. Simultaneously the light in the vestibule came on, casting a glow through the open front door.

Decker heard expressions of approval from the policemen checking the outside of the house.

'Finally,' Esperanza said. 'It looks like Public Service of New Mexico managed to find the problem with your electricity. Would you tell Officer Sanchez where the switches are for the outside lights?'

Decker's throat felt scratchy, as if he'd been inhaling dust. 'Just inside the front door.'

Sanchez put on a pair of latex gloves and entered the house. In a moment, lights gleamed along the courtyard wall and under the portal that led up to the front door. The next thing, Sanchez had turned on the lights in the living room, their welcome glow streaming through windows, illuminating the courtyard.

'Excellent,' Esperanza said. The lights revealed that he had a 9mm Beretta holstered on his belt. He looked even thinner than he had seemed in the limited illumination from the headlights and flashlights. He had the weathered face of an outdoorsman, his skin swarthy, with a grain like leather. He seemed about to ask a question when a policeman came over and gestured toward a man beyond the open gate, a workman who had *Public Service of New Mexico* stenciled on his coveralls. 'Yes, I want to talk to him. Excuse me,' he told Decker, then headed toward the workman.

The Hansons looked overwhelmed by all the activity.

'Would you follow me, please?' an officer asked them. 'I need to ask you some questions.'

'Anything we can do to help.'

'Thank you,' Decker said again. 'I owe you.'

Esperanza passed them as he returned. 'You'll be more comfortable if we talk about this inside,' he told Decker. 'Your feet must be cold.'

'What? My feet?'

'You're not wearing any shoes.'

Decker peered down at his bare feet on the courtyard's bricks. 'So much has been going on, I forgot.'

'And you'll want to put on some clothes instead of that overcoat.'

'There was shooting in the bedroom.'

Esperanza looked puzzled by the apparent change of topic.

154

'And in the walk-in closet,' Decker said.

'Yes?' Esperanza studied him.

'Those are the only places where I keep clothes.'

Now Esperanza understood. 'That's right. Until the lab crew finishes in the bedroom, I'm afraid you can't touch anything in there.' Studying Decker harder, Esperanza gestured for them to go into the house.

2

'They cut off the electricity at the pole next to your house,' Esperanza said.

He and Decker were sitting at the kitchen table while policemen, a forensics crew, and the medical examiner checked the bedroom and laundry room areas. There were flashes, police photographers taking pictures. Decker's eardrums were still in pain, but the ringing had diminished. He was able to hear the harsh scrape of equipment being unpacked, a babble of voices, a man saying something about 'a war zone'.

'The pole's thirty yards off the gravel road behind some trees,' Esperanza said. 'No street lights. Widely separated houses. In the middle of the night, nobody would have seen a man climb the pole and cut the line. The same thing with the phone line. They cut it at the box at the side of the house.'

Despite the overcoat Decker wore, the aftermath of adrenaline continued to make him shiver. He stared toward the living room, where investigators came in and out. Beth, he kept thinking. What was happening at the hospital? Was Beth all right?

'The men who broke in had ID in their wallets,' Esperanza said. 'We'll check their background. Maybe that'll tell us what this is all about. But . . . Mr Decker, what do *you* think this is about?'

Yes, that's the question, isn't it? Decker thought. What in God's name is this about? Throughout the attack, he had been so busy controlling his surprise and protecting Beth that he hadn't had time to analyze the implications. Who the hell were these men? Why had they broken in? Despite his bewilderment, he was certain about two things – the attack had something to do with his former life, and for reasons of national security, there was no way he could tell Esperanza *anything* about that former life.

Decker made himself look mystified. 'I assumed they were burglars.'

'House burglars usually work alone or in pairs,' Esperanza said. 'Sometimes in threes. But never in my experience, four of them. Not unless they intend to steal something big, furniture, for example, but in that case they use a van and we haven't found one. In fact, we haven't found *any* vehicle that seems out of place in the neighborhood. What's more, they chose the wrong time to break into your house. Last evening was the start of Fiesta. Most people go out for the celebration. The smart thing would have been for them to watch to see if you left the house and *then* to break in as soon as it got dark. These guys were smart enough to cut the phone and power lines. I don't see why they weren't also smart enough to get their timing right.'

Decker's face felt haggard. Tense and exhausted, he rubbed his forehead. 'Maybe they weren't thinking clearly. Maybe they were on drugs. Who the hell knows the way burglars think?'

'Burglars with a sawed-off shotgun, two Uzis, and a MAC-10. What did those men expect they were going to have to deal with in here, a SWAT team?'

'Sergeant, I used to work in Alexandria, Virginia. I traveled into Washington a lot. From what I heard on TV and read in the newspaper, it seemed every drug dealer and carjacker had a MAC-10 or an Uzi. For them, submachine guns were a status symbol.'

'Back east. But this is New Mexico. How long have you lived here?'

'About a year and a quarter.'

'So you're still learning. Or maybe you've already realized, they don't call this the City Different for nothing. Out here, in a lot of ways, this is still the wild west. We do things the old-fashioned way. If we want to shoot somebody, we use a handgun or maybe a hunting rifle. In my fifteen years of being a policeman, I've never come across a crime involving this many assault weapons. Incidentally, Mr Decker—'

'Yes?'

'Were you ever in law enforcement?'

'Law enforcement? No. I sell real estate. What makes you think—'

'When Officer Sanchez found you, he said you acted as if you understood police procedure and how an officer feels in a potentially dangerous situation. He said you emphasized that you'd have your hands up when you left the laundry room, that you'd show your hands first before you stepped into view. That's very unusual behavior.'

Decker rubbed his aching forehead. 'It just seemed logical. I was afraid the officer might think I was a threat.'

'And when I told you to put some clothes on, you took for granted you couldn't go into the bedroom to get them, not until the forensics crew was finished in there.'

'That seemed logical, too. I guess I've seen a lot of crime shows on TV.'

'And where did you learn to shoot so well?'

'In the military.'

'Ah,' Esperanza said.

'Look, I need to know about my friend.'

Esperanza nodded.

'I'm so worried about her I can hardly concentrate.'

Esperanza nodded again. 'I tell you what, why don't we stop by the hospital on our way to the police station?'

'Police station?' Decker said.

'So you can make your statement.'

'Isn't that what I'm doing now?'

'The one at the station is official.'

A phone, Decker thought. He needed to get to a payphone and call his former employers. He had to tell them what had happened. He had to find out how they wanted to handle this.

A policeman came into the kitchen. 'Sergeant, the medical examiner says it's all right now for Mr Decker to go into the bedroom to get some clothes.'

Decker stood.

'While we're in there, let's do a walk-through,' Esperanza said. 'It would be helpful if you showed us exactly how it happened. Also . . .'

'Yes?'

'I know it'll be difficult, but this is hardly an ordinary situation. It would save a lot of time if we knew right away rather than waited until tomorrow.'

'I don't understand what you mean,' Decker said. 'What do you want me to do?'

'Look at the faces.'

'What?'

'Of the bodies. Here, instead of in the morgue. Maybe you can identify them. Before, in the dark, you couldn't have seen what they looked like. Now that the lights are back on . . .'

Decker *wanted* to look at the bodies in case he recognized them, but he had to pretend to be reluctant. 'I don't think my stomach would— I'd throw up.'

'You're not obligated. There are alternatives. The forensics crew is taking photographs. You can examine those. Or look at the bodies later in the morgue. But photographs don't always provide a good likeness, and rigor mortis might distort the features of the corpses so they don't seem familiar to you even if you've crossed paths with them before. Right now, though, not long after the attack, there's always a possibility that . . .'

Decker couldn't stop thinking about Beth. He had to get to the hospital. Continuing to feign reluctance, he said, 'God help me. Yes, I'll look at them.'

3

Wearing jeans and a gray cotton sweater, Decker sat in a rigid chair in the almost deserted emergency-ward waiting room at St Vincent's Hospital. A clock on the wall showed that it was almost six-thirty. The fluorescent lights in the ceiling hurt his eyes. To the left, outside the door to the waiting room, Esperanza was talking to a policeman who stood next to a teenage boy with a bruised face who was strapped to a gurney. Esperanza's battered boots, faded jeans, shoulder-long hair, and leather cowboy hat made him look like anything except a police detective.

As a hospital attendant wheeled the gurney through electronically controlled swinging doors that led into the emergency ward, Esperanza entered the brightly lit waiting area. His long legs and lanky frame gave him a graceful stride that reminded Decker of a panther. The detective pointed toward the gurney. 'An accident victim. Drunk driving. Fiesta weekend. Typical. Any news about your friend?'

'No. The receptionist said a doctor would come out to see me.' Decker slumped lower in his chair. His head felt as if someone had tied a strap around it. He rubbed his face, feeling scratchy beard stubble, smelling gunpowder on his hands. He kept thinking about Beth.

159

'Sometimes, under stress, memory can take a while,' Esperanza said. 'You're sure the bodies you looked at didn't seem familiar?'

'To the best of my knowledge, I've never seen them before.' The cloying coppery smell of blood still lingered in Decker's nostrils. The dead men had all appeared to be in their twenties. They were husky, wore dark outdoor clothes, and had Mediterranean features. Possibly Greek. Maybe French. Or were they— The previous evening, at the Fiesta party, Decker had brooded about his last assignment for the agency. Rome. Could the olive-skinned gunmen have been Italian? Did the attack on his house have something to do with what had happened in Rome a year and a quarter ago? If only Esperanza would leave him alone long enough so he could make a phone call.

'Mr Decker, the reason I asked you if you'd ever been in law enforcement is, I can't get over what you managed to do. Four men break in with assault weapons. They blow the hell out of your house. And you manage to kill all four of them with a handgun. Doesn't that seem strange to you?'

'*Everything* about this is strange. I still can't believe—'

'Most people would have been so overwhelmed with fear, they'd have hidden when they heard someone breaking in.'

'That's why Beth and I ran to the walk-in closet.'

'But not before you grabbed the pistol you keep in your bedside drawer. You're a realtor, you mentioned.'

'Yes.'

'Why would you feel the need to keep a pistol by your bed?'

'Home protection.'

'Well, it's been my experience that pistols for home protection don't do much good,' Esperanza said. 'Because the owners themselves aren't any good with them. Family members end up getting shot. Innocent bystanders get hit. Oh, we have plenty of gun clubs in the area. And there are plenty of hunters.

But I don't care how often you've practiced with a pistol at the firing range or how frequently you've gone hunting – when four men come at you with heavy artillery, you're lucky if you have time to piss your pants from fright before they kill you.'

'I was scared, all right.'

'But it didn't impair your abilities. If you'd been in law enforcement, if you'd been tested under fire, I could understand.'

'I told you I was in the military.'

'Yes.' The weathered creases around Esperanza's eyes deepened. 'You did tell me that. What was your outfit?'

'The Rangers. Look, I don't know what you're getting at,' Decker said impatiently. 'The Army taught me to handle a pistol, and when the time came, I was lucky enough to remember how to use it. You're making me feel as if I did something *wrong*. Is it a crime to defend myself and my friend against a gang that breaks into my house and starts shooting? Everything's turned upside down. The crooks are the good guys, and decent citizens are—'

'Mr Decker, I'm not saying you did anything wrong. There'll have to be an inquest and you'll have to testify. That's the law. All shootings, even justified ones, have to be investigated to the fullest. But the truth is, I admire your resourcefulness and your presence of mind. Not many ordinary citizens would have survived what you went through. For that matter, I'm not sure *I'd* have been able to handle myself any better in your circumstance.'

'Then I don't get it. If you're not saying I did anything wrong, what *are* you saying?'

'I'm just making observations.'

'Well, this is *my* observation. The only reason I'm alive is I got angry. *Furious*. Those bastards broke into my *home*. The sons of bitches. They shot my friend. They . . . I got so angry I stopped being afraid. All I wanted was to protect Beth, and by God, I managed that. I'm *proud* of that. I don't know if I should admit that to you, but I *am* proud. And this might not be the sort of thing to tell a police officer, either, but I will anyhow. If I had to, I'd do the same damned thing over again and be proud of it. Because I stopped the bastards from killing Beth.'

'You're a remarkable man, Mr Decker.'

'Hey, I'm no hero.'

'I didn't say that.'

'All I am is awfully lucky.'

'Right.'

A doctor appeared at the entrance to the waiting room. He was short and slight, in his thirties, wearing hospital greens and a stethoscope around his neck. He had small round spectacles. 'Is one of you Stephen Decker?'

Decker quickly stood. 'Can you tell me how my friend is doing?'

'She sustained a flesh wound just below her shoulder. The bleeding has been stopped. The wound has been sterilized and sutured. She's responding to treatment. Barring unforeseen complications, she ought to recover satisfactorily.'

Decker closed his eyes and murmured, 'Thank God.'

'Yes, there's a lot to give thanks for,' the doctor said. 'When your friend arrived at the hospital, she was in shock. Her blood pressure was low. Her pulse was erratic. Fortunately her life signs are back to normal.'

Back to normal? Decker thought. He worried that things would never be back to normal. 'When will she be able to go home?'

'I don't know yet. We'll see how well she continues to improve.'

'Can I see her?'

'She needs rest. I can't let you stay long.'

Esperanza stepped forward. 'Is she alert enough to make a statement to the police?'

The doctor shook his head. 'If I didn't think it was therapeutic for her to see Mr Decker, I wouldn't allow even him to visit.'

4

Beth looked pasty. Her dark hair, normally lush-looking, was tangled, without a sheen. Her eyes were sunken.

Under the circumstances, Decker thought, she had never seemed more beautiful.

After the doctor left, Decker shut the door, muting noises from the corridor. He studied Beth a moment longer, felt a tightness in his throat, came over to the bed, held the hand that wasn't in a sling, then leaned down and kissed her.

'How are you feeling?' He took care not to brush against the intravenous tube leading into her left arm.

Beth shrugged listlessly, obviously affected by sedation.

'The doctor says you're coming along fine,' Decker said.

Beth tried to speak, but Decker couldn't make out what she said.

Beth tried once more, licked her dry lips, then pointed toward a plastic cup filled with water. It had a curved straw, which Decker placed between her lips. She sipped.

'How are *you?*' she whispered hoarsely.

'Shook up.'

'Yeah,' Beth said with effort.

'How's the shoulder?'

'Sore.' Her eyelids looked heavy.

'I bet.'

'I hate to imagine what it'll feel like—' Beth winced.

163

' . . . when the painkillers wear off.' For a moment, she managed to tighten her fingers around his hand. Then her grip weakened. She was having trouble keeping her eyes open. 'Thank you.'

'I would never let anything happen to you.'

'I know,' Beth said.

'I love you.'

Decker could barely hear what she said next.

'Who . . . ?'

Decker completed the question he took for granted she was trying to ask. 'Who were they? I don't know.' He felt as if ashes were in his mouth. All he could think of was that the woman he had devoted his life to wouldn't be in the hospital if not for him. 'But believe me, I damned well intend to find out.'

Not that Beth heard him. Her dark-rimmed eyes drooped shut. She had drifted off to sleep.

5

Lack of sleep made Decker's own eyes feel pained by the glare of the morning sun as Esperanza drove him along Camino Lindo. The time was almost nine-thirty. They had spent the last two hours at the police station. Now Esperanza was taking him home.

'I'm sorry about all the inconvenience,' the sinewy detective said, 'but the judge at the inquest will want to make sure I eliminated all kinds of absolutely ridiculous possibilities.'

Decker concentrated to conceal his apprehension. It was alarmingly obvious to him that the threat against him had not been canceled merely because he'd killed the four men who had attacked him. He had to find out why they'd been sent and who had sent them. For all he knew, another hit team was already keeping him under surveillance. As a TV-news van passed the police car, presumably having taken footage of Decker's house, Decker decided that it would seem natural for him to turn and watch the van recede along the road. That tactic was a good way to check to be certain he wasn't being followed, without at the same time making Esperanza any more inquisitive.

'One ridiculous possibility would be you're a drug dealer who's had a falling out with your friends,' Esperanza said. 'You haven't kept your promises to them. You haven't delivered money you owe them. So they decide to make an example of you and send four guys to blow you away. But you're a resourceful guy. You get them first. Then you arrange things to look as if you're an innocent man who barely managed to save his life.'

'Including getting my friend shot.'

'Well, this is merely a hypothetical possibility.' Esperanza gestured offhandedly. 'It's one of a variety of theories the judge will want to make sure I've considered and eliminated.' The detective stopped the police car on the road outside Decker's house, unable to park in the driveway because a van and two other police cars blocked it. 'Looks like the forensics team isn't finished. That shower you said you wanted will have to be postponed a little longer.'

'For a couple of reasons. I just remembered – one of the men who broke in shot the water heater apart. You'd better drive me down to the next house.'

Esperanza looked puzzled for a moment, the creases in his forehead adding to the leathery grain of his narrow handsome face. Then he nodded with understanding. 'That's right – you mentioned your friend lived next to you.'

'I have a key,' Decker said.

As they drove past several curious bystanders who had

gathered at the side of the road and showed obvious interest in the police car, Decker couldn't help wondering, his muscles rigid, if any of them was a threat to him.

'When you were living in Alexandria, Virginia, what was the name of the real-estate company you worked for?' Esperanza asked.

'The Rawley-Hackman Agency.'

'Do you remember their telephone number?'

'I haven't used it in more than a year, but I think so.' Decker pretended to jog his memory, then dictated the number while Esperanza wrote it down. 'But I don't see why it's necessary to involve them.'

'Just a standard background check.'

'Sergeant, you're beginning to make me feel like a criminal.'

'Am I?' Esperanza tapped his fingers on the steering wheel. 'If you think of anything you've forgotten to tell me, I'll be at your house.'

6

Exhausted, Decker locked Beth's front door behind him and leaned against it. Tense, he listened to the adobe-smothered stillness of the house. At once he went into the living room and picked up the telephone. Under normal circumstances, he would have waited until he had a chance to get to a payphone, but he didn't have the luxury of waiting, and as he kept reminding himself, nothing was normal any longer. In an attempt at security, he reversed the charges, preventing a record of the call from showing up on Beth's telephone bill.

'Rawley-Hackman Agency,' a smooth male voice said.

'I have a collect call from Martin Kowalsky,' the operator said. 'Will you accept the charges?'

Martin Kowalsky, the name Decker had given the operator, was a code for an emergency.

'Yes,' the voice said immediately. 'I'll accept.'

'Go ahead, Mr Kowalsky.'

Decker could not be sure that the operator didn't continue to listen. 'Does your console show the number I'm using?' he asked the voice on the other end.

'Of course.'

'Call me right back.'

Ten seconds later, the phone rang. 'Hello.'

'Martin Kowalsky?'

'My identification number is eight, seven, four, four, five.'

Decker heard what sounded like fingers tapping numbers on a computer keyboard.

'Stephen Decker?'

'Yes.'

'Our records show that you severed your employment with us a year ago in June. Why are you re-establishing contact?'

'Because four men tried to kill me last night.'

The voice didn't respond for a moment. 'Repeat that.'

Decker did.

'I'm transferring you.'

The next male voice had a sharp edge of authority. 'Tell me everything.'

With practiced economy, Decker finished in five minutes, the details precise and vivid, his urgent tone reinforcing their effect.

'You believe the attack was related to your former employment with us?' the official asked.

'It's the most obvious explanation. Look, there's a chance the shooters were Italian. My last assignment was in Italy. In Rome. It was a disaster. Check the file.'

'It's on my monitor as we speak. Your connection between

last night's attack and what happened in Rome is awfully tenuous.'

'It's the only connection I can make at the moment. I want you to look into this. I don't have the resources to—'

'But you're not our responsibility any longer,' the voice said firmly.

'Hey, you sure thought I was when I quit. You were all over me. I figured your security checks would never stop. Damn it, two months ago, you were still keeping me under surveillance. So drop the bullshit and listen carefully. There's a detective in charge of investigating the attack on me. His name is Esperanza, and it's obvious he thinks something isn't right about my story. So far I've managed to distract him, but if something happens to me, if another hit team manages to finish the job the first bunch started, he'll be that much more determined. He might find out a hell of a lot more than you think is possible.'

'We'll see that he backs off.'

'You'd better,' Decker said, adding with force, 'I've always been loyal. I expect the same from you. Get me some backup. Find out who sent those men after me.'

The voice didn't answer for a moment. 'I have the number you're calling from on my monitor. Is your location secure enough for me to call you there?'

'No. I'll have to call *you* back.'

'Six hours.' The man hung up.

Decker immediately set down the phone and was surprised when it rang. Frowning, he answered it. 'Yes?'

'I gather you haven't had a chance to take your shower.' The caller's cadenced voice, almost musical, was instantly recognizable – Esperanza.

'That's right. How did you know?'

'Your line's been busy. I've been trying to get in touch with you.'

'I had to contact some clients to cancel some showings.'

'And are you finished? I hope so – because I want you to meet me at your house. I have some information that will interest you.'

7

'The IDs of the men you shot indicate they came from Denver,' Esperanza said.

He and Decker were in the living room. In the background, the investigating team was leaving, carrying equipment out to the van and the two police cars.

'But Denver's five hundred miles from here,' Esperanza continued. 'That's an awful long way for them to have come just to break into a house and steal. They could have done that in Colorado.'

'Maybe they were passing through Santa Fe, and they ran out of money,' Decker said.

'That still doesn't explain the automatic weapons or why they opened fire so quickly.'

'It could be they were startled when they realized someone was in the house.'

'And it could be Denver's a false trail,' Esperanza said. 'The Denver police department did some checking for me. No one using any of the names on those IDs is a resident at those addresses. In fact, three of the addresses *don't exist*. The fourth is a mortuary.'

'Somebody had a grim sense of humor.'

'And access to authentic-looking bogus credit cards and drivers' licenses. So we have to dig deeper,' Esperanza said. 'I've sent their fingerprints to the FBI. It'll take a day or two before we know if the Feds can match the prints with any they have on file. Meanwhile, I've alerted the Bureau of Alcohol, Tobacco, and Firearms. The serial numbers on the two Uzis and the MAC-10 had been burned off with acid, but ATF has ways to try to bring back the numbers. If they can, maybe the numbers will point us in a direction. Where the guns were bought, for example. Or more likely, stolen. But that's not why I wanted to talk to you.'

Decker waited, apprehensive.

'Let's take a walk. I want to show you something in back of your house.'

Show me what? Decker thought. Uneasy, he went with Esperanza along the corridor past the entrance to the master bedroom. The bodies had been removed. The stench of cordite still hung in the air. Sunlight blazed through the corridor's solar-gain windows, one of which had been shattered by a bullet. The sunlight made vivid the considerable amount of blood that had congealed, turning black, on the corridor's tiles. Decker glanced toward the bedroom and saw the bullet-gutted mattress and pillows. Black graphite fingerprint powder seemed everywhere. It rubbed off on Esperanza's hand as he turned the knob on the door at the end of the hallway.

'You heard them pick this lock.' Esperanza stepped out into a small garden of yuccas, roses, and low evergreens. 'That was after they climbed over the wall to this courtyard.'

Esperanza gestured for Decker to peer over the chest-high courtyard wall. 'See where the scrubgrass on the other side has been crushed? There are numerous footprints in the sand beyond the grass. Those footprints match the outline of the shoes the intruders wore.'

Esperanza moved farther along the wall and climbed over where he wouldn't disturb the tracks he had pointed out. He waited for Decker to follow.

Squinting from the brilliant sunlight, Decker jumped down

near two lines of yellow police-crime-scene tape that had been strung among piñon trees to isolate the footprints.

'You have a good-sized lot.' Esperanza's boots made a crunching sound on the pebbly ground as he walked parallel to the tracks, leading Decker down a steep slope. They passed among yuccas, piñons, and a dense swathe of waist-high chamisa bushes, their seeds having turned a mustard color typical of them in September.

All the while, Esperanza kept pointing toward the tracks. He and Decker climbed down past junipers on the increasingly steep slope. At the bottom, they followed the tracks along a ditch and onto a poplar-lined road that Decker recognized as Fort Connor Lane. The footprints were no longer in evidence, but wheelgrooves were dug into the gravel, as if a vehicle had sped away.

'That walk took us longer than I expected,' Esperanza said. 'A couple of times, we almost lost our footing.'

Decker nodded, waiting for him to make his point.

'In daylight. Imagine how long and difficult it would have been at night. Why did they go to all the trouble? Take a look along this road. The houses are expensive Widely separated. Easy targets. So why would those four men drive here, get out of their vehicle, refuse to make life easy for themselves, and instead decide to hike all over God's creation? From down here, we can't even see if there are any houses above us.'

'I don't get your point,' Decker said.

'Your house wasn't chosen at random. It was exactly the one they wanted. You were the intended target.'

'What? But that's crazy. Why would anybody want to kill me?'

'Exactly.' Esperanza's dark gaze intensified. 'You're holding something back.'

'Nothing,' Decker insisted. 'I've told you everything I can think of.'

'Then think about this. Someone drove their vehicle away. Suppose he comes back with another group of men to finish the job?'

'Are you trying to scare me, Sergeant?'

'I'm putting a policeman on guard at your house.'

8

Decker had never felt so naked as when he took off his clothes and stepped into his shower. Not wanting to be outside his house any more than was absolutely necessary, he had abandoned the idea of returning to Beth's place so he could clean up there. He would have to make do with the cold water coming from his shower, a small discomfort compared to his urgent need to rid himself of the sticky feel of sweat and death that clung to him. Shivering, he washed his hair and body as fast as he could. His muscles were painfully tense.

Quickly, he shaved, the cold water making the razor irritate his face. He put on loafers, khaki pants, and a camel shirt, the colors chosen because they were muted and wouldn't draw attention to him. Wishing that the police hadn't confiscated his pistol, regretting that he hadn't bought two, he picked up a shopping bag of clothes that he had taken from Beth's bedroom closet after he had made his phone call at her house. He tried not to look at the dried blood on his hallway floor as he carried the bag into his living room, where Officer Sanchez was waiting.

'I need to go to the hospital to visit my friend,' Decker said.

'I'll drive you.'

The stocky policeman went past the courtyard and into the

driveway. After looking around, he gestured that it was all right for Decker to come out and get in the police car. Troubled by a group of curious onlookers who were gathered on the road, pointing toward his house, Decker didn't feel reassured, but Sanchez's precaution was better than nothing. If only I had a gun, Decker thought.

He wasn't fooled by the explanation that Esperanza had given for putting Decker under police guard. Sanchez wasn't staying with Decker only to provide protection; the policeman's presence also guaranteed that Decker wouldn't suddenly leave town before Esperanza got some answers. Six hours, Decker thought. The intelligence official whom Decker had spoken to on the phone had said to call back in six hours. But six hours seemed an eternity.

As Sanchez steered onto St Michael's Drive, heading toward the hospital, Decker glanced through the rear window to see if anyone was following.

'Nervous?' Sanchez asked.

'Esperanza has me jumping at shadows. Aren't *you* nervous? You seem a little heavier than when I first saw you. It looks to me like you're wearing a bullet-resistant vest under your uniform.'

'We wear these all the time.'

'Sure you do.'

At the hospital, Sanchez avoided the parking lot and stopped at an out-of-the-way door, then scanned the area before saying it was all right to go inside. On the third floor, the heavy set policeman hitched up his gunbelt and stood watch outside Beth's room while Decker went in.

9

'How are you?' Decker studied Beth in the hospital bed, his heart filled with pity and sorrow. Again he blamed himself for having been indirectly responsible for what had happened to her.

Beth managed a smile. 'A little better.'

'Well, you look *much* better.' Decker kissed her cheek, trying not to jostle the sling on her right arm, noting that the intravenous line had been removed.

'Liar,' Beth said.

'Really. You look beautiful.'

'You have a great bedside manner.'

Although Beth's hair remained gritty, the tangles had been combed from it. The pallor had faded from her tan cheeks, as had a lot of the dark areas around her eyes. The blue-gray eyes themselves had regained some of their brightness. Her loveliness was reasserting itself.

'I can't tell you how worried I was about you.' Decker touched her cheek.

'Hey, I'm tough.'

'That's an understatement. How's the pain?'

'It throbs like hell. Did you learn anything? Did the police find out who broke into your house?'

'No.' Decker avoided her gaze.

'Tell me all of it,' Beth insisted.

'I don't know what you mean.'

'I've gotten to know you better than you think,' Beth said. 'You're keeping something from me.'

' . . . This might not be the time to go into this.'

'I'm asking you not to hide things from me.'

Decker exhaled. 'The detective in charge of the investigation . . . His name is Esperanza . . . feels that this wasn't a random event, that those men broke in specifically to kill me.'

Beth's eyes widened.

'I can't imagine a reason anyone would want to kill me,' Decker lied. 'But Esperanza thinks that, well, I ought to be careful for a while until he figures out what's going on. There's a policeman with me. Outside in the hallway. He drove me here. He's sort of . . . I guess you could call him . . .'

'What?'

'My bodyguard. And . . .'

'Tell me *everything*.'

Decker looked deeply into her eyes. 'You mean too much to me. I don't want to put you in danger a second time. When you're released from the hospital, I don't think we should see each other for a while.'

'Shouldn't see each other?' Beth winced, sitting straighter.

'What if you were struck by another bullet meant for me? It's too dangerous. We've got to stay apart until Esperanza gets the answers he wants, until he says the risk is over.'

'But this is insane.'

Without warning, the door opened. Decker turned sharply, not knowing what to expect, relieved when he saw the short slight doctor whom he had met when Beth was admitted to the hospital.

'Ah,' the doctor said, adjusting his spectacles. 'Mr Decker. You must be as pleased as I am by Ms Dwyer's recovery.'

Decker tried not to reveal the intense emotions his conversation with Beth had produced. 'Yes, she's recovering better than I hoped.'

The doctor walked over to Beth. 'In fact, I'm so pleased that I'm going to release you.'

Beth looked as if she hadn't heard him correctly. 'Release me?' She blinked. 'Now? Are you serious?'

175

'Absolutely. Why? You don't seem happy about—'

'I'm delighted.' Beth glanced meaningfully at Decker. 'It's just that what happened has been so depressing . . .'

'Well, now you have some good news,' the doctor said. 'Resting in your own bed, with familiar things around you, you'll be at the top of your form in no time.'

'In no time,' Beth echoed, glancing again at Decker.

'I stopped by your house and brought you some clothes.' Decker gave her the shopping bag he'd been holding. 'Nothing fancy. Jeans. A pullover. Tennis shoes and socks. Underwear.' The latter reference made him feel selfconscious.

'I'll have a nurse bring you a wheelchair,' the doctor said.

'But I'm able to walk,' Beth said.

The doctor shook his head. 'Our insurance won't let you leave the hospital unless you're in a wheelchair. After that, you can do as you like.'

'Can I at least dress myself without a nurse watching?'

'With an injured arm? Are you sure you can do it?'

'Yes.' Beth checked that her hospital gown was fastened tightly, then allowed the doctor and Decker to help her out of bed. 'There. You see.' Beth stood on her own, looking slightly off balance because of the sling on her right arm. 'I can manage.'

'I'll help with your clothes,' Decker said.

'Steve, I . . .'

'What?'

'I'm not feeling very attractive at the moment. In fact, I'm so grungy I'm embarrassed.' She blushed. 'I could use a little privacy.'

'There's no need to be embarrassed. But if you want privacy, sure, I'll be waiting outside in the hallway. When you're ready, the policeman will drive us home. If you do need help, though . . .'

'You can bet I'll let you know.'

10

After Sanchez checked the parking lot, Decker nervously guided Beth through the hospital's side entrance. On guard against any threatening movements in the out-of-the-way area, Decker helped Beth from the wheelchair into the back seat of the police car, then quickly closed the door and got in the front.

'Why aren't you sitting back here with me?' Beth asked as the police car pulled away.

Decker didn't answer.

'Oh.' Her voice dropped as she realized. 'You're keeping a distance between us in case . . .'

'I'm having second thoughts about even being in the same car with you,' Decker said. 'If Esperanza's right, there'll be another attempt against me, and I don't want to put you at risk. I can't bear the thought that something might happen to you because of me.' On edge, he kept studying the cars behind him.

'And I can't bear the thought of being apart from you,' Beth said. 'Are you really determined that we shouldn't see each other until this is over?'

'If I could think of another option that was safe, I'd take it,' Decker said.

'We could run away and hide.'

Sanchez looked back at her. 'Sergeant Esperanza wouldn't appreciate that. In fact, I can guarantee he'd do everything possible to discourage you.'

'That's part of your job right now, isn't it?' Decker asked. 'To make sure I don't leave the area?'

No response.

'It might be a good idea to avoid returning along St Michael's Drive,' Decker said. 'Take an alternate route so we don't follow a predictable pattern.'

Sanchez looked strangely at him. 'You sound as if this isn't the first time you thought you were being watched.'

'An alternative route just seemed a logical precaution.' Decker turned to Beth. 'We'll let you off at your house. You told me you had business back east, that you were leaving tomorrow. This is a good time for it. I know you don't feel like traveling with your arm the way it is, but you'll be able to rest when you get to New York. In fact, it would be a good idea if you stayed with relatives when your business meetings were over. Make it a long visit. And I think you should leave sooner. This afternoon.'

Beth looked overwhelmed.

'It's the only sure way,' Decker said. 'I still can't believe Esperanza's right, but in the event that he is, someone wanting to hurt me could use you as a weapon, maybe kidnap you.'

'*Kidnap* me?'

'It has to be considered as a possibility.'

'Jesus, Steve.'

'We can keep in touch by phone, and the moment Esperanza thinks it's safe, you can come back.'

'Stay away?'

'Maybe it won't be for a long time. Maybe it'll just be a little while.'

They lapsed into an awkward silence as Sanchez pulled into Beth's driveway and parked the cruiser protectively sideways in front of the gate to her walled courtyard.

Beth winced when Decker helped her out of the back seat. While Sanchez waited in the police car, they entered the courtyard and paused beneath the shadows of the portal, looking into each other's eyes.

'This has got to be a mistake,' Beth said. 'I feel as if I'm having a nightmare and I'll wake up in your arms and none of this will have happened.'

Decker shook his head.

'Can you think of *any* reason someone would want to kill you?' Beth asked.

'I've asked myself that question a hundred times. A *thousand* times. I can't think of an answer,' Decker lied. He studied her face intensely. 'If I'm not going to see you for a while, I want to make sure I remember every detail of your face.'

He leaned close, kissing her lips, trying to be gentle, to avoid her injured shoulder.

Regardless of her wound, Beth used her free arm to hold him close against her, to kiss him as if trying to possess him, even as she winced from the pressure against her shoulder.

She rested her cheek against his, whispering urgently, 'Run away with me.'

'No. I can't.'

She leaned back, her eyes imploring as fiercely as her voice. '*Please.*'

'Sanchez just told you, the police would stop us.'

'If you truly loved me . . .'

'It's *because* I love you that I can't risk putting you in danger. Suppose we did manage to fool the police and run away. Suppose we were followed by whoever is after me. We'd always be looking over our shoulders. I won't do that to you. I love you too much to ruin your life.'

'One last time – please, come with me.'

Decker shook his head firmly.

'I'll miss you more than you know.'

'Just keep reminding yourself, this won't be forever,' Decker said. 'In time . . . with luck soon . . . we'll be together again. When you get to wherever you're going, use a payphone to call

me. We'll work out a way to keep in touch. And . . .' Decker
breathed deeply. 'There are so many details to be settled. I'll ask
Esperanza to have a policeman drive you to the airport. Also—'

Beth put a finger to his lips. 'I'm sure you'll take care of
everything.' Reluctantly, she added, 'I'll phone your house when
I've made flight arrangements.'

'Do you need help getting your suitcases ready?'

'Most of my stuff is already packed.'

Decker kissed her a final time.

'Remember the best day we ever had together,' Beth said.

'There'll be many more.' Decker waited until he had his last
glimpse of Beth going into the house. Only after she closed the
door did he turn and walk back to the cruiser.

11

'*I want to talk to you.*' Esperanza was waiting in Decker's
driveway when the cruiser pulled in. His normally relaxed lean
features were rigid with fury. 'I want to know why you lied to
me!'

'Lied?'

Esperanza stared past Decker toward bystanders on the road.
'*Inside.*'

'If you'd tell me what's bothering you.'

'*Inside.*'

Decker lifted his hands in a surrendering motion. 'Whatever
you say.'

Esperanza slammed the door shut behind them after they
entered. They faced each other in the living room.

'I asked you if you were holding anything back. You said
you'd told me everything you could think of.' Esperanza's
breathing was strident.

'That's right.'

'Well, you ought to see a doctor – you're having serious memory problems,' Esperanza said. 'Otherwise, you wouldn't have overlooked mentioning something as important as your connection with the FBI.'

'The FBI?' Decker asked in genuine surprise.

'Damn it, are you also having hearing problems? Yeah! The FBI! The head of the Santa Fe bureau called me an hour ago and said he wanted to have a little chat. What could he possibly have in mind? I wondered. Something to do with Los Alamos or the Sandia labs? A national security problem? Or maybe an interstate crime spree? So imagine my surprise when I met him at his office and he started talking about the attack on your house.'

Decker didn't trust himself to speak.

'It's a federal matter now, did you know that? *Federal*. Why, I could barely keep my mouth from hanging open when he told me all about what happened last night. He knew details only Sanchez and I and a few other policemen knew. How the hell did he get that information? It's not like he *asked* about last night, sort of professional curiosity. He didn't need to ask. He *told* me. And then he told me something else – that the FBI would appreciate it if I let them handle the case from now on.'

Decker remained still, fearing that any reaction he made would cause Esperanza to become more agitated.

'The attack on your house involves extremely sensitive matters, I was informed. Information about the FBI's interest in the attack is passed out on a need-to-know basis and I do not need to know, I was assured. If I persisted in remaining attached to the case, I would cause untold harm, I was warned.' Esperanza's eyes were ablaze with anger. 'Fine, I said. I mean, hey, I wouldn't want to cause untold harm. God forbid. I'm as good a team player as the next man. My hands are off the case.'

Esperanza stalked toward Decker. 'But that doesn't mean I can't nose around *un*officially, and it certainly doesn't mean I can't demand a private explanation from you! Who the hell *are* you? What really happened last night? Why didn't you keep me from making a fool of myself by telling me from the start to go talk to the FBI?'

Whump.

With a roar, the house shook.

12

Decker and Esperanza frowned at each other as a deafening rumble shuddered through them.

'What the—' Windows rattled. Dishes clattered. Decker felt a change in air pressure, as if cotton batting had been pushed into his ears.

'Something blew up!' Esperanza said. 'It came from—'

'Down the street! Jesus, you don't suppose—' Decker lunged toward the front door and yanked it open just as Sanchez, who had been waiting outside, ran into the courtyard.

'The house next door!' Sanchez said, pointing, agitated. 'It—'

Another roar shook them, the rumbling shockwave of a second explosion knocking Decker off balance. 'Beth!' Regaining his footing, he charged past Sanchez, through the open gate, and into the driveway. To his right, above the piñons and junipers that shielded Beth's house, black smoke billowed. Wreckage cascaded. Even from a hundred yards away, Decker heard the whoosh of flames.

'*Beth!*' Vaguely aware that Esperanza and Sanchez were next to him, Decker raced to help her. He ignored the police car. He ignored the road. His throat raw from screaming Beth's name, he chose the most direct route, charged to the right, crossed his driveway, and scrambled among piñon trees.

'BETH!' Branches scraped his arms. Sand crunched beneath his shoes. Esperanza shouted to him. But all Decker really heard was the fierce rush of his breathing as he swerved around a farther tree, the flames and dark smoke looming closer before him.

As the trees ended, he reached a waist-high wooden fence, gripped a post, vaulted a rail, and landed on Beth's property. The fiery, smoke-obscured wreckage of the house was spread before him. The bitter stench of burning wood surged into his nostrils, searing his throat and lungs, making him cough.

'*BETH!*' The whoosh of the flames was so loud that he couldn't hear himself scream her name. Fractured adobe bricks were strewn everywhere. He stumbled over them. Smoke stung his eyes. Abruptly a breeze caused the smoke to shift, showing him that not all of the house was on fire. A corner section at the back had not yet been engulfed. Beth's bedroom was in that section.

Esperanza grasped his shoulder, trying to stop him. Decker shoved his hand away and rushed toward the back. He squirmed over a waist-high wall, crossed a wreckage-littered patio, and reached one of the bedroom windows. The force of the explosions had blown the glass out, leaving jagged edges that he broke off with a chunk of adobe he found at his feet.

The effort made him breathe hoarsely. As smoke billowed out, he swallowed some of it, strained to control his coughing, and peered through the window. 'Beth!' Again, Esperanza grabbed him. Again, Decker shoved him away.

'Leave me alone!' Decker screamed. 'Beth needs me!' He pulled himself through the window, tumbled to the floor, and banged his shoulder on more wreckage. Smoke surrounded him. He lurched toward the bed but found it empty. Coughing more violently, he groped along the floor, hoping to find Beth if she had collapsed. He felt his way toward the bathroom, bumped against the closed door, and became excited by the thought that Beth had taken shelter there, but when he tugged the door open, he had a heartsinking chance, before the smoke swept in, to see that the bathroom's tub and shower stall were empty.

His vision blurred. He felt heat and recoiled from flames that filled the bedroom doorway. At the same time, he was pressed down by the force of other flames that roared from the ceiling. He fell to the floor and crawled, struggling to breathe. He reached the window, fought to stand, and shoved his head through the opening, trying to pull himself outside. Something crashed behind him. Heat swept over his legs. At once something else crashed. Beams must be falling, he thought in dismay. The roof's about to collapse. Heat pressed against his hips. Frantic, he pulled and pushed and fell outward through the window.

Hands grabbed him, dragging him fiercely over wreckage as flames followed Decker through the window. The hands belonged to Esperanza, who clutched Decker's jacket, jerked him to his feet, and shoved him over the waist-high wall.

Decker felt weightless. Immediately he landed hard on the opposite side of the wall, rolled, and struck the base of a piñon tree. Esperanza dropped next to him, pursued by flames that ignited the tree. As the branches crackled, fire erupting, Esperanza dragged Decker farther away.

Another tree burst into flames.

'We have to keep going!' Esperanza shouted.

Decker stared back at the house. The smoke-spewing wreckage shimmered from the intense heat. 'Beth's in there!'

'There's nothing more you can do to help her! We have to get farther away!'

Listing, Decker fought to get air in his lungs. He stifled the urge to vomit and staggered with Esperanza through smoke down the treed slope at the rear of Beth's house. Again, he stared back at the inferno. 'Christ, what am I going to do? *Beth!*' he kept screaming. 'BETH!'

SIX

1

Decker sat numbly on the hard-packed dirt of Camino Lindo, his back against the right rear wheel of a paramedic truck, breathing through an oxygen mask. The gas was dry and bitter, or maybe the bitterness was because of the smoke he had inhaled – he didn't know. He heard the oxygen hiss from a tank beside him, a paramedic checking the pressure gauge on top. He heard the rumble of engines, fire trucks, police cars, other emergency vehicles. He heard firemen shouting to each other as they sprayed water from numerous hoses onto the smoking wreckage of Beth's house.

My fault, he thought. All my fault.

He must have said it out loud, because the paramedic asked, 'What?' frowned with concern, and took the mask from Decker's face. 'Are you all right? Do you think you're going to throw up?'

Decker shook his head, the movement aggravating a monumental headache, making him wince.

'What were you trying to tell us?'

'Nothing.'

'That's not true,' Esperanza said next to him. 'You said, "My fault. All my fault." ' The detective's grime-covered face had an oval impression around his nose and mouth from an oxygen mask that he had taken away. 'Don't blame yourself. This isn't your fault. You couldn't have anticipated this.'

'Bullshit. I was worried she might have been in danger

because she was close to me.' Decker spat, his phlegm specked with soot. 'I never should have let her go home. Damn it, I never should have—'

'Hold still,' the paramedic said. He had pushed up Decker's pant-legs and was examining the skin of his calves. 'You're lucky. The fire scorched your pants but didn't set them on fire. The hair on your legs is singed. And on your arms. Your head. Another few seconds in there and . . . I'm not sure I would have been as brave.'

Decker's tone was full of self-ridicule. 'Brave. Like hell. I didn't save her.'

'But you nearly got killed trying. You did everything you could,' Esperanza emphasized.

'Everything?' Decker coughed deeply, painfully. 'If I'd been thinking, I would have insisted she stay under guard at the hospital.'

'Here, drink this,' the paramedic said.

Decker sipped from a bottle of water. Drops of liquid rolled down his chin, leaving streaks in the soot on his face. 'I should have anticipated how easy it would be for them to get into *her* house while everyone was watching *my* house. If I'd gone inside when we brought her home, the explosions would have gotten both of us.'

Esperanza's dark brown eyes became somber – what Decker had said troubled him. About to respond, he was distracted by the wailing sirens of another police car and a fire truck arriving on the scene.

Decker sipped more water, then stared toward the chaos of firemen hosing the rubble. 'Jesus.' He dropped the water bottle and raised his hands to his face. His shoulders heaved painfully as tears welled from his eyes. He felt as if he was being choked. Grief cramped his chest. 'Oh, Jesus, Beth, what am I going to do without you?'

He felt Esperanza's arm around him.

'All my fault. All my damned fault,' Decker said through his tears.

He heard an ambulance attendant whisper, 'We'd better get him to the hospital.'

'No!' Decker's voice was strained. 'I want to stay and help find the bastards who did this!'

'How do you suppose they set off the bombs?' Esperanza asked.

'What?' Bewilderment clouded Decker's senses. He tried to focus on Esperanza's question. Concentrate, he told himself. Get control. You can't find whoever did this if you're hysterical. 'Some kind of remote device.'

'Electronic detonators set off by a radio signal.'

'Yes.' Decker wiped tears from his raw red eyes. Beth, he kept thinking. Dear God, what am I going to do without you? All my fault. 'A timer wouldn't be practical. They wouldn't know what time to set it for, when anybody would be home.'

Esperanza looked more troubled.

'It would have to be somebody watching the house, holding a detonator, waiting for the right time to push the button,' Decker said. 'Maybe someone with binoculars on Sun Mountain. Maybe one of the people lingering on the road, pretending to be interested in what happened last night.'

'I have police officers talking to everybody in the area,' Esperanza said.

'Too late. Whoever pushed the button is long gone.'

'Or maybe an electronic signal in the area happened to have the same frequency the detonators were set to. Maybe the bombs went off by mistake,' Esperanza said.

'No. The detonators would have needed a sequence of two different frequencies in order for them to go off. They would have been set to frequencies that weren't common in this area.'

'You seem to know an awful lot about this,' Esperanza said.

'I read about this stuff somewhere. A lot of it's just common sense.'

'Is it?'

Someone was approaching, footsteps heavy. Decker looked up and saw Sanchez stop in front of them.

'The fire chief says the wreckage has cooled enough for him to get close,' Sanchez told Esperanza. 'According to him, there wouldn't have been so much fire unless the bombs were incendiaries.'

'I figured that much already.' With effort, Esperanza stood. His long hair was singed. His jeans and denim shirt were grimy, laced with holes made by sparks. 'What can the fire chief tell us that we *don't* know?'

'He and his crew have started searching for the body. He says, with the adobe walls and the brick and tile floors, there wasn't as much to burn as in a wood-frame house. That'll make the search easier. So far they haven't found any sign of her.'

'Is there anything else?' Esperanza sounded frustrated.

'Yes, but—' Sanchez glanced at Decker, obviously not comfortable speaking in front of him.

'What is it?' Decker came to his feet. Adrenaline shot through him. 'What aren't you saying?'

Sanchez turned to Esperanza. 'Maybe we should go over to the cruiser. There's something we need to talk about.'

'No,' Decker said. 'You're not keeping *anything* from me. Whatever you have to say, you say it right here.'

Sanchez looked uncertainly toward Esperanza. 'Is that okay with you?'

Esperanza raised his shoulders. 'Maybe Mr Decker will share what *he* knows with us if *we* share with him. What have you got?'

'Something weird. You told me to assign officers to question people in the area – neighbors who might have been outside, someone who might have been walking by, busybodies who've been hanging around, curious about what happened last night, anybody who might have seen the explosions.'

Esperanza anticipated. 'And our men found someone who can help us?'

'Well, I think it's a complication more than a help,' Sanchez said.

'Damn it, what did you learn?' Decker stepped closer. 'What are you trying to hide from me?'

'Down on Fort Connor Lane, the street below and behind these houses, a woman was looking for a lost dog. Just before the explosions, she was startled by someone hurrying down through the trees and bushes on the slope.'

'Whoever set off the bombs,' Decker said. 'Does the woman remember well enough to provide a description?'

'Yes. The person she saw was another woman.'

Decker felt as if he'd been jabbed.

'Carrying a suitcase,' the policeman said.

'What?'

'Attractive, in her early thirties, with long auburn hair, wearing jeans and a pullover. Her right arm was under the pullover, as if the arm had been injured.'

Decker put a hand against the paramedic truck. The ground seemed to shift. He felt dizzy, his legs unsteady, his sanity tilting. 'But you just described—'

'Beth Dwyer. That's right,' Sanchez said. 'The woman looking for her dog says there was a car parked on Fort Connor Lane. A man was inside. When he saw the woman with the suitcase, he hurried out, put her suitcase in the trunk, and helped her into the car. That's when the bombs went off, when they were driving away.'

'I don't understand,' Decker said. 'This doesn't make sense. How could—'

A fireman came over, taking his wide-brimmed metal hat off, dripping sweat from his soot-smeared face, reaching for a bottle of water a paramedic offered him. 'There's still no sign of a victim,' he told Esperanza.

Decker's heartbeat became sickeningly fast. His mind swirled. 'But why would . . . Beth's *alive*? What was she doing on the slope? Who the hell was in the car?'

2

It seemed impossible. Beth hadn't been killed! A welter of relief and hope coursed through him. But so did confusion and dismay about her mystifying behavior.

'How did you meet Beth Dwyer?' Esperanza asked. They faced each other in Decker's living room.

'She came to my office. She wanted to buy a house.' This can't be happening, Decker thought, slumping on his sofa.

'When was this?'

'Two months ago. In July.' I'm losing my mind, Decker thought.

'Was she local?'

'No.'

'Where did she come from?'

'Back east.' Decker's headache was excruciating.

'Which city?'

'Some place outside New York.'

'Why did she move to Santa Fe?'

'Her husband died in January. Cancer. She wanted to get away from bad memories, to start a new life.' Just as *I* wanted to start a new life, Decker thought.

'This is an expensive district,' Esperanza said. 'How could she afford to buy her house?'

'Her husband had a sizeable life-insurance policy.'

'Must have been hefty. What was his occupation?'

'I don't know.'

Esperanza looked confused. 'I assumed you were intimate.'

'Yes.'

'And yet there are several basic things about her past that you don't know.'

'I didn't want to ask too many questions,' Decker said. 'With her husband dead less than a year, I didn't want to raise disturbing memories.'

'Such as where she used to live? How disturbing would that have been for her to tell you?'

'I just didn't think to ask.' It was another lie. Decker knew exactly why he hadn't asked. In his former life, he had made it his business to elicit every possible scrap of personal information from people he had just met, never knowing when that information might prove useful. But from the moment he had arrived in Santa Fe, beginning his new life, reinventing himself, he had been determined to shut out his former calculating ways.

'Was the husband's insurance policy large enough to support her after she bought the house next door to you?'

'She earned a living as an artist,' Decker said.

'Oh? What gallery?'

'In New York.'

'But what name?'

'I don't know,' Decker repeated.

'Imagine that.'

'I met the man who runs the gallery. He came to visit. His name is Dale Hawkins.'

'When was this?'

'Thursday. The first of September.'

'How can you be so specific?'

'It was only nine days ago. I remember because that was the day Beth closed the deal on her house.' But Decker had another reason for remembering so quickly – that night, he and Beth had first made love. Beth! he mentally screamed. What in God's name is going on? Why were you running down the slope in back of your house? Who was the man waiting for you in the car?

'Mr Decker.'

'I'm sorry. I—' Decker blinked, realizing that his attention had drifted, that Esperanza had continued speaking to him.

'You said someone with a remote-control detonator must have been watching the house.'

'That's right.'

'Why didn't that person set off the bombs when you were with Ms Dwyer outside her house?'

'Unless I went inside, it wouldn't have been one hundred percent certain that the bombs would have done the job.'

'So the spotter decided to wait until you left before setting off the bombs?' Esperanza asked. 'Does that tactic make sense?'

Decker felt a chill.

'If you were the target,' Esperanza added.

'*Beth* was the target?' Decker's chill became so intense that it made him shiver. 'You're saying that this afternoon and last night, they weren't after *me*?'

'She was obviously afraid of something. Otherwise, she wouldn't have been running down the back slope of her house.'

Decker's face tingled. 'They were after *Beth*? Jesus.' Nothing in his experience – not in military special operations, not in anti-terrorist intelligence work – could compare with what he was going through. He had never felt so emotionally threatened. But then, until he came to Santa Fe, he had never put down his defensive mechanisms and allowed himself to be emotionally vulnerable.

'A while ago, you spoke about the radio frequencies used to set off bombs by remote control,' Esperanza said. 'Where did you learn so much about how to blow up a building?'

Decker wasn't paying attention. He was too busy analyzing implications. For over a year, he had been in a state of denial, convinced that all he needed to be content were a total unsuspicious openness to the present and an equally total rejection of the calculating habits of his former life. But now he embraced those habits with a resolution that startled him. He picked up the telephone book, found the listing he wanted, and urgently pressed numbers.

'Mr Decker, what are you doing?'

'Phoning St Vincent's Hospital.'

Esperanza looked baffled.

When a receptionist answered, Decker said, 'Please put me through to whatever nurses' station is responsible for room 3116.'

When someone else answered, Decker said, 'You had a gunshot victim, Beth Dwyer, who was just released. I'd like to speak to any of the nurses who took care of her.'

'One moment.'

Someone else picked up the phone. 'Yes, I helped take care of Beth Dwyer,' a pleasant-voiced woman said. 'Of course, I didn't come on duty until seven. Other nurses would have taken care of her before that.'

'This is one of the police officers investigating her shooting.'

'Hey,' Esperanza demanded, 'what do you think you're doing?'

Decker held up a hand, gesturing for Esperanza to give him a chance. 'Did she have any visitors?'

'Only a male friend of hers.'

That was probably me, Decker thought. But he was finished taking things for granted. 'What did the man look like?'

'Tall, well-built, around forty.'

'Sandy hair?'

'As I remember. He was good looking in a rugged sort of way. I didn't see anybody else.'

'What about phone calls?'

'Oh, she made plenty of those.'

'What?'

'She received several, too. The phone was ringing constantly for a while. If I was in her room, she wouldn't speak to whoever was calling until I left.'

Decker's chest felt heavy. 'Thank you,' he managed to tell the nurse. 'You've been very helpful.' Pensive, he set down the phone.

'What was *that* about?' Esperanza asked. 'Do you know the penalty for impersonating a police officer?'

'Beth made and received several calls. But to my knowledge, I'm the only close friend she has in town. So who was she calling, and who was calling her?'

'If her calls were long distance and she didn't reverse the charges, there'll be a record of the numbers she called,' Esperanza said.

'Get it. But I have a suspicion the calls were local – that she was talking to the man who was waiting on Fort Connor Lane to pick her up. When I brought her some clothes so she'd have something to wear when she left the hospital, she told me she felt so grungy she was embarrassed to get dressed in front of me. She asked me to wait outside in the corridor. Given her injury and the fact that she might have needed help, I thought it was an impractical time to be modest, but I let it go. Now it's my guess she took the opportunity to make a final call to the man and tell him she was being released – to confirm what time he'd be waiting for her. But who the hell *was* he?'

In addition to Decker's other confusing overwhelming

emotions – relief that Beth was alive, bewilderment about her behavior – a new one suddenly intruded: jealousy. Dear God, is it possible? he thought. Could Beth have had a secret lover? Could she have been seeing someone else all the time I knew her? Questions tumbled frantically through his mind. How would she have met him? Is he someone who followed her from back east? Someone from her past?

'The man who was waiting in the car – did the woman who saw him get a good enough look to provide a description?' Decker asked.

'Sanchez would know.'

As Decker started toward the front door, in a rush to get outside to where Sanchez was guarding the house, the front door opened abruptly.

Sanchez appeared, startling Decker. 'Two men who claim to be friends of yours want to see you.'

'Probably neighbors or people I work with. Tell them I'll talk to them later. Listen, there's something I need to ask you.'

'These men are very insistent,' Sanchez said. 'They emphasized that they're *old* friends of yours, very old friends. They say their names are Hal and Ben.'

3

'Hal and—' Decker tried not to show his surprise. 'Yes.' His reflexes tightened. 'I know them. Let them in.'

Hal and Ben were the two operatives who had taken him into custody in the St Regis lobby after his bitter resignation the previous year. They had questioned him about his motives, had finally decided that he wasn't a threat to security, and had allowed him to proceed to the sanctuary of Santa Fe – with an implicit warning that his anger about what had happened in

Rome had better not prompt him to tell tales out of school.

Now he had to assume that they were the investigators his former employer had sent in response to his emergency telephone call about the attack on his house. As they appeared in the doorway, Decker noted that they didn't look much different than the last time he had seen them – trim and tall, about one hundred and ninety pounds and six feet, close to Decker's age, forty-one, their features hard, their eyes wary. About the only distinction between them was that Hal's hair was dark brown and combed straight back while Ben's was red and cut short. They wore jackets, khaki pants, and sturdy street shoes. After scanning the living room, they assessed Esperanza and focused on Decker.

'What's going on?' Hal asked. 'Why the policeman outside? What happened down the road?'

'It's a long story. This is Sergeant Esperanza. Sergeant, meet Hal Webber and Ben Eiseley.' The last names were fictitious, matching false identification that Decker knew they customarily carried. 'We hung around with each other when I worked in Virginia. They told me they planned to come out this way one of these weekends, but I guess it slipped my mind that it was going to be Fiesta weekend.'

'Sure,' Esperanza said, obviously not buying the story. He shook hands with them, comparing their trim-hipped, strong-shouldered build to Decker's similar physique. 'Are these more real-estate salesmen who know about setting bombs off by remote control?'

Hal looked puzzled. 'Bombs? Is that what happened next door? The place exploded?'

'Sergeant, would you give me a moment to be alone with my friends?' Decker started to guide Hal and Ben toward a door that led to a small barbecue area off the kitchen.

'No,' Esperanza said.

Decker stopped and looked back at him. 'Excuse me?'

'No. I *won't* give you a moment to be alone with them.' Esperanza's weathered face hardened. 'From the start, you've been evasive and uncooperative. I won't tolerate it any longer.'

'I thought you said you'd been asked by the FBI to stay away from the case.'

'The attack on your house. Not the explosions next door.'

'The FBI?' Ben asked, puzzled.

'Whatever you need to tell these men to bring them up to speed, you tell them in front of me,' Esperanza said. 'Bring *me* up to speed.'

'The FBI?' Ben said again. 'I don't get it. What does the FBI have to do with this?'

'Sergeant, I really do need to speak to these men alone,' Decker said.

'I'll arrest you.'

'On what charge? A good lawyer would have me out of jail by tonight,' Decker said.

'On Saturday of Fiesta weekend? Your lawyer would have a hell of a problem finding a judge to listen to him,' Esperanza said sharply. 'You wouldn't be out of jail until tomorrow, maybe Monday, and I don't think you want to lose that much time. So pretend I'm not here. What do you want to tell these men?'

Time, Decker thought, anxious. I've got to start looking for Beth right away. I can't afford to lose two days. Frantic, he felt torn between conflicting motives. Until now, he had been determined to protect his former employer from being implicated in the investigation, but other, more urgent priorities now insisted – he had to find Beth; he had to find out who wanted to kill her.

'I used to work for the US government.'

'Hey, be careful,' Ben told Decker.

'I don't have a choice.'

'The government?' Esperanza came to attention. 'You're talking about—'

'Nothing I can't deny,' Decker said. 'These men were associates of mine. They're here to help find out if the attack last night had anything to do with sensitive matters I was involved with.'

'Take it easy,' Hal told Decker.

'That's as specific as I'm going to get,' Decker told Esperanza, his gaze intense.

Esperanza's gaze was equally intense. Slowly, the detective's lean features became less rigid. He nodded.

Decker turned to Hal. 'You got here sooner than I expected.'

'We were in Dallas. We had the company jet. It's less than a two-hour flight.'

'Thanks for coming.'

'Well, it seemed the only way,' Ben said. 'We were told telephone contact with you wasn't secure. We wanted to touch base, clear up some confusion about something you said when you reported the attack, and then get in touch with the local feds.'

'Which you've already done,' Esperanza said. 'Talked to the FBI.'

'No,' Hal said with concern.

'Not in person but over the phone,' Esperanza said.

'No,' Hal said with greater concern.

'But the head of the local FBI office spoke to me this morning and made an official request to take over investigating last night's attack,' Esperanza said.

'You mentioned that earlier, but I didn't understand what you were talking about,' Ben said. '*No one* on our end has talked to the feds yet. We wanted a first-hand look before deciding if we had to involve them.'

Decker felt a deepening premonition, a quickening throughout his nervous system.

Esperanza anticipated the question for which Decker

urgently needed an answer. 'Then, if *you* didn't ask for federal intervention, who in God's name did?'

4

Steering sharply from Old Santa Fe Trail onto Paseo de Peralta, Sanchez drove the police car as quickly as he could without sounding the siren in the congestion of downtown Fiesta traffic. Stark-faced, Hal sat in front with him. Conscious of his rapidly beating heart, Decker hunched between Ben and Esperanza in the back.

Esperanza finished a hasty conversation on a cellular telephone, then pressed a button that broke the connection. 'He says he'll be waiting for us.'

'What if he doesn't tell us what we want to know?' Decker asked.

'In that case, I'll have to make some phone calls to Virginia,' Ben said. 'Sooner or later, he *will* tell us. I guarantee it.'

'Sooner,' Decker said. 'It better be sooner. It's been two hours since Beth ran down that slope and got in that car. She could be in Albuquerque by now. Hell, if she went directly to the airport, she could be on a plane to anywhere.'

'Let's find out.' Esperanza pressed buttons on the cellular phone.

'Who are you calling?'

'Security at Albuquerque's airport.'

'What if she used the airport in Santa Fe?' Hal asked.

'I'll call there next. The local airport has only a few small passenger flights. Prop jobs. It won't be hard to find out if she was on one of them.'

Someone answered on the other end of the line – Esperanza started talking.

Meanwhile, Decker turned to Ben. For a disturbing moment, he suffered a kind of double focus in which he was still being questioned by Ben and Hal as they drove him through Manhattan the previous year. Or maybe that debriefing had never stopped and what he was going through now was a waking nightmare.

'Ben, when you arrived at my house, you said you wanted to clear up some confusion about something I mentioned when I reported last night's attack. What were you talking about?'

Ben pulled a piece of paper from his pocket. 'This is a faxed transcript of part of your phoned-in report.' Ben ran a finger down the page. 'The case officer you spoke to said, "But you're not our responsibility any longer." You replied, "Hey, you sure thought I was when I quit. You were all over me. I figured your security checks would never stop. Damn it, two months ago, you were still keeping me under surveillance." '

Decker nodded, feeling a swirl of *déjà vu* as his words were read back to him. 'So what's the problem?'

'The case officer didn't comment at the time, but he had no idea what you meant by your last statement. He doublechecked your file. No one from our organization has been maintaining surveillance on you.'

'But that's not true,' Decker said. 'Two months ago, I saw a team. I—'

'At the start, when you first came to Santa Fe, we kept a watch on you, yes,' Ben said. 'But then it seemed easier and cheaper to monitor your financial records. If you suddenly had more money than your new occupation could explain, we would have been all over you, wondering if you'd been selling secrets for cash. But everything about your income has been copacetic. You seemed to have gotten over your attitude toward the problems that made you quit. There wasn't any need for visual surveillance. Whoever was watching you, the team definitely wasn't from us.'

'You expect me to believe Brian McKittrick decided to watch me on his free time when he wasn't working for you?'

'Brian McKittrick?' Hal asked sharply. 'What are you talking about?'

'*I told you I saw him.*'

'Two months ago?'

'McKittrick was in charge of the surveillance team,' Decker said.

'But McKittrick hasn't worked for us since February.'

Decker was speechless.

'His father died in December,' Ben said. 'With no one to protect the son, your complaints about him began to sink in. He screwed up on two other assignments. The organization dumped him.'

Esperanza put his hand over the mouthpiece on the cellular phone. 'Can you guys keep it quiet? I can hardly hear. Luis?' He leaned forward toward Sanchez. 'The Albuquerque police want to know if we've got a description of the car Beth Dwyer drove off in. Did the eyewitness give you one?'

'The old lady didn't know much about cars.' Sanchez steered around a crowded curve on Paseo de Peralta. 'She said it was big, it looked new, and it was gray.'

'That's all?'

'Afraid so.'

'Swell. Just swell,' Esperanza said. 'What about the man who was driving? Did she get a look at him when he hurried out to put Beth Dwyer's suitcase in the trunk?'

'When it comes to noticing *people*, this woman has twenty-twenty vision. The guy was in his early thirties. Tall. Built solidly. Reminded her of a football player. Square jaw. Blond hair.'

'Square jaw? Blond—' Decker frowned.

'What's wrong?'

'Reminded her of a football player? That sounds like—'

'You know somebody who looks like that?'

'It can't be.' Decker felt breathless. What he'd just heard didn't make sense. *Nothing* made sense. 'Brian McKittrick. The description fits Brian McKittrick. But if he isn't working for *you*,' Decker told Ben, 'who *is* he working for?'

5

Decker didn't wait for Sanchez to brake to a full stop in a no-parking zone before he rushed out of the police car toward a long, three-story-high, clay-colored government building. Flanked by Esperanza, Hal, and Ben, he ran up wide concrete steps to a row of glass doors, in the middle of which a fortyish man of medium height and weight, with well-trimmed hair and short sideburns, waited for them outside. The man wore slacks and a blue sport coat. A pager was hooked to his belt. He carried a cellular telephone.

'This better be good. I was at a Fiesta party.' The man pulled out a set of keys and prepared to unlock one of the doors. His sober gaze was directed toward Esperanza, who hadn't had an opportunity to change his singed soot-covered shirt and jeans. 'What happened to you? On the phone, you said this has something to do with what we discussed this morning.'

'We don't have time to go up to your office,' Decker said. 'We're hoping you can tell us what we need right here.'

The man lowered his keys from the door and frowned. 'And just who are *you*?'

'Stephen Decker – the man whose house was attacked,' Esperanza said. 'Mr Decker, this is FBI senior resident agent John Miller.'

Decker immediately asked, 'Why did you intervene in

Sergeant Esperanza's investigation of the attack?'

Miller was caught by surprise. He took a moment before replying, 'That's confidential.'

'It looks as if the attack wasn't against me but against a woman I've been seeing. My neighbor. Her name is Elizabeth Dwyer. She calls herself Beth. Does that name mean anything to you?'

This time, Miller didn't pause. 'I'm not prepared to discuss the matter.'

'Her house blew up this afternoon.'

Miller reacted as if he'd been slapped. 'What?'

'Have I finally got your attention? Are you prepared to discuss the matter *now*? Why did you intervene in the investigation about the attack on me?'

'Elizabeth Dwyer's house blew up?' Startled, Miller turned toward Esperanza. 'Was she there? Was she killed?'

'Apparently not,' Esperanza said. 'We haven't found a body. Someone who looked like her was seen getting in a car on Fort Connor Lane a few seconds before the explosions.'

'Why didn't you tell me this when you called?'

'I'm telling you now.'

Miller glared. 'I don't like being manipulated.'

'And I don't like being shot at,' Decker interrupted. 'Who's trying to kill Beth Dwyer? What do you know about a man named Brian McKittrick? How are you mixed up in all this?'

'No comment,' Miller said flatly. 'This conversation is over.'

'Not until you give me some answers.'

'And if I don't?' Miller asked. 'What are you going to do if I *don't* give you answers?'

'Doesn't it matter to you that Beth's life is in danger?'

'Whether it does or not is none of your business.'

Decker felt heat surging through his veins. As he returned the agent's glare, he wanted to slam Miller against the door. Beth!

he kept thinking. Whoever wanted to kill her might have caught up to her by now. But this son of a bitch didn't seem to care.

'Well?' Miller asked.

Decker took a step backward. He told himself to calm down. He told himself that it wouldn't do Beth any good if he got himself arrested for assaulting an FBI agent. Calm down, he repeated, his chest heaving.

'Smart,' Miller said.

'We need to talk about this,' Esperanza said.

'No,' Miller said, 'we don't. Excuse me. I have several important phone calls to make.' He opened the door and walked into the building. With an angry glance through the window, he locked the door, then turned away.

'When this is over, he and I *will* talk,' Decker said.

6

As Decker got out of the police car in his driveway, he peered dismally up Camino Lindo toward the remaining fire trucks and the smoking ruin of Beth's house. Onlookers crowded the side of the road. A TV crew had a camera aimed toward the wreckage.

'Sorry.' Remaining in the police car, Esperanza made a gesture of futility.

Heartsick, Decker was too preoccupied to respond.

'I'll keep working on him,' Esperanza said. 'Maybe he'll let something slip.'

'Sure,' Decker said without conviction. He had never felt so helpless. Hal and Ben stood next to him.

'I'll keep prodding the Albuquerque police and airport security,' Esperanza said.

'Maybe Beth and McKittrick drove toward Denver or

Flagstaff,' Decker said. 'Hell, there's no way to guess *which* way they went.'

'Well, if I hear anything, I'll let you know. Just make sure you return the favor. Here's my card.' Esperanza wrote something on it. 'I'm giving you my home telephone number.'

Decker nodded.

The dark-blue police car pulled away, turned to avoid the congestion of fire trucks and onlookers at Beth's house, and went back the way it had come.

Squinting from the westerly sun, Decker watched the cruiser raise dust as it receded along Camino Lindo.

'He's not obligated to tell us anything,' Hal said. 'In fact, he has to be suspicious about us. Certainly, he can't just take our word that we're somehow connected to the intelligence community.'

'Affirmative,' Ben added. 'Right now, he'll do everything he can to check our backgrounds. Not that he'll learn anything.'

'At least, he knew enough not to identify you as intelligence officers to that FBI agent,' Decker said. 'Given the FBI's turf wars with other agencies, Miller would have revealed even less than he did.'

'Even less? Hey, he didn't tell us *anything*,' Hal said.

'Not true.' Decker watched the police car completely disappear, then turned to open his courtyard gate. 'Miller's interest in Beth confirms that she was the real target, and when I mentioned Brian McKittrick, I saw a look of recognition in Miller's eyes. Oh, he knows something, all right. Not that it does *us* any good.'

Hal and Ben looked uncomfortable.

'What's the problem?' Decker asked.

' "Us",' Hal said.

'What do you mean?'

'We were sent here to do damage control if what happened

last night was related to any of your former assignments,' Ben said.

'And?'

'It wasn't.' Ben looked down, scuffing the gravel driveway with his shoes. 'Whatever Beth Dwyer's problem is, *your* problem is personal. We're not authorized to help you.'

Decker didn't say anything.

'As soon as we report in, we'll be recalled,' Ben said.

Decker still didn't say anything.

'Honestly,' Hal said, 'it's out of our hands.'

'Then, damn it, get in your car and leave,' Decker said. 'I'll do this without you.'

'How?'

'There has to be another way. Whatever it is, I'll find it. Get out of here.'

'No hard feelings?' Hal asked.

'Do I sound like I have hard feelings?' Decker said bitterly. He entered his courtyard and slumped on a bench beneath the portal, murmuring despondently, thinking, If Esperanza doesn't learn anything from the Albuquerque airport, if he decides to hold back on anything he does learn . . . The words 'dead end' passed through Decker's mind. He automatically applied their literal meaning to Beth. Was she being threatened at this moment? Why was she with McKittrick? Why had she lied? 'Something.' Decker impatiently tapped his right hand against the bench. 'There has to be something I've missed, another way to connect with her.'

Decker heard footsteps enter the courtyard. He looked up to find Hal standing next to him.

'Did she ever mention that she'd like to go to any particular place?' Hal asked.

'No. Only that she wanted to close the door on her life back east. I thought you were leaving.'

'No rush.'

'Isn't there?' Frustrated, Decker imagined Brian McKittrick driving Beth along Fort Connor Lane as she felt the rumble of the explosions that blew her house apart on the street above her. If only the old woman who had seen the car drive away had gotten the license number. Numbers, he was thinking. Maybe the record of the telephone calls Beth made from her hospital room would provide a direction in which to search.

Or calls she made from her *home* phone, Decker thought. I'll have to remind Esperanza to check on that. But Decker's skepticism about Esperanza continued to make him uneasy. What if Esperanza holds back information?

'There has to be another way,' Decker said again. 'What alternatives are there to trace her? It can't be through her paintings. She never told me the name of the New York gallery she used. There are hundreds and hundreds of galleries there. Given the time pressure, it would take too long to contact every one of them. Anyway, for all I know, the gallery was a lie and Beth never sold *any* paintings. The only proof was the art dealer I met, Dale Hawkins, and he might not have been who Beth said he was. If only I'd thought to make a note of the license number on the car he parked outside her house. But I didn't have a reason to be suspicious.'

When Decker looked up, Hal and Ben were watching him strangely. 'Are you okay?'

'What do you mean?'

'You're gesturing and muttering to yourself.'

'The car,' Decker said.

'Excuse me?'

'The car Hawkins was driving. That's it!'

'What are you talking about?'

'Dale Hawkins was driving a rental.' Decker stood, excited. 'When I passed the front window, I looked in and saw the envelope for the rental agreement on the front seat. I'm pretty sure it was Avis. And I'm *very* sure the date was September first because that was when Beth closed the deal on her house. A blue Chevrolet Cavalier. If Dale Hawkins flew into Albuquerque as he claimed, he would have rented the car at the airport. He would have needed to show his driver's license and a credit card. I can find out his home address.' Decker's excitement suddenly was smothered. 'Assuming Esperanza tells me what he learns from the car rental company.'

Decker looked long and hard at Hal and Ben.

'I'm probably going to regret this,' Hal said.

'What are you talking about?'

'I guess I can wait a while to let headquarters know that what happened last night has nothing to do with business.'

'You're going to help me?'

'Do you remember when the three of us worked together in Beirut?' Hal asked unexpectedly.

'How could I forget?'

On March 16, 1984, the Shiite terrorist group, Hizbullah, had kidnapped CIA station chief, William Buckley. Decker, Hal, and Ben had been part of a task force, trying to find where Buckley was being held prisoner. Decker's part in the search had lasted until September when he had been transferred to anti-terrorist activities in Germany. The intensity of those hot summer months and the determination of the task force were seared in his memory. Buckley was never located. A year later, on October 11, 1985, Hizbullah announced Buckley's death.

'Down the street from the task force headquarters, there was a little zoo,' Hal said. 'Do you remember *that*?'

'Certainly. I don't know how many animals the zoo had before the civil war broke out, but when we arrived, the only ones left were a leopard, a giraffe, and a bear. The bear hadn't adjusted to the climate. It was pathetic.'

'Then a sniper from one of the factions decided to make a game of shooting at whoever went out to feed the animals. The sniper killed the caretaker. In the next two days, he popped off four volunteers. The animals began to starve.'

'I remember that, too.' Decker felt a constriction in his throat.

'One night, you disappeared. When you came back in the morning, you said you were going to take food and water out to the animals. I tried to stop you. I warned you the sniper would like nothing better than to kill an American. You told me you had taken care of the sniper. He wasn't going to be a problem any longer. Of course, another sniper might have replaced him and shot at you, but that didn't seem to bother you. You were determined to make sure the animals weren't suffering.'

The courtyard became silent.

'Why did you mention that?' Decker asked.

'Because *I* thought about going out to track down that sniper,' Hal said. 'But I never worked up the nerve. I envied you for having done what *I* should have. Funny, huh? Beirut was a pit of human misery, but we were worried about those three animals. Of course, it didn't make any difference. A mortar shell killed them the next day.'

'But they didn't die hungry,' Decker said.

'That's right. You're a stand-up guy. Show me where the nearest payphone is,' Hal said. 'I'll tell headquarters we're still looking into things. I'll ask them to use their computer network to find out who rented a blue Chevrolet Cavalier from Avis at the Albuquerque airport on September first. There was probably more than one Cavalier. A good thing it's not a big airport.'

'Hal?'

'What?

' . . . Thanks.'

213

7

Decker struggled with painful emotions as he stared out the rear window of the Ford Taurus that Hal and Ben had rented when they drove up from Albuquerque earlier in the day. That seemed an eternity ago. What he saw through the car's rear window was the diminishing vista of the Sangre de Cristo mountains, of yellowing aspen in the ski basin, of adobe houses nestled into foothills, of piñons and junipers and the crimson glow of a high-desert sunset. For the first time since he had arrived more than a year ago, he was leaving Santa Fe. Oh, he had driven out of the city limits before – to go fishing or white-water rafting or on sightseeing expeditions to Taos. But those day trips had somehow seemed an extension of Santa Fe, and after all, they had been brief, and he had known that he would soon be coming back.

Now, however, he was truly leaving – for how long he had no idea, or whether he would in fact be coming back. Certainly, he wanted to come back, with all his heart, the sooner the better, but the issue was, would he be *able* to come back? Would the search upon which he had embarked create pitfalls that *prevented* him from coming back? Would he *survive* to come back? During his numerous missions in military special operations and later as an intelligence operative, he had remained alive in part because he had a professional's ability to distinguish between acceptable risks and foolhardy ones. But being a professional required more than just making judgments based on training, experience, and ability. It demanded a particular attitude – a balance between commitment and objectivity. Decker had resigned from intelligence work because he no longer had the commitment and was sick of an objectivity that left him feeling detached from everything around him.

But he definitely felt committed now, more than at any time

in his life. He was totally, passionately, obsessively determined to find Beth. His love for her was infinite. She was the focus of his life. He would risk anything to catch up to her.

Anything? he asked himself, and his answer was immediate. Yes. Because if he wasn't able to find Beth, if he wasn't able to resolve the overwhelming tensions that seized him, he wouldn't be able to continue with anything else. His life would have no meaning. He would be lost.

As he peered morosely out the Taurus's side window, noting how the sunset's crimson had intensified, almost blood red, he heard Hal in the front seat saying something, repeating his name.

'What is it?'

'Do people around here always drive this crazy, or is it just because of the holiday weekend?'

'No. Traffic's always this crazy,' Decker said, only partly attending to the conversation.

'I thought New York and Los Angeles had terrible drivers. But I've never seen anything like this. They come up right behind my rear bumper at sixty-five miles an hour. I can see them in my rearview mirror glaring at me because I'm not going eighty. They veer out into the passing lane without using their signal, then veer back into *my* lane, again without signaling, this time almost scraping my *front* bumper. Then they race ahead to crowd the next car. Sure, in New York and Los Angeles, they crowd you, too, but that's because everybody's in gridlock. Here, there's plenty of space ahead and behind me, but they *still* crowd you. What the hell's going on?'

Decker didn't answer. He was peering through the back window again, noting that the foothills and adobe houses had gotten even smaller. He was beginning to feel as if he were plummeting away from them. The race track flashed by. Then the Taurus began the climb to the peak of La Bajada hill and the start of the two-thousand-foot southward drop toward Albuquerque.

'Saturday night,' Hal said. 'The guy might not be home.'

'Then I'll wait until he comes back,' Decker said.

'We'll all wait,' Ben said.

Emotion made it difficult for Decker to speak. 'Thanks. I appreciate this.'

'But I don't know how long I can keep stalling headquarters,' Hal said.

'You've already been a great help.'

'Maybe. We'll soon find out if what I learned really does help.'

When Hal had driven to a payphone in Santa Fe, he had requested information from his employer's computer system. The system had covert links to every civilian data bank in the United States and with remarkable speed was able to inform Hal that while several blue Chevrolet Cavaliers served as rental cars at the Albuquerque airport, all but one had been rented prior to Thursday, September 1. The remaining Cavalier had indeed been rented on September 1, at 10:13 in the morning, but the name of the renter had not been Dale Hawkins, as Decker had hoped. Instead, the name had been Randolph Green, and his address had not been in or around New York City, as would have been the case for Dale Hawkins, but rather the address had been in Albuquerque itself.

'Randolph Green,' Hal said, driving farther from Santa Fe, almost to the crest of the hill. 'Who do you suppose he is?'

'And why does a man who lives in Albuquerque go out to the airport to rent a car?' Decker turned from the diminishing crimson sunset. 'That's what makes me think we're on the right track.'

'Or at least the only track that's promising,' Ben said.

'But why would Beth lie about his name?' Decker shook his

head. In a way, the question was naive – he already knew part of the answer. Beth had lied for the same reason she hadn't told him she thought *she* was the real target of last night's attack, for the same reason she hadn't told him that Brian McKittrick would be waiting on Fort Connor Lane to pick her up. Throughout her relationship with me, Decker thought, she's been hiding something. The relationship itself had been a lie.

No! he insisted. It *can't* have been a lie. How could anything that powerful have been a sham? Wouldn't I have seen the deception in her eyes? Wouldn't I have noticed hesitancy or calculation, *something* in her manner that would have given her away? I used to be a master of calculation. She couldn't possibly have fooled me. The emotion she showed toward me was real, the tenderness, the passion, the caring, the . . . Decker was about to use the word 'love' when it occurred to him that he couldn't recall an occasion when Beth had told him directly that she loved him. He had said it to her often enough. But had she ever initiated the statement or echoed it when he said it to her? Trying as hard as he could, he was unable to remember.

Other memories came readily – the first time he and Beth had made love, sinking to the brick floor of her studio, uncertain, tentative, awestruck, wanting, caressing, exploring. That, also, had been on September 1, after he had met 'Dale Hawkins', after Beth had shown Decker her paintings. An avalanche of doubting questions threatened to crush Decker's sanity. Had Beth actually painted them? Was Beth Dwyer her true name? Was her husband in fact dead? For that matter, had she ever been married? What was her relationship with Brian McKittrick? It couldn't possibly be a coincidence that McKittrick knew *both* Decker and Beth.

Madness, Decker thought. Sweat beaded on his upper lip. He felt off balance. Nothing was as it seemed. Everything he had taken for granted was called into question. He had a persistent sense of falling and almost wished that he had never resigned from intelligence work. At least, back then, he had known the rules. Deception was the norm, and he had never been fooled by the lies presented to him. Now, in his determination to believe that life didn't have to be based on deception, he had finally been deceived.

Then why, he asked himself, did he feel so determined to catch up to Beth? To protect the woman he loved? Or was his motive the need to demand explanations from the woman who had lied to him? Confusion was the only thing about which he was certain – and the fact that, for whatever reason, he would never rest until he found Beth. He would die trying.

Ben was talking to him again. 'When that detective – what's his name? Esperanza? – figures out you've left town, he'll be mad as hell. He'll have the state police looking for you.'

'For all of us,' Hal added. 'He saw this rental car parked in front of Steve's house. He can describe it.'

'Yes,' Decker said. 'He'll come looking for me.'

The Taurus crested the hill and began the long descent toward Albuquerque. As Santa Fe vanished, Decker turned to study the dark uncertainties that faced him.

SEVEN

1

After the Hispanic-pueblo design of the buildings in Santa Fe, the peaked roofs and brick or wood exteriors of the conventional structures in Albuquerque seemed unusual. While Santa Fe had a few Victorian houses, Albuquerque had many, and they too looked unusual to Decker, as did the even more numerous ranch houses, one of which was Randolph Green's.

It took an hour to find the address. Decker, Hal, and Ben had to stop at three different service stations off Highway 25 before they found one that had a map of Albuquerque. The map wasn't as detailed as they would have liked and they had to drive slowly, watching for street signs, but they finally reached their destination in the flatlands on the west side of the city. Chama Street consisted of modest ranch houses, whose lawns, shade trees, and hedges made Decker feel as if he'd been transported into a midwestern suburb. Again he had a dizzying sense of unreality.

'That's the address,' Hal said, driving past a house that seemed no different from any of the others.

The time was after ten p.m. Sunset had ended quite a while ago. Except for widely spaced street lights and a few illuminated windows in homes, the neighborhood was dark, residents presumably out enjoying their Saturday night. Green's house had a light on in a room at the back and on the porch.

'Maybe he's home – maybe he isn't,' Ben said. 'Those lights

221

might be intended to discourage burglars.'

'Drive around the block,' Decker said. 'Let's make sure there aren't any surprises.'

There weren't. The neighborhood appeared as perfectly ordinary as Green's house.

'Maybe we've made a mistake,' Hal said. 'This doesn't exactly seem like a hotbed of danger.'

'It's the only lead we've got.' Decker struggled to maintain hope. 'I want to ask Green why he had to go all the way to the airport to rent a car.'

Hal parked down the street.

Decker waited until the Taurus's headlights had been extinguished before he got out. He wanted the cover of darkness. But as he started to walk back toward Green's house, Hal opened the trunk.

'Just a minute,' Hal told him softly, and handed him something. Decker recognized the feel of a packet of lockpick tools.

Then Hal handed him something else, and Decker definitely didn't need to ask him what *it* was. The feel of the object was all too familiar – a semiautomatic pistol.

'Nine millimeter,' Hal said even more softly. 'A Beretta. Here's a sound suppressor for it.' Hal was taking items out of a suitcase. Ben was helping himself.

'But how did you get through airport security?'

'Didn't need to.'

Decker nodded. 'I remember now. Back at the house, you mentioned you'd used a company jet.'

'All set?' Ben asked.

After glancing around to make sure he wasn't seen, Decker removed the pistol's magazine, checked that it was fully loaded, replaced the magazine, and worked the slide on top of the weapon, inserting a round into the firing chamber. Carefully, he lowered the pistol's hammer, didn't bother to engage the safety catch, and shoved the weapon under his belt, concealing it beneath a tan windbreaker that he had put on along with dark sneakers, fresh jeans, and a clean denim shirt. Although he had done his best to shower off the soot in his hair and on his skin, the cold water had not done a good job. He still had a faint odor of smoke about him. 'Ready.'

'How do you want to do this?' Ben asked. 'If Green's at home, he might not be by himself. He might have a family. He might be innocent. Or he might be rooming with a bunch of guys who love to sit around with automatic weapons. In either case, we can't just barge in.'

'Watch the house from here. I'll have a look,' Decker said.

'But you might need backup.'

'You said yourself this isn't business. Since this is *my* show, I'll take the risk.'

'We're not doing this for business reasons.'

'Believe me, if I need help, I'll let you know.'

As Hal shut the trunk, Decker walked with deceptive calm along the shadowy sidewalk, warily scanning the houses on both sides of the street as he approached Green's. No one was in sight. He passed Green's house, turned left onto the yard of the house beyond it – that house was completely dark – and moved along a wooden fence, staying low until he reached the back. He had been concerned that there might be a dog at this house or at Green's, but neither backyard had a dog house and he didn't hear any barking. The night was still. While he worked to control his tension, he smelled the unfamiliar sweetness of new-mown grass.

The light at the back of Green's house came from a window, sending a rectangular glow into the murky backyard. No figures moved inside the house. From Decker's position, he had a view of the back of Green's single-car garage. Moving slowly to minimize any slight noise he made, he climbed the waist-high fence and dropped to the opposite lawn. Immediately he pressed himself against the back of the garage, blending with shadows. When no one responded to his entry into the yard, he peered through the garage's back window, the light at the rear of Green's house allowing him to see that the garage was empty.

Immediately he crept toward bushes at the back of the house and stooped beneath a dark window, listening for voices, music, a television show, anything to indicate that someone was inside. Silence. Satisfying himself that a hedge and some trees concealed him from the house in back of this one, he emerged from shadows and warily listened at Green's back door. No sounds from within. He approached the illuminated window and listened beneath it. Nothing.

He assessed the situation. If Green lived alone, the empty garage suggested he had gone out. But what if Green shared the house with others and not everyone had left? Or what if Green didn't have a car and that was why he had rented the Cavalier on September 1?

Damn it, I don't have time to rethink everything, Decker told himself. I've got to find Beth! In his former life, he would have backed off and maintained surveillance on the house, waiting until he had a chance to confront Green under controllable circumstances. But this was Decker's *present* life, and his heart pounded with the certainty that Beth was in danger, that she needed his help. There had to be an explanation for why she had lied to him. For all he knew, at this very moment she was about to be killed in Green's house.

He hadn't seen any signs warning potential intruders that the house was equipped with a security system. Usually, such signs were displayed in prominent areas. None of the windows in back had a 'protected by' sticker. On the off chance that Green had forgotten to lock the back door, Decker tried it. No luck. He reached into his jacket pocket, pulled out the packet of lockpick tools, and in thirty seconds had freed the lock. He could have done it much quicker, but he had to work cautiously, making as little noise as possible so as not to alert anyone who might be inside. He was suddenly conscious of the irony that last night someone else had tried to be cautious while picking *his* lock.

Drawing the Beretta, he crouched, opened the door, and aimed toward what he discovered was a small kitchen. The light he had seen was above the sink. As quickly as soundlessness would allow, he crept through the otherwise dark house, checking every room, grateful that there was only one level and that the house didn't have a basement. He found no one.

He went out through the rear door, emerged onto the murky front sidewalk without being noticed, and in five minutes was back inside, this time accompanied by Hal and Ben. The moment Decker locked the door behind them, he said, 'So let's find out who the hell Randolph Green is. When I searched earlier, I didn't find any children's clothing or toys. I didn't find any dresses. Green lives alone or with a man.'

'I'll search the master bedroom,' Hal said.

'If there's another bedroom, I'll take it,' Ben said.

'There is,' Decker said. 'And I'll take the study.'

'Maybe not.' Hal frowned.

'What's wrong?'

'Headlights coming into the driveway.'

2

Decker felt a shock. Through a side window in the kitchen, he saw the gleam of approaching headlights and heard a car engine. The vehicle wasn't close enough for anyone inside it to have a direct view into the kitchen, but it *would* be that close in a matter of seconds. Decker, Hal, and Ben ducked below the window and peered around hurriedly.

'Let me handle this. Don't let anyone see your faces unless it can't be avoided,' Decker said. 'If this turns out to be nothing, I don't want you identified for breaking and entering.' He retreated through an archway on the right, concealing himself in the darkness of the living room. Hal and Ben took a hallway on the left that led to the study and the bedrooms.

Outside, what sounded like a garage door made a rumbling noise. A few seconds later, the car engine stopped. The garage door made another rumbling noise.

Pressed next to a bookshelf in the living room, Decker felt sweat trickle down his chest as he listened to the rasp of a key in the back door's lock. The door was opened. A single pair of footsteps came in. The door made a scraping sound as it was shut. The lock was twisted back into place – and Decker stepped into the kitchen, ready with his handgun.

His reaction to the person he saw was a mixture of relief, confusion, and anger. Decker was well aware that his determination had led him to take risks that he never would have considered in his former life. There was every possibility that Randolph Green was a perfectly law-abiding citizen, that it was only coincidence that the man had rented a blue Chevrolet Cavalier from the Albuquerque airport on September 1. In that case, what if Green panicked at the sight of Decker's handgun? What if something went horribly wrong and Green was fatally injured? Even if Green wasn't injured, Decker had broken the law by invading Green's home, and Decker didn't have his former employer to convince the local police to overlook the crime if he was caught.

His misgivings vanished as the man who had just entered the kitchen swung in surprise toward the sound of Decker's footsteps. Stunned by the sight of Decker's pistol, the man lunged his right hand beneath the navy blazer he wore. Decker got to him before he had a chance to pull a revolver all the way free. Kicking the man's legs from under him, Decker simultaneously yanked the man's right hand toward the ceiling, twisted the man's wrist sharply, and pried the revolver from his grasp.

The man grunted in pain as he hit the floor. Decker slid the revolver away and hurriedly searched the man while pressing the Beretta against the man's forehead. Reassuring himself that the man had no other weapons, Decker took the man's wallet and stepped back, continuing to aim the Beretta down at him. At the same time, he heard urgent footsteps in the corridor at his back as Hal and Ben rushed into the room.

'Are you okay?' Ben aimed his own Beretta.

'As okay as I can be, considering how pissed off I am.' Decker gestured down toward the slender fiftyish man with soft features and thinning, partially gray hair. The only detail that had changed since Decker had last seen him was that the man's skin had been pale ten days ago but now had some color from the desert sun. 'Let me introduce you to the art dealer who claims to sell Beth's paintings – Dale Hawkins. Long time no see, Dale. How's business?'

Hawkins glared up from where he was sprawled on the floor. 'What the hell do you think you're doing? Do you have any idea—'

Decker kicked him. When Hawkins finished groaning, Decker said, 'I asked you a question, Dale. How's business? It must not be too good if you had to leave your gallery in New York? Or is your real name Randolph Green? I'm really confused about all this, Dale, and when I get confused, I get angry. When I get angry, I—'

Decker pulled out a kitchen drawer and dropped its heavy contents on him, making Hawkins groan and clutch his arm.

'Talk to me, Dale. Eventually you will, so you might as well save yourself a world of hurt in the meantime.'

'You don't know what—'

When Decker threw a toaster at Hawkins, it struck his thigh. The man contorted his face in pain, not knowing which part of his body to clutch.

'Don't make me impatient.' Decker poured water into a pot, set it on the stove, and turned on the burner. 'In case you're wondering, that isn't for coffee. Ever had a third-degree burn? They say scalding is the worst. I'm really serious about this, Dale. Pay attention. What . . . is . . . your . . . connection . . . to . . . Beth . . . Dwyer?'

Hawkins continued to hold his thigh in pain. 'Look in my wallet.'

'What?'

'My wallet. You've got it in your hand. Look in it.'

'There's something about Beth in here?' Not wanting to take his eyes off Hawkins, Decker tossed the wallet to Ben. 'See what he's talking about.'

Ben opened the wallet, studied its contents, and frowned.

'What's the matter?' Decker asked. 'He lied? There's nothing about Beth?'

'Not that I can find.' Ben looked extremely troubled. 'But assuming that this ID isn't bogus, Randolph Green is his real name.'

'So? What's the problem?'

'According to this—' Ben held up a badge. 'He's a United States marshal.'

3

'*A marshal?*' Decker's thoughts swirled. 'No. That doesn't

make sense. What would a US marshal have to do with—?'

'Quiet,' Ben said.

'What's—?'

'I heard something.' Ben stared toward the window in the back door. 'Jesus.' He raised his pistol. 'Get down! Someone's outside!' In that instant, he jerked backward, his forehead spraying blood from the force of a gunshot.

Decker flinched, his ears ringing from the blast that shattered the window on the back door. Sensing Hal dive to the floor, Decker did the same, aiming toward the back door, frantically shifting his aim to the window above the kitchen sink, then to the windows on each side of the room. Shocked, he couldn't allow himself to react to Ben's death. Grief would come later, *strong* grief, but for now, training controlled him. He had only one imperative – to stay alive.

Squirming fiercely backward, hoping to seek cover in the darkness of the living room, Decker shouted at the man whom he still thought of as Dale Hawkins. 'Who's shooting at us? Tell them to hold their fire!'

But Hawkins had a look of absolute incomprehension.

Decker heard angry voices beyond the back door. He heard glass shatter at the front. As he spun to aim in that direction, intense detonations threatened to burst his eardrums. One, two, three, four. Almost passing out, Decker shoved his hands to his ears and then his eyes, desperate to shield them, because the concussions were matched by blinding flashes that seared past his eyeballs into his brain.

Moaning reflexively, unable to stop his nervous system's automatic response to such intense pain, he fell to the floor, powerless against the flash-bang grenades that were intended to disable without permanently harming. In a turbulent recess of his mind, Decker knew what was happening – he had used flash-bangs on many occasions.

But knowledge was no defense against primal panic. Before he had a chance to overcome his pain and reacquire his presence of mind, his gun was kicked from his hand. Deaf and blind, he was grabbed and yanked to his feet. He was shoved out a door. He fell on a sidewalk and was dragged to his feet. Hands pushed him off a curb. Suddenly weightless, he was thrown to the right. He landed hard on a metal floor, felt other bodies being hurled in with him, and vaguely realized that he must be in a vehicle. A van, he thought, dazed. The metal floor tilted as men scrambled in. With several jolts, doors were slammed. The van sped away.

4

'You searched them?' a gruff voice demanded.

'In the house.'

'Do it again.'

'But we've got all their weapons.'

'I told you, do it again. I don't want any more surprises.'

Disoriented, Decker felt hands pawing over him, rolling him over, pressing, probing. His traumatized vision had begun to correct itself. His ears rang painfully so that the voices he heard seemed to come from a distance.

'He's clean,' another gruff voice said.

'So are the others.'

'Okay,' the first voice said. He sounded as if he had gravel stuck in his throat. 'It's time for show and tell. Hey.'

The van made a swerving motion, presumably turning a corner. Its engine roared louder. Decker had the sensation of increased speed.

'Hey,' the gravelly voice repeated.

Decker felt movement beside him.

'That's right. You. I'm talking to you.'

Decker scrunched his eyelids shut, then opened them again, blinking, his sight improving. Bright spots in his vision began to dissolve. They were replaced by oncoming headlights that glared through a windshield. A *lot* of headlights. Freeway traffic. Decker saw that he had been right to believe he was in a van. The rear compartment in which he lay had no seats. Three men with handguns faced him. They were crouched at the front end of the vehicle. Beyond them were a driver and a man in the passenger seat, who had his head turned, staring back.

'Yes, *you*,' the man with the gravelly voice repeated. Flanked by gunmen, he was husky with thick dark hair and a sallow complexion, olive-like. In his thirties. Wearing expensive shoes, well-cut slacks, a designer shirt, and a tailored windbreaker, all of them dark. Decker noted that the other men in the van had a similar appearance.

Ready with his weapon, the man leaned forward and nudged someone lying next to Decker. When Decker looked, he saw that it was the man he thought of as Dale Hawkins.

'You, for Christ's sake,' the man said. 'Sit up. Pay attention.'

Dazed, Hawkins pushed himself to a sitting position and slumped against the side of the van.

Although the ringing was still painful, Decker's eardrums felt less compromised. He was able to hear the driver complain, 'Another one! Jesus, these drivers are nuts. What are they, drunk? They think this is Indianapolis. They keep cutting in front of me. Any closer, they'd have my front bumper as a souvenir.'

The man who seemed in charge didn't pay attention to the driver but instead kept staring at Hawkins, who was on Decker's left. On Decker's right, Hal sat up slowly.

'So this is how it works,' the husky man said. 'We know Decker has no idea where the woman is. Otherwise, he wouldn't be running around trying to find her. But he must think *you* know where she is.' The man gestured forcefully toward Hawkins. 'Otherwise he wouldn't have driven all the way from Santa Fe to Albuquerque to break into your house and question you when you came home.'

The roiling breathless effects of adrenaline seized Decker's body. Everything was happening terribly fast, but despite the light-headedness and nausea that resulted when neither a fight nor flight response was possible, Decker struggled to keep his presence of mind, to pay attention to as many details as he could.

He continued to be struck by the man's dark eyes, strong features, and olive-like complexion. Italian, he decided. The group was Italian. The same as last night. Rome. This all goes back to what happened in Rome, he thought with a chill. But how?

'I'll make it simple for you,' the man in charge told Hawkins. 'Tell *me* what Decker wanted you to tell him.'

With a curse, the van's driver swerved sharply as another car cut in front of him.

'Where is Diana Scolari?' the man in charge asked.

For a moment, Decker was certain that his traumatized eardrums were playing tricks on him, distorting the sound of words. Beth Dwyer. Surely that's what the man had asked. Where is Beth Dwyer? But the movement of the man's lips did not match Beth's name. Diana Scolari. *That* was the name the man had used. But who the hell was Diana Scolari?

'I don't know,' Hawkins said. His skin had turned gray with fear. His speech was forced as if his mouth was dry. 'I have no idea where she is.'

The man in charge shook his head with disappointment. 'I told you I wanted to make this simple for you. I asked you a question. You're supposed to give me the answer I need. No muss, no fuss.'

The man picked up a tire iron, raised it, and whacked it against Hawkins's shin.

Hawkins screamed, clutching his leg.

'And if you do what you're told, no pain,' the man in charge said. 'But you're not cooperating. Do you honestly expect me to believe that the US marshal –' He held up Hawkins's badge. '– assigned to make sure that Diana Scolari settles herself into Santa Fe doesn't know where she's run to?' The man whacked the tire iron near Hawkins's other leg, causing the floor to rumble, making Hawkins wince. 'Do you think I'm that stupid?'

Hawkins's throat sounded parched as he insisted, 'But I wasn't the only one. There was a team of us. We took turns checking in with her, so none of us would stand out. I haven't seen her since the first of the month.'

The husky man again whacked the tire iron against the metal floor. '*But you knew she ran off today.*'

'Yes.' Hawkins swallowed with difficulty.

Whack! The tire iron struck the floor yet again. 'Which means you've been in contact with the rest of the team. Do you expect me to believe you weren't told where the rest of the team has got her holed up?'

'That information is on a need-to-know basis. They told me I didn't need to know.' Hawkins's voice sounded like sandpaper.

'Oh, did they really? Well, that's too bad for you, because if you don't know anything, you're useless, and I might as well kill you.' The man pointed his handgun at Hal. 'I know who Decker is. But who are *you*?'

'Nobody.'

'Then what good are you?' The man's weapon had a sound suppressor. The pistol made the muffled report of a hand striking a pillow.

Hal fell back and lay still.

Decker's heartbeat lurched.

The sudden silence in the van was emphasized by the roar of traffic outside. The driver swerved, avoiding a car that changed lanes without warning. 'These jerks. I don't believe it. They think this is a stockcar race. They're out of their minds.'

The husky man continued to ignore the driver, concentrating hard on Hawkins. 'Do I have your full attention now? One down. Next comes Decker. And after that, guess who?'

'You'll kill me anyway,' Hawkins said. 'Why should I tell you anything?'

'Hey, if you cooperate, we'll tie you up and stick you in a shed somewhere. We need to keep you quiet only until Monday. After that, it won't matter.'

'How do I know I can believe you?'

'Look at this face. Would it lie to you?'

'What happens Monday?' Decker asked. He remembered that Beth had planned to fly east on Sunday.

'Did I ask you to butt in?' the husky man demanded.

Decker shook his head.

'You're already on my list,' the gunman said. 'If it hadn't been for you, we would have gotten the bitch last night. We would have been back in Jersey by now. The boss wouldn't have gone ballistic at us for missing her again this afternoon. We wouldn't have to be spending our Saturday night driving around goddamn Albuquerque with you two.'

The reference to New Jersey increased the burning in Decker's stomach. It was absolutely clear to him that the gunman would not have revealed any personal detail unless, despite his promises to the contrary, he had every intention of killing Decker and Hawkins.

The gunman pressed his pistol against Hawkins's forehead. 'Maybe you still haven't grasped the situation. Maybe you don't realize what my boss will do to me if I don't solve his problem.'

'Please,' Hawkins said. 'Listen to me. I don't know what to

tell you. At the end of August, I was transferred from Philadelphia to Albuquerque. Diana Scolari was my first assignment in this area. Other marshals were already involved. *They* knew the details. I wasn't in the loop.'

At once Decker thought he might have found a way to postpone his execution. '*I* know her better than Hawkins does.'

The gunman swung his pistol toward Decker's face. 'Didn't I tell you about butting in?'

Decker nodded.

'If you know so damned much about her, why don't you know where she's gone? We had orders to tail you. After the bunch of you left the house to drive to the FBI office, Rudy here put a homing device under the back bumper of the car your friends rented, the one you drove to Albuquerque tonight. We've been following you. It's obvious you're running around looking for her.'

Decker didn't respond.

'Say something!' the gunman barked.

'If I knew what this was about, I might be able to remember something she said, something she let slip, something that gives away where she might have gone,' Decker said.

'And out of the goodness of your heart, you'd tell me.'

'To get out of this alive. Hey, I'm as pissed off at her as *you* are,' Decker said.

'Man, I doubt it.'

The van swerved again.

'She lied to me,' Decker said. 'Diana Scolari? She told me her name was Beth Dwyer. She told me her husband died from cancer back in January. She told me she'd come to Santa Fe to start a new life.'

'Oh, her husband died all right,' the gunman said bitterly. 'But it wasn't from cancer. She blew his brains out.'

Surprise made Decker gape. 'What?'

'She's a better shot than I am. She ought to be. Joey taught her.'

Joey? Decker thought. He wanted urgently to ask who Joey was, but he didn't dare, needing to seem to be giving information rather than getting it.

'And how did she tell you she could afford that house?' the gunman asked.

'Her husband's insurance police.'

The gunman laughed once, angrily. 'Yeah, Joey had an insurance policy, all right. It was in hundred-dollar bills in several bags in his safe at the house. Over two million dollars. After she blew his brains out, she took everything.'

The van swerved sharply, making everybody lurch.

'Hey!' The gunman turned in fury toward the driver. 'If you can't handle this thing, Frank will.'

'I'm telling you,' the man behind the wheel said, 'I've never seen drivers like this. Everybody's got these big pickup trucks, and they cut in front of me like it's some kind of game to see how close they can get without hitting me. This makes the Long Island Expressway seem like a drive in the country.'

'Just do what you're told. I'm sick of screwups. That's all this rotten job has been. One long screwup.'

As the gunman swung back toward Decker, Decker didn't show his startled reaction when he felt slight movement next to him. On his right. From Hal. Concealed by the shadows at the rear of the van, Hal pressed a finger against the side of Decker's ankle to show that the gunshot hadn't killed him. Decker could think of only one reason Hal would do that – to warn Decker that Hal might try something.

The gunman aimed his pistol at Decker. 'So, all right, loverboy. I'm a reasonable man.'

One of his companions snickered.

'Hey, I am,' the gunman said. 'Give me a little credit. So

here's my proposition. On the odd chance that you had a suspicion you wanted confirmed by this marshal, I'll give you thirty seconds to give me your best guess where she is. Make it good. Because if you don't sell me, it's bye-bye. Maybe by then this marshal will have figured out how serious I am.'

Sweat streaked Decker's face. 'She told me she was going back to New York on Sunday.'

'Of course. To testify on Monday. Twenty-five seconds left.'

'Then you know where to try to intercept her – wherever she's testifying.'

'Decker, after two attempts on her life, the feds won't risk exposing her now until she's got as much security as the president. The point is to get to her while they're still confused, *before* they get organized. Twenty seconds.'

I have to do something, Decker thought, frantic. I can't just let him shoot me. I have to—

His reflexes tightened as something made a muffled shrill noise in the gunman's windbreaker. A cellular telephone.

The gunman muttered, taking out a small slim telephone, pressing a button. 'Yeah, who is this?' The gunman listened. 'Damn it, Nick's going to be furious. We missed her again. The police radio said she got out of the house before it blew up. We're trying to find her . . . *You?* She went to *you?* Where did you take her? Well, I'll be . . . That close to home. Did you phone Nick? Will he take care of it? I don't mind telling you I was getting nervous . . . . We'll catch the first plane back. In the meantime, I've been talking to an old pal of yours, asking him if he has any last words. Anything you want to pass on? . . . Right.' With a grin, the gunman handed the phone to Decker.

Confused, Decker took it. ' . . . Hello?'

The voice on the other end was one that he hadn't heard in over a year, but its sullen tone was instantly recognizable. 'Decker, I wish to God I could be there to see you get it.'

'*McKittrick?*'

'You ruined my life,' the voice said.

'Listen to me.'

'You destroyed my career.'

'No. That isn't true. Tell these guys to take me to where you are. We need to meet. We need to talk about this,' Decker said.

'My father would have been proud of me.'

'McKittrick, I need to know about Beth.'

'But you had to interfere. You had to prove how smart you are.'

'Where is she?'

'You wanted all the credit.'

'*Why did she run away with you? What have you done with her?*'

'Nothing compared to what I'm *going* to do. And what those men do to *you* – I hope they make it last a long time.'

'McKittrick!'

'*Now* who's so damned smart?'

Decker heard a click, dead air, a dial tone. Slowly, in despair, he lowered the telephone.

The gunman kept grinning. 'Before I gave you the phone, your old buddy said to tell you, "*Arrivederci, Roma*."' He laughed and raised his pistol. 'Where was I? Fifteen seconds? Ten? Oh, to hell with it.'

But as the gunman's finger tightened on the trigger, Hal managed sufficient strength to make his move. Despite his wound, he kicked his foot up, deflecting the weapon. The muffled report of the pistol sent a bullet bursting through the van's roof.

Decker threw the telephone as hard as he could, striking the gunman between the eyes. At the same time, he lunged for the pistol, knocking the husky man off balance, jolting against the two men who flanked him. In the confinement of the van, bodies slammed against bodies.

'What's going on back there?' The driver looked over his shoulder toward the commotion. The van swerved.

Bodies lurched against each other. Decker kicked one of the gunmen in the groin while he struggled for the husky man's pistol. At once someone else was struggling next to him. Hawkins. The marshal struck one of the gunmen in the face and fought to pry his weapon away. In front, the gunman in the passenger seat started climbing over the low barrier to get to the back. The husky man fired again, another bullet bursting through the roof, as Decker shoved and the entire group thrust forward. The press of bodies knocked the gunman in front back into the passenger seat. The struggling bodies thrust even farther forward, toppling over the barrier, sprawling into the front, squeezing the driver against the steering wheel.

'No!' the driver screamed as the van struck the rear of a pickup truck. He stomped the brake pedal and tried to swing the steering wheel to avoid hitting the truck again, but the weight of several squirming men wedged him against the steering wheel and he didn't have the leverage to turn it. Out of control, the driver could only watch in horror as the van veered into the next lane, broadsided a car, tipped, fell onto its right side, slid forward, grazed another vehicle, and careened violently to the side of the freeway, striking barrels, smashing through a barrier, shattering the windshield, walloping to a dizzying sickening stop.

Decker's breath was knocked out of him. He lay motionless among a jumble of other motionless men, stunned, seeing double for a moment. He wondered why he was blinking up at the van's left side instead of the ceiling, then realized that the van had overturned and the left side *was* the ceiling. Time seemed to have halted. With a shock, it resumed, fear urging him into action as he smelled gasoline. The fumes were cloyingly thick. My God, he thought, the gas tank must have ruptured.

He groped to move, pushing a body off him. Fear propelled him. Headlights gleamed through the broken windshield. Hal. Have to get Hal out with me. Have to find Hawkins. With a start, he realized that it was Hawkins he had pushed off him and that Hawkins's blank gaze in tandem with the grotesque position of his head made it obvious his neck was broken. Hal! Where is—? One of the gunmen groaned. As Decker searched for Hal, his mind cleared enough for him to understand that the front doors were jammed with bodies and that the van had fallen onto its side door. Amid overpowering gasoline fumes, feeling trapped, Decker prayed that the back doors hadn't been jammed.

Another gunman groaned. One of them weakly raised an arm. Decker groped on his hands and knees toward the back and found himself staring down at Hal, whose mouth – revealed by headlights rushing past the broken windshield – was open, trickling blood.

His eyes were open also, sightless. But maybe he's just knocked out! Maybe he's not dead! Decker fumbled to try to find a pulse, not succeeding.

With a curse, one of the gunmen gained more strength. Simultaneously Decker smelled something else besides gasoline. Smoke. The van was hazy with it, making Decker cough. The van's going to blow up, he realized, and scrambled toward the back doors. His abrupt movement caused the van to tilt toward the rear. Why? What was it resting on? He reached the back doors. Because the van was on its side, the doors were horizontal. Gripping the bottom latch, turning it fiercely, he exhaled in triumph when it moved, grateful that it wasn't jammed. He pushed the bottom door open and squirmed out onto it, again feeling the van tilt. Unexpectedly he slid downward. In a frenzy, he grabbed the edge of the back door just before he would have tumbled toward the headlights of cars speeding below him.

He gasped as he understood that the van must have crashed through barriers on a section of the freeway that was being repaired. That section was on a bridge. The back end of the van projected into space, delicately balanced on the sideless rim of the bridge. He was dangling over a busy underpass, oncoming traffic roaring beneath him. If he let go, he would probably break his legs when he hit the highway twenty feet below him. Not that the pain would matter. He would be killed an instant later when a vehicle struck him.

He struggled to pull himself back up, but, responding to each of his motions, the van bobbed. It threatened to tilt all the way over and topple with him onto the underpass, crushing him. His heart pounded so fast that it made him nauseous. He stopped his frenzied attempt to climb back into the overturned van and instead hung motionless from the horizontal back door, calculating whether he could reach beneath the back of the van and clutch the rim of the bridge, whether he could grope along the bridge until he came to the side. Beneath him, wreckage blocked one of the lanes. Horns blared as the traffic in the blocked lane swerved between vehicles in the open lane. Meanwhile, the van bobbed again as a sound above him made him flinch.

The sound came from labored breathing as someone crawled to the back of the van. The husky man who had interrogated him peered down in stupefaction, his face covered with blood. Obviously disoriented, the man seemed paralyzed by the rush of headlights beneath him. Then the man saw Decker hanging from the open rear door, and his senses returned to him. He pawed at his clothes, evidently looking for his pistol. Realizing he had dropped it, he swung toward the van's interior. Again, the van bobbed.

Whump. A bright flickering light burst into view at the front. Fire! Decker thought. The gasoline had ignited. Any second, the fuel tank would explode. The van would blow apart in flames. The husky man quickly reappeared, pursued by the fire spreading rapidly toward him. In panic, he started to climb out onto the open door, then seemed to realized that the door wouldn't hold both Decker and himself. Screaming, he raised a pistol he had picked up, aiming at Decker.

No choice, Decker thought. He peered down, saw a transport truck passing beneath him, released his grip, and plummeted as the gunman shot at him. At the same time, the fuel tank erupted, flames enveloping the gunman. Then all Decker saw was the moving transport truck beneath him. Its driver had been forced to reduce speed as he avoided the wreckage in one lane, squeezing between vehicles in the next lane. With a gasp, Decker struck the sixteen-wheeler's roof and instinctively buckled his knees as he had been taught in jump school. If he hadn't rolled, if he had somehow remained upright, his chest and head would have been whacked against the top of the overpass. Coming out of his roll, propelled by the force of his fall and the momentum of the truck, Decker slammed his hands against the roof of the truck and clawed to find a seam, a ridge, *anything* to stop him from sliding. The rumbling darkness of the tunnel contributed to his dizziness. He felt his feet slipping off the back of the truck. Behind him, vaguely, he had the sense of a flaming body that streaked from the bridge and hit the highway, more horns blaring, the crunch of impact. But all he paid attention to was the speed with which his knees, thighs, groin, and chest slid off the back of the transport truck. He pressed his fingers harder against the roof, felt himself about to fly into space, imagined his impact on the freeway just before the crushing force with which the vehicle behind him would strike him . . . and then he snagged the top edge of the truck's rear door. Immediately his left hand lost its grip. He clung more desperately with his right, again snagged his left hand onto the top edge of the door, banged his knees against the center of the door, and touched the huge latch with the bottom of his left sneaker.

The truck sped from the tunnel. Decker heard an explosive crash behind him. Even without looking back, he knew what had happened. The burning van had cascaded off the bridge and struck the remaining open lane on the freeway. Horns blared. Metal crashed against metal. Glass shattered.

The truck's speed diminished, its driver veering off the freeway toward a breakdown lane. The sideview mirrors must have shown the driver the flames and explosion on the lane behind him. Now he was pulling over to stop and see what had happened. The more the truck reduced its speed, the better Decker was able to hang on. The moment the truck eased to a halt, Decker released his grip and dropped to the gravel at the side of the freeway. He vaulted the freeway's guardrail and disappeared into the darkness near a used-car lot before the driver walked to the rear of the truck and stared back toward the inferno.

5

'I'll pay you to drive me to Santa Fe.'

Decker was outside a convenience store/gas station. Amid the harsh glare of arc lights, he spoke to three street kids who had just returned to their bright red, dark-windowed, low-slung Ford, carrying two twelve-packs of beer.

'Man, we're busy,' the first kid said.

'Yeah, we're havin' a party,' the second kid said.

'Yeah, we're drivin' around, havin' a party,' the third kid said.

As one, the three of them snickered.

'You'll be able to have a much better party with the hundred dollars I'm willing to pay for a ride to Santa Fe,' Decker said.

The three kids scowled at him.

'A hundred?' the first kid asked.

'You heard me.'

'It ain't enough,' the second kid said.

'What *is* enough?'

'*Two* hundred,' the third kid said.

Again, they all snickered.

'All right,' Decker said.

The three kids scowled harder.

'Hey, what happened to you?' the first kid asked.

'I was in a car accident.'

'Looks more like you were in a fight,' the second kid said.

'Like you *lost* the fight,' the third kid said.

They bent over, laughing.

'Let's see your money,' the first kid said.

Decker showed them the cash he had gotten from his bank's automatic teller machine before leaving Santa Fe earlier in the day. 'So are you giving me a ride, or aren't you?'

'Oh, yeah, we're givin' you a ride, all right,' the second kid said.

But half the distance to Santa Fe, they turned off the Interstate onto a murky side road.

'What's this?'

'A detour.'

'Short cut.'

'Rest stop.'

They snickered uncontrollably as they showed him their knives.

'Give us your money, man,' the first kid said.

'Not just the two hundred,' the second kid added.

'*All* of it,' the third kid demanded.

'You picked the absolutely worst time to do this,' Decker said.

He broke their arms, legs, and jaws. Leaving them unconscious in the darkness of the desert, he got in the car and revved the engine, roaring back toward the Interstate, racing toward Santa Fe.

6

Beth. Decker was hunched over the Ford's steering wheel, gripping it tightly, staring fiercely ahead toward the dark freeway. Beth. His foot was heavy on the accelerator. Although he was determined not to attract the attention of the police by driving faster than the sixty-five-mile-an-hour speed limit, he was appalled to discover that he was doing seventy-five every time he glanced down at the speedometer. He had to go slower. If he was stopped in a stolen car . . .

Beth, he kept repeating. Why did you lie to me? Who *are* you? Who on earth is Diana Scolari?

A clock on the Ford's dashboard told Decker that the time was shortly after one in the morning, but he felt as if it was much later. His head throbbed from fatigue. His eyes were raw, as if sand had been thrown into them. More, his body ached from the bruises and scrapes he had suffered during the fight in the van and the subsequent accident. Dropping onto the transport truck had jolted him to his core. For the past year, he had deluded himself that by exercising regularly, jogging and playing tennis for example, he had kept in adequate physical condition. But now he realized that he had been coasting. He hadn't been maintaining a professional level of preparedness.

For what? he raged. I left that life behind me. I reinvented myself. What did I need to be prepared for?

Everything! he insisted as he sped past a pickup truck, his headlights blazing. I was crazy to let my guard down! *Beth*, he inwardly screamed.

Or maybe he screamed Beth's name out loud. His throat felt strained, his vocal cords tense. *Why did you lie to me?* Shot your husband? Took two million dollars from a safe your husband had in the house? What the— Had the gunman told the truth? Was *anybody* telling the truth? What about McKittrick? How was he involved in this?

Now he definitely *was* screaming Beth's name out loud, the angry outburst amplified by the Ford's interior. As he urged the Ford up the long dark curve of La Bajada hill, exhaustion and pain caused him to be overwhelmed by the confusion of emotions surging through him. He couldn't separate them, couldn't tell them apart. Was it love he felt, the certainty that there had to be a valid explanation, that Beth would provide the explanation, convincing him when he found her? Or were his emotions the opposite – hate, anger, betrayal? Did he want to save Beth?

Or did he want to catch up to her and punish her?

The Ford rushed to the crest of the hill, and in turmoil, he suddenly faced the lights of Santa Fe. The English translation of the city's Spanish name struck him with its bitter irony: holy faith. He had to have – he prayed for – faith.

EIGHT

1

Decker's house seemed like a stranger's. Having wiped his fingerprints from the stolen car and left it on a dirt road off Old Pecos Trail, he ran wearily through the darkness toward his home, but despairingly he felt no identification with it. For the past year and a quarter, it had been his sanctuary, the symbol of his new life, and now it was merely a place, no different from the apartment he had given up in Alexandria, Virginia.

Wary, he checked for surveillance on it, detected none, but still felt the need to be cautious, approaching up the piñon-treed slope behind it, as last night's attackers had done. Fumbling with his key in the gloom beneath a rear portal, he unlocked his back door and eased inside. In case the police might drive by and see any lights he turned on, he didn't reach for a switch, just quickly locked the door behind him and used the moonlight streaming through the wall of windows at the back to guide him into his ravaged bedroom. Litter was everywhere. The stench of cordite remained. *That* now was the symbol of his life.

For the third time in less then twelve hours, he took a cold shower and put on fresh clothes. *This* time, he packed a small travel bag. He gathered his few items of jewelry – a gold bracelet, a gold chain, a jade ring. He never wore these. They were a vestige from his former life, objects that he could barter if he ran out of money in an emergency. The same was true for the pouch of twelve gold coins that he had thrown disgustedly into a drawer when he moved in. He had intended to cash them in or store them in a safe-deposit box but had not gotten around to doing either. Now he added his jewelry to the coins in the pouch and set the pouch among the clothes in his travel bag.

Almost ready. He carried the bag to the door that led to his garage. That door was off the kitchen. He grudgingly paused to open the refrigerator, slap together and wolf down a ham-and-cheese sandwich, and gulp what was left in a carton of skim milk. Wiping drops from his mouth, he went into his study and checked his answering machine in hopes that there would be a message from Beth. What he heard instead were reporters wanting to talk to him about the attack on his house and the bombing next door. Several friends from work had also left messages, surprised about what they had learned on the news. There were a half dozen messages from Esperanza. 'Decker, as soon as you hear this, phone me. I've been trying to get in touch with you. By God, if you've left town . . .' Solemn, Decker returned to the kitchen, picked up his travel bag, and went out to his garage. His Jeep Cherokee's powerful engine starting without hesitation, he roared away into the night.

2

'Uh. Just a . . . What time is . . . ?'

Holding his carphone to his ear as he drove, Decker said, 'Esperanza?'

'*Decker*?' The detective's groggy voice immediately sounded alert. 'Where have—'

'We need to talk.'

'You're damned right we need to talk.'

'Your home phone number is on the business card you gave me but not your address. How do I get to where you live?'

Decker listened. 'Yes, I know where that is.'

Eight minutes later, Decker pulled into a dimly lit trailer court on the south side of town, the sort of unglamorous district that tourists roaming the glitzy shops on the Plaza weren't aware existed. A pickup truck and a motorcycle were parked on a shadowy dirt driveway next to a trailer. Yuccas studded the gravel area in front. A flower garden hugged the front wall. Esperanza, wearing black sweat pants and a top, his long dark hair hanging to his shoulders, sat under a pale yellow light that illuminated three concrete steps that led up to the metal front door.

When Decker started to get out of the Jeep, Esperanza gestured for him to stay put, walked over, and climbed in, shutting the passenger door. 'Your phone call woke my wife.'

'Sorry.'

'That's what *I* said. It didn't help the problems she and I are having.'

Esperanza's personal remark came as a surprise. Decker had been so preoccupied by his own problems that he hadn't thought about what kind of life Esperanza had outside his job. The detective seemed so objective and professional, he gave the impression he was like that twenty-four hours a day. Decker would never have guessed that the man had problems of his own.

'She keeps telling me I don't earn enough for the risks I take and the hours I put in,' Esperanza said. 'She wants me to quit the force. Guess what she wants me to be? You'll love the coincidence.'

Decker thought a moment. 'A real-estate broker?'

'Give the man a cigar. Do *you* get calls in the middle of the night?'

Decker shook his head.

'But in your former line of work, I bet you did. And for damned sure, *tonight* you did. I went over to your house several times. You weren't around. I kept phoning. All I got was your answering machine. Funny how a person can jump to conclusions. I had a notion you'd left town. If you didn't show by tomorrow morning, I was going to put out an APB for you. Where the hell have you been?'

'Out walking.'

'Since four in the afternoon? That's almost ten hours.'

'I stopped and sat a while.'

'*Quite* a while.'

'I had a lot to think about.'

'Like what?'

Decker looked squarely into Esperanza's eyes. 'I'm going after her.'

Esperanza's gaze was equally challenging. 'Even though I want you here in case I have more questions?'

'I've told you everything I can. This is a courtesy visit. So there aren't any misunderstandings. So you know exactly what I'm up to. *I'm going after her.*'

'And where exactly do you think she's gone?'

Decker ignored the question. 'I'm telling you my plans because I don't want you to put out that APB you mentioned. I don't want to have to worry that the police are looking for me.'

'And in exchange? Why on earth should I agree to this?'

Decker ignored those questions, too. 'Did the Albuquerque airport mention any sign of Beth and McKittrick?'

Esperanza stared at him in amazement, then broke out into bitter laughter. 'You really expect me to help? From the start, you told me as little as possible, but I'm supposed to share what I know?'

'Do whatever you want.'

'I intend to. Right now, what I want is for you to come into the house.'

Decker straightened. 'You expect me to stay here while you

phone for a patrol car to take me to the station?'

'No. I expect you to stay while I get dressed. Wherever *you're* going, *I'm* going. Whether you like it or not, you've got company. I'm tired of being jerked around. You obviously know a lot more than you're letting on. From now on, you and I are going to be like Siamese twins until you give me some answers.'

'Believe me, I wish I had them.'

'Get out of the car.' Esperanza opened his passenger door.

'Her real name isn't Beth Dwyer,' Decker said. 'It's Diana Scolari.'

Esperanza froze as he was getting out.

'Does that name mean anything to you?' Decker asked.

'No.'

'US marshals were watching her. She was supposed to fly to New York and testify about something on Monday. I can think of only one explanation that fits.'

'The Federal Witness Protection Program.'

'Yes.'

Esperanza got back into the Cherokee. 'When did you find this out?'

'Tonight.'

'How?'

'You don't want to know. But if you're serious about helping, there's a man you can tell me how to find.'

3

Decker rang the bell a fourth time, banged on the door, and was pleased to see a light come on inside the house. He and Esperanza had tried phoning, but after four rings, they had gotten only an answering machine. Assuming the man Decker needed to talk to hadn't left town in the twelve hours since they had last seen him, they had decided to go directly to where Esperanza knew he lived. It was a modest adobe on a side street off Zia Road, a low wall enclosing well-tended shrubs. Like many districts in Santa Fe, there weren't any street lights. Taking care to step back from the door when its overhead light came on, showing themselves so they wouldn't seem to be threatening, Decker and Esperanza waited for the door to open.

FBI Agent John Miller challenged them from the shadows behind an open window. '*Who's out there? What do you want?*'

'It's Sergeant Esperanza.'

'Esperanza? Why the— It's almost four in the morning. What are *you* doing here?'

'I have something I need to talk to you about.'

'Can't this wait until a decent hour?'

'It's urgent.'

'That's what you said this afternoon. I haven't forgotten how you tried to set me up.'

'You'll be setting *yourself* up if you don't listen this time.'

'Who's that with you?'

'The man who was with me this afternoon.'

'Shit.'

More lights came on in the house. The scrape of a lock being turned was followed by the creak of the front door as Miller opened it. He wore boxer shorts and a T-shirt that showed his athletically lean arms and legs. His rumpled hair and whisker stubble contrasted with his bureaucratically neat appearance the previous afternoon. 'I have a guest,' he said. Blocking the entrance to the house, he pointed toward a closed door at the end of a short hallway. Miller was divorced, Esperanza had told Decker. 'She's not used to people pounding on the door at four in the morning. This had better be good.'

'I want to know about Diana Scolari,' Decker said.

'Who?' Miller gave him a deadpan.

'Diana Scolari.'

Miller pretended to look confused. 'Never heard of her.' He started to close the door. 'If that's all you came here about—'

Decker blocked the door with his shoe. 'Diana Scolari is Beth Dwyer's real name.'

Miller stared down at where Decker's shoe blocked the door. 'I don't know what you're talking about.'

'She's in the Federal Witness Protection Program.'

Miller's eyes changed focus, sharper, more alert.

'That's what the attack on *my* house and the explosions at *her* house were about,' Decker said.

'I still don't know what you're getting at.'

'Granted, the FBI isn't as directly involved with the Witness Protection Program as it used to be,' Decker said. 'The US Marshals Service is mostly in charge. But you and they work closely enough together that they would have told you if they were relocating a major witness to Santa Fe. On the other hand, the local police would *not* have been told. It *wasn't necessary* for them to be told. The fewer people who knew the better.'

Miller's features became harder. 'Assuming what you say is correct, why should I admit anything to *you*?'

'Brian McKittrick,' Decker said.

Miller stopped trying to close the door.

'He's the man who picked up Beth when she ran from her house just before it blew up,' Decker said.

Miller's suspicion was obvious. 'How do you know this man?'

'I used to work with him.'

'That's a stretch. You're telling me you used to be a US marshal?'

'Marshal?' Decker didn't understand what Miller was referring to. At once the implications struck him. '*McKittrick is a US marshal?*'

Having unintentionally given away information, Miller looked chagrined.

'No,' Decker said. 'I never worked for the Marshals Service.' Pressed for time, he had to take Miller by surprise. 'I knew McKittrick when we worked together in the CIA.'

It had the appropriate effect. Startled, Miller assessed Decker with new awareness. He turned to Esperanza, then looked at Decker again, and gestured for them to come in. 'We need to talk.'

4

Like the exterior of the house, Miller's living room was modest: a plain sofa and chair, a small coffee table, a twenty-inch television. Everything was scrupulously clean and ordered. Decker noticed a .38 revolver on a bookshelf and suspected that Miller had been holding it when he peered out his window to see who was pounding on his door.

'I don't suppose you can prove you worked for the agency,' Miller said.

'Not at the moment. We didn't exactly use badges and business cards.'

'Then why should I believe you?' Miller frowned toward Esperanza. 'Do *you* believe him?'

Esperanza nodded.

'Why?'

'You haven't been with him since this time yesterday. The way he handles himself in a crisis, it's obvious he's a professional, and I don't mean at selling real estate.'

'We'll see.' Miller returned his attention to Decker. 'What do you know about Brian McKittrick?'

'He's the most fucked-up operative I ever worked with.'

Miller stepped closer.

'Wouldn't obey orders,' Decker said. 'Thought his team members were scheming against him. Took serious action without permission. Exceeded his authority at every opportunity. The assignment I shared with him ended as a disaster because of him. Numerous casualties. It was almost an international incident.'

Miller studied him, as if debating how candid he wanted to be. At last, exhaling, he sat wearily in the chair opposite Decker. 'It's not giving anything important away if I admit I've heard rumors about McKittrick. Nothing to do with the CIA. I didn't know anything about that. His behavior as a marshal. That's what I heard rumors about. He's a hot dog. Thinks he knows better than his superiors. Doesn't obey the chain of command. Violates procedure. I never understood how he got into the Marshals Service.'

'I can make a good guess,' Decker said. 'The agency must have given him first-rate recommendations when they let him go. In exchange for his not embarrassing them by revealing details about the disaster he was involved in.'

'But if McKittrick caused the disaster, he would have been harming himself if he talked about it.'

'Not if he convinced himself he wasn't to blame,' Decker said. 'McKittrick has a reality problem. When he does something wrong, he manages to delude himself that it's always someone else's fault.'

Esperanza leaned forward. 'You sound especially bitter about that.'

'*I* was the one he blamed. I resigned from government work because of him – and now the son of a bitch is back in my life.'

'By coincidence.'

'No. I can't believe it's a coincidence that Beth just happened to buy the house next to mine. Not if McKittrick was in charge

257

of her protection. The only way the scenario makes sense is if McKittrick kept tabs on me after I quit the agency. He knew I was in Santa Fe. He had a witness to relocate. He did a little more investigating and found out the house next to mine was for sale. Perfect. Why not put Beth next to me? She'd have a next-door neighbor as extra protection, an unwitting bodyguard.'

Miller thought about it. 'The tactic might have been cynical, but it does make sense.'

'Cynical doesn't begin to describe it. I was *used*,' Decker said. 'And if I'm not mistaken, *Beth* was used. I think McKittrick went over to the other side.'

'*What?*'

Decker vividly remembered his telephone conversation with McKittrick. 'I think McKittrick told the mob how to find her, provided they killed me in the bargain. I think he blames me for the CIA's decision to kick him out. I think he's a sick bastard who planned to ruin my life from the moment he was assigned to help turn Diana Scolari into Beth Dwyer.'

5

The small living room became silent.

'That's a serious accusation.' Miller bit his lower lip. 'Can you *prove* any of this?'

'No.' Decker didn't dare tell him about what had happened in the van.

'How did you find out that Beth Dwyer's real name is Diana Scolari?'

'I can't tell you.'

'Why not?'

Decker didn't respond.

'Listen very carefully.' Miller stood. 'You are in possession of information indicating there was a serious breach of security in the protection of an important government witness. I am ordering you to tell me how you came by this information.'

'I'm not at liberty to say.'

Miller glared. 'I'll teach you about liberty.' He picked up the telephone. 'You'll be giving up your liberty for quite a while until you tell me what I want to know.'

'No. You're making a mistake,' Decker said.

Miller glared harder. '*I'm* not the one who's making a mistake.'

'Put down the phone. Please. All that matters is saving Beth's life.'

Miller swung toward Esperanza. 'Do you hear this bullshit?'

'Yes. For the past twenty-four hours, he's been playing mindgames on me,' Esperanza said. 'What worries me is, he's beginning to make sense. Beth Dwyer's safety *is* the priority. If Decker cut corners to get his information, I'm prepared to deal with that later, provided it doesn't compromise me.'

'Plausible deniability,' Decker said.

'What?'

'That's what we used to call it in the agency.'

'How about calling it "accessory to a felony"?' Miller asked.

'Tell me what Beth Dwyer was going to testify about.'

Miller wasn't prepared for the abrupt change of topic.

'Did she really shoot her husband in the head and get away with two million dollars of mob money?' Decker asked.

Miller gestured fiercely. 'Where the hell did you learn this stuff?'

But Decker ignored the outburst. He was too busy recalling something the gunman had said on the telephone. ('*Nick's going to be furious.*')

'A man called Nick is involved,' Decker said. 'Do you know who that is? What's his last name?'

Miller blinked in astonishment. 'It's worse than I thought. There'll have to be a complete review of witness-relocation security procedures.'

'Beth's in danger,' Decker said with force. 'If we share what we know, we might be able to save her life.'

'Diana Scolari.'

'I don't know anything about Diana Scolari. The woman I care about is Beth Dwyer. *Tell me about her.*'

Miller stared toward the darkness beyond his window. He stared at his hands. He stared at Decker. 'Diana Scolari is the wife – or used to be the wife until someone shot the son of a bitch in the head – of Joey Scolari, the chief enforcer for the Giordano family in New York City. We estimate that Joey was responsible for at least forty mob executions during his eight-year tenure. He was a very busy man. But he didn't complain. The money was excellent and, just as important, he loved his work.'

Decker listened, distressed.

'Three years ago, Joey met the woman you know as Beth Dwyer. Her unmarried name was Diana Berlanti, and she was working as an activity director on a cruise ship in the Caribbean, where Joey had decided to put himself on display to give himself an alibi while one of his lieutenants eliminated a problem back in New York. Diana attracted his attention. Understand, he was a good-looking guy, stylish dresser, knew what to say to women. They normally fell all over him, so it wasn't any surprise that Diana didn't tell him to get lost when he started making advances. One thing led to another. They were married three months later. The courtship was convenient for him. He arranged it so they kept going back to the Caribbean. It gave him a chance to have a natural-seeming reason to visit certain islands that have banks with numbered accounts and no objection to laundering money. Same with the honeymoon.'

Decker felt sick.

'It's important to emphasize that, according to Diana, she had no idea of Joey's real occupation. She claims he told her he was in the restaurant business – which is true enough; Joey did own several restaurants as part of the same money-laundering scheme. Anyhow, time passed, and – no surprise, Joey's attention span was limited – he started to get tired of her. For a while, they lived in his penthouse in the city, but when he needed the place for his extracurricular activities, he put Diana in a big house with walls around it across the river in one of those mob bedroom communities in New Jersey. Plenty of guards. To keep her safe, he claimed. Actually they were to keep her from going back to the penthouse and catching him with his girlfriends. But an equally important reason for the guards was to make sure she didn't get any ideas about moving out after the numerous times he beat her up.'

Decker's temples throbbed.

'And I mean he beat her up *a lot*,' Miller said. 'Because Diana had started asking questions not only about his fidelity but also about his business. You know how intelligent she is. It didn't take her long to realize what Joey really did, what kind of monster he was. So now she had a big problem. If she tried to leave – and there wasn't much hope of success with so many guards – she was certain he'd kill her. If she stayed and he suspected she was noticing too much, he'd kill her also. Her temporary solution was to pretend to lose interest in his women and his business, to pretend to be compliant. She spent her days doing what under other circumstances would have given her a great deal of pleasure – painting. Joey got a kick out of that, found it amusing. Sometimes, after he beat her up, he would build a big fire in the den and force her to watch him burn her favorite paintings.'

'Jesus,' Decker said. 'Why did the bastard marry her?'

'Obviously for the pleasure of possessing someone he could

hurt. As I said, Joey was a monster. Until nine months ago, in January, when someone solved her problem by blowing Joey's brains out. Or maybe *she* did it. There are two conflicting stories. Diana claims she was outside in the back of the estate, painting a winter scene, when she heard a shot in the house. Cautious, not knowing what to expect, she took her time going inside. Her assumption was that whatever had happened, Joey and the guards would take care of it. Her first surprise was to find the guards gone. Her second surprise was to find Joey dead in his study, his brains across his desk, his safe open. That safe normally held a considerable amount of cash, she knew. She'd seen bags of it delivered from time to time. She'd caught a glimpse of Joey putting it away. She'd overheard references to amounts. Her best guess was that two million dollars was missing. The implications of that didn't strike her at the time. All she cared about was taking the opportunity to escape. She didn't even bother to pack, just threw on an overcoat, grabbed Joey's keys, and drove away.'

'To the Justice Department,' Decker said.

'What other direction did she have? She knew the mob would be looking for her after she disappeared. But she figured their motive would be to keep her from talking. She didn't realize until later that Joey's godfather blamed her for the death, that the mob figured *she* killed Joey and took the money. It was a matter of family pride now. *Blood* pride. Revenge.'

Decker nodded. 'So the Justice Department spent months debriefing her, relocated her with a new identity in Santa Fe, and finally summoned her back to New York to testify.'

'Under protection.'

'You mean *McKittrick's* protection.'

'Unfortunately.'

'What a goddamn mess,' Esperanza said.

'You still haven't told me who Nick is,' Decker said.

'Nick Giordano, the head of the family, Joey's godfather. Joey's birth father was Nick's best friend. When Joey's parents were killed in a mob attempt to kill Nick, Nick raised Joey as his own. That's what I meant about blood pride. To Nick, it's a matter of personal honor – family in the strictest sense – to find and punish her. Now it's *your* turn,' Miller said. 'How is what I just told you going to help save Diana Scolari's life?'

Decker didn't speak for a moment. 'It looks like I have only one choice.'

'What are you talking about? *What* choice?'

'I'm suddenly very tired. I'm going home.'

'How the hell is *that* going to help your girlfriend?'

'I'll phone you when I wake up. Maybe you'll have more information by then.' Decker turned toward Esperanza. 'I'll drop you off.'

6

'Don't bother taking me home,' Esperanza said as Decker put the Cherokee into gear and sped from Miller's house.

'Then where do you want me to take you?' Decker veered around a shadowy corner.

'Just figure I'm along for the ride.'

'What do you think that will accomplish?'

'Maybe I'll keep you out of trouble,' Esperanza said. 'Where are your friends?'

'Friends?' The thought of Hal and Ben made Decker's mouth taste of ashes.

'You sound as if you don't really have many.'

'I have a lot of acquaintances.'

'I was referring to the two men who showed up at your house this afternoon.'

'I know who you're referring to. They left town.' The taste of ashes was matched by an aching sensation – in his chest and at his eyes.

'So soon?' Esperanza asked. 'After they went to all the trouble to get here so quickly?'

'My former employer decided what was happening here had nothing to do with business.' The murky streets were almost deserted. Headlights blazing, Decker pressed his foot on the accelerator.

'Do you think it's a good idea exceeding the speed limit with a police officer in the car?'

'I can't think of anyone I'd rather exceed it with. If a cruiser stops us, show your badge – explain we're on the way to an emergency.'

'I lied to you,' Esperanza said. 'I did have the State Police and the Albuquerque PD looking for you.'

Decker felt a cold spot on his spine.

'I gave them the license number and the description of the Taurus your friends were driving. The car was found near a crime scene on Chama Street in Albuquerque around eleven o'clock tonight. The neighbors complained about what they thought were gunshots and explosions. Turned out the neighbors were right. A man whose ID referred to him as Ben Eiseley was found shot to death on the kitchen floor of the house the neighbors complained about. We have no idea where Hal is.'

For an instant, Decker could no longer repress his grief. The memory of the shocked expression on Ben's face as the bullet struck him, blood spewing from his head, seized Decker. Suddenly it was as if he had never come to Santa Fe, as if he had never tried to distance himself from his former life. He thought about how Hal had been shot in the chest and yet had still managed the strength to kick the man who had shot him. This wasn't their fight! Decker thought. I should have insisted they back off. But I asked for their help. They died because of me. It's my fault!'

'They must have been given another assignment while they were out here,' Decker said as calmly as he could.

'You don't seem affected by what happened to Ben.'

'In my own way.'

'I've never met anyone like you,' Esperanza said. 'Aren't you curious about what he was doing there and where his partner is?'

'Let me ask *you* a question,' Decker said angrily. 'Why did you wait so long to tell me you'd put out a police alert about me?'

'I wanted the right moment. To make a point. You need me,' Esperanza said. 'Security at the Albuquerque airport has your name. The officers are watching for a man of your description. The minute you try to buy a ticket, you'll be stopped. If you want to fly to New York, you need me to call off the alert, and I charge a price for doing that. You're going to have to let me come along.'

'Fly to New York? What makes you think I—'

'Decker, just once, for Christ's sake, quit playing mindgames with me, will you?'

'Why would you want to go to New York?'

'Let's say tomorrow's my day off and and my wife and I could use a little distance from each other.' Esperanza gestured with frustration. 'Or let's say being with you is a definite learning experience, and I'm not ready to let the classes end. Or maybe, let's say – and this is really far out – let's say I'm a cop because I'm a sucker for helping people. Dumb idea, huh? Right now, I can't think of anybody who needs help more than Beth Dwyer. I want to help you save her. I've got a feeling you're the only person who really knows how to do that.'

7

The roar of the eastward-bound jet vibrated through the fuselage. Sunlight blazed through the window, making Decker's weary eyes feel stabbed. As flight attendants came down the aisle, handing out coffee and a sweet roll, his stomach pained him, reminding him of the stomach problems that he used to have when he was an operative. It's all coming back, he told himself.

Esperanza sat next to him, the only other passenger in the row. 'I regret I've never met Beth Dwyer. She must be very special.'

Decker stared out the window at the high-desert landscape he was leaving, the mountains, the arroyos, the Rio Grande, the green of piñon trees against the yellow, orange, and red of the land. He couldn't help being reminded of his ambivalent feelings when he had first arrived, his concern that he might have been making a mistake. Now, after more than a year, he was flying away, and again he felt ambivalent, again wondered if he was making a mistake.

'Yes,' Decker said, 'very special.'

'You must love her very much.'

'That depends. It may be –' Decker had trouble speaking. '– that I also hate her.'

'Hate?'

'She should have told me about her background,' Decker said.

'At the start, she probably thought it was none of your business.'

'And what about later, after she and I were involved?' Decker insisted.

'Maybe she was afraid to tell you, afraid you'd react as you're reacting now.'

'If she loved me, she would have trusted me.'

'Ah,' Esperanza said. 'I'm beginning to understand. You're worried that maybe *she* doesn't love *you*.'

'I've always let business control my personal life,' Decker said. 'I have never been in love, not truly. Until I met Beth Dwyer, I had never allowed myself to experience—' Decker hesitated. 'Passion.'

Esperanza furrowed his brow.

'When I did commit, when I gave myself, it was totally. Beth became the absolute focus of my life. If I was merely a convenience to her . . .' Decker's voice dropped toward despair.

'Suppose you do find out that she didn't care about you, that you *were* just an unwitting bodyguard. What will you do about it?'

Decker didn't answer.

Esperanza persisted. 'Would you still save her?'

'In spite of everything?'

'Yes.'

'In spite of all my suspicions, all my fear that she betrayed me, my anger because of my fear?'

'Yes.'

'I'd go through hell for her. God help me, I still love her.'

NINE

1

It was raining when Decker arrived in New York, a strong steady downpour that was one measure of how foreign Manhattan felt to him after New Mexico's arid climate. The unaccustomed humidity was palpable. After having lived for fifteen months at almost a mile and a half above sea level, he felt an atmospheric pressure that reinforced the emotional pressure inside him. Accustomed to being able to see for hundreds of miles, he felt constricted by skyscrapers. And by people: the total population of New Mexico was one and a half million, but that many people lived within the twenty-two square miles of Manhattan alone, and that didn't count the hundreds of thousands who commuted to the island to work, with the consequence that Decker was conscious – as he had never been until he experienced New Mexico's peace and expansiveness – of New York's intense noise and congestion.

Esperanza stared in fascination out the taxi's rain-beaded windows.

'Never been here?' Decker asked.

'The only big cities I've been to are Denver, Phoenix, and Los Angeles. They're low. They sprawl. Here, everything's jammed together, crammed on top of each other.'

'Yeah, we're not in the wide open spaces any longer.'

The taxi let them off at the Essex Street Market on the Lower East Side. The large brick building was closed. As Decker

271

carried his travel bag into the shelter of one of the doorways, his headache increased. Although the sleep he had managed to get on the airplane had not been enough to relieve his weariness, nervous energy kept him going. Fear for Beth fueled him.

Esperanza peered into the deserted market, then glanced at the shops on the other side of the street. 'Is our hotel in this area?'

'We don't have one. We don't have time to check into one.'

'But you made a phone call at the airport. I thought you were making a reservation.'

Decker shook his head; the movement aggravated his headache, but he was too obsessed to notice. He waited until the taxi drove out of sight. Then he left the market's doorway and began walking north through the rain. 'I was making an appointment with someone.'

'Nearby?'

'A couple of blocks.'

'Then why didn't you let the taxi take us straight to him?'

'Because I didn't want the taxi driver to know my business. Look, I'm afraid this isn't going to work. There's too much to explain, and not enough time,' Decker said impatiently. 'You've been very helpful. You called off the New Mexico police alert on me. You got me through airport security in Albuquerque. I wouldn't be here without you. Thank you. I mean that. Really. But you have to understand – our partnership ends right here. Take a taxi to midtown. Enjoy the city.'

'In the rain?'

'See a show. Have a nice meal.'

'I kind of doubt New York meals come with red and green salsa.'

'Give yourself a little vacation. Then fly back tomorrow morning. Your department must be wondering where you've gone.'

'They won't know I've left. I told you, this is my day off.'

'What about tomorrow?'

'I'll call in sick.'

'You don't have jurisdiction here,' Decker said. 'Do yourself a favor. Get back to New Mexico as soon as possible.'

'No.'

'You won't be able to follow me. Two minutes from now, you won't have any idea how I got away from you.'

'But you won't do that.'

'Oh? What makes you think so?'

'Because you can't be sure you won't need me.'

2

The bar – on First Avenue, near Delancey – looked to be on the verge of going out of business. In its windows, liquor advertisements had faded almost to illegibility. The windows themselves were so grimy that they couldn't be seen through. Several letters in its neon sign were burned out, so that instead of BENNIE'S, it now read BE E'S. A derelict holding a whiskey bottle in a paper bag slumped on the sidewalk next to the entrance, mindless of the downpour.

Frustrated by the rush of time, Decker crossed the street toward the bar. He was followed by Esperanza, whose cowboy hat had been replaced by an inconspicuous Yankees baseball cap that they had bought from a souvenir stand along the way. His long hair had been tied back so that it, too, was less noticeable. About to go into the bar, Decker made Esperanza pause at the entrance, letting the derelict, who wasn't a derelict, get a good look at them.

'Bennie's expecting us,' Decker said.

The derelict nodded.

Decker and Esperanza went into the bar, which was hazy with cigarette smoke. Given its shabby exterior, the place was surprisingly busy, its noise level high because of a football game on a big-screen television.

Decker went directly to the husky bartender. 'Is Bennie around?'

'Ain't seen him.'

'I phoned earlier and made an appointment.'

'Says who?'

Decker used the pseudonym, 'Charles Laird.'

'Why didn't you say so?' The bartender gestured toward the far end of the counter. 'Bennie's waiting for you in his office. Leave your bag with me.'

Decker nodded, handing him the small suitcase, putting twenty dollars on the counter. 'This is for the beer we didn't have.'

He led Esperanza toward the closed door at the end of the counter, then halted.

'What's the matter?' Esperanza asked. 'Why don't you go ahead and knock?'

'There's a formality we have to get through first. I hope you don't mind being groped.'

Four broad-shouldered men turned from playing pool at a table next to the door. Eyes cold, they searched Decker and Esperanza roughly and thoroughly. With a final check of both men's ankles, not finding any microphones or weapons, they nodded curtly in dismissal and went back to playing pool. They didn't find anything suspicious because, at Decker's insistence, Esperanza had left his badge and handgun locked in Decker's Jeep Cherokee at the Albuquerque airport. Decker was determined that, if he and Esperanza had to do any shooting, it wouldn't be with a weapon that could be traced to either of them.

Only now did Decker knock on the door. Hearing a muffled voice behind it, he opened it and faced a narrow cluttered office, in which an overweight man with a striped shirt, a bow-tie, and suspenders sat at a desk. The man was elderly. He had a bald head and a silvery mustache. A polished-brass cane lay across the top of his desk.

'How are you, Bennie?' Decker asked.

'On a diet. Can't seem to lose this weight. Doctor's orders. And what about you, Charles?'

'I've got trouble.'

Bennie nodded wisely, each movement of his head squeezing his double chins together. 'No one ever comes to me otherwise.'

'This is a friend of mine.' Decker indicated Esperanza.

Bennie listlessly raised a hand.

'My friend has to make a phone call.'

'Right over there.' Bennie pointed to a payphone in a corner.

'It's still linked to a payphone in Jersey City?'

'That's where anyone tracing the call will think you are,' Bennie said.

Decker gestured to Esperanza that it was okay for him to make the call. As agreed, it would be to Miller in Santa Fe to find out if there was any news about Beth and McKittrick. Decker had phoned him several times en route, desperate to know if Beth was still alive. So far, there wasn't any news.

'Sit down,' Bennie told Decker as Esperanza put coins in the payphone. 'How can I help?'

Decker positioned himself in a chair across from Bennie, knowing that a shotgun was under the intervening desk. 'Thank you. You were always cooperative when I needed help before.'

'It amused me,' Bennie said. 'A change of pace, doing something for my government.'

Decker understood. Although it was commonly thought that the CIA had a mandate limiting it to overseas operations, the fact was that it maintained offices in various major American cities and did on occasion carry out domestic operations, but in theory not without first obeying a presidential order to alert the FBI. It had been with the cooperation of the Bureau that Decker had consulted with Bennie three years earlier and been given a fake identity as a mob member associated with Bennie. The purpose was to enable Decker to infiltrate a foreign terrorist network that was trying to disrupt the United States by using organized crime to flood the country with fake hundred-dollar bills.

'I'm sure the government was most appreciative,' Decker said.

'Well, it doesn't come around and bother me anymore.' Bennie shrugged listlessly. 'And after all, it *was* in my self-interest. What's bad for the economy is bad for *my* business, too.' He smiled slightly.

'This time, I can't offer you incentives, I'm afraid.'

'Oh?' Bennie looked suspicious.

'I don't have anything to do with the government these days. I have a personal favor to ask you.'

'Favor?' Bennie grimaced.

In the background, Decker heard Esperanza speaking into the payphone, his tone somber as he asked questions.

'What kind of favor?' Bennie obviously dreaded the answer.

'I need to know how to contact Nick Giordano.'

Bennie's cheeks normally had a touch of pink. Now they turned pale. 'No. Don't tell me any more. I don't want to be involved with any involvement *you* have with Nick Giordano.'

'I swear to you, this has nothing to do with the government.'

Bennie's formerly listless gestures were now animated. 'I don't care! I don't want to know anything about it!'

Decker leaned forward. 'And I *don't want* you to know anything about it.'

Bennie stopped suddenly in mid-gesture. '*Don't want* me to know?'

'All I'm asking for is a simple piece of information. How do I get in touch with Nick Giordano? Not the owner of the restaurant where he likes to eat. Not one of his lieutenants. Not his attorney. *Him. You* won't have to introduce us. *You* won't be directly involved in any way. I'll take the responsibility for making contact. Giordano will never know who told me how to get in touch with him.'

Bennie stared at Decker as if trying to understand a foreign language. 'What possible reason would make me want to do this?'

Esperanza's telephone conversation ended. He turned toward Decker.

'Any news?' Decker's stomach cramped.

'No.'

'Thank God. At least, she hasn't been reported dead. I've still got hope.'

'She?' Bennie raised his thick eyebrows.

'A friend of mine. I'm trying to find her. She's in trouble.'

'And Nick Giordano can help get her *out* of trouble?' Bennie asked.

'He definitely has the power to do that,' Decker said. 'That's what I need to talk to him about.'

'You still haven't given me a reason to help you.'

'I love this woman, Bennie. I want you to do this because I love her.'

'You're making a joke, right?'

'Am I laughing?'

'Please. I'm a businessman.'

'Then here's another reason. Nick Giordano has a special interest in this woman. He thinks she killed Joey Scolari.'

Bennie flinched. 'You're talking about *Diana* Scolari? Joey's

277

wife? Jesus, Nick has everybody looking for her.'

'Well, it might be I can help him find her.'

'Make sense. If you love her, why would you turn her over to Nick?'

'So she won't have to run for the rest of her life.'

'Of course not. She'll be dead. You're still not making sense.'

'Then maybe *this* will make sense,' Decker said. 'If Nick Giordano is happy with the way my conversation with him turns out, he might want to reward anybody who showed the good judgment to make the conversation happen.'

Bennie scowled, calculating.

3

The phone on the other end rang only once before a man's raspy voice said, 'You'd better have a damned good reason for calling this number.'

Immediately Decker heard the beep of an answering machine and dictated his message. 'This is Steve Decker. My name ought to be familiar to you. Your people were watching me in Santa Fe. I have something important I need to discuss with Mr Giordano. It concerns Diana Scolari and the murder of her husband. It also concerns a US marshal named Brian McKittrick. I'll call back in thirty minutes.'

Decker put the phone back on its hook and stepped from the littered glass booth into the dusky rain, approaching Esperanza who stood in the doorway of a closed appliance store.

'Getting tired of following me?'

'Not when you're taking me to such interesting places.'

4

The flower shop was on Grand Street. OPEN SUNDAYS AND HOLIDAYS, a sign on the door announced. A bell rang when Decker opened the door and stepped into the shop. The funeral-home scent of flowers surrounded him. Curious, Esperanza glanced around at the closed-circuit television cameras above the abundant colorful displays, then turned toward the sound of footsteps.

A matronly middle-aged woman, wearing gardener's gloves and a smock, came out of a back room. 'I'm sorry. It's almost seven. My assistant was supposed to lock the door. We're closed.'

'I guess I lost track of the time,' Decker said. 'It's been a while since I did business with you.' He picked up a pen and a business card on the counter, wrote something, then showed it to the woman. 'This is my account number, and this is how my name is spelled.'

'One minute while I examine our records.'

The woman returned to the back room and closed the door behind her. A mirror next to that door was two-way, Decker knew. An armed man watched him from behind it, he also knew, just as two other armed men in the basement watched the monitors of the closed-circuit cameras.

Not letting his troubled thoughts show, he pretended to be interested in various attractive corsages that were visible behind the glass doors of a cooler. He was appalled by the disarming ease with which he was slipping back into his former life.

Esperanza glanced at his watch. 'Ten minutes until you have to make that phone call.'

The woman came back into the display room.

'Mr Evans, our records show that you left a deposit with us two years ago.'

'Yes. I've come to close out the account.'

'Our records also show that you always ordered a particular type of flower.'

279

'Two dozen yellow roses.'

'Correct. Please, step into our display room.'

The small room was to the left of the counter. It had photographs on the walls, showing the numerous flower arrangements the shop could provide. It also had a plain table and two wooden chairs at which Decker and Esperanza sat after Decker closed and locked the door. Esperanza parted his lips to say something but was interrupted when the matronly woman came in through another door, set a briefcase on the table, and left.

The moment the door clicked shut, Decker opened the briefcase. Esperanza leaned forward, seeing objects cushioned within niches cut into plastic foam: a Walther .380 pistol, an extra magazine, a box of ammunition, and two small electronic objects, the purpose of which wasn't obvious.

Decker couldn't subdue his self-loathing. 'I hoped I had touched this stuff for the last time.'

5

'You'd better have a damned good reason for calling this number.'

Beep.

'This is Steve Decker again. I have something important I need to discuss with Mr Giordano. It concerns Diana Scolari and—'

A man picked up the phone on the other end. His voice had the arrogant tone of someone accustomed to giving orders. 'What do you know about Diana Scolari?'

'I need to speak to Mr Giordano.'

'*I'm* Mr Giordano,' the man said angrily.

'Not *Nick* Giordano. Your voice sounds too young.'

'My father doesn't take calls from people he doesn't know. Tell me about Diana Scolari.'

'And Brian McKittrick.'

'Is that name supposed to mean something to me?'

'Put your father on.'

'Anything you have to say about Diana Scolari, you can say to *me*.'

Decker hung up, waited two minutes, then put additional coins in the payphone and pressed the same numbers.

This time, there wasn't an answering machine. Instead, halfway through the first ring, a hoarse elderly male voice said, 'Nick Giordano.'

'I was just talking to your son about Diana Scolari.'

'And Brian McKittrick.' The voice sounded strained. 'My son says you also mentioned Brian McKittrick.'

'That's right.'

'How do I know you're not a cop?'

'When we meet, you can search me to make sure I'm not wearing a wire.'

'That still won't mean you're not a cop.'

'Hey, if you're that paranoid, maybe there's no point in trying to arrange a meeting.'

For a moment, the line was silent. 'Where are you?'

'Lower Manhattan.'

'Stand on the Fifth Avenue side of the Flatiron Building. A car will be there to pick you up in an hour. How will the driver know it's you?'

Decker glanced at Esperanza. 'I'll be holding two dozen yellow roses.'

6

In a coffee shop just down Fifth Avenue from the Flatiron Building, Decker stayed silent until the waiter brought their order and left. They had chosen a far corner table. The place wasn't busy. Even so, Decker made sure no one was looking in his direction before he leaned down, opened his travel bag, and removed a small object that he had earlier taken from the briefcase at the flower shop. The object was metal, the size of a match box.

'What *is* that thing?' Esperanza asked.

'It sends out a homing signal. And this –' Decker reached into his travel bag and withdrew a metal box the size of a pack of cigarettes '– receives it, as long as the signal doesn't come from farther than a mile. Traffic moves south on Fifth Avenue past the Flatiron Building. You'll be waiting in a taxi north of here – at Madison Square Park. After I get into the car Giordano sends for me, give me fifteen seconds so you won't be obvious, then follow. The receiver operates visually. This needle points to the left, right, or straight ahead, depending on which direction the signal is coming from. This gauge tells you from one to ten how close you are, ten being the closest.' Decker flicked a switch and put the receiver ahead of the transmitter. 'Yes. The system's working. Take the receiver. If something goes wrong, our rendezvous is in front of this coffee shop at the top of each hour. But if I don't show up by six tomorrow night, get back to Santa Fe as fast as you can.' Decker glanced at his watch. 'It's almost time. Let's go.'

'What about your bag?'

'Keep it.' The bag contained the pistol, the spare magazine, and the box of ammunition. Decker knew he'd be searched. There was no way he was going to spook Giordano by trying to carry a weapon to a meeting with him. 'Ten minutes after I arrive at wherever I'm being taken, phone the number Bennie gave me. Ask to speak to me. Make it sound as if bad things will happen if I don't come to the phone.'

'And?'

'Follow my lead when I talk to you.'

They reached the exit from the coffee shop.

'You won't have any trouble catching a cab around here.'

'Decker.'

'What?'

'Are you sure about this?'

'No.'

'Then maybe there's another way.'

'The last thing I want to do is go out there. But I'm running out of time. Maybe I've *already* run out of time. I don't know where else to go except straight to the source of the problem.'

Esperanza hesitated. 'Good luck.'

'Beth needs it more than me.'

'But what if—'

'They've already killed her?'

'Yes.'

'Then what happens to me doesn't matter.'

A minute later, during which Decker hoped that Esperanza had time to hail a cab, he stepped into the darkening rain and turned right, walking toward the Flatiron Building. Worried about what McKittrick might be doing to Beth, Decker couldn't help being reminded of the similar rain that had fallen the night McKittrick shot his father in Rome.

He reached the Flatiron Building five minutes ahead of schedule and stood in the shelter of another doorway, holding the yellow roses in plain view. His emotions were complicated: various levels of doubt, fear, and apprehension. But only the doubt applied to himself. The rest were outwardly directed: fear for Beth, apprehension about what might already have happened to her. But most of all, he felt seized with determination. It was the first time he had ever engaged in a mission in which the mission truly meant more to him than his own life.

He recalled something Beth had told him two nights earlier,

Fiesta Friday, after they had left the film producer's party and driven back to Decker's house – their last moment of normalcy, it seemed at the time, although Decker now realized that *nothing* about their relationship had been normal. Moonlight through his bedroom windows had gleamed on them, making their bodies resemble ivory, while they made love – the bittersweet memory made him feel hollow. Afterward, as they lay next to each other, side by side, Decker's arms around her, his chest against her back, his groin against her hips, his knees against hers, legs bent, in a spoon position, she had lapsed into so long a silence that he thought she had fallen asleep. He remembered inhaling the fragrance of her hair. When she spoke, her hesitant voice had been so soft that he barely heard it.

'When I was a little girl,' she murmured, 'my mother and father had terrible fights.'

She lapsed into silence again.

Decker waited.

'I never knew what the fights were about,' Beth had continued softly, not without tension. 'I still don't. Infidelity. Money problems. Drinking. Whatever. Every night, they screamed at each other. Sometimes it was worse than just screaming. They threw things. They hit each other. The fights were especially horrible on holidays. Thanksgiving. Christmas. My mother would prepare a big meal. Then, just before dinner, something would happen to make them start yelling at each other again. My father would storm out of the house. My mother and I would eat dinner alone, and all the while she would tell me what a rotten bastard he was.'

More silence. Decker knew enough not to prompt her, sensing that whatever she wanted to say was so private she had to reveal it at her own pace.

'When the fights got worse than I could bear, I begged my parents to stop. I pushed at my father, trying to get him to stop hitting my mother. All that did was make him turn against *me*,' Beth finally continued. 'I still have a mental image of my father's fist coming at me. I was afraid he would kill me. This happened at night. I ran into my bedroom and tried to figure out where to hide. The shouts in the living room got louder. I stuffed my pillows, one in front of the other, under my bed covers to make it seem as if I was sleeping there. I must have seen that trick on television or something. Then I crawled under the bed, and that's where I slept, hoping I was protected from my father if he came in to stab me. I slept that way every night after that.'

Beth's shoulders heaved slightly, in a way that made Decker think she was sobbing. 'Was *your* childhood like that?' she asked.

'No. My father was a career soldier. He was rigid, very much into discipline and control. But he was never violent with me.'

' Lucky.' In the darkness, Beth wiped at her eyes. 'I used to read stories about knights and fair ladies, King Arthur, that sort of thing. I kept dreaming that I was in those stories, that I had a knight to protect me. Even as a kid, I was good at drawing. I used to make sketches of what I thought the knight would look like.' Covers rustling, Beth turned to him, her face now in moonlight, tears glinting on her cheeks. 'If I could draw that knight again, he'd look like you. You make me feel safe. I don't need to sleep under the bed anymore.'

Two hours later, the hit team had broken into the house.

7

Rain gusting at Decker's face brought him out of his memory. Racked with emotion, he studied the traffic that sped through puddles past the Flatiron Building. Conflicting questions tortured him. Had the story Beth told him been true, or had she been setting her hook deeper, lying to elicit more sympathy from him, programming him to protect her regardless of the threat? It came down to what he had been brooding about since yesterday when he had learned that she had deceived him about her background. Did she love him, or had she been using him? He *had* to know. He *had* to find her and learn the truth, although if the truth wasn't what he wanted to hear, he didn't know what he would do, for the fact was, *he* loved *her* completely.

Headlights piercing the rain, a gray Oldsmobile veered out of traffic and stopped at the curb before him. The car's back door opened and one of Giordano's soldiers got out, indicating with a stiff motion of his head that he wanted Decker to get in the car. Muscles compacting, determination strengthening, Decker approached him, holding a bunch of roses with each hand.

'That's right.' The man, who had a large chest, broad shoulders, and a suit that was too tight, smirked. 'You keep your hands around those flowers while I search you.'

'On the street? With that police car coming?'

'Get in the car.'

Calculating, Decker saw that there were two men in the front and another man in the back. As he got in, feeling the first man coming after him, pressing against him, he kept the matchbox-sized transmitter along with the stems of the flowers in the palm of his right hand. As the driver pulled away from the curb, tires splashing, the man in the passenger seat aimed a pistol at Decker. The two men in back searched him.

'He's clean.'

'What about those flowers?'

The men pulled the roses from Decker's clenched hands, so preoccupied that they didn't notice the small transmitter he continued to conceal in his cupped right palm.

'Whatever you want with the boss, it better be good,' one of the men said. 'I've never seen Nick this pissed off.'

'Hey, what stinks in here?' another man asked.

'It's them flowers. They smell like a cheap funeral.'

'Maybe *this* guy's funeral.' The man on Decker's left chuckled as he rolled down the window and tossed out the battered roses.

8

Throughout the drive, Decker didn't speak. For their part, the men ignored him. As they talked among themselves about football, women, and casinos on Indian reservations – safe topics, nothing that would incriminate them – Decker kept wondering if Esperanza had managed to follow in a cab, if the transmitter and the receiver were working, if the driver would notice he was being tailed. He kept telling himself that he had to have faith.

The time was just after eight p.m. The rain had thickened, dusk becoming night. Headlights piercing the downpour, the driver took several streets at random as an evasion tactic, then proceeded north on the crowded Henry Hudson Parkway, eventually turning west onto the George Washington Bridge. On the New Jersey side, he headed north again, this time on the Palisades Parkway. An hour after picking up Decker, he turned left into the sleepy town of Alpine.

The men in the car sat tensely straighter as the driver went through the almost non-existent downtown area, then steered to the right, took several more turns, and at last came to a quiet, thickly treed, tastefully but brightly lit section of large houses on half-acre lots. High fences made from wrought iron topped with spikes separated the lots. The car pulled into a driveway and stopped before an imposing metal gate, where the driver leaned out into the rain and spoke into an intercom. 'It's Rudy. We've got him.'

The gate parted to the right and left, providing a gap through which the driver proceeded. Glancing back through the rain-beaded rear window, Decker saw the gate close as soon as the Oldsmobile had cleared it. He didn't see any headlights of a taxi that might·be following. The car went along a curved driveway and stopped before a brick three-story home with numerous gables and chimneys. After the low, round-edged, flat-roofed adobe houses that Decker was used to, the mansion seemed surreal. Arc lights illuminated the grounds. Decker noted that the trees were a distance from the house and that all the shrubs were low. Any invader who managed to get past what Decker assumed were state-of-the-art intrusion detectors along the fence wouldn't have any cover as he tried to reach the house.

'Showtime,' the man on Decker's left said. He opened his door, got out, and waited for Decker. 'Move it. Don't keep him waiting.'

Decker didn't say a word when his arm was grabbed. In fact he welcomed the gesture. It gave him an excuse to pretend to trip as he was tugged through the rain toward the wide stone steps that led into the house. Falling near a bush, he slipped the small homing device under it, then let the man pull him to his feet and into the house. His heart seemed surrounded by ice.

The first thing he noticed was an armed guard in a corner of the spacious, marble-floored foyer. The second thing he noticed was a pit bull behind the guard. After that, he barely had time to look for other possible exits as he was hurried along an oak-paneled hallway, through double doors, and into a thickly carpeted study.

The wall opposite Decker had leather-bound books. The wall to the right had framed family pictures. The wall to the left had glass cabinets, in each of which were vases. The center of the room was dominated by a wide antique desk, behind which a compact man of about seventy, wearing an expensive dark-blue suit, exhaled cigar smoke and squinted at Decker. The man had severely pinched features, dominated by a cleft chin and a furrow down each cheek. His deep tan emphasized his short but thick white hair.

Sitting in front of the desk, turning to look at Decker, was a man in his thirties, but the contrast involved more than age. The younger man wore trendy clothes that seemed garish compared to the elderly man's conservative suit. The younger man wore conspicuous jewelry whereas the older man had none to be seen. The younger man looked less fit than the older man, his body slightly puffy as if lately he had given up exercise in favor of drinking.

'Did you search him?' the elderly man asked the guards who had brought in Decker. The raspy voice sounded like the one Decker had heard on the phone, the man who claimed to be Nick Giordano.

'When we picked him up,' a guard said.

'I'm still not satisfied. This guy's clothes are wet. Get him a robe or something.'

'Yes, sir.'

Giordano assessed Decker. 'Well, what are you waiting for?'

'I don't understand.'

'Take off your clothes.'

'What?'

'You've got a hearing problem? Take off your clothes. I want to make sure you're not wearing a wire. Buttons, belt buckles, zippers, I don't trust any of them, not when it comes to a guy who used to be a spook.'

'Brian McKittrick must have told you a lot about me.'

'The son of a bitch,' the younger man said.

'Frank,' Giordano said in warning. 'Shut up until we know he's not wired.'

'You're actually serious about my clothes?' Decker asked.

Giordano didn't answer, only glared.

'If this is how you get your kicks.'

'Hey.' The younger man stood angrily. 'You think you can come into my father's home and insult him?'

'Frank,' Giordano said again.

The young man was poised to slap Decker's face. He stared at his father and backed away.

Decker took off his sports coat.

Giordano nodded. 'Good. It's always smart to cooperate.'

As Decker took off his shirt, he watched Giordano walk over to the vases in their glass cabinets.

'Do you know anything about porcelain?' Giordano asked.

The question was so unexpected that Decker shook his head in confusion. 'You mean like bone china?' Grim, Decker removed his shoes and socks.

'That's one type of porcelain. It's called bone china because it's made from powdered bones.'

Even grimmer, Decker unbuckled, unzipped, and took off his pants. His exposed skin prickled.

'Everything,' Giordano ordered.

Decker slipped off his briefs. His testicles shrank toward his groin. He stood with as much dignity as he could muster, keeping his arms at his sides. 'What's next? A cavity search? Do you do it personally?'

The younger man looked furious. 'You want one, big mouth?'

'Frank,' Giordano again repeated in warning.

A guard came in with a white terry-cloth robe.

'Give it to him.' Giordano gestured with his cigar. 'Take his clothes to the car.'

As the man obeyed, Decker put on the robe. Its hem came down to his knees, its wide sleeves just below his elbows. Tying its belt, he was reminded of the *gi* he had worn when he learned martial arts.

Giordano picked up a vase that had the shape of a heron, the bird's head upright, its beak open. 'Look at how light seems to shine through it. Listen when I tap it with my finger. It resonates, almost like crystal.'

'Fascinating,' Decker said unenthusiastically.

'A hell of a lot more than you know. These vases are my trophies,' Giordano said. 'They warn my enemies –' His face became flushed. '– *not to fuck with me*. Bone china. Powdered bones.' Giordano held the bird-shaped vase close to Decker. 'Say hello to Luigi. *He* tried to fuck with me, so I had his flesh burned off with acid, then his bones ground up and made into this. I put him in my trophy case. Like everyone else who tried to fuck with me.' Giordano hurled the vase toward the room's large fireplace, the porcelain shattering.

'Now Luigi's just garbage!' Giordano said. 'And *you'll* end up just like him if *you* try to fuck with me, too. So answer this question very carefully. *What do you have to tell me about Diana Scolari?*'

9

The shrill ringing of a phone punctuated the tension in the room.

Giordano and his son exchanged troubled glances.

'Maybe it's McKittrick,' Frank said.

'It damned well better be.' Giordano picked up the phone. '*Talk to me.*' He frowned. 'Who the hell—' He stared at Decker. '*Who?* What makes you think he's—'

'That'll be for me,' Decker said. 'It's a friend of mine,

checking on my welfare.' He took the phone from Giordano and spoke into it. 'So you found the place all right.'

'Almost didn't,' Esperanza's somber voice said on the other end. 'It was tough staying far enough back so your driver wouldn't see the taxi's headlights. It was also tough finding a phone.'

'Where are you?'

'Outside the post office – on what passes for the main drag.'

'Call back in another five minutes.' Decker set the phone on its cradle and turned to Giordano. 'Just a precaution.'

'You think some guy on the phone is going to save your ass if I think you're out of line?'

'No.' Decker shrugged. 'But before I died, I'd have the satisfaction of knowing that my friend would get in touch with other friends and you'd soon be joining me.'

The room became silent. Even the rain lancing against the French doors seemed suddenly muted.

'Nobody threatens my father,' Frank said.

'That stuff about Luigi sure sounded like your father was threatening *me*,' Decker said. 'I came here in good faith to discuss a mutual problem. Instead of being treated with respect, I was forced to—'

'Mutual problem?' Giordano asked.

'Diana Scolari.' Decker paused, focusing his emotion. Everything depended on what he said next. 'I want to kill her for you.'

Giordano stared.

Frank stepped forward. 'For what she did to Joey, there are *plenty* of us who want to kill her.'

Decker's expression remained rigid. He didn't dare show the relief that flooded through him. Frank had used the present tense. Beth was still alive.

'You expect me to believe you want to kill her after you've been screwing her?' Giordano asked.

'She lied to me. She used me.'

'Too damned bad.'

'For her. I'm going to find her. I'm going to give her what she deserves.'

'And we're supposed to tell you where she is?' Frank asked.

'And where *Brian McKittrick* is. *He* used me, too. *He* set me up. It isn't the first time. He's going to pay.'

'Well, you can get in line for him, as well,' Frank said. 'A lot of us are looking for *both* of them.'

'Looking for— I thought he was working for you.'

'That's what *we* thought. He was supposed to report in yesterday. Not a word. Is he back working for the US Marshals Service? If she shows up in that courtroom tomorrow—'

'Frank,' Giordano said, 'how many times do I have to tell you to shut your mouth?'

'You don't have any secrets from me,' Decker said. 'I know she's supposed to testify against you tomorrow. If I could find out where she is, I'd solve your problem for you. She'd let me get close enough to—'

The phone rang again.

This time, Giordano and Frank kept their full concentration on Decker.

'That'll be your friend again,' Giordano said. 'Get rid of him.'

Decker picked up the phone.

'Give me Nick,' a New-England-accented voice demanded smugly.

Brian McKittrick.

10

Time seemed suspended.

As Decker's pulse faltered, he urgently lowered his voice,

hoping that McKittrick wouldn't recognize it. 'Is the woman still alive?'

'You're damned right. And she's going to stay that way unless I get a million dollars by midnight. If I don't get the money, she goes into that courtroom tomorrow.'

'Where are you?'

'Who *is* this? If I don't hear Nick's voice in ten seconds, I'm hanging up.'

'No! Wait. Don't do anything. Here he is.'

Decker handed the phone to Giordano, whose eyebrows were raised in question. 'It's McKittrick.'

'*What?*' Giordano grabbed the phone. 'You son of a bitch, you were supposed to call me yesterday. Where—? Stop. Don't answer right away. Is your phone secure? Use that voice scrambler I gave you. Turn it on.' Giordano flicked a switch on a black box next to his phone – a voice scrambler presumably calibrated to the same code as McKittrick's scrambler. 'Now talk to me, you bastard.'

Decker stepped away from the desk. Frank and the guards, the fourth member of whom had come back, were riveted by Giordano's savage expression as he shouted into the phone.

'*A million dollars?* Are you out of your mind? I already paid you two hundred thousand ... It wasn't enough? Is your *life* enough? I told you what I do to smart guys who try to mess with me. Here's the best deal anybody ever offered you. Do the job you promised. Prove to me you did it. *I'll forget this conversation happened.*'

To the left of the guards, parallel to them but not wanting to arouse their suspicions by stepping behind them, Decker scanned the room and focused his attention on the fireplace.

Giordano listened to the phone, shocked. 'You dumb bastard, you're really serious. You're going to hold me up for a million bucks ... I *don't need reminding* her testimony can put me away for life.' Giordano's expression became even more fierce. 'Yes, I know where that is. But midnight's too soon. I need more time. I need to . . . I'm not stalling. I'm not trying to doublecross you. All I want is to solve my problem. I'm telling the truth. I'm not sure I can get the money by midnight . . . Here's a gesture of good faith. The guy you talked to at the start of your call – he's the guy you wanted us to take out in Santa Fe as part of the deal. Your buddy, Steve Decker.'

As Giordano and everyone else in the room looked at him, Decker's reflexes tightened.

'He paid us a visit. Called me up and wanted to come over for a heart-to-heart. He's standing right in front of me. Want to come over and visit? . . . No? Don't you trust me? . . . Okay, here's my offer. We'll do him for you. You prove the woman's dead. I'll prove Decker's dead. You'll get the million. But I can't get you the money by midnight.' Giordano scowled. 'No. Wait. Don't.' He slammed the phone onto its cradle. 'Bastard hung up on me. Midnight. Says midnight or it's no deal. Thinks I'll pull a fast one if I've got more time.'

'Where are we supposed to meet him?' Frank asked angrily.

'The scenic lookout two miles north of here.'

'In Palisades State Park?'

Giordano nodded. 'The bastard's right here in the neighborhood. We leave the money and Decker behind the refreshment stand.'

'And McKittrick leaves the woman?'

'No. He says he *won't* do the job until he's positive we don't try to follow him after he leaves with the money.'

'Shit.'

Giordano turned toward the wall of leather-bound books. He pressed a portion of the wall, releasing a catch.

'You're actually going to give him the money?' Frank asked.

'What choice do I have? I don't have time to second-guess

him. Diana Scolari can't be allowed to go into that courtroom tomorrow. I'll deal with McKittrick later. He can't hide forever. But right now—' When Giordano tugged, the large bookshelf slid away from the wall, revealing a safe. He quickly worked the combination, yanked open the door, and pulled out bundles of cash, setting the rubber-banded packets onto the desk. 'There's a briefcase in that closet.'

'Suppose McKittrick takes the money and *still* lets her testify.' Frank went for the briefcase. 'Or suppose he asks for more cash tomorrow morning.'

'Then I'll give him more cash! I won't spend the rest of my life in prison!'

'We can try to follow him,' Frank said. 'Or we can grab him when he shows up to get the money. Believe me, *I'll* make him tell us where the woman is.'

'*But what if he dies before he talks?* I can't take the risk. I'm seventy years old. Prison would kill me.'

For the third time, the phone rang.

'Maybe that's McKittrick again.' Giordano grabbed it. 'Talk to me.' He frowned toward Frank. 'I can't understand a word he's saying. He must have turned his scrambler off.' Furious, Giordano switched his own scrambler off, then blurted into the phone, 'I told you . . . Who? Decker? For Christ's sake, he isn't here anymore. Quit calling about him. He's gone. One of my men drove him back to the city . . . Shut up and listen. *He's gone.*'

Giordano slammed down the phone and told Decker, 'So much for your insurance policy. Think you can threaten *me*, huh?' He turned to the guards. 'Take this prick out to the cliffs and do him.'

Decker's stomach felt frozen.

'Just before midnight, dump him behind the refreshment stand at the scenic overlook. Frank'll be there by then with the money,' Giordano said.

'*I'll* be there?' Frank asked in surprise.

'Who else am I going to trust with the money?'

'I thought *we* were taking it.'

'Are you nuts? *You're* not the one who might be indicted tomorrow. If I get caught being involved in this ... Hey,' Giordano told the guards, 'what are you hanging around for? I said take him out and do him.'

The pressure in his chest intensifying, Decker saw one of the guards reach beneath his suit coat to pull out a gun. Decker's body was like a spring wound to its tightest coil. The coil was suddenly released. While Giordano had been arguing with McKittrick on the phone, Decker had choreographed what abruptly happened now. Next to the fireplace, he had noticed a set of tools. With eyeblink speed, he grabbed the long thin heavy log pick and whipped it around, striking the guard in the throat. The guard's larynx made an audible crack. His windpipe swelling shut, in agony, unable to breathe, the guard dropped his pistol and clutched his throat. He fell back against another guard, who was already dead, falling from the impact with which Decker had struck the top of his skull with the metal tool. As a third guard tried to pull a pistol from beneath his suit, Decker threw the pick with such force that it speared the guard's chest. The next thing, Decker was diving to the floor, grabbing the pistol that the first guard had dropped, shooting the fourth guard, shooting Giordano, shooting ...

But the only other target was Frank, and Frank wasn't in the room any longer. Using the hanging draperies to protect himself from broken glass, Frank had lunged against a French door, smashed through its windows, and disappeared past the draperies into the storm. Decker fired but missed. He barely had time to register that the briefcase was gone from the desk before the guard who had been speared managed to brace himself against a chair and aim his pistol.

Decker shot him. Decker shot the guard who had been at the front door and now rushed into the room. Decker shot the pit bull who charged in after him. He had never felt such a fury. Pausing only for the second it took him to flick off the lights, he ran toward the French doors. Wind gusted through the broken glass, billowing the draperies into the room. He thought of the arc lights outside and the lack of cover near the house. He imagined Frank aiming from behind one of the few large trees that Giordano's security staff had permitted. Even if Decker managed to shoot out the arc lights, his white robe would be an obvious target in the darkness. He tugged it off and threw it on the floor. But his skin, although tan, was pale compared to the night. His body, too, would be an obvious target in the darkness.

What am I going to do? It'll soon be midnight. I have to get to that scenic lookout. Grabbing a second pistol from one of the fallen guards, Decker spun and rushed into the hallway. At the same moment, to the right, a guard burst into the hallway through a door at the back. Decker shot him.

Rain swept in through the open door. Decker reached the exit, pressed himself next to the door, and peered toward the arc-lit grounds at the back of the house. Seeing no sign of Frank, he ducked back out of sight and flinched as a bullet from out there blasted away part of the doorjamb. He noticed a row of light switches and flicked them all, sending this portion of the house and the grounds into darkness.

Immediately he charged through the open door and raced across rain-soaked grass toward a series of low shrubs that he had seen before he shut off the arc lights. The rain felt shockingly cold on his nakedness. He dropped flat behind the first shrub and squirmed forward as a bullet tore up lawn behind him. He reached another shrub, and unexpectedly, his chest and groin were no longer pressed against soft grass. Instead, he was in a flower bed, crawling across stalks and mud. The stalks scraped his skin. Mud. He smeared it onto his face. He rolled in it, trying to coat himself, to conceal his skin. He knew that the rain would soon wash off the camouflage. He had to move quickly.

Now! He surged to his feet, almost falling on the slick grass as he scrambled toward the cover of a large tree. The tree seemed to expand, its trunk becoming double. A figure whirled in surprise, lurching away from the trunk. As Decker dove to the spongy lawn, the figure fired toward where Decker had been, the muzzle flash disorienting, the bullet zipping above Decker. Decker shot three times, saw the figure drop, and darted closer, taking cover behind the tree.

Had he shot Frank? Staring toward the fallen man, he could see enough to determine that the man wore a suit. Frank had not.

Where *is* he? The shots will alarm the neighbors. The police will soon be here. If I don't get my hands on Frank before then, I'll never have the chance. I've got to get away from here before the police arrive. I can't save Beth if I'm in jail.

From the other side of the house, he heard a rumble, a garage door opening. Frank isn't hiding out here, waiting to shoot me! Decker realized. He ran for the garage!

Decker knew that there might be other guards, that they might be aiming at him from the darkness, but he couldn't let that hold him back. He didn't have time for caution. With the father dead, there was no certainty that Frank would go through with the plan to give McKittrick the money. What would be the point? Beth's testimony wasn't against Frank. He might keep the money and tell McKittrick to do whatever he wanted with Beth. She wasn't important anymore. McKittrick would have no choice except to kill Beth to keep her from telling the authorities about him.

Hearing a car engine, Decker raced toward the open back door of the house. Someone shot from the darkness, a bullet walloping next to Decker as he rushed into the house, but he didn't return fire. His only thought was to reach the front and hope to get a shot at Frank when he drove past toward the gate. He threw open the door and crouched naked, aiming.

Headlights flashed. A large dark sedan, a Cadillac, rushed past, a blur in the rainswept night. Decker fired, hearing glass shatter. The car roared toward the gate. Decker fired again, hearing a bullet puncture metal. Abruptly he heard another sound: the drone of the gate as it started to open. And yet another sound: sirens in the distance.

The Oldsmobile remained in front of the house, where the gunmen had left it after bringing Decker from Manhattan. As the Cadillac's taillights receded toward the gate, Decker raced down the steps toward the Oldsmobile. He yanked open the driver's door, stared in frantic hope, and saw that the key had been left in the ignition.

The interior light made him a target. Stooping to get in and slam the door to shut off the light, he heard footsteps behind him. Caught off balance, he spun, aiming toward the open front door, where the hulking shadows of two guards suddenly loomed into view, their handguns raised. At the same time, he was terribly conscious of urgent footsteps on the opposite side of the Oldsmobile. Another guard! He was trapped. The guard on the opposite side of the car shot at him, his handgun roaring once, twice, bullets zipping over Decker's head, and Decker didn't have a chance to pull the trigger of his own weapon before the two guards at the open front door lurched backward. Two more shots dropped them, and with a shock, Decker understood that it wasn't a guard on the opposite side of the Cadillac. It was—

Esperanza shouted, 'Are you all right?'

'Yes! Get in! You're driving!'

'*What happened to your clothes?*'

'No time to explain! Get in and drive!'

Hearing the fast-approaching sirens, Decker scurried toward a bush on the right side of the front steps.

'Where are you going?' Esperanza shouted, throwing Decker's travel bag into the Olds, sliding behind the steering wheel.

Decker fumbled beneath branches. He scrabbled and clawed to find what he was looking for, finally snagging it: the tiny transmitter that he had hidden under the bush when he had pretended to fall after his arrival here. He opened the Oldsmobile's rear door and leapt in, yelling, 'Frank Giordano's in the car that just left! We have to catch up to him!'

Before Decker could slam the door behind him, Esperanza had started the car, put it into gear, and stomped the accelerator, swerving along the curved driveway toward the front gate. The gate was closing. Beyond it, the Cadillac's taillights disappeared to the right. To the left, the sirens were louder. Straight ahead, the gap between the right and left portions of the gate became narrower.

'Hang on!' Esperanza shouted. The Oldsmobile roared into the gap. The left portion of the gate scraped along the car's side. The right portion struck the car's other side, and for an instant, Decker feared that the car would be jammed to a stop. Instead, when Esperanza stomped even harder on the accelerator, the Oldsmobile rocketed through the opening with such force that the two portions of the gate were twisted and yanked off their moorings. Decker heard them clatter on the wet pavement behind him. Esperanza swung the steering wheel. Tires skidding through puddles, throwing up water, the Oldsmobile slid sideways onto the murky road, straightened, and roared after the Cadillac.

'Damned good!' Decker said. Shivering, he remembered that Giordano had told a bodyguard to put his clothes in the car.

Checking the back seat, he found them.

'Comes from learning to drive on mountain roads,' Esperanza said, speeding after the Cadillac. 'When I was thirteen.'

Decker pulled on his underwear and trousers, chilled by their dampness. Simultaneously he stared out the rear window in search of the flashing lights of police cars. Despite the nearness of the sirens, the night remained dark. Without warning, the night became even darker as Esperanza extinguished the Oldsmobile's lights.

'No point in letting our taillights tell the police where we're headed,' Esperanza said.

A half block in front, the Cadillac's brake lights came on as Frank swerved to the left around a corner. The moment he disappeared, flashing lights sped into view behind Decker. Sirens wailing, police cars stopped at Giordano's estate.

'They haven't spotted us yet, but they will,' Decker said, hastily putting on his shirt. 'They'll see our brake lights the moment you slow down to go around that corner.'

'Who said anything about slowing down?' Esperanza slid into the intersection, steering furiously, almost careening over the curb, straightening, vanishing from the police cars. 'I used to do a little drag racing. When I was fourteen.'

'What did you do when you were *fifteen*? Race in demolition derbies?' Decker reached for his shoes and socks. 'Jesus, except for the Cadillac, I can't see a thing. You'd better turn on the headlights now.'

Narrowly missing a car parked at the side of the road, Esperanza breathed out sharply. 'I agree.' The lights came on. 'That doesn't help much. How do you work the windshield wipers on this thing? Is this the switch? No. How about *this* one?' The wipers started flapping.

Ahead, the Cadillac swerved to the left around another corner.

Esperanza increased speed, braked at the last minute, and veered through the intersection. Midway through the turn, streaking through a puddle, his tires lost their grip on an oily section of pavement. He jolted up on the curb, scraped past a light pole that snapped off the right sideview mirror, and lurched back onto the street.

'No, when I was fifteen, I was *stealing* cars, not racing them,' Esperanza said.

'How did you show up at the house?'

'When the guy on the phone told me you were gone, I knew there was trouble. I checked the receiver you gave me. The homing signal was constant, so I figured the guy was lying and you were still at Giordano's place. But whatever was going on, I was useless in that phone booth. So I had the taxi drive me to the house. That's when I heard shots from inside.'

'When we left, I didn't see the taxi outside.'

'The driver thought there was something suspicious about me. He spotted the receiver and kept asking me if I was following somebody. The second he heard the shots, he made me pay him, ordered me to get out of the cab, and sped away. The only thing I could think to do was climb the fence and find out what was going on.'

'And take the pistol from my travel bag.'

'A good thing for you I did.'

'I owe you.'

'Don't worry – I'll figure out a way for you to repay me. Tell me what happened at the house.'

Decker didn't answer.

Esperanza persisted. 'What was the shooting about?'

'I have to keep reminding myself you're a policeman,' Decker said. 'I'm not sure it's a good idea to go into details.'

With the next sharp turn, the Cadillac led them onto the town's deserted main road. They sped through the rain past the few shops in the shadowy business area.

'In a minute, he'll be on the Interstate,' Decker said.

'I can't catch up to him before that.' Esperanza tried to increase speed but almost lost control of the Olds. 'Is Nick Giordano dead?'

'Yes.' Decker's mouth was dry.

'Self-defense?'

'That's definitely what it felt like to me.'

'Then what's the problem? Are you worried that the police will think you went out there intending to kill him? That you planned to get rid of him from the moment you left Santa Fe?'

'If that thought occurred to you, it'll occur to *them*,' Decker said.

'It would certainly be a direct way of solving Diana Scolari's problems.'

'Beth Dwyer. Her name's Beth Dwyer. I'm trying to save Beth Dwyer. *Up ahead*.' Decker pointed urgently toward a swiftly moving stream of glaring headlights. '*There's the entrance to the Interstate*.'

The Caddy's brakelights flashed as Frank Giordano slowed, trying to navigate the curve that would lead him down the Interstate's access ramp. He braked too hard and lost control of the car. The Caddy spun violently.

'Jesus,' Esperanza said. The Oldsmobile hurtled toward the spinning Caddy, which magnified with alarming speed. 'We're going to hit him!'

Esperanza tapped the brakes. They gripped but not enough. He tapped them again, then pressed them, speeding nearer to the Caddy. At once a gust of wind hit the Olds, and Esperanza lost control on the rain-slick pavement. The car drifted, its back end suddenly at the front. It spun.

Decker had the disorienting vision of the ever-larger spinning Caddy appearing like flashes of a strobelight through the Olds's front windshield, it too spinning. At once the Caddy wasn't there anymore. It must have gone off the road, Decker thought, frantic. Simultaneously the Oldsmobile lurched. The texture of the surface beneath the car became soft and mushy. Grass! The Olds's right rear fender struck something. Decker's upper and lower teeth were knocked together. Outside, metal crumbled. A taillight shattered. The Olds jerked to a stop.

'Are you okay?' Esperanza's voice shook.

'Yes! *Where's Giordano?*'

'I see his headlights!' Esperanza gunned the engine, urging the Olds away from the tree it had spun into, fishtailing across the edge of a muddy field, aiming toward the Interstate's access ramp. Ahead, the Caddy roared out of a ditch and sped toward the chaos of traffic on the Interstate.

'You killed the father.' Esperanza's breathing was strident. 'If you kill the son, Beth Dwyer's problems are over. There's no one to pay off the contract on her. Giordano's men will stop hunting her.'

'You sound like you don't approve of my methods.'

'I'm just making observations.'

Ahead, Giordano sped onto the Interstate, forcing other cars to veer out of his way. Horns blared.

'Giordano has a million dollars in that car,' Decker said.

'*What?*'

'It's a payoff to Brian McKittrick, the price for killing Beth. Ninety minutes from now, he expects it to be delivered to him.'

Esperanza raced onto the Interstate after the Cadillac. 'But what if it isn't? Maybe he'll let her go.'

'No. McKittrick's crazy enough to kill her out of spite,' Decker said. 'The money has to be delivered to him. Maybe I can use it to get him to lead me to Beth. As it is, Frank obviously has no intention of delivering the money. He's heading south. The drop-off site is a couple of miles north of here.'

Despite the downpour, Esperanza risked pushing the accelerator to seventy, veered into the passing lane, and surged forward, approaching the Cadillac five cars ahead in the right lane. Rain pelted the windshield. The wipers could hardly clear it. Unable to go faster because of the car ahead of him, Giordano veered into the passing lane and accelerated. The Cadillac's spray struck the Oldsmobile's windshield and made it impossible for Esperanza to see. With a curse, he swerved into a break in traffic in the right lane, only four car lengths away now.

Inexplicably Giordano slowed, dropping back. In a moment, the Cadillac was parallel to the Oldsmobile. The Cadillac's passenger window was down. Giordano raised his right arm.

'He's going to shoot!' Decker yelled.

Esperanza tapped the brakes. When Giordano fired, the Olds had dropped back just enough that the bullet passed in front of the windshield.

Giordano reduced speed more, dropping back farther, trying for another shot.

Decker lunged toward the floor to grab the pistol that he'd thrown into the car when they left Giordano's house. Giordano fired. The bullet punched a hole in the driver's-side window, zipped past Esperanza's head, and crashed through the far side window in the back. In front, a section of the safety glass disintegrated into jagged pellets, spraying Esperanza's face.

'I can't see!' Esperanza shouted.

The Olds wavered.

Giordano aimed again.

Decker fired. The report inside the closed space was agonizing, like hands being slammed against Decker's ears. There hadn't been time to open the back window. The bullet blasted a hole in the glass, passed through Giordano's open front window, and blew a chunk out of his windshield. Giordano flinched and, instead of firing, had to use both hands to correct his steering.

The Olds wavered again as Esperanza struggled to see. Decker bent frantically over the front seat and grabbed the steering wheel. About to hit a car in front, he swung sharply to the left, crossed into the passing lane, and slammed against Giordano's Cadillac.

'Keep your foot on the accelerator!' he yelled to Esperanza.

'What are you doing?' In a sightless frenzy, Esperanza pawed chunks of glass from around his eyes.

Bent over the front seat, Decker steered harder toward the Caddy, walloping against it. He thought he heard Giordano scream. The third time Decker whacked the Caddy, he forced it off the road. In terror, Giordano veered toward the grassy centerstrip, hurtled down a slight embankment, and surged up an incline toward approaching headlights in the opposite lanes.

Decker followed, almost parallel to the Caddy, feeling a jolt as the Olds left the Interstate. He cringed from the loose feel of the steering on rain-soaked grass. His stomach dropped as the Oldsmobile rose, and suddenly he was streaking diagonally past headlights speeding toward him.

'Brake!' Decker yelled to Esperanza. *'Hard!'*

The Olds had hurtled across two lanes of traffic before the brakes engaged. The wheels skidded, shrieking across wet pavement, throwing up gravel on the shoulder. Horns blaring, traffic rushed past. Ahead, Giordano skidded sideways, crushed bushes, snapped through saplings, and disappeared down a rainswept slope.

Decker swung the steering wheel in a furious effort to avoid going straight down the slope. He had no idea how steep the drop was or what would be at the bottom. All he did know was that they had to reduce speed even more. 'Keep your foot on the brake!' he yelled to Esperanza.

The Olds skidded nearer to the drop. Veering, Decker swung the steering wheel harder, gravel flying. Afraid that the Olds would flip over, he was equally afraid of a head-on impact against a tree. The Olds spun, its tail end pointing toward the slope where the Caddy had disappeared, and suddenly halted, banging Decker's ribs against the seat he leaned against.

'Jesus,' Decker said. 'Are you all right?'

'I think so.' Esperanza pawed more chunks of glass from his blood-smeared face. 'I'm starting to see. Thank God, my eyes weren't cut.'

'I'm going after him!' Decker grabbed his pistol and raced from the Olds, assaulted by cold lancing rain. Vaguely aware that headlights were pulling off the Interstate behind him, a car stopping to investigate what seemed to be a terrible accident, he ignored the distraction and studied the dark wooded slope.

The Caddy's headlights blazed upward from it, as if the car had twisted going down the slope and was now resting on its back end. Decker didn't dare make himself a clear target by going straight ahead and exposing himself to the Caddy's headlights. Instead, he hurried to the right, entered the darkness of the rainswept trees, and climbed warily down a steep slippery slope. After what he judged to be thirty feet, he reached the bottom, turned left, and crept toward the glow of the Caddy's upended headlights, ready with his pistol.

11

Branches snapped. Rain hissing down through the thickly leaved trees obscured the sound. Decker listened harder. There! Another branch had snapped. Near the car.

Decker crouched, trying to blend with the undergrowth. A shadow moved through the trees. Partially silhouetted by the illumination from the Caddy, a man lurched into view. He held his stomach and bent forward, stumbling. Groaning, the figure lost his balance and staggered to Decker's right, away from the lights of the car, swallowed by the dark woods, but not before Decker saw that what the man had been clutching wasn't his stomach but instead the briefcase.

Decker crept through the trees after him. Although he didn't have much time, he didn't dare hurry. He couldn't afford to make mistakes. At once other noises unnerved him: voices behind him, on the top of the slope. Risking a glance backward, Decker saw rain glinting through several flashlight beams that were aimed down toward the Cadillac. A car had stopped as he went down the slope. Other vehicles must have stopped, also. He could only pray that one of them had not been a police car.

Shifting deeper into the woods, Decker followed the route he thought Giordano had taken. Behind him, people climbed awkwardly down the slope, shuffling through bushes, bending branches, talking loudly. The commotion they made prevented Decker from hearing any noises that Giordano might make ahead of him. He had to avoid the flashlights, stooping, trying to conceal himself in the undergrowth, searching. The money, he thought. I can't get to Beth if I don't have the money.

He took a tentative step forward into the darkness and at once felt nothing beneath his shoe. Another slope. About to fall, his momentum tugging him over, he grabbed a tree and dangled, then struggled back onto a slippery stretch of rock. Rain streamed down his neck, his clothes clinging coldly to him. He breathed deeply, trying to steady himself. He had no way of knowing how far down the drop went, but its pitch was extremely steep. If Giordano had toppled over, it would be impossible to climb down and find him in the dark.

Back at the Cadillac, the flashlights scanned the trees. They'll spread out and try to find the driver, Decker thought. If Giordano didn't go over the edge, if he's still alive, he'll move as far from those flashlights as he can. But which way? Forced to make an arbitrary decision, Decker turned to the right.

If not for the chest-high branch that he had to stoop under, the rock that Giordano clutched would have struck Decker's skull instead of his bent-over back. The pain of the blow was matched by its surprise. Dazed, Decker was knocked to the ground, dropping his pistol. In a frenzy, Giordano attacked from the darkness. Decker rolled, feeling the fierce rush of air as the rock passed his head and struck the wet ground with a muffled wallop. He kicked, knocking Giordano's legs from under him. Giordano's full weight landed on him, almost knocking his wind out. Squirming, Decker felt the edge of the steep slope next to him. As Giordano raised the rock to strike it at Decker's face, Decker grabbed Giordano's wrist to stop the blow. At the same time, he felt the ground give way beneath him. He and Giordano were suddenly in the air, falling through the darkness, striking an outcrop, rolling, falling again. With shocking abruptness, they jolted to a stop.

Despite being out of breath, Decker couldn't allow himself to hesitate. He struck at Giordano, who lay next to him, but in the dark, his blow glanced off Giordano's shoulder. Giordano had kept his grip on the rock, and although his aim was hampered by the darkness, he managed to graze Decker's ribs, almost doubling him over. The additional pain made Decker furious. He came to his feet and chopped with the side of his hand, but Giordano stumbled back, avoiding the blow, and swung with the rock. Decker felt the brush of wind as the rock barely missed his face. Wanting to get close to block the next blow, he lunged through the darkness, thrust Giordano back, and heard him gasp when they struck something. Giordano stiffened, his arms outstretched. He trembled. His breath sounded like a leak coming out of an innertube. Then his arms sank, his body becoming motionless, and the only hiss was that of the rain.

Decker didn't understand. Straining to catch his breath, he braced himself to continue the struggle. Slowly, he realized that Giordano was dead.

But somehow the body was still standing.

'I told you I heard something!' a man yelled. Flashlight beams arced through the storm-shrouded trees. Footsteps pounded close to the rim of the slope down which Decker had fallen.

I can't let them see him! Decker thought. He rushed toward where Giordano remained eerily upright. Tugging, he felt resistance and understood sickly that Giordano had been impaled on the jagged stump of a broken-off branch.

The voices and footsteps rushed closer. Have to get him out of sight, Decker thought. Lowering Giordano's dead weight to the ground, about to drag him deeper into the murky trees, Decker became paralyzed by a flashlight beam that caught him squarely as it glared down from the bluff.

'Hey!' a man yelled.

'I found him!' Decker shouted. 'I thought I heard a noise down here! I managed to climb down! I found him!'

'Holy—' another man yelled, aiming a flashlight. 'Look at all the blood!'

'*Can you find a pulse? Is he alive?*' someone else yelled.

'I don't know!' Decker shouted. The glare of the flashlights hurt his eyes. 'I think what I heard was him falling! The drop must have killed him!'

'But there's a chance he might be alive! We have to get an ambulance!'

'His neck might be broken! We don't dare move him!' Rain streaked down Decker's face. 'Is anybody up there a doctor?'

'We need an ambulance!'

Guided by their flashlights, several men were working down past trees on the muddy slope.

'Why did he come this way?' A man reached the bottom. 'Couldn't he see the Interstate back there?'

'He must have banged his head in the wreck!' Decker said. 'He was probably delirious!'

'Jesus, look at him!' One of the men turned away.

'He must have hit something when he fell!'

'*But what about the woman he was with?*' Decker said.

'*Woman?*'

'I heard her voice!' Decker said. 'She sounded like she was hurt! Where *is* she?'

'Everybody!' a man yelled. 'Keep looking! Someone else is out here! A woman!'

The group split apart, scanning their flashlights, quickly searching.

Taking advantage of the chaos, Decker retreated into the darkness. He climbed the slope, slipping in the mud, grabbing exposed tree roots, bracing his shoes on outcrops of rock. Any minute, the group would wonder what had become of him. He had to get away before they suspected he wasn't part of the search team. But I can't leave without Giordano's briefcase. It wasn't with him when he fell. Where *is* it? If the searchers get their hands on the money, there's no way I can save Beth.

Heart pounding, Decker reached the top and spotted more flashlight beams near the wrecked Cadillac. Temporarily he was concealed by undergrowth, but the searchers might soon investigate this area. Breathing hard, he crouched, trying to get his bearings. Where had Giordano attacked him? Was it to the right or the left? Decker swung to stare down toward what in the darkness he could barely tell was Giordano's body. He replayed the struggle at the bottom of the slope. He calculated where they had landed. To reach that area, they would have had to fall from Decker's left. Giordano must have attacked from—

Decker squirmed on his hands and knees through the underbrush. At the same time, flashlights started coming in his direction. No! Decker thought. He had never felt such a powerful surge of adrenaline. He didn't think his pulse had ever been so rapid. Pressure built behind his ears. The briefcase. Have to find the briefcase. Need the briefcase. Can't save Beth without the briefcase.

He had almost crawled past it before he realized what he had touched. Fearing that his heart would surely burst from relief, he grabbed the briefcase. At the same time, his foot nudged something behind him near the edge of the slope. His pistol. He had dropped it when Giordano struck him with the rock. As he shoved the pistol into his jacket, he dared to hope that things might actually work out. He still had a chance to save Beth.

But not if the flashlights came any closer. What if one of them belonged to a policeman? His clothes smeared with mud, Decker crawled farther through the undergrowth, straining not to make noise. He came to where he thought he had initially descended into the trees. Staring behind him, he waited for the flashlights to shift toward an area away from him. The first chance he got, he crept swiftly up through the trees and paused at the edge of the Interstate. Vehicles rushed by in the rain, tires hissing, headlights glaring. On the shoulder, several cars had stopped. Most of them were empty, their occupants presumably having gone into the trees to help search for survivors of the wreck. One of the cars was a police cruiser, Decker saw in dismay, but it too was empty, although probably not for long.

The police car was next to the Oldsmobile. Esperanza sat in the Olds, slumped behind the steering wheel. Even from a distance, it was obvious that his face was bloody. I can't wait any longer, Decker thought. He quickly emerged from the trees, tried to use his body to shield the briefcase from anyone looking at him from the trees, and walked swiftly along the side of the Interstate.

Esperanza straightened as Decker got in the Olds.

'Can you see to drive?'

'Yes.'

'Go.'

Esperanza turned the ignition key, put the Olds in gear, and sped out into traffic. 'You look like hell.'

'I wasn't dressed for the occasion.' Decker stared behind him to see if they were being followed. It didn't seem so.

'I wasn't sure when or if you'd come back,' Esperanza said.

'And *I* wasn't sure if you'd stay with the car. You did the right thing.'

'I'd make a good getaway driver. In fact, I *was* a good getaway driver.'

Decker looked at him.

'When I was sixteen,' Esperanza said. 'You've got the briefcase.'

'Yes.'

'What about Frank Giordano?'

Decker didn't answer.

'Then Beth Dwyer has one less problem.'

'It was self-defense,' Decker said.

'I didn't suggest otherwise.'

'I needed the briefcase.'

'A million dollars. With that kind of money, some men wouldn't think about saving anybody.'

'Without Beth, I wouldn't save *myself*.'

TEN

1

'Jesus, Decker, this is crazy. If you're not careful, you'll end up killing yourself,' Esperanza tensely murmured, lower than a whisper. 'Or else you're giving McKittrick the chance to do it for you.' But they had argued about Decker's intentions for the last hour, and Decker had made clear his determination. This was the way McKittrick expected the dropoff to happen, and by God, this was the way it was *going* to happen.

Decker felt Esperanza lean into the back seat of the Oldsmobile. He felt Esperanza grab his shoulders and tug him out into the rain. His instructions to Esperanza had been to avoid being gentle, to be as rough as someone would expect a hitman to be with the corpse of someone he had just killed.

Esperanza obeyed, making no attempt to ease the impact of Decker's body onto the ground. Pain jolted through him, but he didn't show it, just remained limp as Esperanza dragged him through a puddle. Although Decker kept his eyes shut, he imagined the scene: the battered Oldsmobile next to the refreshment building at the scenic lookout. A little before midnight, in the rain, it was very unlikely that any motorists would have stopped to admire the view from the Palisades. In good weather, the view from the lookout showed the lights of boats on the Hudson and the expansive glow of Hastings and Yonkers across the river, but in bad weather like this, it would show only gloom. On the off-chance that a driver might pull in

319

to rest for a few minutes, Esperanza had parked the Oldsmobile sideways toward the entrance to the lookout, preventing anyone on the Interstate from seeing what appeared to be a corpse being dragged around to the back of the refreshment building.

Decker heard Esperanza grunt, then felt the squishy impact as Esperanza dropped him into a muddy puddle. Limp, he allowed his body to roll and ended on his left side in the puddle. Peering through half-open eyelids, he saw what appeared to be garbage cans in the darkness behind the building. He heard Esperanza run through the puddle back to the car and quickly return. He saw Esperanza set the briefcase against the rear of the building. Then Esperanza disappeared. In a moment, Decker heard car doors being shut, an engine revving, the splash of tires as Esperanza drove away. The engine became fainter. Then all Decker heard was the distant drone of traffic on the Interstate. and the pelt of rain on the clear plastic bag tied over his head.

'Giordano's deal with McKittrick was the money and my corpse,' Decker had insisted while he and Esperanza drove anxiously from town to town, worried about the time they were losing, desperate to find a convenience store. They had started their search at ten-thirty. Then the time was eleven, then eleven-fifteen. 'We have to be there by midnight.' Twice, the stores they did find open had not had all the materials Decker needed. At eleven-thirty, they had finally gotten what they needed. Esperanza had parked on a deserted country lane and done what was necessary.

'Why can't I leave the money along with a note, supposedly from Giordano, that says he won't kill you until McKittrick makes good on his promise?' Esperanza had tied clothes-line rope around Decker's ankles.

'Because I don't want to do anything to make him suspicious. Be sure the knots are in plain view. It'll be dark behind that building. I want it to be obvious to him that I've been tied up.'

320

'But this way, if he isn't convinced you're dead, you won't have a chance to defend yourself.' Esperanza tied Decker's arms behind his back.

'That's what I'm hoping will convince him. He won't believe I willingly made myself completely vulnerable to him.'

'Does this knot hurt?'

'It doesn't matter whether it hurts. Make it real. Make it look as if I couldn't possibly be alive and not show any reaction to the way I've been tied. *He has to believe I'm dead*.'

'You *might be* dead by the time he gets to you. Decker, this plastic bag scares the hell out of me.'

'That's the point. It might even scare *him*. I'm counting on it to be the finishing touch. Mark me up. Hurry.'

Needing something that looked like blood, Decker had used what a pathologist once explained to him were the easiest materials to obtain to fake it – colorless corn syrup and red food dye.

'Make it look as if they really enjoyed beating me,' Decker insisted.

'They mashed your lips. They messed up your jaw.' Esperanza had applied the mixture.

'Hurry. We've only got fifteen minutes to get to the drop-off site.'

Esperanza quickly tied the bag around Decker's neck and then murmured a Spanish prayer as Decker inhaled and forced the bag to collapse around his head, the plastic clinging to his face, sticking to his skin, stuffing Decker's nostrils and his mouth. Immediately Esperanza poked a tiny hole in the plastic that filled Decker's mouth and hurriedly inserted a cutoff piece of a drinking straw, which Decker gripped between his teeth, allowing him to breathe without breaking the vacuum that made the plastic bag stick to his face.

'My God, Decker, does it work? Can you get enough air?'

Decker had managed to nod slightly.

'The way that bag sticks to your face, you look like a corpse.'

Good, Decker thought as he lay in the muddy puddle, in the dark, behind the refreshment building, listening to the rain pelt the plastic bag. Provided that he breathed shallowly, slowly, and calmly, the small amount of air he got through the straw was enough to allow him to remain alive. But with each slight inhalation, panic tried to force itself through his fierce resolve. With each imperceptible exhalation, his heart wanted to beat faster, demanding more oxygen. The cord that secured the bag around his neck was tight enough to dig into the skin – Decker had insisted on that, also. Everything absolutely had to look convincing. And *feel* so – the cold rain would lower Decker's exterior temperature, making his skin feel like that of a corpse losing body heat. If McKittrick for one moment doubted that Decker was a corpse, he would put a bullet through Decker's head and settle the matter.

The danger was that McKittrick would shoot him no matter what, but Decker was counting on the grotesque appearance of his face to make McKittrick decide that further violence wasn't necessary. If McKittrick felt for a pulse on Decker's wrists, he wouldn't find one, the tight ropes having sharply reduced the flow of blood. He could try to feel for a pulse along Decker's neck, but to do so, McKittrick would have to untie the cord that secured the plastic bag – time-consuming and disgusting. That left pressing a palm against the ribs over Decker's heart, but he wasn't likely to do that, either, because Decker had landed on his left side – to feel the ribs over Decker's heart, McKittrick would have to turn the body over and press his hand against the repulsive mud that adhered to Decker's clothes.

It was still a great risk. 'Insane,' as Esperanza had kept telling him. 'You're going to get yourself killed.' But what was the alternative? If the dropoff didn't occur exactly as McKittrick expected, if Decker's body wasn't there as promised, McKittrick might become suspicious enough not to take the money, fearing that the briefcase was boobytrapped. But the money was what Decker's plan was all about, the money and the homing device that Decker had hidden with the money. If McKittrick didn't take the money, Decker would have no way to follow him to where Beth was being held captive. No matter how Decker analyzed it, there wasn't an alternative. McKittrick *had* to find Decker's corpse.

'Do you love Beth that much?' Esperanza had asked before he tied the plastic bag over Decker's head. 'To risk your life for her so completely?'

'I'd go to hell for her.'

'To learn the truth about her feelings toward you?' Esperanza had looked strangely at him. 'This isn't about love. It's about pride.'

'It's about hope. If I can't trust love, nothing matters. Put that straw in my mouth. Tie the bag.'

'Decker, you're the most remarkable man I ever met.'

'No, I'm a fool.'

Lying in the puddle, breathing slightly, fighting panic, mustering all the discipline of which he was capable, Decker struggled against the temptation to second-guess himself. As his lungs demanded more air, he thought perhaps there *had* been another way. Was it possible that all he wanted was to show Beth the lengths he would go to demonstrate how much he loved her?

Desperately needing to distract himself, he recalled the first time he had seen her, two months ago . . . Could it have been only that recently? It seemed forever . . . in the lobby of the real-estate office – how she had turned toward him, how his heart rhythm had changed. Never before in his life had he felt such instant attraction. In his imagination, he saw her again vividly, her lush auburn hair reflecting the light, her tanned skin glowing with health, her athletic figure making him selfconscious about the contour of her breasts and hips. He was spellbound by her elegant chin, her high cheekbones, her model's forehead. He imagined stepping close to her, and suddenly his imagination shifted to the evening they had first made love, her blue-gray eyes and sensual lips so close they were a blur. He kissed her neck, drawing his tongue along her skin, tasting salt, sun, and something primal. He smelled her musk. When he entered her, it was as if all his life he had been only half of a person, but now he was complete, not only physically but emotionally, spiritually, filled with wellbeing, at last blessed with a purpose – to build a life with her, to share, to be one.

2

In a rush, his senses returned to the present – because, amid the distant drone of traffic and the pelting of the rain, he heard sounds from the bluff behind him. Although the plastic bag muffled his hearing, apprehension heightened his awareness. The sounds he heard were labored breathing, footsteps slipping on wet rocks, branches being snapped.

Dear God, Decker thought. He had been waiting to hear a car pull off the Interstate and approach this section of the scenic lookout. But McKittrick had been here all along, below the guardrail, hiding on the slope. He must have seen Esperanza drag me behind the building, Decker told himself. He must have seen Esperanza dump me into the puddle, leave the briefcase, and drive away. If Esperanza had said just one word to me, if he had made any attempt to cushion me, McKittrick would have realized instantly that this was a trap. He would have shot us.

Decker shivered from the understanding of how close he had come to dying. The cold rain made him shiver, also, and at once he strained to subdue the reflex. He didn't dare move. He had to achieve the appearance of lifelessness. In the past, when he had been about to embark on a dangerous assignment, he had relied on meditation to calm himself. Now he did so again. Concentrating deeply, he fought to purge himself of emotion, of fear, of longing, of apprehension, of need.

But his imagination could not be denied. He envisioned McKittrick peering over the rainswept bluff and scowling at the darkness. McKittrick would be nervous, wet, cold, impatient to finish this and escape. He would be holding a weapon and prepared to shoot at the slightest provocation. He might have a flashlight. He might risk exposing himself by turning it on and aiming the light at the ropes around Decker's arms and legs. If so, he would definitely let the light linger on the plastic bag that covered Decker's head.

Footsteps touched down on wet gravel, as if McKittrick had stepped over the guardrail. This was the moment, Decker knew, when McKittrick might shoot to make sure that Decker was in fact dead. Simultaneously, to prevent his chest from moving even slightly, Decker stopped breathing. His lungs immediately demanded more air. The suffocating pressure in his chest began to build. His oxygen-starved muscles ached with intensifying need.

The footsteps paused near him. Decker had prepared himself and showed no reaction when a shoe pushed at his upright shoulder flipping him onto his back. Through closed eyelids, Decker was able to see the filtered glare from a flashlight as McKittrick studied the plastic bag's seal against Decker's face. Decker had shifted the cutoff section of straw toward a corner of his mouth and inhaled imperceptibly so that the bag was deeper past his lips. He felt light-headed. Desperate to breathe, he concentrated on kissing Beth; his mind filled only with her. Swirling, he felt swallowed by her.

McKittrick grunted, perhaps with satisfaction. At once the flashlight was extinguished. His lungs threatening to burst, Decker heard quick footsteps through water as McKittrick presumably hurried toward the briefcase. But now other sounds confused Decker, clicks, scrapes, aggravating his apprehension. *What were those sounds? What was McKittrick doing?*

Understanding came in a rush. McKittrick was transferring the money to another container, suspicious that Giordano might have put a homing device in the briefcase. Good instincts, but Decker had anticipated. The homing device wasn't secured to the briefcase. Decker had used a knife to cut out the interior of one of the packets of cash. He had inserted the homing device and then had resecured the rubber bands around the packet so it appeared no different from any of the others.

Decker heard McKittrick grunt again, this time with effort. Something flipped through the air, then clattered down the bluff. The briefcase, Decker realized. McKittrick had thrown it away. He didn't want to leave any indication that this area behind the restrooms had been used as a drop site. But if he had thrown away the briefcase—

Jesus, he's going to do the same with me. Decker barely kept his oxygen-deprived body from showing his panic as McKittrick grabbed his shoulders, dragged him violently backward, roughly hefted him up, and doubled him over the guardrail. No! Decker mentally screamed. The next instant, he felt weightless. His body struck something. He flipped off it and again felt weightless. His bound arms hit something beneath him. Unable to restrain the impulse, he moaned in pain. *Had McKittrick heard him?* He toppled, rolled, hit something else, imagined that he was about to begin the long, deadly fall all the way from the Palisades bluff to the Hudson River, and suddenly jolted to an agonizing halt, his head banging against something.

Dazed, he felt something liquid inside the plastic bag. I'm

bleeding! The hot sticky fluid streamed from a cut on his forehead and began to fill the plastic bag. No! He didn't care if McKittrick now saw him move. There wasn't a choice. *He had to breathe*. The plan had been for McKittrick to take the money, leave Decker, and hurry away. At that point, Decker would have reinserted the piece of straw in the hole in the bag and breathed as best he could until Esperanza – alerted by the moving needle on the receiver that the money had been taken – returned to free him. But Decker had never once considered that McKittrick might try to dispose of the body. Decker would never have attempted the plan if the terrifying thought had occurred to him. I'm going to die. The cord that was tied around his neck, securing the plastic bag to his face, dug into his skin, making him feel strangled.

Frantic for air, he worked the piece of straw from the corner of his mouth and poked it through the hole in the bag . . . or tried to – he couldn't find the opening. Unable to control his body, he exhaled forcefully, expanding the bag, and with equal force, totally unwilled, he inhaled. This time, the bag filled his nose and mouth. Like a living thing, it gripped tightly to his skin. The makeup and blood beneath it caused it to stick fast. Esperanza will never find me in time!

Thrashing, he turned in the rain toward whatever he had landed on and rubbed his face along whatever it was that supported him, searching for anything that was sharp, a branch, a jagged outcrop of rock, *anything* that would snag the plastic bag and tear it open. The surface was wet and slick. He banged his head against something – a rock – ignored the pain, and continued squirming. But he felt in slow motion. The blood that continued to slick his face and fill the plastic bag gave him the sensation of drowning. For all he knew, his movements were about to topple him over a precipice. What difference did it make? He was doomed if he didn't . . .

A stakelike object snagged the plastic bag. His consciousness graying, he feebly jerked his head to the left, felt the bag tear, and used a final burst of strength to twist his head even farther to the left. The tear increased. He felt a chill wind against his forehead, the cold rain on his brow. But the plastic still stuck to his nose and mouth. He tried to breathe through the tiny hole at his mouth, but his efforts had twisted the plastic and sealed the hole. He thought he was going to choke on the piece of drinking straw in his mouth. I have to get the bag off my head! Feeling as if something inside him were going to burst, as if he were about to sink into a deep black pit, he made one last attempt to snag the bag on the sharp object, scraped his right cheek, and tore the bag totally open.

When he spat out the piece of drinking straw and breathed, wind seemed to shriek down his throat. The rush of cold air into his lungs was unbelievably sweet. His chest pumped convulsively. He lay on his back, trembling, gulping air, and tried to adjust to the realization that he was alive.

3

Alive, but for how long? Decker asked himself in dismay. Esperanza might not find me. If I stay out in the cold rain much longer, I'll get hypothermia. I'll die from exposure. Turning so that his face was toward the black sky, he tasted sweet rain, breathing hungrily, trying not to be alarmed by the force with which he shuddered and the pressure it put on his bound arms and legs. How long have I been down here? Has McKittrick gone? Did he hear me groan when I landed?

He waited in dread that a dark shape would clamber down the bluff toward him, that McKittrick would turn on his flashlight, grin, and aim his pistol. Indeed, all of a sudden, Decker did see a flashlight glaring at the top of the bluff, the beam moving toward the refreshment building, toward the guardrail, toward the refreshment building again, and responding to the faith that he had felt growing in him, Decker shouted, or tried to shout, 'Esperanza.' The word came out hoarsely, as if he had been swallowing gravel. He tried again, harder. 'Esperanza!' This time, the flashlight beam froze toward the guardrail. A moment later, it blazed down the bluff, and Decker was able to see that the drop here was on an incline, a series of bush-and-tree-studded levels that angled down toward the eventual sheer fall to the river.

'Over here!' Decker shouted. The flashlight beam streaked along the ledge toward him. Not far enough. 'Here!' At last, the flashlight found him. But did it belong to Esperanza? Faith, Decker thought. I've got to have faith.

'Decker?'

Esperanza! Thanking God, Decker felt his heart pound less furiously as the familiar tall lanky figure climbed over the guardrail and began a hurried descent.

'Be careful,' Decker said.

Esperanza's cowboy boots slipped off a rock. 'Holy—' He steadied himself, scurried lower, and crouched, using his flashlight to study Decker's face. 'There's blood all over you. Are you all right?'

'I have to be.'

Esperanza swiftly cut the rope that held Decker's arms behind him. With equal speed, he cut the rope that bound Decker's legs. Although Decker's muscles were cramped, he luxuriated in his ability to move.

'Hold still while I work on these knots,' Esperanza said. 'Damn, the rain soaked into the rope and swelled it. I can't get—'

'We don't have time,' Decker said. 'We have to get to the car.

The homing signal is good for only a mile. *Help me up*.'

With effort, struggling not to lose his own balance, Esperanza helped him to stand.

'The circulation's almost gone from my hands and feet. You'll have to pull me up,' Decker said.

Grunting, straining, they worked up the slope.

'I parked about a hundred yards north on the shoulder of the Interstate,' Esperanza said. 'No headlights turned in to the lookout. It was after midnight. I was beginning to think he wasn't going to show up. But all of a sudden the needle on the receiver moved – the homing device was in motion. I backed along the Interstate's shoulder to get to you as fast as I could.'

'McKittrick was hiding on a ledge.' Decker reached the guardrail, gasping with effort, climbing over. 'He must have escaped through the trees. His car must be parked south of here or farther north than where *you* were. Hurry.'

Splashing through puddles, Esperanza reached the shadowy Oldsmobile before Decker did. He grabbed the receiver off the front seat. 'I'm still getting a signal,' he said excitedly. 'The needle says he's driving north.'

Decker slumped into the front seat, managed to slam the door, and felt his body lurch against the seat as Esperanza tromped the accelerator. The Oldsmobile tore up gravel and fishtailed across the soaked parking area, speeding toward the rain-streaked headlights on the Interstate.

4

'The signal's weak!' Decker stared at the illuminated dial on the receiver. His wet clothes clung to him.

Esperanza drove even faster. Barely taking the time to turn on the windshield wipers, he spotted a break in traffic, roared onto the Interstate, and began passing cars.

'Jesus, I'm freezing.' Decker pawed at the switch for the car's heater. With the awkward, almost senseless fingers of his right hand, he fumbled to saw Esperanza's knife across the knot that secured the rope to his left wrist. He studied the dial on the receiver. 'The signal's stronger.' The needle shifted. 'Watch! He's off the Interstate. He's to the left of us up ahead!'

Quicker than expected, the Oldsmobile's headlights revealed a rain-obscured offramp, a sign for Route 9.

'It parallels the Interstate,' Decker said. 'The needle says he's reversed direction! He's heading south.' Decker barely avoided nicking himself as the knife sliced all the way through the rope on his wrist. Blood tingled into the veins of his left hand. He massaged the painful groove that the rope had made on his wrists.

'You told me to make it look real,' Esperanza said.

'Hey, I'm still alive. I'm not complaining.'

At the end of the offramp, Esperanza veered left across the bridge over the Interstate and sped left again, accessing Route 9, hurrying south, approaching a string of taillights.

'The signal's even stronger!' Decker said. 'Slow down. He could be in any of these cars ahead of us.' He severed the rope around his other wrist. Blood flowing into his hand made his fingers less awkward, allowing him to cut harder and faster at the coils around his ankles.

Despite the hot air from the car's heater, he continued to shudder. Troubled thoughts tortured him. What if McKittrick had already killed Beth? Or what if McKittrick guessed that he was being followed and discovered where the homing device was, throwing it away? No! I can't have gone through this for nothing! Beth *has* to be alive.

'The needle says he's turning again. To the right. Heading west.'

Esperanza nodded. 'Four cars in front, I see headlights turning. I'll slow down, so he doesn't see us turn after him.'

Anticipation bolstered Decker's strength. He wiped his forehead and looked at his hand, disturbed by the crimson on his palm. Not corn syrup mixed with red food dye. Coppery-smelling, this was unmistakably the real thing.

'I don't know how much help it will be, but here's a clean handkerchief I found in the glove compartment,' Esperanza said. 'Try to stop the bleeding.' As he followed McKittrick, steering to the right off Route 9, passing a sign that read ROCKMAN ROAD, Esperanza flicked off his headlights. 'No point in advertising. I can barely see his taillights in the rain, so I'm sure he can't see *us* at all.'

'But you're driving blind.'

'Not for long.' Esperanza turned left into a lane, re-illuminated his headlights, made a U-turn, and drove back onto Rockman Road, steering left, again following McKittrick. 'In case he's watching his rearview mirror, which I'd certainly be doing in *his* place, he'll see headlights pull onto the road from his left, which is the wrong direction for anyone to be following him from the Interstate. He won't be suspicious.'

'You're very good at this,' Decker said.

'I'd better be. When I was a kid, I ran with gangs. I had a lot of practice in following and *being* followed.'

'What straightened you out?'

'I met a police officer who got through to me.'

'He must be proud of the way you turned out.'

'He died last year. A drunk with an attitude shot him.'

A blinding flash was followed by a rumble that shook the car.

'Now we're getting lightning and thunder. The storm's worse,' Decker said.

'Shit.' But it wasn't clear if Esperanza referred to the storm or his memories.

The next time lightning flashed, he pointed. 'I see a car.'

'The signal on the receiver is strong. The needle's straight ahead,' Decker said. 'That must be McKittrick.'

'Time to pull off the road. I don't want him getting suspicious.' Past a sign for the town of Closter, Esperanza let McKittrick proceed straight ahead while he himself turned to the right, went around a block, and came back onto Rockman Road. By then, the headlights of other cars had gone by and filled the space between the Oldsmobile and McKittrick's vehicle.

'The receiver indicates he's still ahead of us.' Decker's cold wet clothes continued to make him shiver. Tension made his muscles ache. The places on his back and chest where he had landed falling down the bluff were swollen, throbbing. It didn't matter. Pain didn't matter. Only Beth did. 'No, wait. The needle's moving. He's turning to the right.'

'Yes, I see his lights going off the road,' Esperanza said. 'I don't want to spook him by following him right away. Let's pass where he turned and see where he's going. He might be trying an evasion tactic.'

Having gone through the quiet heart of town, they reached the even quieter outskirts, and now, as lightning flashed, they saw where McKittrick had turned: a modest one-story motel. A red neon sign announced PALISADES INN. Attached plain units – about twenty of them, Decker judged – stretched back toward a murky area away from the street. As the Oldsmobile went by, Decker scrunched down out of sight, in case McKittrick was glancing toward the sparse traffic that had followed him.

Then the motel was behind the Oldsmobile, and Decker slowly straightened. 'The needle on the receiver indicates that McKittrick isn't moving.'

'How do you want to handle this?'

'Park off the street some place. Let's go back and see what he's doing.'

Thunder shook the car as Decker picked up the pistol that he had taken from one of the guards at Giordano's estate. He watched Esperanza pocket the Walther. 'We'd better take the receiver with us. In case this is a trick and he starts to move again.'

'And then?' Esperanza asked.

'A damned good question.' Decker got out of the car and was instantly reassaulted by rain. For an angry moment, he remembered the cold rain that had been falling the night he had followed McKittrick into the trap in the courtyard in Rome. Then Esperanza was next to him, his baseball cap dripping water, his drenched long hair sticking to his neck. In the glare from passing headlights, Esperanza's face looked leaner than usual, his nose and jaw more pronounced, reminding Decker of a raptor.

5

Rather than show themselves at the front of the building, they moved cautiously along an alley that led to the back. Decker noted that the units were made of cinderblock and that there weren't any rear exits. The only windows on the alley side were small and made of thick opaque glass bricks that would be extremely difficult to break.

Skirting the back of the motel, Decker and Esperanza concealed themselves behind a Dumpster bin and studied the front of the units. The needle on the receiver continued to indicate that the homing device was in one of them. Although eight of the twenty units had a vehicle in front, only four of them had lights glowing beyond closed draperies. Two of those units were next to each other, near the Dumpster bin that Decker hid behind. Decker didn't need the receiver to tell him that the signal came from one of those latter units. A car in front of them, a blue Pontiac, made sporadic ticking sounds as its engine cooled. Rain pelting on the Pontiac's warm hood vaporized into mist.

Hurry, Decker thought. If Beth's in one of those rooms, McKittrick might be tempted to kill her as soon as he's back with the money. Or if he checks the money and finds the homing device, he might panic and kill Beth before he tries to escape.

'Wait here,' Decker whispered to Esperanza. 'Back me up.' He moved as silently as he could through puddles and paused next to the softly lit window of the last unit in the row. An intense flash of lightning made him feel naked. A deep burst of thunder shook him. The night again concealed him. Uneasy, he noted that the draperies didn't meet fully, and he was able to see through a narrow gap into a room – a double bed, a cheap dresser, a television bolted to the wall. Except for a suitcase on the bed, it seemed unoccupied. In the middle of the wall to the left, a door was open, appearing to allow access to the room next to it.

Decker stiffened at more lightning and thunder, then shifted toward the next window. Despite the noise of the storm, he was able to hear voices, although he couldn't distinguish what they said. A man was talking, then a woman. The male voice might have been McKittrick's, the female voice Beth's. Hard to tell. Maybe what Decker heard was only a conversation on the television. Unexpectedly, someone else spoke, a man with a severely distorted, deep, hoarse voice, and Decker was briefly confused until he realized that if Beth was in there, someone would have had to guard her while McKittrick went for the money. He imagined Beth tied to a chair, a loosened gag dangling from her mouth. He imagined the gag being reapplied and Beth struggling, her eyes bulging as McKittrick strangled her.

Do something! he told himself. After noting the room number on the door, he hurried back to Esperanza and explained what he intended to do. Then, staying among shadows, he rushed to the street, where he remembered having seen a payphone at a closed gas station across from the motel. Quickly, he inserted coins and pressed numbers.

'Information,' a woman said. 'For what city, please?'

'Closter, New Jersey. I need the number for the Palisades Inn.'

In a moment, a computerized monotonous voice said, 'The number is . . .'

Decker memorized the number, hung up, put in more coins, and pressed buttons.

After three rings, a weary male voice answered, almost sighing, 'Palisades Inn.'

'Give me room nineteen.'

The clerk didn't acknowledge the request. Instead, Decker heard a click, then a ring and another ring as the call was put through. He imagined McKittrick swinging toward the phone, his burly features expressing a mixture of surprise and puzzlement. After all, who would be calling him? Who would know that he was at that motel? McKittrick would be debating whether it was smart to answer.

The phone kept ringing. Ten times. Eleven times.

The clerk finally interrupted. 'Sir, they're not answering. Maybe they're not in.'

'Keep trying.'

'But maybe they're trying to sleep.'

'This is an emergency.'

The clerk sighed wearily. Again Decker heard a click. The phone on the other end rang, then rang again.

'Hello.' McKittrick's voice was hesitant, at half-volume, as if by speaking softly he hoped that his voice would not be recognizable.

'If you use your common sense,' Decker said, 'there's still a chance you'll get out of this alive.'

The line became silent. The only sound Decker heard was the rain against the phone booth.

'Decker?' McKittrick sounded as if he doubted his sanity.

'It's been a long time since we talked, Brian.'

'But it can't be. You're *dead*. How—'

'It's not *my* death I called to talk about, Brian.'

'Jesus.'

'Prayer's a good idea, but I'm in a better position to help you than Jesus is.'

'Where are you?'

'Come on, Brian. I'm the guy who wrote the book on tradecraft. I don't volunteer information. The next thing, you'll be asking how I found out where you are and how many people are with me. But all you need to concern yourself about is you've got the money and I want Beth Dwyer.'

The line became silent again.

'If she's dead, Brian, you don't have any way to bargain with me.'

'No.' Brian made a tense swallowing sound. 'She isn't dead.'

Decker felt a sinking sensation, one of relief. 'Let me talk to her.'

'This is very complicated, Decker.'

'It used to be. But tonight, things got simpler. Nick and Frank Giordano are dead.'

'How the hell—'

'Trust me, Brian. They're not in the equation any longer. No one's hunting Beth Dwyer. You can keep the money and let her go. How you got the money will be our secret.'

McKittrick hesitated, his tense breathing audible. 'Why should I believe you?'

'Think about it, Brian. If the Giordanos were still alive, I

337

wouldn't be talking to you. That would really have been my corpse at the drop site.'

McKittrick breathed harder.

'And it wouldn't be *me* on the phone,' Decker said. 'It would be *them* breaking through your motel-room door.'

Decker heard what sounded like McKittrick's hand being put over the phone's mouthpiece. He heard muffled voices. He waited, shivering from his wet clothes and his bone-deep dread that McKittrick would do something to Beth.

On the other end, something brushed against the phone's mouthpiece, and McKittrick was talking again. 'I need convincing.'

'You're *stalling*, Brian. You're going to try to leave while I'm talking to you. I'm not alone. The moment you show yourself at the door, there'll be shooting, and I guarantee if Beth gets hurt, you'll find out the hard way you can't spend a million dollars in hell.'

Pause. Another round of muffled voices. McKittrick's voice was strained when he came back on the line. 'How can I be sure you'll let me go if I give you Diana Scolari?'

'*Beth Dwyer*,' Decker said. 'This might be a new idea to you, Brian. Integrity. I never go back on my word. When I worked for Langley, that's how I was able to make deals. People knew they could count on me. And this is the most important deal I ever wanted to make.'

From Decker's vantage point in the phone booth, he could see across the street toward the motel units stretching back toward the Dumpster bin. He could see Esperanza hiding behind that bin, watching the two motel units. He could see both windows go dark.

'Why did you turn off the lights, Brian?'

'Jesus, you're that close?'

'Don't try something stupid. You're planning to use Beth as a shield and bet that I won't risk shooting. Think. Even if I did let you escape with her, are you prepared to use her as a shield for the rest of your life? That plastic bag over my head back at the drop site proves I'm ready to take any risk for her. I would never stop hunting you.'

No response.

'Just keep focused on the million dollars, Brian. No one can prove how you got it. No one will want it back. It's yours to spend once you drive away from here.'

'Provided you let me leave.'

'Provided *you* leave *Beth*. This conversation is pointless if you don't prove to me she's alive. *Let me talk to her*.'

Decker listened to the phone so hard that he didn't hear the pelting of the rain. Then he couldn't help hearing the thunder that rattled the glass of the phone booth and the greater thunder of his heart.

The phone made a sound as if it was being moved.

'Steve?'

Decker's knees felt weak. Despite all his determination, he now realized that he had not totally believed he would ever hear Beth's voice again.

'Thank God,' Decker blurted.

'I can't believe it's you. How did—'

'I don't have time to explain. Are you all right?'

'Scared to death. But they haven't hurt me.' The voice was faint and weak, trembling with nervousness, but he couldn't fail to recognize it. He recalled the first time Beth had spoken to him and how he had been reminded of wind chimes and champagne.

'I love you,' Decker said. 'I'm going to get you out of there. How many people are with you?'

Abruptly the phone made a bumping sound, and McKittrick was talking. 'So now you know she's still alive. How am *I* going to get out of here alive?'

'Turn on the lights. Open the draperies.'

'*What?*'

'Put Beth in plain sight at the window. Come out with the money. Get in the car. All the while, keep your pistol aimed at her. That way, you know I won't try a move against you.'

'Until I'm on the street and I can't see to shoot her anymore. Then you'll try to kill me.'

'You've got to have faith,' Decker said.

'Bullshit.'

'Because *I* have faith. I'll show you how much faith I really have. You know you'll be safe after you leave Beth in the room because *I'll* be with you in the car. *I'll* be your hostage. Down the road, when you're sure no one's following, you can let me out, and we'll be even.'

Silence again. Thunder.

'You're joking,' McKittrick said.

'I've never been more serious.'

'How do you know I won't kill you?'

'I don't,' Decker said. 'But if you do, I have friends who will hunt you down. I'm willing to gamble you want this to end here and now. I mean it, Brian. Give me Beth. Keep the money. You'll never hear from me again.'

McKittrick didn't speak for a while. Decker imagined him calculating.

With a muffled voice, McKittrick spoke to someone else in the motel room. 'All right,' he said to Decker. 'Give us five minutes. Then we're coming out. I expect you to be waiting with your hands up at my car.'

'You've got a deal, Brian. But in case you're tempted to go back on the bargain, just remember – someone else will be aiming at you.'

6

Mouth parched with fear, Decker hung up the phone and stepped out into the rain. His chill increased as he hurried across the street and into the motel's dark parking lot, staying within shadows, concealing himself. At the back, he came up behind the Dumpster bin, and using a whisper that was muffled by the rain, he explained to Esperanza the deal he had made.

'You're taking a hell of a risk,' Esperanza said.

'So what else is new?'

'*Cojones*, man.'

'He won't kill me. He doesn't want to spend the rest of his life running.'

'From your imaginary friends.'

'Well, I sort of thought *you'd* go after him if he killed me.'

'Yes.' Esperanza thought about it. 'Yes, I would.'

The lights came on beyond the closed draperies in unit nineteen.

'I can't let him find a weapon on me. Here's my pistol,' Decker said. 'Don't hesitate to shoot him if things go bad.'

'It would be my pleasure,' Esperanza said.

'When I tell you to, pick up that empty bottle by your feet and throw it toward the front of the motel. Throw it high so he doesn't know where you are.'

Trying to avoid revealing where Esperanza was hiding, Decker crept back into the darkness and emerged from the shadows of a different area of the parking lot. With his hands up, he stepped through puddles toward the Pontiac in front of unit nineteen.

The draperies parted, like curtains in a theater. Decker's body felt disturbingly out of rhythm when he saw what was revealed. Beth was tied to a chair, her mouth stuffed with a gag. Her blue-gray eyes looked wild with fright. Her hair was disheveled. Her oval face was tight, her high cheekbones pressing against skin made pale by fear. But then she saw him through the window, and Decker was moved by the affection that replaced the fear in her eyes, by the trusting way she looked at him. The relief she felt, her confidence in him, were obvious. She had faith that he was the hero she had dreamed about when she was a child, *her* hero, that he would save her.

From the left, concealed by the cinderblock column between the window and the door, a person stretched out an arm, pointing a hand toward Beth's temple. The hand held a cocked revolver.

Tensing, Decker heard a noise at the door, the lock being freed, the handle being turned. Light spilled from a narrow gap.

'Decker?' McKittrick didn't show himself.

'I'm at your car – where I said I would be.'

The door came fully open. McKittrick stepped into view, the beefy shoulders of his thirtyish football-player's body silhouetted by the light. He looked a little more heavy in the chest than when Decker had last seen him. His blond hair was cut even shorter than Decker remembered, emphasizing his squared-off rugged features. His eyes reminded Decker of a pig's.

Aiming a pistol, McKittrick smiled. For a dismaying moment, Decker feared that McKittrick would shoot. But McKittrick stepped from the open door, grabbed Decker, and thrust him across the still warm hood of the Pontiac.

'You'd better not be armed, old buddy.' McKittrick searched him roughly, all the while pressing the barrel of his pistol against the back of Decker's neck.

'No weapon,' Decker said. 'I made a deal. I'll stick to it.' With his cheek pressed against the Pontiac's wet hood, Decker was able to see sideways toward the illuminated window and the revolver aimed at Beth. He blinked repeatedly to clear his vision as cold rain pelted his face.

Beth squirmed in terror.

McKittrick stopped his rough search and stepped back. 'My, my, my, you really did it. You gave yourself up to me. So sure of yourself. What makes you think I won't shoot you in the head?'

'I told you – I've got backup.'

'Yeah, sure, right. From who? The FBI? This isn't their style. From Langley? This doesn't involve national security. Why would *they* care?'

'I have friends.'

'Hey, I've been *watching* you, remember? In Santa Fe, you don't have *any* friends, none you would trust to back you up.'

'From the old days.'

'Like hell.'

'*Make a noise,*' Decker called to Esperanza in the darkness.

McKittrick flinched as the empty bottle plummeted onto the pavement near the entrance to the motel. Glass shattered.

McKittrick scowled and continued to aim at Decker. 'For all I know, that's a wino you paid to throw that bottle.'

'The point is, you *don't* know,' Decker said. 'Why take the risk?'

'I'm going to be so damned happy to have you out of my life.'

For a panicked moment, Decker feared that McKittrick was going to pull the trigger.

Instead, McKittrick shouted toward the open door, 'Let's go!'

A figure appeared – of medium height, wearing a black oversized raincoat and a rubber rainhat, the wide brim of which drooped down and concealed the person's features. Whoever it was had a suitcase in his left hand while he continued to aim the revolver at Beth in the window.

McKittrick opened the Pontiac's back door so the man in the raincoat could throw the suitcase into the car. Only when the man got into the back did McKittrick open the Pontiac's driver's door and tell Decker to slide across. The man in back sat behind

Decker and aimed at his head while McKittrick got behind the steering wheel, all the while aiming at Beth.

'Slick.' McKittrick chuckled. 'No muss, no fuss. And now, old buddy, you get what you wanted.' His tone became sober. 'We take you for a ride.'

McKittrick started the Pontiac, switched on its headlights, and went into reverse. The headlights blazed at Beth. Through the distortion of rain streaming down the windshield, Decker watched her trying to struggle against her ropes and turn her head to shield her eyes from the glare of the headlights. As the Pontiac continued backing up, she seemed to get smaller. McKittrick put the car into forward, steered, and pulled away from the motel unit. Grateful that Beth was safe but simultaneously feeling alone and hollow, Decker turned to catch his last glimpse of her struggling against the ropes that bound her to the chair. She stared with heartbreaking melancholy in his direction, afraid now for him.

'Who would have guessed?' McKittrick drove onto the gloomy street outside the motel and headed to the right. 'A romantic.'

Decker didn't say anything.

'She must really have gotten to you,' McKittrick said.

Decker still didn't respond.

'Hey.' McKittrick took his eyes off the road and aimed his pistol at Decker's face. 'This is a goddamned conversation.'

'Yes,' Decker said. 'She got to me.'

McKittrick muttered with contempt, then glanced back at the road. He studied his rearview mirror. 'No headlights. Nobody's following.'

'Did she know who I was when I first met her?' Decker asked.

'What?'

'Was she only using me for extra protection?'

'You're something. All that pose about being a professional, about keeping control, and you ruin your life over a woman.'

'That's not the way I look at it.'

'How the hell *do* you look at it?'

'I didn't ruin my life,' Decker said. 'I found it.'

'Not for long. You want to talk about ruined lives?' McKittrick snapped. 'You ruined *mine*. If it hadn't been for you, I'd still be working for the Agency. I would have been promoted. My father would have been proud of me. I wouldn't have had to take this shit job with the Marshals Service, protecting gangsters.' McKittrick raised his voice. 'I could still be in Rome!'

The man in the back seat said something – a gravelly, guttural statement that was too distorted for Decker to understand it. Decker had heard the puzzlingly grotesque voice before – when he listened outside McKittrick's room. But there was something about it that made it naggingly familiar, as if he had heard it even earlier. McKittrick was obviously familiar with it and knew immediately what was being said.

'I *won't* shut up!' McKittrick said. 'I'm not giving anything away! He knows as well as I do, he couldn't stand for me to be successful! He shouldn't have interfered! If he'd let me do things *my* way, I would have been a hero!'

'Heroes don't let themselves get mixed up with scum like Giordano.'

'Hey, since the good guys decided to kick me out, I thought I'd see how the *bad* guys treated me. A hell of a lot better, thank you very much. I'm beginning to think there's not a whole lot of difference.' McKittrick laughed. 'And the money is definitely an improvement.'

'But you turned against Giordano.'

'I finally realized there's only one side in any of this – mine. And you're on the *wrong* side. Now it's payback time.' McKittrick held up an object. For a moment, Decker thought it was a weapon. Then he recognized the homing device. 'I'm not as sloppy as you think. After you phoned, I kept asking myself, how did you find me? Back at the drop site, I threw the briefcase away, just in case it was bugged. But I never thought of the money itself. So I went through every bundle, and guess what I found in a hollow you cut out.'

McKittrick pressed a button that lowered the driver's window. Furious, he hurled the homing device into a ditch that he sped past. 'So who's the smart guy now? Whoever's with you won't be able to follow. You're mine.'

McKittrick turned onto a side road, pulled onto the tree-lined shoulder, stopped, and shut off the Pontiac's headlights. In the darkness, rain drummed on the roof. The rapid flapping of the windshield wipers was matched by the beat of Decker's heart as lightning flashed and he saw McKittrick aiming a pistol at him.

'I can hide for quite a while on a million dollars,' McKittrick said. 'But I don't have to hide at all if you're not chasing me.'

McKittrick steadied his finger on the trigger.

'We had a bargain,' Decker said.

'Yeah, and I bet you meant to keep your end of it. Get out of the car.'

Decker's tension increased.

'*Get out of the car*,' McKittrick repeated. 'Do it. Open the door.'

Decker eased away from McKittrick, putting his hand on the passenger door. The moment he opened the latch and stepped out, McKittrick would shoot him, he knew. Frantic, he tried to think of a way to escape. He could attempt to distract McKittrick and get his hands on the pistol, but that still left the man in the back seat, who would fire the moment Decker made an aggressive move. I can dive for the ditch, he thought. In the night and the rain, they might not be able to get a good shot at me.

Muscles cramping, he eased the door open, praying, ready to scramble out.

'Does she really love you?' McKittrick asked. 'Was she aware of who you were? Was she using you?'

'Yes, that's what I want to know,' Decker said.

'Ask her.'

'What?'

'Go back and ask her.'

'What are you talking about?'

The smugness had returned to McKittrick's voice. He was playing a game, but Decker couldn't tell what the game was. 'I'm keeping my part of the bargain. You're free. Go back to Diana Scolari. Find out if she's worth the price you were willing to pay.'

'For *Beth Dwyer*.'

'You really are a goddamned romantic.'

The instant Decker's shoes touched the rainsoaked side of the road, McKittrick stomped the gas pedal, and the Pontiac roared away from Decker, barely missing his feet. As the door slammed shut from the force of the Pontiac's acceleration, McKittrick laughed. Then the car's taillights receded rapidly. Decker was alone in the dark and the rain.

ELEVEN

1

The realization of what had just happened didn't immediately take possession of Decker. He seemed to exist in a dream. Shuddering from the numbness of the shock that he had not been killed, he doubted the reality that McKittrick had let him go. McKittrick's disturbing laughter echoed in his mind. Something was wrong.

But Decker didn't have time to think about it. He was too busy turning, racing back toward the dim lights of Closter. Despite his exhaustion from too little sleep and not enough food, despite the pain from his numerous injuries and the chill of his wet clothes further draining his strength, it seemed to him that he had never run faster or with a fiercer resolve. The storm gusted at him, but he ignored it, charging through the darkness. He stretched his legs to their maximum. His lungs heaved. Nothing could stop him from getting to Beth. In his frenzy, he neared the town's limits. He had a wavering glimpse of the Oldsmobile, where Esperanza had parked it off the street near the motel. Then the motel loomed, its red neon sign shimmering. Almost delirious, he charged around the corner, mustered a last burst of speed, and surged past darkened units toward the light gleaming from room nineteen's open door.

Inside, Beth was slumped on the side of the bed. Esperanza held a glass of water to her lips. The gag and the ropes were on the floor. Aside from those details, every object in the room

351

might as well have been invisible. Decker's attention was riveted on Beth. Her long auburn hair was tangled, her eyes sunken, her cheeks gaunt. He hurried to her, fell to his knees, and tenderly raised his hands to her face. Only vaguely did he have an idea of his unrecognizable appearance, of his drenched hair stuck flat to his skull, of the scrapes on his face oozing blood, of his soaked torn clothes smeared with mud. Nothing mattered except that Beth was safe.

'Are . . . ?' His voice was so hoarse, so strained by emotion, that it startled him. 'Are you all right? Did they hurt you?'

'No.' Beth quivered. She seemed to be doubting her sanity. 'You're bleeding. Your face is . . .'

Decker felt pain in his eyes and throat and realized that he was sobbing.

'Lie down, Decker,' Esperanza said. 'You're in worse shape than Beth is.'

Decker tasted the salt from his tears as he put his arms around Beth and held her as gently as his powerful emotions would allow. This was the moment he had been waiting for. All of his determination and suffering had been directed toward this instant.

'You're hurt,' Beth said.

'It doesn't matter.' He kissed her, never wanting to let her go. 'I can't tell you how worried I was. Are you sure you're all right?'

'Yes. They didn't hit me. The ropes and the gag were the hardest part. And the thirst. I couldn't get enough water.'

'I mean it, Decker,' Esperanza said. 'You look awful. You better lie down.'

But instead of obeying, Decker took the glass of water and urged Beth to sip more of it. He kept repeating in amazement, 'You're alive,' as if in the darkest portion of his soul he had questioned whether he would in fact be able to save her.

'I was so scared.'

'Don't think about it.' Decker lovingly stroked her tangled hair. 'It's over now. McKittrick's gone.'

'And the woman.'

'Woman?'

'She terrified me.'

Decker leaned back, studying Beth in confusion. '*What* woman?'

'With McKittrick.'

Decker felt his stomach turn cold. 'But all I saw was a man.'

'In the raincoat. With the rainhat.'

A chill spread through his already chilled body. 'That was a *woman*?'

Beth shuddered. 'She was beautiful. But her voice was grotesque. She had something wrong with her throat. A puckered hole. A scar, as if she'd been struck with something there.'

Decker now understood why the guttural repugnant voice had been familiar. However distorted, there had been something about it that suggested an accent. An *Italian* accent. 'Listen carefully. Was she tall? Trim hips? Short dark hair? Did she look Italian?'

'Yes. How did—'

'My God, did McKittrick ever call her by name? Did he use the name—'

'Renata.'

'We have to get out of here.' Decker stood, drawing Beth to her feet, looking frantically around the room.

'What's wrong?'

'Did she leave anything? A suitcase? A package?'

'When they were getting ready to go, she took a shopping bag into the other room but she never brought it back.'

'*We have to get out of here,*' Decker shouted, urging Beth and

Esperanza toward the open door. 'She's an expert in explosives. I'm afraid it's a bomb!'

He pushed them outside into the rain, fearfully recalling another rainstorm fifteen months ago when he had crouched behind a crate in a courtyard in Rome.

Renata had detonated a bomb in an upper apartment. As wreckage cascaded from the fourth balcony, the ferocity of the flames illuminated the courtyard. Decker's peripheral vision detected motion in the far left corner of the courtyard, near the door that he and McKittrick had come through. But the motion wasn't from McKittrick. The figure that emerged from the shadows of a stairway was Renata. Holding a pistol equipped with a sound-suppressor, she shot repeatedly toward the courtyard, all the while running toward the open doorway. Behind the crate, Decker sprawled on wet cobblestones and squirmed forward on his elbows and knees. He reached the side of the crate, caught a glimpse of Renata nearing the exit, aimed through the rain, and shot twice. His first bullet struck the wall behind her. His second hit her in the throat. She clutched her windpipe, blood spewing. As her brothers dragged her out of sight into the dark street, Decker knew that their efforts to save her were worthless. The wound would cause her throat to squeeze shut. Death from asphyxiation would occur in just a few minutes.

But *she hadn't died*, Decker realized in horror. In the weeks and months to come, McKittrick must have gone looking for her. Had she and McKittrick gotten together? Had she convinced him that she wasn't his enemy, that the Agency had used him worse than *she* had? Had *she* been directing this?

'Run!' Decker screamed. 'Get behind the Dumpster bin!' Hearing Esperanza racing next to him, he urged Beth ahead of him and suddenly felt himself being lifted off his feet by a force of air that had the impact of a giant fist. The burst of light and the roar that enveloped him were as if the heart of the electrical storm had condensed and struck him. He was weightless, couldn't see, couldn't hear, couldn't feel until with shocking immediacy he slammed onto the wet pavement behind the Dumpster bin. He rolled onto Beth to shield her from the wreckage falling around them. Something glanced off his shoulder, making him wince. Something banged near his head. Glass shattered all around him.

Then the shockwave had passed, and he was conscious of the painful ringing in his ears, of the rain, of people shouting from nearby buildings, of Beth moving under him. She coughed, and he feared that he might be smothering her. Dazed, he gathered the strength to roll off her, hardly aware of the chunks of cinderblock that lay around them.

'Are you hurt?'

'My leg.'

Hands shaking, he checked it. The light from a fire in the remnants of the motel rooms showed him a thick shard of wood projecting from her right thigh. He pulled it out, alarmed by how much blood pulsed from the wound. 'A tourniquet. You need a—' He tugged off his belt and cinched it around the flesh above the jagged hole in her leg.

Someone groaned. A shadow moved behind the Dumpster bin. Slowly, a figure sat up, and Decker shook with relief, knowing that Esperanza was still alive.

'Decker!'

The voice didn't come from Esperanza. The ringing in Decker's ears was so great that he had trouble identifying the direction from which the voice shouted.

'*Decker!*'

Then Decker understood, and he stared past the reflection of flames on the pools of water in the parking lot. In the street out front, McKittrick's Pontiac idled. Prevented by wreckage from entering the lot, the car was positioned so the driver's window faced the motel. McKittrick must have followed Decker back to town. His features contorted with rage, he leaned out the open window, holding up a detonator, screaming, 'I could have set it off when you were inside! But that would have been too easy! I'm just getting started! Keep looking behind you! One night, when you least expect it, we'll blow you and your bitch apart!'

In the distance, a siren wailed. McKittrick raised something else, and Decker had just enough strength to roll with Beth toward the protection of the Dumpster bin before McKittrick fired an automatic weapon, bullets slamming against the metal container. Behind the bin, Esperanza pulled out a pistol and shot back. The next thing, Decker heard tires squealing on wet pavement, and McKittrick's Pontiac roared away.

2

A second siren joined the first.

'We have to get out of here,' Esperanza said.

'Help me with Beth.'

Each man took an arm, lifting her, struggling to hurry with her into the darkness at the back of the motel. A crowd had begun to gather. Decker brushed past two men who ran from an apartment building behind the motel.

'What happened?' one of them shouted.

'A propane tank blew up!' Decker told him.

'Do you need help?'

'No! We're taking this woman to a hospital! Look for other survivors!' Holding Beth, Decker couldn't help feeling her wince with each hurried step he took.

In the murky alley on the opposite side of the motel, he and Esperanza paused just before they reached the street, waiting while several people raced past toward the fire. Immediately they carried Beth unseen along the street toward where the Oldsmobile was parked.

'Drive!' Decker said. 'I'll stay in the back with her!'

Slamming his door, Esperanza turned the ignition key. On the rear seat, Decker steadied Beth to keep her from rolling onto the floor. The Oldsmobile sped away.

'How *is* she?' Esperanza asked.

'The tourniquet has the bleeding stopped, but I've got to release it. She'll get gangrene if blood doesn't circulate through her leg.' Alarmed by a spurt of blood when he loosened the belt, Decker quickly reached into his travel bag on the floor in the back, and grabbed a shirt, shoving it against the wound, creating a pressure bandage. He leaned close to Beth where she lay on the back seat. 'Are you sick to your stomach? Are you seeing double?'

'Dizzy.'

'Hang on. We'll get you to a doctor.'

'*Where?*' Esperanza asked.

'Back in Manhattan. We were headed west when we came into Closter. Take the next left turn and the next left turn after that.'

'To go east. Back to the Interstate,' Esperanza said.

'Yes. And then south.' Decker stroked Beth's cheek. 'Don't be afraid. I'm here. I'll take care of you. You're going to be all right.'

Beth squeezed his hand. 'McKittrick's insane.'

'Worse than in Rome,' Decker said.

'Rome?' Esperanza frowned back at him. 'What are you talking about?'

Decker hesitated. He had been determined to stay quiet about

357

Rome. But Beth and Esperanza had nearly been killed because of what had happened there. They had a right to know the truth. Their lives might depend on it. So he told them . . . about the twenty-three dead Americans . . . about Renata, McKittrick, and that rainy courtyard where Renata had been shot.

'She's a *terrorist*?' Esperanza said.

'McKittrick fell in love with her,' Decker explained. 'After the operation in Rome went to hell, he refused to believe she had tricked him. I think he went after her to make her tell him the truth, but she convinced him she really did love him, and now she's using him again. To get at me. To get her hands on the money Giordano gave him.'

'She hates you.' Beth hardly managed the strength to speak. 'All she could talk about was getting even. She's obsessed with making you suffer.'

'Take it easy. Don't try to talk.'

'No. This is important. Listen. She kept ranting to McKittrick about something you did to her brothers. What did you do?'

'*Brothers?*' Decker jerked his head back. Again he suffered the nightmarish memory of what had happened in that courtyard in Rome.

As wreckage from Renata's bomb had cascaded, a movement to Decker's right had made him turn. A thin, dark-haired man in his early twenties, one of Renata's brothers, rose from behind garbage cans. The man hadn't been prepared for Renata to detonate the bomb so soon. Although he had a pistol, he didn't aim at Decker – his attention was totally distracted by a scream on the other side of the courtyard. With gaping dismay, the young man saw one of his brothers swatting at flames on his clothes and in his hair that had been ignited by the falling, burning wreckage.

Decker shot them both.

* * *

'It's a blood feud,' Decker said, appalled. A wave of nausea swept through him as he understood that Renata hated him even more than McKittrick did. Decker imagined them reinforcing each other's malice, feeding off it, becoming more obsessed with paying him back. But how to get even? They must have debated it endlessly. What revenge would be the most satisfying? They could have just gunned me down in a drive-by shooting, Decker thought. The trouble is, merely killing me wouldn't have been good enough. They wanted to make me afraid. They wanted to make me suffer.

But Decker wasn't only thinking this. Beth's shocked expression made him realize that he was saying it out loud. He couldn't stop himself. His anguished thoughts kept pouring out. 'Nothing would have happened in Santa Fe if McKittrick and Renata hadn't been fixated on me. McKittrick had been forced out of the CIA, but the official story was, he quit. On paper, he looked impressive enough for the US Marshals Service to accept him. He'd been keeping track of where I was living. When you were assigned to him and when he found out the house next to mine was for sale, the plan came together.'

Decker braced himself. His ordeal of saving Beth had been aimed toward this moment, and now the moment had come. He couldn't put off the question any longer. He had to know. 'Were you aware of my background when you first met me?'

Her eyes still shut, Beth didn't answer. Her chest heaved, agitated.

'Before you came to my office, did McKittrick tell you I'd worked for the CIA? Did he instruct you to play up to me, to do your best to make me feel close to you so I'd want to spend all my spare time with you and, in effect, be your next-door-neighbor bodyguard?'

Beth remained silent, breathing with difficulty.

'That would have been their revenge,' Decker said. 'To manipulate me into falling in love with you, then to betray you to the mob. By destroying your life, they hoped to destroy mine. And the mob would pay them for their pleasure.'

'I see lights,' Esperanza interrupted, steering swiftly around a corner. 'That's the Interstate ahead.'

'I have to know, Beth. *Did McKittrick tell you to try to make me fall in love with you?*'

She still didn't answer. How could he make her tell him the truth? Abruptly, as they reached the Interstate, the glare of passing headlights spilled into the backseat, showing Decker that Beth hadn't closed her eyes because she was trying to avoid his gaze. Her body was limp, her breathing now shallow. She had passed out.

3

It was three a.m. when Esperanza, following Decker's directions, sped to a stop at the brownstone on Manhattan's West 82nd Street. That late at night, the affluent neighborhood was quiet, the rainy street deserted. No one was around to see Decker and Esperanza carry Beth from the car and into the brownstone's vestibule. Worried by her increasing weakness, Decker pressed the intercom button for apartment eight. As he anticipated, instead of having to push the button several times and wait for a sleepy voice to ask what he wanted, he received an immediate response. The person upstairs had been alerted by an emergency phone call Decker had made from a service station along the Interstate. A buzzer sounded, the signal that the lock on the vestibule's inner door had been electronically released.

Decker and Esperanza hurried through, found the elevator waiting for them, and went up to the fourth floor, frustrated by the elevator's slow rise. The moment the elevator's door opened, a man wearing rumpled clothes that made him look as if he had dressed quickly hurried from an apartment and helped to carry Beth inside. The man was tall and exceedingly thin with a high forehead and a salt-and-pepper mustache. Decker heard a noise behind him and turned to see a heavy set woman with gray hair and a worried look shut and lock the door behind them.

The man directed Decker and Esperanza to the left into a brightly lit kitchen, where a plastic sheet had been spread across the table, other sheets on the floor. Surgical instruments were laid out on a protected counter. Water boiled on the stove. The woman, who wore hospital greens, blurted to Decker, 'Wash your hands.'

Decker obeyed, crowding with the man and the woman at the sink, using a bottle of bitter-smelling liquid to disinfect his hands. The woman helped the man put on a surgical mask, a Plexiglas face shield, and latex gloves, then gestured for Decker to help *her* put on a mask, shield, and gloves. Without pausing, the woman used scissors to cut Beth's blood stained slacks, exposing her right leg all the way up to her underwear. Now that the pressure bandage was removed, the jagged hole spurted blood.

'When did this happen?' The doctor pressed a gloved finger against the flesh next to the wound. The bleeding stopped.

'Forty minutes ago,' Decker said. Rainwater dripped from him onto the plastic sheet on the floor.

'How soon did you restrict the flow of blood?'

'Almost immediately.'

'You saved her life.'

While the woman used surgical sponges to wipe blood from the wound, the doctor swabbed alcohol onto Beth's injured leg, then gave her an injection. But despite what the doctor explained was a painkiller, Beth moaned when the doctor used surgical tweezers to examine the interior of the wound and determine if there was any debris inside.

'I can't be certain. This will have to be quick and crude, just to get the bleeding stopped. She needs an X-ray. Intravenous fluids. Possibly microsurgery if the femoral artery was nicked.' The doctor gave Beth another injection, this time of what he explained was an antibiotic. 'But she'll need more antibiotics on a regular schedule after she leaves here.'

The woman swabbed the wound with a brownish disinfectant while the doctor peered close to the wound, studying it with spectacles, one lens of which had a small additional lens that he swiveled into place. As soon as the woman finished disinfecting the area around the wound, she put a finger where the doctor had been applying pressure, allowing him to begin suturing.

'You shouldn't have called me,' the doctor complained to Decker as he worked.

'I didn't have a choice.' Decker studied Beth, whose face, moist with rain and sweat, was the gray of porridge.

'But you're not with the organization any longer,' the doctor said.

'I didn't know you had heard.'

'Evidently. Otherwise, you wouldn't have presumed to contact me.'

'I meant what I said. I didn't have a choice. Besides, if you knew I wasn't sanctioned, you didn't have to agree to help me.' Decker held Beth's hand. Her fingers clutched his as if she was drowning.

'In that respect, *I'm* the one who didn't have a choice.' The doctor continued suturing. 'As you so vividly told me on the phone, you intended to cause trouble in this building if I didn't help.'

'I doubt the neighbors would have approved of your sideline.'

The woman peered up angrily from where she assisted. 'You contaminated our *home*. You know where the clinic is. You could have—'

'There wasn't time,' Decker said. 'You once treated *me* here.'

'That was an *exception.*'

'I know of *other* exceptions you made. For a generous fee. I assume that's another reason you agreed to help.'

The doctor frowned up from the sutures he applied. 'What generous fee did you have in mind?'

'In my travel bag, I have an eighteen-carat gold chain, a gold bracelet, a jade ring, and a dozen gold coins.'

'Not money?' The doctor frowned harder.

'They're worth around twelve thousand dollars. Put them in a sock for when times get tough. Believe me, they come in handy if you have to leave the country in a hurry and you can't trust going to a bank.'

'That hasn't been a problem of ours.'

'To date,' Decker said. 'I suggest you do the best job you can on this woman.'

'Are you threatening me?'

'You must have misunderstood. I was cheering you on.'

The doctor frowned even more severely, then concentrated on applying more sutures. 'Under the circumstances, my fee for this procedure is twenty thousand dollars.'

'What?'

'I consider the items you mentioned only a down payment.' The doctor straightened, no longer working. 'Is my fee a problem?'

Decker stared at the half-closed hole in Beth's leg. 'No.'

'I thought not.' The doctor resumed working. 'Where are the items?'

'Over here. In my travel bag.' Decker turned toward where he had dropped it when he helped carry Beth into the kitchen.

'And what about the remaining amount?'

'You'll get it.'

'How can I be certain?'

'You have my word. If that isn't good enough—'

Esperanza interrupted the tension. 'Look, I feel useless just standing here. There must be something I can do to help.'

'The blood in the hallway and the elevator,' the woman said. 'The neighbors will call the police if they see it. Clean it up.'

Her peremptory tone suggested that she thought she was speaking to an Hispanic servant, but although Esperanza's dark eyes flashed, he only responded, 'What can I use?'

'Under the sink, there's a bucket, rags, and disinfectant. Make sure you wear rubber gloves.'

As Esperanza gathered the materials and left, the woman applied a blood-pressure cuff to Beth's left arm. She studied the gauge. Air stopped hissing from the cuff.

'What are the numbers?' Decker asked.

'A hundred over sixty.'

Normal was one-hundred-and-twenty over eighty. 'Low, but not in the danger zone.'

The woman nodded. 'She's very lucky.'

'Yeah, you can see how lucky she looks.'

'You don't look so good yourself.'

The phone rang, its jangle so intrusive that Decker, the doctor, and his wife tensed, staring at it. It was mounted to the wall, next to the Sub-Zero refrigerator. It rang again.

'Who'd be calling at this hour?'

'I have a patient in intensive care.' The doctor continued working. 'I left instructions for the hospital to phone me if the patient's condition worsened. When *you* called, that's what I thought it would be about.' He held up his blood-smeared gloves and gestured toward those on his wife. 'But I can't answer the phone with these.'

It rang again.

'And I don't want you to stop what you're doing.' Decker picked up the phone. 'Hello.'

'Awfully predictable, Decker.'

Hearing McKittrick's smug voice, Decker stopped breathing. He clutched the phone with knuckle-whitening force.

'What's the matter?' McKittrick asked on the other end. 'Not feeling sociable? Don't want to talk. No problem. I'll carry the conversation for both of us.'

'Who is it?' the doctor asked.

Decker held up his free hand, warning the man to be quiet.

'Maybe I'm not the idiot you thought I was, huh?' McKittrick asked. 'When I saw you cinching your belt around the woman's leg, I said to myself, where's the logical place he'll take her? And by God, I was right. I was watching from a doorway down the street when you arrived. You must have forgotten *I* was taught about this place, too. All of a sudden, you're as predictable as hell. You know what I think?'

Decker didn't answer.

'I asked you a question,' McKittrick demanded. 'You'd better talk to me, or I'm going to make this much worse than I planned.'

'All right. What are you thinking?'

'I think you're losing your touch.'

'I'm tired of this,' Decker said. 'Pay attention. Our deal still holds. Leave us alone. I won't give you another thought.'

'Is that a fact?'

'I won't come after you.'

'It seems to me, old buddy, that you're missing the point. *I'm* coming after *you*.'

'You mean you and *Renata*.'

365

'So you figured out who that was in the car?'

'Your tradecraft didn't use to be this good. She's been teaching you.'

'Yeah? Well, she also wants to teach *you* something, Decker – what it's like to lose somebody you love. Look out the window. Toward the front of the building.'

Click. The connection was broken.

4

Slowly, Decker lowered the phone.

'Who *was* that?' the doctor insisted.

Look out the window? Decker asked himself in dismay. Why? So I'll show myself? So I'll make myself a target? Sickeningly, he remembered that Esperanza wasn't in the room. He had left the apartment to clean the blood from the hallway and the elevator. Had he started in the lobby? Had McKittrick—?

'Esperanza!' Decker raced from the kitchen. He yanked the front door open and hurried out into the corridor, hoping to see Esperanza but finding the area deserted. The needle above the closed elevator door indicated that the compartment was at the ground floor. About to push the UP button, Decker recalled how slow the elevator had been. He charged down the stairs.

'*Esperanza!*' Decker took the steps three at a time, the impact of his shoes echoing in the stairwell. He reached the third floor and then the second. 'ESPERANZA!' He thought he heard a muffled voice shout a reply. Yelling, 'Get out of the lobby! Take cover!' Decker jumped down a half-dozen steps toward the final floor. He heard a heavy clatter, as if a pail was being dropped. 'McKittrick and Renata are outside! Get up the stairs!' He swung toward the final continuation of the stairwell, reached the midway landing, swung again, and was shocked to see Esperanza staring up at him, not moving.

Decker leapt, diving down the remainder of the stairs, colliding against Esperanza's chest, knocking him past the open door of the elevator toward an alcove in the lobby.

Immediately the lobby was filled with blazing thunder. A deafening blast from the street disintegrated the lobby's glass door. Striking the floor with Esperanza, Decker was aware of shrapnel zipping through the air, chunks of wood, metal, and glass hurtling past him, objects slamming against the walls. Then the lobby became unnaturally still, as if the air had been sucked out of it. Certainly that was how Decker felt, out of breath. Lying next to Esperanza in the alcove, he tried to get his chest to work, to take in air. Slowly, painfully, he managed.

Through smoke, he peered up, seeing shards of glass embedded in the walls. He risked a glance beyond the lobby's gaping entrance toward where they had parked the Oldsmobile hurriedly in a no-parking space in front of the building. The car, the source of the explosion, was now a twisted, gutted, flaming wreck.

'Jesus,' Esperanza said.

'Hurry. Up the stairs.'

They struggled to stand. As Decker lurched toward the stairs, he looked to the side and saw a figure – silhouetted by the flames, obscured by the smoke – rush past the entrance. The figure threw something. Hearing it strike the floor, Decker charged up the stairwell with Esperanza. The object made a bouncing sound. Decker reached the midway landing and swung with Esperanza toward the continuation of the stairs. Below, the object whacked against something, metal against wood. The elevator? The doors had been open. Had the grenade landed in—

The explosion sent a shockwave through the stairwell,

slamming Decker and Esperanza to their hands and knees. The shockwave was amplified by the confines of the elevator shaft, blowing up and down as well as to the side, making the stairwell shudder, cracking the exterior wall of the shaft. Plaster collapsed. Flames filled the lobby, smoke drifting upward.

With greater effort, Decker and Esperanza straightened, climbing. At the next landing, the door to the elevator had been blown apart. Hurrying past the gaping shaft, Decker saw flames and smoke in there. He whirled as an apartment door was yanked open. An elderly man in pajamas rushed out to see what had happened, his eyes wide with shock when he saw the flames and smoke. An alarm started blaring.

'There's been an explosion!' Decker yelled. 'The lobby's on fire! Is there another way out of the building?'

The man's lips moved three times before he managed to make a sound. 'The fire escape in back.'

'Use it!'

Decker climbed higher, following Esperanza who hadn't paused. At the next floor, other occupants of the building hurried out, dismayed by the smoke that was rising.

'Phone the fire department!' Decker yelled as he passed them. 'The elevator's been gutted! The stairway's in flames! Use the fire escape!'

He lost count of the floors. Expecting *3*, he reached *4*. The door to the doctor's apartment was open. Rushing into the kitchen, he found Esperanza arguing with the doctor.

'She can't be moved!' the doctor protested. 'Her stitches will pull open!'

'To hell with the stitches! If she stays here, she'll burn to death! We'll *all* burn to death!'

'There's supposed to be a fire escape!' Decker said. '*Where is it?*'

The doctor pointed along the corridor. 'Through the window in the spare bedroom.'

Decker leaned close to Beth. 'We have to lift you. I'm afraid this is going to hurt.'

'McKittrick's out there?'

'He meant what he said at the motel. He and Renata are hunting me. Sooner than I expected.'

'Do what you have to.' Beth licked her dry lips. 'I can handle the pain.'

'I'll get the window open,' Esperanza said.

'Help us,' Decker told the doctor and his wife.

Startling him, the phone rang again.

This time, Decker had no doubt who was calling. He grabbed it, shouting, 'You've had your fun! For Christ's sake, stop!'

'But we've only just started,' McKittrick said. 'Try to make this more interesting, will you? So far you've done everything we anticipated. Who's an idiot now?' McKittrick broke out into bellowing laughter.

Decker slammed down the phone and spun toward Beth, noting the thick plastic sheet she lay upon. 'Is that strong enough to hold her?'

'There's one way to find out.' Esperanza came back from opening the window in the guest room. 'You take the head. I'll take the feet.' Using the plastic sheet, they lifted Beth off the table and carried her from the kitchen.

The doctor went out to the hallway and hurried back, appalled. 'There are flames in the stairwell and the elevator shaft.'

'I told you we need help!' Esperanza looked angrily over his shoulder as he carried the section of the sheet that supported Beth's legs.

'Get the jewelry,' the doctor told his wife, and rushed from the room.

'And don't forget the gold coins, you bastard!' Decker shouted. Bent over, moving backward, holding the portion of the sheet that supported Beth's shoulders, he worked into the bedroom. After bumping painfully against the back wall, he turned and stared out through the open window, its curtains blowing inward from the force of the rain. A night-shrouded fire escape led down the back of the building to what may have been an interior garden. He heard panicked residents of the building rushing awkwardly down the metal fire escape.

'Predictable,' Decker said. 'That's where Renata and McKittrick expect us to go.'

'What are you talking about?' Esperanza asked.

'It's a trap. McKittrick knows about this place. He's had time to check the layout. He and Renata will be waiting down there for us.'

'But we can't stay here! We'll be trapped in the fire!'

'There's another way.'

'Up,' Beth said.

Decker nodded. 'Exactly.'

Esperanza looked incredulous.

'To the roof,' Decker said. 'We'll move across several buildings, reach another fire escape near the end of the block, and use *it*. McKittrick won't know where we've gone.'

'But what if the flames spread through other buildings and cut us off?' Esperanza asked.

'No choice,' Decker said. 'We'll be easy targets if we try to carry Beth down this fire escape.' He eased Beth headfirst through the window until her back was supported by the window sill. Then he squirmed out past her, feeling cold rain pelt him again as he guided her farther through the window. In a moment, Beth was lying on the wet slick metal platform, rain striking her face.

Decker touched her forehead. 'How are you doing?'

'Never better.'

'Right.'

'I don't deserve you.'

'Wrong.' Decker kissed her cheek.

Esperanza scrambled out to join them. 'Whatever was in that bomb, it must have been powerful. The flames are spreading fast. The front of the apartment's on fire.'

Decker peered through the rain toward the top of the building not far above them. 'We'd better get up there before the flames reach the roof.' As they lifted Beth, Decker heard approaching sirens.

'There'll be police cars as well as fire trucks.' Esperanza followed Decker up the fire escape. 'McKittrick and Renata won't try anything against us in front of the police.'

'Or they'll count on the confusion.' Decker carried Beth higher. 'The police won't have time to realize what's happening.'

Flames burst from a lower window, illuminating them on the metal stairs.

'Jesus, now they've seen us.' Decker tensed, anticipating the impact of a bullet into his chest.

'Maybe not.' Esperanza hurried to work higher. 'Or if they did, it might not be obvious we're going up instead of down.'

They came to a landing. Beth groaned as Decker was forced to turn her awkwardly to start up the final section toward the roof. His shoes slipped on the slick wet metal, making him stumble, almost dropping her.

'We're close.'

The fire roared.

'Just a little farther.'

The sirens reached a crescendo on the opposite side of the building. Backing up, Decker felt his hips bump against the roof's waist-high parapet. At the limit of his energy, he stretched one leg and then the other over the parapet, hefted Beth over, waited for Esperanza to follow, and finally set Beth down. Breathing fast, he slumped.

'Are you okay?' Esperanza stooped next to him.

'Need a little rest is all.'

'I can't guess why.' Esperanza squinted through the rain. 'At least this parapet keeps us from being targets.'

Decker's arms and legs were numb with fatigue. 'McKittrick and Renata will wonder why we're not coming down. We have to get away from here before they figure out what we're doing.'

'Take another minute to catch your breath,' Beth murmured.

'No time.'

Beth tried to raise herself. 'Maybe I can walk.'

'No. You'd rip out your stitches. You'd bleed to death.' Decker calculated: to the left, there were only a few buildings before the end of the block. The fire escapes there would be too close to where McKittrick and Renata waited below. To the right, though, there were more than enough roofs to get them away from the area.

Decker crouched and lifted Beth. He waited for Esperanza to do the same, then backed away from the parapet, guided by lights in other buildings and the reflection of flames bursting from the windows of the brownstone.

'Behind you,' Esperanza said. 'A ventilation duct.'

Decker veered around the waist-high obstacle, turning his head to avoid inhaling the thick smoke spewing out.

'The housing for the elevator pulleys,' Esperanza warned.

Decker veered around that as well, alarmed that he could see flames through cracks in the housing.

'It's spreading faster.'

More sirens wailed at the front of the building.

Decker glanced behind him and saw that the next building was one story taller. '*How are we going to—*'

'On my right,' Esperanza said. 'A metal ladder bolted to the wall.'

Decker backed against the ladder. 'The only way I can think to do this is—' He struggled to breathe. 'Beth, I don't have the strength to carry you over my shoulder. Do you think you can stand on your uninjured leg?'

'Anything.'

'I'll climb up while Esperanza steadies you. When I lean down, you reach up. I'll lift you by your hands.' Decker mentally corrected himself – by her *left* arm, the one that hadn't been wounded in Santa Fe.

After he and Esperanza helped her to stand, propping her against the brick wall, Decker gripped the ladder and mustered the effort to climb to the next roof. At the top, his back pelted by rain, he leaned over the edge. 'Ready?'

Decker strained to lift her. He almost panicked when he discovered that his strength was failing, that he was able to raise her only a few feet.

Amazingly, the effort became easier.

'I'm resting my good leg on a rung in the ladder,' Beth said. 'Just pull me up a little at a time.'

Decker grimaced, lifting harder. Slowly, rung after rung, Beth came up. Decker moved his grip from her hand to her upper arm and shoulder, pulling higher. Then he saw the murky outline of her drenched head, put his arms under hers, and hoisted her onto the roof. He set her down and sprawled beside her.

Esperanza's shoes thrummed on the metal ladder. In a rush, he was at the top, the plastic sheet tucked under his arm. Behind him, flames spewed from ventilator ducts and the housing for the elevator pulleys. The fire escape was engulfed by smoke.

'Even if we wanted to, we can't go back that way,' Decker said.

They spread out the plastic sheet, set Beth onto it, and lifted her, making their way through another maze of ducts and housings. Decker stumbled over a pipe. He bumped past a TV antenna.

The reflection of flames revealed the edge of the building and the drop down to the next one.

'It won't be long now,' Decker said.

A thunderous shockwave hit him, jolting him off his feet. Unable to keep a grip on Beth, he landed next to her, hearing her scream. Only then did he have time to realize—

It hadn't been thunder.

It had been another bomb.

The detonation echoed through the night. Trembling, Decker lay on his chest, drew his pistol, and stared ahead toward where a shed-like protrusion from the roof had disintegrated.

A voice yelled, 'You're being predictable again!'

Jesus, Decker thought. McKittrick's on the roof!

'Walked right into it again, didn't you?' McKittrick yelled. 'I gave you fair warning, and you still did what I expected! You're not as goddamned smart as you think you are!'

'Let it go!' Decker shouted. 'Our business with each other is over!'

'Not until you're dead!'

The voice came from somewhere to the left. It sounded as if McKittrick was hiding behind the elevator housing. Fingers tight on his pistol, Decker rose to a crouch, preparing to charge. 'The police heard that explosion, McKittrick! Now they know this is more than a fire! They'll seal off the area and check everybody who tries to leave! You won't get away!'

'They'll think it was combustibles blowing up in the building!'

Combustibles? Decker frowned. It wasn't the kind of word McKittrick would normally use, but it definitely was a word he would learn from a bomb expert. There wasn't any doubt – Renata was teaching him.

And she was somewhere close.

'Paint cans! Turpentine! Cleaning fluid!' McKittrick yelled. 'At a fire, the police worry about that stuff a lot! Now they'll be afraid something else will blow up! They'll keep their distance!'

Behind Decker, flames burst from the lower roof. We can't go back, and the fires will soon reach us if we stay here, he thought. 'Esperanza?' he whispered.

'Ready when you are. Which side do you want?'

'Left.'

'I'll flank you.'

'Now.' Decker sprinted through puddles toward a large ventilation duct, then toward another. But as he prepared to charge toward the elevator housing, it ceased to exist. A brilliant roar blasted it into pieces. Decker was thrown flat, chunks of wreckage flying over him, clattering around him.

'You guessed *wrong*, Decker! That's not where I am! And I'm not to your right, either! Where your friend's trying to sneak up on me!'

A moment later, in that direction, a blast tore a huge chunk out of the roof. Decker thought he heard a scream, but whether it was from Esperanza or occupants of the building, he couldn't tell.

He felt paralyzed, uncertain where to move. McKittrick must have set charges all over this roof and the next ones, he thought. But how would McKittrick have had time if he was calling from a payphone?

The appalling answer was immediate and obvious. McKittrick *hadn't* been using a payphone. He had been calling from a *cellular* phone. From the roof. While he was placing the charges. That must have been Renata who blew up the Oldsmobile in front of the building and then threw the fire bomb into the lobby. *She's* down in the courtyard. That way, whichever direction we chose, up or down, we were trapped.

Are trapped, Decker thought. The fire's behind us. McKittrick's ahead of us.

What about the fire escape on *this* building? Decker wondered desperately as the flames roared louder. If we can get onto it . . . Too obvious. I have to assume McKittrick rigged explosives on *it*, as well. Even if he didn't, we'd still be trapped between Renata in the courtyard and McKittrick on the roof.

With no apparent alternative, Decker rose to attempt another frantic charge toward McKittrick's voice. But the moment he did, a blast heaved the roof in front of him, knocking him back down, tearing another huge chunk from the building.

'Naughty, naughty, asshole! You didn't ask, "May I?" '

Where *is* he? Decker thought in dismay. If McKittrick was on this roof, he wouldn't be setting off bombs that he'd hidden here. He couldn't guarantee that he wouldn't blow himself up along with me. Then *where*?

Again the answer was immediate. On the *next* roof. The reflection of flames revealed that the next roof was lower. McKittrick must be on a ladder bolted to the wall or on a crate or some kind of maintenance structure. Hidden, he can peer over the top of the wall, then duck down when he sets off a bomb.

Decker aimed, saw what might have been a head inching up from the darkness beyond the building, started to pull the trigger, and stopped when he realized that what he had seen was only a wavering shadow caused by the flames.

Behind him, the blaze surged closer, its progress barely impeded by the storm.

'So what's it going to be?' McKittrick yelled. 'Are you going to wait to get barbecued? Or do you have the guts to try to come for me?'

Yeah, I'm coming for you, Decker thought fiercely. The way to do it was directly in front of him, courtesy of McKittrick – the hole that the last bomb had blown in the roof.

Responding to a sickening flow of heat from the roof behind him, Decker squirmed through puddles, reached the dark hole, gripped its sides, lowered his legs, dangled, and dropped.

5

He imagined jagged planks from the roof, pointing upright, about to impale him. What he struck instead was a table that collapsed from the force of his landing and threw him to the side where he struck a padded chair that tilted, tumbling him to the wreckage-strewn floor. At least, those were the objects he *thought* he struck – the room's draperies were closed; the darkness was almost absolute.

From above, through the hole in the roof, he heard McKittrick yell, '*Don't think you can hide from me, Decker!*'

In pain, Decker struggled to his feet and pawed his way through the darkness of the room, trying to find an exit. Fire alarms blared. He touched a light switch, but he didn't dare turn it on – the abrupt illumination through the hole in the roof would make it obvious where he had gone. Heart speeding, he touched a doorknob, twisted it, and pulled the door open, but when he groped beyond it, he bumped into pungent-smelling clothes and discovered that he had opened a closet.

'*Decker?*' McKittrick yelled from above. '*If you're behind that ventilator duct—*'

An explosion shook the apartment, plaster falling. Urgent, Decker found another door, opened it, and felt a rush of excitement when he saw dim lights through windows. He was at the end of a corridor. Peering down from a rain-beaded

377

window, he saw the chaos of fire trucks, police cars, and emergency workers at the front of the building. Lights flashed; motors rumbled; sirens wailed. Pajama-clad occupants of other buildings were hurrying out, the entrances not yet filled with flames.

Smoke swirled around him. Unable to pause to rest, he turned and hurried along the corridor to reach the back of the apartment. He passed an open door that led to murky stairs and assumed that the people who lived in this apartment had hurried out.

That possible escape route was useless to him. It didn't matter if he saved himself. He had to save Beth and Esperanza. Before the smell of fresh paint warned him, he banged against paint cans, a rolled-up dropcloth, and a ladder. Stumbling on, he reached the rear of the building and discovered that the window to the fire escape wasn't in a guest bedroom but instead at the end of the corridor.

He thrust the window upward and crawled out onto a slippery metal platform. Flames spewing from the windows in the building to his right reflected off the fire escape. He prayed that Renata would not see him from below as he squinted through the rain toward the fire escape on the undamaged brownstone to his *left*. He had hoped that the two fire escapes would be close enough that he could leap from one to the other, but now, in despair, he was forced to accept the reality that his plan was hopeless. The other fire escape was at least twenty feet away. Even under the best of circumstances, in daylight, in peak condition, he couldn't possibly reach it.

Beth's going to die up there, he told himself.

Screaming silently that there had to be a way, he squirmed back into the apartment. The smoke was thicker, making him bend over, coughing. He entered a bedroom off the corridor and opened its window, leaning out. He was now closer to the other building's fire escape. It looked to be no more than ten feet away, but he still couldn't hope to leap from this window and reach the landing.

There has to be a way!

With a chill, he knew what it was. He ran back to the corridor. Flames had started to eat through the wall. Avoiding the paint cans, he picked up the ladder that he had almost tripped over, and guided it into the bedroom. Please, God, let it be long enough. Fighting for strength, he pushed it through the open window and aimed it toward the next building's fire escape.

Please!

The scrape of wood against metal made him flinch. The tip of the ladder grated as it passed over the railing on the fire-escape platform. Had McKittrick heard?

Something roared. Another explosion? Were Beth and Esperanza already dead?

No time! Decker crawled from the window and pulled himself flat across the rungs of the ladder. Rain had already slicked it. The ladder bent under his weight. It began to waver. He imagined it giving way. He shut out the nightmare of his splattering impact against the concrete of the courtyard and focused his complete attention on the fire escape he was nearing. His hands shook. Rain made him blink. Wind twisted the ladder. *No.* He stretched his left arm to its limit, strained to reach the railing, and at once, a stronger gust of wind shifted the ladder completely.

The ladder's tip scraped free of the railing. As Decker felt the vertiginous suck of gravity and began to drop with the ladder, he leapt through the darkness. His left hand grabbed the railing. But he almost lost his hold on the wet slippery metal. He flung up his other arm, snagged the fingers of his right hand around the railing, and hung breathlessly.

The ladder crashed below him. Someone down there shouted. Had McKittrick heard? Would he understand what the sounds meant? Would he come to investigate?

Dangling, straining his arms, Decker slowly pulled himself up. Rain lashed against his face. Wincing, he pulled himself higher. The railing scraped against his chest. He bent over and toppled onto the platform.

The metal-vibrating sound he caused made him flinch. Trembling, he came to his feet and drew his pistol from where he had shoved it into his pants pocket. Staring toward the roof, prepared to shoot, he crept up the last section of steps. He had never felt this exhausted. But his determination refused to surrender.

He reached the top and scanned the roof. McKittrick was to the left, three quarters of the way along a wall that led up to the roof upon which Beth and Esperanza were trapped. Halfway up a ladder bolted to the wall, McKittrick peered over the top, able to use a remote-control detonator to set off bombs without fear of injuring himself.

Decker stalked through the rain toward him.

'*Where the hell are you?*' McKittrick screamed toward the other roof. 'Answer me, or I'll blow your bitch all across Manhattan! She's lying right next to a packet of C-4! All I have to do is press this button!'

More than anything, Decker wanted to shoot, to pull the trigger again and again, but he didn't dare, for fear that McKittrick would retain the strength to press the detonator and kill Beth seconds before Decker could save her.

The clatter of heavy footsteps on the fire escape made him drop toward the cover of a ventilation duct. Indifferent to the noise they made, murky figures charged into view at the top of the metal steps. McKittrick whirled toward what now obviously were three firemen, their protective hats dripping water, their heavy rubber coats and boots slick with rain, reflecting the flames. With his left arm hooked around a rung in the ladder, McKittrick used his right to draw a pistol from his belt. He shot all three. Two of them fell where they were. The third stumbled back, toppling off the edge of the roof. The roar of the flames obscured the crack of the shots and the fireman's plummeting scream.

With his left arm still hooked around the ladder, McKittrick fumbled to put his pistol back under his belt. His left hand held the detonator. Taking advantage of McKittrick's distraction, Decker scrambled from behind the ventilation duct, reached the bottom of the ladder, and jumped, clawing his fingers toward the detonator. He hooked it, and as he dropped, he wrenched it from McKittrick's grasp, nearly yanking McKittrick off the ladder. McKittrick cursed and tried to raise his pistol again but found that it had snagged on his belt. When Decker fired, it was too late – McKittrick had given up trying to take out his pistol and instead had jumped from the ladder. As Decker's bullet slammed against the wall, McKittrick collided with Decker, sprawling with him onto the roof, rolling through puddles.

Decker's hands were full, his left with the detonator, his right with his pistol, his position too awkward for him to aim the weapon. Tumbling onto Decker, McKittrick punched and grabbed for the detonator. Decker kneed him and rolled to gain the distance to aim, but the blow to McKittrick's groin had not been solid, and McKittrick's pain was not great enough to prevent him from scuttling after Decker, striking him again, chopping at his right wrist, knocking the pistol from his hand. The weapon splashed into a puddle, and as McKittrick dove for it, Decker managed a glancing kick that knocked McKittrick away from the weapon.

Decker staggered backward. He bumped against the parapet and nearly toppled over. McKittrick groped again for the pistol

under his belt. Decker had no idea where his own pistol had
fallen. With a firm grip on the detonator, he pivoted to take
cover on the fire escape, felt his shoe slip off something that one
of the firemen had dropped, understood what it was, picked up
the fire ax with his free hand, and hurled it toward McKittrick
as McKittrick freed his pistol from his belt.

Decker heard McKittrick laugh. The next thing, Decker
heard the whack of the ax against McKittrick's face. At first,
Decker thought it was the blunt top that had struck McKittrick.
But the ax didn't drop. It stayed in place, projecting from
McKittrick's forehead. McKittrick wavered as if drunk, then
fell.

But that was not certain enough. Decker lurched forward,
picked up McKittrick's handgun, hoped that the roar of the fire
would conceal the noise, and shot him three times in the head.

6

'Decker!'

He was so unnerved he didn't at first realize that Esperanza
was shouting to him.

'Decker!'

Turning, he saw Esperanza on the roof where McKittrick had
set off the explosives. Behind Esperanza, flames rose, hissing in
the rain.

Decker took a step but faltered. Shock and fatigue had finally
caught up to him. But he couldn't stop. Not when he was so
close to saving Beth. Delirious, he reached the ladder. He didn't
know how he got to the top. He and Esperanza made their way
around gaping holes in the roof and found Beth crawling in a
desperate effort to get away from the fire. Behind her, the plastic
sheet she had been lying on burst into flames.

As Decker helped to lift her, flames revealed the further damage that had been done to him. 'McKittrick's dead.'

Beth murmured, 'Thank God.'

'But we still have to worry about Renata.' Supporting Beth on each side, he and Esperanza stumbled away from the heat of the blaze toward the ladder.

Again, Decker's consciousness faded. He didn't recall getting Beth to the bottom of the ladder, but he retained sufficient presence of mind to stop and lean Beth against Esperanza when he came abreast of McKittrick's body.

'What's the matter?' Esperanza asked. 'Why are you stopping?'

Too weary to explain, Decker searched through McKittrick's wet clothing and found what he needed: McKittrick's car key. On the phone, McKittrick had bragged about watching from down the street when Decker arrived at the brownstone. They had a good chance of finding the Pontiac McKittrick had used.

But that wasn't all he had to find. McKittrick had knocked Decker's pistol from his grasp. It couldn't be left behind. He tried to recreate the pattern of the fight and stumbled over where it had fallen into a puddle. But after putting it beneath his belt, he grudgingly understood that he still had something to do. Dizzy, he wavered. 'It's never over.'

'What are you talking about?'

'McKittrick. We can't leave him like this. I don't want him to be identified.'

McKittrick's dead weight was awkward as they carried the body toward the ladder. Esperanza climbed up onto the roof. With effort, Decker hefted the body to him, then climbed up after it. They grabbed McKittrick's arms and legs, moved as close to the flames as they dared, and heaved. The body disappeared into the fire. Decker threw the ax after him.

All the while, he was fearful of Renata. Wary, he and

Esperanza returned to where they had set Beth down. They continued with her across the roof, determined to use the farthest fire escape, one that wouldn't take them down toward where they thought Renata was waiting for them.

'Maybe there's another way,' Esperanza said. He guided them toward a shed-like structure on the next roof, but when he tried to open its door, he found it locked. 'Turn your faces.' Standing on an angle so his bullets wouldn't ricochet toward him, Esperanza fired repeatedly toward the wood around the lock. That section of the door disintegrated, the door jolting open when Esperanza kicked it.

Inside, away from the rain, the dimly lit stairwell was empty. There was no sound of occupants rushing down the stairs.

'They couldn't have helped but hear the sirens. The building must have been evacuated,' Decker said.

'But the fire hasn't reached this far. It's safe to use the elevator,' Esperanza said.

The elevator took them down to the ground floor. When they emerged onto the cluttered chaos of the street, overpowered by the din of engines and water being sprayed and people shouting, they struggled to make their way through the crowd. Flashing lights made them squint.

'We've got an injured woman here,' Esperanza said. 'Let us through.'

They squeezed to the right along the sidewalk, passed a fire truck, and avoided paramedics who rushed toward someone on the opposite side of the truck. Decker felt Beth wince each time he moved with her.

'There's the Pontiac,' Esperanza said.

It was near the corner, a recent model, blue, apparently the one McKittrick had been driving. When Decker tried to insert the key in the passenger door, it fit.

Thirty seconds later, Beth was lying on the back seat, Decker was kneeling on the floor next to her, and Esperanza was behind the steering wheel. An ambulance blocked the way. 'Hold Beth steady,' Esperanza said.

'What are you going to do?'

'Take a detour.' Esperanza started the engine, put the Pontiac in gear, and swung the steering wheel severely to the right. Pressing the accelerator, he jolted up onto the sidewalk.

Beth moaned from the impact. Decker leaned against her, working to keep her from sliding off the seat. Pedestrians scattered as Esperanza aimed the Pontiac along the sidewalk, reached the corner, and jounced down off the curb.

Beth groaned, her pain more severe.

'That'll do it.' Esperanza glanced in his rearview mirror, sped to the next corner, and turned. 'No one's following us. All you have to do now is relax, folks. Enjoy the ride.'

Decker didn't need encouragement. He was so exhausted that breathing was an effort Worse, he couldn't control his shivering, partly because of the aftermath of adrenaline but mostly, he knew, because of his bone-deep chill from having been in the rain for so long.

'Esperanza?'

'What?'

'Find us a place to stay. Fast.'

'Is something—'

'I'm think I'm starting to get —' Decker's voice was unsteady. ' – hypothermia.'

'Jesus.'

'I have to get out of these wet clothes.'

'Put your hands under your armpits. Don't go to sleep. Is there a blanket or anything back there?'

'No.' Decker's teeth chattered.

'All I can do for now is put on the heater,' Esperanza said. 'I'll find a take-out place and get hot coffee. Hang on, Decker.'

'Hang on? Sure. To myself. I'm hugging myself so hard I—'

'Hug *me*,' Beth said. 'Closer. Try to use my body heat.'

But no matter how tightly he pressed himself against her, her voice seemed to come from far away.

TWELVE

1

Decker dreamed of Renata, of a tall thin dark-haired woman with a grotesque voice and a gaping hole in her throat. He thought that the figure looming over him was Renata about to crush his head with a rock, but just before he prepared to strike at her, his mind became lucid enough for him to realize that it wasn't Renata but Beth who leaned over him, and that the object wasn't a rock but a washcloth.

Someone else was with her – Esperanza – holding him down. 'Take it easy. You're safe. We're trying to help you.'

Decker blinked repeatedly, groggy, as if hungover, trying to understand what was happening. His body ached. His arms and face stung. His muscles throbbed. He had the worst headache of his life. In the background, pale sunlight struggled past the edges of closed draperies.

'Where—'

'A motel outside Jersey City.'

As Decker scanned the gloomy interior, he was reminded disturbingly of the motel where McKittrick had held Beth prisoner.

'How long— What time is—'

'Almost seven in the evening.' Beth, who sat next to him, her weight on her good leg, put the washcloth on his forehead. It had been soaked in steaming hot water. Decker instantly absorbed the heat.

'This is the kind of place that doesn't ask questions about people checking in,' Esperanza said. 'The units are behind the office. The clerk can't see who goes into the rooms.'

Like the motel where McKittrick had held Beth prisoner, Decker thought again, uneasy.

'We got here about six in the morning,' Beth said. 'Counting time in the car, you've been sleeping almost thirteen hours. You had me scared that you wouldn't wake up.'

Esperanza pointed toward the bathroom. 'I had a lot of trouble getting your clothes off and putting you into the tub. With hypothermia, the water has to be tepid to start with. I increased the temperature slowly. When your color was better, I pulled you out, dried you off, and put you in bed with all three blankets I found on the shelf. Beth managed to get out of her wet clothes, dried off, and got in bed next to you, helping to keep you warm. I poured hot coffee into you. Man, I've never seen anybody so exhausted.'

Beth kept wiping Decker's face. 'Or so bruised and cut up. Your face won't stop bleeding.'

'I've had easier nights.' Decker's mouth felt dry. 'I could use . . . a drink of water.'

'It'll have to be *hot* water,' Esperanza said. 'Sorry, but I want to make sure you've got your body heat back.' He poured steaming water from a thermos into a Styrofoam cup and brought it to Decker's lips. 'Careful.'

It tasted worse than Decker had expected. 'Put a tea bag in it. Where'd you get . . . ?' Decker pointed toward the thermos.

'I've been busy. While you rested, I did some shopping. I've got food and clothes, crutches for Beth and—'

'You left us alone?' Decker asked in alarm.

'Beth had your handgun. She's in pain, but she was able to sit in that chair and watch the door. There didn't seem a reason not to get what we needed.'

Decker tried to sit up. '*Renata*. That's your reason.'

'She couldn't possibly have followed us,' Esperanza said. 'I was extra careful. Whenever I had the slightest doubt, I went around the block or down an alley. I would have noticed any headlights following us.'

'*We* were able to follow McKittrick,' Decker said.

'Because we had a homing device. Does it seem likely to you that McKittrick and Renata would have put a homing device in their own car? She didn't even have a car to follow us.'

'She could have stolen one.'

'Assuming she knew that we weren't on the roof any longer, that we'd stolen *her* car. Even then, by the time she hot-wired a vehicle, we'd have been long gone. She couldn't have known which way we went. Relax, Decker. She's not a threat.'

'For the moment.'

It wasn't Decker but Beth who made the comment.

'She *will* be, though,' Beth added, somber.

'Yes,' Decker said. 'If Renata went to all this trouble to get even with me for killing two of her brothers, she won't stop now. She'll be all the more determined.'

'Especially since we have the money,' Beth said.

Decker was too confused to speak. He looked at Esperanza.

'After we got to this motel,' Esperanza said, 'while you and Beth were resting, I checked the Pontiac's trunk. Along with enough explosives to blow up the Statue of Liberty, I found *that*.' Esperanza pointed toward a bulging flight bag on the floor by the bed. 'The million dollars.'

'Holy—' Decker's weariness made him dizzy again.

'Stop trying to sit up,' Beth said. 'You're turning pale. Stay down.'

'Renata *will* come looking for us.' As Decker closed his eyes, giving way to exhaustion, he reached to touch Beth, but his consciousness dimmed, and he didn't feel his hand fall.

2

The next time he wakened, the room was totally dark. He continued to feel groggy. His body still ached. But he had to move – he needed to use the bathroom. Unfamiliar with the motel room, he bumped into a wall, banging his shoulder, before he oriented himself, entered the bathroom, shut the door, and only then turned on the light, not wanting to wake Beth. His image in the mirror was shocking, not just the bruises and scratches but the deep blue circles around his eyes and the gauntness of his beard-stubbled cheeks.

After relieving himself, he hoped that the flushing of the toilet wouldn't disturb Beth. But when he turned off the light and opened the door, he discovered that the main room's lights were on. Beth was sitting up in the bed where she had been sleeping next to him. Esperanza was propped up against a pillow in another bed.

'Sorry,' Decker said.

'You didn't wake us,' Esperanza said.

'We've been waiting for you to get up,' Beth said. 'How do you feel?'

'The way I look.' Decker limped toward Beth. 'How about *you*? How do *you* feel?'

Beth shifted her position and winced. 'My leg is swollen. It throbs. But the wound doesn't look infected.'

'At least that's one thing in our favor.' Decker slumped on the bed and wrapped a blanket around him. He rubbed his temples. 'What time is it?'

'Two a.m.' Esperanza put on trousers and got out of bed. 'Do you feel alert enough to discuss some things?'

'My throat's awfully dry.' Decker managed to hold up his hands as if defending himself. 'But I don't want any of that damned hot water.'

'I bought some Gatorade. How about that? Get some electrolytes back in your system.'

'Perfect.'

It was orange-flavored, and Decker drank a quarter of the bottle before he stopped himself.

'How about something to eat?' Esperanza asked.

'My stomach's not working, but I'd better try to get something down.'

Esperanza opened a small portable cooler. 'I've got packaged sandwiches – tuna, chicken, salami.'

'Chicken.'

'Catch.'

Decker surprised himself by managing to do so. He peeled the plastic wrap off the sandwich and bit into tasteless white bread and cardboard-like chicken. 'Delicious.'

'Nothing but the best for you.'

'We have to decide what to do.' Beth's solemn tone contrasted with Esperanza's attempt at humor.

Decker looked at her and tenderly grasped her hand. 'Yes. The Justice Department won't be happy that you didn't show up to testify. They'll be looking for you.'

'I took care of it,' Beth said.

'Took care of—' Decker felt troubled. 'I don't understand.'

'Esperanza drove me to a payphone. I called my contact at the Justice Department and found out I don't have to testify. The Grand Jury was meeting to indict Nick Giordano, but since he's dead, the Justice Department says there's no point in going further.' Beth hesitated. 'You killed *Frank* Giordano, also?'

Decker didn't say anything.

'For me?'

'Keep reminding yourself that you're in the presence of a police officer,' Decker said.

Esperanza glanced at his hands. 'Maybe this would be a good time for me to take a walk.'

'I didn't mean to—'

'No offense taken. You two have a lot to talk about. You could use some time alone.' Esperanza put on his boots, grabbed a shirt, nodded, and went outside.

Beth waited until the door was closed. 'Esperanza gave me an idea of what you went through last night.' She reached for his hand. 'I'll never be able to thank you enough.'

'All you have to do is love me.'

Beth cocked her head in surprise. 'You make it sound as if that's something I have to talk myself into. I *do* love you.'

She had never told him that before. The longed-for words thrilled him, flooding him with warmth. With emotion-pained eyes, he studied her. There was little resemblance between the enticing woman he had known in Santa Fe and the pale, gaunt-cheeked, hollow-eyed, straggly-haired woman before him. This was the woman he had suffered for. Risked his life for. Several times. Been prepared to go *anywhere* and do *anything* to save.

His throat felt cramped. 'You're beautiful.'

Welcome color came into her cheeks.

'I couldn't have gone on living without you,' Decker said.

Beth inhaled sharply, audibly. She looked at him as if she had never truly seen him before, then hugged him, their embrace painful because of their injuries but intense and forceful all the same. 'I don't deserve you.'

Beth had told him that earlier, when Decker had helped her onto the fire escape at the doctor's apartment. Was 'don't deserve you' another way of expressing affection, or did she literally mean that she felt undeserving – because she had used him and now felt ashamed?

'What's wrong?' Beth asked.

'Nothing.'

'But—'

'We have a lot of details to take care of,' Decker said quickly. 'Did your contact in the Justice Department ask about McKittrick?'

'Did he ever.' Beth looked puzzled by the sudden change of topic, by the way intimacy had given way to practicality. 'I told him I thought McKittrick was the man who let the Giordanos know I was hiding in Santa Fe. I said that I'd been suspicious about McKittrick from the start and when we got to New York I slipped away from him. I told them I had no idea where he was.'

'Keep telling them that,' Decker said. 'When McKittrick's body is found in the wreckage from the fire, the authorities will have trouble identifying it. Because they don't know whose dental records to compare it to, they might not *ever* be able to identify it. His disappearance will be a mystery. It'll look as if he ran away to avoid going to prison. The main thing is, don't show any hesitation. Never vary from your story that you don't know anything about what happened to him.'

'I'll need to account for where I've been since Saturday afternoon when I left Santa Fe,' Beth said.

'I'll make a phone call. A former associate of mine lives in Manhattan and owes me a favor. If the Justice Department wants an alibi, he'll give you one. They'll want to know your relationship with him. Tell them I mentioned him to you in Santa Fe, that he was an old friend and I wanted you to look him up when you got to New York. It was natural for you to run to him after you got away from McKittrick.'

'That still leaves another problem . . . you.'

'I don't understand.'

'Esperanza and I don't have to worry about our fingerprints being identified. The Oldsmobile was destroyed by fire. So were the motel room in Closter and the doctor's apartment in Manhattan. But what about *your* fingerprints? While you were asleep, we switched on the television so we could find out how the authorities were reacting to what happened last night. The FBI has stepped into the investigation of the Giordano deaths. There are reports that they've isolated fingerprints on a murder weapon left at Nick Giordano's house. A log pick.' Beth seemed disturbed by the brutal implications of the weapon.

'And?'

'The authorities think it was a mob slaying, a war between rival gangs. But when they identify your prints—'

'They'll find the prints are registered to a man who died fifteen years ago.'

Beth stared.

'Where would you like to live?' Decker asked.

'Live?' Beth seemed puzzled by another sudden change of topic. 'Back in Santa Fe, of course.'

'With me?'

'Yes.'

'I don't think that's a good idea,' Decker said.

'But the mob isn't looking for me anymore.'

'Renata is.' Decker paused, letting silence emphasize what he had said. 'As long as I'm alive, Renata might use you to get at me. You'll be in danger.'

Beth became paler than she already was.

'Nothing's changed,' Decker said. 'So I'll ask you again, Where would you like to live?'

Something in Beth's eyes seemed to die.

'If we split up,' Decker said.

'Split up?' Beth looked bewildered. 'But why on earth would—'

'If we had a very public argument back in Santa Fe, at noon in Escalera or some other popular restaurant, if word got around that we weren't an item any longer, Renata might decide there's no point in doing something to you, because she wouldn't be torturing me if she killed someone I didn't care about.'

Beth's bewilderment intensified.

'In fact,' Decker said, giving her a way out, wanting to learn the truth, 'the more I think about it, the more I'm convinced Renata would leave you alone if we broke up.'

'But—' Beth's voice didn't want to work. No sound came out.

'It would have to be convincing,' Decker said. 'I could accuse you of knowing who I was from the start of our relationship. I could make a scene about how you only pretended to love me, how you bribed me with sex, how all you wanted was a bodyguard living next door to you and sometimes in your house. In your bed.'

Beth started weeping.

'I could tell everybody that I'd been a fool, that I'd risked my life for nothing. If Renata was keeping tabs on me, she'd hear about the argument. She'd believe it. Especially if I left Santa Fe but you stayed.'

Beth wept harder.

'Who killed your husband?' Decker asked.

Beth didn't answer.

'I suppose we could make up a theory,' Decker said, 'about someone in the organization, maybe one of his guards, shooting him, taking the money, and blaming it on you. Another theory would be that Nick Giordano's son, Frank, was so jealous of the attention his father gave to your husband that he decided to set matters straight and blame it on you.' Decker waited. 'Which theory do *you* like?'

Beth wiped at her eyes. 'Neither.'

'Then—'

'*I* did it,' Beth said.

Decker straightened.

'*I* shot my husband,' Beth said. 'The son of a bitch won't ever beat me again.'

'You took the money?'

'Yes.'

'That's how you could afford the house in Santa Fe?'

'Yes. The money's in a numbered bank account in the Bahamas. The Justice Department couldn't get their hands on it, so they let me support myself with it – especially since they wanted my testimony.'

'Did you know who I was before you met me?'

'Yes.'

'Then you *did* use me.'

'For about forty-eight hours. I didn't know I'd be so attracted to you. I certainly didn't expect to fall in love with you.'

Blood trickled from one of the open gashes on Decker's face. 'I wish I could believe you.'

'I've always had an inclination to live in the South of France,' Beth said unexpectedly.

Now it was Decker who wasn't prepared. 'Excuse me?'

'Not the Riviera. Inland,' Beth said. 'Southwestern France. The Pyrenees. I once read an article about them in a travel magazine. The photographs of the valleys, with pastures and forests and streams running down from the mountains, were incredibly beautiful. I think I could do some good painting there . . . Provided you're with me.'

'Knowing that you'd be putting your life in danger, that Renata would want to use you to get at me?'

'Yes.'

'For the rest of your days, always looking over your shoulder?'

'Without you –' Beth touched the blood trickling from the gash on his face. ' – I'd have nothing to look *ahead* to.'

'In that case,' Decker said, 'we're going back to Santa Fe.'

3

'Are you sure this is a good idea?' Esperanza asked.

'No. But it makes more sense to me than the alternatives,' Decker said. They were in the clamorous crowded expanse of Newark International Airport. Decker had just come back from the United Airlines counter, rejoining Esperanza and Beth, where they waited for him in an alcove near restrooms and schedule-of-flights monitors. He handed out tickets. 'I've got us on an 8:30 flight. We switch planes in Denver and arrive in Albuquerque at 12:48 this afternoon.'

'These seats aren't together,' Beth said.

'Two of them are. One of us will have to sit farther back.'

'I will,' Esperanza said. 'I'll check to see if any passengers show unusual interest in you.'

'With my crutches, I'm afraid I can't help being noticed,' Beth said.

'And the scratches on my face definitely attracted attention from the woman at the United counter.' Decker looked around to make sure they weren't being overheard. 'But I don't see how Renata could anticipate which airport we would use. I'm not worried that she's in the area. When we get back to Santa Fe, that's when we start worrying.'

'You're sure she'll be waiting for us there?' Beth asked.

'What other choice does she have? She needs to start somewhere to find us, and Santa Fe is her best bet. She knows if I'm not coming back, I'll need to sell my house and transfer my bank account. She'll want to be around to persuade the realtor or the bank manager to tell her where the money is being sent.'

Beth frowned toward passengers hurrying past, as if afraid that Renata would suddenly lunge from among them. 'But that information is confidential. She can't just walk into the real-estate agency or the bank and expect someone to tell her your new address.'

'I was thinking more along the lines of a gun to the head when the realtor or the bank manager came home from work,' Decker said. 'Renata's an expert at terrorizing. In addition to hating me because I killed her brothers, she has the incentive of the million dollars of her money that I've got in this carry-on bag. She'll do everything possible to get even. In her place, I'd be waiting in Santa Fe until I knew in which direction to start hunting.'

Esperanza glanced at his watch. 'We'd better head to the gate.'

Uneasy about showing themselves, they left the alcove and started through the crowd, each man flanking Beth to make sure no one jostled against her as she used her crutches. Not that she looked unsteady. Although she hadn't been given much opportunity to practice with the crutches, her natural physical abilities had made it possible for her to develop a confident stride.

Decker felt a surge of admiration for her. She looked determined, oblivious to her pain, ready to do whatever was necessary.

And what about *you*? Decker asked himself. You've been through a hell of a lot. Are *you* ready?

For anything.

But he wasn't being entirely truthful with himself. Now that the immediate practical details had been taken care of, he didn't have anything to distract him from his emotions. He couldn't adjust to the reality that Beth was next to him. He had a squirming sensation of incompleteness if he wasn't with her. Even the brief time he had been away to buy the plane tickets had been exceedingly uncomfortable for him.

Ready for anything? he repeated to himself as he walked with

Beth and Esperanza toward the line at the security checkpoint. Not quite everything. *I'm not ready for Beth to be hurt again. I'm not ready to learn that she still might be lying to me about her feelings for me. I'm not ready to discover that I've been a fool.*

At the security checkpoint, he hung back, letting Esperanza and Beth go through a minute before he did in case the ten thousand one-hundred-dollar bills in his carry-on looked suspicious to the guard checking the X-ray monitor. If Decker was asked to open the bag, he would have a hard time explaining to the authorities how he had acquired a million dollars. The security officers would immediately assume that the money had something to do with drugs, and he didn't want Beth or Esperanza to appear to be associated with him. The X-ray monitor showed the outlines of non-metallic objects as well as metal ones, so, to make the bills look less obvious, Decker had removed the rubber bands around the stacks and jumbled them in the large bag, adding a dirty shirt, a note pad and pen, a toilet kit, a deck of cards, a newspaper, and a paperback novel. With luck, the X-ray guard wouldn't pay any attention to the visual chaos once he satisfied himself that the bag did not contain a weapon.

A woman ahead of Decker set her purse on the monitor's conveyor belt, then stepped through the metal detector with no trouble. His pulse rate increasing, Decker took her place, setting the heavy bag onto the belt. The X-ray guard looked strangely at him. Ignoring the attention he received, Decker put his diver's watch and his car keys into a basket that a uniformed woman in charge of the metal detector took from him. Decker wasn't worried that the metal detector would find a weapon on him – he and Esperanza had taken care to disassemble their handguns and drop them into a sewer before they set out toward the airport. Nonetheless, he didn't want to take the chance of any metal object, no matter how innocent, setting off the detector and drawing further attention to him.

'What happened to your face?' the female guard asked.

'Car accident.' Decker stepped through the metal detector. The machine remained silent.

'Looks painful,' the guard said.

'It could have been worse.' Decker took his watch and car keys. 'The drunk who ran the red light and hit me went to the morgue.'

'Lucky. You'd better take care.'

'Believe me, I'm trying.' Decker walked toward the conveyor belt that led from the X-ray monitor. But his chest tightened when he saw that the belt wasn't moving. The guard in charge of the monitor had stopped the conveyor while he took a solemn look at the fuzzy image of what was in Decker's carry-on.

Decker waited, a traveler who had a plane to catch but who was trying to be reasonable about security, even though there obviously couldn't possibly be anything wrong with that carry-on.

The guard scowled, looking closer at the monitor.

Decker heard pounding behind his ears.

With a shrug, the guard pressed a button that re-engaged the conveyor belt. The carry-on emerged from the machine.

'Your face makes me sore just to look at it,' the guard said.

'It feels even worse than it looks.' Decker picked up the million dollars and walked with other passengers along the concourse.

He stopped at a payphone, asked the information operator for the airport's number, then pressed buttons for the number he was given. 'Airport security, please.'

Pause. Click. 'Security,' a smooth-voiced man said.

'Check your parking area for a Pontiac, this year's make, dark blue.' Decker gave the license number. 'Have you got all that? Did you write it down?'

'Yes, but—'

'You'll find explosives in the trunk.'

'*What?*'

'Not connected to a detonator. The car is safe, but you'd better be careful, all the same.'

'*Who—*'

'This isn't a threat to the airport. It's just that I find myself with a lot of C-4 on my hands, and I can't think of a safer way to surrender it.'

'But—'

'Have a nice day.' Decker broke the connection. Before leaving the Pontiac in the parking area, he had rubbed a soapy washcloth over any sections where they might have left fingerprints. Normally, he would have left the car where street kids would soon steal it, but he didn't want them screwing around with the explosives. By the time the Pontiac and the C-4 were found, he would be on his way to Denver.

He walked swiftly toward the gate, where Beth and Esperanza waited anxiously for him.

'You took so long I got worried,' Beth said.

Decker noticed the glance she directed toward his carry-on. Is the money what she really cares about? he wondered. 'I was beginning to feel a little tense myself.'

'They've already started boarding,' Esperanza said. 'My seat number was called. I'd better get moving.'

Decker nodded. He had spent so much time with Esperanza the past few days that he felt odd being separated from him. 'See you in Denver.'

'Right.'

As Esperanza followed passengers down the jetway, Beth gave Decker an affectionate smile. 'We've never traveled together. This will be the start of a whole lot of new experiences for us.'

'As long as they're better than what happened since Friday night.' Decker tried to make it sound like a joke.

'*Anything* would be better.'

'Let's hope.' But what if it gets even worse? Decker wondered.

Beth glanced toward the check-in counter. 'They're calling our seat numbers.'

'Let's go. I'm sure you can use a rest from those crutches.' Heading back to Santa Fe, am I doing the right thing? Decker brooded. Am I absolutely sure this is going to work?

At the jetway, a United agent took Beth's ticket. 'Do you need assistance boarding the aircraft?'

'My friend will help me.' Beth looked fondly toward Decker.

'We'll be fine,' Decker told the agent, and surrendered his boarding pass. He followed Beth into the confinement of the jetway. It's not too late to change the plan, he warned himself.

But he felt carried along by the line of passengers. Two minutes later, they were in their seats midway along the aircraft. A flight attendant took Beth's crutches and stored them in the plane's garment-bag compartment. Decker and Beth fastened their seatbelts. The million dollars was stowed at his feet.

I can *still* change my mind, he thought. Maybe Beth was right. Maybe the South of France *is* where we ought to be going.

But something he and Beth had talked about at the motel kept coming back to him. He had asked Beth if she was willing to stay with him, knowing that she would be putting her life in danger, that Renata would try to use her to get at him. For the rest of Beth's time with Decker, she would always be looking over her shoulder. Beth's answer had been, 'Without you, I'd have nothing to look *ahead* to.'

Let's find out if she means it, Decker thought. I want to settle this *now*.

The 737 pulled away from the terminal, taxiing toward the runway. Beth clasped his hand.

'I've missed you,' she whispered.

Decker gently squeezed her fingers. 'More than you can ever know, I missed you.'

'Wrong,' Beth said. Engines whined outside their window. 'What you did these last few days – I have a very definite idea of what you feel for me.' Beth snuggled against him as the 737 took off.

4

By the time the jet leveled off at thirty-two thousand feet, Decker was surprised to find that he was having trouble making small talk with her, the first time this had happened in their relationship. Their chitchat sounded hollow compared to the substantive matters he wanted to discuss with her but couldn't because of the risk that passengers around them would overhear. He was grateful when the flight attendant brought breakfast, a cheese-and-mushroom omelette that he devoured. In part, he was ravenous, his appetite having kicked in. But in part, also, he wanted to use the food as a distraction from the need to keep up conversation. After the meal, refusing coffee, he apologized for being exhausted.

'Don't feel you have to entertain me,' Beth said. 'You earned a rest. Take a nap. In fact, I think I'll join you.'

She tilted her seat back just as he did, then leaned her head against his shoulder.

Decker crossed his arms and closed his eyes. But sleep did not come readily. His emotions continued to divide him. The intensity of the long ordeal he had been through left him restless, his body exhausted but his nerves on edge, as if he was having withdrawal symptoms from a physical dependence on the rush of adrenaline. These sensations reminded him of the way he had once felt after his missions for the military and the Agency. Action could be addictive. In his youth, he had craved it. The 'high' of surviving a mission had made ordinary life unacceptable, producing an eagerness to go on other missions, to overcome fear in order to replicate the euphoria of coming back alive. Eventually, he had recognized the self-destructiveness of this dependency. When he had settled in Santa Fe, he had been convinced that peace was all he wanted.

As a consequence, he was puzzled by his eagerness to pursue his conflict with Renata. Granted, from one point of view, it didn't make sense to prolong the tension of waiting for her to attack him. If he could control the circumstances under which Renata came after him, he would be hunting her as much as she would be hunting him. The sooner he confronted her, the better. But from another point of view, his eagerness troubled him, making him worry that he was becoming what he had used to be.

5

'We're not exactly sneaking back into New Mexico. How do we know Renata won't be in the concourse, watching whoever gets off this flight?' Esperanza asked. He had joined Decker and Beth where they remained in their seats, waiting for the other passengers to disembark at the Albuquerque airport. No one was near them. They could speak without fear of being overheard.

'That's not the way she would handle it,' Decker said. 'In an airport as small as this, someone hanging around day after day, doing nothing but watch incoming flights, would attract the attention of a security officer.'

'But Renata wouldn't have to do it by herself. She could hire someone to watch with her. They could take shifts,' Esperanza said.

'That part I agree with. She probably does have help by now. When she was using McKittrick –' Decker glanced toward Beth, wondering if *she* had used *him* just as Renata had used McKittrick. ' – Renata would have kept her friends at a distance, to prevent McKittrick from getting jealous. But once McKittrick was out of the picture, she would have brought in the rest of her terrorist group from Rome.' Decker lifted his carry-on from the compartment at his feet. 'A million dollars is worth the effort. Oh, they're here all right, and they're taking turns, but they're not watching the incoming flights.'

'Then what *are* they doing?'

A flight attendant interrupted, bringing Beth her crutches.

Beth thanked the woman, and the three of them started forward.

'I'll explain when we're by ourselves.' Decker turned to Beth. 'Those stitches will have to be looked at. The first thing we'll do is get you to a doctor.' He shook his head. 'No, I'm wrong. The first thing we have to do is rent a car.'

'Rent?' Esperanza asked. 'But you left your Jeep Cherokee in the airport's parking garage.'

'Where it's going to stay for a while,' Decker said. He waited until there was no one around them on the jetway before he told Esperanza, 'Your badge and your service pistol are locked in my car. Can you do without them for another day?'

'The sooner I get them back, the better. Why can't we use your car?' Immediately Esperanza answered his own question. 'Renata knows your Jeep. You think she might have rigged it with explosives?'

'And risk blowing up the million dollars in this bag? I don't think so. As much as she wants revenge, it has to be sweet. It's no good if it costs her – certainly not *this* much. My car will be perfectly safe . . . Except for the homing device she'll have planted on it.'

6

Midday sunlight blazed as Decker drove the rented gray Buick Skylark from the Avis lot next to the Albuquerque airport. He steered along the curved road past the four-story parking garage, then glanced at the two large metal silhouettes of race horses on the lawn in front of the airport, remembering the misgivings with which he had first seen those horses more than a year ago when he had begun his pilgrimage to Santa Fe. Now, after his longest time away from Santa Fe since then, he was returning, and his emotions were much more complex.

He steered around another curve, reached a wide grass-divided thoroughfare that led to and from the airport, and pointed toward a fourteen-story glass-and-stucco Best Western hotel on the right side of the road, silhouetted against the Sandia mountains. 'Somewhere in that hotel, Renata or one of her friends is watching a homing-device receiver, waiting for a needle to move and warn them my car is leaving the parking garage. Whoever it is will hurry down to a car that's positioned for an easy exit from the hotel's parking area. My car will be followed as it passes the hotel. The person in the car will have a cellular phone and pass the word to the rest of the group, some of whom will have no doubt set up shop in Santa Fe. The person following me will take for granted that cellular-phone conversations can be overheard by the wrong people, so the conversation will be in code, at regular intervals, all the way behind me to Santa Fe. Once I get to where I'm going, they'll move quickly to get their hands on me. There's no reason for them to wait. After all, I won't have had time to set up any defenses. Immediate action will be their best tactic. If I'm carrying the money, they won't have to torture me for information about where I put the million. But they'll torture me, anyhow. For the pleasure of it. Or rather Renata will do the torturing. I don't know where she'll want to start first – my balls or my throat. Probably the former, because if she goes for my throat, which I'm sure is what she would really like to do, to get even for what I did to *her*, I won't be able to give her the satisfaction of hearing me scream.'

Beth was in the back seat, her injured leg stretched out. Esperanza sat in front in the passenger seat. They looked at Decker as if the strain of what he had been through was affecting his behavior.

'You make it sound too vivid,' Beth said.

'And what makes you so sure about the homing device and the Best Western hotel?' Esperanza asked.

'Because that's the way *I* would do it,' Decker said.

'Why not the Airport Inn or the Village Inn or one of these other motels farther down?'

'Too small. Too hard for someone not to attract attention. Whoever's watching the homing-device receiver will want to be inconspicuous.'

'If you're that certain, I can ask the Albuquerque police to check the rooms in the Best Western.'

'Without a search warrant? And without the police tipping their hand? Whoever's watching the receiver will have a lookout, someone outside the hotel checking to see if police arrive. Renata and her friends would disappear. I'd lose my best chance of anticipating them.'

'You're worrying me,' Beth said.

'Why?' Decker steered from the airport thoroughfare and headed down Gibson, approaching the ramp onto Interstate 25.

'You're different. You sound as if you welcome the challenge, as if you're enjoying this.'

'Maybe I'm reverting.'

'What?'

'If you and I are going to survive this, I *have* to revert. I don't have another choice. I have to become what I used to be – before I arrived in Santa Fe. That's why McKittrick picked me to be your next-door neighbor, isn't it?' Decker asked. 'That's why you moved in next to me. Because of what I used to be.'

7

As the rented Buick crested La Bajada hill and Santa Fe was suddenly spread out before him, the Sangre de Cristo mountains hulking in the background, Decker felt no surge of excitement, no delight in having returned. Instead, what he felt was an unexpected emptiness. So much had happened to him since he had left. The clay-colored, flat-roofed, Hispanic-pueblo structures of Santa Fe seemed as exotic as ever. The round-edged adobe-style homes seemed to glow warmly, the September afternoon amazingly clear and brilliant, no smog, visibility for hundreds of miles, the land of the dancing sun.

But Decker felt apart from it all, remote. He didn't have a sense of coming home. He was merely revisiting a place where he happened to live. The detachment reminded him of when he had worked for the Agency and returned from assignments to his apartment in Virginia. It was the same detachment that he had felt so many times before, in London, Paris, and Athens, in Brussels, Berlin, and Cairo, the last time in Rome – because on all his missions, wherever he had traveled, he had not dared to identify with his surroundings for fear that he would let down his guard. If he was going to survive, he couldn't permit distractions. From that point of view, he *had* come home.

8

'The stitches are nicely done,' the stoop-shouldered red-haired doctor said.

'I'm relieved to hear it,' Decker said. The doctor was a former client with whom he occasionally socialized. 'Thanks for agreeing to see us without an appointment.'

The doctor shrugged. 'I had two no-shows this afternoon.' He continued to examine the wound in Beth's thigh. 'I don't like this area of redness around the stitches. What caused the injury?'

'A car accident,' Decker said before Beth could answer.

'You were with her? Is that how you hurt your face?'

'It was a lousy end to a vacation.'

'At least *you* didn't need stitches.' The doctor returned his attention to Beth. 'The redness suggests that the wound is developing an infection. Were you given an anti-tetanus injection?'

'I wasn't alert enough to remember.'

'It must have slipped the other doctor's mind,' Decker said bitterly.

'Then it's due.' After giving Beth the shot, the doctor rebandaged the wound. 'I'll write a prescription for some antibiotics. Do you want something for the pain?'

'Please.'

'Here. This ought to take care of it.' The doctor finished writing and handed her two pieces of paper. 'You can shower, but I don't want you soaking the wound in a tub. If the tissue becomes too soft, the stitches might pull out. Call me in three days. I want to make sure the infection doesn't spread.'

'Thanks.' Wincing, Beth eased off the examination table and pulled up her loose-fitting slacks, buckling them. In order to avoid attracting suspicion, Friday night's bullet wound to the fleshy part of her shoulder had not been mentioned. That wound had no redness around it, but if an infection was brewing there, the antibiotics for the wound in her thigh would handle it.

'Glad to help. Steve, I'm in the market for more rental properties. Got any that might interest me? I'm free Saturday afternoon.'

'I could be tied up. I'll get back to you.' Decker opened the door to the examination room and let Beth use her crutches to go ahead of him to where Esperanza waited in the lobby. Decker told them, 'I'll be out in a minute,' then shut the door and turned to the doctor. 'Uh, Jeff?'

'What is it? You want me to check those contusions on your face?'

'They're not what's on my mind.'

'Then—'

'I'm afraid this will sound a little melodramatic, but I wonder if you can make sure our visit to you stays a secret.'

'Why would—'

'It's delicate. Embarrassing, in fact. My friend's in the middle of getting a divorce. It could get nasty if the husband knew that she and I were seeing each other. Someone might call or come around, identifying himself as her husband or a private investigator or whatever, wanting to know about medical treatment you gave her. I'd hate for him to find out that she and I had been here together.'

'My office isn't in the habit of handing out that kind of information,' Jeff said stiffly.

'I didn't think it was. But my friend's husband can be

awfully persuasive.' Decker picked up the bag containing the money.

'He certainly won't get any information from me.'

'Thanks, Jeff. I appreciate this.' As he left the examination room, he had the sense that the doctor disapproved of the circumstances Decker claimed to be in. He stopped at the receptionist's counter. 'I'll pay cash.'

'The patient's name?'

'Brenda Scott.'

It was highly unlikely that Renata would try to check every doctor in Santa Fe to see if Beth received the medical treatment Renata would suspect she might require. But thoroughness had always been Decker's trademark. He had deliberately avoided taking Beth to his personal physician or to the emergency ward at St Vincent's Hospital or to the Lovelace Health System offices. Those were obvious places that Renata could easily have someone watch to see if Beth and, by extension, Decker were back in town. Decker's precautions were possibly excessive, but old habits now controlled him.

9

The trailer with its yucca-studded gravel area in front looked oddly different from the way it had when Decker had seen it a few days earlier. Correction, Decker told himself. Nights. You saw it in the middle of the night. It's bound to look different. As he parked the rented Buick at the curb, he glanced at the stunted marigolds in the narrow flower garden that hugged the front wall.

'Do you think it's safe for you to show up here?' Esperanza asked. 'Renata or one of her friends might be watching where I live.'

'Not a chance,' Decker said. 'Renata didn't get a good look at you the other night.'

Esperanza, too, was studying the trailer as if there was something oddly different about it. What's making him nervous? Decker wondered. Does he truly think Renata is in the area? Or is it because— Decker remembered Esperanza's references to the arguments he was having with his wife. Maybe Esperanza was uneasy about being reunited with her.

'You took all kinds of risks by coming with me. I owe you big time.' Decker extended his hand.

'Yes.' Beth squirmed to lean forward. 'You saved my life. I can never repay you. To say "thanks" doesn't come close to expressing my gratitude.'

Esperanza continued to stare at the trailer. '*I'm* the one who should be saying "thanks".'

Decker furrowed his brow. 'I don't get your point.'

'You asked me why I wanted to come along.' Esperanza turned, directing a steady gaze at him. 'I told you I needed some time away from my wife. I told you I was a sucker for wanting to get people out of trouble.'

'I remember,' Decker said.

'I also told you I'd never met anybody like you before. Hanging around with you was an education.'

'I remember that, too.'

'People get set in their ways.' Esperanza hesitated. 'For quite a while now, I've been feeling dead inside.'

Decker was caught by surprise.

'When I ran with gangs, I knew there had to be something more than just going nowhere in a hurry, raising hell, but I couldn't figure out what it was. Then the policeman I told you about changed my way of seeing things. I joined the force, to be like him, so I could make a difference, so I could do some good.' Esperanza's voice was taut with emotion. 'But sometimes, no matter how much good you try to do, all the shit you see in this world can get you down, especially the needless pain people put each other through.'

'I still don't—'

'I didn't think I'd ever get excited about anything again. But trying to keep pace with you these past few days . . . Well, something happened. . . . I felt alive. Oh, I was scared out of my mind by what we did. Some of it was plain damned insane and suicidal. But at the time—'

'It seemed like the thing to do.'

'Yeah.' Esperanza grinned. 'It seemed like the thing to do. Maybe I'm like you. Maybe I'm reverting.' He stared at the trailer again and sobered. 'I guess it's time.' He opened the passenger door and swung his cowboy boots out onto the gravel.

As Decker watched the lanky long-haired detective walk pensively toward the trailer's three front steps, he realized part of the reason the trailer seemed different. There had been a motorcycle and a pickup truck in the driveway a couple of nights ago. Now only the motorcycle remained.

When Esperanza disappeared inside, Decker turned to Beth. 'Tonight's going to be rough. We'll have to put you in a hotel somewhere out of town.'

Despite her discomfort, Beth straightened in alarm. 'No. I won't be separated from you.'

'Why?'

Uneasy, Beth didn't answer.

'Are you saying you don't feel safe away from me?' Decker shook his head. 'That might have been what you felt when you were living next door to me, but you're going to have to break yourself of that attitude. Right now, it's a lot smarter for you to stay as far away from me as possible.'

'That's not what I'm thinking,' Beth said.

'What *are* you thinking?'

David Morrell

'You wouldn't be in this mess if it wasn't for me. I'm not going to let you try to get out of it alone.'

'There'll be shooting.'

'I *know* how to shoot.'

'So you explained.' Remembering that Beth had killed her husband and emptied his wall safe, Decker glanced beside him toward the bag containing the million dollars. Is the money what she wants? Is that her motive for staying close?

'Why are you angry at me?' Beth asked.

Decker wasn't prepared for the question. 'Angry? What makes you think I'm—'

'If you were any colder to me, I'd have frostbite.'

Decker stared toward Esperanza's trailer. Stared toward his hands. Stared toward Beth. 'You shouldn't have lied to me.'

'About being in the Witness Protection Program? I was under strict orders not to tell you.'

'Orders from McKittrick?'

'Look, after I was shot, after I got out of the hospital, when you and I talked in my courtyard, I tried to tell you as much as I could. I begged you to go away and hide with me. But you insisted I go without you.'

'I figured that would be the safest thing for you in case another hit team came after me,' Decker said. 'If I'd known you were in the Witness Protection Program, I would have handled it a different way.'

'Different? How?'

'Then I *would* have gone with you,' Decker said. 'To help protect you. In *that* case, I'd have run into McKittrick, realized what was happening, and saved you and me from the nightmare we went through.'

'So it's still my fault? Is that what you're saying?'

'I don't think I used the word "fault". I—'

'What about all the lies *you* told *me* about what you did

416

before you came to Santa Fe, about how you got those bullet scars? It seems to me there was plenty of lying on both sides.'

'I can't just go around telling people I used to work for the CIA.'

'I'm not just anybody,' Beth said. 'Didn't you trust me?'

'Well . . .'

'Didn't you *love* me enough to trust me?'

'It was a reflex from the old days. I was never good at trusting people. Trust can get you killed. But that argument cuts both ways. Evidently you didn't love *me* enough to trust *me* with the truth about your background.'

Beth sounded discouraged. 'Maybe you're right. Maybe there wasn't enough love to go around.' She leaned back, exhausted. 'What was I expecting? We spent two months together. Of that, we were lovers for only eight days before—' She shuddered. 'People's lives don't change in eight days.'

'They can. Mine changed in a couple of minutes when I decided to move to Santa Fe.'

'But it *didn't* change.'

'What are you talking about?'

'You said it yourself. You're back to where you started. To what you once were.' Tears trickled down Beth's cheeks. 'Because of me.'

Decker couldn't help himself. He wanted to lean over the seat and clasp Beth's hand, to lean farther and hug her.

But before he could act on the impulse, she said, 'If you want to end our relationship, tell me.'

'End it?' Now that the ultimate topic had been raised, Decker wasn't ready. 'I'm not sure . . . I wasn't—'

'Because I won't tolerate having you accuse me of taking advantage of you. I lied to you about my background because I was under strict orders to keep it a secret. Even then, I was tempted to tell you, but I was worried that you'd run from me if you knew the truth.'

'I would never have run.'

'That remains to be seen. But that's all the explanation you're going to get from me. Accept it or not. One thing's for sure – I don't intend to stay in any hotel room while you face Renata by yourself. *You* risked your life for *me*. If I have to do the same to prove myself, that's what I'm willing to do.'

Decker felt overwhelmed.

'So what's it going to be?' Beth asked. 'Are you going to forgive me for lying to you? *I'm* prepared to forgive *you*. Do you want to make a fresh start?'

'If it's possible.' Emotion was tearing Decker apart.

'Anything's possible if you try.'

'If we both try.' Decker's voice broke. 'Yes.'

At once Decker's attention was distracted by the sound of Esperanza's front door being opened. Esperanza came out. The lean detective had put on fresh jeans, a denim shirt, and a stetson. A semiautomatic pistol was holstered on his right hip. But something in his expression indicated that more than his outward appearance had changed since he went in the house.

Esperanza's boots crunched on gravel as he approached the Buick.

'Are you all right?' Decker asked. 'Your eyes look—'

'She isn't here.'

'Your wife? You mean she's at work or—'

'Gone.'

'What?'

'She left. The trailer's empty. The furniture. The pots and pans. Her clothes. All gone, even a cactus I had on the kitchen counter. She took everything, except for my jeans and a few of my shirts.'

'Jesus,' Decker said.

'I was a while coming out because I had to phone around to find out where she went. She's staying with her sister in Albuquerque.'

'I am really sorry.'

It seemed that Esperanza didn't hear him. 'She doesn't want to see me. She doesn't want to talk to me.'

'All because you wouldn't quit your job as a police officer?'

'She kept saying I was married to my job. Sure, we were having problems, but she didn't have to leave. We could have worked things out.'

For the first time, Esperanza seemed fully aware of Decker and Beth. He glanced toward the back and noticed the strained expression on Beth's face. 'Looks like I'm not the only one with some things to work out.'

'We've been playing catch-up,' Beth said. 'Truth or consequences.'

'Yeah, that's the name of a good New Mexican town, all right.' Esperanza got into the car. 'Let's do it.'

'Do . . . ?' Decker asked in confusion.

'Finish what we started with Renata.'

'But this isn't your fight any longer. Stay here and try to settle things with your wife.'

'I don't walk away from my friends.'

Friends? Decker suffered a pang of grief as he remembered the price that Hal and Ben had paid for being his friends. Again he tried to dissuade Esperanza. 'No. Where you work? Where you're known? That's crazy. If there's trouble, we won't be able to cover it up the way we did in New York and New Jersey. Word will get around. At the very least, you'll lose your job.'

'Maybe that's what I finally want. Come on, Decker, start the car. Renata's waiting.'

10

A buzzer sounded as Decker entered the store. The sickly sweet smell of gun oil hung in the air. Racks of rifles, shotguns, and other hunting equipment stretched before him.

The shop was called The Frontiersman, and it had been the first store Decker went to when he had arrived in Santa Fe fifteen months earlier. To Decker's left, a clerk came to attention behind a glass counter of handguns, assessing him. The clerk appeared to be the same stocky sunburned man, wearing the same red plaid work shirt and the same Colt .45 semiautomatic pistol, who had waited on him before. Decker felt a vortex sucking him backward and downward.

'Yes, sir?'

Decker walked over. 'Some friends and I are making plans to go hunting. I need to pick up some things.'

'Whatever you need, we've either got it or we can order it.'

Decker didn't have time to wait five days for the mandatory background check on anyone who applied to purchase a handgun. A rifle could be obtained on the spot. Before Congress passed the assault-weapon ban, Decker would merely have chosen several AR-15s, the civilian version of the US military's M-16, commonly available in most gunshops until the ban. Now his choices weren't as easy. 'A Remington bolt-action .270.'

'Got it.'

'A Winchester lever-action .30-30. Short barrel – twenty-four inches.'

'No problem.'

'Two double-barrel shotguns, ten gauge.'

'No can do. The heaviest double barrels I've got are twelve gauge. Made by Stoeger.'

'Fine. I need a modified choke on the shotguns.'

'No problem there.' The clerk was writing a list.

'Short barrels on them.'

'Yep. Anything else?'

'A .22 semiautomatic rifle.'

'Ruger all right? Comes with a ten-round magazine.'

'Got any thirty-round magazines?'

'Three. Get them while they last. The government's threatening to outlaw them.'

'Give me all three. Two boxes of ammunition for each weapon. Buckshot for the shotguns. Three good hunting knives. Three camouflage suits, two large, one medium. Three sets of polypropylene long underwear. Three sets of dark cotton gloves. A tube of face camouflage. Two collapsible camp shovels. A dozen canteens – those Army-surplus metal ones. Your best first-aid kit.'

'A dozen canteens? You must have a lot of friends. Sounds like you're going to have yourself quite a time. You've covered almost everything – distance, midrange, up close.' The clerk joked, 'Why, the only thing you haven't included is a bow and arrows.'

'Good idea,' Decker said.

11

The total came to just under seventeen hundred dollars. Decker was concerned that Renata had contacts who could provide her with information from the computers of credit-card companies, so he didn't dare use his Visa card and warn her he was in town buying weapons. Instead, he invented a story about having had a big win at the blackjack tables in Las Vegas and paid cash. He needn't have worried that the seventeen one-hundred dollar bills would attract attention. This was New Mexico. When it came to weapons, how you paid for them and what you did with them was nobody else's business. The clerk hadn't even made a comment about the scrapes on Decker's face. Guns and personal remarks didn't mix.

It took Decker several trips to take all the equipment to the Buick. He would have asked Esperanza to come in and help him, but Esperanza had said he was known in the gun shop. In case of trouble, Decker didn't want Esperanza to be linked with him and a large purchase of weapons.

'Jesus, Decker, it looks like you're going to start a war. What's *this*? A bow and arrows?'

'And if that doesn't work against Renata and her gang, I'll piss on them.'

Esperanza started laughing.

'That's the stuff. Keep loose,' Decker said.

They closed the trunk and got in the car.

Beth waited in the back seat, her eyes still red from her conversation with Decker outside Esperanza's trailer. She made an obvious effort to rouse her spirits and be part of the group. 'What were you laughing about?'

'A bad joke.' Decker repeated it.

Beth shook her head and chuckled slightly. 'Sounds like a guy thing.'

'How come you bought so many canteens?' Esperanza asked. 'One for each of us. But what about the other nine?'

'Actually we're going to fill all twelve with plant fertilizer and fuel oil.'

'What the hell does that do?'

'Makes a damned good bomb.' Decker checked his watch and started the car. 'We'd better move it. It's almost four-thirty. We're running out of daylight.'

12

An hour later, after several other purchases, Decker steered off Cerrillos Road onto Interstate 25, but this time, he took the northbound route, heading in the opposite direction from Albuquerque.

'Why are we leaving town?' Agitated, Beth leaned forward. 'I told you I won't let you put me in an out-of-the-way motel. I won't be left out.'

'That's not why we're leaving town. Have you ever heard the expression, "There's no law west of the Pecos"?'

Beth looked mystified by the relevance of the comment. 'I seem to . . . In old westerns, or maybe in a history about the Southwest.'

'Well, the Pecos the expression refers to is the Pecos River, and that's where we're headed.'

Twenty minutes later, he turned to the left onto State Road 50 and shortly afterward reached the town of Pecos, whose architecture was dominated by traditional wood-sided peaked structures in sharp contrast with the stuccoed flat-roofed Hispanic-pueblo buildings in Santa Fe. He turned to the left again. Past Monastery Lake where he had gone fishing for trout his first summer in the area, then past the monastery for which the lake was named, he drove up an increasingly steep winding road that was bordered by tall pine trees. The sun had descended behind the looming western bluffs, casting the rugged scenery into shadow.

'We're going up into the Pecos Wilderness Area,' Decker said. 'That's the Pecos River on our right. In spots, it's only about twenty feet wide. You can't always see it because of the trees and rocks, but you can definitely hear it. What it lacks in size, it gains in speed.'

'This road is almost deserted,' Beth said. 'Why did we come up here?'

'This is a fishing area. Back among the trees, you might have seen a few cabins. After Labor Day, they're mostly unoccupied.' Decker pointed ahead. 'And once in a while, someone decides to sell.'

On the right, past a curve, a sign attached to a post read, EDNA FREED REALTY, then in smaller letters, *Contact Stephen Decker*, followed by a phone number.

Directly beyond the sign, Decker turned off the road, entered an opening among the fir trees, rumbled over a narrow wooden bridge above the river, and drove up a dirt lane to a clearing in front of a gray log cabin, whose sloped roof was rusted metal. The small building, surrounded by dense trees and bushes, was perched on a shadowy ridge not far above the clearing; it faced the turnoff from the country road; log steps were cut into the slope, leading up to the weathered front door.

'Just your basic home away from home,' Beth said.

'I've been trying to sell this place for the past six months,' Decker said. 'The key's in a lock box attached to the front door.'

Beth got out of the car, braced herself on her crutches, and shivered. 'I was warm in town, but it certainly gets chilly up here once the sun is low.'

'And damp from the river,' Decker said. 'That's why I bought thermal underwear for each of us. Before we get started, we'd better put them on.'

'Thermal underwear? But we won't be outside that long, will we?'

'Maybe all night.'

Beth looked surprised.

'There's a lot to do.' Decker opened the Buick's trunk. 'Put on these cotton gloves and help us load these weapons. Make sure you don't leave fingerprints on anything, including the ammunition. Do you know how to use a shotgun?'

'I do.'

'Someday you'll have to tell me how you learned. Your injured shoulder won't stand the shock of the recoil, of course. It would also make you awkward if you had to work a lever or a pump action to chamber a new round. That's why I bought double-barreled shotguns. The side-by-sides are wide and flat enough, they won't roll around if you set them on a log. You can lie down behind the log and shoot without raising the guns to aim them. You'll be able to get two shots per weapon. Opening the breach to reload isn't hard.'

'And what log did you have in mind?' Beth gamely asked, surprising him.

'I'm not sure. Esperanza and I are going to walk around and get a feel for the layout. Ask yourself what Renata and her friends will do when they get here tonight. How they'll approach. What cover they'll find most inviting. Then try to think of a position that gives you an advantage over them. It'll be dark in an hour. After that, after we've got our equipment assembled, we'll start rehearsing.'

13

And then, too frustratingly soon, it was time to go. Just before nine o'clock, in thickening darkness, Decker told Esperanza, 'The last flights of the evening will soon be arriving at the Albuquerque airport. We can't wait any longer. Do you think you can finish the rest of the preparations on your own?'

The cool night air chilled Esperanza's breath so that vapor could be seen coming from his mouth. 'How long will you be?'

'Expect us around midnight.'

'I'll be ready. You'd better not forget this.' Esperanza handed him the carry-on bag that had contained the million dollars but that now contained old newspapers they had found in the cabin.

The money was in a duffel bag at Esperanza's feet.

'Right,' Decker said. 'The plan won't work if Renata doesn't think I have the money.'

'And without me beside you,' Beth said.

'That's right, too,' Decker said. 'If Renata doesn't see us together, she'll wonder why we split up. She'll begin to suspect I'm keeping you out of danger while I lead her into a trap.'

'Imagine,' Beth said. 'And here, all the time, I thought you decided to bring me along because of the pleasure of my company.'

The remark made Decker feel as if he'd been stuck by a needle. Was her joke good-natured or— Not knowing what to say, he helped her into the front of the car, pushed back the passenger seat so that she had more room for her injured leg, then put her crutches in the back. Finally, when he got in beside her and shut his door, he thought of what to say. 'If we can get through this . . . If we can get to know each other . . .'

'I thought we already *did* know each other.'

'But who did I get to know? Are you Beth Dwyer or Diana Scolari?'

'Didn't *you* ever use fake names?'

Decker didn't know what to say to that, either. He started the Buick, nodded tensely to Esperanza, and made a U-turn in the clearing. His headlights flashing past dense pine trees, he drove down the lane, over the bridge, and onto the deserted road to Pecos. They were on their way.

But neither of them spoke until they were back on Interstate 25, passing Santa Fe, heading toward Albuquerque.

'Ask me,' Beth said.

'Ask . . . ?'

'Anything. Everything.' Her voice was heavy with emotion.

'That's a big order.'

'Damn it, try. By the time we get to the airport, I want to

know where we stand with each other.'

Decker increased speed, passing a pickup truck, trying to keep his speed under seventy-five.

'A relationship doesn't survive on its own,' Beth said. 'You have to work at it.'

'All right.' Decker hesitated, concentrating on the dark highway he sped along, feeling in a tunnel. 'You once told me something about your childhood. You said your parents had such violent arguments that you were afraid your father would burst into your bedroom and kill you while you slept. You said you arranged your pillows to make them look as if you were under the covers and then you slept under the bed, so he'd attack the pillows but not be able to get at you . . . Is that story true?'

'Yes. Did you suspect I lied to make you feel protective toward me?'

Decker didn't respond.

Beth frowned with growing concern. 'Is that the way you think – that people are constantly trying to manipulate you?'

'It's the way I *used* to think – before I came to Santa Fe.'

'And now you're back to your old habits.'

'Suspicion kept me alive. The fact is, if I had *kept* my old habits, if I hadn't let my guard down . . .' He didn't like where his logic was taking him and let the sentence dangle.

'You wouldn't have fallen in love with me. Is that what you wish?'

'I didn't say that. I'm not sure *what* I wanted to say. If I *hadn't* fallen in love with you, Renata would still be after me. *That* wouldn't have changed. I . . .' Decker's confusion tortured him. 'But I *did* fall in love with you, and if I could go back and do it all over again, if I *could* change the past . . .'

'Yes?' Beth sounded afraid.

'I'd do everything the same.'

Beth exhaled audibly. 'Then you believe me.'

'Everything comes down to trust.'

'And faith,' Beth said.

Decker's hands ached on the steering wheel. 'A *lot* of faith.'

14

Apprehensive, Decker left the Buick in the brightly lit rental-car lot next to the Albuquerque airport and walked with Beth into the terminal. On the second level, near the incoming baggage area, he surrendered the car keys to the Avis clerk, provided information about mileage and how much fuel was in the car, paid cash, and folded his receipt in his pocket.

'Catching a late plane out?' the clerk asked.

'Yes. We tried to make our vacation last as long as possible.'

'Come back to the Land of Enchantment.'

'We certainly will.'

Out of sight from the Avis counter, Decker guided Beth into a crowd that was descending from the terminal's upper levels, where the evening's final flights were arriving. Trying to make it seem as if he and Beth had just flown in, they went with the crowd down the escalator to the terminal's bottom level and out into the parking garage.

'And now it begins,' Decker murmured.

The sodium arc lights in the garage cast an eerie yellow glow. Although Decker was certain that none of Renata's group would have risked attracting the attention of security guards by hanging around the airport's arrival gates, he couldn't be as confident that a surveillance team was not in the garage, watching his Cherokee. The garage wasn't as carefully guarded as the airport was. Once in a while, a patrol car went through, but the team would see it coming and pretend to be loading luggage into a vehicle, then go back to watching as soon as the patrol car was gone. But if a surveillance team *was* in the garage, it was doubtful they would try to abduct Decker and Beth in so public a place, with only one exit from the airport. Travelers getting into nearby vehicles would see the attack and get a license number, then alert a security officer, who would phone ahead and arrange to have the road from the airport blocked. No, with too many opportunities for the attempted abduction to go wrong, the surveillance team would want to wait for privacy. In the meantime, they would use a cellular telephone to report to Renata that they had seen Decker carrying a bag that matched the description of the one containing the million dollars. Renata would be lulled into thinking that Decker didn't suspect she was in the area. After all, if he thought he was in immediate danger, he wouldn't be carrying the bagful of money, would he? He would have hidden it.

The Cherokee was to the left at the top of the stairs on the garage's second level. Decker unlocked the car, helped Beth into the front seat, threw the bag and her crutches into the back, and hurriedly got in, locking the doors, inserting his ignition key.

He hesitated.

'What are you waiting for?' Beth asked.

Decker stared at his right hand where it was about to turn the key. Sweat beaded his brow. 'Now is when we find out whether I'm right or wrong that Renata didn't rig this car with explosives.'

'Well, if you're wrong, we'll never know,' Beth said. 'To hell with it. We were talking about faith. Do it. Turn the key.'

Decker actually smiled as he obeyed. Waiting for the explosion that would blow the car apart, he heard the roar of the engine. 'Yes!' He backed out of the parking space and drove as quickly as safety allowed past travelers putting luggage into their cars, any of whom might be his enemy. A half-minute later, he was leaving the garage, stopping at one of the collection booths, paying the attendant, and joining the stream of cars speeding from the airport. Headlights glared.

His heart pounded furiously as he rounded a curve and pointed toward the lights gleaming in almost every window of the fourteen-story Best Western hotel. 'Right now, there's a lot of activity in one of those rooms. The needle on their homing-device monitor is telling them this car is in motion.' He wanted to increase speed but stopped the impulse when he saw the roof lights of a police car in front of him.

'I'm so nervous, I can't stop my knees from shaking,' Beth said.

'Concentrate on controlling your fear.'

'I can't.'

'You *have* to.'

Ahead, the police car turned a corner.

Decker lifted the hatch on the storage compartment that separated the two front seats. He took Esperanza's service pistol from where Esperanza had left it in the car when they had flown to New York. 'They'll be out of their room now, hurrying toward the hotel's parking lot.'

'How do *you* stop from being afraid?'

'I don't.'

'But you just said—'

'To control it, not stop it. Fear's a survival mechanism. It gives you strength. It makes you alert. It can save your life, but only if you keep it under control. If *it* controls *you*, it'll get you killed.'

Beth studied him hard. 'Obviously I've got a lot to learn about you.'

'The same here. It's like everything that happened with us before the attack on my house last Friday night was our honeymoon. Now the marriage has begun.' Decker sped onto the

Interstate, merging with a chaos of headlights. 'They've had time to reach the hotel's parking lot. They're getting in their vehicles.'

'Honeymoon? Marriage? . . . Was what you just said a proposal?'

' . . . Would that be such a bad idea?'

'I'd always disappoint you. I could never be the ideal woman you risked your life for.'

'That makes us even. I'm definitely not the ideal man.'

'You're giving a good imitation of that hero I told you I dreamed about as a little girl.'

'Heroes are fools. Heroes get themselves killed.' Decker increased speed to keep pace with traffic, which was doing sixty-five in a fifty-five-mile-an-hour zone. 'Renata and her friends will be rushing toward the Interstate now. The homing-device monitor will tell them which direction I've taken. I have to keep ahead of them. I can't let them pull abreast of me and force me off a deserted section of the highway.'

'Do you mind talking?'

'Now?'

'Will it distract you? If it doesn't, talking would help me not to be so afraid.'

'In that case, talk.'

'What's your worst fault?'

'Excuse me?'

'You were courting me all summer, showing me your best side. What's your worst?'

'You tell me *yours*.' Decker squinted toward the confusion of headlights in his rearview mirrow, watching for any vehicle that approached more rapidly than the others.

'I asked first.'

'You're serious?'

'Very.'

As the speed limit changed to sixty-five, Decker reluctantly began.

15

He told her that his father had been a career officer in the military and that the family had lived on bases all over the United States, moving frequently. 'I grew up learning not to get attached to people or places.' He told her that his father had not been demonstrative with affection and in fact had seemed to be embarrassed about showing any emotion, whether it was anger, sadness, or joy. 'I learned to hide what I felt.' He told her that when he entered the military, a logical choice for the son of a career officer, the special-operations training he received gave him further reinforcement in controlling his emotions.

'I had an instructor who took a liking to me and spent time talking with me on our off-hours. We used to get into philosophical discussions, a lot of which had to do with how to survive inhuman situations and yet not become inhuman. How to react to killing someone, for example. Or how to try to handle seeing a buddy get killed. He showed me something in a book about the mind and emotions that I've never forgotten.'

Decker kept glancing apprehensively toward the headlights in his rearview mirror. Traffic was becoming sparse. Nonetheless, he stayed in the passing lane, not wanting to be impeded by the occasional cars on his right.

'What was it he showed you?' Beth asked.

' "When we make fateful decisions, fate will inevitably occur. We all have emotions. Emotions themselves don't compromise us. But our thoughts about our emotions *will* compromise us if those thoughts aren't disciplined. Training controls our thoughts. Thoughts control our emotions." '

'It sounds like he was trying to put so many buffers over your emotions that you barely felt them.'

'Filters. The idea was to interpret my emotions so that they were always in my best interest. For instance –' Decker tasted something bitter. ' – Saturday night two friends of mine were killed.'

'Helping you try to find me?' Beth looked sickened.

'My grief for them threatened to overwhelm me, but I told myself I didn't have time. I had to postpone my grief until I could mourn for them properly. I couldn't mourn for them in the future if I didn't concentrate right then on staying alive. I *still* haven't found time to mourn for them.'

Beth repeated a statement from the quote he had given her. ' "Thoughts control our emotions." '

'That's how I lived.' Again, Decker checked the rearview mirror. Headlights approached with alarming speed. He rolled down his driver's window. Then he veered into the no-passing lane, held the steering wheel with his left hand, gripped Esperanza's pistol with his right, and prepared to fire if the vehicle coming up on his left attempted to ram him sideways off this barren section of the Interstate.

The vehicle's headlights were on their brightest setting, their intense reflection in Decker's rearview mirror almost blinding. Decker reduced speed abruptly so that the vehicle would surge past him before the driver had a chance to put on the brakes. But the vehicle not only rushed past; it continued speeding into the distance, its outline that of a huge pickup truck. Its red taillights receded into the darkness.

'He must be doing ninety,' Decker said. 'If I give him a little distance and then match his speed, that truck will run interference for me with any state trooper parked at the side of the Interstate. The trooper will see the truck first and go after *it*. I'll have time to reduce speed and slip past.'

The interior of the car became quiet.

'So,' Beth said at last, 'emotions make you uncomfortable? You certainly fooled me this summer.'

'Because I was making a conscious effort to change. To open up and allow myself to feel. When you walked into my office that first day, I was ready, for the first time in my life, to fall in love.'

'And now you feel betrayed because the woman you fell in love with wasn't the woman she said she was.'

Decker didn't respond.

Beth continued, 'You're thinking it might be safer to go back to what you were, to distance yourself and not allow any emotions that might make you vulnerable.'

'The notion occurred to me.'

'And?'

'To hell with my pride.' Decker squeezed her hand. 'You asked me if I wanted to make a fresh start. Yes. Because the alternative scares me to death. I don't want to lose you. I'd go crazy if I couldn't spend the rest of my life with you . . . I guess I'm *not* reverting, after all.'

You'd *better* revert, he told himself. You have to get both of us through this night alive.

16

Tension produced the familiar aching pressure in his stomach that he had suffered when he worked for the Agency. The omelette he had eaten that morning on the plane remained in his stomach and burned like acid, as did the quick take-out burgers and fries that he had grabbed for everyone while picking up equipment during the afternoon. Just like old times, he thought.

He wondered how close his pursuers were to him and what

they were deciding. Did they have members of their group waiting ahead of them in Santa Fe? Maybe only a few of Renata's friends had been stationed at the Best Western hotel, not enough to attempt an interception. Maybe they had used a cellular telephone to call ahead and arrange for reinforcements. Or maybe Decker was wrong and his car didn't have a homing device hidden in it. Maybe his plan was useless. No, he told himself emphatically. I've been doing this for a lot of years. I know how this is done. Given the circumstances, I *know* how Renata would behave.

Well, he thought dismally, isn't it nice to be certain?

When he passed the three exits to Santa Fe, continuing to speed along Interstate 25, it amused him to imagine the confusion his pursuers would be feeling, their frantic discussions as they tried to figure out why he hadn't stopped and where he was going. They would all be after him now, though, the ones in Santa Fe as well as those who had followed him from Albuquerque. Of that, he was sure, just as he was sure that he had not yet faced his biggest risks of the night – the isolation of State Road 50, for example.

It was two-lane, dark, narrow, and winding, with sporadic tiny communities along it but mostly shadowy scrub brush and trees. It offered perfect opportunities for his pursuers to force him off the road, with no one to see what happened. He couldn't possibly keep driving as fast as he did on the Interstate. At the first sharp curve, he would overturn his car. In places, even forty-five miles an hour was extreme. He hunched forward, peering at the darkness beyond his headlights, trying to gain every second he could on the straight, reducing speed, steering tensely around turns, once again accelerating.

'I can't risk taking my eyes off the road to check the rearview mirror,' he told Beth. 'Look behind us. Do you see any headlights?'

'No. Wait, now I do.'

'What?'

'Coming around the last curve. One— I'm wrong – it looks like *two* cars. The second just came around the curve.'

'Jesus.'

'They don't seem to be gaining on us. Why would they hold back? Maybe it's not them,' Beth said.

'Or maybe they want to know what they're getting into before they make their move. Ahead of us.'

'Lights.'

'Yes. We've reached Pecos.'

Near midnight on a Tuesday night, there was almost no activity. Decker reduced his speed as much as he dared, turned left onto the quiet main street, and proceeded north toward the mountains.

'I don't see the headlights anymore,' Beth said. 'The cars must belong to people who live in town.'

'Maybe.' As soon as the glow of the sleepy town was behind him, Decker again picked up speed, climbing the dark narrow road into the wilderness area. 'Or maybe the cars do belong to Renata and her gang, and they're holding back, not wanting to make it obvious they're following us. They must be curious what we're doing up here.'

In the darkness, the dense pine trees formed what seemed to be an impenetrable wall.

'It doesn't look very welcoming,' Beth said.

'Good. Renata will conclude the only reason anybody would come up here is to hide. We're getting closer. Almost there. Just a few more—'

17

He nearly shot past the *Contact Stephen Decker* realty sign before he reduced speed enough to turn into the barely visible break between fir trees. Terribly aware that he could be trapping Beth and himself as much as he was attempting to trap Renata, he crossed the wooden bridge above the roar of the swift, narrow Pecos River, entered the gloomy clearing, parked in front of the steps up to the house, and turned off the engine. Only then did he push in the knob for his headlights – the sequence activated a feature that kept his lights on for an additional two minutes.

With the aid of those lights, he got Beth's crutches and the carry-on bag from the back seat. He felt a desperate compulsion to hurry, but he didn't dare give in to it. If Renata and her gang drove past and saw him rushing up to the cabin, they would immediately suspect that he knew he was being followed, that he anticipated their arrival, that they were being set up. Tensely repressing his impatience, he allowed himself to look as weary as he felt. Following Beth up the log steps, he reached a metal box attached to the cabin's doorknob. The lights from his car provided just enough illumination for him to use his key to unlock the box. He opened the lid, took out the key to the cabin, unlocked the door, and helped Beth inside.

The moment the door was closed and locked, the lights turned on, Decker responded to the urgency swelling inside him. The blinds were already drawn on the cabin, so no one outside could see him support Beth while she dropped her crutches and picked up camouflage coveralls that Decker had bought at the gun shop. She pulled them on over her slacks and blouse. As soon as she tugged up the zipper and took back her crutches, Decker hurriedly put on his own camouflage coveralls. Before leaving the cabin to go to the airport, they had already put on the polypropylene long underwear he had bought. Now Decker smeared Beth's face and then his own with dark grease from a tube of camouflage coloring. When they had rehearsed these movements early in the evening, they had gotten ready in just under two minutes, but now it seemed tensely to Decker that they were taking much longer. Hurry, he thought. To avoid leaving fingerprints, they put on dark cotton gloves, thin enough to be able to shoot with, thick enough to provide some warmth. When Decker switched on a small radio, a Country and Western singer started wailing about 'livin' and lovin' and leavin' and . . .' Decker kept the lights on, helped Beth out the back door, shut it behind him, and risked pausing in the chill darkness long enough to stroke her arm with encouragement and affection.

She trembled, but she did what had to be done, what they had rehearsed, disappearing to the left of the cabin.

Impressed by her courage, Decker went to the right. At the front of the cabin, his headlights had gone off. Away from the glow of the cabin's windows, the darkness thickened. Then Decker's eyes adjusted, the moon and the unimaginable amount of stars, typically brilliant in the high country, giving the night a paradoxical gentle glow.

When Decker and Esperanza had walked around the property, assessing it from a tactical point of view, they had decided to make use of a game trail concealed by dense bushes at the back of the cabin. Unseen from the road, Beth was now moving along that trail and would soon reach a thick tree that the trail went around. There, Beth would lower herself to the forest floor, squirm down a slope through bushes, and reach a shallow pit that Esperanza had dug, where the two double-barrel shotguns lay on a log, ready for her to use.

Meanwhile, Decker crept through the darkness to a similar shallow pit that he himself had dug, using one of the camp shovels he had bought at the gunshop. Even wearing three layers of clothing, he felt the dampness of the ground. Lying behind a log, concealed by bushes, he groped around but couldn't find what he was looking for. His pulse skipped nervously until he finally touched the lever-action Winchester .30-30. The powerful weapon was designed for mid-range use in brush country such as this. It held six rounds in its magazine and one in the firing chamber, and could be shot as rapidly as the well-oiled lever behind the trigger could be worked up and down.

Next to the rifle was a car battery, one of the other items he had purchased before leaving Santa Fe. And next to the battery were twelve pairs of electrical wires, the ends of which were exposed. These wires led to canteens that were filled with fuel oil and a type of plant fertilizer, the main component of which was ammonium nitrate. Mixed in the proper ratio, the ingredients produced an explosive. To add bite, Decker had cut open several shotgun shells and poured in buckshot and gunpowder from them. To make a detonator for each bomb, he had broken the outer glass from twelve one-hundred-watt light bulbs, taking care not to use too much force and destroy the filament on the inside. He had gripped the metal stem of each bulb and inserted a filament into each canteen. Two wires were then taped to the stem of each bulb. The canteens were buried at strategic spots and covered with leaves. The pairs of wires, concealed in a like manner, led to the car battery next to Decker. The wires were arranged left to right in a pattern that matched where the canteens were located. If Decker chose a pair and pressed one end to the battery's positive pole while pressing the other end to the negative pole, he would complete a circuit that caused the light-bulb filament to burn and detonate the bomb.

He was ready. Down the lane and across the narrow Pecos River, on the other side of the road, Esperanza was hiding in the forest. He would have seen Decker drive onto the property and would be waiting for Renata and her friends to arrive. Common sense dictated that, when their homing-device receiver warned them that Decker had turned off the road, they wouldn't just follow him into the lane without first taking care to find out what trouble they might be getting into. Rather, they would pass the entrance to the lane, drive a prudent distance up the road, and park, proceeding cautiously back to the lane. They would want to avoid the bottleneck of the lane, but they wouldn't be able to, because the only other way to get onto the property was by crossing the swift river, and in the darkness, that maneuver was too risky.

The moment Renata and her group were off the road and moving into the lane, Esperanza would emerge from cover and disable their vehicles so that, if the group had a premonition and hurried back to the cars, they wouldn't be able to escape. There would probably be two vehicles – one for the surveillance team at the airport, the other for the team in Santa Fe. As soon as Esperanza had made them inoperable by cramming a twig into the stem valve of several tires, the slight hiss of escaping air muffled by the roar of the river, he would stalk the group, using the .22 semiautomatic rifle with its thirty-round magazine and two other magazines secured beneath his belt, attacking from the rear when the shooting started. Although light, the .22 had several advantages – it was relatively silent, it had a large ammunition capacity, and it could fire with extreme rapidity. These qualities would be useful in a short-range, hit-and-run action. The canteens would be exploding; Beth would be using the shotgun; Decker would be firing the Winchester, with the Remington bolt-action as a backup. If everything went as planned, Renata and her group would be dead within thirty seconds.

The trouble is, Decker thought, Murphy's Law had a way of interfering with plans. Whatever *can* go wrong, *will* go wrong.

And there were a lot of question marks in this plan. Would Renata and all of her group go up the lane at the same time? Would they sense a trap and check to make sure that no one was sneaking up behind them? Would Beth be able to control her reactions and fire at the right time as they had rehearsed it? For that matter, would fear paralyze her, preventing her from firing at all? Or would—

18

Decker heard a noise that sounded like a branch being snapped. He nervously held his breath, not wanting even that slight sound to interfere with his hearing. Pressed hard against the dank ground, he listened, trying to filter out the faint Country and Western music from the radio in the cabin, ignoring the muffled rush of the river, waiting for the sound to be repeated. It seemed to have come from near the lane, but he couldn't assume that a human being had made it. This close to the wilderness area, there were plenty of nocturnal animals. The noise might not indicate a threat.

He couldn't help wondering how Beth had reacted to it. Would she be able to control her fear? He kept straining to assure himself that her presence was necessary. If she hadn't come along, Renata might have suspected that Decker was planning a trap and didn't want to put Beth in danger. At the same time, Decker kept arguing with himself that maybe Beth's presence wasn't absolutely necessary. Maybe he shouldn't have involved her. Maybe he had demanded too much from her.

She doesn't have to prove anything to me.

You sure made it seem that way.

Stop, he told himself. There is only one thing you should be concentrating on, and that is getting through this night alive.

Getting *Beth* through this night alive.

When he failed to hear a repetition of the sound, he exhaled slowly. The cabin was to his right, the glow of lights through its windows. But he took care not to compromise his night vision by glancing in that direction. Instead, he focused his gaze straight ahead toward the road, the bridge, the lane, and the clearing. The lights in the cabin would provide a beacon for anyone sneaking up and make it hard for a stalker to adjust his or her night vision to check the darkness around the cabin. Conversely, the spill from those lights, adding to the illumination from the brilliant moonglow and starlight, were to Decker's advantage, easy on his eyes, at the periphery of his vision. He had the sense that he was peering through a gigantic light-enhancing lens.

Crickets screeched. A new mournful song about open doors and empty hearts played faintly on the cabin's radio. At once Decker stiffened, again hearing the sound of a branch being snapped. This time, he had no doubt that the sound had come from near the lane, from the trees and bushes to the right of it. Had Renata and her gang managed to cross the bridge without his having seen their silhouettes? That didn't seem likely – unless they had crossed the bridge before he reached this shallow pit. But the bridge had been out of his sight for only a few minutes. Did it make sense that Renata would have had time to drive by (he hadn't seen any passing headlights), conclude that he was parked up the lane, stop, reconnoiter the area, and cross the bridge before he came out of the cabin? She and her group would have had to rush to the point of recklessness. That wasn't Renata's style.

But when Decker heard the noise a third time, he picked up the Winchester. It suddenly occurred to him that Beth would be doing the same thing, gripping one of the shotguns, but would she have the discipline not to pull the trigger until it was absolutely necessary? If she panicked and fired too soon, before her targets were in range, she would ruin the trap and probably get herself killed. During the ride up from Albuquerque, Decker had emphasized this danger, urging her to remember that a shotgun was a short-range weapon, that she mustn't shoot until Decker did and she had obvious targets in the clearing. The devastating spray of buckshot would make up for any problem that her injured shoulder gave her in aiming, especially if she discharged all four barrels in rapid succession.

Remember what I told you, Beth. Hold your fire.

Decker waited. Nothing. No further sound of a branch being snapped. What he judged to be five minutes passed, and still the sound was not repeated. He couldn't look at his watch. It was in his pocket. Before arriving at the cabin, he had made certain that he and Beth took off their watches and put them away, lest the luminous dials reveal their position in the darkness.

What he judged to be *ten* minutes passed. He had talked to Beth about how it felt to lie motionless possibly for hours, about subduing impatience, about ignoring the past and the future. Get in the moment and *stay* in the moment. Tell yourself that you're in a contest, that the other side is going to move before *you* do. At the Albuquerque airport, Decker had insisted that they both use a restroom, even though neither of them felt an urge, pointing out that at night when they were lying in the forest, a full bladder could make them uncomfortable enough that they might lose their concentration. Getting up to a squat to relieve oneself was out of the question – the movement would attract attention. The only option was to relieve oneself in one's clothes, and that definitely resulted in loss of concentration.

Fifteen minutes. Twenty. No more suspicious sounds. No signs of activity on the moonbathed lane or in the murky bushes next to it. Patience, Decker told himself. But a part of him began to wonder if his logic had been valid. Perhaps Renata had not hidden a homing device on his car. Perhaps Renata wasn't anywhere in the area.

19

The night's chill enveloped Decker, but he felt an even greater chill when the forest moved. A section of it, something low, about the size of someone crouching, shifted warily from bush to bush. But the movement wasn't near the lane, not where Decker had expected it to be. Instead, dismayingly, the figure was already halfway around the tree-rimmed edge of the clearing, creeping toward the cabin. How did he get so far without my seeing him? Decker thought in alarm.

Where are the others?

His chill intensified as he saw another figure near the first one. *This* figure seemed not to be skirting the edge of the clearing but, instead, to be emerging from deep within the forest, as if coming from the north rather than from the west, from the bridge. The only explanation would have to be that they had found another way across the river.

But how? I checked the river for a hundred yards up the road, as far as the group was likely to drive before stopping. There weren't any logs across the river, any footbridges, any boulders that might serve as stepping stones.

As a third figure emerged from the forest halfway around the clearing, Decker fought to subdue a wave of nausea, understanding what must have happened. After parking, the group had separated. Some had come southward down the road to guard the exit from the lane, to make sure Decker stayed put. But the others had hiked *northward*, a direction Decker had not anticipated. Higher up the road, they had come to another property and used its bridge to cross the river. The properties in this area tended to be a quarter mile apart. Decker had never imagined that in the night, feeling pressure, Renata and her group would hike so far out of their way. They had taken so long to get to the clearing because they had crept south through dense forest, moving with laborious slowness to make as little noise as possible. Members of the group would be emerging from the forest behind the house, also, doing their best to encircle it.

Behind Decker.

Behind *Beth*.

He imagined an enemy creeping onto her, both of them caught by surprise but the killer reacting more quickly, shooting Beth before she had a chance to defend herself. Decker came close to shifting instantly out of his hiding place and crawling hurriedly through the dark underbrush to get to her and defend her. But he couldn't allow himself to give in to the impulse. He would be endangering Beth as well as himself if he acted prematurely, without sufficient information. The trouble was, when he did have that information, it might be too late.

His hesitation saved his life as, behind him, sickeningly close, a twig snapped. He felt his heart seem to swell and rise toward his throat, choking him, as a shoe made a crunching sound on fallen pine needles. Slowly, a painstaking quarter-inch at a time, he turned his head. Carefully. With agonizing deliberateness. For all he knew, a weapon was being aimed at him, but he couldn't risk making a sudden move to look. If he hadn't been noticed, a backward jerk of his head would give him away, *would* make him a target.

Sweat broke out on his forehead. Little by little, the shadowy woods behind him came into view. Another footstep easing down on crunchy pine needles made him inwardly flinch. The speed of his pulse made him feel lightheaded as he saw a figure ten feet away. Renata? No. Too heavy. Shoulders too broad. The figure was male, holding a rifle, his back to Decker. Facing the cabin, the man sank down, eerily vanishing among bushes. Decker imagined the scene from the man's point of view. Music in the cabin. Lights beyond closed blinds. Part of Decker's preparations had been to set up timers for the lamps and the radio, so that one by one they would go off within the next hour. That realistic touch would make Renata and her friends confident that they had trapped their quarry.

On the other side of the clearing, the three figures were no longer visible. Presumably they had spread out, flanking the cabin, preparing to attack it simultaneously. Will they wait until the lights are out and they think we're asleep, or will they hurl stun grenades through the windows and break in right now?

When they rush through the trees, will they stumble onto Beth?

Decker's original plan had depended on the group being caught together after they crossed the bridge and tried to sneak up the lane, devastated by explosions, simultaneously coming under gunfire from three positions. Now, the only way he could think of to retain the element of surprise was—

Slowly, he squirmed from the pit. Feeling before him, he checked for anything that might cause him to make a noise. His movements were almost as gradual as when he had turned his head. He eased through a narrow space between two bushes, approaching the spot where the figure had sank down. The figure's attention would be centered on the cabin. The others would be staring at it as well, not looking in this direction. It had been twelve years since Decker had used a blade to kill a man. Gripping one of the hunting knives that he had bought at the gun shop and that he had earlier placed next to the Winchester at the side of the pit, he shifted through more bushes.

There. Five feet ahead. Braced on one knee. Holding a rifle. Watching the house.

When we make fateful decisions, fate will inevitably occur.

Without hesitation, Decker lunged. His left hand whipped in front of the gunman to seize his nostrils and mouth, the cotton glove helping to muffle any sound the figure made as Decker jerked him backward and slashed his throat, severing his jugular vein and his voice box.

Emotions themselves don't compromise us. But our thoughts about our emotions will *compromise us if those thoughts aren't disciplined.*

Blood gushed, hot, viscous. The man stiffened . . . trembled . . . became dead weight. Decker eased the corpse silently to the ground. Moonlight revealed a wisp of what resembled steam at the dead man's gaping throat.

Training controls our thoughts. Thoughts control our emotions.

20

Hearing his hammer-like pulse behind his ears, Decker knelt behind bushes, straining to detect a sign of where the other figures prepared to make their move. Were there more he didn't know about? Someone would be at the road, guarding the exit from the lane. And what about the property a quarter mile south of here? Decker's hunters would have seen it as they passed it, pursuing Decker's Jeep Cherokee. Had some of Renata's group returned to it, crossing the bridge *down there*, approaching the cabin from *that* direction? Maybe that was how the dead man at Decker's feet had reached this side of the clearing.

What *can* go wrong, *will* go wrong. The group must have had a plan before they approached the cabin. But how would they have communicated to synchronize their movements? Lapel microphones and earplug receivers were a possibility, although it was doubtful that the group would want to risk making even a whisper of a noise. Decker checked the corpse's ears and jacket and verified his doubt, not finding any miniature two-way radio equipment.

What other way could they synchronize their attack? Feeling along the corpse's left wrist, Decker found a watch, but one that had no luminous hands that might give away his position. Instead of a glass face, it had a metal hatch, and when Decker raised it, the only way he could tell the time in the darkness was to remove a glove, then touch the long minute hand, the short hour hand, and the palpable numbers along the notched rim. Familiar with this type of watch, Decker felt the minute hand jerk forward and quickly determined that the time was five minutes to one.

Would the attack on the cabin occur at one o'clock? Decker didn't have much time to get ready. He put on his glove, wiped his fingerprint off the watch, and crawled back through bushes with as much speed as silence permitted, returning to the dank shallow pit, which more and more reminded him of a grave. There, he felt along the row of wires and selected two pairs that were on the extreme right. He separated the pairs, holding one pair in his left hand, the other in his right, ready to touch one exposed tip from each pair to the positive pole of the car battery, the other exposed tips to the negative pole.

Despite the night's cold air, sweat oozed from the camouflage grease on his forehead. He concentrated on the cabin, grudgingly aware that the lights in the windows ruined his night vision. Since touching the watch on the corpse's wrist, he had been counting, estimating that four minutes and thirty seconds had passed, that the attack on the cabin would begin in just about—

He was fifteen seconds off. Windows shattered. Eye-searing flashes and ear-torturing roars from stun grenades erupted within the cabin. Dark figures holding rifles scrambled from the cover of bushes, two crashing through the front door, one through the back. Presumably the man whom Decker had killed would have joined the solitary figure barging through the back door, but that solitary figure (perhaps it was Renata) was so intent on the attack that he (she) didn't seem to notice that the partner hadn't shown up to help.

From the pit, Decker saw urgent shadows that the cabin's lights cast on the window blinds. Angry motions. Shouts. A curse. Not finding anyone in the cabin, the attackers knew that they had been tricked, that they were in a trap. They would be desperate to get out of the cabin before the trap was sprung. Another curse. The shadows frantically retreated. Decker flicked his gaze back and forth to the front and back doors of the cabin. Would they all rush out one entrance, or would they split up as they had going in?

The latter. Seeing a lone figure rush from the back, Decker instantly pressed wires to the poles on the battery. Night became day. The ground beneath the figure heaved in a thunderous blaze, spewing earth, buckshot, and fragments of metal from the canteen. The figure arched through the air. Immediately the two killers rushing from the front door faltered at the sound of the blast. Decker pressed the other pair of wires to the battery's poles, and the resultant explosion was even more powerful than the first, a fiery roar that tore a crater in the earth and catapulted the screaming figures down the steps toward Decker's car. The cabin's windows were shattered. Flames seethed up the outside walls.

Squinting from the ferocity of the blaze, Decker dropped the wires and picked up the Winchester. As rapidly as he could work the lever, he shot toward the back of the cabin, strafing the area where the lone figure had fallen. The unmistakable blast from a shotgun told him that Beth was shooting at the figures who had landed in the clearing near her. Another blast. Another. Another.

If there were more attackers in the area, the noise from the shotguns, not to mention the muzzle flashes, would reveal Beth's position. She had been instructed to grab both shotguns and roll fifteen feet to her right, where another pit had been dug. There, a box of shotgun shells waited for her. Hurrying, she would reload and fire again, continuing to switch locations.

But Decker didn't have time to think about that. He had to have faith that Beth was following the plan. For his part, he fired the seventh and final round that the Winchester held, dropped the rifle, pulled out Esperanza's 9mm Beretta, and tried to stay among shadows as he stalked through bushes toward where the lone figure had fallen. The closer he came to the burning cabin, the more impossible it was for him to be concealed by darkness. But the illumination from the flames had the benefit of revealing a figure on the ground. Decker shot, the figure jerking when the bullet struck his (her) head.

Hearing more roars from Beth's shotgun, Decker rushed forward, aimed down while he shoved the corpse over with his shoe, and failed to see what he had been hoping for. The face below him was not a woman's, not Renata's, instead that of one of her brothers whom Decker had spoken to in the Rome cafe fifteen months ago, when McKittrick had introduced Decker to Renata.

Decker pivoted, feeling exposed, eager to retreat from the burning cabin to the darkness of the woods. At the same time, he was seized by a compulsion to get to Beth, to help her, to discover if either of the two figures she was shooting at (and perhaps had killed) was Renata. He wondered anxiously what was happening with Esperanza. Had Esperanza eliminated the guards whom Decker assumed had been stationed on the road, on the other side of the bridge, at the exit from the lane? But Decker had to believe that Esperanza could take care of himself whereas Beth, as superbly as she had behaved, might now be close to panic.

Even though his choice put him at risk, Decker ran along the side of the burning cabin, planning to find cover at the front and shoot toward the figures who had landed in the clearing, near Decker's car. If they were still alive, they would be concentrating on where Beth was shooting from. Decker could take them by surprise.

But a bullet whizzing past, walloping into the cabin, took *Decker* by surprise. It came from his left, from the section of woods where he had been hiding. The man Decker had killed must have had a companion, who hadn't been as efficient in making his way through the woods from the property to the south. Decker sprawled to the ground and rolled toward a wide sheltering pine tree. A bullet tore up dirt behind him, the muzzle flash coming from the left of the tree. Decker scrambled to the right, circling the tree, shooting toward where he had seen the muzzle flash. Immediately he dove farther to the right, saw another flash, and aimed toward it, but before he could pull the trigger, he heard someone scream.

21

The scream belonged to Beth. Despite the rumble of flames from the burning cabin, Decker heard a disturbance behind him, at the edge of the clearing, bushes rustling, branches being snapped, the sounds of a struggle.

Beth screamed again. Then someone yelled what might have been Decker's name. Not Beth. The voice was grotesque, deep, gravelly, and distorted. Again it yelled what might have been Decker's name, and Decker now was absolutely certain that the guttural voice belonged to Renata. Wary of the gunman in the murky trees ahead of him, risking a glance behind him, Decker

451

confirmed his grave fear. A black-jumpsuited woman, with hair cut short like a boy's, with a tall slim sensuous figure, held Beth captive in the clearing, the left arm around Beth's throat, the right arm holding the barrel of a pistol to Beth's right temple.

Renata.

Even at a distance of thirty yards, the rage in her dark eyes was obvious. Her left arm encircled Beth's throat so tightly that Beth's features were twisted, her mouth forced open, grimacing, gasping for air. Beth clawed at Renata's arm, struggling to get free, but the injuries to her right leg and shoulder robbed her of strength and stability. Indeed her right leg had collapsed beneath her. She almost dangled from Renata's stranglehold, in danger of being choked to death.

'Decker!' Renata yelled, the voice so guttural that Decker had trouble deciphering the words. 'Throw down your gun! Get down here! Now! Or I'll kill her!'

Desperation paralyzed him.

'Do it!' Renata screamed hoarsely. 'Now!'

Decker's hesitation was broken when Renata cocked the pistol. Even with the noise of the fire, he thought he heard only one thing – the snick of the hammer being pulled back. Hearing it wasn't possible, of course. Renata was too far away. But in Decker's imagination, it sounded dismayingly vivid, as if the gun was at his own head.

'No! Wait!' Decker yelled.

'Do what I say if you want her to live!'

Beth managed to squeeze out a few strangled words. 'Steve, save yourself!'

'Shut the hell up!' Renata increased the pressure of her arm around Beth's throat. Beth's face became more distorted, her eyes bulging, her color darkening. Renata yelled to Decker, 'Do it, or I won't bother shooting her! I'll break her neck! I'll leave her paralyzed for the rest of her life!'

Unnervingly aware of the gunman somewhere in the forest behind him, Decker calculated his chances of shooting Renata. With a handgun? In firelight? At thirty yards? With his chest heaving and his hands shaking as much they were? Impossible. Even if Decker tried it, the moment he raised his gun to aim, Renata would have sufficient warning to pull the trigger and blow Beth's brains out.

'You have three seconds!' Renata yelled. 'One! Two!'

Decker saw Renata's right arm move. He imagined her finger tightening on the trigger. 'Wait!' he screamed again.

'Now!'

'*I'm coming out!*'

Although the blaze from the cabin warmed Decker's right side, the area between his shoulder blades felt ominously cold as he thought of the gunman in the forest training a weapon on him while he emerged from the shadows of the pine tree.

He raised his hands.

'Drop your pistol!' Renata shouted, her voice grotesque as if something had been wedged in her throat.

Decker obeyed, the pistol thunking onto the forest floor. He walked closer, feeling wobbly in his legs, dreading the impact that would topple him when the gunman behind him shot him in the back. But dying was better than seeing Beth die. He didn't want to remain alive without her.

Arms high, he reached the slope to the clearing, eased down it sideways, passed his car, and saw the bodies of the two men who had been caught in the explosion at the front of the cabin. He stopped in front of Renata.

'Look, you bastard,' Renata growled, pointing at the corpses. 'See what she did. See *this*.' Her formerly alluring face was made repulsive by the hate that distorted it. 'See what *you* did!' She raised her chin so that, in the light from the burning cabin, Decker was able to see the ugly puckered bullet-wound scar at the front of Renata's throat, near her voice box. 'There's a bigger scar in the back!'

Decker could barely understand her. His mind worked urgently to keep translating.

'You killed my brothers! *What do you think I should do to you?*'

Decker didn't have an answer.

'Should I blow a hole in *your* throat? Should I blow a hole in *her* throat? Where's my money?'

'In the carry-on bag I found in your car in New York.'

'Where's the damned carry-on bag? When I drove past the lane, I saw you taking it into the cabin.'

Decker nodded. 'That's where I left it.' He glanced toward the blazing cabin.

'You didn't bring it out with you?'

'No.'

'You *left* it in there?'

'That's what I said.'

'*My million dollars?*'

'Minus a couple of thousand I spent on equipment.'

'You're *lying*.'

Decker glanced again toward the flames, trying to prolong the conversation. 'Afraid not.'

'Then prove it,' Renata snapped.

'What are you talking about? How could I possibly prove it?'

'Bring me the money.'

'What?'

'Go in there and get my money.'

'In the fire? I wouldn't have a chance.'

'You want to talk about taking a chance? This is the only chance you're going to get. Go in the cabin and . . . get . . . my . . . money.'

The flames roared.

'No,' Decker said.

'Then I'll make *her* go in for it.' Renata dragged Beth across the clearing toward the stairs up to the cabin. At the same time, she yelled toward the dark forest behind the burning cabin, 'Pietro! Get down here! Guard him!'

Beth's eyelids fluttered. Her hands stopped fighting to pull away Renata's arm. Her face an alarming color, she went limp, the pressure around her neck so severe that she lost consciousness.

'Pietro!' Renata yanked Beth up several log steps. 'Where are you? I said come down here!'

The flames roared higher, covering the exterior of the cabin, filling the interior with churning smoke and a fierce crimson glow.

Renata jerked Beth to the top of the steps and halted, repulsed by the savagery of the heat. She released Beth's throat and straightened her to shove her into the flames.

Decker could no longer restrain himself. Even though he knew he'd be shot, he charged wildly toward the steps, desperate to help Beth.

'Pietro!'

Decker reached the first step.

'Shoot him, Pietro!'

Decker was halfway up.

Shoving Beth toward the flames, Renata simultaneously turned to aim at Decker.

The barrel of her pistol was leveled at Decker's face as a hand from behind her came crashing down on the pistol. The hand belonged to Beth, who had only pretended to lose consciousness. After Renata had pushed her, she had lurched toward the flames, staggered back, pivoted, and flung her weight onto Renata. She wedged her thumb between the pistol's hammer and its firing pin an instant before Renata pulled the

---

trigger, the hammer's powerful spring driving the hammer into Beth's flesh. Beth's unexpected weight caused Renata to lose her balance. The two women tumbled down the steps, rolling, twisting, bumping, striking Decker, carrying him with them.

They jolted to a stop at the bottom, the three of them tangled on the ground. Beth's thumb was still wedged beneath the pistol's hammer. She tried to yank the pistol out of Renata's grasp but didn't have the strength. For her part, Renata gave a mighty jerk to the weapon and wrenched it free, ripping Beth's thumb open. Flat on the ground, his arms caught beneath the two women, Decker couldn't move as Renata swung the pistol at him. Wincing, in agony, Beth rolled over Decker, clutched the pistol, and struggled to deflect the gun.

The ground heaved, the explosive in one of the canteens detonating, a blazing roar erupting from the far side of the clearing. A second explosion, a little closer, tore up a crater. A third explosion, halfway across the clearing, threw Beth and Renata back from the shockwave. A fourth explosion, nearer than halfway, deafened Decker. Someone was setting off the canteens in sequence, marching the explosions across the area.

Smoke drifted over Decker. Stunned, he took a moment to recover from the surprise and force of the detonations. In a frenzy, he rolled through the smoke to find and help Beth. But he wasn't quick enough. Amid the smoke, he heard a shot, a second, a third. He screamed and lurched forward, hearing a fourth shot, a fifth, a sixth. The shots were directly in front of him. A seventh. An eighth. A breeze caused the smoke to clear, and as Decker heard a ninth shot, he gaped down at Renata and Beth locked in what might have been an embrace.

'Beth!'

A tenth shot.

In a rage, Decker stormed toward Renata and yanked her away, ready to snap her arm so she'd drop her pistol, to crack her ribs, to smash her nose and gouge out her eyes, to punish her for killing Beth. But the dead weight he held, the blood oozing from numerous holes in Renata's body, dribbling from her lips, showed him how much he had been mistaken. It wasn't Renata who had been shooting but, rather, Beth.

22

Beth's eyes communicated an emotion close to hysteria. She was about to shoot an eleventh time but then realized that Decker was in the way and slowly lowered the weapon, then sank to the ground.

Surrounded by smoke, Decker dropped Renata and hurried to her.

'There wasn't anything wrong with my *left* arm,' Beth murmured in what sounded almost like triumph.

'How bad are you hurt?' Decker quickly wrapped a handkerchief around her gashed bleeding thumb.

'Sore all over. God, I hope there aren't any more of them.'

'There was one in the forest. He should have moved against us by now.'

'He's dead,' a voice said from the other side of the drifting smoke.

Decker looked up.

'They're *all* dead.' Silhouetted by the flames from the cabin, Esperanza stepped specter-like from the smoke. A rifle was slung over his shoulder. In his right hand, he held the bow Decker had bought. In his left, he held a quiver of arrows.

'When the explosions went off at the cabin, I shot two men who were guarding the exit from the lane,' Esperanza said. 'Back that far, the .22 didn't make enough noise to be heard with all the other commotion. But I couldn't use it on the man

Renata called Pietro. He and I were too close to the clearing. She might have heard *those* shots, realized you weren't alone, panicked, and killed both of you before she had planned to.' Esperanza held up the bow. 'So I used this. No noise. Good thing you bought it.'

'Good thing you know how to use it.'

'I meant to tell you. Every fall, during bow season, I head up into the mountains and go hunting. I haven't failed to bring back a deer since I was fourteen.'

'It was you who set off the explosions?' Decker asked.

'Renata was going to shoot you. I couldn't think of anything else to do. I couldn't take a shot at her with you and Beth in the way. I couldn't get to you fast enough to grab her. I needed some kind of diversion, something that would startle everyone and give you a chance to recover sooner than *she* did.'

'It's Beth who recovered first.' Decker looked at her with admiration. 'Help me get her into the car.'

The moment she lay in the back seat, Esperanza anticipated what Decker was going to say next. 'Clean the area?'

'Get everything we can. The authorities in Pecos will be up here to investigate the explosions. That fire will lead them right to this cabin. We don't have much time.'

Decker ran to get Beth's shotguns while Esperanza threw the .22, the bow, and the quiver into the Cherokee's storage compartment. The firearms were important because their serial numbers could be traced to the store where Decker had bought them and eventually traced to him. When Decker returned with the shotguns, Esperanza was disappearing into the forest, presumably getting the Winchester and the car battery. Decker dug up the remaining canteens. He pulled out the light-bulb filaments, gathered the wires, and set everything into the back of the car. Meanwhile, Esperanza had returned with the equipment from Decker's hiding place.

'I'll get the money from where I buried it,' Esperanza said. 'What else?'

'The Remington bolt-action. It's in the pit we dug near the bridge.'

'I'll get that, too,' Esperanza said.

'Beth's crutches. The hunting knives.'

'We'd better make sure we collect all the boxes of ammunition. And the arrow I shot.'

'. . . Esperanza.'

'What?'

'I had to use your handgun. Two shell casings are in the bushes up there.'

'Jesus.' In the firelight, Esperanza seemed to turn pale. 'I loaded it before all this happened. I wasn't wearing gloves. My fingerprints will be on those casings.'

'I'll do everything I can to find them,' Decker said. 'Here are my car keys. Get the money, the knives, the Remington, and the boxes of ammunition. Drive Beth and yourself the hell away from here. I'll keep searching until the last minute, until police cars are pulling into the lane.'

Esperanza didn't respond, only stared at him.

'Go,' Decker said, then raced up the slope toward the trees and bushes on the right of the burning cabin. One of the shots from Esperanza's pistol had been next to a large pine tree, just about—

Here! Decker thought. He tried to re-enact what he had done, how he had dropped to the ground when the gunman shot at him from deeper in the woods, how he had scrambled to the right of the tree, how he had knelt and pulled the trigger and—

The ejected shell casing would have flipped through the air and landed about three or four feet from—

Firelight reflected off something small and metallic. Breathing fiercely, exhaling in triumph, Decker dropped to his knees and found one of the 9mm casings he was searching for. Only one more to go. As he surged to his feet, he discovered Esperanza hurrying toward him.

'Leave,' Decker said.

'Not without you.'

'But—'

'Show me where to look,' Esperanza said.

Skirting the flames from the cabin, they rushed toward the back and ignored the corpse of the man Decker had shot in the head, totally consumed by the hunt for the other casing.

'It could be there or maybe over there.' Decker's chest heaved.

'The undergrowth's too thick.' Esperanza got down, crawling, tracing his hands along the ground. 'Even with the firelight, there are too many shadows.'

'We have to find it!'

'Listen.'

'What?'

'Sirens.'

'Shit.'

'They're faint. Quite a distance away.'

'Not for long.' Decker searched harder beneath bushes, pawing in a frenzy over the murky ground. 'Go. Get in the car. Leave. There's no point in *all* of us being caught.'

'Or *any* of us. Forget the casing,' Esperanza said. 'Come with me to the car.'

'If they find the casing, if they manage to lift prints from it—'

'Partial prints. Probably smudged.'

'You hope. You'd never be able to explain what a casing with your prints was doing up here.' Decker searched among dead leaves.

'I'll claim someone stole my pistol.'

'Would *you* believe that story?'

'Not likely.'

'Then—'

'I don't care.' Esperanza crawled beneath bushes. 'Just because I might be implicated, that doesn't mean you and Beth have to be. Let's get out of—'

'Found it! Oh, sweet Christ, I found it.' Decker leapt to his feet and showed Esperanza the precious casing. 'I never believed I'd—'

They charged from the bushes and raced toward the car, scrambling down the slope so fast that they almost tripped and fell. Esperanza still had the car keys. He slid behind the steering wheel while Decker dove into the back seat with Beth. Before Decker could slam the door, Esperanza had the car in gear and was making a rapid turn in the clearing, throwing up dirt. Barely taking the time to flick on the headlights, he sped down the lane, bounced over the bridge, and veered swiftly onto the dark country road.

'Have we got everything? The money? All the weapons?' Decker asked, his voice loud enough to be heard above the walloping din of his heart.

'I can't think of anything we left behind.' Esperanza pressed his foot on the accelerator.

'Then we got away with it,' Decker said.

'Except for—' Esperanza pointed toward the growing wail of sirens in the darkness before him.

He slowed down and turned off the headlights.

'What are you doing?' Decker asked.

'Bringing back memories of when I was a kid.' Esperanza swerved into the lane of the property a quarter-mile below the burning cabin. The flames rose high enough to be seen from a distance. Hiding the car in the undergrowth, Esperanza turned off the engine and peered through shadowy trees toward the

461

road. The headlights and flashing emergency lights of a fire engine and several police cars rushed past, their outlines a blur, their sirens shrieking.

'Just like old times,' Esperanza said. Immediately he restarted the car and backed out onto the road, turning on his headlights only when forced to.

Twice more, they had to veer into a lane to stop from being seen by passing emergency vehicles. The second time, Decker and Esperanza paused long enough to get out of the car and strip off their camouflage suits. Beth winced when Decker took off hers. Using the inside of the suits, they wiped the camouflage grease from their faces, then spread the suits over the weapons in the back and covered everything with a car blanket. When they got to Pecos or when they reached Santa Fe, they wouldn't attract attention now if a police car pulled up next to them.

Decker stroked Beth's head. 'Feeling any better?'

'My mouth's awfully dry.'

'We'll get you some water as soon as we can. Let me check those pulled stitches . . . You're bleeding, but only a little. You don't need to worry. You're going to be all right.'

'The pulled stitches will make the scars worse.'

'I hate to agree with you, but yes.'

'Now we'll have matching sets.'

Decker took a moment before he realized that, despite her pain, Beth was doing her best to grin.

'Like the bullet-wound scars you showed me,' Beth said. 'But mine will be bigger.'

'You are something else,' Decker said.

23

Forty minutes later, Esperanza turned off Interstate 25 onto Old

Pecos Trail and then onto Rodeo Road, heading toward the side street upon which he had his trailer. The time was almost two-thirty. The late-night streets were deserted.

'In the morning, I'll drive into the desert and burn the weapons, our gloves, and our camouflage suits, along with the fuel oil and fertilizer in the canteens,' Decker said. 'I bought the Remington for long-distance shooting, but we never did use it. It's safe to keep. Why don't you take it, Esperanza? Take the bow and the arrows, too.'

'And half the money,' Beth said.

'I can't,' Esperanza said.

'Why not? If you don't spend the money right away, if you dribble it out a little at a time, no one will suspect you have it,' Decker said. 'You won't need to explain how you came to have a half-million dollars.'

'That figure has a wonderful sound to it,' Esperanza admitted.

'I can arrange for you to have a numbered account in a bank in the Bahamas,' Beth said.

'I bet you can.'

'Then you'll take the money?'

'No.'

'Why not?' Decker repeated, puzzled.

'The last few days, I killed several men for what I thought were valid reasons. But if I took the money, if I profited, I don't think I would ever stop feeling dirty.'

The car became silent.

'What about *you*, Decker?' Esperanza asked. 'Will *you* keep the money?'

'I know a good use for it.'

'Such as?'

'If I talk about it, it might not work out.'

'Sounds mysterious,' Beth said.

'You'll soon know.'

'Well, while I'm waiting, I'd like you to ease my worries about something.'

Decker looked concerned. 'What?'

'The gun dealer you went to. If the crime lab establishes that the metal fragments from the bombs came from canteens, if he reads that in the newspaper, won't he remember a man who bought several firearms and *twelve* canteens the day before the attack?'

'Possibly,' Decker said.

'Then why aren't *you* worried?'

'Because I'm going to contact my former employer and report that Renata has finally been taken care of – with extreme denial, as McKittrick liked to call it. Given the catastrophe she caused in Rome, my former employer will want to make sure that it isn't connected to what happened at the cabin, that *I'm* not connected to it. My former employer will use national security as an excuse to discourage local law enforcement from investigating.'

'I'll certainly cooperate,' Esperanza said. 'But just in case they're a little slow, I'm the detective who would normally be assigned to talk to the gun dealer. I can tell you right now that any link between you and what happened in Pecos is purely coincidental.'

'Speaking of local law enforcement . . .' Decker leaned forward from the back to open the storage compartment between the front seats. 'Here's your badge.'

'Finally.'

'And your pistol.'

'Back where it belongs.' But the lightness in Esperanza's tone changed to melancholy as he parked in front of his trailer. 'The question is, where do *I* belong? The place doesn't feel like a home anymore. It sure looks empty.'

'I'm sorry about your wife leaving. I wish there was something we could do to help,' Beth said.

'Phone from time to time. Let me know the two of you are all right.'

'We'll do more than phone,' Decker said. 'You'll be seeing a lot of us.'

'Sure.' But Esperanza sounded preoccupied as he left the key in the ignition and got out of the car.

'Good luck.'

Esperanza didn't reply. He walked slowly across the gravel area in front of the trailer. It wasn't until he disappeared inside that Decker got into the driver's seat and turned the ignition key.

'Let's go home,' Decker said.

24

In contrast with his feelings of detachment when he had returned to Santa Fe from New York, Decker now did feel at home. As he headed into the driveway, he scanned the dark, low, sprawling outline of his adobe compound and said to himself, 'This is mine.'

He must have said it out loud.

'Of course, this is yours,' Beth said, puzzled. 'You've been living here for fifteen months.'

'It's hard to explain,' he said in amazement. 'I was afraid I had made a mistake.'

The driveway curved along the side of the house to the carport in back, where a sensor light came on, guiding the way. Decker helped Beth out of the Cherokee.

She leaned against him. 'What about me? Did you make a mistake about me?'

Coyotes howled on Sun Mountain.

465

'The night after I first met you,' Decker said, 'I stood out here and listened to those coyotes and wished that you were next to me.'

'Now I am.'

'Now you are.' Decker kissed her.

In a while, he unlocked the back door, turned on the kitchen light, and helped Beth inside, holding her crutches. 'We'll use the guest room. The master bedroom still looks like the aftermath of a small war. Can I get you anything?'

'Tea.'

While water boiled, Decker found a bag of chocolate-chip cookies and set them on a saucer. Under the circumstances, the cookies looked pathetic. No one ate.

'There isn't any hot water for a bath, I'm afraid,' Decker said.

Beth nodded wearily. 'I remember the heater was destroyed during Friday night's attack.'

'I'll put fresh bandages on your stitches. I'm sure you could use a pain pill.'

Beth nodded again, exhausted.

'Will you be all right here alone?'

'Why?' Beth straightened, unsettled. 'Where are you going?'

'I want to get rid of that stuff in the back of the car. The sooner, the better.'

'I'll go with you.'

'No. Rest.'

'But when will you be back?'

'Maybe not until after dawn.'

'I won't be separated from you.'

'But—'

'There's nothing to discuss,' Beth said. 'I'm going with you.'

25

In the gray of false dawn, as Decker dropped the camouflage suits and the gloves into a pile in a hollow twenty miles into the desert west of Santa Fe, he glanced at Beth. Arms crossed over a sweater he had given her, she leaned her back against the front passenger door of the Cherokee and watched him. He came back for the canteens filled with plant fertilizer and fuel oil, dumping their contents over the garments, the sharp smell flaring his nostrils. He threw down the arrow that Esperanza had used to kill the man in the forest. He added the .22, the .30-30, and the shotgun, sparing only the .270 because it hadn't been used. A fire wouldn't destroy the serial numbers on the weapons, but it would make them inoperable. If someone by chance found them in the various isolated places where he intended to bury them, they would be discarded as garbage. Decker used the claw end of a hammer to punch holes into the canteens so that no fumes would remain inside and possibly set off an explosion. Because fuel oil burned slowly, he poured gasoline over the pile. Then he struck a match, set fire to the entire book of matches, and threw the book onto the pile. With a whoosh, the gasoline and the fuel oil ignited, engulfing the garments and the weapons, thrusting a pillar of fire and smoke toward the brightening sky.

Decker walked over to Beth, put his arm around her, and watched the blaze.

'What's that story in Greek mythology? About the bird rising from the ashes?' Beth asked. 'The phoenix?'

'It's about rebirth,' Decker said.

'That's what Renata's name means in English, isn't it? Rebirth?'

'The thought occurred to me.'

'But is it really?' Beth asked. 'A rebirth?'

'It is if we want it to be.'

Behind them, the sun eased above the Sangre de Cristo mountains.

'How do you stand it?' Beth asked. 'Last night. What we were forced to do.'

'That's what I was trying to explain earlier. To survive, I was taught to deny any emotions that aren't practical.'

'I can't do that.' Beth trembled. 'When I killed my husband . . . as much as he needed to be killed . . . I threw up for three days afterward.'

'You did what you had to. *We* did what *we* had to. Right now, as bad as I feel, I can't get over the fact that we're here, that I've got my arm around you—'

'That we're alive,' Beth said.

'Yes.'

'You wondered how I learned about firearms.'

'You don't need to tell me anything about your past,' Decker said.

'But I want to. I *have* to. Joey made me learn,' Beth said. 'He had guns all over the house, a shooting range in his basement. He used to make me go down and watch him shoot.'

The flames and smoke stretched higher.

'Joey knew how much I hated it. Even though I wore ear protectors, every gunshot made me flinch. That made him laugh. Then he thought it would be really hilarious to make *me* do the shooting – .357 magnums, .45s. The most powerful handguns. All the way up to .44 magnums. Sometimes, I think he taught me how to shoot because he loved the thrill of knowing all those loaded guns were around me, taunting me, daring me to try to use one against him. He went to great pains to make me understand the hell he would put me through if I was ever foolish enough to try. Then he made me learn to use shotguns. Louder. With a more punishing recoil. That's what I used to kill him,' Beth said. 'A shotgun.'

'Hush.'

'A double barrel. The same type I used tonight.'

'Hush.' Decker kissed a tear from her cheek. 'From now on, the past doesn't exist.'

'Does that mean *your* past doesn't exist, also?'

'What are you getting at?'

'Did you lose the openness you found here? Have you truly reverted? Have you sealed yourself off again and gone back to feeling apart from things?'

'Not apart from you,' Decker said. 'Not apart from *this*.' He gestured toward the sun above the mountains, toward the aspen starting to turn yellow in the ski basin, toward the green of the piñon trees in the foothills and the mustard-colored chamisa in the red and orange of the brilliant high desert. 'But there are things in my life that I do feel apart from, that I don't want you to know about, that I don't want to have to remember.'

'Believe me, I feel the same way.'

'I'll never ask you about those things,' Decker said, 'and you never have to tell me about them, not if you don't want to. I can only imagine the fear and confusion you must have felt, coming to Santa Fe, trying to hide from the mob, knowing I had skills to help you. You saw me as a savior, and you grabbed for me. Was that using me? If it was, I'm glad you did – because I never would have met you otherwise. Even if I had known you were using me, I would have *wanted* you to use me.'

Decker reached into the back of his car and pulled out the travel bag containing the million dollars. 'For a time, after I rescued you, I thought you were staying with me because of this.'

Decker carried the bag toward the fire.

Beth looked startled. 'What are you going to do?'

'I told you I had a good use for this. I'm going to destroy the past.'

'*You're going to burn the money?*'

'Esperanza was right. If we spent it, we'd always feel dirty.'

Decker held the bag over the fire.

'*A million dollars?*' Beth asked.

'Blood money. Would it really matter to you if I burned it?'

'You're testing me?'

The bottom of the bag started smoldering.

'I want to get rid of the past,' Decker said.

Beth hesitated. Flames danced along the bottom of the bag.

'Last chance,' Decker said.

'Do it,' Beth said.

'You're sure?'

'Throw it in the fire.' Beth walked toward him. 'For us, the past stops right now.'

She kissed him. When Decker dropped the bag into the flames, neither of them looked at it. The kiss went on and on, It took Decker's breath away.

Long Lost

David Morrell

Brad Denning's brother Petey is long lost.

Frozen in time as a skinny nine-year-old bicycling away from his uncaring older brother, Petey haunts Brad's consciousness. To this day, within his prosperous life, Brad knows with certainty that he was responsible for the boy's disappearance. He knows how much his mother and father suffered and that nothing can ever bring Petey back – until a stranger walks into Brad's life.

Suddenly Brad is confronted by a man who claims to be his brother and whose tale is one of wandering, pain, and survival. As Brad gradually puts aside his suspicions, Petey makes himself at home in Brad's life. Then everything is shattered. Petey again disappears. Only this time, he's taken Brad's wife and child with him.

Building to a high-voltage, haunting climax, *Long Lost* is a novel of shocking intensity that also brilliantly explores the ties that bind us to our past. It is the finest work yet by David Morrell, the master of high-action suspense.

'Exciting, pacey and everything an aficionado could want or need' *Independent on Sunday*

Praise for David Morrell's international bestsellers:

'Tight, colourful, fast-moving, and packed with tension' Stephen King

'David Morrell is a master of suspense. He wields it like a stiletto – knows just where to stick it and how to turn it. If you're reading Morrell, you're sitting on the edge of your seat' Michael Connelly

0 7472 6696 4

headline

Burnt Sienna

David Morrell

Now a famous artist, ex-Marine, Chase Malone, has built a new, isolated life, and spends his days painting. But then billionaire arms merchant Derek Bellasar offers a huge commission for two portraits of his wife, Sienna. Malone never accepts commissions, refusing to paint to another's dictates, but Bellasar won't take no for an answer. Before long, Malone's beach is bulldozed, his favourite restaurant closed, and the gallery displaying his works taken over.

Confused and angry, Malone vows to get revenge. Then an old friend from the Marines asks him to take the commission. Jeb, now a CIA agent fighting Bellasar's ever-increasing power, sees this as his one chance to get close to him. It is also Sienna's one chance for survival. She doesn't know she is Bellasar's fourth wife, and that each of the other three died mysteriously in an accident just after her beauty had been immortalized by a renowned artist.

Malone is quickly overwhelmed by Sienna and saving her life soon becomes his only goal. Once on the run, however, he finds that a woman as beautiful as Sienna is impossible to hide . . .

'Tight, colourful, fast-moving and packed with tension' Stephen King

'Fresh, inventive, gripping suspense. Morrell plays by his own rules and leaves you dazzled' Dean Koontz

'The story grabs you by the short hairs of your soul and your brain and does not let go. It's a rich and obsessive novel' James Ellroy

0 7472 6695 6

headline

Black Evening

David Morrell

From the American heartland to the edge of Hell, David Morrell, bestselling author of the classics FIRST BLOOD and THE BROTHERHOOD OF THE ROSE, presents a career-spanning examination into his own life – and the fears we all share. From his first published short fiction to his latest, award-winning stories including:

THE BEAUTIFUL UNCUT HAIR OF GRAVES

Winner, Best Novella, Horror Writers of America Award: your parents die suddenly, leaving adoption papers dated at your birthday. You investigate – but every official document has vanished, along with your biological mother . . .

ORANGE IS FOR ANGUISH, BLUE FOR INSANITY

Winner, Best Novella, Horror Writers of America Award: the Beautiful landscapes of a master's paintings hold deeper meanings, hiding unearthly horrors . . .

Praise for BLACK EVENING:

'Showcase[s] Morrell's ability to capture pure, hard-driving suspense, often culminating in unspeakable tragedy or bizarre discovery' *Publishers Weekly*

Praise for David Morrell's other international bestsellers:

'Fresh, inventive, gripping suspense. Morrell plays by his own rules and leaves you dazzled' Dean Koontz

'Tight, colourful, fast-moving, and packed with tension' Stephen King

0 7472 6697 2

headline